FIRST COLONY - BOOKS 1 - 3

KEN LOZITO

ACOUSTICAL BOOKS LLC

Published by Acoustical Books, LLC

KenLozito.com

Cover design by Jeff Brown

IF YOU WOULD LIKE TO BE NOTIFIED WHEN MY NEXT BOOK IS RELEASED VISIT

WWW.KENLOZITO.COM

ISBN: 978-1-945223-27-3

GENESIS

FIRST COLONY - BOOK 1

1

THE FREIGHTER WAITED for clearance to make its final approach to Chronos Station while Connor Gates and his squad hid in a shipping container in the vast belly of the vessel. Connor glanced at his men. They were the most famous squad that no one outside the NA Command had ever heard of. Officially they didn't exist. For hundreds of years, black ops military platoons had celebrated a long tradition of working in the shadows, and their effectiveness was measured by the undetected execution of their missions. Even within the shadowy confines of black ops, Connor's Ghosts were a bit of a legend. When failure was not an option, it was the Ghosts who were given the toughest missions. Connor had been the CO of the Ghosts for ten years—not even a blip in the prolonged lifetimes of people in this day and age.

"We're patched in, Colonel," Sawyer said.

Connor used his implants to access the open comms channel on the bridge.

"Freighter JEC 2701, hold your approach while we validate the codes for your ship," the harbormaster said.

"Copy. We'll hold the approach," the freighter's helmsman replied.

A sub-screen appeared on Connor's heads-up display that showed the ship's codes being matched up with the records being transferred from the lunar shipping yards.

The station comms channel was muted by someone on the freighter's bridge, and Connor heard the helmsman speaking.

"Captain, with as many deliveries as we make to this station, you'd think they'd give us a warmer welcome," said the helmsman.

"They're following standard protocol," said the captain.

"Yeah, but targeting us with their weapons systems every time we come here is a bit much. It's not like we're part of the Syndicate or anything," said the helmsman.

"And here I thought you couldn't wait for some shore leave on a luxurious seventh-generation deep-space station," said the captain.

Connor muted the comms channels and clenched his teeth at the mention of the Syndicate. He'd been hunting them for the past five years, patiently working his way closer to the vast crime family that had the power to challenge the nation-states of old.

The soldier next to Connor checked his weapon while he waited. "If they only knew the head of the Syndicate had taken up residence on this station," Major Kasey Douglass said.

Kasey had been Connor's second in command for almost as long as he'd been hunting the Syndicate.

"Only if our intel is good. Remember Sandy Springs?" Connor asked.

Kasey nodded. "Kinda hard to forget that crapstorm of an op."

"This is the right place. I know it. A civilian space station that has weapons capabilities to defend itself from attack matches his MO," Connor said.

"You still think the entire Syndicate is run by just one person?"

"It is," Connor said.

"But we don't have a name for this guy," Kasey said.

"We have his location. He's smart. Even if we'd come here with combat shuttles under stealth, we would have run the risk of alerting him. And even though the Sandy Springs op was a disaster, we learned a lot," Connor said.

"Yeah, not to trust the chain of command in our own org. We're completely off the reservation with this. No backup," Kasey said.

"Had to be this way. I couldn't risk the mission becoming compromised. Besides, it's not like we're breaking any rules. I do have authority to conduct this mission," Connor said.

"I won't argue about authority, but this is a civilian station—and not just any civilian station. This is Chronos. Only the most affluent dignitaries, ambassadors, and heads of corporations use this place as their go-to spot. If we have an incident here, it could hurt us. We should report the op to COMCENT," Kasey said.

Connor regarded Kasey for a moment. The major was doing his job, voicing his concerns to his commanding officer. "Your concerns are noted, but this is still a comms blackout op. COMCENT will be notified after the op is complete, Major," Connor replied.

"Of course, Colonel," Kasey said and let the matter drop.

They all knew why they were there. The Syndicate had a significant research and development operation that did not abide by the Earth's R&D accords, freely testing anything and everything on human subjects regardless of sex, age, or ethnic origin. Some of the research stations they'd shut down throughout the solar system still gave him nightmares as he recalled cross-species genetic experimentation that created horrific monsters that were set loose to test how well their experiments had worked. The Syndicate had become the NA Command's highest priority, but the real work fell into black ops command channels. The Syndicate was among the most ruthless organizations in history. They had little regard for human life and operated above the law. The fact that they'd set up operations at a place like Chronos Station was a testament to their practices in maximizing collateral damage.

The harbormaster cleared the freighter to dock, and within the hour the large freighter was being guided to its docking slip. The Ghosts waited in silent anticipation. Once the ship docked, they could move under the cover of offloading activities. No one would suspect that one of the shipping containers carried an infiltration force.

"Wil, are you in the station's systems yet?" Connor asked.

Wil Reisman waved his hands around, working through an interface that only he could see. "I'm in but only with transit access. We can get schematics and access the maglev transport, but I'm not in the secure Mosi system, Colonel."

"Good. Those systems are closely monitored. I don't want them tipped off to our presence," Connor said.

"I've uploaded the station's schematics to our suit computers," Reisman said.

Connor brought up the schematics, and his suit computer showed a one hundred percent match for what they had on record. He inputted the latest intelligence overlay, and a path highlighted to a destination called Rabbit's Foot.

"Send coded message to Bravo Squad. The op is a go," Connor said.

The ship's status showed that it was docked and the automated loaders would begin offloading the shipping containers to the station. Connor glanced at Tiegan, waiting for his tech ops specialist to give them the go-ahead.

Large lifts came for the priority pallets first, and Connor felt himself shift to zero gravity until their shipping container was brought within the station's gravitational field. He engaged his combat suit's camo-mode, which rendered them invisible to anyone watching, as well as to the station's sensors. The secure latch of the shipping container's door popped open and Connor pushed his way out, dropping down sixty meters to the ground. His combat suit absorbed the shock of his landing, and he quickly moved to the side while the rest of the squad came down and took up positions on the space dock.

The space dock was a massive open area through which all ship traffic to the station was routed. Freighters like the one they'd stowed away on docked in a designated area away from civilian transports.

"Contact," Denton said.

Connor looked over and saw a standard Bosheir Security Mech patrolling the dock. The large mech could either be piloted by a person or engaged in patrol mode, allowing the mech's AI or pilot to remotely operate the machine. Large cannons gleamed on the mech's metallic forearms, and its head swiveled in their direction.

"Hold. It's a T-series 10-01 and can't detect us," Reisman said.

Connor waited. Samson had the mech in his sights, his heavy rocket launcher ready to go if needed, but the mech turned away from them and stalked off.

The Ghosts headed in the direction the mech had gone, watching as work drones went about unloading the shipping containers after transfer off the ship. The heavily armed soldiers systematically moved forward two by two, with the first group clearing the area before the next group came up and took point. Most of them were armed with a third generation M32 pulse rifle with grenade launcher. The compact firearm packed quite a punch for its size and was ideal for close-quarters combat.

The few actual dockworkers in the area didn't notice them as they made their way across the docks and entered one of the large freight elevators.

"Reisman, we need those markings," Connor said.

His intelligence officer worked through the options on his holo-interface while Connor kept a careful watch on the elevator's progress toward one of Chronos Station's many common areas. An empty elevator would certainly be noticed by the local security office.

"Okay, time to blend in with the locals," Reisman said. He gestured with his hand as if flinging something at his squad mates. Within moments their combat suits produced a realistic-looking hologram of someone who lived on the station.

Samson growled. "Come on, man. You turned me into a pregnant woman."

The others grinned. Connor glanced down at his own combat suit and saw that Reisman had assigned him the hologram of Chronos Station security force personnel—black armor and a helmet that only showed his jawline underneath the visor.

"That's the way it goes, Samson. This time you drew the short straw. Congratulations! You're about eight months pregnant," Reisman said.

Samson turned toward Hank. "What are you laughing at? You got stuck with the grandma this time."

Connor glanced around at all of them to be sure there were no abnormalities in anyone's hologram. "Alright, by the numbers. Check each other out," Connor said.

The disguises were preconfigured for operations that brought them among civilians, and they used forms that put the casual onlooker off guard. Not many people would look twice at a pregnant woman or an elderly couple.

Connor checked Kasey, whose outward appearance resembled a morbidly obese man. Maintaining the hologram was taxing on their combat suit computers and couldn't be sustained for more than a few hours.

The elevator doors opened and the Ghosts exited. They followed a few corridors and were ushered through a security checkpoint. They didn't carry any heavy ordnance, and the scanners wouldn't be able to detect the ceramic composite that made up their combat suits. They did, however, need to store their weapons so they couldn't be detected.

The squad divided as they made their way across an expansive common area. Chronos Station sported blue skies and a parklike setting for its patrons. Though Connor couldn't smell the air, he imagined it was as fresh as if he were standing on a forested pathway back on Earth. Chronos Station was among the largest in the solar system and was restricted to the more affluent population. There was enough space for everyone and hardly any crowds, so the risk of someone accidentally brushing past the hologram and actually bumping into them was almost nonexistent.

The Ghosts converged on the platform for the maglev trains. Maglev trains didn't make any noise, and the top-of-the-line inertia dampeners gave no indication that they were traveling nearly five hundred kilometers an hour. The train cars were luxurious, and Connor noticed a few squad members glance longingly toward the food stations. Being topside on an op was a rare treat. Usually, they traveled through the bowels of a location and stayed out of sight, but there was no doubt the Syndicate would have ample security monitors watching all those entry points. Connor was wagering that their unorthodox approach would get them close enough to where the head of the Syndicate kept himself that their surprise attack would make escape all but impossible.

A flickering of light caught Connor's eye and he turned toward it. Samson's hologram was slipping, and Connor's mouth tightened. No one else on the train seemed to have noticed, so Connor walked over and gestured for Kasey to follow him. They were joined by two of the others as they circled around Samson. Reisman went over to Samson and swore.

Connor glanced behind him and saw Reisman working on Samson's combat suit. The hologram was nowhere to be seen. Perfect. He just wanted this to run smoothly, and having a damn suit processor fail on them wasn't that.

Kasey cleared his throat, and Connor turned back around. A small boy was looking at him, and his gaze narrowed suspiciously.

Connor waved. "Hello there, Citizen," he said, using the deepest official voice he could muster.

The boy's eyes widened and he backed away a few steps. Then he turned around and darted over to his family.

"Check this out," Kasey said, gesturing toward the wallscreen.

The image of a massive spaceship under construction at the Martian shipyards was displayed and a commentator began to speak:

The Ark—humanity's valiant effort to reach beyond the confines of our solar system to establish the first interstellar colony out among the stars. We're now just weeks away from the Ark's christening, Earth's first interstellar colony ship will begin the longest journey ever embarked upon by mankind—a journey that began over a hundred years ago in 2105 when the star XPA6 was first observed among a group that held our best hope of an Earth-sized planet. Probes were sent out to see if any of these stars could support life as we experience it here on Earth. In 2182 we finally got our answer and the Ark program was born. Now, in 2217, three hundred thousand people will embark on a journey that will take eighty-four years to complete...

Connor stopped listening and glanced at the info-terminal beneath the wallscreen. The train was approaching their stop. "You have twenty-five seconds to get it fixed," he whispered.

The boy returned with a teenage girl who was probably his older sister, followed by his parents. The boy was gesturing toward them.

Connor stopped himself from shaking his head. He hadn't come all this way to be pestered by an overprivileged eleven-year-old brat. Connor faced them and put as much stern into his stance as he could while the others stood poised to knock out the family with stunners if they became a problem.

Just look away, kid, Connor pleaded in his mind.

The train came to a stop and Connor felt someone tap his shoulder.

"I'm feeling much better now. Thank you," Samson said, but his voice sounded like that of a woman.

"I'm glad to hear it," Connor replied.

The boy rubbed the back of his head as if he wasn't quite sure what he'd seen while his father ushered him off the train. Connor motioned for his squad to wait a few seconds and then they exited the train as well.

"Commander, I bypassed a bad processor branch, but the hologram's gonna overload it if we can't find cover in a few minutes," Reisman said.

"Understood," Connor replied.

They quickly left the platform and headed toward a nearby service tunnel. His nav computer noted the change in their path and updated the time-to-destination on his helmet's heads-up display.

With Reisman close behind, Samson went ahead to the maintenance tunnels, where they overrode the locking mechanism and went inside. They locked the door behind them and Connor hoped the unauthorized access hadn't been detected. One by one they disengaged the holograms and their combat suits returned to a deep gunmetal-gray color.

Connor retrieved his M32 from his storage compartment and the others did the same. Now was the time for speed, so they blazed a path through the maintenance tunnels that were normally frequented by maintenance bots. The bots hardly registered that they were in the tunnel with them, most likely due to the bots' rudimentary recognition systems determining the Ghosts' combat suits were just more bots on maintenance duty.

The Syndicate's stronghold was in the middle level of the station toward the interior. This was the part of the station that would be least vulnerable to attack. Connor had studied the station's schematics and knew all the ins and outs for this section. He'd seen enough military installations to recognize the design, even with the lavish furnishings. According to the schematics, they were on the premises of a luxurious hotel.

They came to a stop outside a maintenance door. Connor was certain it was being monitored, so he gestured for Reisman.

The tech specialist moved forward. "Nothing to see here. Just another lowly maintenance bot trudging along," Reisman muttered.

The door retracted into the ceiling, and the Ghosts went through to a nearby station where two guards were posted. The guards glanced over toward the open door, and when no maintenance bot came through, one of them went over to investigate.

The guard peered through the door and activated his comlink. "Central, we have a maintenance door open on Deck 19, but no bot has come through. Do you have any bots on sensors?"

The guard stepped through the doorway. The door shut, and he turned and banged at it from the other side.

Connor engaged the charge they'd placed and the banging stopped. The Ghosts then waited while the second guard came out of the station to investigate. As he stepped away, Connor fired a stunner dart into the guard's exposed neck, the shock of which caused the guard to drop to the ground, unconscious.

"Station 19, do you copy?"

Connor glanced at Reisman, who nodded that he was okay to speak.

"We're here, Central. That door is shut now and won't open. We'll need to schedule a repair crew to come check it out," Connor said. The hacked signal disguised his voice based on the speech patterns recorded from when the guard had spoken earlier.

"Confirm. Repair crew will be sent out. Carry on."

The comlink signal deactivated, and Connor looked at Reisman. "Good work," he said and looked over at Kasey. "Any word from Bravo Squad?"

Kasey shook his head. "Negative, sir."

"Alright, we go on. You're cleared to only engage hostiles, so if you don't see a weapon, we can't use ours. Clear?" Connor said.

The squad replied that they understood.

"Okay, Samson, you're on point with Jefferson and Oslo," Connor said. "Reisman, you're with me. Kasey, you're with the others."

Samson was six feet eight inches tall and a bear of man. Connor had seen him fire a T49 assault rifle in each hand while maintaining accuracy.

Samson led them forward, and Jefferson covered him. Oslo was just behind. The trio moved forward on point, and the rest of the squad followed in pairs. They left the maintenance tunnels behind and made their way through the lower levels of the hotel, stopping at a service elevator and waiting while Reisman overrode the controls so they could get to the sixtieth floor.

Reisman stopped what he was doing and looked at Connor. "Special access required, even to put in the floor number. If I override it, they'll likely detect it."

Connor's brows pulled together in thought. "What about the fifty-ninth floor? Can you get us close?"

Reisman checked. "Ah, there it is. Fifty-eighth floor is still under construction."

"Perfect," Connor said.

Reisman punched in the new destination and the service elevator began its ascent. Connor would have preferred to break the squads up into six-man teams lest one of them got pinned down, but he chose speed over caution for this op. He checked the comms status for Bravo Squad, which was being led by Denton, but there was nothing. He had doubled up for this op, breaking their platoon into two squads. They had separate ships and approach vectors, but even with comms blackout there still should have been at least an encoded check-in. Connor frowned and felt the hairs on the back of his neck stand on end—a feeling he'd get when an op was about to go south.

The service elevator stopped and the Ghosts readied their weapons. When the doors pulled apart, a dark, half-finished floor could be seen beyond. Samson checked his corner while Jefferson checked the other. Both men ducked out of the elevator with two more Ghosts behind them. The rest of them followed, and Connor scanned the area ahead. There were large stacks of construction materials amid offline machinery. Connor narrowed his gaze and switched to enhanced view, cycling through different bands until the area came alive with soldiers wearing combat suits just like theirs.

"Take cover!" Connor cried and lunged behind the nearest construction vehicle.

The rest of the Ghosts scattered toward cover as the Syndicate soldiers opened fire. The head of the Syndicate had known they were coming for them. This whole op had been a trap.

2

BLISTERING weapons fire tore into the machine Connor hid behind. The Ghosts were seasoned professionals who were at home on any battlefield, whether on a ship, on a space station, or in the jungles of South America. They spread out and took cover, returning fire while they evaluated the battlefield.

Connor set his ammo to frag grenades, stuck his M32 rifle around the corner, and saw where two enemy soldiers huddled behind a stack of metal beams. He angled the rifle up and his targeting computer identified the proper angle. Connor fired a grenade.

The Syndicate was down two soldiers.

Samson unleashed his T49 at full auto, and Jefferson did the same. Connor moved to the other end of the machinery he was using for cover, and Kasey came to his side. Across from them was a crane. He needed to get over to it so he could flank their attackers.

"I'll cover you," Kasey said and brought up his pulse rifle.

Connor sprinted across amidst a hailstorm of deadly fire from Syndicate mercenaries while Kasey provided covering fire as promised. Connor felt several shots glance off his armor as he slammed into the crane and circled around, flanking the four-man firing team that kept Kasey pinned. Connor aimed and fired his M32, taking out two Syndicate soldiers, then ducked back behind the crane as the remaining two soldiers fired their weapons at him and Kasey seized the opportunity to take them out.

Connor opened a storage compartment in the leg of his suit and pulled out two drone spheres, flinging them up into the air and activating them. The drones split apart. One zoomed directly over the enemy while the other went across the battlefield. The active drones sent data back to Connor's combat suit.

"This was a trap, but I think we got here sooner than they expected," Kasey said.

"We'll continue to flank them and stay out of the choke points," Connor said.

He sent his orders over the secure comlink and the Ghosts moved forward. The Syndicate soldiers were likely ex-military, and their tactics might have worked on a different platoon.

"Jefferson's down," Oslo shouted.

"I'm coming," Malarkey said over the comlink.

Connor watched as his medic hugged the ground and crawled toward Jefferson. Samson bellowed as he provided covering fire. Connor and Kasey continued up the side, using massive metal girders for cover. They'd flanked the soldiers that had Samson and others pinned down, and the two groups ping-ponged the Syndicate soldiers. Agility was essential for blazing through the battlefield.

Malarkey opened a comlink to Connor. "Jefferson's gone, sir. They hit him with something that ate through his armor—"

Malarkey stopped speaking and started screaming.

"Commander, Malarkey and Woods are down," Sawyer said.

Connor swore, hating what he was about to do. "Bring out the NESS and avoid Malarkey and Woods."

The nano-robotic explosive seeker swarm, NESS, was a last-resort weapon that could level the whole floor. Oslo pulled out a metal canister and keyed in the activation code on the panel, then hurled the canister past the Syndicate soldiers and tumbled away. A weaponized nano-robotic swarm burst from the canister.

"I've sent the clean-and-sweep protocol, sir," Kasey said.

There was a bright flash, and the bodies of their fallen soldiers disintegrated. There could be no trace of the Ghosts having been here. Connor heard Samson growl as he kept firing his weapon at full auto. There were more reinforcements bolstering the Syndicate ranks.

"Damn it! Where is the NESS?" Connor demanded.

"Online now, sir. It'll be in position in twenty seconds," Tiegan replied.

The NESS interface came online, and as commanding officer, Connor had to be the one to authorize its use. But the Syndicate soldiers had stopped firing their weapons, so Connor brought up the drone feeds. A woman stood in the middle of an open area and stared defiantly at the drones.

Connor sent out the cease-fire signal to his team.

"The fabled Ghost Platoon. I must admit I'm impressed with your performance. You did much better than that other team," the woman said.

Connor ignored the bait and stayed behind cover. "Then you know it's hopeless. We've got you. The Syndicate is finished," he said and peeked around the corner.

The woman looked to be in her mid-forties and wore a blue business suit, but due to the possibility of prolonging, there was no way for Connor to tell how old she was. She could have been anywhere from a hundred to two hundred years old, and there wasn't an ounce of fear in her cold gaze hidden under a mask of amusement.

"Did you really think that if you came here and destroyed this place the Syndicate would just disappear? That I have no contingency plans?"

"I'd call it a good start. I'll find whoever your successor is and take them out as well. You see, your operations at Sandy Springs got the attention of some pretty powerful people, and I'm authorized to take you out," Connor said.

The minimum time required for the NESS to move the pieces into position was twenty seconds, but this conversation was allowing it to probe deeper into the structure of the building.

The woman smiled. "Tell me, Connor, which R&D company do you think came up with the NESS?"

Kasey glanced at him and Connor's eyes widened. She knew his name.

"Are you saying you invented the NESS?" Connor asked.

He stayed focused but also kept wondering how the hell this bitch knew his name.

"Connor Gates, rank colonel, commanding officer of the Ghosts Special Forces Platoon in service of the North American Union Alliance. Believe me when I tell you that there isn't a member of your platoon we don't have detailed files on," the woman said.

Connor took a shot, aiming a foot above the woman's head. The woman's form wavered for a moment and the hologram vanished. In her place was a large mech that dropped its stealth field.

"You know an awful lot about me," Connor said.

"Indeed we do. You can call me RJ," the same woman's voice said from the mech's speakers.

"Okay, RJ, you must know there's no way you're walking out of here alive," Connor said.

RJ laughed. "You've been at a disadvantage since you started hunting the Syndicate because your small mind cannot grasp what the Syndicate actually is. We're everywhere. There isn't a part of your world that isn't touched by us."

"I think you have an over-bloated sense of self-worth, pretty common in megalomaniacs. I've taken a few down in my career, and I'm ready to add you to the list," Connor said.

He brought the NESS interface up on his suit computers and was about to activate the device. The rest of the Ghosts continued to identify targets and escape routes.

"I wouldn't do that if I were you," RJ said.

"You're not me," Connor replied.

"If you engage the NESS, you'll destroy this entire station, not just this floor as you were expecting. I know the rules of engagement, Colonel, and your authorization to take me out doesn't include the wholesale slaughter of millions of people," RJ said.

The NESS they'd brought with them didn't have anywhere near the ordnance to destroy the station.

"Some might consider the price worth it," Connor bluffed.

"Your military record says otherwise."

"If you were willing to destroy this station, you would have done it already, unless we really did catch you off guard and you're stalling for time," Connor said.

He opened up a comlink to Reisman. "Can you confirm what she's saying?"

"I've been trying since she first mentioned it, sir. I've got nothing. The NESS has been deployed and has converged on the support structure of this floor."

"Why don't you come out from where you're hiding?" RJ said. "I've ordered my forces not to fire on you."

Connor shook his head. "You'll have to forgive me if I don't take your word for it."

He checked the status of the other Ghosts. They'd all lined up shots on the large mech. If he gave the order, that mech would be taken out in seconds.

"You're still trying to figure out whether I'm telling you the truth. I will admit you've been a thorn in my side for longer than most. I'll tell you what. I know your tech specialist is trying to determine whether my threat to the station is real or not. I'll save him the trouble," RJ said.

Connor glanced over at Reisman and his eyes became as wide as saucers. "There's a NESS deployed station wide. It's on every level!"

Connor's gut clenched. They were in a stalemate. His mind raced, trying to find some way he could achieve their objective and not lose the station. The NESS required specialized encrypted protocols that couldn't be copied. Reisman was good, but no one could break it. RJ's thumb was on the trigger to take out the entire station.

"We walk away and—" Connor began.

"Not quite as ruthless as your reputation says you are. You're the first person in a hundred years to be in my presence and able to inflict physical harm, and the thought of killing millions of people shatters your resolve? This encounter hasn't been as illuminating as I'd hoped it would be," RJ said.

The large mech took several steps back.

"Why? Because I won't play your game?" Connor asked.

The mech stopped. "You've been playing my game, Colonel, for the past five years. Granted, your presence here denotes a hole in our security that will soon be rectified."

"Sir, the NESS field is being activated," Reisman said.

"What are you doing! I already said I'd let you go," Connor shouted.

He came out from cover and pointed his weapon at the head of the Syndicate. The mech kept moving backward and Connor fired his weapon. "Is that all this was? A way for you to test your security?"

"Goodbye, Colonel. We won't be meeting again," RJ said.

Syndicate troops resumed firing on them and Connor scrambled behind cover. He emptied his mag of frag grenades, laying fiery waste to the Syndicate troops, and then pulled back toward Reisman.

"Can you block the signal?" Connor asked.

Reisman shook his head. "According to this, the signal was sent before we even got to the station. It's been on a timer . . ." His voice trailed off as if he couldn't believe what he was seeing.

Connor tried to access the station's systems, looking for a way to signal the evacuation protocols.

"Sir, we need to fall back," Kasey said.

Connor glanced the way RJ had gone.

"There's a way out if we go this way," Kasey said.

Connor looked where Kasey was gesturing. The path lay in the opposite direction. This whole thing had been staged, and the worst part was that RJ wanted them to escape. Connor turned back toward where the Syndicate forces had retreated and screamed.

Kasey grabbed him and spun him around, putting his head inches from Connor's own. "Listen to me. You found her once. If we get out of here, we can find her again."

Kasey let go of him, and Connor looked at Reisman. "Try and signal the evacuation using any protocols you can find. Use anything to signal that something is wrong with the station."

Connor gave the order for them to retreat, and the acid taste of bile crept up his throat. They quickly made their way to the edge of the floor as the NESS triggered the explosions, stemming from the far side of Chronos Station.

"Combat shuttle en route," Kasey informed them.

Samson placed breaching explosives on the outer walls of the station. Once they detonated, a containment field would become active that would prevent the atmosphere from escaping, but the field wouldn't prevent them from leaving.

"We can wait to be picked up. Use your suit jets to get clear of the station and head toward the rendezvous point marked on your heads-up display," Connor said.

The Ghosts leaped out of the gaping hole, and Connor waited for them to go. He kept glancing at the Chronos Station info terminal feed, which showed the number of residences numbered in the millions. Powerless to stop the destruction, Connor felt the crushing weight of the soon-to-be-dead pressing in on him. With one last glance at the station's interior, he leaped away from Chronos Station.

3

THE COMBAT SHUTTLE'S autopilot honed in on their beacons and found the remains of the Ghosts. They'd never heard from Bravo Squad. The NESS detonated on Chronos Station, having used its advanced targeting artificial intelligence to position all the pieces at the weakest points. Something as large as a space station that was home to millions of people would have taken weeks for the NESS to deploy. When the NESS went active, there were fiery explosions that were instantly expunged by the fire suppression systems of the station. What killed all the people was the collapse of the station's superstructure, which overwhelmed any redundancy systems in place.

"Anything show up on the scanners?" Connor asked.

He'd hoped there would be some evidence of a ship leaving, but a debris field as massive as Chronos Station had overwhelmed the combat shuttle scanners.

"Negative, Commander," Reisman said.

Connor nodded, having expected as much despite his fool's hope for a break. The remaining Ghosts lined the shuttle, looking as shocked as he felt. Connor had to address them.

"Men," Connor said, "we've lost some of our own today—Jefferson, Malarkey, Oslo, Denton . . ." Connor went on to list all twelve members of Bravo Squad, and each name was like a punch to the throat. "I want you all to know— and this is on the record—that I take full responsibility for what happened. I've punched in the coordinates for the shuttle to return to COMCENT."

"With all due respect, sir, that's bullshit," Samson said.

"The Syndicate laid a trap for us. We were there. There was no way they were going to let us go without blowing the station," Reisman said.

Connor fixed them all with a stern glare. "My op. My objective. My command. My responsibility."

The Ghosts looked at him with mixed expressions.

Kasey cleared his throat. "Why don't we take a few minutes to calm down and then decide our next steps?"

"The decision has been made. You'll get a new CO and they'll likely promote you, Kasey," Connor said.

Kasey was about to respond when klaxon alarms signaled a target lock on their shuttle.

Reisman raced back to the shuttle's cockpit.

"Sir, the Battleship Carrier *Indianapolis* is two hundred thousand kilometers from our starboard bow. They're hailing us," Reisman said.

"Open a channel," Connor said.

"Combat Shuttle *Trident*, you're to change your heading to the following coordinates. Failure to comply will be considered an act of aggression that will be dealt with swiftly. *Indianapolis* out."

"They've sent us an intercept course," Reisman said.

Connor reviewed the coordinates. "Follow it," he said. They couldn't outrun a Barracuda-class battleship carrier. He glanced at Kasey. "What do you make of this?"

Kasey looked at the coordinates and frowned. "They don't want us coming in through the main hangar."

"Who's the CO of the *Indianapolis*?" Connor asked.

"We're locked out, sir. Once I put in the new coordinates, they took control of the shuttle's navigation systems and everything else," Reisman said, thrusting his hands in the air helplessly.

"*After* the new coordinates were entered?" Connor asked.

"Affirmative, sir," Reisman said.

Kasey leaned over. "What do you think it means?"

"I think it was a test, but without knowing who's in command, there's no way for us to know for sure," Connor replied.

Kasey frowned and gestured for Connor to step aside so the others couldn't hear them. "They're all thinking it, so I've got to say it."

Connor's brows pushed forward. "Captain."

"Not now. I'm speaking to you as a friend. I can't let you take the fall for this," Kasey said.

"You objected to this whole op because of the civilian presence. I wouldn't listen," Connor said and shushed Kasey as he began to speak. "I appreciate what you're trying to do, but I made the call and this is my burden to bear."

Kasey glared at him.

"Uh, sir, they're guiding us to a small cargo bay on the port side," Reisman said.

"Acknowledged," Connor replied.

The combat shuttle quickly closed in on the battleship carrier, and Connor glanced out the shuttle's windows. He'd begun his military career serving aboard a carrier like this. The NA Alliance Space Navy was a mix of the military branches of old, with each performing their specialized tasks. He'd first been recruited into the special forces and then into the Ghosts. Black ops had been his home for much of his career, so it was fitting that it was all coming to an end on a ship like this.

As the combat shuttle was remotely guided in, Connor started to make his way toward the rear of the shuttle but stopped as Kasey spoke.

"Officer on deck," Kasey bellowed and stood at attention.

The rest of the Ghosts came to their feet and saluted Connor, and although he wasn't one for emotions, his throat thickened at the gesture. They'd bled together, and some of them had died along the way. Connor returned the salute and headed for the back of the shuttle where the hatch was. The shuttle came to a stop and the rear doors opened. Connor expected to be greeted by a company of troops ordered to take them all into custody. Instead, there was only the *Indianapolis's* executive officer, along with five soldiers.

Connor stepped off the shuttle and saluted the XO, who was an older man, appearing to be a bit out of breath. The soldiers kept checking the area and hardly paid any attention at all to the Ghosts.

"Colonel Gates?" the XO asked.

"Yes, sir."

"I'm Captain Tung Yep. We don't have much time. If you and your team will please follow me," the captain said.

Captain Tung Yep didn't wait for a reply and turned around, walking away. Connor jogged to catch up with him.

"Are you the commanding officer of this ship, sir?" Connor asked.

"No," Captain Tung Yep said. "My orders are to retrieve you and your team and escort you to cargo bay D97. I don't have time for questions."

Connor didn't press the captain for any more information since he doubted he'd get anything useful. The rest of the Ghosts followed him. They'd been allowed to keep their weapons, so they weren't being taken into custody for the moment.

"Captain, I'm prepared to make a full report regarding the events on Chronos Station," Connor said.

Captain Tung Yep was leading them through a series of darkened corridors whose ambient lighting came on when their presence was detected.

"Stop right there, Colonel. Not another word," Captain Tung Yep said. "I can't know anything else about who you are other than to confirm your identity and then deliver you into someone else's custody. If you tell me anything about the events that have transpired in the last twenty-four hours, it will be considered an act of treason and I'll be forced to take you and your men into custody while an official investigation is launched."

Connor nodded, finally understanding why the captain didn't want to hear what he had to say. He'd been involved in enough missions that fell into the military "gray area" to recognize when the rules were being bent, but he had no idea who his mysterious benefactor was.

Captain Tung Yep came to a stop in front of a pair of wide doors. He gave his authorization and the door opened to a dimly lit room beyond.

"Colonel, this is where I leave you," the captain said, and then he and his five-soldier escort disappeared down a nearby corridor.

For a moment, Connor hovered in the doorway. The cavernous room beyond was some sort of storage area.

"Step inside, Colonel Gates," a voice called from inside.

The voice sounded wizened, carrying a tough rasp to it as if the owner of the voice had been in command longer than Connor had been alive.

Connor stepped inside and was quickly followed by the rest of the Ghosts. A few of them whispered to each other.

"You can leave your weapons in the containers to the side," the voice said.

Connor saw the faint outline of a man standing just outside the lighted area.

Connor frowned. "Of course. Right after you step into the light."

"You always were a stubborn pain in the ass, Gates. Can't you just do as you're told?"

An old man stepped into the light. Four thick gold bars rested on his sleeves.

"Admiral, sir," Connor said and stood at attention.

The Ghosts instantly followed Connor's example.

Fleet Admiral Mitch Wilkinson stepped before Connor and regarded him for a moment. "You know, if you'd joined the space navy and transferred under my command when I asked you to all those years ago, you'd have avoided this mess," the admiral said. "At ease."

Knowing better than to question the orders of a flag officer, Connor's squad went over to the storage containers and stowed their weapons. Kasey took Connor's M32 from him.

"You know me, sir. I learned from the best," Connor said.

He hadn't seen Wilkinson in almost twenty years. Wilkinson had served with Connor's father.

Admiral Wilkinson looked over at the Ghosts. "Combat suits too," he said and gestured for Connor to do the same.

Connor went over to his team and engaged the shutdown protocols for his combat suit. The armored unit split down the chest and opened. Connor stepped out and immediately became aware of his lack of personal hygiene over the last thirty-six hours.

"Come on back. I'm sure you're nice and ripe, but it's certainly not going to kill me," Admiral Wilkinson said.

Connor went back over to the admiral. "I'm sure you didn't just happen to be in the neighborhood, sir."

"No, you're right about that. The destruction of Chronos Station is going to have swift repercussions. It's only a matter of time before a scapegoat is targeted."

"How would anyone even know we were involved?" Connor asked.

"You think the Syndicate is beyond releasing the names of you and your team to the public?"

Connor went cold. If working in black ops had taught him anything it was that keeping your identity secret was paramount—both for your protection and that of your loved ones.

"There's no way the alliance military will condone the actions that led to the station being destroyed. You'll be branded terrorists, hunted down, tossed in jail, and probably executed for treason."

Connor felt heat rush to his face. It was like explosions were going off in his head. An image of his son, Sean, came to the forefront of his mind. The last time he'd seen him he'd been three years old, and that had been eight years ago. He glanced over at his team. They were all in danger. Some of them had families.

"Now before you do anything stupid, you and what remains of your team need to follow me," Admiral Wilkinson said.

4

CONNOR FOLLOWED ADMIRAL WILKINSON. More lights came on, revealing a massive warehouse filled with storage containers that were marked with a golden sunburst.

"Recognize it?" Wilkinson asked.

Connor shook his head. "No, sir."

The admiral nodded. "Never mind that. Why don't you tell me what really happened on Chronos Station."

Connor followed the admiral through a maze of storage containers all marked with the golden sunburst. He filled Wilkinson in on the op, figuring at this point he had nothing to lose. It was a break in protocol, but all black ops teams accepted the fact that there might be a time when COMCENT needed to disavow all knowledge of them and the operation they were part of. Flag officers like Admiral Wilkinson were privy to knowledge that most others wouldn't be. It came with the job. Connor broke down his recent activities in his hunt for the Syndicate—from the pieces of intelligence they'd gathered that put them on the path to Chronos Station to getting inside and storming the Syndicate stronghold.

They reached the edge of the warehouse, where there were several rooms, and Connor recognized a mobile medical unit setup. The people inside wore blue uniforms with a gold caduceus on the shoulders. One of the men walked over to them.

"We're ready for them, sir," the man said. He was of Asian ancestry, but he spoke as if he'd grown up south of the Mason-Dixon line.

"Connor, this is Lieutenant Kim. He needs to do a quick check of you and your men," Wilkinson said.

Connor frowned. "We're not due for med checks. What's this all about?"

"Just a precaution. I'll be across the hall, waiting for you," Wilkinson said and entered an office.

"Shouldn't keep the old man waiting, sir," Lieutenant Kim said and gestured to the room.

Connor nodded for his squad to go inside and then followed. Doctor Kim pulled him out of the line to go first, saying the admiral had specified that Connor be checked first. Connor followed the doctor to one of the exam tables and granted access to his biochip. Within moments, all his medical history appeared on the doctor's mobile holoscreen. Lieutenant Kim flipped through the history and noted Connor's vital signs, which confirmed his excellent health. The doctor brought up a secondary screen that looked to have information about Connor's physiology. The information on the screen went by so quickly that Connor couldn't read it. A panel hissed opened from the bottom of a cabinet, and cold vapor licked the edges. Lieutenant Kim reached inside and pulled out a medical injection gun. Inside the small tank was blue liquid.

"What's that, Doc?" Connor asked.

"It's a booster shot for your nanites. Your records showed you were out of date."

The doctor came over and pressed the metal tip against the side of Connor's neck, squeezing the trigger and pushing the actuator forward, forcing the cocktail of blue liquid past his skin.

"You're all set. We'll check out the rest of your team, but the admiral's waiting for you," Lieutenant Kim said.

Connor rubbed his neck and glanced over at Kasey and the others. In response, Kasey jutted his chin up once with a slight raise of his brows. It was something he'd always done to let Connor know everything was fine.

Connor looked at the rest of the team calmly awaiting their turn to be checked by the doctors. More than a few looked over in his direction. He'd been their CO for years and they'd been through hell together, and yet today he felt he'd let them down. He kept going over the events that had led to the standoff with the head of the Syndicate. He doubted RJ was even her name. And was the person behind the voice even a woman? In hindsight, he kept thinking that instead of hunting his prey, he'd been led by the nose. He left the room and stood out in the hall. His breath quickened and he balled his hands into fists.

Connor heard slow footsteps from across the hall, and Admiral Wilkinson's steely-eyed gaze regarded him. There was neither judgment nor compassion in Wilkinson's slate-blue eyes—just an acknowledgment shared by those who were in command. Lives were always on the line, and today, lives had been lost. A lot of them.

Wilkinson waved him inside the office. News feeds showed on the wallscreen.

"Have you heard about this?" Wilkinson asked and gestured toward the screen.

Connor looked over and the feed showed a commentator on a ship in one of Earth's oceans.

"We've studied almost every square kilometer of our solar system, built colonies on Mars and Venus and space stations among the outer planets, and we're still making discoveries back home. We're only scratching the surface of the secrets in our own oceans," Wilkinson said.

Connor glanced at the screen again and then back at the admiral. "Permission to speak freely, sir."

"Granted."

"Why did you bring us here?"

Wilkinson waved his hand and the news feed stopped. He then gestured for Connor to sit down while he took his own seat.

"There're no two ways about it. You're in the shit. As deep as one can go. Before we go into all that, what were your future plans?"

Connor's mouth hung open. "My future plans? Millions of people are dead and you want to ask me about future plans?"

"I had my intelligence analyst pull your records from the shuttle. They sent me the information you intended to file in your report. A mass-destruction NESS was deployed throughout Chronos Station. The NESS was brought online and activated, causing catastrophic destruction to the station. Nowhere does this report say it was you who detonated the thing, and I know a team like yours doesn't bring enough ordnance to destroy an entire space station," Wilkinson said.

"She used the transponder codes from our own NESS so when the salvage teams go through the wreckage, all fingers will be pointed at me and my team," Connor said.

"You think you're the first person to get kicked in the balls?"

"I don't know how you can equate me getting kicked in the balls with millions of people dying. If I had the bitch in my sights right now, I'd pull the trigger, no hesitation," Connor said.

Admiral Wilkinson sucked in a deep breath. "I need to know who you have left on Earth."

"Why do you want to know?"

Wilkinson let out a bitter laugh. "Stubborn right to the end. Your father was the same way. You're so angry you can hardly see straight and realize that I'm trying to help you. If you have anyone on Earth who's important to you, I need to know so they can be protected."

Connor swallowed hard. "Alyssa, my ex, and our son, Sean."

"I need more than names. I need last known locations. When was the last time you spoke to them?"

Connor's mind raced as he tried to think of the last time he'd seen his son. "It's been a few years," he said, his own voice sounding rough.

"How old is Sean now?"

Connor frowned. "He'd be eleven years old now."

A deep pang crushed Connor's chest. The primal need to protect his son that only showed itself in the quiet moments between missions pushed its way to the forefront of his mind.

"You haven't seen your son in years?" Wilkinson asked, unable to keep the disbelief from his voice.

"He needed a father who was going to be there for him, not someone who was away on deployment eleven months out of the year . . ."

Wilkinson shook his head. "A boy deserves to have a father in his life, even if that father is married to the mission."

Connor's vision swam as if he were looking down a long tunnel. A spike of adrenaline pushed the darkness back and he felt as if he were sinking into the chair. "What have you done to me?"

Connor looked toward the door where his team was and surged to his feet. He took a step and stumbled to the floor.

The admiral knelt down beside him. "Try to relax."

"The doctor didn't give me a booster shot," Connor said, his words slurring as if he were drunk on too much whiskey.

He tried to crawl, but his arms and legs wouldn't move. The last thing that registered in his mind was the southern drawl of Lieutenant Kim speaking.

Admiral Wilkinson rose to his feet and looked down at the unconscious form of Connor Gates. He'd promised David that he'd look after his son, which had been all but impossible with Connor choosing to join the special forces.

"It took them all a while to go down," Doctor Kim said and waved for his staff to come in and retrieve Connor.

"To be expected. The Ghosts would no doubt all have been using the latest implants and nanite technology that aren't available anywhere else," Wilkinson said. "Your staff . . . have they been briefed?"

"Of course, sir, as you specified. We were never here and none of this happened," Lieutenant Kim said. "But can I ask you a question, sir?"

"Go ahead."

"I just don't understand why."

Wilkinson sighed and regarded the doctor. "I've served the NA Alliance for a long time. Life for the cause, but sometimes the laws and procedures we fight to protect aren't good enough to effectively judge our soldiers. The Ghosts deserved better than what they were going to get."

"I don't understand. Are you so certain they would have been implicated, much less convicted of a crime?"

"The Syndicate has a lot of influence, and I'm unwilling to take the chance, not when I have a debt to pay."

Stasis tubes were being lined up in the hallway.

"Sir, what happens to them now?" Lieutenant Kim asked.

"You and your staff have done a great service, but your task is done," Wilkinson said.

The lieutenant's eyes widened, and Wilkinson was once again struck by a doctor's sense of entitlement. "We can't just leave them here. They need to be monitored . . ." The lieutenant's voice trailed off as a squad of soldiers without rank or insignia marched down the hallway.

"They'll be taken care of, I promise," Wilkinson said.

The mobile medical unit left them, and Wilkinson made a mental note to have them watched to be sure they kept their mouths shut.

One of the soldiers approached. "We're here to transport the cargo, sir."

"One minute," Wilkinson said, and the soldier stepped to the side.

Wilkinson reached into his pocket and withdrew a data storage stick. He walked over to Connor's stasis tube and opened the access panel, glancing at the stick that held the recorded message he'd hastily done while Connor was in with the doctors. After a moment he shoved it inside and closed the panel. He'd done all he could.

Wilkinson turned around. "Daniels," he said, "take these containers to the Ark Project and mark them for transfer to permanent storage. At no time are these containers to be out of your care until they're permanently stowed. Is that clear?"

"Absolutely, sir. We'll report back to you when it's finished," Daniels said.

Wilkinson knew the soldier could be trusted, but he still had a lot of favors to call in to make this work. He would have liked to have done more. Lord knows Connor deserved better than this, and he hoped that one day Connor would forgive him for what was about to happen. But . . . better to ask forgiveness than permission.

"Carry on," Wilkinson said and returned to the small office.

"Ship's log," Wilkinson said. The ship's computer chimed, indicating the log was open. "*Indianapolis* was the first ship to find the wreckage of Chronos Station. Preliminary scans indicate there were no survivors or ships detected nearby. We'll be conducting an investigation and reporting our findings.

"Computer, package the log and beam a transmission back to COMCENT."

5

CONNOR FELT something tugging him from a deep sleep. The more awake he became, the more he became aware of the tingling pain he felt in his hands and feet. It felt as if his eyes were pinned down by steel weights and refused all his attempts to open them. There was something hard in his throat. He heard the sound of muffled voices speaking but couldn't understand them. Connor tried to cough, and his throat muscles worked to expel the hard rod that was in his mouth. He raised his hands, but someone held him down. The tube in his throat was yanked out. He winced and coughed weakly, spitting out a foul-tasting liquid as someone helped roll him to his side.

"Give yourself a few moments to adjust. We've just pulled you from stasis," a woman's voice said.

Connor couldn't tell if he was just having a really bad dream or if he'd awakened to a nightmare where he was trapped in his own body, unable to move.

"Can he answer questions yet?" a man's voice shrilled.

Though Connor couldn't open his eyes, the man's tone grated on his nerves.

"Not yet, Dr. Baker. He's only just come around," the woman said.

Connor heard someone stomp across the floor.

"I don't know how this could have happened. Dr. Peter Faulkner, the eminent planetary scientist, was supposed to be in his pod. That's not him," the man said.

Sounds of footsteps stomped closer to Connor.

"Hey, can you hear me? We need to know your name."

"Doctor, please. He just needs a few minutes for the stasis drugs to wear off. We've got revival protocols to follow. Perhaps you should step outside."

"Don't get snippy with me, Kara."

"Of course, Dr. Baker," Kara said.

Connor was gently rolled onto his back, and the bed he was in started to rise. It was hard to think. He pushed his eyes open, and it was like trying to see through thick syrup. Connor squeezed his eyes shut and moaned. Someone pressed a cool wet towel on his face and wiped the gooey substance from his eyes. Connor opened them and saw a young woman looking down at him. She smiled.

"Take it easy and give the revival cocktail some time to work. You're likely to feel a bit off until it starts to kick in," Kara said.

Connor cleared his throat. Everything about his body felt wrong.

"Drink this. It will help," Kara said and put a straw in his mouth.

Connor sucked down the liquid, which contained a faint trace of cinnamon. He drank a few mouthfuls and coughed because his throat refused to work properly. A thin man with beady eyes glared at him.

"Do you know where you are?"

"Doctor—" Kara began.

Dr. Baker swung his beady eyes toward the woman. "Thank you, Kara. I'll take it from here. I'm sure you have other patients to check on."

Kara glanced at Connor regretfully. "I'll be just outside," she said and left the room.

Dr. Baker walked to the side of the bed, snapping his fingers in front of Connor's face and then by his ears. He shined a bright light in Connor's face. Connor tried to raise his arm, and the doctor glanced down.

"Motor control and response to stimuli are normal," Dr. Baker said. He leaned down. "So I know you can hear me. I don't know who the hell you are, but you'd better start answering questions."

"What are you talking about?" Connor said, his voice sounding gravelly in his own ears.

"This is taking too long," Dr. Baker said and crossed the room. He pulled a syringe from a container and filled it with clear liquid from a vial.

Connor tried to wave the doctor off, but he was too weak.

"Now, this will sting a little," Dr. Baker said and jabbed the thick needle into Connor's thigh.

White fiery pain shot through his system as if there were lightning burning through his veins. Connor screamed and grabbed the doctor by his shirt, pulling him in. Dr. Baker's eyes widened, and Connor growled as he shoved the doctor across the room. Whatever the doctor had given him had made him able to move, so Connor stood up as the doctor turned around. He limped over and grabbed the doctor, pulling him off balance while driving his knee into the doctor's chest.

"I'm sick of doctors sticking me with stuff, asshole," Connor said.

He shoved the stunned doctor into the wall, and the beady-eyed tyrant collapsed to the floor.

Connor became aware of a sharp pain in his thigh and saw that the syringe was still in his leg. He yanked it out and clutched it like a knife. "Let's see how you like being stuck."

Connor charged across the room, fist raised, but the door to the room opened and someone tackled him to the floor. Strong hands grabbed his arm, and he let go of the syringe. A man in a blue uniform tried to pin Connor down, but Connor twisted around and punched the guy in the stomach multiple times, then drove his palm up into the man's face. The man fell off him and Connor was on his feet instantly. There were screams coming from the hallway, and a wave of dizziness washed over him. Something hit him in the back, and a jolt of electricity brought Connor to his knees. He collapsed forward and his cheek slapped against the floor. A small amount of drool escaped his mouth and he groaned.

"What's going on here?" someone asked with the voice of authority.

"I'm sorry, Dr. Quinn. I left him alone with Dr. Baker and then I heard shouting coming from the room," Kara said.

"Alright. Let's get him up in that bed. Get the restraints on him," Dr. Quinn said.

Connor felt himself being lifted and taken back to his bed. Metallic straps raced across his body, securing him in place. He lay there, knowing the effects of the stunner used on him would only last for a short while. He watched as they carried Dr. Baker out and felt a small bit of satisfaction when he saw blood dripping down the doctor's face from a shallow gash on his forehead. He was really starting to hate doctors. Connor closed his eyes and drifted off to sleep.

Later on, Connor woke up again. He was alone in the room and the metallic restraints were still wrapped around his body so he couldn't move. The door opened and an older woman walked in, her long brown hair pulled back. She regarded him like a mother would a misbehaving child.

"You're awake. Have you calmed down?"

Connor nodded. He didn't know how long he'd slept, but he felt more refreshed than he had before.

"Good. I'm Ashley Quinn, head medical doctor on the Ark."

Great. Another damn doctor. "As long as you don't go sticking me with any needles, we'll get along fine," Connor said.

Ashley's lips curved. "Dr. Baker's bedside manner leaves much to be desired. I'm sorry about that."

"You can say that again," Connor replied.

He tried to stretch, but the restraints kept him in place.

"I'll make you a deal. I won't stick you with any needles unless you give me the okay, and I'll even let you out of those restraints if you promise not to attack anyone else. Deal?" Ashley said.

Connor nodded.

Ashley pressed her lips together. "I need to hear you say it."

Connor blew out a breath. "I promise. Why are you treating me like a child?"

"Vocalization of a promise has a higher success rate," Ashley said.

She tapped a few commands into her tablet computer and the metallic restraints retracted back into the bed.

Connor raised his arms and stretched, letting out a large yawn followed by a sigh. He hated being tied down. He glanced at the doctor. She was a handsome woman, and her confident gaze held none of the telltale signs of inexperience, despite her outward appearance. A wedding ring gleamed from her left hand.

"Where am I?" Connor asked.

"That's the real question, isn't it? I'm afraid it's going to take a bit of explaining," Ashley said and regarded him for a moment. "You look like you could stand stretching your legs a bit. Would you like to take a short walk?"

Connor looked down at his appearance. He had on a white close-knit unitard that strained against his muscles.

Ashley turned around and opened a cabinet door, pulling out some clothes, along with a pair of slippers, and tossing them on the bed. "I'll step outside while you get dressed. Then we can talk about where we are. And I'd like to find out more about you and what you remember."

Dr. Quinn turned and left the room. Connor glanced at the door as it shut and sighed. He pulled off the unitard and took a quick sniff. A musky scent assaulted his nostrils, and he flung the unitard into a container marked for laundry. He really wanted to take a shower and wash, but there was no bathroom in the room. He put on the gray shirt and sweatpants Dr. Quinn had found. The synthetic cotton felt soft against his skin. He slipped his feet into the slippers and headed for the door.

Connor stepped out into a long hallway where people were walking about from room to room. All of them were wearing some kind of blue uniform with a golden sunburst patch on the shoulder. He frowned, trying to remember where he'd seen that symbol before, but the vague memory remained stubbornly out of reach. To his left were two men with shock-sticks on their belts. The looks they gave him were neither challenging nor relenting.

"My office is up this way on the left," Dr. Quinn said.

Connor glanced at the two men and raised his eyebrows.

"You did cause quite a ruckus when they woke you up. Tim and Theo are here just in case," Dr. Quinn said.

Connor nodded, and they started walking down the hallway. He glanced inside some of the rooms and they all had stasis pods in them. None of the rooms had windows, so he couldn't use that to determine where he was. Connor found that the more he walked, the less stiff he became.

"I can have lunch brought up if you're hungry," Dr. Quinn said.

Connor frowned. "Why are you trying to be nice to me? It's not that I don't appreciate it, but . . ."

"I've found that common courtesy can go a long way, and I think we've gotten off on the wrong foot," Dr. Quinn said.

She opened a door to an office with a wide desk. Behind the desk was a window, but it was grayed out, so he couldn't see outside.

"Have a seat," she said and told Tim and Theo to wait outside.

Connor sat down in one of the plush chairs on the opposite side of the desk. Dr. Quinn sat down on the business side and opened up an info terminal.

"Okay, is this where the interrogation begins, Dr. Quinn?" Connor asked.

"No need to be so formal. You can call me Ashley if you want," she said and seemed to consider him for a moment. "If I had to guess, I'd say you've served in the military."

Connor didn't reply.

"I need to ask you a couple of questions before we get to explaining where we are. First, can you tell me the year?" Ashley asked.

"It's 2217," Connor said.

Ashley noted his answer. "Will you tell me your name?"

"Gates, Connor."

"So you *are* in the military," Ashley said.

"I'm not at liberty to say, ma'am."

Ashley smiled. "Ma'am. That's one I don't hear too often anymore," she said and entered his name into the info terminal. She waited a moment and then glanced at him. "It says here that you were NA Alliance Special Forces and you were killed in action."

Connor frowned and his gaze narrowed.

"Here, look," Ashley said and tapped a few commands in so a holoscreen appeared over the desk for him to see.

Connor's eyes widened. He was looking at his own service record, which was supposed to be sealed since he was black ops and the CO of the Ghosts.

Ashley pulled a data stick out from a drawer in her desk. "We found this in the storage unit of your pod for personal effects. Any idea what's on it? We tried to have a look, but it seems encoded for you."

Connor took the data stick from Ashley and looked at it. "I've never seen this before."

"It's fine. One of the side effects of long-term stasis is that sometimes your memory takes a little while to catch up."

"Long term? How long have I been in stasis?" Connor asked.

"We'll get to that, I promise," Ashley said.

"How about we get to it now? How long have I been in stasis?"

Ashley pressed her lips together. "It's been a while, but—"

Connor rose to his feet. "I want a straight answer right now."

He glanced at the information on the screen. "You shouldn't have access to that information. *I* don't even have access to it, which means you must be part of the NA Alliance Intelligence, high up in the chain of command. My commanding officer is Colonel Benjamin Crouse of the seventy-third brigade—" Connor stopped speaking. The image of an older man with gunmetal-gray hair appeared in his mind as if he were standing over him.

"You've just remembered something, haven't you?" Ashley asked.

"Admiral Wilkinson," Connor said.

Ashley entered the name in the search bar. "Admiral Mitch Wilkinson, CO of the Battleship Carrier *Indianapolis* from the years 2197 through 2220 . . . shit," she said.

"Twenty-two twenty! What the hell are you talking about? Have I been in stasis for three damn years?"

"Connor, please calm down. I'll tell you everything you want to know. Please, just sit down," Ashley said.

The door to her office opened and Tim stuck his beefy head in. Connor's breath came in gasps.

Three years in stasis. Fuck!

Tim and Theo hovered in the doorway.

"Connor, look at me. Never mind them. It's just you and me," Ashley said.

Connor swung his gaze toward her. "How long have I been in stasis?"

Ashley swallowed. "Two hundred years."

Connor frowned and tilted his head to the side as if he hadn't heard her. "Two hundred years? Is that what you said?"

Ashley held her hand up imploringly. "I know this is a lot to take in. You've been in stasis for two hundred years and eight months."

Connor couldn't catch his breath, and he clamped his hand down on the chair. Small sparkles of light flashed in his vision as he fought to remain conscious. He glanced at Ashley. "Please tell me this is some kind of joke."

"I wish it were a joke, but you've been in stasis for two hundred years like the rest of us," Ashley said.

Connor had spent a bulk of his career reading people and had a sense of whether he was being lied to or not. Everything in his gut told him Ashley was telling the truth.

"You've been in stasis for two hundred years too?" Connor asked.

Ashley nodded.

Connor started laughing and looked back at Tim and Theo hovering in the doorway. "You almost had me going. Did Wilkinson put you up to this?"

Ashley frowned. "No, I already told you I wasn't lying."

Connor craned his neck to see if anyone was behind Tim and Theo. "Is Kasey out there? Or Reisman?"

He took a step toward the door and Tim held up his hand.

"Clear window," Ashley said.

Connor turned around and looked out the window, which displayed a view of the black canopy of space on one side and a blue planet on the other. Instinctively, his eyes searched for the continents he expected to see, but the land masses were all out of place. A fuzzy area at the bottom of the window cleared last. Surrounding the planet were several distinct rings that resembled a vast expanse of highway made of light.

Connor slowly walked toward the window and gazed at the alien world. He turned toward Ashley, his mouth wide open.

"We're sixty light-years from Earth. The astronomers have an alpha-numeric designation for the star system, if you'd like to know it," Ashley said.

Connor looked back out the wide window. Off to the side and in the distance was a large cigar-shaped ship.

"What ship is that?" Connor asked.

"That's the *Galileo*. It's a seed ship, and it's been here for twenty-five years," Ashley said.

Connor brought his hands up to his head and raked them through his short hair. He couldn't stop looking out the window, but at the same time he couldn't believe what he was seeing. He felt his knees go weak and he leaned against the wall. Connor closed his eyes and felt like he was going to be sick.

Ashley came to his side and put her hand on his shoulder. "Just breathe. Everything is going to be fine."

Connor's mouth went dry and he couldn't catch his breath. He looked over at the door, where Tim and Theo looked back at him sympathetically. Connor gulped some air and sprinted toward the door. Tim and Theo drew back in surprise as Connor tucked his shoulder in and barreled through them. The two men went down like bowling pins and Connor darted off, running down the hallway. There was shouting behind him, but he hardly heard it. He had to keep moving. This must be a mistake or maybe some psychological form of interrogation. The Syndicate was known for their ruthless interrogation techniques. They could have put this whole sham together, but to what purpose? The Ghosts were an effective special ops team, but they didn't harbor any specific intelligence the Syndicate couldn't get through other means.

Connor ran down the long white hallway. He glanced inside some of the rooms as he passed, and the ones with windows all showed an Earth-like planet with rings around it.

Two hundred years!

Connor rounded a corner and kept going. This hallway had people in it.

"Get out of the way!" Connor shouted.

The people in the hallway scrambled out of reach. He glanced behind and saw a group of men chasing him, all armed with stun batons. He had to find a way out of there. If this was a ship, there must be a hangar, or if he was locked away in some secret facility then there must be a communications array he could use to send a signal out to COMCENT. They would dispatch a team to pick him up. Were Kasey and the other Ghosts here?

The hallway opened into a small atrium with large windows. The alien planet was outside, and Connor stopped running. Nearby, a mother stood holding a child in her arms while the child pointed out the window.

"Is that our new home?" the child asked in an awestruck voice.

The mother smiled and nodded. "It sure is. That's our new home. We'll get to go down to the surface soon."

Connor gasped and his gaze darted around, looking for some way to escape.

"There he is!"

Connor spun around as a group of men closed in on him.

The leader put his stun baton back on his belt and held out his hands. "I know you're scared. I'm here to help you. Just come back with us."

"Stay away from me," Connor said.

The child started to cry as the mother and child ran away from him.

"Just stay back," Connor said.

"Alright, I'm staying back. Just calm down, buddy. You got a name?"

Connor looked at the man and took the measure of the other men. They held the stun batons like they knew how to use them. Connor took a step toward one.

"We'll use the stunners if we have to. Don't make us."

With five men facing him, they thought they had the advantage. Connor had faced worse odds. He darted in, taking one of them by surprise, then clamped down on the man's wrist and swung the stunner toward the other man closing in on them. Connor dragged the man around while twisting his wrist. He took the stunner and jammed it into the man's side.

Two down.

Connor heard a stunner being swung through the air and ducked out of the way. He rolled forward and came to his feet, swinging his own stunner at the man, and the glowing tip smacked against his face.

Three down.

The remaining two men kept their distance.

"There's nowhere for you to go."

Behind the men was a hallway that led out of the atrium. "Get out of the way," Connor said.

"It's not gonna happen."

"You can't stop me," Connor said.

"Maybe not," said the man, and he looked behind Connor, "but she can."

Connor spun around to find Ashley Quinn standing there. She gave him a disapproving look as she jabbed a stunner into his stomach.

Connor felt hot pain spread from his middle as he sank to the floor.

"I thought you said you wouldn't be any trouble," Ashley said.

No words would come as the darkness closed in.

6

CONNOR WOKE up strapped to the bed again. He shook his head and sighed. Dr. Quinn entered the room and stared down at him with a quizzical brow raised. He assumed that Ashley was a mother because only mothers could pack so much disapproval into an expression. Connor glanced down at his arm to see an IV plugged into his vein.

"I have you on a mild sedative," Ashley said.

He felt a bit calmer, but that meant he was off his guard.

"You still don't believe what I told you," Ashley said.

Connor pressed his lips together and shook his head. "Just go ahead and do what you're going to do."

Ashley tilted her head to the side with a slightly bemused expression. "What is it you think I'm going to do to you?"

"I don't know. You tell me."

Ashley shook her head. "Well, I had to stick you with a needle to hook up the IV bag, so I broke my promise. But you were unconscious and unable to put up much of a fight."

Connor looked away at the wall.

"I had no idea you military types were so mistrusting. What is it you did in the military?"

"Don't you already know? You have my records."

"Yeah, but they didn't make much sense to me. I'd much rather hear about it from you. Anyway, there were a lot of references to something called the Syndicate," Ashley said.

"Are you really going to tell me you're not part of the Syndicate?"

Ashley laughed as if the idea were the most absurd thing she'd ever heard. "You make it sound so sinister, but no, I'm not part of any syndicate."

"Sure," Connor said.

"You've looked out the window of my office and you were in the atrium. You saw the planet," Ashley said.

"I saw an image of a planet. For all I know, you put that image up there to fool me."

"Why on Earth would I do something like that?"

"To keep me off balance and lull me into a sense of confidence so I'll give you information," Connor said.

"I think you give me too much credit, but since we're talking, do you know how you came to be in a stasis pod in the first place?" Ashley asked.

Connor's thoughts screeched to a halt and he frowned, unable to remember.

"The pod that you were in was supposed to be occupied by Dr. Peter Faulkner. He's a planetary scientist whose help we really could use right about now and a close personal friend of Dr. Baker's. The man you beat up," Ashley said.

"I think we can both agree he had it coming," Connor replied.

"Some would agree. But given the circumstances, I think we all could be given a bit of leniency for some of our behaviors. You know, like running around the Ark like a madman, scaring a child and his mother half to death. That sort of thing," Ashley said.

Connor thought about it for a moment. Why would the Syndicate go through all that trouble? Could they be trying to brainwash him?

"Someone really did a number on you. I can see you still don't believe me," Ashley said.

She grabbed her tablet computer and typed some things in, reading the screen for a few moments and then looking up at him. "Counterintelligence and counterinsurgency. You've been trained not to take anything at face value."

Connor shrugged as best he could from within his restraints.

"No response to that? Okay. Have you heard of the Ark program?" Ashley asked.

Connor frowned in thought. A wall seemed to give way in his mind and the floodgates holding back his memories opened. Within moments he remembered Admiral Wilkinson drugging him, and he looked at Ashley in alarm. Could she be telling him the truth?

"You've just remembered something else, haven't you?" Ashley said, peering at him intently. She came closer to the bed. "I wish you would just trust me. I'm telling you the truth."

There was a knock at the door. Ashley walked over and opened it.

"I heard someone finally knocked Baker on his ass and I just wanted to thank them in person."

"Lenora, please. That's not very professional."

A woman with brilliantly blue eyes and long auburn hair walked in. She looked at Connor and then at the straps but didn't seem surprised.

"Another one not taking the news very well," she said.

Ashley stood next to her. "Lenora Bishop, this is Connor Gates. I'm afraid his being here is something of a surprise to everyone, including Connor."

Lenora glanced at Ashley, and her big blue eyes widened when she looked back at him. Her full lips made a circle, and Connor found himself fixated on Lenora's beautiful face.

"Oh my god, I'm so . . . wow," Lenora said. "I can't believe it. How the hell could this have happened? I thought all the pods were vetted before entering storage on the Ark."

Ashley shrugged. "Evidently something slipped through the vetting process."

Lenora looked back at Connor. "You're just gonna have to deal with it. We slept for two hundred years, and like it or not, you're gonna be part of humanity's first interstellar colony."

The edges of Connor's lips curved upward. "We'll see."

Lenora leaned in and looked at him intently. "Oh, you're a stubborn one."

"I've been called worse."

"I'll bet," Lenora said.

"What do you do here?" Connor asked.

"Well, everyone does a little bit of everything, but my specialty is archaeology," Lenora said.

Connor glanced at Ashley, who gave him a nod. "Why would they bring an archaeologist on an interstellar colony mission?"

"Are you kidding me? Why wouldn't they? We had no idea what we were going to find. All the probe sent back was that the conditions were within Earth norms, so humans could survive here. And in the end, we didn't end up anywhere near where we were supposed to go. So you ask why bring an archaeologist on a colony mission? And the answer is to get the answers to the tough questions," Lenora said.

Connor smiled and found himself enjoying the sound of her voice. "Like what?" he asked.

"Just wait until you get down to the surface. We've found remnants of an alien civilization. And I'm not talking about evidence of parasitic life. I'm talking about a species that built something. A whole civilization," Lenora said.

"So there are aliens on this planet?"

Lenora frowned. "Technically, yes. They're just not the ones we found ruins for. We're still looking. Anyway, I have to go. It was nice to meet you, and I do hope to see you on the surface someday."

Lenora left the room and Connor watched her go.

"Lenora has a lot of energy," Ashley said.

"She certainly does," Connor said.

Ashley regarded him for a moment. "You still don't believe it, do you? Not fully. Okay, let's try this again. I'll take the restraints off and you need to cooperate. I'm not sure what the long-term effects are of repeated stunning, and I don't want to go look it up."

The straps retracted and Connor was free. He didn't know what to think.

"Come on, let's go," Ashley said.

"Where to now? Another window for me to look out of?"

"I'd like to introduce you to my husband, Tobias," Ashley said.

Connor decided to cooperate. He'd tried running and it had landed him right back in restraints. If this was the Syndicate trying to brainwash him, he figured he'd see how far they were willing to go.

"Sounds good. I can't wait to meet him," Connor said.

7

CONNOR FOLLOWED Ashley out of the room and saw Tim and Theo waiting outside.

"Gentlemen," Connor said in greeting.

He expected a warning look or some indication that the two men wanted some kind of payback for what he'd done to them, but there wasn't anything.

"Feeling better?" Tim asked.

Connor glanced at Ashley and then back at the two men. "Worlds. Hey listen, about before . . ."

Theo smiled, revealing a great big set of pearly whites in contrast to his dark skin. "Looking forward to next time. There's a pickup football game on the surface. You might want to think about joining up."

"I'll think about it," Connor said.

The Syndicate was pulling out all the stops to convince him he was shanghaied on a ship that was some sixty light-years from Earth, so Connor dutifully followed as Ashley led him through a series of hallways with no shortage of people busy doing a number of tasks.

"Are you taking me to the bridge?" Connor asked.

"Goodness no. The Ark is the biggest ship we've ever built. No, I'm taking you to one of the hangar decks nearby," Ashley said.

If they were taking him to a real hangar deck, they couldn't be too concerned with him escaping. "Is your husband a doctor too?"

"No, Tobias is the governor of the colony," Ashley said.

"Governor? Really?"

Ashley ignored his dubious tone. "Of course. Can't set up a colony without some kind of government. Once we're established, we'll hold elections and stuff, but that won't be until everyone is awakened and the colony is established on the surface of the planet."

Connor let out a slight chuckle.

"I know you're having doubts. I can't even imagine what this must be like for you. Just try to keep an open mind, okay?" Ashley said.

She led him through a series of doors that ended in a command center. There were multiple rows of workstations about with teams working. There were also windows on the far side of the command center that overlooked a massive hangar bay.

Connor stopped in his tracks, his mouth agape. He looked around, taking a few steps forward. Throughout his career he had been conditioned to take in information and adapt as needed, but nothing had prepared him for this. If this was the Syndicate trying to brainwash him, he felt like it was beginning to work.

Ashley waited patiently for him with a knowing smile. "Come on, I want you to meet Tobias. He's in the conference room over here."

Connor glanced back at his escorts, Tim and Theo, and they gave him encouraging nods.

"You could have warned me," Connor said.

Tim grinned. "And ruin the surprise? You wouldn't have believed us anyway."

Connor followed Ashley across the command center and into a conference room. In the middle of the room was a long table that had a holoscreen outlined in translucent amber lines to give it definition. An older man with salt-and-pepper-colored hair stood in front of it. Next to him were three younger men, not much more than boys.

"Tobias," Ashley called as they approached.

Tobias was sipping coffee from a mug and turned at her call. He hastily put his mug down and stuck out his hand. "Hi there, I'm Tobias Quinn."

Connor shook the proffered hand and introduced himself.

Tobias gestured toward each of the young men in turn. "This is Noah and Lars, and this is my son, Sean."

Connor blanched at the mention of Sean.

Tobias glanced at his wife. "Did I say something wrong?"

"No," Connor said. "I have a son named Sean."

Tobias's expression became somber. "I'm so sorry."

Connor clamped down on his emotions, but his heart was thumping like a rabbit. He needed to keep it together. "It's not your fault," Connor said and looked at the three young men. "Nice to meet you."

They returned the sentiment in kind.

"Could you guys give us a few minutes?" Tobias said to the young men, then turned back to Connor. "I bet you could use a drink."

Connor looked at him. "Yeah, I think that would be good."

Tobias walked over to the side and pulled out a metal container. He grabbed a couple of glasses and poured two fingers of dark amber liquid into each.

Tobias handed a glass to his wife and then to Connor. "Kentucky bourbon. A little taste of home," Tobias said.

Connor downed the bourbon in one swallow, and it blazed a path down his throat. Warmth spread across his chest as he felt the alcohol immediately start to do its thing.

"I'd offer you another, but then I'd start getting that look from my wife. You know, that look that tells you you're heading into trouble," Tobias said.

"Careful now," Ashley warned and gave Connor a wink.

"Okay, let's get to it," Tobias said. "You were found in Peter Faulkner's pod and you have no recollection of how you got there. Judging by your reaction to being on the Ark, I feel it's safe to say that you had nothing to do with being stowed away. Sound fair to you?"

Connor put his cup down on the table. "I didn't sneak aboard this ship. In fact, I'd only heard of the Ark a few days . . . well, let's just say recently."

Tobias nodded. "What's the last thing you remember?"

"I'm not at liberty . . ." Connor's voice trailed off and he frowned. "I'm not sure if any of that matters anymore."

"Sam, can you bring up anything we have about Connor Gates?" Tobias asked.

"Of course. One moment," a generic male's voice said through speakers on the ceiling.

"Sam is our artificial intelligence for data reference and research, both of which are crucial to us building a life here," Tobias said.

Connor's service record appeared on the holoscreen. As he read through it, words at the bottom of the screen appeared in bold red lettering like a punch to his gut.

"KIA - DV. Guilty of the destruction of Chronos Station and the deaths of . . ." Tobias read aloud and looked at Connor.

"Five million people," Connor finished.

He stepped closer to the holoscreen and read through the report on Chronos Station. Connor felt like acid was gathering in his stomach. The report painted Connor and the Ghosts as an elite military outfit that had gone rogue.

"What does DV mean?" Ashley asked.

"Disavowed. It means the NA Alliance Congressional Council separated themselves from me when our operation to bring down the Syndicate went bad," Connor said.

He looked at Ashley and Tobias, who both waited for him to continue.

"My team and I were on Chronos Station, but it was the Syndicate and not my team that caused the destruction," Connor said.

He told them about his hunt for the Syndicate and how it had led them to Chronos Station and the Syndicate's leader.

"So someone stashed you aboard the Ark," Tobias said.

"Evidently," Connor said.

Ashley walked over and handed him the data stick. "I think those answers could be on here," she said.

"Where'd that come from?" Tobias asked.

"It was in the storage compartment for his pod," Ashley said.

Connor looked down at the black data stick. "Is there somewhere I can look at what's on here?"

Tobias regarded him for a moment. "Yes, right here. Ordinarily I'd offer you a bit of privacy, but I think we all need to be on the same page regarding how you got here. Wouldn't you agree?"

"I don't have anything to hide," Connor said.

Tobias gestured for him to put the data stick into the analysis tray. The tray glowed, and a liquid metal probe came out of a small panel. Small bolts of electricity leaped to the stick. The liquid metal formed a receptacle, and the data stick plugged inside. A command window appeared on the holoscreen:

VOICE PRINT ID - NAME - RANK - BRANCH

"Connor Gates, Colonel, North American Alliance Military, Special Forces."

VERIFIED.

Admiral Mitch Wilkinson's face appeared on a video log file that opened automatically. Connor glanced at the date on the file and noted that it was from the year 2217. He started the video.

"Connor, by now you must be twenty-five light-years from Earth and have figured out that it was I who put you on the Ark. I'll do what I can for the rest of the Ghosts. I'm not sure whether I can get them on the Ark, but rest assured that I'll see to it that they're safe. I imagine you're quite angry and confused. Well, that can't be helped, and by the time you get this it will be over eighty years into the future. Even with prolonged life spans, I'll be dead and gone by then.

"I imagine you'll have a few choice words about what I did to you, but I couldn't stand by and watch the son of my dear friend get thrown to the lions for a crime he didn't commit. I had to act and couldn't wait for confirmation of what the NA Alliance and the Syndicate would do. We had a special delivery to make for the Ark program, and its special nature required that it be carried out under military control. You were going to be made the scapegoat for the destruction of Chronos Station. Hell, you probably already knew that part before you even saw this message. Seems strange to me that you'll view these events as if reading from the historical records, but for you it'll feel like it was yesterday. I'm sorry for that, but as I said, it couldn't be helped.

"I know you intended to reconnect with your son and possibly your wife. That won't happen now, and I know you'll hate having the choice taken from you. I'll watch over Sean for you, and he'll know his father was a hero and not the terrorist that will no doubt be portrayed by the news outlets." Wilkinson looked away from the camera as Connor heard his own voice. Wilkinson switched off the video.

There were so many emotions vying for attention that Connor felt numb. He *had* wanted to reconnect with Sean and had always assumed there would be time. If this journey had taken the Ark two hundred years, Sean would now be an old man. Connor couldn't even send him a message to tell him he was still alive and that he loved him.

"Sam, are there any records for Sean or Alyssa Gates?" Connor asked.

"Apologies, but I have no records of either of them," the AI said.

"They might have had to change their identities," Ashley said.

Ashley had a point. If the Syndicate was hunting for him, they could have targeted his family in hopes that it would bring him out of hiding.

"I'll never know," Connor said, swallowing hard.

"We can keep looking through the records. I'll make sure you have the access you need to do so," Tobias said.

Connor wanted to thank them, but he couldn't muster up the effort. His mind was reeling from what Wilkinson had done.

"Wilkinson was a flag officer. He'd have had the resources to get you aboard the Ark and he'd also have been able to protect your family," Tobias said.

"I hope so, for their sakes," Connor said and rested his hands on his hips. His mind was racing so much if felt like there was pressure building inside his ears.

"Perhaps you need some rest. Give yourself some time—" Ashley began.

"No," Connor said. "I need . . . something to do. I need to move around." He glanced at Tobias. "I need a job."

Tobias nodded. "Your case is a rather unique situation. There are always transports going down to the colony. Perhaps if I have someone give you a tour there and I follow up with you in a few days we can discuss things like next steps."

"I appreciate it. I have another question, if you don't mind," Connor said.

"You're entitled to as many as you want," Tobias said.

"Wilkinson said the rest of my team might be aboard the Ark somewhere. Is there any way we can find them?"

Tobias's eyes widened and he blew out a breath. "We have three hundred thousand colonists, most of whom are still in stasis. I can have some of my people look into it, see if there was any evidence of tampering with Peter Faulkner's pod, which could point us to other pods. That will take some time. Alternatively, we'll know when we bring the other colonists out of stasis."

"When will that be?" Connor asked.

"I think that kind of question will be best answered if I tell you about the Ark program itself. I trust you know that we're not where we'd planned on being and our journey took about a hundred years longer than anticipated," Tobias said.

Connor nodded.

Tobias gestured for Connor to sit down, and Tobias joined him.

"I have to step away for a few minutes. Be back in a bit," Ashley said.

Connor watched her leave and looked back at Tobias.

"The Ark program. There are hours of vids you could watch, but I'll give you a quick rundown," Tobias said and brought up a small holo-interface so he could control the screen. A star map appeared. "This is the Earth and our star system, and over here, roughly twenty-five light-years away, is where we were supposed to go."

The star map expanded, showing a line from Earth to another star with the designation HD-Alpha-2. "We sent a probe there and some other places about two hundred years ago, looking for a place we could send the first interstellar colony. The information sent back about the planets surrounding HD-Alpha-2 was the most promising. It was time for the next stage of the ongoing project— securing funding and convincing the general public that an interstellar colony was something we could achieve. We received overwhelming support. The original plans called for a colony of five thousand. Instead, we had millions of people who wanted to be a part of the Ark. We eventually settled on three hundred thousand souls."

"So you built a big ship and just set off toward this star system?" Connor asked.

"Not quite that simple. The Ark was one massive ship, but it was also made up of smaller ships that we could use once we got to our destination. There was also a seed ship that went ahead of us," Tobias said.

Connor glanced around. "What ship are we on?"

"This is the Ark. The seed ship had no human presence aboard. It was completely run by machines and thus could travel at much faster speeds than the Ark. The seed ship was to get here first and start running experiments and studying our future home. This way, when we finally arrived we could hit the ground running," Tobias said.

Connor studied the star map and nodded. "I'm with you so far. What went wrong?"

"Nothing went wrong," Tobias said.

Connor pressed his lips together in a thoughtful frown. "You didn't arrive at HD-Alpha-2, so something had to have gone wrong."

"Sam, show us our current position in relation to Earth," Tobias said.

The view of the star map expanded out farther and showed a course change and a distance of sixty light-years from Earth. There were glowing points along the track the Ark had taken to the star system they were currently at.

"What are those glowing points?" Connor asked.

"Good question. In basic terms, they're communications buoys we dropped along our path here. They allowed the ship to send and receive data bursts back from Earth. This way, if there were advancements in technology that would be useful to us, they were packaged and sent to us," Tobias said.

"So you dropped these comms buoys and they just send and receive data? How do they hold their position? What happens if a few of them get damaged? Wouldn't the whole thing just break down?" Connor asked.

"The buoys do more than just send and receive data. There are redundancies in place by design. They keep track of their neighboring buoys so when a new one is added, it lets the others know that another link in the chain has been added. If some are damaged or have become inoperable, the nearest buoys will shift position and try to contact the next buoy up the chain. This will continue until communication is reestablished. It's important to remember that we're talking about communication in interstellar terms. The data bursts, while faster than any ship we have, can't go faster than the speed of light," Tobias said.

Connor poured himself a cup of coffee and took a sip while he considered what Tobias had said. "So if we're sixty light-years from Earth, at the very minimum any message sent from Earth today would take sixty years to reach us here."

"Exactly. We've had communications from Earth, but they're quite old, and we receive the messages, or info-dumps, a piece at a time. Only when it's completed can we see what's in the message," Tobias said.

"I'm with you so far," Connor said and peered at the spot on the map where the Ark had changed course.

"Approximately twenty years into our journey, the ship's computers received a major update from Space Command Central. This update contained a new course heading, as well as updated protocols for the ship's systems to follow," Tobias said.

"Did they say why?"

Tobias frowned and looked to be deciding how he should say what he was about to say. "We're still piecing together what happened. We think they might have learned something about our destination and decided that the best recourse was to redirect us to another star system."

Connor considered this. He'd been on ops where the chain of command had updated their objectives, and what seemed random to a new recruit made sense later on. The Ark program wasn't a military operation though.

"What could they have found that would make them send us to a star system they knew so little about?" Connor asked.

"Well, they knew we had the seed ship so wherever they sent us we wouldn't be completely in the dark once we reached our destination. There could have been advancements in deep space observation that led them to do this, or something could have gone terribly wrong with HD-Alpha-2," Tobias said.

"How is it that we didn't run out of resources along the way?" Connor asked.

"Another good question. In terms of power, we have plenty. The Ark has multiple fusion reactors aboard that will eventually be brought to the planet's surface," Tobias said.

"Yeah, but you need materials to build the comms buoys, for instance. Even if you had a surplus of materials, it couldn't have been enough for almost triple the amount you thought you'd need," Connor said.

"Our tech platforms include onboard robotic fabricators. Once we deviated from our original course, the seed ship would have identified things such as asteroids that would be viable candidates for the Ark's use. Once we were within the vicinity of one, our own robotic workforce would use the same retrieval techniques we used to mine the asteroid field beyond the orbit of Mars. They'd bring the specimens close and extract the resources we needed," Tobias said.

"I didn't know so much automation had been part of the design for the Ark," Connor said.

"There were a lot of people involved. The intent for the colony was to be self-sufficient, so we needed the capacity to gather the materials we'd need to build our new home," Tobias said.

"I understand that part. But the automation involved in keeping this ship going for a hundred and twenty years beyond what it was designed for is something else entirely. We're lucky to even be alive," Connor said.

"Well, we made it, certainly. But as you said, we're operating outside of the original design specifications. Systems did wear out, and when we first woke up there was a lot for us to do to get where we are today," Tobias said.

"How many people are awake?"

"About twenty thousand. Most are on the surface of the planet. We can't just wake everyone at once or we'll have severe shortages of things like food and water. The people on the surface are setting up farms and living spaces. Each group contributes in preparation for the next. That part hasn't changed, even if the landscape has," Tobias said.

"When Ashley first showed me the planet, I thought it was fake," Connor said.

Tobias brought up a three-dimensional image of the planet. "Now that we know more about you, I can understand why you'd think that."

Tobias bridged his fingers together in front of his chest. "I'm very sorry for what happened to you, Connor," Tobias said. "I can't imagine what you must be thinking right now. It's going to take you some time to adjust. Have a look around the colony. There's no shortage of things that need to be done, problems that need to be solved. Think about where you'd fit in here. In essence, this is a second chance for you should you choose to see it that way."

Connor had more questions about the colony and the events that had led the Ark here. At times during his conversation with Tobias, he felt as if his mind were spinning. He didn't know what to think or how to feel. Perhaps a tour of the colony would help.

The mere thought of his wife and son were enough to thicken his throat. He hadn't seen them in years, but he'd always assumed there would be time to reconnect with them. He wondered what had happened to the other Ghosts. Were they here, frozen in stasis? Or had they lived out their lives quietly thanks to Wilkinson? Connor might never know all the answers to those questions, but he intended to find out as much as he could.

The door to the conference room opened, and Ashley Quinn walked back in. Tobias came to his feet and Connor followed suit.

Ashley came over to them and spoke to Connor. "There's a transport leaving for the planet. Lars, Noah, and our son, Sean, are going down."

"Oh, Lars is going too. That's good," Tobias said. "Lars Mallory is the son of Franklin Mallory, who's our head of security. If you're up for going down to the surface, I think checking in with Franklin would be good. He can set you up with a couple of tour guides over the next few days."

Connor nodded. "I just want to thank you both. I really don't know what to say. I think going down to the planet is a good idea."

Ashley smiled. "Good, I'm glad. Lars is just outside the door. Once you get down there you'll be set up with some clothes, and there's a colony initiation program to help familiarize you with . . . everything. I'll be coming down planet-side tomorrow and I'll find you."

CONNOR LEFT THE ROOM, and Ashley let the door close before facing her husband.

"Well, what do you think?" she asked.

"I meant what I said. I can't imagine what this must be like for him, and at the same time I'm wondering if there are any more people in the same boat as him," Tobias said.

"We can initiate a search, but we really won't know until we open up each stasis pod and look inside. Did you tell him everything about the messages from Earth?"

"I think he has enough on his mind right now. We don't even fully understand what they mean," Tobias said.

"We've been here six months and we still don't fully understand why they changed course. I never would have thought such a massive override was possible," Ashley said.

"Do you think there is a psychological profile on him somewhere? Each person who was part of the Ark program had to go through a selection process, and despite what information we were able to retrieve on Connor, so far it's minuscule compared with our other colonists," Tobias said.

"I'll look, and Franklin will be evaluating him to be sure Connor's not a danger to himself or others," Ashley said.

Tobias eyed her for a moment. "You like him, don't you?"

Ashley smiled. "Yes."

"He reminds you of John, doesn't he?"

Ashley looked away. "A little bit. My brother was military for life."

"Connor is special forces. We know that much at least. There's almost no mention of the Ghosts he referred to, so he must have been part of some black ops group. Those groups generally don't include the nice guys."

"Given some of the local wildlife on the planet, that may be a good thing," Ashley said.

"Has there been another attack?"

Ashley shook her head. "No. They would have told you if there was. It'll be interesting to see what Connor thinks of our new home."

"Ever the mother of us all. Okay, let's get back to work," Tobias said.

Ashley kissed him on the cheek.

"Will I see you for dinner tonight?" Tobias asked.

"Only if you're very lucky," Ashley said, grinning, and they left the conference room.

8

As CONNOR LEFT the conference room, he had the feeling that Ashley and Tobias needed to discuss a few things, probably about him. Taken at face value, Tobias and Ashley seemed like genuinely good people. They had a job to do, regardless of the circumstances of his own unanticipated presence on the Ark.

Connor needed to get away and welcomed the opportunity to get some fresh air. Even before the Ghosts' last mission, it had been a while since he'd been planet-side on Earth. A deep pang seized his chest and he felt his throat thicken as he thought about Wilkinson's last message. The admiral must have recorded it while Connor had been with the doctors, which meant that there must not have been a lot of time for Wilkinson to throw all this together. The more Connor thought about it, the more he wanted to know about the circumstances that had led the Battleship Carrier *Indianapolis* to intercept their combat shuttle. Had Wilkinson known about the mission to Chronos Station beforehand? He couldn't have found out about it in the time they'd just happened to discover the combat shuttle the Ghosts had used. There was too much coincidence there for Connor's tastes. He didn't know whether to hate the old admiral or thank him. Wilkinson had seemed sincere in his message, and he'd served with Connor's father in the military. Connor still had no idea how Wilkinson had smuggled him aboard the Ark.

More than once he found himself looking for Kasey or Reisman. One of the reasons the Ghosts had been so successful was that Connor took the feedback from his team very seriously. In the end, the decision was always his and the team knew that, but he always tried to give his team the opportunity to share their expert opinions.

Connor approached a trio of young men who appeared to be in their late teens. Prolonging treatments could fool most people, but there was an unmistakable youthful vigor in the eyes of each.

"I'll be tagging along with you down to the colony," Connor said.

The tallest of the trio had straw-colored hair and blue eyes. He greeted Connor. "I'm Lars Mallory, Mr. Gates."

There weren't many people Connor had to look up to, but Lars was among the few. His broad shoulders and muscular body had the look of someone who was extremely active.

"You can call me Connor."

"Is it true you were a colonel in the special forces?" asked the shortest of the trio.

He had long brown hair tied back in a ponytail and his eyes were alight with excitement. Connor guessed he didn't get out much, considering his pale complexion.

"Sorry, I'm Noah. As you may have guessed, this is my ship," Noah said with a grin.

"The Genesis story," Connor said.

"Yup. Are you a religious type?"

"No, religion and I don't mix well," Connor said.

Noah's brows pulled together. "None of them?"

"Never mind him. He studies religions as a hobby. I'm Sean, by the way," said a sandy-haired youth with freckles on his face. His skin was bronzed by the sun.

"It's fine. I don't mind speaking about it," Connor said.

Noah's eyes lit up.

"How about we hold off on the theological discussion until we get on the cargo carrier shuttle," Lars said.

The trio was eager to get back to the planet, and Connor followed them into the hangar.

"So what do you guys do planet-side?" Connor asked.

Lars answered first. "Since we're eighteen, we get to rotate through different occupations in addition to our chosen professions. I'm back in Field Operations and Security, which is headed up by my father."

Connor nodded and looked at the other two.

Noah adjusted the straps of the pack he was carrying. "No field work for me. I work with the different scientists and help get their systems up and running. I also get to visit all the FORBs and set those systems up as well. Connect them back to the compound. That sort of thing."

"FORBs?" Connor asked.

"Forward Operating Research Bases. They're away from the main compound. Some of them are accessible via land transports and we need to fly to others. Someday, when we build the maglev train lines, they'll all be connected," Noah said.

Connor looked at Sean, who wouldn't make eye contact with him. "And you?"

Sean pressed his lips together in annoyance. "I rotate through like the others," he said and quickened his pace to march ahead of them.

"Did I say something wrong?" Connor asked.

"Nah, Sean always gets sensitive about that stuff. With his dad being the governor and all, that usually impacts what Sean gets to do," Noah said.

Lars led them to a cargo carrier that was fully loaded with equipment containers. They checked in with the deck officer and were allowed aboard. The deck officer scanned Connor's palm and then informed him that he'd get ID tags at the compound. Since Connor didn't have any belongings, he took his seat and strapped himself in.

Noah stored his gear and took the seat next to Connor.

"You never answered my question," Noah said.

Connor knew he hadn't answered the question about whether he was in the military and had hoped they'd let it go. Apparently not. "Yes, I was."

Noah's eyes widened. "Wow, are you able to talk about the missions you've been on? Have you been on a lot of them? Were they dangerous?"

"No, and I'm not at liberty to say," Connor said.

Noah's eyes drew downward in disappointment.

"So you set up systems, right?" Connor asked Noah, and he nodded in reply. "Are you any good with getting information off of the Ark's computer systems?"

"There are none better. The Ark systems are linked with the compound's. What is it you'd like to find out?"

"I have a list of things. I guess they'd be considered historical records now," Connor said.

"That wouldn't be a problem—" Noah began.

A woman in the row ahead cleared her throat and poked her auburn-haired head over the seat. "I didn't realize you had so much free time, Noah Barker," Lenora said. She glanced at Connor and gave him a wink.

"I don't, Dr. Bishop," Noah stammered.

"Are you sure?" Lenora asked and pursed her lips in thought. "Because it's been two weeks and our data link still isn't working right at FORB 97."

Noah nodded. "I know I've kept you waiting, but I've been working on it. There's something local that's interfering with the signal, and I'm working on a solution. We're trying additional sensors to bolster it."

"Uh huh," Lenora said, sounding unconvinced. "Then you won't mind accompanying me out to 97 to check out the systems yourself. I think you've done all you can from the compound."

Noah's face paled and then he sighed. "Oh, joy," he said.

Lenora smiled at Connor. "You could come too. You look like you'd make yourself useful."

Connor suspected Lenora would put anyone she could find to work for her. And with those eyelashes, he was sure many found it hard to say no to her.

"I'm sorry, Dr. Bishop, but Mr. Gates will be going through orientation for the next few days," Lars said.

Lenora shrugged, turned around, and sat in her seat.

Noah cleared his throat. "So you really don't believe in any religion?"

The carrier left the hangar, and Connor craned his neck to look out the window at the Ark. The Ark was the biggest ship he'd ever seen. They could have lined up all the battleship carriers in the NA Alliance fleet and they wouldn't have reached the end of the massive ship.

He turned back around. "Not one. Atheism isn't that uncommon anymore."

"The things I've read say that most people in the military do have faith in a religion. It's a pretty interesting statistic that pivots toward belief, especially for those with combat experience," Noah said.

"Religions are a destructive force responsible for thousands of years of war and bloodshed that stifled mankind's growth and prosperity. I don't need to believe there's a super being watching me in order to adhere to a moral code," Connor said.

"So you'd blame the institutions of religion because of the actions of certain members?"

"The scripture they follow is flawed and filled with contradictions. You can't preach tolerance and also have a clause in there that implies 'join us or die—if you don't believe what we believe, you'll go to a mythical hell.' That's all crap people use to control other people," Connor said.

"Religions have had to change a lot in the past few hundred years and acknowledge the flaws of their earlier practices," Noah said.

"Did God tell them to do that? Or was it common sense?" Connor asked.

"That's the real question, isn't it?"

"They had no choice. People were leaving them in droves. The old standards didn't make any sense. I don't have anything against anyone who chooses to have faith in something. Just don't try and push those viewpoints on me. I've spent a bulk of my career dealing with groups that thought they were divine in some way, be it with some crazy concept or luring people in with empty promises. The patterns are there, even if you strip away all the shiny things people like," Connor said.

Noah nodded. "Interesting viewpoint. People are so passionate about it regardless of what they believe."

"I think the framework of religion had a significant purpose in our history, but it's something we're meant to outgrow, that we *should* outgrow. Yet I still see those same tactics used to subvert people, whether it's religion or corporations," Connor said.

"So you don't like the institutions of religion, but God is okay?" Noah asked.

"One and the same for me. You're born, you live, and you die. That's it," Connor said.

"You must be the life of the party," Lenora called out.

Connor snorted. "So, did we bring two of each species from Earth on the ship?"

"We have the genetic materials for most species in the cryolabs, but we're years away from using any of that stuff," Noah said.

"And rightfully so. We can't go changing the ecosystem here to make this place seem more like Earth. We have to adjust to life here," Lenora said.

"If you tell me I can't have a dog, I'll never get to FORB 97," Noah said.

Lenora laughed. "If you fix the issue, I'll personally see to it that you get a puppy from the first litter."

"Hey, Lenora, how does religion fit into *your* line of work?" Connor asked.

Lenora twisted around and eyed him. "You're gonna burn," she said and laughed.

Connor chuckled.

"In all seriousness," Lenora said, "I'm a scientist. I believe there's an order to the universe that we don't fully understand. Just because we understand some mysteries doesn't mean we can do away with others. Call it whatever you want, but I don't think that you and I are here by accident."

Connor settled back in his seat and watched as they closed in on the planet. He hadn't seen distinct continents, only one large mass that stretched a long distance. There were vast mountain ranges that created a spider-work of peaks from one side of the vast continent to the other.

"We're heading toward the western reaches. It's heavily forested, with lots of freshwater springs. They still need to be purified, of course," Noah said.

"Have you explored much of the continent? It reminds me of the old references to the supercontinent Pangea," Connor said.

"The seed ship provided much of the survey data we have. There are strings of islands that go across the oceans, but we've only been exploring the western reaches of the continent. Don't forget there are only about twenty thousand of us awake at the moment," Noah said.

"How'd the site for the main compound get picked?" Connor asked.

"Oh, it was the Ark's artificial intelligence that took the data gathered from the seed ship and ran it through some pretty complex data models. We sent out probes of our own, along with survey crews, and Governor Quinn chose the first site," Noah said.

"Do you have family at the compound?" Connor asked.

Noah's features darkened. "No," he said.

The cargo carrier plunged through the upper atmosphere and leveled off its approach. Connor didn't press Noah for any more information. There was so much he didn't know about the planet. He kept thinking about different things he'd taken for granted on Earth and then wondered what it was going to truly be like on this planet. He recalled Lenora mentioning something about alien ruins, so there would have been an intelligent civilization that had evolved during the planet's history. If there were only ruins left, they must have died out for some reason.

Connor's stomach growled and he smacked his lips, thinking about real food and how he'd never have another beer and burger in Tub's Bar at the Wings Airfield in Colorado. His mind charged down the path of all the things he'd never have again, and at the same time, he looked around at the people in the cargo carrier and thought how they'd all volunteered to be part of the Ark program. They'd chosen to leave Earth and the other colonies in the solar system behind. How does one make that kind of decision? And yet, three hundred thousand colonists had been picked to be on the Ark.

Connor glanced out the window and saw that the landscape was much closer than it had been. They were flying over a vast lush forest that formed a treetop canopy. Their velocity was too fast for Connor to see the landscape in any detail, but a tree was a tree. As he took in the scenery, he kept thinking about what had happened to the Ark mission and how someone back on Earth had overridden the Ark's destination and added another hundred and twenty years to their trip so they could come here.

The compound was easy to spot, and the pilot circled around it once before making the final approach. Connor couldn't imagine that they did this for each flight down here and thought perhaps they'd done it for his benefit. He wasn't used to nice gestures like that. Until recently, his line of work frequently put him at odds with people who wanted to kill him.

The compound was a pretty large campus of buildings and farming areas. There was enough perimeter fencing to surround a small city.

The cargo carrier maneuvered to the landing strip, and the pilot set the large ship down. Connor pushed himself to his feet and felt a wave of dizziness creep over him.

"The planet's a bit bigger than Earth, but it won't take you long to adjust," Lars said.

"We can just breathe the air here?" Connor asked.

"Part of the revival cocktail you were given included an immune system booster to help it acclimate to the environment. You'll need to get treatments at least once every month since they're always discovering something new that hasn't been addressed, but it's a close match to Earth," Lars said.

Connor waited as the others gathered their belongings and he started to feel empty-handed. More than once he thought about his T49 assault rifle. Being armed was part of the life he'd led, and his lack of a weapon made him feel exposed.

The rear doors of the cargo carrier swung down, and a blast of humid air blew inside. The air smelled like a mix of sweet and musky, as if they were in a springtime bloom after a long winter. Were there any seasons? There must be. How long did they last?

Connor stepped outside and shielded his eyes from the bright sunlight. Lars handed him a pair of sunglasses and apologized for forgetting to do so earlier. Connor didn't really need the sunglasses because he had military-grade implants with a full nanite suite, but since they'd been offline for over two hundred years he didn't want to try turning them on again just yet.

To the south, the rings that surrounded the planet appeared gray but still clearly defined.

"What time is it?" Connor asked.

"The cycles are a bit different here, but a day takes a little over twenty-five hours and months are . . ." Noah's voice trailed off. "Don't worry about it. You'll cover all that stuff in orientation, and then you'll struggle to remember it like the rest of us. A year on this planet is three hundred and ninety days. I've been awake for almost four months and I still have trouble keeping it straight," Noah said.

"So when's Christmas?"

Noah glanced at him and chuckled.

"Everyone likes Christmas," Connor said.

He glanced around the airfield and saw a perimeter fence that looked quite robust and tall, considering the distance.

Lars followed his line of sight. "Thirty feet high and electrified to deter some of the local predators from coming around."

Connor frowned in thought. They'd surrounded the entire compound with a thirty-foot-tall electric fence, which made him wonder what they were trying to keep out. But it felt good to have his feet on solid ground again, and Connor recalled that they'd only started bringing people to the surface six months ago.

Noah and Sean hopped onto a ground transport vehicle that took them away while Connor followed Lars to the Field Operations and Security buildings located just off the airfield. There was no shortage of buildings that looked to be constructed of previously fabricated parts. Connor wondered how long it would be before they built a real city at this location.

The area was flat and looked to be the same elevation beyond the perimeter walls, which would be easily defended. He expected the Forward Operating Research Bases to be comparably constructed but on a much smaller scale.

Connor noted that Field Ops personnel had comlinks attached to their ears. The comlinks hugged the ridgeline of the ear and rested against the head. Everywhere he looked he saw the same green jumpsuit and assumed this was the uniform of security personnel. The people they'd passed also noted Connor's clothing, which marked him as a newbie.

Inside the building, Connor followed Lars through a series of hallways leading to the interior. Cool, conditioned air blew through the air vents. They eventually stopped at an office outside what looked like a typical military command center. Connor glanced through the window. People were working at various workstations and there were large wallscreens that showed critical system statuses. He saw a reference to team deployment and some kind of schedule he didn't understand.

After gaining permission to do so, Lars took him into the office of Franklin Mallory. Connor noted that he was an older version of his son—nearly six foot five and broad-shouldered—but Franklin had a thick beard.

Franklin closed the video call he was on and came over to them. "Hello there. Franklin Mallory, head of security here."

Connor shook his hand and then took a seat.

"How was the trip down?" Franklin asked his son.

"Uneventful, as always," Lars said.

"Just what I like to hear. Charles has something for you in the pit, and I'll see you later for dinner. There are some things I need to talk to you about," Franklin said to his son.

Lars glanced at Connor.

"Thanks for getting me here. I appreciate it," Connor said.

Lars nodded and left the room. Franklin called for his son to close the door on his way out.

"So, I hear you're our unexpected colonist," Franklin said.

"So it seems. I think we can lay some things out on the table," Connor said.

"I bet it's your job to evaluate whether I'm going to be any trouble. Does that sound about right?"

Franklin shrugged. "I told Tobias and Ashley I would evaluate you like I do anyone else, but I'm sure you understand that yours is a special case."

"How special?" Connor asked.

"You mean beyond the fact that someone snuck you onto the Ark? You're not the run-of-the-mill colonist, I'll tell you that. Everyone else chose to be here."

"Alright then, level with me," Connor said.

"You served in the military. There are few of us here," Franklin said.

"Where did you serve?"

"I was a colonel in the Military Police Division. They wanted someone who was good at organizing our security forces and investigations," Franklin said.

Connor didn't say anything, but he kept thinking that Franklin Mallory had zero combat experience.

"There aren't that many people from the military here. Tobias was adamant about having a police force equipped to keep the peace but not an actual military fighting force. I think they didn't want any tensions from the previous few hundred years before we left Earth to follow us here," Franklin said.

Now Connor understood. Despite the wishes of Tobias and the mission architects, *he* had shown up—an active member of elite special forces with more combat experience than anyone else here.

"So are they worried I'm going to get people to start fighting or something?" Connor asked.

"Colonists were vetted to determine whether they would thrive on a frontier-type colony. Candidates were tested to see if they could cope psychologically with a real break from home. Even our colonies in the solar system pretty much functioned as an extension of Earth, whereas things here would be different," Franklin said.

"Please don't tell me you came all this way and didn't bring a means to defend yourselves," Connor said.

Franklin chuckled. "Even though we don't have warships or grand carrier vessels, we can defend ourselves. Our tech and manufacturing platforms could enable us to build those things, but it's not the primary reason for being here."

"So where do I fit in?" Connor asked.

"The plan is still the same. You'll go through the basic orientation program, as well as go on a tour of the facilities. Tobias hopes you'll figure out your own place here."

"And you?"

Franklin regarded him for a moment. "I'm here in case you have trouble."

Connor didn't feel as if he were being threatened. Franklin had a job to do and was laying out the facts so they'd be on the same page.

"I'll assign personal escorts you are to take with you wherever you go," Franklin said.

Connor rolled his eyes. "You say I'm free to do what I want, but you're assigning me babysitters. How long will that last?"

"As long as I feel it's necessary," Franklin said.

Connor sighed.

"I looked at the records we have on file for you. You mentioned to Tobias that you led a platoon?" Franklin asked.

"We were part of the elite special forces battalion for the NA Alliance. I commanded multiple squads and our call sign was Ghosts," Connor said.

"I've never heard of them, and I can't find any record of a group like that existing in the military."

Connor smirked. "That's because we did our jobs right. We had the high-risk missions that carried a high mortality rate for other groups. We hunted terrorist groups and rogue research outposts, but I focused primarily on a group that called themselves the Syndicate."

"That's something I'd like to hear more about," Franklin said.

Connor pressed his lips together. Officially, he wasn't supposed to divulge any information about the Ghosts to anyone outside their squad unless clearance was given by his commanding officer. It was one of the driving forces that had put a huge wedge between Connor and his ex-wife, Alyssa. She hadn't tolerated the confidentiality of his work.

"You do realize that you're not in the military anymore," Franklin said.

"I understand. Old habits die hard, I guess," Connor said.

Franklin shrugged. "Fair enough. So we'll need to get you sorted out. I'll have living quarters assigned to you that are befitting your former rank as an officer."

It was an olive branch, plain and simple. "I appreciate that," Connor said.

"I think someone with your experience could be extremely valuable in terms of what we're trying to do here. So as you go through the basic orientation, if you have ideas about things we can do better, I encourage you to share them," Franklin said.

"What about leaving the compound?" Connor asked.

"It's not safe to go off by yourself. We assign a small team of armed escorts to our field scientists," Franklin said.

"What's out there?"

"Some local predators are giving us some trouble. Pack hunters mainly, but there are others as well. We're still learning about the ecosystems here, and well . . . we're the aliens," Franklin said.

"I met an archaeologist on the Ark who said some ruins had been found," Connor said.

"Lenora Bishop. Yeah, she's keen to study the ruins. She believes that understanding the planet's history is the key to our future here." Franklin regarded him for a moment. "Lenora has turned more than a few heads here, so if she's caught your eye, you might have to stand in line."

Connor laughed. Lenora was a beautiful woman, but that wasn't what he had in mind, and said so.

Franklin held up his hands. "We're here to colonize, which includes making lots of babies."

Connor felt the blood drain from his face.

Franklin frowned for a moment. "Oh, dammit! I didn't think. I'm sorry. I read that you left a family behind. This must be difficult for you since there're so many families here and there'll be more. It's probably too soon to think about it, but there are also many people who aren't married. New life and new beginnings."

"I have a son . . . He'd be two hundred and eleven years old by now," Connor said.

"Wife?"

"Only for a while. Didn't cope too well with military life," Connor said.

"Takes a special kind of person to cope with it, and I bet it was even harder with the type of work you were doing," Franklin said.

"How does orientation work?" Connor asked.

"There are some basic classes and video instruction that I'm sure you'll breeze through. There are also qualifications for using land or air transport, but given your credentials, you'll know more about them than the local experts. There are field guides we can upload to your personal digital assistant," Franklin said.

"I do need to see a doctor. I have ZX-64 implants with a full suite of nanites. They're likely dormant, but I haven't switched them back on," Connor said.

Franklin's eyes widened. "Was your entire platoon outfitted with them?"

Connor nodded. "Allowed for swift communication and system interface capabilities regardless of how secure they were."

"I know who'd be interested in that. His name is Dr. Amir Marashi. He'd be the best one to help. You'll likely need to go into one of the med scanners. He'll want to reverse-engineer your implants if they can't find a reference to them in our data-libraries. Did Noah Barker come down with you?" Franklin asked.

"Yes."

"I know he's young, but he's one of the good ones. He's some kind of prodigy. Excels at pattern recognition and a bunch of other words that I have no idea what they mean. If you come across something you need help finding, he's your best asset. Navigating the archives can be a real bear sometimes. The AI helps but can be finicky at times," Franklin said and rose from his chair. "Also, your guides are there to assist you as well as keep an eye on you, so feel free to ask them questions. I'm assigning Corporal Diaz to you, and he'll rotate out with someone else."

"So am I free to go anywhere I want?" Connor asked.

"Inside the compound, yes, unless there are danger signs. There are some places we restrict access to, like the power station and weapons depot, that sort of thing, but think of yourself as a civilian," Franklin said.

Connor didn't know why, but thinking of himself as a civilian seemed harder than thinking of himself as a colonist. He'd been a colonel and now he was here.

"Diaz will show you where your quarters are, and you can get cleaned up. Your orientation begins tomorrow. Check in with me in a few days. Sooner, if you want to," Franklin said.

"How would I find you?"

"Your escorts will know, and once you get situated you'll find it's not that difficult to find the person you're looking for," Franklin said.

Connor left the office and found Corporal Diaz waiting for him outside. Diaz was short and built like a tank, with thick muscles.

"I'll take you to your quarters, sir," Diaz said.

Connor followed him, but he had every intention of exploring the compound. His quarters were in one of the temporary housing units located near the Field Operations and Security Headquarters. His accommodation was a one-room studio apartment that didn't have a kitchen, but he did have his own bathroom. Diaz explained that he'd only need to stay there for a few weeks before more permanent housing was built. Inside there was a bed and a dresser. On the bed was a pack that was full of clothing his size. Diaz left him alone, saying he'd be just outside.

Connor stifled a yawn and sat on the bed. Deciding to lie back just to see what the bed felt like, he was asleep in moments.

9

THE NEXT DAY a sharp knock on his door woke Connor from a deep sleep. He stumbled toward the door, but years of training quickly pushed back early morning disorientation. He opened the door to Corporal Diaz.

"Good morning, sir. Once I realized you were asleep, I left you alone. The revival cocktail can leave you groggy for a few days while your body acclimates to the planet. You have about an hour before your orientation begins," Diaz said.

Connor mumbled something about getting dressed.

"There's a shower in there. Don't be afraid to use it," Diaz said and chuckled.

Connor lifted up his arm and caught a whiff of foul odor. Laughing, he shut the door on Diaz and began to get ready for the day. In the shower, he blasted his body with hot water, feeling that there was nothing like a hot shower to make him feel like a new person. After his shower, Connor got dressed. His jumpsuits were all gray and had the golden sunburst on the sleeve. He put on thick black boots, and the smart mold inside contoured to the shape of his feet, providing superior support. He checked his appearance in the mirror and took a deep breath.

"New beginnings."

Connor walked outside, and Corporal Diaz joined him. Connor arched an eyebrow. "How come you got stuck with babysitting duty?"

Diaz laughed. "Just lucky, I guess. I'll take you to the cafeteria to get some food. I know I'm hungry."

They started walking. The clothing they'd given Connor was quite comfortable, reminding him of his army fatigues—thick and durable.

"I don't understand the color codes of the uniforms. I assume green is for your division," Connor said.

"There isn't much to it, and it will most likely go away, except ours and any other government entity. Gray, like yours, is for generalist and people who are new," Diaz said.

Connor smelled food cooking before they reached the cafeteria, and his mouth started watering. They went inside and there were food stations set up along a buffet. Connor headed directly over to the omelet station and asked for a ginormous, four-egg omelet with bacon and onions and peppers.

"Make it good. My friend hasn't eaten in a while," Diaz said. "Hell, I'll take one too."

The cook reached for a large pan and heated up the oil. Connor watched as he sautéed the vegetables and then added bacon. After a minute, he poured on the eggs and shook the pan vigorously, then set it down and added cheese. Saliva gushed inside Connor's mouth.

Connor held out his plate as the precious omelet slid off the pan. He grabbed a cup of coffee and sat down at one of the empty tables, crushing the omelet in minutes. It hadn't stood a chance. Diaz joined him and Connor sipped his coffee.

Diaz whistled. "Did you even taste it?"

"You bet. Part of me wants another one, but I don't think I could fit it in," Connor said and took another sip of his coffee. "How long have you been here?"

Diaz finished chewing his food. "I was one of the early ones who came with the survey teams."

"So what made you decide to leave Earth behind?" Connor asked.

"That was easy. Traveling to another world. Come on, man, that's the stuff, right there," Diaz said.

"Which unit did you serve in?" Connor asked, playing a hunch.

"I was airborne division . . ." Diaz said, then frowned. "How'd you know?"

"If you're in the service long enough, you just know. It also makes sense for Mallory to have a former military person keeping an eye on me," Connor said.

They left the cafeteria and Diaz told him they were going to Central Processing for orientation. They took a two-seater all-terrain vehicle that had roll bars and thick knobby tires. The only sound the dark-green-colored ATV made was the thick tires on the ground.

"Do you like it here?" Connor asked.

"What's not to like about a new world to explore? Any chance I get to head to the FORBs, I take it. I have to say there are some strange-looking creatures here."

"Doesn't it bother you that this wasn't the original destination?"

Diaz shrugged. "Not really. I mean, when we first woke up a lot of people were freaking out, but we're here. We're not going to turn around and head back home. New Earth is here."

Connor shook his head. "I hope they come up with a better name than that."

"Oh, anyone can submit a suggestion for the name of this place, but Governor Quinn said they wouldn't decide on a permanent name until everyone is out of stasis," Diaz said.

"I guess that's fair," Connor said and caught sight of the perimeter fences in the distance.

Diaz took him to a large tent and parked the ATV. Connor climbed out and they headed inside. There were chairs lined up and a big screen at the front. "Time to go to school," Diaz said.

There were fifty other people in gray jumpsuits, and Connor sat in the back. To his surprise, Diaz sat next to him.

A man in a blue uniform stood up in the front and smiled at them in greeting. "Welcome to your orientation. My name is Rich, and I'm going to tell you about our new home. By now, you've been told that this wasn't the original planet we were supposed to colonize. At a precise point during our journey, we received an update from Earth that changed the Ark's course. We're still piecing together why, but it may be years before we have a complete understanding. For now, I take comfort in believing that the reason was quite simple. They were looking out for us, and we're here.

"This planet is close to Earth in size and is quite conducive to supporting life. And the rings, of course," Rich said and looked around at all of them, "are really quite something. There's also a moon here. Planetary scientists have known for quite some time how important a moon is for stabilizing planetary tilt and how tidal shifts are required for life like ours to flourish on any planet. There are life forms on this planet that are similar to what we've seen on Earth, and there are some with striking differences. There are vast forests and jungles if you go to the southern reaches of the supercontinent. Deserts and prairies. The list goes on and on. Have a look at some of the birds we've observed."

An image came on the large wallscreen showing the leathery wings of a bat-like creature that had a hooked beak like a hawk and a large protrusion covering its head.

"We think the creature's large head is for extra cranial capacity, and we have scientists who are studying them now. They have an excellent sense of direction, and when a flock of them takes to the skies, it's truly a sight to behold. While their wings look leathery, they are in fact multilayers of translucent fibers. These things have double-jointed shoulder sockets that allow them to change how their wings work. They're able to lock their wings into position for lengthy glides that don't strain their muscles," Rich said.

One of the newcomers raised their hand. "How did you learn so much about them if we've only been here a short time?"

"Excellent question," Rich said and repeated it so everyone else could hear. "We've done field studies, but much of our research was gathered from drones. We've been careful not to disrupt their habitats and migration patterns. But if you want to see something truly strange, check this out."

The next image showed a creature that looked like evolution hadn't been able to decide what it was supposed to be. It stood on two clawed feet that bore a striking resemblance to a rooster's. There were two arms and four fingers with black claws, a tail that reached the ground, and small feathered wings. It had a small round head covered in dark hair, large dark eyes, and a mouth full of teeth.

"They're nocturnal. Some of our younger colonists insist on calling them nightcrawlers. Their wings enable them to fly short distances and they'll eat just about anything from small rodents to a variety of plants. They sing at night, which we think is part of their mating ritual. They average between one to two feet in height and, believe it or not, are most active during a full moon," Rich said.

The speaker paused to take a drink of water. "We could spend weeks learning about all the different animals here, but we're not going to do that. Your personal digital assistants—"

There were several chuckles from the crowd and Rich smiled. "I know—a very old reference. Your PDA is equipped with a vast encyclopedia of knowledge that interfaces with most equipment, so if you're out and about and you see something you're not sure is dangerous, this can tell you."

Connor shook his head, thinking that if any of the colonists encountered something truly dangerous, they might not have the time to wait for the all-clear from their PDAs.

"As part of your orientation, we'll go out beyond the fence and acquaint you with the area. I'm not going to lie to you. Like Earth, there are some dangerous predators out there. It's important to remember not to let your preconceived notions about an animal fool you. It may look like a friendly cousin back on Earth but may be a dangerous predator here. The next images I'm going to show you are to make you aware of some of those predators," Rich said and took a breath. "Honestly, this one creeps me out a little bit."

The image showed four smaller pictures of a large tree limb. A long powerful tail coiled around it and was connected to a large armored body with four hairy legs that each ended in a claw. A beard made up of tentacles adorned a face with fearsome dark eyes and savage-looking canine teeth.

"If you spot this up in the trees, get the hell out of there because there are likely more of them. The creature uses ambush-predator tactics, so once it loses its surprise advantage, there's only a small chance of it chasing you. The armor is tough and, like everything else here, warrants closer study. We learn more every day, so check your PDAs frequently for any updates," Rich said.

Connor raised his hand, and Rich nodded for him to speak. "What predator is the perimeter fence meant to keep out?"

"There are some large herbivores that sometimes come near here, and they draw in some pack hunters. One of them looks like a giant centipede that has a pair of pinchers. They move pretty fast but are easily deterred with subsonic frequency transmissions. It drives them away. There's another one to be aware of, however," Rich said and put another picture on the wallscreen. "This resembles a prehistoric bear, but they roam together in packs and move more like wolves. There's usually an alpha, and they range in size from between six hundred to eight hundred pounds. They're capable of running long distances. We find them mostly on the open plains, but our drones have seen them in the forests as well. We call them berwolf," Rich said.

Connor glanced around the room and saw that many of the people looked scared.

"It's going to take some getting used to. The fauna here is sometimes bigger and more exotic than what we're familiar with, but in time this place will become familiar too," Rich said.

Connor had more questions but he didn't want to scare the group any more than they already were.

A woman raised her hand. "Has anyone been attacked?"

Rich nodded. "Yes, they have. There have even been some deaths. This is why we don't leave the compound without an armed escort."

The murmurings of several people swept across the room.

"I get it. You're new and some of this stuff is scary, but think about it. Anyone who lived out in the wilds back on Earth never went out without some kind of protection. The same principles apply here. That's why your next class will be in small arms training so you can protect yourselves and your loved ones," Rich said.

Diaz leaned over toward Connor. "I'm pretty sure you can skip that one."

"What do they arm them with?" Connor asked.

"Mostly deterrents like sonic-type weapons. Just enough to get the thing to pause and go off in another direction," Diaz said.

"What happens if it doesn't?"

"We do have gauss rifles and plasma pistols, some heavier stuff, but we're not handing those out to the general colonist," Diaz said.

The other new colonists rose to their feet, and Connor did the same.

"Rich," Diaz called out. "My buddy, Connor, here, is already checked out of the next training sessions. We'll regroup with you later on."

Rich waved to them and then led the other colonists through the exit near the wallscreen.

"What do we do now?" Connor asked.

"You have an appointment with Dr. Marashi," Diaz said and smiled. "Then I get to clear you for weapons training myself. That will be fun."

They left the tent, and Diaz drove them to the neurological research facility. These buildings were also made up of prefab parts that had just needed to be put together. They went to the front desk and were told where Dr. Marashi's office was, which they found after a short walk.

Dr. Amir Marashi was an extremely thin man with a thick dark beard.

"Hello there, Connor. I was told to expect you," Dr. Marashi said. "Ashley warned me of your aversion to needles, so I'll assure you that we won't be needing any today."

Diaz glanced at Connor questioningly.

"I'll tell you about it later," Connor said.

"Let's get you loaded up onto the table and see what the med scanner can tell us about the state of your implants," Dr. Marashi said.

Connor climbed onto the table and lay down. "Do you have the restart protocols for the ZX-64?"

"Not exactly, but let's take a look first," Dr. Marashi said. "I assure you I won't do anything without your consent first."

Connor nearly grinned. He guessed his reputation had preceded him. A large robotic arm extended from the ceiling, and Amir told him to lie still while a broad-spectrum laser pulsed from the end of the arm and proceeded to scan his body. A holoscreen appeared nearby that displayed an image of the results as they came up. The scan went on for a few minutes and then stopped.

Connor sat up and watched as Dr. Marashi examined the information on the screen.

"The good news is that the nanites are intact. The scans show—and your biochip confirms—that their integrity hasn't been compromised due to the abnormally long stasis period," Dr. Marashi said.

"And the bad news?" Connor asked.

"I wouldn't call it bad news. I just can't be exactly sure what will happen if you re-enable your implants, but they'll more than likely function normally. Once active, the startup protocols should signal a diagnostic of your nanites with all the fail-safes designed to keep them from harming a person. The thing is, we can't be sure. Even if we fabricated another set of the ZX-64 series implants to the exact specifications, there's no way for me to reproduce what's already occurred," Dr. Marashi said.

Connor considered what the doctor had said for a moment. "Well, if anything were to go wrong, then I'd be in the right place."

"Brain implants are nothing new. We've been using them for over two hundred years. The fact that yours are designed for military application shouldn't affect that, but there is a degree of risk involved that I needed to make you aware of. An alternative I can offer you is to surgically remove them," Dr. Marashi said.

Connor frowned. He didn't like the idea of surgery. "I'm going to turn them on. If something goes wrong, you can always yank them out."

"I must warn you that the risk of turning them back on also extends to your brain," Dr. Marashi said.

"So what do you recommend?" Connor asked.

"I'd say you'll be fine."

"Turn 'em back on, doc," Connor said.

Dr. Marashi brought up a separate holo-interface on his console. "Okay, I'm going to send the startup protocols. You should experience the same sensations as when they were first installed."

Connor lay back down on the bed and told Amir to send the signal. There was a long pause, and Connor braced himself. Then he felt an extension of his consciousness come back online in the form of a disorienting buzz in the back of his mind. The throbbing in his head quickly gained in intensity. Connor squeezed his eyes shut and arched his back.

"What's wrong with him?" Diaz asked.

"His nanites are coming back online," Amir answered.

Connor cried out.

"He's in pain. Is this normal?" Diaz asked.

Connor's muscles went rigid as a strange pins-and-needles sensation spread throughout his body. His breath came in gasps and he focused on his breathing. Thankfully, the pain in his head slowly went away and he began to relax. He opened his eyes, and a familiar internal heads-up display overlaid his field of vision. He took several long blinks and felt his leg muscles twitch.

"I'd forgotten how painful that could be," Connor said.

"Are you alright?" Diaz asked.

"I think so," Connor said.

His implants were showing that they were online. Everything he was looking at was immediately classified, and his implants searched for the nearest network connection.

"I'm showing that your implants are online and the nanite activation sequence is progressing," Dr. Marashi said.

Diaz frowned. "How long does it take?"

"It can take a day to cycle through all of them," Connor said, and Dr. Marashi nodded.

"I'd offer you something for the pain, but your nanites should be taking care of that," Dr. Marashi said.

Connor nodded.

"You've got healing nanites that just stay in your system?" Diaz asked.

"Yeah, they've saved a lot of lives," Connor said.

Diaz looked at the doctor. "Can you reverse-engineer that? The healing nanites we use are temporary and just cycle out of a person's system."

"I'll look into it, but I'm not sure they're entirely safe," Dr. Marashi said and looked at Connor. "If you're willing to be scanned again, I think that—coupled with some test sequences for the implant-to-nanite interface—would reveal a lot about how they work," Dr. Marashi said.

"Go ahead, doctor," Connor said.

The deep-level scan took almost thirty minutes to complete. Dr. Marashi told Connor to use his implants, and Connor opened a connection to the compound's computer network. He spent the time trying to learn what had happened to the rest of the Ghosts, but there wasn't a trace of them. Wilkinson had covered his tracks well. He thought about looking up his son but changed his mind at the last second. He wasn't ready to face that just yet.

"Finished for now. If you wouldn't mind, please come back in a few days or at least forward me a diagnostic report of your implant's performance. I'd like to be sure there aren't any problems with the nanites. Meanwhile, I'll dig through the archives we have to see what the side effects were for prolonged nanite exposure," Dr. Marashi said.

Connor thanked him, and they left the neurological research building.

Diaz glanced at him. "You sure you're alright? You looked like you were in a lot of pain."

"I'm fine. The nanites do a good job managing the pain. What I'd really like to do is go for some target practice," Connor said.

Diaz let out a hungry laugh and they hopped back into the ATV.

Now that his internal heads-up display was active, he felt more like his old self and caught himself looking for Kasey and Reisman from Ghosts Squad. Thinking about them reminded him of the men who had died under his command on Chronos Station—Jefferson, who was calm and kept his shit together even in the stickiest of situations, and Malarkey, who was one of the medics serving with the Ghosts. Connor could always count on Malarkey to risk life and limb if there was a chance that one of them could be saved. He kept looking around for them, wanting those men near him—anything to create the illusion that he was home, even if it was just for a moment.

10

THE COMMUNICATOR on the ATV chimed, and Diaz hit the button. "Go ahead," Diaz said.

"Hey, Diaz, Vic here. Where you heading?"

"Sweet Victoria, your voice is enough to brighten anyone's day. I'm just taking my friend Connor to the firing range," Diaz said.

There was a pause and a chuckle. "Do you think you can swing by section seventy-three? I'm showing unauthorized access to the perimeter fences over there."

"You know I'd do anything for you, but aren't Mills and his group on patrol?" Diaz said.

"They're on their way, but they haven't checked in. Also, it's not far from the outer farms that have the new fruit you like," Victoria said.

Diaz looked over at Connor. "She gets me."

"If I get some, does that mean we can share that tasty fruit tonight?" Diaz asked.

"Stop being a pain and just do what I ask you to do," Victoria said.

"Roger that. I'll see you tonight," Diaz said and laughed.

The comms channel closed, and Diaz turned the ATV around.

"What's going on?" Connor asked.

"We started planting some local crops outside the fence and sometimes people take it upon themselves to go out there and harvest it. There should be guys out there working the field nearby, but I think Victoria just likes the sound of my voice," Diaz said.

"You guys together?" Connor asked.

"Every chance I get," Diaz said.

They headed toward the perimeter fence. There was an open area near the fence, and Connor could only glimpse what was on the other side.

"Do me a favor and reach behind us into the storage locker. There should be a CAR-74 semiautomatic hunting rifle in there," Diaz said.

Connor twisted around in his seat and opened the storage locker. Inside was a black rifle. He pulled it out and sat back in his seat. When he activated the gun's interface, it barked an alarm saying he wasn't authorized.

Diaz glanced over and nodded. "You're not cleared yet. Inside the glove compartment is an SD-15 you can use."

Connor opened the compartment and saw a bulky handheld weapon with a stubby barrel.

"That's the one. Activate it now so it's charged. The SD-15 is a sonic deterrent system capable of firing short-range frequency bursts. Have you used one before?" Diaz asked.

Connor held the SD in his hand and gave it a once-over. "I've used something like it. Are you expecting trouble?"

"Oh, you know, rather have it and not need it than need it and not have it," Diaz said.

They approached the perimeter gates and the guard immediately waved them through. Once through the gate, Connor held on while Diaz hooked the steering wheel to the left and put on the speed. There were at least a hundred yards between the perimeter fence and the edge of the forest. Everything from the plants to the trees was big and thick, and some of the plants were a variety of colors other than the dominant green. A short distance from them was a large ATV off to the side with four Field Operations security people working around it.

Diaz slowed down and stopped. "Hey there, boys. What seems to be the problem?"

The men were huddled around the ATV, which had a series of holes over the engine compartment. One of them turned around. The name Mills was written on his shirt.

"Vic got you here to check out activity on seventy-three?" Mills asked.

"That's right. She thought you were farther away," Diaz answered and introduced Connor.

"One of those berwolf shot out of the forest and sank his teeth into the engine compartment. He hit one of the power cables and got the shock of his life. Then he took off running back into the forest," Mills said.

"Are your comms down? Need me to radio in for a field mechanic?" Diaz offered.

"Nah, we got a spare cable here and we're changing it out. I think we've got a group of kids that decided to make a fruit run. Charlie's crew. Caught sight of some of them, but that's when that berwolf decided to try chewing on our ATV," Mills said.

"You're lucky it wasn't one of the big ones," Diaz said. "How many kids with Charlie?"

"Definitely saw four of them," Mills confirmed.

"Alright, we'll check it out," Diaz said.

They drove away, and Connor kept an eye on the forest. "Do your ATVs get attacked often?"

Diaz shook his head. "Nah, don't think that's happened before. A few months back I was in one of the more armored ones and was caught out there while a pack of those berwolfs was attacking a herd of herbivores. Other than a few glances at my vehicle, they didn't do anything to me."

Connor looked ahead of them and then back at the forest. "You should call in for backup," Connor said.

Diaz glanced over at him. "Why?"

"Pack hunters don't do anything without a reason. What if the animal Mills encountered was a scout and he just wanted to slow down the response for the real target?" Connor said.

Diaz's mouth formed a grim line and he activated the communicator. "Hey there, Vic. We found Mills. Their vehicle was having an issue with a power cable that's being replaced. Is there anyone else out here who can provide backup? Mills had a lone berwolf try to take a chunk out of his ATV," Diaz said.

"One moment," Victoria said.

They drove on, and Connor kept a sharp lookout. "How old are these kids?"

"Typical teenagers, like sixteen and seventeen. Mostly boys hang out with Charlie, but I've seen the occasional group of girls go with them as well," Diaz said.

The perimeter fence curved, and they went around the corner. Ahead of them was a plowed field that was lined with tall plants. Large yellow pods were bending the branches over.

"What's the status on that backup?" Diaz said.

"The section chief wants to know if you have visual confirmation of berwolfs in the area," Victoria said.

"Mills' report isn't good enough? We're at the crop fields now, and no, I don't see any of them, but that doesn't mean anything," Diaz said.

Connor set his implants on tracking mode and his vision became sharper. They were at a higher vantage point, and Connor saw workers with some machinery on the other side of the field several hundred meters from them. He peered at the area about halfway to the workers and his HUD showed an anomaly. Connor focused his attention on it and recognized the head-bobs of six distinct shapes.

"I've got 'em," Connor said. "About halfway to those workers, more toward the forest than the fence."

Diaz glanced at him in surprise. He gestured for the rifle and looked through the scope. After about a minute he'd found them too. "How the hell did you see that far?" Diaz asked.

"Implants," Connor said and scanned along the forest line. "Crap, looks like one of those berwolfs is following those kids. It's keeping its distance though."

Diaz slammed his palm on the communicator. "I have visual confirmation of a berwolf in the area. Now send us some damn backup," he said and closed the channel. "Switch it to broadband and try to get in touch with those guys. We've got to move," Diaz said.

Diaz gunned the ATV, and Connor held on while trying to operate the communicator. "They're not responding."

Diaz swore and started banging on the horn. They were closing in on the kids but the berwolf was still a lot closer. Connor unbuckled his seat belt and stood up while grabbing onto the roll bar. The ATV had large tires and he was able to see over the line of crops while standing. One of the kids turned around. The blaring horn startled the berwolf, who craned its thick neck around to peer in their direction. Connor pointed the SD-15 at it and fired. An invisible force flattened a swath toward the creature, but they were out of range. Connor glanced toward the teenagers, who were already running.

"Bring me in closer toward that thing," Connor said.

"Alright, I got you," Diaz said.

The ATV lurched toward the right and Connor aimed the SD-15 again. This time the creature turned around and started running.

"What's it doing?" Diaz asked.

"It's running along the tree line. Damn, those things are fast," Connor said.

Diaz took them out of the crops and was able to go much faster. Connor looked over to the left and saw that the bobbing heads of the teenagers were almost to the fence.

"Can they get through the fence over there?" Connor asked.

"The next gate is up ahead near those workers," Diaz said.

The berwolf cut to the right and dashed into the forest. Diaz eased up on the accelerator while Connor scanned the area. It was like the thing had disappeared, but everything in Connor's gut told him this wasn't over. Where was the main pack?

They were almost to the workforce and the security detail assigned to them. Hearing the commotion, the workers gathered by the security detail. Connor pressed his lips together at the way things were being run here. It was miracle they'd survived this long.

Diaz brought the ATV to a stop, and he and Connor climbed out of the vehicle.

"Time to go. We've got berwolfs in the area," Diaz said.

One of the workers glanced fearfully toward the forest. "We're almost done."

"Well, get done," Diaz said.

The security detail closed in, and a woman with the name J. Scott on her shirt spoke first. "Did you say you saw a berwolf? We haven't seen anything all day."

Connor shook his head. He'd seen this before. Guard duty was tedious when it was uneventful, which led to the people on duty not paying attention. Two men from the detail turned around and approached the forest. Diaz kept speaking with Scott.

"Looks like Mills is finally going to join us," Diaz said.

Connor glanced behind and saw the large ATV almost upon them.

"Hey, we got nothing over here," one of the men said.

Connor turned back around. An alarm flashed on his internal heads-up display and then a large brown creature burst from the trees, snarling, and snatched one of the men backwards. The man screamed as he was dragged into the forest. The other man froze.

"We have to go get him!" Scott said.

"She's right," Mills said. "Everyone on Scott. Now!"

"No, wait," Connor said, but the Field Operations security people didn't hear him.

All eight of them ran into the forest, including Diaz. Connor followed behind. "Go slowly and stagger your approach."

Mills glanced over at him and noted Connor's gray apparel. "We know what we're doing," he said.

Diaz paused. "Maybe we should listen to him. He's—"

Diaz was cut off by the screams of the man who'd been dragged off. The way forward showed the forest closing in on them, and Connor kept looking for more of the berwolfs. He stomped over to Diaz.

"You have to listen to me. This is a trap. The berwolfs are laying a trap for us," Connor said.

Diaz's eyes widened.

"They're bringing this group to a choke point and then they're going to close in on all sides," Connor said.

"How could you know what they're going to do?" Diaz said.

"Where'd this guy come from?" Mills said. "Diaz, take the civilian back to the compound."

Diaz frowned and looked at Connor for a moment. "What if he's right?"

"You guys can trail behind if you want. Steve is one of my guys, and I'm going to get him," Scott said and quickened her pace.

Mills shook his head and followed along with the others.

Diaz looked at Connor. "What can we do? We can't let them go off alone," he said and started to follow.

Connor grabbed his arm. "Not that way. Let's circle around and flank them."

Diaz frowned and then nodded.

Connor set a quick pace. He checked the area as they angled their approach, circling around the others, who were calling out for Steve. Connor glanced back at Diaz and kept a sharp lookout, his face intense. They moved quickly in short bursts, stopping to check the area until eventually they were level with the other team, which was a short distance from them. Connor slowed down, and they moved quietly through the forest. He heard a deep grunt from a large creature, and Connor became still. He raised his fist and pointed to where he'd heard the noise. A berwolf was less than thirty meters from them, its muscular square head jutting out and its gaze fixed on the security detail. There was an answering grunt, followed by several more. He caught sight of the other team, which the berwolfs were about to attack.

Connor bellowed a loud roar and fired his weapon. Sonic bursts tore through the forest. Diaz fired his gun, aiming low so as not to hit the other team. The berwolfs reared in surprise and started running forward. Connor charged ahead and kept firing his weapon. He heard several screams and weapons fire from the other team. Connor ran past the others, pursuing the fleeing berwolfs, and then stopped. The terrain sloped upward, and two berwolfs had stopped on the ridgeline. They turned around. Connor stood up and had his weapon pointed at them but knew they were too far for him to reach, so he lowered it. The berwolfs regarded him in the cold, calculating way that a hunter used to measure the threat of another hunter. After a few moments the berwolfs turned around and ran down the other side of the ridge, away from them. There were several high-pitched yipping sounds and the answering calls by others. The sounds faded as the berwolfs headed off.

Diaz called out to him, and Connor ran back toward the others. They were gathered around two men who had wounds on their legs. At the rate they were bleeding, Connor knew the main artery in the inner thigh had been missed. They'd live.

"He's dead!" J. Scott cried over Steve's body.

There were several large gashes on Steve's arms and shoulder, but the killing blow had come from the wound on his neck.

Mills stormed over to Connor. "I've got two wounded people because of you. You made them go right into us."

"They were about to attack. I took the element of surprise from them. Otherwise you'd all be dead," Connor said.

Mills swung his gaze to Diaz. "Who the hell is this guy? Never mind that," he said and glared at Connor. "You're coming with me. Bind him and toss him in the back of the ATV."

Connor's brows pushed forward and he clenched his teeth. Two of Mills' men came over and one had his weapon pointed at Connor. "Drop the weapon, sir," he said.

Connor blew out a breath and let the SD-15 fall to the ground. The other man started to come over with the bindings, but Diaz intercepted them. "Give me those things," Diaz said and tossed the bindings on the ground. "I'll take him back to headquarters and Mallory can decide what to do."

"Whatever, as long as he gets there. I'll be there shortly," Mills said.

The other men set up a perimeter while they called in med evac for the wounded men.

Diaz glanced at Connor. "Let's go," he said.

As Connor followed Diaz, he kept going over the berwolf encounter in his mind and tried to think of something he could have done differently. They'd been ready to attack. Connor knew his actions had been correct, but would Mallory see it that way?

"They were about to die. You saw it," Connor said.

Diaz looked shaken up and didn't answer him.

"How many of you have died like this?" Connor asked.

Diaz glared back at him. "You don't know what you're talking about. You could have just gotten lucky back there."

"You know it wasn't luck. It was a trap," Connor said.

"Yeah, how did you know?"

"Because it's how I've conducted operations before—pick off one of the weaker ones along the edge and pull the rest of your enemy away from their stronghold, then take them out. Pack hunters have been doing the same thing for millions of years," Connor said.

Diaz shook his head and cursed. "Dammit, this is going to be a real shit-storm."

Connor glanced up and saw a drone. The drone's serial number appeared on Connor's heads-up display, and he noted it for later. An emergency transport carrier flew overhead toward where the others were in the forest. Everything he'd seen so far spoke volumes as to how unprepared Field Operations and Security was at dealing with the challenges they faced.

They climbed back into the ATV, and Connor started making lists in his mind. Diaz didn't say anything to him as they went back through the gates.

"What about those kids?" Connor asked.

Diaz stopped the ATV and waved one of the guards over. "We saw a group of kids outside the fence. Did they make it back inside?"

The guard checked his tablet and nodded. "Yeah, they're at the next sector waiting to be taken back to the compound. They're pretty shaken up."

Diaz thanked the guard and drove away. Halfway to their destination, Diaz broke his silence. "Look, I gotta have a good think about what happened. It's been quiet along the fences for a while. I'm not saying I think you're wrong, but I have to go through the events in my mind to make sure we did the right thing."

An alert flashed on Diaz's PDA, and he thumbed through the interface.

"What is it?" Connor asked.

"You're overdue for your next scheduled orientation class," Diaz said.

Orientation was the furthest thing from Connor's mind. "I think they'll be able to carry on without me. Take me back to Frank Mallory and let's get this sorted out before Mills thinks I've gone rogue."

11

DIAZ KEPT DRIVING and every now and then shook his head as if he were having a conversation with himself. Connor remained quiet. Twenty minutes later they were back at the Field Operations and Security Headquarters. Diaz stowed the rifle in the ATV's storage compartment and led Connor inside.

"Hey," Connor said. "Thanks for sticking up for me back there."

Diaz nodded, and they headed to Franklin Mallory's office.

A short while later they stood outside the office and waited. Mallory's assistant wouldn't let them pass because he was on a call. Connor peeked inside the command center.

"Let's go inside," Diaz said and told the assistant they'd be next door.

The door slid open to the hustle of those working in the command center. Diaz walked over to the nearest workstation, where an older woman sat. She had on a headset, and Diaz tapped her on the shoulder.

"You causing trouble again, Juan?" she asked with a grin.

"Hey there, Alverez, this is Connor," Diaz said. "We had a couple of our guys get hurt. Have you had any updates from the med evac team that was dispatched?"

"I'll check," Alverez said.

Her fingers zipped through the interface with practiced precision. "Here it is. I'm showing three—oh no! Looks like one person was killed. The other two made it to the medical center and are receiving treatment."

Diaz thanked her and they headed back to wait outside Franklin's office. They couldn't see inside, but Connor definitely heard raised voices.

"That sounds like Mills. Could he have gotten here ahead of us?" Connor asked.

"Probably hitched a ride with the med evac," Diaz said.

"Screw this," Connor said and stormed toward the door. He wasn't about to let Mills go on about how his people were attacked because of him.

Franklin's assistant tried to step into his way. Connor quickly weaved his way around the young man and opened the door. Franklin was sitting behind his desk and Mills was pacing around in front, his hands balled into fists. Mills stopped speaking and turned around, his face contorting in anger at the sight of Connor.

Connor ignored Mills and walked inside the office. Diaz followed.

Mallory's skinny assistant came in. "I tried to stop them, sir."

"It's alright, Gabe," Franklin said to his assistant and then looked at Connor. "I hear you're having a hell of a first day."

The door to Mallory's office shut.

Connor strode to Franklin's desk right in Mills' designated pacing stretch. "I hope you'll give me a chance to explain—"

"Explain what?" Mills snarled. "How you're responsible for two of my people getting critically injured? Or the fact that you caused a pack of berwolfs to charge at my team?"

Connor went rigid and swung his cold gaze toward Mills. Mills took a step back. "Cut me off again and you'll be eating out of a straw for the next few months."

Mills tucked his chin in and his nostrils flared.

Franklin stood up. "Alright, let's settle down."

Despite how satisfying it would have been to follow through with his threat to Mills, Connor looked at Mallory.

"Damon, why don't you go get a cup of coffee?" Franklin said.

"With all due respect, sir, he needs to hear what I have to say," Connor said.

"Fine, let's sit down then. Juan, you take the middle seat," Franklin said.

Diaz moved in front of the middle chair and adjusted his belt. The corporal only sat down after Mills and Connor did.

Franklin settled back down behind his desk. "Juan, why don't you give me your take on what happened outside the fence first."

Diaz laid out the facts of the day's events and left nothing out, recounting without a hint of conjecture. Diaz simply stated the facts as he saw them. More than once Franklin's gaze slid toward Connor, but he couldn't get a sense as to what the head of Field Operations was thinking.

"How did you know the berwolfs were laying out a trap?" Franklin asked.

"When you've been involved in as many missions as I have, you learn to see the signs. Otherwise you'll end up dead," Connor said.

"For Christ's sake. Do we really need to listen to this?" Mills asked.

"You don't know who you're talking to, Damon," Franklin said. "Connor Gates led an elite special forces team. I've had some time to look up some of his operations . . . well, the AI pointed me in the right direction by running an analysis of news headlines and found a pattern of events that were tied to Connor's reported whereabouts. So if the man says you were being ambushed, I'm inclined to believe him," Franklin said.

Mills pressed his lips together and glanced over at Connor.

"Don't take my word for it. Take a look at the drone feed we have," Franklin said.

An aerial video started playing on the wallscreen off to the side. It showed Diaz driving the ATV and Connor shooting the SD-15 to startle the berwolf that was stalking the kids. A secondary drone feed showed four other berwolfs just inside the tree line. Those berwolfs sprinted further into the forest, where the drone lost the visual. Franklin forwarded the video to where the first man was taken by the berwolf and dragged into the woods. Connor watched the security detail plunge into the forest despite his protests and he and Diaz circling around to flank the hunters. By the time they'd finish the video feed, Mills looked pale and at a loss for words.

"Paints a different picture, doesn't it? I think you owe Connor your thanks for saving your lives," Franklin said.

"Drone feeds are one thing, but being there is another," Mills said.

Connor cleared his throat. "Why don't the security details have access to the drone feeds? I know I didn't spot the drone until after the berwolfs had left."

"We rely on the tech on duty at Command Central to patch us the feed if they see something suspicious. The drones themselves don't have any type of combat-suite AI that can alert soldiers to an enemy nearby," Franklin said.

"The berwolfs have never done anything like this before," Diaz said.

"They're nothing but stupid animals that just got lucky," Mills said.

"You're wrong. They're quite intelligent, and you'll see more attacks like these in the future until we figure out why," Connor said.

"What makes you say that?" Franklin asked.

"They were probing defenses. Are there records of them showing up along the perimeter? Especially by the gates or where you have other crops outside the fence. Any place where people are likely to visit regularly," Connor asked.

Connor glanced around, and none of them knew the answer.

"I think this is something to look into, Damon," Franklin said to Mills.

"It looks like the kids were the original target, but we disrupted their approach, so they changed tactics. This was a coordinated attack. I'm no expert on animal behavior. Do you know someone on staff who can advise us on predatory behaviors? If you do, they should be brought in to give their opinion," Connor said.

Franklin nodded. "I'll bring someone in and have them evaluate the video. Another good suggestion. You look like you've got more to say."

"You might not like it," Connor warned.

"My pride probably won't, but if it saves lives, I can put that aside," Franklin said.

Both Mills and Diaz watched him, waiting for him to speak.

"Your protocols for dealing with field personnel are full of holes. They should be standardized to convey the importance of the communication at the outset. The operator who contacted Diaz either didn't know or didn't convey the level of suspicious activity, then acted as if Diaz could have refused the request," Connor said.

"I wouldn't have done that," Diaz said quickly.

"I know, but one thing that keeps getting drilled into my head is that this isn't Earth. We're the aliens. We need to remember one thing above all. Lives are at stake. Command Central didn't know where Mills or his crew were when they contacted us. We only learned that Mills' ATV had been attacked by a berwolf when we saw them pulled off the path repairing their own vehicle. That should have been reported," Connor said.

Mills frowned. "It was just a power cable, something we could easily replace."

Connor shook his head. "This is how lives are lost. Status updates, regardless of whether you think them trivial, need to be communicated back to Command Central so if you're overdue they can send a team out to investigate. What if the berwolfs had attacked you? I know you're armed, but what if one of you had gotten hurt or dragged off into the forest like what happened with the other team?" Connor asked.

"We'd radio to COMCENT for backup," Mills said.

"Really? Like you did when the other team had a team member get dragged into the forest? I'm not trying to insult you, but I don't believe it. But let's say for the sake of argument that you did just that. Then the people at Command Central, who didn't know where you were in the first place, would have to scramble to find someone to get out there to help you," Connor said and looked at Franklin. "There needs to be a clear chain of command and concrete protocols that your field teams and leaders follow to the letter. In addition, you need an emergency response team ready for deployment to deal with issues as they arise. Also, what about the kids who were out there? It was dumb luck that they even survived. While Diaz and I were trying to find that berwolf, we should have sent an update about those kids so when Mills came in behind us he could have checked on them before reaching the other team," Connor said.

Franklin pressed his lips together in thought. "You make a lot of good points."

Mills blew out a breath. "This is overkill, Franklin."

"Hold on a second, Damon," Franklin said. "Go on, Connor."

"I would need time to evaluate the teams you've got together. I'm not sure if you have any advisories that are communicated to your field teams. If you have techs monitoring drones, why aren't they putting out a daily report on the activity they see? Based on what I saw today, it seems like you need an experienced direct-action force. Otherwise, you're going to lose more people until we properly evaluate the threat an animal like the berwolf poses," Connor said.

Mills laughed bitterly. "I can see you coming from a mile away. You come in here and dazzle them with your evaluation, all so you can lead a team of your own."

"Clearly you need the help," Connor said.

Mills rose to his feet and glared toward Franklin. "I don't have to sit here and listen to this. I want this taken up to Tobias for review. Until then, I have a compound to secure," he said and walked out of the office.

Franklin rubbed his fingertips on his desk and then looked at Connor. "I'm trying to remember that I asked for your opinion."

"You've got it. I'm not going to lie to you. The protocols being used here are entirely too lax," Connor said.

"And you don't pull any punches, it seems," Franklin said.

"What's Mills' role?" Connor asked.

"He's my second in command. So all that stuff you pointed out about how we've been doing things is basically like a slap in the face," Franklin said.

"I'm not trying to insult anybody," Connor said, and Franklin gave him a dubious look. "Fine, only a little bit, but lives are at stake."

"What would you propose I do? Just assign you a team and say have at it?"

"Well, for one, you can give some serious thought to the communications protocols and make your people use them. They need to be formalized. I think that'll have the greatest impact to start with. As for me, you need a highly skilled direct-action team," Connor said.

"Like your Ghosts?"

"No, I don't think so. We were mainly used for counterterrorism and intelligence gathering, as well as high-risk, high-reward missions. Some of the methodologies will carry over, but not all of it. Tobias told me to come down here and find a place in the colony. I think I found it," Connor said.

Franklin sucked in a deep breath and sighed. "You're awfully quiet there, Juan."

"Thinking about everything Connor just said, sir," Diaz said.

"And?" Franklin asked.

"I agree with him, sir. All of it, including my part."

Franklin nodded. "I'm not going to make any decisions right now. I'll talk to Tobias about this and your suggestions. In the meantime, I want you to finish orientation and have Diaz continue showing you around Field Operations."

"Sir, I have duty—"

"It's canceled. I'll have someone else take over," Franklin said. "As for you, Connor, continue your evaluation and come up with a real proposal for this new team and anything you think we could improve here."

Connor nodded. "I'll need access to personnel files."

"I can't just grant that kind of access, but I can work on it. For now, work with Juan. Oh, and I meant what I said before. You saved a lot of lives today. I know Mills doesn't see it yet, but he will. Eventually," Franklin said.

They left Mallory's office, and Connor was still trying to come to grips with what had happened. He hadn't gone in there with the goal of establishing a new security response team for the colony. He'd just pointed out all the flaws he'd seen with their current system and how he thought they should fix it. Is this what he even wanted? He didn't have a choice about being here, but everything beyond that was up to him. He glanced at the people who worked at the Field Operations Headquarters. They were just people trying to do the best job they could. Mallory had mentioned the lack of military personnel on staff. Who were these people? And were they even qualified to be doing the jobs they were being called upon to do? Connor glanced at Diaz. If Connor had to guess about Diaz's background, he would pin him as an infantryman for the Marines. He'd followed Connor's lead and his actions denoted some combat training. Ideally, he'd like to find more people like Juan Diaz, but the situation on this new world would definitely influence the makeup of the team he had in mind. Like it or not, he'd need the expertise of noncombatants.

Diaz took him back to orientation and Connor tried to pay attention, but in his mind he was already moving forward. Never one for sitting idly by, he had spent the bulk of his life throwing himself at his objectives, and this was no different. At least back home he'd had the chain of command to rely on, but here on New Earth *he* was all he had, and he'd need to convince Franklin and Tobias that they needed him more than they knew.

12

DURING THE NEXT FEW DAYS, Connor settled into a routine of attending the orientation required by all new colonists and working with Diaz in the off hours. Diaz had become a voice of reason, fulfilling a role once occupied by Kasey Douglass from the Ghosts. Diaz was adamant that Connor first needed to learn how they operated at the Field Operations Headquarters before making recommendations, and Connor conceded the point.

The colony's orientation program only lasted for a few days and was meant to give colonists a brief introduction to the planet, as well as a vision of what they could become. Basic system access was easily understood. Connor breezed through the qualification tests to demonstrate that he understood the materials presented to him. It was implied that the colonists would receive more of an introduction from their designated faction for work. The priorities of the colony were to learn as much as they could about their new home and build new habitats so more colonists could be brought down from the Ark.

He and Diaz had just finished eating dinner. The vatery was able to produce any kind of meat they wanted and had been the solution for producing animal proteins for human consumption on Earth for hundreds of years. Noah had pointed out that there hadn't been an actual slaughterhouse on Earth for a hundred and fifty years.

"So in terms of equipment for the field teams, is this all you've got? Or is there stuff in storage that hasn't been brought down yet?" Connor asked.

Diaz groaned and took the last bite of his pork chop, savoring it. He surrendered his fork to his empty plate and wiped his mouth. "Connor, enough already. We've been at this for days. I need a break. Do you understand what I mean when I say I need a break?"

"I'm afraid I have no idea," Connor said mockingly.

Diaz sighed. "I have needs, Connor, needs that can't be fulfilled if you keep me trapped working late another night. Needs! Do you get me?"

Connor laughed. "Victoria off duty tonight?"

"Yes! So can we just take the night off? I know we have to meet with Tobias tomorrow and Damon will be there and all that. We can have an early start, but tonight, Connor, tonight I have to unleash the beast," Diaz said.

"Alright, go feed the beast. I'll see you tomorrow at oh six hundred," Connor said.

Diaz shot to his feet and grabbed both their trays. "How about oh six thirty?"

Connor chuckled. "Fine. Go have fun," he said.

It was his fourth day on the planet and he'd been working almost around the clock getting up to speed about how the colony worked. Diaz had been with him through most of it, and he could hardly fault the guy for wanting to take a day off.

"Hey there, rookie. Is this seat taken?"

Lenora sat down without waiting for an answer. She smiled at him while enjoying a vanilla ice cream cone.

"You didn't bring any for me?" Connor asked and then took a sip of his water.

Lenora stuck out her cone for a second and then snatched it back. "Why, Mr. Gates, I don't think I know you well enough to be giving you a sample from my ice cream cone."

Connor started coughing as the water went down the wrong pipe, and he felt a flush sweep across his face.

"I do believe I took your breath away," Lenora said and giggled.

Connor had to fight to keep from coughing, but there was still a tickle right on the cusp. "You do accents too?"

He let out one final cough and then glanced at his water, weighing whether he should risk taking another drink.

"My mother is from Atlanta and my father was from New York," Lenora said.

Connor nodded. "Want to take a walk?"

Lenora nodded.

They left the cafeteria. Nightfall had descended on New Earth and the sky was full of stars. Nearby there were a couple of people playing acoustic guitars and singing.

"How are things going at that research base?" Connor asked.

"Great, now that Noah got our systems up and running. Had to bring him back here earlier today, so I thought I'd stick around and head back out tomorrow morning," Lenora said.

"You flew him back here alone?" Connor asked.

"Yeah," she said and took another lick of her ice cream. "I decided early on that I wasn't going to wait for a pilot to take me where I needed to go, so I earned my flight clearance before going to sleep on the Ark," Lenora said.

"I thought all travel outside the compound required a security detail."

"Are you gonna turn me in?"

"It's for your protection."

Lenora's eyes widened. "You *do* care," she said.

Connor rolled his eyes.

"I appreciate your concern, but our security people were escorting some field ops near our base. Noah had to get back in time for some big meeting tomorrow," Lenora said.

"Oh, that's probably my fault then. I asked for him to be there. I'm meeting with Tobias tomorrow."

"So I have you to thank for dragging me away from my work," Lenora said.

"Who says you get to keep Noah all to yourself?"

Lenora smiled widely, and Connor found himself looking longer than he should have. She punched him in the arm. "I knew I liked you ever since you laid Barker out on his ass. So we're sixty light-years away from Earth instead of twenty-five. Big deal. Doesn't give him the right to be a jerk."

"You're not bothered by it?"

Lenora shook her head. "No, we were never going back to Earth. This place is incredible—a field scientist's dream."

"But still, the people back home didn't change the Ark mission on some whim. A lot of work had to have gone into it, and I wish I could understand why," Connor said.

"You and a lot of other people. For me, I'm going to concentrate on being here."

The band nearby began singing again and Lenora finished her ice cream cone.

"Since you're here, have you noticed any strange activity in your neck of the woods?" Connor asked.

"What do you mean?"

"A few days ago there was a berwolf attack," Connor said and told her what had happened.

Lenora frowned and shook her head. "There aren't any berwolfs out in our area, but I'll let my team know. We do see these . . . they're almost like a primate but different. They seem to show up now and then. They don't get close or attack or anything like that, but they do make their presence known."

"A primate? You mean like a monkey?"

"Something like it. This place certainly has a different mix of species than we had on Earth, and then at other times it seems quite similar," Lenora said.

Connor stifled a yawn.

"Jeez, am I putting you to sleep already?" Lenora asked.

"I'm so sorry. No, not at all. I've been putting in a lot of late nights," Connor said.

The light from the campfire cast a silhouette of Lenora's long hair. She yawned widely.

"Yawns are contagious," she said. "So, what's this meeting about?"

"I have some recommendations about how Field Operations and Security should run," Connor said.

Lenora laughed. "Now you're bumping heads with Damon Mills. You better watch your step."

"How come?"

"Damon has a lot of support from Field Operations."

"I don't have anything against him personally, but the way they run things is going to get people killed," Connor said.

Lenora sighed. "That's it right there. Direct. Straight to the point. Sometimes that can make people dig in their heels and resist all the good advice in the world."

"So you're saying I should be more tactful."

Lenora shrugged. "Couldn't hurt, and you might gain an ally instead of making another enemy."

Connor frowned in thought.

Lenora yawned again. "I'm gonna go. I intended to get my ship loaded with additional supplies before I set off tomorrow."

"Pursuing the alien ruins?"

"You bet. You know, if you get bored here you could always come out to our little research base and check things out. Tell us how secure we aren't," Lenora said with a grin.

"I'd like that. I might even be more tactful by then," Connor said.

Lenora left him, and Connor headed back to his quarters. It had been a long time since he'd just sat down and spoken with a woman—at least one not in the military. The last time he'd done something like this was with his ex-wife, and she'd given him an ultimatum. Alyssa had been domineering from the start, but he got the sense that Lenora was not like that at all. She seemed to state her opinion and then trust that you'd be smart enough to figure it out on your own.

Connor entered his quarters and sat down on the bed, closing his eyes and trying to build a picture of what his son looked like. The boy he remembered was three years old. He'd kept pictures of him in his office at their base near Earth, but he'd never interacted with him after he left. He'd just checked in on him from time to time. He'd often been tempted to reconnect with his son and be in Sean's life again, but the events on Chronos Station had changed all that, and now he was here on a planet sixty light-years from Earth, trying to picture what his son looked like. He recalled staying away because he'd felt that it was the right thing to do. So why did he feel like such a failure as a father? He couldn't even send him a message telling him how he felt and listen as Sean yelled at him for leaving. Connor deserved that, but now there would be no reconnection, no closure where his son was concerned. All Connor was left with was an ocean of regret and a new life to build. He didn't feel like he deserved it. His failure as a father and his inability to take down the Syndicate made him feel hollow inside. Millions of people had died. He'd followed the breadcrumbs that led to Chronos Station and then recklessly stormed it. If he hadn't, would all those people still be alive? If he'd done things by the book, would his last encounter with the Syndicate have ended any differently? He lay back on his bed with his feet still on the floor and slept.

13

CONNOR WOKE up to a fist pounding on the door and Diaz's muffled voice shouting that it was after seven a.m. He shot up in bed and scrambled to open the door.

"Wow, you overslept," Diaz said with entirely too much delight.

"Yeah, I know," Connor muttered.

"And you're still in the same clothes you were in last night," Diaz said.

Connor glared at the corporal. "It's not like I have a closet full of clothes."

He only had four gray jumpsuits, which he was getting tired of. He just wanted some regular clothes or something other than gray.

"Don't worry, they're making clothes for you, unless you want all your stuff to have some other name on it," Diaz said.

Connor quickly washed his face and ran his fingers through his short hair, then put on his last clean gray jumpsuit. Would it be so hard to get a pair of pants? That shouldn't be hard.

"Come on, we should have just enough time to get some breakfast," Diaz said.

Connor glanced at his watch. He'd slept ten hours and felt completely refreshed. The doctor had told him it would take a few days to adjust to the reactivation of his implants, and he'd been right. Now he should only need a few hours' sleep a night.

They headed toward the cafeteria and met up with Noah.

"I heard you got the comms issues sorted out at that research base," Connor said.

"If by sorted out you mean I reconfigured the signal so the intensity is an order of magnitude above what should be required, then yeah, I guess I fixed it. You must have run into Dr. Bishop last night. Do *not* let her fly you anywhere," Noah said.

"Rough flight?" Connor asked and stuck a piece of bacon in his mouth.

Noah shivered. "You could say that. She scraped the bottom of the ship on the trees. Said she thought she saw the tip of an obelisk or something like that."

"Did you get a chance to look at the proposal I sent you?" Connor asked.

"Yeah, about the drones. It's possible, but we still need to define what the recognition software should recognize as dangerous versus what's benign," Noah said.

"How long will that take?"

"You know, you're starting to sound like the other department heads around here. I'll give you the same answer I give them. If you can get the request prioritized, you'll be moved to the top of my list. Otherwise, you'll have to wait," Noah said.

Diaz snorted. "Didn't you just get back from the research base?"

Noah nodded.

"How'd that become a priority?" Diaz asked.

"Oh, well, it's Dr. Bishop . . ."

Diaz frowned. "Oh, so a pretty doctor gets priority, but we don't?"

Noah's eyes widened. "No . . . Uh, no way. Have you met her? She's scary as hell. She basically kidnapped me."

Diaz glanced at Connor, unconvinced. "I don't know. Being kidnapped by a pretty doctor doesn't sound so bad to me."

Diaz was stoic for a moment and then burst out laughing. "But seriously . . ."

"Alright, leave him alone," Connor said and looked at Noah. "I get it. I'm pretty sure I can get to the top of that list."

Noah's eyebrows rose.

Connor didn't say anything else about it. They left the cafeteria and headed toward the Field Operations and Security Headquarters.

"So let me get this straight," Diaz said to Connor. "After I left you last night, you had dessert with the pretty doctor?"

"We talked for a bit," Connor said.

"Yeah, but did you have any dessert?" Diaz said.

"Shut the hell up." Connor chuckled, and Diaz started laughing.

"So, no dessert," Diaz said and slapped a beefy hand on Noah's shoulder. "I bet he'd like to though."

Noah was at a rare loss for words.

The playful banter all but ceased as they went inside the headquarters. Connor had spent a lot of time here when not attending orientation classes. He really needed to spend more time here, but Damon was pushing for Connor's request to form his own team for Field Operations to be rejected.

Ashley Quinn met them just inside and asked to speak to Connor alone for a minute. Diaz changed his whole demeanor when he saw her and treated her like his long-lost mother.

"I thought you said you'd stay out of trouble, and you found some on the first day. Thankfully, the past few days have been free of incidents," Ashley said.

"Hello, Dr. Quinn," Connor said.

"Don't give me that. It's Ashley now and forever. I got enough people calling me Dr. Quinn."

"Fine," Connor said. "Have you been able to . . . Is there anyone else . . ."

"Don't start stammering on me now. Spit it out."

"Did you find anyone else on the Ark like me? Who wasn't supposed to be there?" Connor asked.

Ashley's smile faltered. "No. We're still looking, but it's going to take a while."

Connor nodded and tried to hide his disappointment. He'd had a fool's hope that perhaps the rest of the Ghosts had been put into stasis along with him.

"So you think you've figured out what you want to do for the colony?" Ashley asked.

"I already made the suggestion. Now I'll find out whether or not they'll let me do it," Connor said.

Ashley nodded. "Tobias and the rest of the people who first conceived of the colony had a specific vision of what it was supposed to be. I don't think they anticipated some of the challenges we're facing."

"So you think they'll grant the request?"

"I think they'll let you make your case. Some of the things you suggested about communications and updates from those in the field made a lot of sense. Damon eventually came around to it. But what you're asking to create could be the beginning of something else that you probably don't even intend," Ashley said.

Connor frowned, trying to think of something but couldn't.

"You're asking to create a highly trained and highly capable group of people. Some might perceive it as a threat or that it might be misused in some way," Ashley said.

Connor shook his head in exasperation. "No, I don't want to take over the colony."

Ashley smiled. "I didn't think you did, but keep that in mind when you're speaking to the folks inside."

They headed to a small auditorium, and Connor stopped just inside the doorway. There were at least a hundred people in attendance. The walls and furnishings all had the uniform prefab look of something that was designed purely for function rather than aesthetics.

"Are all these people department heads?" Connor asked.

"No, this is an open forum. Tobias will want consensus before a decision is made," Ashley said and regarded him for a moment. "Does speaking in front of a crowd bother you?"

"No, not at all. It just wasn't what I was expecting." Connor frowned. "Does a public forum really get to decide matters of security?"

"No of course not, but their opinions matter. If they get to voice them here and feel that their concerns have been heard, it could stave off problems down the line," Ashley said.

Connor frowned in thought. He had only been expecting to speak to a few people and hadn't expected to be required to sway the public to his proposal.

The ground sloped downward toward a stage, and there were a couple of chairs set off to the side. Damon Mills and Franklin Mallory sat in two of the seats on stage.

Connor followed Ashley onto the stage, where she sat next to her husband. Connor took a moment to greet Tobias and acknowledge the other people sitting with him. There was a woman sitting next to Ashley who had red-rimmed eyes and a flushed face. Her gaze narrowed when she saw him looking at her.

Franklin waved him over from the other side of the stage and Connor sat down next to him.

"Are you ready?" Franklin asked.

"Always," Connor said with a confidence he didn't really feel.

He tended to do better speaking to other people like him, people who'd had similar training as him and he could speak to using a common frame of reference. He glanced over at Damon, who coolly returned his gaze. Connor took a deep breath and accepted that this was the arena in which he'd have to fight for what he believed. He hadn't given any thought to what he'd do if his request was denied.

Connor glanced at the first row of people and saw Lenora sitting there. Her long auburn hair hung down in front of her shoulders. She gave him a smile and slight nod of her head. Nearby, Diaz and Noah sat together. Diaz gave him a thumbs-up and a small fist pump.

Tobias stood up and went to the center podium. "Thank you all for coming," he said.

The ongoing discussions stopped and the room became quiet.

"I know we're all quite busy, so I'll be brief. There was an incident earlier this week involving a pack of berwolfs, and we lost Steven Bernstein of the Field Operations and Security group. Steven is survived by his wife, Grace, who is with us today. I'd like everyone to stand up and observe a moment of silence in remembrance of Steven, who made the ultimate sacrifice to keep others safe," Tobias said.

Connor came to his feet and bowed his head. He wasn't a religious man, but he believed wholeheartedly in honoring the sacrifice of those who wore the uniform. He looked over at the grieving widow sitting on the other side of the stage. Ashley had her arm around the widow's shoulders, consoling her.

"The events that transpired were something new, something we hadn't noticed before, and this was pointed out by one of our new colonists to whom I will introduce you in a minute. Franklin Mallory has had Field Operations and Security operating at a heightened state of readiness since the incident. In that time we've observed more berwolfs in the area. We consulted with Dr. Edwin Cummings and showed him the captured drone videos of the attack, as well as the eyewitness testimonies of the people who were there," Tobias said.

Connor frowned. No one had contacted him.

"I'll make Edwin's report available for everyone to review, but on the high level, the berwolfs executed a coordinated attack that demonstrated just how cunning a predator they can be. At this time, we don't know why they're targeting us, but we've made understanding the berwolfs one of our top priorities. Now,

Franklin Mallory is going to come up here and speak about the changes that are happening at Field Operations," Tobias said.

Franklin stood up and went over to the podium. "I know many of you are quite concerned with this latest development. I won't sugarcoat it for any of you. This attack caught us almost entirely off guard. No, strike that, it *did* catch us off guard. One man, who is not part of Field Operations, made a huge difference that day and is responsible for saving the lives of the six teenagers who were the berwolfs' original targets. His name is Connor Gates, and he was not part of the Ark program. How he came to be aboard the Ark is a mystery even to Connor. I've met and spoken with Connor at length. So have Tobias and Ashley, and we know that Connor's presence here, while a mystery, was a stroke of luck for those six teenagers who are alive today. You see, Connor has a unique background. Back home he was part of an elite special forces group in the North American Alliance military. I'm telling you this because we all volunteered to be part of the Ark program. We're explorers and pioneers. Back on Earth, there was a shroud of secrecy that was prevalent in most facets of government, including the colonies of the solar system. That's not what we want to do here, which is why I'm disclosing the unique circumstances of how Connor came to be here in the first place. We can all agree that our journey to this planet has been nothing if not extraordinary. So when he comes up here to speak, please give his request careful consideration," Franklin said.

Connor stood up, and Franklin came over to him. "You could have warned me," Connor said.

Franklin shrugged. "You're here now."

Connor approached the podium and gazed out at the crowd. He took a deep breath, and remembering Lenora's advice about using tact, he glanced over at the grieving widow.

"Mrs. Bernstein, I didn't know your husband. I have no idea what kind of man he was, but I know what it takes to put on a uniform and put your life at risk every day for the safety of others, and I know the terrible toll it takes on the loved ones who are left behind. I offer you my sincerest condolences for your loss and my solemn vow to work my hardest to help prevent something like this from happening again," Connor said.

Tears streamed down Grace's face, but she held her head high and refused to let her grief steal her resolve. Connor turned to address the crowd. "I'm an outsider. I figured I'd get that out of the way right off the bat. I wasn't supposed to be here. Until a week ago, the only thing I knew about the Ark program was an infomercial I saw in a transit tube on a space station. Next thing I knew, I was here. I'm not going into the details of my past, and if you must know the details, you can come to me directly or see Tobias," Connor said and gestured toward the governor. "Some of the things I'm going to say will appear harsh and have been met with heavy resistance from those who've been here longer than I have.

"I've spent the bulk of my career evaluating enemy forces and overcoming obstacles. What I saw in the berwolf attack was a strategic execution used by predators but also by people with training similar to mine. We need to adapt if we're to survive here." Connor stepped away from the podium and took a few steps closer to the audience. "If I were you, I'd be thinking: why should I listen to this guy? He can't possibly know what he's talking about. I get it. I'm new and I haven't proven myself to you yet. I wasn't alone the other day when the attack happened. Corporal Diaz was escorting me around that day. He was there and was just as pivotal to the survival of those kids. Since then, I've been learning about how Field Operations and Security conducts its work and achieves its primary objective, which is to keep all of you safe. I'm not going to stand up here and list a bunch of flaws and start pointing fingers at anyone. I've made my suggestions to Franklin, who's considering them. I'm hoping my suggestions will help save lives because that's what this is all about—keeping you alive and keeping the people at Field Operations alive. What I've come prepared to speak about is a new team that is to be part of Field Operations, although I thought my audience was just going to be Tobias," Connor said.

There were a few chuckles from the audience.

"See, I'm still learning too. My proposal is to form a new division within Field Operations with the purpose of providing support to Field Ops teams both here in the compound and out at the research bases. I would like a team of volunteers to train and make into a highly specialized direct-action force, the purpose of which is providing rescue operations and field reconnaissance so that at some point in the future we don't need to live behind a wall," Connor said.

Damon Mills stood up. "How is what you're proposing different than what we already have? I have teams already designated for those jobs."

"I don't think this is the right place for that discussion," Connor replied.

"Why is that? Is it because you don't have an answer to the question?" Damon said coldly.

"Because that discussion is best served between professionals," Connor said.

"Okay, so you don't have an answer then," Damon said and sat down.

Connor gritted his teeth. He'd wanted to keep this civil. "I'll answer the question. Your methods and protocols are putting people's lives at risk. More tragedies like what happened to Steve Bernstein will happen. It's not a matter of *if*, it's a matter of *when,* unless we adapt. How many will have to die before you admit you're not equal to the task that's been given to you? With the right training, you could be."

Damon shot to his feet, his face purple with rage. "This is outrageous! How dare you imply that Steve's death is because of me?"

"I didn't say it was because of you. But the fact that you and the other team plunged headlong into the berwolf trap didn't help. Instead of one tragedy, we might have had eight. I told you to wait, and instead you did just as the berwolfs wanted you to do," Connor said.

Damon took a step closer and stopped himself. "One of those things took a member of my team. I wasn't just going to let that happen. No one in Field Ops would do such a thing."

"That's good. There *should* be that kind of camaraderie in our line of work. I'm not questioning the courage of your team. I'm questioning how you handled the situation. A real team that's been properly trained stands a better chance of changing the outcome the next time the berwolfs, or some other creature, attacks," Connor said.

"Right. So how would you have done it?"

"The team I have in mind would be comprised of specialists equipped to deal with the situation. I would have used the drones, set my sharpshooters up high. They don't need to go running through the forest to get a clear shot. I'd have had the rest of my team stagger their approach so we'd cover each other while we went in and got our man," Connor said.

Damon shook his head. "Sounds good while we're here, but out there it's different. If another of my men got taken tomorrow, I'd go in there and get him as quick as I could."

"You'd prefer to go on with business as usual. If you do that, more people will die," Connor said and turned toward the audience. "Is Dr. Cummings here?"

A short balding man stood up in the crowd and raised his hand.

"Just a quick question for you. In nature, once predators begin probing defenses, do they simply go away?" Connor asked.

Dr. Cummings glanced over at Tobias, who nodded for him to answer. "Predators have been known to stalk their prey for extended periods of time. However, when a predator believes there is a competing predator encroaching on their territory, some will never leave and will fight to preserve what's theirs. They'll keep coming until the threat is annihilated or they cannot perceive a way to overcome the stronger predator."

"You see, Damon, it's not me. These are facts based on what we learned back home, except that the predators here seem more intelligent than what we had back home. Why else would they incapacitate your ATV before moving in on their intended target?" Connor said.

Mills shook his head and looked away.

"I'm not asking to take over Field Operations. I'm asking to train a new team as a proof of concept that will help secure the colony."

Tobias stood up and came over to Connor. "I think we understand what you're asking for, and I have a suggestion of my own for how best to handle this. Damon, you supervise field operations and will continue to do so, executing your duties as you see fit. I need you, but I also want you to consider what Connor has said."

Damon glared at Connor, then gave a jerk of his head.

"I'm going to give Connor's proposal of forming a new team a chance. I believe that in the original request Connor called them a platoon. This is on a provisional basis to get a better idea of how such a team would perform," Tobias said. "Now, who has questions?"

"I have a question," Damon said. "Where do you intend to get your volunteers? I won't order any of my people to do this because it's not something I'd do myself."

"I only want volunteers. I'll speak to various Field Operations personnel in groups," Connor said and then turned toward the audience. "I will also be coming to your respective divisions because we'll need the expertise of people like you and your departments to provide consultancies. Not all consultancies can be done from the safety of the compound."

Multiple people began shouting their displeasure at this request.

Lenora stood up. "This is a perfectly reasonable request. Don't you see that this is for our own protection? He's not asking you to join the army. He's asking for at least one member of your staff to be field qualified in the event they need your help. The better those guys can do their jobs, the safer we all are. I know when I go out in the field the security details that are assigned to my group do an excellent job at trying to keep us safe. But if someone like Mr. Gates can offer something better and lower the risk to our lives, we should give him our support. If you don't, you forfeit your right to complain when it's you out in the field and it's your life on the line."

Connor's mouth hung open and he took a moment to recover. "Thank you."

Lenora sat back down.

"Just remember, the motivation for all of this is to save lives. I'm not going to force anyone out into the field. This is our new home. We have to adapt to it, and that means sharing some of the burdens, which includes risk."

"Thank you, Connor. You've certainly given us some things to think about. That's it for today's session. I hope you all have a wonderful day," Tobias said.

Connor leaned in so Tobias could hear him. "I still need to speak with you."

Tobias nodded. "I expected as much. Once the audience leaves we can talk."

It didn't take long for the audience to start emptying out. Lenora waved to him and left. Connor felt a soft tap on his shoulder and turned around.

Grace Bernstein stared up at him. "Is what you said true? If Steven had been part of your group, would he have survived?" she asked.

Connor saw the anguish in her eyes and the longing for some fleeting hope that could give her husband back to her.

"No, ma'am, I can't make that guarantee. No one can," Connor said softly.

Grace nodded and then allowed herself to be guided away.

"Nice performance," Damon said. "Just now, I mean."

Connor glared at the man, and his knuckles ached to strike the man's jaw. "You're a piece of work."

"You're the one selling these people on something you can't deliver. A life without fences here on this planet isn't possible," Damon said.

"We'll see," Connor replied.

"You've only been here a few days. Talk to me after you've been here as long as I have. You don't know the half of it. You act as if the berwolfs are the worst things waiting for us out there," Damon said.

Before Connor could reply, Franklin called them over. Juan Diaz and Noah Barker were standing with him, along with Tobias and Ashley Quinn.

They all went into a nearby conference room located behind the stage. A fresh pot of coffee waited for them, and they all sat down.

"Governor, I don't see why we need to indulge this request. There's a lot more to worry about—bigger things than the local wildlife," Damon said.

Connor frowned in confusion. What was Damon talking about?

Tobias held up his hand. "Not now, Damon. The decision's been made," the governor said and turned to Connor. "Alright, Connor, we're all ears. What is it you want to do?"

"I'll need a designated space to train my team," Connor said.

"We can provide space here at the compound—" Tobias began, but stopped when he noticed Connor shaking his head.

"Not here. I need to train them away from here. There are too many distractions, too much comfort. Are all the forward operating research bases in use?" Connor asked.

Tobias pinched his lips together and looked over at Franklin.

"How far away did you want to go?" Franklin asked.

"Doesn't have to be on the frontier or anything like that. Just more than a few days' walk from here," Connor said.

"Are you serious? What are you going to do with this team?" Damon asked.

"I'm going to train them, make them into a cohesive unit that's highly disciplined and able to adapt to new situations," Connor replied.

"You mean you're turning them into soldiers," Damon said.

"If that's what it takes, but you can't argue with the thousands of years of history backing me up. Were you a soldier?" Connor asked.

Damon shook his head. "No, I was in law enforcement."

Connor held in his surprise. Tobias had people with only a law enforcement background running security for the whole damn compound? Mallory was a good man, but he had to know he was getting in over his head.

Franklin cleared his throat. "How many people do you intend to bring?"

"Ideally between thirty and fifty, but I'll start with as few as ten. There'll be some who will quit and there'll be some who won't make the cut. We'll need some equipment and supplies, but we'll be somewhat self-sufficient," Connor said.

"We have a research base just twelve kilometers away that's underutilized. You'd need to share it with the field team that's there, but I think it could work if we had a barracks there. What else?" Franklin said.

"Weapons. Diaz informed me that you restrict their use and prefer to use deterrent-type force like the SD-15s. Nonlethal weapons have their uses, but there comes a time when a deterrent isn't enough and more than one predator will need to be put down to make them leave us alone," Connor said.

"That is out of the question," Tobias said.

"You need to reconsider because no matter how we frame it, we're the invaders here. I prefer a peaceful resolution, but sometimes it comes down to them or us, and we need to be prepared. Locking up the military-grade weaponry isn't going to prevent that. Please, Tobias, trust me to do my job. My team needs not only to learn how to use the weapons we have, but they must be comfortable with them. But I'm not going to have them annihilate a species so we can be comfortable," Connor said.

Tobias drew in a breath and glanced at his wife. "I don't like this, but I'll give you clearance for them."

"The other thing I'll need is priority access to engineering teams and Noah," Connor said.

Noah had been nodding and listening, then gave a start when his name was mentioned. "Me? What do you need me for?"

"To help us with some of our technological hurdles," Connor said.

"I'm happy to help you, Connor, you know that, but there are so many people waiting for me already with projects of their own," Noah said.

"Do those projects directly impact the survivability of the people involved?" Connor asked.

Noah swallowed hard and looked at Tobias helplessly.

Franklin cleared his throat. "We have some engineers on staff who can help."

"I'm sure they're very good, but I need the best, and by most accounts I've heard, that's Noah," Connor said.

Franklin looked at Tobias. "How about we designate a chunk of Noah's allocation to what Connor needs each week and take it from there?"

"Don't I get a say in this?" Noah asked.

Tobias smiled. "Of course, go right ahead."

"What do you need that you think only I can do?" Noah asked.

"For starters, we'll need changes to the standard Field Operations equipment that will require upgrades to things like suit computers. I want to be able to deploy my own drones and have them fly reconnaissance that's patched directly to us and not Command Central. And about three or four more things," Connor said.

Noah looked intrigued. "I'm sure I can do some of that an—"

"We'll work something out," Tobias said, cutting Noah off.

"I need command authority within Field Operations and Security," Connor said.

"Why?" Tobias asked.

"We're going to be working together, and I don't need anyone having to run to someone like Mills to see whether they should follow an order from me when we're out in the field," Connor said.

Tobias glanced at Franklin, eyebrows raised.

"It's done," Franklin said.

"That's it? You're just giving him command authority?" Damon snarled.

Franklin's brows pushed forward. "The man was a colonel in the NA Alliance military with decades of experience commanding platoons like the one he's proposing. What more do you need?"

Damon clamped his mouth shut and just shook his head.

"How's this going to work?" Tobias asked. "Officially, Field Operations and Security isn't a military by itself. It's more of a law enforcement agency mixed with the old-style park rangers."

"Well, we'll need a new division then, one that'll provide the framework Connor needs to put his team together so we can all work in concert," Franklin said.

"I'll consider it. For now, you're Search and Rescue," Tobias said.

"I'd like you to transfer Corporal Diaz under my command," Connor said.

"Now wait just a damn minute," Damon snarled.

"Hold on a minute," Diaz said. "I volunteer. I've been working with Connor all week. I want to join his team, and to be honest, Connor is going to need all the help he can get." Diaz turned to Damon. "Meaning no disrespect to you, sir, but I think it would be the best fit for me."

Damon's nostrils flared. "Fine," he said and looked at Franklin. "Are we done?"

"Not yet," Connor said. "I'll want to speak to your direct reports tomorrow morning."

Damon looked like he was about to spew fire. "Tobias, I want to confirm that I have the authority to block transfers of individuals whose roles are critical to Field Operations."

"I'll leave that to Franklin," Tobias said.

"I'll give final approval for any transfers, but you can certainly bring me your concerns," Franklin said.

Connor tried not to smile, and that seemed to infuriate Damon more. The Field Operations commander left them, and Tobias blew out a low whistle.

"He'll come around," Franklin said. "Mills is a good man."

Connor didn't say anything, but he wasn't convinced that he and Damon could work together. The man was territorial and took everything personally—not the best traits in a commander.

"Well then, I wish you luck with this," Tobias said to Connor.

"I appreciate the show of support. I know this can't be easy," Connor said.

"Why? Because you're not supposed to be here?" Tobias asked.

"That's part of it."

"We'll see what happens," Tobias said.

"Come on, Connor," Franklin said. "Let's get you set up. I'll find a place at headquarters for you and Diaz to work while you get this up and running."

"Thank you. Oh, one more thing for Tobias," Connor said. "Mills is right. There are only so many people I can pilfer from Field Ops before it becomes a problem. I know you have a schedule for waking up the colonists on the Ark, but can you prioritize certain types of individuals? Former military experience would be good, people like Diaz who have infantry experience, anyone with hunting and survival experience. People like that."

Tobias glanced at his wife. "You said he wouldn't be trouble, and now he's treating the people on the Ark like a mail order catalog."

Ashley gave him a playful slap on the shoulder. "No one said starting a colony would be easy, love."

"I'll see what I can do," Tobias said.

"Really? I've been asking for additional personnel and you've been putting me off, but Connor gets special treatment." Franklin laughed and looked at Connor. "Tomorrow you get to try to convince a bunch of people who are settled to leave all that behind for a while to be trained in a job they might not want," Franklin said.

"Sometimes people will surprise you," Connor said.

They left the auditorium conference room, and Connor was already making lists in his head. He pulled Diaz and Noah aside.

"Thanks, guys. If you know someone who would be a good fit for the team, I want to know about it. Don't be shy about it either, Noah," Connor said.

"Wait. I'm just on loan," Noah said.

Connor grinned. "For now."

"But I'm not a soldier," Noah protested.

"Neither was I," Connor said. "Don't look so scared. I want your input on the technical stuff, and I'll show you things like how to shoot a rifle. It'll be fun. Plus you'll gain a valuable perspective by doing some fieldwork."

Noah considered it for a moment and then nodded.

"Let's get to it," Connor said.

Now the real work would begin. Building the team he had in mind wasn't going to be easy. He and Diaz had their work cut out for them, but it was a start —at least for now.

14

In the weeks that followed, Connor worked nearly around the clock. He only needed a few hours' sleep in order to function, which was one of the benefits of the nanite suite he had. Dr. Marashi had taken a sample of the nanites from Connor's blood to see if he could duplicate them. Long-term exposure carried a risk of the body rejecting the nanites, rendering them ineffectual. The nanites Connor had in his system were experimental and cutting edge, which was why only his old platoon had access to them. They'd needed to cycle them at least once a year to avoid complications. Since Dr. Marashi hadn't been able to reproduce the nanites, Connor was reluctant to let them go. They simply offered him too many advantages, including quick healing abilities, for him to go back to living without them.

"Are you sure about this?" Diaz asked, glancing down at the three chevrons that adorned the arms of his uniform.

"If I wasn't sure, you wouldn't be here," Connor said.

Field Operations had a similar command structure as the NA Alliance military, which Connor attributed more to Franklin Mallory than Tobias Quinn. Quinn was adamant about not having anything that functioned as a military, believing that having standing militaries created as many problems as it solved.

"I have to say I really didn't think Mallory would go for the change in plans," Diaz said.

"You saw that research base. It wasn't going to work," Connor replied.

They were standing in Connor's temporary office at the Field Operations Headquarters. The interactive wallscreen had lists of supplies and personnel records of the squad they'd put together.

"That's another thing. We easily had more volunteers. Why aren't we taking everyone we can get?" Diaz asked.

"This is only the first bunch. Search and Rescue is just the two of us right now. A dozen recruits is a good start," Connor said.

"Mallory was surprised by the short list," Diaz said.

"I'd thought of bringing more recruits and then whittling them down, but there simply aren't enough people to go around for that. We can replace anyone on the team if it comes to that," Connor said.

Diaz glanced at the list of recruits. "You better keep that backup list handy, Colonel."

Mallory had reinstated Connor's previous rank, which made him equal to Chief Mills and second in rank to Mallory himself. Whereas Mills had multiple squads totaling nearly three hundred people in Field Operations and Security, Connor just had himself, Diaz, and twelve recruits.

There was a knock on the office door, and Diaz went to open it.

"We have a visitor, sir," Diaz said.

Sean Quinn was standing outside. The sandy-haired youth waved from the doorway, and Connor gestured for him to come inside.

"What can I do for you?" Connor asked.

Sean walked in and did a pretty good impression of standing at attention. "I'd like to join Search and Rescue, sir."

Diaz's mouth rounded in surprise, but since he stood behind the governor's son, only Connor could see.

"Why?" Connor asked.

"There have been more incidents with the berwolfs stalking the teams—not only here, but at some of the research bases. You were right, sir, and I want to join you so I can help do something about it," Sean said.

Connor regarded the youth for a moment. He had a few freckles on his face and his tanned skin indicated that he spent much of his time outside, but there was still that uncertainty in his gaze that suggested Sean was running from something.

"How old are you?" Connor asked.

Sean's shoulders slumped. "Seventeen, sir."

"You're too young for this. Come back to me next year," Connor said and walked behind his desk, giving the young man a moment to school his features.

"Sir, I'll be eighteen in just a few weeks. What difference will the time make?"

"Not much from your perspective. What matters is where we draw the line. Do your parents know you're here, asking for this?" Connor asked.

Sean's eyes flashed angrily. "No, sir."

"Do you think they'd give their consent for you to do something like this?"

"I'm not sure, sir."

"What do you think we're going to be doing?" Connor asked.

"Helping people out, being the strongest of the strong, the best trained, sir."

"You can be all those things without joining Search and Rescue," Connor said.

Diaz opened the door and the busy sounds from the corridor beyond echoed inside.

Sean stood in the same spot, his gaze on the floor. "Please, sir."

Connor shook his head. "Look at me. What we're doing is dangerous. I'm not running a day camp where you get to 'find' yourself to determine whether you're worth something. You can 'find' yourself without me. Go out there and make a difference and then, maybe, I'll consider letting you join. Now get out of here."

Sean sucked in a breath and fled.

Diaz closed the door and made a low whistling sound. "Is this what you're gonna be like once we get to our camp?"

Connor shook his head. "Worse. Besides, I don't have time for that right now."

Another knock came as the door opened and Noah stuck his head inside. "Am I interrupting?"

"Not at all. Come inside," Connor said.

"I have good news. The drones you asked for are ready," Noah said.

"Excellent! Are they in the supply crates?" Connor asked.

"All twenty-five of them are being loaded as we speak," Noah said.

"Great, so you're coming with us then," Connor said.

"I'll be out there in a few days. Mills has me doing some things for Field Ops now," Noah said.

With the onset of Search and Rescue, Damon Mills had suddenly begun making changes to Field Ops, improving their response times and security.

"Mills has plenty of engineers working for him," Connor said.

Noah glanced over at the wallscreen. "And I see you have one, too."

Connor caught Noah's gaze lingering on the list. "Is there something I should know?"

Noah shook his head. "It's nothing. I'll be working on the suit upgrades for your squad and will come out to the camp when they get delivered."

Connor eyed the young tech specialist. "It's your squad too."

"You're relentless," Noah said and left the room.

"The funny thing is he thinks he has a choice." Diaz snorted.

"Don't be crazy. They all have a choice. They might not like the choices they have, but they'll always have a choice," Connor said.

He killed his open session on the wallscreen and looked around his office. Everything was in its place and there was nothing he'd forgotten. Connor stepped outside the office and heard his name being called.

Franklin Mallory caught up to him. "I thought I'd walk you out."

"I was just coming to your office to let you know we were leaving," Connor said.

Diaz said he'd meet them on the tarmac and quickened his pace.

"So, you're all ready?" Franklin asked.

"As we'll ever be," Connor said.

"I have to be honest. I'd feel a whole lot better if you were going to the research base as we originally planned."

"Isolation is key, for the first few weeks anyway. Most of them have been too comfortable living at the compound," Connor said.

"Yeah, but that camp is rustic, to say the least. I saw on the manifest that you're only bringing one small power generator and a light backup."

"They already know how to operate here. We strip everything away and gradually reintroduce things. Also, it measures their commitment," Connor said.

Franklin nodded. "I know. I know. We've been through this a half dozen times. You'll be off the grid."

"With regular check-ins. Diaz and I have been out to the site and have a pretty good knowledge of the area. We have all the data collected so far, and we've had a Field Ops drone in the area doing reconnaissance," Connor said.

Franklin glanced at him. "You're excited about this, aren't you?"

"Absolutely. And remember our agreement. No inspections for at least a month," Connor said.

They exited the headquarters and climbed into the waiting ground transport that would take him to the airfield.

"I hear the berwolfs have been coming back around," Connor said.

Franklin nodded grimly. "Yes, they have. Some of the new protocols have helped."

Connor was glad to hear it. He hadn't been convinced that Damon Mills would make any changes. "How's Mills handling it?"

"He cares about his people. It's just you he doesn't like," Franklin said.

They arrived at one of the smaller landing areas of the airfield, but there was still quite a bit of traffic going to and from the Ark. Outside a cargo carrier, Sergeant Diaz was shouting at a ragtag group.

"Form a line. Now!" Diaz bellowed. "It's not that hard."

Connor and Franklin walked over. Diaz turned around and snapped a salute. "Search and Rescue trainee squad awaits inspection, sir."

"Thank you, Sergeant," Connor said, returning his salute.

Twelve men and women formed two lines of six, varying in age and experience. Off to the side was a pile of personal items that had no business going to their camp. More than a few of the recruits glanced over at the pile.

"Your stuff will be returned to you once your training is complete. We'll do formal introductions later," Connor said.

"Sir, yes, sir," the squad shouted.

Connor suppressed a smile. Diaz must have given them some preliminary instruction before he arrived. Connor stood next to Diaz and snapped a salute to Mallory.

Franklin regarded them with a nod to a time long gone. "The clock is ticking. I'll let you get to it."

Connor turned toward Diaz. "Get them on board, Sergeant."

"Yes, sir," Diaz said and turned to face the new recruits. "Alright, you heard him. Grab your gear and get on board the ship. Debriefing will occur once we're on site."

"Good luck," Franklin said.

Connor shook his hand. "I'll see you in a few weeks."

Franklin returned to the ground transport, and Connor caught a glimpse of a man standing off to the side. A tele-view of the man appeared on his internal heads-up display. Damon Mills watched him, stone-faced and impossible to read.

Connor regarded Mills for a moment, and though there were a hundred meters between them, it wasn't far enough in Connor's mind.

Connor turned around and walked up the ramp to enter the cargo carrier, the last one to board. He walked past the supply crates, and as he came to his new recruits, their conversations hushed. Connor headed to the cockpit where the pilots sat.

A pilot named Mitchell greeted him. "We're clear for takeoff."

Connor nodded. "Good. Once we're in the air I have a new set of coordinates for you."

"I'm afraid I don't understand," Mitchell said.

"It's fine. You will," Connor said.

The cargo carrier thrusters were engaged and the ship lifted off the ground. Once they were high enough, the carrier sped off.

Connor used his implants to interface with the ship's systems and uploaded the coordinates and his authorization.

The new coordinates appeared on Mitchell's terminal, and the pilot frowned. "I have the new destination, but sir, there isn't any research base at this location."

"I know," Connor said. "We'll also be doing a low-altitude deployment."

"I wasn't aware of that," Mitchell stammered.

"I'm making you aware of it now. Will there be a problem?" Connor asked.

"The passengers aren't equipped for a low-altitude drop, sir."

Connor glanced behind him, making a show of considering what the pilot was saying. "Oh, that. Don't worry about it. They'll be fine. Just get us over those coordinates, dump us out, and go back home."

The pilot nodded. "Yes, sir."

Connor went over to see that Diaz was already wearing a vest with repulsor jets on the back. They were designed for low-altitude jumps. The jets would fire to slow the wearer's descent enough for them to make a soft landing. Connor put his own repulsor vest on and waited.

"Sir, we're approaching the drop zone. I'll just warn the passengers in the cabin of the flight status," Mitchell said.

"That won't be necessary," Connor said.

"But, sir—"

Connor gave him a hard look. "Are they all strapped into their seats?"

The pilot did a quick check of the status of the passengers. "Yes, sir."

"Then when we're over the drop zone, dump them out," Connor said.

He glanced at Diaz and headed to the cargo area.

"You believe that guy?" Connor heard Mitchell ask his copilot when he thought they were away. Connor closed the door. He was facing his new recruits, and the nearest one raised her hand.

"Yes," Connor said.

"How long till we get there, sir?" she asked.

She had thick blond hair and pale skin. The name A. Blake was stenciled into her jacket.

"What did you say?" Connor asked.

He'd heard her, he was just delaying his answer. The recruits nearby were actively listening when suddenly a klaxon alarm sounded and the interior lights changed to red. A few seconds later the cargo bay doors opened and wind roared through the airship. The recruits looked behind them in horror as the locking mechanism holding large storage crates in place shifted and the crates were pulled from the cargo area.

"I can't get my straps undone!" one of the recruits cried.

Connor kicked the emergency lever. The recruits all angled backward and screamed as their seats raced on tracks toward the exit. At the last second, small rockets fired as their seats detached from the ship and they were tossed out of the cargo ship.

The cargo area was clear. Connor glanced across at Diaz, who gave him a thumbs-up. Together they ran down the ramp and jumped into the air. Diaz let out a loud woot and bellowed a laugh almost the whole way to the ground.

15

The wind slapped against Connor's face as he jumped out of the cargo ship and noted multiple chute deployments from his new recruits. Their chairs were bolted together and designed for this type of emergency. He scanned ahead for the hardened cargo crates and made a quick count. Connor looked at Diaz and gave him a thumbs-up. Without parachutes of their own, they quickly overtook his new recruits. The pilots had done their jobs well, because they were right on target, and they approached the wide-open glade he'd designated as the spot for their new camp over a week ago.

He and Diaz used their arms to angle away from each other. Landing with a repulsor jet pack wasn't for the faint of heart. They were required to change the angle of their approach; otherwise, the small repulsor engines would speed them to their deaths. Connor brought his arms in and dove forward. The momentum of his body aligned his feet with the ground below, and he fired his engines for a few moments. He slowed down, but not enough, so he fired his engines again in a controlled burst and his velocity quickly decreased. His feet scraped the ground and he pumped his legs, then killed the jets and ran a short distance before stopping. Diaz landed nearby, and the sergeant immediately started scanning the area. He had his SD-15 in his hand.

Connor kept his SD holstered and patched into the recon drone they had in the area. There were no berwolfs nearby. The cargo crates landed close by, followed by his harried-looking recruits. Some of them had vomit on their shirts.

He did a quick visual. "Alright. Fall in line. Let's go. I haven't got all day. What are you waiting for? Get up!" Connor shouted.

Diaz was on them, coming from the other side, shouting for them to get up. The recruits unstrapped themselves and tried to stand up, but most of them immediately fell because their wobbly legs refused to hold them up.

"On your feet. Line up, people," Connor said.

All twelve recruits lined up, most of them looking completely out of sorts as if they couldn't believe what had just happened.

"Welcome, Lightning Platoon, to Search and Rescue training. Over the next few weeks you will be challenged and tested to see if you have what it takes to be on my team," Connor said. He walked down the line as he spoke. "I know many of you have questions," Connor said.

Five recruits' hands shot into the air.

"Put your hands down," Diaz snapped. "The commander didn't ask you if you had questions. He made a statement."

The recruits reluctantly put their hands down.

"Thank you, Sergeant Diaz," Connor said. "You're wondering where the research base is that you were told about, the one that was just twenty klicks from the compound. I lied."

A recruit glanced over at her fellow recruit, and Connor immediately stepped in front of her. "Is there a problem, Owens?"

Amy Owens had thick dark hair and a plump body. She wasn't overweight, but she'd never be what you'd call slender either. "Uh, no, sir."

"Then why were you looking at Deacon when I was speaking to you?" Connor asked.

Owens glanced over at Deacon.

"Again!" Connor shouted. "Henry Deacon, maybe you can tell me why Owens keeps looking at you during my debrief."

"Sir, I think she's just scared from the drop, sir," Deacon said.

Connor nodded. "Perhaps she likes you. What do you think, Sergeant Diaz?"

Diaz stalked over to them. "I definitely sense some animal magnetism going on here, Commander."

Owens' face flushed.

"Indeed, we got ourselves a real Hot Rod here," Connor said. "In fact, from here on out your name is Hot Rod. How's that sound?"

"Sounds great," Deacon said.

Diaz got up in Deacon's face. "Hot Rod, you're addressing a superior officer. Fifty pushups. Count them off."

Hot Rod dropped and immediately began doing pushups.

Connor went back to Owens. "You're my tech specialist. Is that right, Owens?"

"Yes," Owens said. "Sir, I meant yes, sir, sir."

Diaz was about to start in on her, but Connor held up his hand. "That's alright, Sergeant. We got ourselves a regular Einstein here. Do you know who Einstein is, Owens?" Connor asked.

"Yes, sir. He came up with the theory of relativity, sir," Owens said.

Connor grinned. "Outstanding, Owens, except you forgot one thing. Anyone can spout out the accomplishments of a historical figure. They overlook the fact that he was a man of innovation. You'll be called upon to do complex things with limited resources. Each time you think you don't have what you need, I want you to remember our good friend Albert. What did he have? The man conceived theories that couldn't be proven for over a hundred years after he died. From now on I'm going to call you Einstein."

"Yes, sir," she said.

Connor moved down the line and peered at a lanky young man. Even the man's fingers were long and spindly. His short black hair and tan skin announced his Spanish heritage. "Ramirez, Joseph," Connor said.

"Yes, sir," Ramirez said.

"You are the thinnest man I've ever seen," Connor said and glanced over at Diaz, who repeated the same. "You can almost see his bones. In fact, that's what I'm going to call you. Bones. How's that name sound?"

"It sounds good to me, sir," Bones said.

Connor nodded and moved on to the next recruit. "Elyse Winters, is that your name?" Connor asked.

"Sir, yes, sir," Winters said.

She had blond hair that was tied into a bun and her blue eyes were fixed decidedly ahead.

Connor smiled and pretended to get the chills. "You're one cool customer, Winters. I bet not much shakes that resolve of yours."

"Sir, yes, sir," Winters said.

"Yes, what? You're one cool customer? Or nothing shakes your resolve?"

"Both, sir," Winters said.

Connor grinned and gave Diaz an approving nod. "Very frosty. In fact, that's your new name. In fact, Frost, I want you to drop and give me fifty pushups."

Frost dropped down and immediately started counting off her pushups. Connor couldn't help but be impressed. He'd just thrown them out of a perfectly good cargo ship and they were out in the middle of nowhere, yet Winters, now Frost, followed instructions to the letter. She was a keeper for sure.

Connor glanced at Diaz. "I guess engineers are predisposed to work well under pressure."

"Sir, yes, sir," Winters said while doing her pushups.

"Where are my hunters?" Connor said.

He glanced down the line.

"Over here, sir," a woman said.

Connor walked over to her and glanced at the man next to her. "Donna Marten?"

"Yes, sir," Marten said.

Donna Marten was lean and in great shape. Connor was sure he could give her two hundred pushups and she'd hardly break a sweat.

Connor glanced at the man. "And you're Nate Poe?"

The man had long straight black hair tied back from his face and brown skin. "Yes, sir."

Both hunters were tall—easily six feet.

"First, it's convenient that you guys chose to stand together. Otherwise, I'd have to do this whole song and dance again. Don't you agree?" Connor asked.

Poe frowned. "I guess so, sir."

Connor looked at Marten. "What about you?"

"No, sir," Marten said.

Connor stepped back. "Did the rest of you hear that? Recruit Donna Marten doesn't agree that it was a good idea for her and her fellow hunter to stand together in the line."

"She's got some nerve, sir," Diaz said.

"Nerve indeed. Got ourselves a regular Boone right here. In fact, Marten, that's going to be your new name. Boone," Connor said. "It just so happens that Recruit Boone is absolutely right. It's a terrible idea for my specialists to be so close to one another. Does anyone besides Boone know why?"

"Sir," said a huge man from further down the line.

"Randle, Wayne, go ahead and tell us why," Connor said.

"Because if we're attacked, we run the risk of two people with the same skill sets being lost," Randle said.

Connor nodded. "That's exactly right, Randle. Outstanding. From now on, when we're outside of the camp, you are to stagger yourselves from anyone who has the same specialty as you. We have comlinks, and you can always speak that way. Is that understood?"

"Sir, yes, sir," the recruits replied in unison.

Connor looked back at Randle. "I recognize you from Field Operations."

Randle nodded. "Sir, I was on patrol the day of the berwolf attack, sir."

"That's right. You're one of my weapons specialists. Where is my other weapons specialist?" Connor asked.

"Over here, sir," a man said from further down the line.

"Compton, Neal. Good job, the both of you," Connor said.

"Thank you, sir," they both said.

"It could have been luck, but I'm sure the fact that you both were infantrymen back home had something to do with it," Connor said and walked to the middle of the line. "We'll have to continue the introductions a little bit later. As you can see, we're not at a research base. We're out in the middle of nowhere, roughly fifty kilometers from the compound," he said and looked down the line for his next victim.

"Blake, Allison," Connor said. "What's our situation?"

Blake's brows drew upward and her hazel eyes widened. "I'm not sure, sir," she said softly.

Diaz shook his head. "Recruit! Your commanding officer asked you a question. You will speak loudly and clearly. Now!"

"I'm not sure, sir," Allison said much louder this time.

"Why not?" Connor asked.

Blake started to look at the recruits on either side of her but caught herself. "I'm not sure what you're asking me, sir."

"It's a simple question. What's our situation?" Connor asked.

Blake's chin crumpled and she took shallow breaths.

"Calm down," Connor said. "You're one of my medics, right? Take the same skills you'd use to assess a patient and apply them to us right now."

Blake swallowed hard and she glanced around. "We're exposed out here and it will be dark soon."

Connor smiled. "Excellent. So what do you think we should do?"

"Set up camp, sir?"

"Outstanding," Connor said. "You heard Babyface. We need to set up camp. In that first storage crate, you'll find fencing to set up a perimeter. Split up into two teams and get it set up first."

"Sir, where are we going to sleep tonight?" Compton asked.

Connor's gaze narrowed. "Who said anything about sleeping?" he asked.

"Yes, sir," Compton said.

"Bones and Frost, there's a power generator in one of these crates. Find it and check with Diaz about where to set it up. Then help with the fence," Connor said.

"Dismissed," Diaz shouted. "Time to get to work, people."

Randle walked over to Connor. "Sir, shouldn't some of us be armed in case there are predators around? Some of them start coming out during this time, sir."

"Listen up," Connor said, and the recruits stopped what they were doing. "Sergeant Diaz and I are the only ones cleared for weapons, so the more time we have to spend answering your pitiful questions, the less time we have to keep watch for any predators in the area, which means one of you might become dinner. Now get that fence up."

Randle snapped a salute and ran over to the large container. Connor watched as the recruits started offloading the crate.

"Recruits, if that fence isn't set up within three hours, I'll make sure you'll be sleeping in a tent on the other side," Connor said.

The recruits quickened their pace. Connor knew there weren't any predators in the area, but he wanted to deploy the new drones Noah had given them. He retrieved his tablet computer from his pack and brought up the manifest, found the crate that contained specialized equipment, and entered the security code. There was a snap-hiss sound as the crate opened. Squished inside, looking uncomfortable as hell, was Sean Quinn.

16

CONNOR'S MOUTH HUNG OPEN. Of all the things he'd expected to encounter, a stowaway in a cargo crate wasn't among them.

"Get out of there," Connor said.

Sean climbed out of the crate and winced. His hand went to his side.

"How did you get inside the crate? When did you even have time? I just saw you a little while ago on base," Connor said.

Sean tried to stand up straight and winced again. "After I left your office, I bumped into Noah. He told me he was just coming from the airfield and that you were leaving to begin training the new recruits. So . . . I went to the airfield and snuck aboard."

Connor regarded him for a moment and pushed away his irritation at the utter lack of security at the airfield. "Hard landing in that crate, wasn't it?" he said.

"I didn't know they were going to be dropped out of the ship—" Sean began to say.

"You could have been killed. Those crates are designed to land without a chute. We put chutes on those with delicate equipment. It was dumb luck that you weren't seriously hurt," Connor said.

Sean pressed his side and winced. "I think I might be hurt a little bit."

"And now this is my problem to deal with. I don't want to explain to your parents how their idiot son decided he'd stowed away in a crate because he's having rebellion issues, but you've given me no choice," Connor said.

"Please don't!" Sean pleaded. "Don't do it. I'll do anything you tell me to. Just don't send me back there."

"What's your problem? Why don't you want to go back to the compound? You can do whatever the hell you want there and be someone else's problem," Connor said.

Sean looked away. "No, I can't. I can't do anything."

Connor watched as Sean winced again, and this time his hand rubbed the side of his head.

"Sit down," Connor ordered.

He stepped back and looked over to where the recruits were emptying a storage crate about forty meters from them. "Sergeant Diaz!" Connor shouted.

One of the recruits heard him and told Diaz. Diaz came around the storage crate.

"Send over Babyface. I need a medic," Connor said.

He heard Diaz shout for the recruit to go to Connor, and Recruit Blake ran over. Her pretty face was a grim line of determination, but Connor could tell she was barely coping. She reached them and came to a halt, glanced at Sean sitting on the ground, and then remembered to stand at attention and salute Connor.

"Recruit Babyface, please put your skills as medic to good use and examine Recruit Bling here," Connor said.

"Yes, sir," Babyface replied.

She immediately squatted down and set about assessing Sean Quinn for injuries. Connor stepped around them and searched for the container of drones Noah had packed for them. There were three silver cases marked with the golden sunburst, and Connor pulled them out one at a time, setting them down a short distance from the others. He listened to Blake question Sean and check his injuries. Connor had his back to them, but he could hear everything that they were saying. Despite the shakeup of the circumstances and the fact that they were utterly exposed to New Earth's vibrant ecosystem, the young medic went about her assessment with the practicality that only came from experience.

Connor heard footsteps approaching and turned around.

"Sir, Recruit Bling has some minor bruising of the ribs and a headache that was caused by the jolting he experienced while inside the storage crate, sir," she said.

"Excellent. Return to the others and get the fence set up," Connor ordered.

He looked at Sean, who was sitting on the ground but hastily got to his feet.

"I don't know what I'm going to do with you. We'll have communications up in a little while. In the meantime, there's no way I'm going to let an extra pair of hands go to waste, even ones as dainty as yours. From here on out, you'll be called Bling. While you're here, you will follow my orders without question. Is that understood?"

"Yes, sir," Sean said and tried to keep the smile from his face.

"Now, go report to Sergeant Diaz. He'll put you to work. Tell him I said to give you the dirtiest task he has. Now repeat my order," Connor said.

"Report to Sergeant Diaz and tell him to give me the dirtiest task he has, sir."

"Good. Now leave," Connor said.

The kid ran off to join the others, and Connor put thoughts of him out of his mind. He had other things to worry about. Grabbing the first case, he used his implants to authenticate the lock, and it sprang open. The oval-shaped drones had the look of a decapitated head from a robot. Two optics in the front glowed when he activated the drone. There were also different sensors along the tubes on the side that gave it a more streamlined look, and the metallic compound the hull was made of was light and strong.

Connor checked the drone's status and video-feed output using his implants. A sub window appeared on his internal heads-up display that showed anything he pointed the drone at while the drone's target-awareness computer identified and classified anything that came into view. He set the dark gray drone on the ground and put it in patrol mode. The drone rose up into the air and sped off, hardly making any noise. He uploaded the transponder identification for Diaz's PDA. Connor activated the rest of the drones from all the cases and broke them up into groups. Their patrols would send them into different vicinities outward from the camp. Connor connected to drone seven and set it to locate Diaz. He watched the video feed as the drone made a quick sweep of the camp and quickly identified Sergeant Juan Diaz. Connor acknowledged the recorded success and put the drone in patrol mode. Noah had assured him that the drones could identify the known predators and would alert Connor if anything should happen to be heading toward their camp. Once they set up their small operations center, the recruits would rotate through monitoring duty. He and Diaz would need to review the unknown detections to help the drones' artificial intelligence learn what the misidentified creatures were. It was a pain but definitely worth the effort.

Connor set the empty cases to the side. The drones still had to prove themselves, so he set about doing a patrol of his own just to be sure no berwolfs or anything else were coming to investigate the camp while it was being built. A short while later Diaz caught up to him.

"Excuse me, sir," Diaz said.

They'd agreed that they would maintain formal communications while the recruits were around them.

"Are you aware that we have an extra recruit in our midst, sir?" Diaz asked.

"I am," Connor replied.

"You do realize he's the governor's son, sir?"

"I do," Connor said and waved Diaz closer. "He stored himself in one of the crates. I had to do something with him."

Diaz grinned. "I've got him digging a latrine—that is, of course, until we get the rest of the camp set up."

Connor glanced over at the recruits who were working on building the perimeter fences. He and Diaz had given them the orders and were evaluating how well they could work together. Connor had trained soldiers before, and every task, large and small, was a test. The sooner these recruits learned that, the better.

"How do you think it's going so far?" Connor asked.

"No one has died, sir," Diaz said.

Connor made a face at the sergeant. Diaz grinned and went back over to the recruits, shouting that they'd better get a move on. Connor walked over to his two engineers, who were making excellent progress setting up the power generators.

"Bones, I need you to help out the others with the fence," Connor said.

"Yes, sir," Bones said. He returned his tools to the kit and ran off to help the others.

Elyse Winters, now known as Frost, continued working on the main generator. Frost hardly paid Connor any notice at all and just focused on what she was doing.

There was a loud slam as one of the fence sections hit the ground, and Diaz's shouts could be heard echoing around them. Connor glanced over and saw that several recruits were now doing pushups.

"Sir, may I ask you a question?"

"Go ahead, Frost," Connor said.

"Why did you pick such a remote location to train us, sir?" Frost asked.

"You were in the military before?" Connor asked.

"Yes, sir, same kind of job. Different location, sir."

"Then you already know the answer to that question," Connor said.

"Joe and I . . . uh, Bones and I have served before. We understand the discipline you're trying to instill, but some of the others have no idea, sir," Frost said.

"They'll learn or they'll go back to the compound," Connor said.

"This is done, sir," Frost said and gestured toward the power generator.

Connor thought it would have taken another half hour to put it together, but he looked it over and everything seemed to be in order. Frost engaged the generator's startup sequence and it went through several self-diagnostics before returning the ready status.

"Good work," Connor said.

"Thank you, sir. You wanted the best, sir," Frost said.

She wasn't lacking in confidence. "That remains to be seen. Lay out the wiring for the fence and then rejoin the others," Connor said.

Connor left his engineer and headed toward the others. The fully constructed fence sections were over twelve feet tall, but inside the crate they were folded over and only half that height. Most of the recruits carried the sections together except for Randle and Compton, who each took a section of their own. The progress they were making was painstakingly slow. At the rate they were going, the fence wouldn't be complete until well after nightfall, which was unacceptable.

"I think we have ourselves a competition going on here," Connor said. "Randle, you're strong as a bull. In fact, that's your name now. And Compton is like a bear."

"A grizzly bear, sir," Diaz said.

"Grizzly, I like that. Do you like it, Compton?" Connor asked.

"Yes, sir," he answered.

"Well, see how many sections Bull and Grizzly can handle on their own. Let's see how many they can lift up together. Any bets?" Connor asked.

"I say six sections, sir," said Henry "Hot Rod" Deacon.

"Whatever it is, I know I can equal it, sir," Bones said.

Connor laughed with the rest of them. "The gauntlet has been thrown. Show us what you can do."

Bull went inside the large crate and came out with two sections of fencing.

Each section was ten feet in length. He laid the sections on the ground, one atop the other. Grizzly continued stacking until they had eight sections in a neat pile. Each section weighed about fifty pounds. Neal "Grizzly" Compton and Wayne "Bull" Randle squatted down and easily lifted them up. They carried the fencing a hundred meters from the storage container toward the end of the fence that was already up. By the time they reached the end, both men were gasping and drenched in sweat. They set the sections down and hunched over with their hands on their knees, trying to catch their breath.

"Alright, Bones, you're up. Eight sections," Connor said.

"No problem, sir," Bones said.

"This should be interesting," Connor said and glanced over to see Boone and Nate beginning to offload a section of fencing. "Hold off on that a second. I want everyone to watch how Bones is going to pull this off."

Bones smiled widely. "I'll need one volunteer to help me."

"Now wait a minute," Bull said. "You said you could beat us alone."

"That's not what I said. I said I could equal it," Bones replied.

Bull looked at Connor. "Sir?"

"Let's see what he does," Connor said.

They went back to the storage crate, and Bones stood in the entrance. "Sir, I need one volunteer."

"Me, sir, I'll do it," Blake "Babyface" Allison said and ran forward before anyone could stop her.

Bones frowned for a moment, then shrugged and gestured for her to follow him inside.

The two of them carried out eight more sections of fencing one section at a time and stacked them together. The rest of the recruits looked on with slightly bemused expressions. If Bull and Grizzly—who were both six feet, six inches tall and close to three hundred pounds of solid muscle—had trouble, they assumed that the team of Bones and Babyface certainly couldn't do it.

Bones went back into the storage container and pulled out the straps from inside. The engineer got down on his hands and knees and weaved the cord through the slats at the bottom section of fencing. Babyface helped him and after a few minutes they had multiple crisscross sections weaved throughout. Bones cut the remaining cords into smaller sections and weaved those in, leaving enough slack at the end to make a harness.

Bones called Babyface over and gave her some instructions. She nodded and knelt on the ground. Bones looped the cords around her middle and then crossed them behind her neck, then ran to the other side and got himself set up with a makeshift harness.

"Okay, Blake . . . I mean Babyface, on three we lift together," Bones said.

Bones counted down and then pushed up from a squat to a standing position. Babyface did the same and, much to the recruits' surprise, the stack of fencing rose off the ground, entirely stable.

"Good job!" Boone shouted and clapped.

Bull and Grizzly just stood with their mouths hanging open.

"Okay, one step at a time. Just a walk in the park," Bones said.

Connor watched as the two recruits carried eight fence sections over a hundred meters and set their stack down near the other stack. Both of them were sweating and slightly winded from the effort.

Connor grinned. "You see, brains and brawn can work just fine apart, but together you can accomplish so much more."

Bull went over to Bones. "You've got to show us how you did that."

"It's easy. I can show you," Bones said and led some of the others back toward the storage crate.

Connor saw Babyface watching him, so he gave an approving nod. She beamed at the acknowledgment.

The recruits broke themselves up into two teams. One team carried the fencing sections out from the storage crate while the others set them up and connected the sections together. They progressed much quicker because of it, but Connor knew there was no way they were going to finish in the time he'd given them. They did manage to get well past the midpoint using Bones' new method of carrying. Connor looked around and saw that they were now leaving stacks of fence sections along the perimeter of their new camp. Neither he nor Diaz yelled at them to move faster. They'd achieved each objective he'd set for them, which was to set up the perimeter fence and work quickly and efficiently as a team. To the casual onlooker, what Connor was about to do would seem cruel, but anyone who'd trained soldiers would know it was necessary.

The sun was getting lower in the sky, and his team of recruits lined up. They were grimy and sweaty and starting to smell pretty ripe.

"Recruits, we have a temporary addition to our team. Recruit Bling, get up here and face the squad," Connor said.

Sean Quinn was covered in dirt from the trench he'd dug to serve as their latrine. He stood at attention.

"I see that some of you recognize Recruit Bling, but for those of you who don't know him, his name is Sean Quinn. His father, Tobias, is the governor of our colony and his mother, Ashley, is chief of medicine on the Ark. Bling decided it would be a good idea to store himself in one of the crates, and I didn't find him until after we'd gotten here," Connor said and circled around Sean while addressing the other recruits. "He complained that the other people at the compound give him too much preferential treatment. He wants to join Search and Rescue to be part of something important. He says he's committed to us and to you. Over the next few days, before our next shipment of supplies comes in, I'll need to decide what his level of commitment is. The reason I'm telling you this is because I didn't want anyone to give this young man any preferential treatment, but now I'm not sure I agree with that. He's used to getting special treatment, so I'm going to hold with that tradition. For every mistake Recruit Bling makes, you all will join him in his punishment. For every mistake, lapse in judgment, trip, fall, complaint, or anything else the rest of you do that Sergeant Diaz and myself don't like, Recruit Bling here will do *double* your punishment," Connor said and turned toward Sean Quinn. "How's that sound to you, Bling?"

"Sir, it sounds outstanding, sir," Sean replied.

"Get back in line," Connor said.

Sean scurried back to his place and stumbled into Bull. He whispered a hasty apology and took his place.

"Recruit Bling, come back here," Connor snapped.

Sean ran back to the front.

"Did you understand my order, recruit?" Connor asked.

Sean frowned. "Yes, sir."

"Repeat the order for me," Connor said.

"Sir, you said to get back in line, sir," Sean said.

"That's right. Then why did you assault Recruit Bull?"

Sean's eyes widened. "I'm sorry, sir. It just sort of happened."

"Just sort of happened?" Connor asked and looked at Diaz. "Sergeant Diaz, do you believe in magic?"

"No, sir."

Connor glared at Sean. "I assume you know how to walk straight, is that right?"

"Yes, sir, it won't—"

"Recruit!" Diaz bellowed. "The commander didn't ask for an excuse."

"Sergeant Diaz, what's our standard punishment for this kind of infraction?"

"Fifty pushups, sir," Diaz said.

Connor stood in front of Sean. "That means you get to do a hundred pushups and the rest of you get to do fifty. Count them off right now."

"But, sir—"

"I'm not interested in your opinion!" Connor bellowed. "If I want your opinion, I'll give it to you."

Sean immediately dropped to the ground and started counting off pushups. The rest of the team dropped and began their pushups.

Connor paced in front of them. "I know you've become accustomed to voicing your opinions the moment they become a thought in your brain, but during training we're not interested in your opinions. When you make a mistake, don't offer up excuses and try to tell Sergeant Diaz or myself that it won't happen again. Words are cheap." Connor paused and watched as Recruit Allison struggled with her pushups. She glanced at Connor's feet as he stood by her and doubled her efforts.

"Sergeant Diaz, do you know what an excuse is?" Connor asked.

"I'm sure I do, sir, but I never get tired of hearing you say it," Diaz replied.

"An excuse is another word for failure. No amount of words will erase the failure. Now, you say it," Connor ordered the recruits.

The recruits repeated it, and Connor had them do it again. They finished their pushups, with the exception of Bling.

"The rest of you have a hundred and twenty seconds to use the latrine and return here or you'll join Recruit Bling for more pushups," Connor said.

Half the recruits immediately ran toward the trench at the far side of the camp.

"Excuse me, sir," Owens said.

"Einstein, I don't recall giving you permission to ask me anything. You have your orders," Connor said.

"But, sir, I don't think I can in front of everybody, sir," Owens said.

"Hold on. Recruits, get back here," Connor shouted.

Diaz yelled at the other recruits to get back. Several stumbled back, pulling up their pants and looking annoyed.

"Line up!" Diaz said.

Several glared ahead and refused to look at him.

"The reason you were called back was because Recruit Einstein didn't think she could handle the pressure of relieving herself in front of all of you. Apparently she's pee-pee shy. So now we get to do a little bit of running. Thirty laps, following the fence. You will stay in formation. Recruit Bling, that will be sixty laps for you," Connor said.

Sean turned around and started running.

"Recruits, you heard the man. Fall out!" Diaz said.

Connor led them along the perimeter of the fence and heard the footfalls of the recruits behind him.

"Hey, Bones, how far is thirty laps?" Compton asked.

"Six miles," Bones answered, and several recruits started groaning.

Connor turned around and jogged backwards. "There is no talking on this run, recruits."

The first two miles passed without anyone complaining. The third mile brought on a few groans and the fourth mile added to that.

Diaz pulled out a shock stick from his belt. "If any of you lag behind, you'll get to feel the love from my stunner."

The recruits immediately shut their mouths. At six miles, Connor brought them to a halt. He told Diaz to get them lined up and ran with Sean Quinn.

"Ready to call it quits?" Connor asked.

"No, sir."

"Why not? All you have to do is get to a comlink and make that call. Mommy and Daddy will come and take you home. Acknowledge this was all a big mistake and promise never to do it again," Connor said.

"I won't quit, sir," Sean said.

"Are you sure? I can get communications up in no time," Connor said.

"I'm not gonna quit, sir."

"We'll see, Bling. We'll see," Connor said and stopped running. "If you finish the rest of the run in forty-five minutes, you get to stay for another hour. Otherwise, I'm going to make the call."

Connor watched as Sean quickened his pace.

Connor returned to the others and regarded his recruits for a moment. There were already a few soldiers in the bunch, but by the time he was done, they'd all be much closer to being soldiers than they were right now.

"Let's try this again. You have one hundred and twenty seconds to use the latrine and return here," Connor said.

Diaz repeated the order, and this time the recruits hastened toward the latrine without comment. Diaz walked over to his side.

"Going to be a long night," Diaz said.

"I thought you liked to stay up all night," Connor chided.

"I do, but we don't all have those fancy implants and nanites that let us get by on two hours of sleep," Diaz said.

"I think it's time for a water ration. Would you get the canteens and bring them back here? Take Boone and Einstein to do the heavy lifting," Connor said.

Diaz grinned. "At once, sir. Right away, sir."

Diaz jogged away and called the recruits over to him while Connor made a show of checking his PDA for the time. He had a timer showing on his internal heads-up display, but the recruits couldn't see that. Connor watched as Deacon shouted that their time was running out. The warning was repeated by several of the others. The recruits finished their business and sprinted back toward Connor, lining up in two rows.

"Congratulations, you *just* made it and have proficiently demonstrated your ability to follow simple commands," Connor said.

Relief shone on most of their faces. Elyse Winters had no reaction and neither had Joe Ramirez nor Nate Poe. The three were in the best physical shape of the bunch. Wayne Randle and Neal Compton didn't look that much worse for wear, but during the run Connor had heard them huffing and puffing quite a bit. Connor glanced at Allison Blake, who wore a determined expression.

Diaz returned with Boone and Einstein.

"Go get your water ration and get back in line," Connor said.

The recruits quickly retrieved their canteens, and Wayne Randle drank from it greedily. Joe Ramirez did the same, but none of the other recruits did.

"Bull, do you have trouble hearing? I didn't read in your file that you had issues with hearing," Connor said.

Randle looked guiltily at the canteen in his hands and closed his eyes for a moment. "No, sir," he said.

"What about you, Bones? Is there something wrong with your hearing that I'm not aware of?" Connor asked.

"No, sir," Ramirez said.

"Come out here and stand in the front. Both of you," Connor said. "The rest of you may drink since you know how to follow orders."

"It seems that both of you need a lesson in following orders again, so we're going to do a little exercise to drive that point home," Connor said.

"Yes, sir," both recruits said in unison.

"Do either of you know what burpees are?" Connor asked.

"No, sir," Ramirez said.

"Yes, sir. It's hands to the ground by your feet, jump your feet back, then do a pushup, bring your feet back in, then jump into the air, sir," Randle said.

Connor smiled and gave an approving nod to Diaz. "Outstanding. Do forty now."

Both men immediately started doing the burpees. Ramirez followed along, awkwardly at first, but then easily got the hang of it. By the time they both reached twenty-five, each man was breathing heavily and had spit up the water they'd drunk.

"As entertaining as this is, we have more work to do," Connor said.

There were several soft groans.

"But if you would like to join Bull and Bones, that can easily be arranged," Connor said.

All groans ceased immediately and there was silence but for the footfalls of Sean Quinn running along the perimeter fence nearby.

"We have four tents to set up. There'll be two cots in one tent. The remaining tents will be divided among you. One tent will have five cots since we're now a team of lucky thirteen. You have one hour to complete this task," Connor said.

There were no comments or questions. The recruits simply followed Diaz to the supply crate that held the tents. Exactly thirty minutes later, Sean Quinn finished his run early. He panted, and Connor regarded him for a minute. To Sean it seemed that Connor was staring at him as a form of intimidation, but what Connor was really doing was giving the young recruit some recovery time.

"That canteen of water contains your water ration," Connor said.

"Yes, sir," Sean said but didn't move. He immediately began doing burpees and counting them off.

Connor watched as Sean used every ounce of his remaining strength toward completing the exercise.

"You got this!" Deacon shouted from where they were assembling the tents.

Sean collapsed at forty up/downs, gasping for breath.

"Get up, Bling. You can do it!" Randle's deep voice bellowed.

The other recruits shouted for Sean to get up.

Connor squatted down. "They believe in you. Do you really want to let them down?"

Sean growled as he came to his feet. "Search and Rescue!" he shouted.

The rest of the recruits cheered, and Connor shared a look with Diaz. Neither one of them cracked a smile, but their chests filled with pride for the young man. When Sean reached eighty he could hardly catch his breath. He was on his hands and knees.

"Go on over and help them get the tents set up," Connor said and walked away.

Randle and Compton ran over to Sean and helped him to his feet. One retrieved a canteen of water and urged him to drink.

Sean Quinn glanced over at Connor with a burning intensity in his eyes. It wasn't until that moment that Connor believed the young man really wanted to be part of the team.

Over the next few hours the recruits had one break to feast on a pack of field rations. There weren't any complaints since they only had five minutes to eat before the next task was given to them. The recruits set up other mobile structures, which were basically tents designed for a purpose. With the power generator up, the perimeter fence had electrical current running through it. It wasn't a constant high-voltage charge since that would have been inefficient, even with the advanced battery capabilities they had. They set up motion sensors that would cause the fence to go full charge if an animal large enough to be a threat was detected.

It was well past midnight, and the recruits were almost asleep on their feet.

"Time for some rack time. Two of you will patrol the perimeter of the fence for the next hour and then the next set will rotate in. You will alert either me or Sergeant Diaz if you see anything suspicious outside our perimeter," Connor said.

"Sir, may I ask a question?" Donna Marten asked.

"Go ahead, Boone," Connor replied.

"Will we be armed for patrol?"

"Negative. Weapons training will be tomorrow. Until I've assessed your abilities, you will not be armed," Connor said.

"Dismissed," Diaz said.

As the recruits walked toward their tents—some of them limping—Connor and Diaz watched. At the last second, Boone and Grizzly headed away from the tent to take the first patrol.

"Go on and get some rack time," Connor said.

"I'll see you in few hours, sir," Diaz said and went to the tent they were sharing.

Connor went to the command tent, where there were several crates of computer equipment waiting to be set up. Noah wouldn't be there for a few days, and Connor was sure that either Ramirez or Winters could set it up, but he wanted at least one monitoring station up and knew he could handle it. It had been a long day for them all, but Connor wasn't the least bit tired. If anything, he was excited to finally be doing something. He believed building his own team was the best way he could contribute to the colony.

Throughout the day he and Diaz had recorded the recruits' strengths and weaknesses, both of which would be tested over the coming days and weeks.

He heard the sound of hushed conversation as Boone and Grizzly walked the perimeter. He hadn't given them specific orders on how to stand watch and was curious to see what each pair of recruits would do. He had one of the drones following them, but doubted the recruits knew the drone was there.

Connor finished setting up the monitoring station and brought it up. Drone feeds began to upload their data, and Connor noticed that they had limited communications capability with the main compound. A chat window opened up.

::*Couldn't wait for me to get there to set up a monitoring station I see,*:: N. Bates said.

"Noah," Connor muttered.

::*SR-Camp is up. Drones are on patrol and checking in,*:: C. Gates said.

::*Sweet! I'll run diagnostics on them when I'm out there in a few days. How's the training going?*:: N. Bates asked.

::*We're missing our second tech specialist,*:: C. Gates replied.

::*Owens is good. I hope you're being nice to her,*:: N. Bates said.

The amber text window became outlined in green.

::*I've encrypted this session,*:: N. Bates said.

Connor frowned. ::*Okay, why?*::

::*We've received a data burst from the space buoy network. If you recall, the data we received from Earth was sent sometime in the past two hundred years,*:: N. Bates said.

::*What did you receive?*::

::*Only the header of the data burst, which had a reference called EOD-Extinction*

Critical Alpha. What follows is a set of programming instructions for the Ark,:: N. Bates said.

::*Are you trying to play a joke on me?*::

::*It's tempting, but no. There's also a mention of M. Wilkinson.*::

Connor felt something sink into the pit of his stomach. ::*Can you send me what you have?*::

::*No, it's too much for this connection. I only have a partial dump because access to buoy transmissions is restricted until they're reviewed by the Governor's office,*:: N. Bates said.

Connor leaned back in his chair and rubbed his chin. ::*Okay, show me what you've got when you get here in a few days. I would suggest not showing this around to anyone else.*::

::*You don't have to tell me twice.*::

::*I need you to do something for me. Sean Quinn stored himself in one of our crates. He requested to join the Search and Rescue squad, which I initially refused. Since he's here, I have him training with the rest. Can you send a message to Ashley?*:: C. Gates asked.

::*Oh boy, that's not good. I'll let her know.*::

The chat session ended, and Connor thought about the partial data dump from the space buoy network. Tobias normally had a policy for transparency, so why would any information received from Earth be restricted? He recalled some of the conversations on the Ark and that Ashley and Tobias had explained how their mission had been overwritten to bring them here instead of their original destination. That override added over a hundred years to the mission.

Connor got up from his seat and stepped outside the tent, looking over at the tents nearby and thinking about Sean Quinn. Could Sean know something about why the mission had been changed? Did he know why Tobias was keeping information from the colony? Was that the reason Sean was determined to join Connor's new team? Or was he just doing what normal teenage kids who are on the cusp of adulthood and carving out their own niche in the world do?

Connor looked up at the night sky. A blanket of stars shined along with the moon. His gaze was then drawn to the south, where the ring that surrounded the planet brightened the night sky. Connor doubted there was ever a pitch-black night on this planet. The surrounding area was alive with chirping insects, and when Connor closed his eyes, he could almost imagine he was back on Earth, but the rhythm of sounds from the nightly critters was of a different cadence, and his brain kept registering that fact.

Connor walked over to one of the armored storage crates and placed his hand on the palm reader. At the same time, he used his implants to engage the locking interface with his biometric information and the lock disengaged. Connor pulled the large doors open. Inside was a mobile armory that held a variety of weapons they'd be training with in the coming weeks. It had taken a fair amount of negotiating with Tobias, but Connor had been able to access the weapons manifest from the Ark. Tobias may have no intention of starting a formal military, but that didn't mean he couldn't arm one if it came down to it. Someone had the foresight to include military-grade assault rifles and other types of weapons.

Connor unloaded the weapons crates he wanted to use with the recruits and stacked them just outside the container. There was only so much time he'd allocated for training these recruits who'd ostensibly come with at least some experience in a field he needed for Search and Rescue.

Connor heard two recruits walking along the perimeter fence. When they noticed him, they jogged over.

"Do you need some help, sir?" Deacon asked.

It appeared that Connor had been working long enough for a shift change. "Grab a crate and follow me," Connor said.

Deacon and Poe each took a crate, and Connor grabbed the last one. He led them over to the command tent, where he'd set up the monitoring station, and put his case down. The others put theirs down next to his.

Connor thanked them, and they returned to their patrol. Connor went to his tent just as Diaz was leaving.

"I was just coming to find you," Diaz said.

"I set up a monitoring station and there are three crates of CAR-74s in the tent," Connor said.

Diaz nodded. "Couldn't you get the mess tent set up and get some eggs going?"

"We'll see how they perform today. If they earn it, they'll get a hot meal at the end. If not, then more rations," Connor said and went inside the tent.

He sat down on his cot, removed his boots, lay down, and shut his eyes. The last time he'd trained recruits like this he'd had a staff of twelve instructors with rotations. Here, he and Diaz just had each other. He thought about the Ghosts. More than once, images of Kasey and Reisman came to mind, along with Samson and Oslo. Randle and Compton reminded him a lot of Samson and Oslo, who'd carried heavy weapons in his unit. Connor went to sleep dreaming about lost friends and family. The Ghosts had been both to him. Today he'd kept comparing the recruits to the professional level of the elite special forces that made up the Ghosts. Perhaps he was being too hard on them, but the more ruthless side of Connor dismissed such thoughts. They trained because they'd be called upon to deal with the most dangerous of situations. They'd be facing the unknown, and in order to do that, they'd all need to perform at their best. This meant Connor had to push the recruits past their limits to see what they were truly capable of.

17

CONNOR SLEPT for two hours and woke up completely refreshed. He glanced outside the tent and saw that the sun was starting to rise, and he heard Diaz let out a hearty laugh. Connor put on his boots and didn't have to smell his underarms to know he smelled just as bad as the recruits. It had never bothered him before and certainly wasn't going to today. He put on a fresh shirt and went outside.

Diaz had the recruits lined up, and he turned around to face Connor.

"Good morning, Commander," the entire team said.

"Good morning," Connor replied.

Diaz's eyes were gleaming.

"Report, Sergeant."

"Quiet night. All is secure, Commander," Diaz replied.

"Excellent. Let's start our morning with some PT," Connor said.

Blake went pale, and Owens swayed on her feet. For the next hour Connor led them through various exercises, and he and Diaz performed them right along with the recruits. Sean Quinn stood with the others. Despite all the extra physical activity, he kept up with them. Connor led them on a six-mile run inside the perimeter fence, which he was already getting tired of. Running around in circles had never been his thing. Soon it would be time for their morning exercises to be performed outside the protective confines of the fence.

They ate breakfast in the form of field rations. He and Diaz divided the recruits into groups and assigned them tasks for setting up the rest of their camp. The first and foremost was setting up useable porta-toilets. While the latrine Sean had dug yesterday held a certain amusement factor, Connor didn't relish the thought of dropping anchor over a trench again today. He assigned Elyse Winters the task of digging a well, which wasn't as labor intensive as it once was.

Connecting their water supply to their mess hall and showers with a flex-pipe wouldn't take much time at all.

By midafternoon, sore muscles were beginning to stiffen up. Now that they had a fresh supply of water, Connor ended water rationing. They had more field rations as their midday meal, and he promised them that if they continued to perform there would be a hot meal for dinner.

They assembled in the yard away from the tents, and Diaz had them line up.

"We're going to start weapons testing. Inside the crates behind me is the CAR-74 semiautomatic hunting rifle. It's standard issue for Field Operations and is a good, basic firearm," Connor said.

Nate Poe raised his hand, and Connor nodded for him to speak. "Sir, I thought we'd be using weapons with a bit more stopping power. Presumably, Search and Rescue will be going into some of the worst situations. Wouldn't that mean we get to use more powerful firearms, sir?"

"Some of you haven't fired anything but the SD-15 Sonic Hand Blaster, and others have used the CAR-74 and on up to the AR-71 assault rifle. We'll get to the more powerful weapons. The purpose of using the CAR-74 is to teach basic marksmanship and to see if you can even fire a weapon accurately. And weapons testing will require that we leave the safety of the camp. We'll only be going just outside the fence. Either myself or Sergeant Diaz will be keeping watch at all times while we're outside. If you see something, do not fire your weapon at it unless your life is in danger. Instead, let us know," Connor said.

"Yes, sir," the recruits said.

Connor bent over and opened the crate full of the CAR-74 semiautomatic hunting rifles and picked one up. "The compact design should fit comfortably in your hands and uses smart rounds for ammunition. There's a full automatic setting, but you will never go full automatic out in the field. The reason for this is that you would use up all your ammo inside a minute," Connor said.

He proceeded to show them the different features of the rifle, along with safety instructions. Each of the recruits picked up a weapon.

"Sir, I'm not able to turn off the safety setting," Deacon said.

"That's because I don't want you to shoot anyone yet. The only weapons cleared for use are the ones Sergeant Diaz and I are holding. When I authorize you to shoot, you'll be able to disengage the safety on your weapon," Connor said.

They marched to the gate and left the safety of the camp. Connor led them away from the gate and had six of them line up while Diaz kept an eye on the forest nearby. So far, the berwolfs hadn't seen fit to pay them a visit. Connor took a small case from his pack and opened it. Inside were six target drones, which he set to fifty yards away. The drones raced to the configured distance and hovered a foot off the ground. Above the drones, six holographic targets appeared.

"Cute," Poe said.

"Successfully hit the target and the drone will move farther away to a limit of five hundred yards. I will demonstrate," Connor said.

Connor knelt down on one knee and aimed his rifle. He fired one round and hit his target dead center. The drone moved back to seventy-five yards and

Connor repeated the feat. Based on the ease with which Connor hit the target, the drone doubled the distance to a hundred and fifty yards. Connor lay down on the ground and used the legs at the end of the barrel to rest the weapon on. He quickly aimed the rifle and hit the center again. The target was hit two more times—once at three hundred yards and then again at five hundred.

Connor stood up. "Now it's your turn. First group, line up and fire from either a kneeling or ground position."

Nate Poe went to the first position, followed by Donna Marten. Randle and Compton came next, with Elyse Winters and Jo Ramirez next.

Poe and Marten quickly completed the exercise without missing a single shot. Connor expected nothing less from his two hunters. Deacon and Owens took the two open positions. Randle got stuck at three hundred yards but eventually made it to five hundred. Compton also performed the exercise without missing the target.

Deacon got stuck at a hundred and fifty yards and slammed his fist into the ground. "Sir, I believe there's something wrong with my rifle, sir," Deacon said.

Diaz went over and checked the weapon. He took one shot and hit the target. "The only problem here is that you can't shoot straight. Keep at it, Hot Rod."

Allison Blake dropped her rifle, and Connor was on her in seconds. "I won't have another member of this team get shot because you can't hold on to a damn hunting rifle. Fifty burpees now, recruit," Connor ordered.

Sean Quinn went over to her and began performing the burpees alongside her. Connor heard her whisper that she was sorry.

Connor turned his attention back to the others, and Amy Owens was trying to hit her target set at a hundred yards. She was joined by Jackson and Cooper. A few minutes later, Allison Blake returned to the line, and this time she held onto her weapon. She fired a shot at the target and completely missed. Connor lay down next to her and began giving her some guidance. After a few more tries she hit the target at fifty yards and let out a squeal of delight. The drone moved the target to seventy-five yards and Connor left her to it.

Connor had set a hundred-round limit, and Blake didn't make it past a hundred yards, but she was happy to make it that far. Connor knew she hadn't fired any type of firearm before. Sean Quinn was last to go. He lay down on the ground and aimed the CAR-74 hunting rifle as if he'd used one many times before. In five shots he also achieved the five-hundred-yard mark.

Connor stood behind him. "Excellent job, Recruit Bling. Are there any other hidden talents I should know about?"

"No, sir," Sean replied.

Connor had them line up again. "Not bad. For some of you, this was easy. Probably too easy. We'll be practicing each day and all of you will improve. The CAR-74 is a good introductory weapon. We'll only practice with it part of the time and only because it's standard issue for Field Operations. The likelihood of you encountering this weapon again is high, so you will know all its capabilities. Several of you will start on the M-Viper Sniper Rifle," Connor said.

This announcement brought several excited grins.

"When I call your name, I want you to line up next to me," Connor said.

"Yes, sir," the recruits said.

"Boone and Poe, obviously, and Grizzly," Connor said and made a show of surveying the rest. "Bling," he said.

Boone and Grizzly started clapping as the very surprised Sean Quinn joined the others.

"You're now my sharpshooters. You will train with me using the M-Viper and we'll focus on vantage points and other tactics unique to that kind of weapon. Rejoin the others," Connor said. After his sharpshooters got back in line, Connor continued. "Now that you're well rested, we're going to go for a nice run. From here on out you'll be armed everywhere you go. For today, it's going to be the CAR-74, and tomorrow it will be something different. Before we start our run, I'll open up the floor for a couple of questions," Connor said.

"Sir," Owens said. "What does CAR stand for in the CAR-74?"

"Good question. CAR stands for civilian assault rifle and the number is the series number," Connor said.

Deacon smiled and raised his hand. "Sir, is dinner soon? I'm starting to get hungry."

This brought more than a few laughs from the other recruits.

"Thanks for volunteering, Hot Rod," Connor said.

Deacon's face became pale. "Sir?"

"You've just volunteered for cleanup duty in our mess hall for the next two days. It comes with the added benefit of eating last," Connor said.

"Yes, sir," Deacon said.

"Recruits, be sure the safety on your rifles is on. Our run is going to be a little more scenic this time," Connor said.

He nodded to Diaz.

"Recruits, form two lines," Diaz ordered.

Connor took point. He had the surveillance drones in patrol mode, but there hadn't been enough time to allow the system to mature. Regardless, they were armed, and he and Diaz had already been to the area they were going to run to before they brought the recruits here. Connor set off at a slow pace down a rough trail that took them into the forest. As the forest thickened, shafts of sunlight poked through the canopy high above them. Connor glanced up and saw several creatures moving near the treetops. Their long arms were used to grasp thick vines and swing among the dizzying heights. Connor pulled up a drone feed on his internal heads-up display to get a closer look at them. The tree creatures looked to have thick skin that was a mix of grays to pale yellow stripes going to their elongated, three-fingered hands. Each finger looked as thick as his forearm. The lower half of the creatures' bodies split into two thick tails. Their ears ended in a point on either side of their reptilian faces. One of the creatures carried a smaller version of itself. The creature swung its young onto its back, where it held on, and then the group followed Connor and the recruits from the lofty heights of the treetops.

"We've got company," Randle said.

"Bull, put your gun down," Marten hissed at him.

"Won't they attack us?" Randle asked, clutching the weapon to his chest.

"No, they're just watching us," Marten said.

"Boone is right, you should listen to her," Connor said.

Randle lowered his gun and kept running. "Yes, sir."

"What are they called?" Deacon asked.

"They don't have a name, just a designation. TCL, for tree climber, large, and I can't remember the number associated with it. I do know they pretty much stay in the trees but can come onto the ground and use their split tails to move them around," Sean Quinn answered.

The tree climbers kept up with them.

"This is our new home. We need to learn to survive here. As part of our training, we'll be going outside the camp a lot, and eventually we'll be spending multiple nights away from camp," Connor said.

"Oh boy, I can't wait," Deacon said with mock enthusiasm.

"You'll be fine, Hot Rod. I'll protect you," Marten said.

"I always like a strong woman to keep me safe and warm," Deacon replied.

Several of the other recruits laughed. Connor used his implants to connect to a drone ahead of them that was located in an open plain similar to where they'd made their camp. After thirty minutes of navigating the rocky terrain of the forest path, they emerged onto a grassy field. The field led to a shallow valley, and Connor stopped running.

Ramirez gasped and pointed down into the valley. Two hundred yards away moved a herd of long-legged creatures that had thick, muscular bodies on top and were covered in shaggy brown hair.

"They've got to be twenty feet tall, maybe even taller," Ramirez said.

"Look how many of them there are," Blake said.

One of the creatures swung its head toward them. The short tentacles along its mouth gave it a bearded look. The creature blew out a blast of air and the call was taken on by the others.

"We don't want to get any closer," Sean warned. "They'll leave us alone if we don't bother them, but the alphas will defend the herd."

Another creature made a sound that reminded Connor of a deep horn blast. The herd perked up at this and started running away from them.

"Looks like we spooked them," Owens said.

Connor frowned and tried to see if there were any drones on the far side of the valley.

"They're not frightened of us," Marten said. She raised the scope of her rifle and peered across the valley.

Connor couldn't hear anything but the pounding legs of the giant creatures as they sped away.

"How fast can they run?" Randle asked.

"They can get up to a hundred and thirty kilometers an hour on an open field like this," Sean said.

"You know an awful lot about the creatures that live here," Randle said.

"Sergeant Diaz, we might have a planetary expert in our midst," Connor said.

A piercing scream echoed throughout the valley. Across from them, one of the long-legged creatures was pulled down by a group of spotted predators.

They'd darted from the forest on the other side and sunk their claws into it. The predators looked as if they wore the pelt of a leopard that gave way to black skin and two sets of arms.

The long-legged beast had bleated a final cry before the spotted predators silenced it with harsh growls.

Connor looked at Sean. "Know what they are?"

Sean Quinn squinted his eyes and then shook his head.

"Boone?" Connor asked.

"No, sir, we haven't encountered those before," Donna Marten said.

"That's our cue to leave. Sergeant Diaz, take point," Connor said.

They quietly withdrew back into the forest. Connor was about to turn around and follow the others when he caught sight of a spotted predator that wasn't feasting on the fresh kill. It was facing him.

"Shit," Connor said.

He raised his rifle and looked at the creature through his scope, taking off the safety and silently pleading with it not to attack him. It had no element of surprise, and no ambush predator would run across a field to attack its prey when there was a fresh kill waiting to be eaten.

The predator's muscular chest heaved as it drew breath. It had a set of smaller arms, followed by a set of longer arms behind it. The shoulder joint for the second pair of arms angled forward, and Connor was willing to bet that it could use those arms to help it run faster—a lot faster than Connor could ever run, that was for sure. There was no doubt in Connor's mind that the predator was looking at him. There were thick protrusions from the creature's cheekbones, which ended in red, giving it the look of fresh blood from its latest kill. Connor shivered and slowly eased his way backward. He'd thought the berwolfs were the apex predator in this area, but he might have been wrong.

As soon as Connor was within the cover of the trees, he turned around and ran, eager to catch up with the others. He tasked a drone to follow that creature and kept the video feed on his internal heads-up display. It hadn't followed him, but it definitely noticed him. He didn't know if he was seeing the curiosity of encountering a new life form or whether that creature was judging how much of a threat Connor was. Either way, he didn't want to find out, especially since he was armed with only a civilian hunting rifle.

18

That evening they had their first hot meal and the recruits also got their first taste of free time to eat and shower, which they all took advantage of. The only one pressed for time was Henry Deacon, whose comments had landed him on cleanup duty.

They met again for further instruction, as well as information regarding the expectations Connor had for his Search and Rescue platoon. The class environment was more interactive since each recruit had professional experience in their chosen field that applied to what Connor was trying to accomplish with them. Nate Poe and Donna Marten had both been on security details, rotating through the research bases. They had an excellent working knowledge of the creatures and plants they should be careful of and things that weren't a threat. Much to Connor's surprise, Sean Quinn possessed a breadth of knowledge about the planet and its creatures. Admittedly, Connor had mistaken the sandy-haired youth for just another kid, but he'd proven to be intelligent. Given Sean's parents, Connor supposed he shouldn't have been too surprised.

Over the next few days their time was broken down to physical training followed immediately by weapons instruction that included hand-to-hand combat. They also hiked into the forest beyond the camp. There were no reports from the drones about the spotted predator they'd encountered in the valley, but Connor still stayed away from the valley just to be on the safe side until the recruits were more experienced with their weapons.

They'd built elevated platforms inside the camp, where they'd practiced rescue scenarios of extracting trapped victims. As they were completing their second round of PT one day, a small cargo ship flew over the horizon. The wings folded upward and the pilot landed the ship in the marked area of the camp.

The cargo doors opened, and Diaz had the recruits start offloading the containers. Connor approached the side hatch, where Noah Barker exited the ship, followed by Ashley Quinn. Her gaze narrowed when she saw him. Ashley glanced to the side and saw her son offloading the plane. Her gaze softened for a moment and then she turned to Connor.

"Noah explained what happened," Ashley said.

Connor nodded and glanced at Noah. He was carrying a backpack and glanced around the camp as if he were deciding whether he could get back on the ship.

"Welcome to Search and Rescue. You can stow your gear in the tent and then meet up with the rest of the recruits when we assemble," Connor said to him.

Noah, recognizing a dismissal when he heard one, left Connor alone with Ashley.

"Sergeant Diaz," Connor said, "can you send Recruit Bling here?"

Ashley frowned in confusion until she saw her son running toward them. Sean came to a stop and snapped a salute at Connor before standing at attention.

"At ease. Give your mother a hug," Connor said.

Ashley pulled her son into her arms, and Connor took a few steps away to give them some privacy. He glanced over and Ashley was speaking in a stern tone to her son.

Connor caught snippets of the conversation. There were a few "crazies" and "your fathers" worked in.

"Connor, would you come here?" Ashley called.

Connor walked over and she had Sean give them a moment.

"How could you let this happen? This isn't what I want for my son," Ashley said.

"By the time I noticed he was here the ship had already gone back to headquarters. Training my recruits was more important at the time," Connor said and stepped closer. "Look, if he'd been hurt I would have called in a transport for him. He wants to be here. Believe me, I tried to dissuade him from training with us."

Ashley shook her head. "Yes, I'm quite aware of the level of training you're subjecting your recruits to."

Connor frowned. "What's that supposed to mean?"

"Come on, Connor, we've been keeping an eye on you. I'm not disputing your training methods. You have specific goals you're trying to achieve, and as an expert, I recognize that. But as a mother, it's tough to see. Why is Sean given double the punishment? Couldn't you take it easier on him?" Ashley asked.

"No. He locked himself in a storage crate to get away from special treatment. He did that to get away from the fact that you and Tobias are the head of the colony and Sean gets special treatment because of it. The fact that he handles everything I put him through is a clear indication of the man he wishes to become," Connor said.

"I think you underestimate how influential you can be. He's still a boy," Ashley said.

"He's almost eighteen. Old enough to be counted as an adult," Connor said.

Ashley scowled. "What do you know about—" she began to say but stopped herself from speaking.

"You were going to say: What do I know about being a parent? Not nearly as much as you. You know that," Connor said and squelched the pang of regret that threatened to rise up inside him. "But I know about training soldiers. Your son has what it takes."

"We didn't bring him here to become a soldier," Ashley said.

Connor sucked in a deep breath. Ashley's maternal instincts were in high gear, and this was an argument he couldn't win. He turned toward Sean and waved him over.

"Wait. I'm not finished speaking to you," Ashley said.

After nearly a week of being conditioned to follow orders, Sean Quinn was already coming toward them.

"Sean, your mother has made it quite clear that she doesn't want you here. Before you decide what you want to do, there's something I want to say to you," Connor said.

Sean glanced at his mother and then back at Connor. "Yes, sir?"

"You've recognized that you're at a crossroads in your life and that it's time to start forging your own path and have a say in what your life is to become, whether it's here or some other part of the colony. I have one question for you, and whatever you decide will not influence my opinion of you. Understand?" Connor asked.

"Yes, sir," Sean answered.

"Do you want to be known as the governor's son or Sean Quinn? Because the governor's son has no place on the Search and Rescue team, but Sean Quinn can earn a spot. Your actions over the past week have given you the right to try to be here in a more official capacity. That's all I wanted to say. I'll leave you to your mother and wait to hear your decision," Connor said.

Connor started to walk away, but before he could get too far, Sean called out to him.

"Commander, I'd like to stay, sir."

Connor glanced at Ashley. The chief of medicine was seething, but when her son looked at her, she smiled at him.

"I'll tell your father your decision. I don't have to tell you that he won't like it, but I'll share your reasons with him," Ashley said.

Sean's eyes lit up and he gave his mother a peck on the cheek.

"Be . . . careful," Ashley said quietly.

"I promise I'll look after him," Connor said.

"I'm sure you will. Would you mind walking me back to the ship? There's something I'd like to talk to you about," Ashley said.

"Of course," Connor said.

He followed Ashley back to the ship and she led him up the loading ramp beyond where the recruits were finishing offloading the ship. Once they were alone, Ashley spun around and punched Connor right in the stomach.

Connor doubled over, gasping for air. Ashley loomed over him with a satisfied smirk on her face as he straightened up.

"As a mother, you owed me that and you know it," Ashley said.

Connor sighed and nodded. "Alright, I'll give you that, but I meant what I said about your son."

"Oh, I know you believe it. Somehow Sean has come to idolize you. While I do think you're one of the good ones, you have a more dangerous side that I'd rather my son not emulate," Ashley said.

"This is supposed to be a place for fresh starts. I have a past that I won't apologize for. I'm here, and I'm doing the best I can to contribute to the colony."

"I know you are. That's the only reason I'm letting Sean stay here."

"Oh really? I don't think you'd be able to stop him. Not anymore."

The pilot stuck his head out of the cockpit. "Ma'am, we're ready to go."

"That's my cue to leave," Connor said.

"Oh, I do have an update for you. Noah will be here for the duration of the training. And I'm showing that you requested one of the Hellcats for training purposes?" Ashley asked.

"It's a troop carrier vessel that I know is on the Ark. We're Search and Rescue, and I want that to be one of our primary vehicles. We can rotate the ATVs as needed. Most of them know how to operate those anyway, but the Hellcat is different," Connor said.

"Who's cleared to fly it?" Ashley asked.

"Well I am, for one, and Juan Diaz for another. Unless you want to officially transfer a pilot to my group?" Connor asked.

"Nope, not yet. I'll see to it that you get your Hellcat, but it will take a few weeks," Ashley said.

"I appreciate the effort," Connor said.

Ashley narrowed her gaze in mock vehemence. "Don't try using that charm of yours on me. Now get out of here."

Connor laughed and wished her well. He exited the ship and cleared the area, waving to the pilot as he went. The pitch of the repulsor engines increased as more power was pumped into them and the ship rose into the air and sped away.

The recruits were moving the cargo crates over to their supply area.

"Commander," Diaz said.

"What is it, Sergeant?"

"Does this mean Recruit Bling is officially part of the Search and Rescue platoon, sir?"

The nearby recruits, including Sean Quinn, stopped so they could listen.

"Affirmative, Recruit Bling is part of Search and Rescue now," Connor confirmed.

Compton hooted loudly and gave Sean a healthy slap on the back. The sentiment was shared by the other recruits. Diaz walked over to Connor and barked for the recruits to get moving.

"So you're keeping the governor's son here," Diaz said. He spoke quietly so the others couldn't hear.

"He earned it. You know that," Connor said.

"I do, but some might read it as a political move," Diaz said.

"You mean my good friend, Damon Mills?"

"Among some others," Diaz said.

Connor pressed his lips together. "What are you saying? I shouldn't have let Sean stay?"

"No, I agree with you, and it wouldn't matter if I didn't. You'd just do as you please anyway. If something happens to that kid—he gets hurt or killed—then that will be on you," Diaz said.

"If something like that happens to any of them, it will be on me," Connor replied.

"True, but Tobias Quinn can be a dangerous enemy to have. I'm not speaking to you as a sergeant. I'm speaking to you as a friend. Just keep that in mind," Diaz said.

"Well, as your friend I appreciate it," Connor said. "I also doubt we'll get many delays in our equipment requests from here on out."

Diaz's eyes widened and he grinned. "You're a piece of work. And you say you don't play politics."

"I don't. I'm just using the cards I've been dealt," Connor said.

Later that day Connor went into the tent that served as his command center. Noah Barker was hard at work setting up additional systems and checking the ones that they'd put in place.

Noah turned around as Connor came inside. "Who set up this monitoring station? It's like they just jammed all the connections in. Whoever did it didn't know what the hell they were doing. I swear I spend more time going behind people, fixing their mistakes, whereas if they'd just let me do the install in the first place it would work perfectly. I bet it cuts out on you a bunch, doesn't it?" Noah said.

Connor glanced at Diaz, who had followed him inside the tent. The sergeant's stone-faced expression didn't reveal a thing. Only his eyes hinted at the barely contained mirth threatening to break free.

"Is anything broken?" Connor asked.

The monitoring station *had* been cutting out on them, but he hadn't been able to figure out why.

Noah stood up and rubbed his hands together. "Nothing I can't fix. So are you going to tell me?"

"What?" Connor asked.

Noah frowned. "Which of your recruits do I have to thank for botching up this install? They'll need to be trained to do it right."

Connor walked to the other side of the tent and looked away, feeling a flush creep across his face. "That won't be necessary."

"Why not? Look, I won't be that hard on them," Noah said.

Diaz started laughing, unable to contain himself any longer. "*He* put it together," Diaz said when he caught his breath.

Noah's eyes widened. "Oh, my God! I'm sorry—uh, I didn't mean all that. You know I was just being dramatic. It wasn't so bad."

"Just stop," Connor said. "It's not going to crush me that I can't install a monitoring station with the same skill as you. Just fix it so it stops cutting out on us."

"I'm almost done," Noah said.

He ducked behind the workstation and fiddled with the control panel, then came around and powered it on. This time there was no interference registering on the screen.

"Oh good, you've had the drones patrolling," Noah said.

"Yeah, and we stumbled onto a new type of predator. The drones have some footage to upload that I want sent back to the compound," Connor said.

Noah nodded. "They'll be able to upload their stored data now."

"That's good because we were only able to get live feeds from them and nothing prerecorded," Connor said.

"That's because you didn't connect the monitoring station to the storage array," Noah said.

Diaz started laughing again and spread his arms wide when Connor looked over at him.

"You've got to admit, it's pretty funny," Diaz said.

Connor chuckled. "I get it. Oh, and Noah, did you bring the other thing with you?"

Noah feigned ignorance. "I'm not sure what you mean."

"I told Diaz what you showed me—the data burst from the space buoy network," Connor said.

Noah glanced at Diaz and then back at Connor. "I did. You should know that after our little chat, Damon Mills paid me a visit asking about why our chat session was encrypted."

"What did you tell him?"

"I told him you wanted to test the secure communications features of the monitoring station," Noah said.

"Did he believe you?" Connor asked.

Noah shrugged. "I think so. He stopped asking me about it, but he started hanging around wherever I was working. It was enough for me to notice."

"Maybe Mills knows about the data burst somehow," Connor said.

Diaz nodded. "Probably. He and Franklin Mallory were among the first to be awakened on the Ark. They'd definitely be in the know."

"So do you have a full dump of the data burst?" Connor asked.

Noah shook his head. "Just the partial. With Mills hanging around, I didn't want to take a chance and go poking around at the Field Operations Headquarters. So I was thinking . . ."

"You want to work on this here," Connor said.

"It's remote and isolated," Noah replied.

"Show me what you have and then I'll decide," Connor said.

Noah reached into his pack and pulled out his tablet computer. He navigated through the interface and then flicked his hand toward the large holoscreen above the monitoring station.

"Here's the header that has the totally uplifting and non-scary reference to EOD-Extinction Critical Alpha," Noah said.

"EOD," Diaz repeated. "What the hell does that mean?"

Connor stared at the information on the screen. His brows pushed forward in concentration and he glanced at the others. "End of Days," he said.

Noah's face paled. "I've got a bad feeling about this."

"Are you sure the translation is right?" Diaz asked.

"Yes, this first part of the message was in the clear before the main data burst, which is why we're able to read it," Noah said.

"We shouldn't jump to conclusions," Connor said.

"Are you serious? A data burst from Earth that has the words 'extinction' and 'end of days,' and you don't want to jump to conclusions?" Noah asked.

"That's exactly what I'm saying. Something like this could spread like wildfire across the colony. We need to fully understand what's in that data before we decide what to do next," Connor said.

"So if it's bad, can I freak out then?" Noah asked only half-jokingly.

"We'll see. Where's the rest of it?"

"The main data burst has to be decoded. I thought of writing up my own decoder to do the job, but that could take a really long time. So I think I can access it from the Ark's computer system," Noah said.

"They'll detect it," Connor said.

"How do you know?" Noah asked.

"How do you *not* know? You think there won't be a digital trail if you try to access secure information?"

Noah thought about it for a moment. "Okay, I bet if I can just see the framework of the algorithm used to decode communications from the space buoy network, we should be able to see what the rest of the message says."

"Okay, but this is a part-time effort for you. You've missed a week's worth of training and you need to get caught up," Connor said.

Noah looked at both Connor and Diaz in alarm. "I thought I was just consulting with Search and Rescue," he said.

Connor smiled. "Keep telling yourself that. Welcome to the team. Now go put on a uniform like the rest of the recruits."

Noah's laugh became silent as he realized Connor was serious.

"Don't worry, we'll take good care of you," Diaz said.

Noah left the tent.

"This is some next-level stuff," Diaz said.

"Too soon to really know what it means," Connor said. The references did worry him, but it wasn't enough for him to drop everything he was doing and confront Tobias about it. "Whatever it means, it won't change what we're doing here. So let's get back to work."

19

Over the next six weeks, Connor and Diaz trained the first class of Search and Rescue. Franklin Mallory, the Director of Field Operations and Security, visited the camp twice. Both visits had left the director impressed and eager to put them in the field. After Mallory's first visit, the recruits had become preoccupied with giving their camp an official name rather than some alphanumeric designation. The name Camp Gates had been tossed around, but Connor put a stop to that quickly. The next name suggestion came from Blake, who called it Camp Mutt. Blake confessed that she was a dog lover, and as a field biologist as well as a medic, she championed to the idea that genetic diversity led to a superior species. Randle offered his services for providing genetic diversity when it came time to procreate for the sake of the colony. As far as Connor knew, no one had taken him up on his offer.

Connor checked the time and brought up the schedule for the day. He was in the command center working at his terminal. They had an active connection back to the compound, which he authorized the recruits to use at the end of the week so they could contact friends and family. After being completely isolated for six weeks, most recruits welcomed the opportunity. They'd earned it. Their initial training would be completed soon, and Connor already had his eye on at least two of them to lead squads of their own someday.

Noah walked into the tent. He had his travel bag all packed up and ready to go.

"I'm really sorry, sir," Noah said.

Connor glanced at him. "You'll be back."

"I'll just be gone for a few weeks. Dr. Bishop made a huge discovery at the forward operating research base and needs a technical consultant," Noah said.

"She found alien tech," Connor said.

"That's what the report said. She found more ruins built by the civilization that used to be here," Noah said.

"They died out. There are living people here who need us right now. Berwolf ambush attempts have been steadily escalating."

"I know. I see the same reports. They're at the compound and at some of the research bases," Noah said.

"Yeah, so why haven't you requested to take your weapon with you?" Connor asked.

Noah blinked for a while. "I didn't think it was allowed."

"You're field-weapons qualified now, and as long as you're officially a member of my team, you're part of Field Operations. You're authorized to carry your weapon with you. As far as I'm concerned, this is an extended field assignment," Connor said.

Noah smiled. "I didn't . . . Uh, thank you, sir."

Connor feigned sternness. "You'll have to complete survival week with the next class that comes through here."

The smile on Noah's face faltered. "You're joking, right?"

"Do I look like I'm joking?"

Noah swallowed hard and then recovered. "Looking forward to it, sir."

"It won't be as bad as you think it's going to be. By now, going out into the forest isn't the mystery it once was," Connor said.

"That first time you came through the gate while I was on patrol scared the crap out of me. I thought that new predator you found, the ryklars, had learned to open gates," Noah said.

"Haven't seen them in a while. According to the field biologist at the compound, they're predators that follow the herds, so it's likely they just migrate from place to place with the herds," Connor said.

"I've meant to ask why you've been going into the forest at night," Noah said. "I mean, beyond the training you make us do."

"One of the most useful things we can do to adjust to living here is to get to know the planet," Connor said.

Noah snorted. "As long as you're armed with an assault rifle and night vision, along with an additional reconnaissance drone, you're good to go."

"Those things certainly do help."

"So, this survival week you've got planned . . . What equipment are you allowing us to bring?" Noah asked.

Connor raised a brow. "You didn't really think I was going to give anything away. That's a need-to-know, which you don't."

Outside the tent, they heard the approach of a transport ship. The sound from the engines came closer, and Connor frowned.

"Sounds like they're coming in too fast," Connor said.

Noah's eyes widened.

"Lenora!" they both said at the same time.

Connor and Noah raced outside. The camp was larger than it had been when they'd first gotten there to accommodate their Hellcat troop carrier ship, and they'd had to extend the perimeter fence to allow for other drop ships to visit the camp. It was a tight fit for experienced pilots, which Dr. Lenora Bishop, Head of Archaeological Studies, definitely was not.

Connor opened a comlink to the approaching ship.

"Hello, Connor," Lenora said.

"Don't destroy my camp with a bad landing. If you're not comfortable landing here, put the ship down outside the fence and we'll escort you in," Connor said.

"Where's the fun in that?" Lenora said.

The transport ship circled the camp and then approached the landing zone.

Connor glanced at Noah. "Why doesn't she use a pilot?"

"They kept telling her they couldn't fly the ship where she wanted it to go, so she fired them," Noah said.

The transport ship started its descent over the painted white circle and started to drift toward the fence. Connor brought his hands up to his head and winced. That ship could tear a hole in the perimeter fence. At the last second, Lenora course corrected and set it down. Half the landing gear was outside the designated landing area.

Connor ran his palm over his face and blew out a breath. "Are you sure you want to go with her? It might be safer out in the forest. You could take your chances with the local predators."

Noah's face was already pale from watching Lenora's nearly catastrophic landing attempt. "I'll be right back," he said and hastened away.

Lenora stepped out the side door of the ship and her auburn hair surrounded her head like a mane of pure femininity. She saw him and waved. Connor walked over and nearly forgot how she almost just destroyed his camp. Her cupid's-bow lips lifted into a playful smirk as he got closer.

"You stuck the landing," Connor said.

"You should have seen the last one I did," Lenora said.

She glanced around the camp and saw that the recruits were doing various exercises. One group was rappelling down an elevated platform while the others were using the repulsor vests. Connor noted that Neal Compton was the victim being lowered in a harness from the fifty-foot-tall platform. Owens, Jackson, and Cooper were slowly lowering Compton's three-hundred-pound body.

"Things have really come along here," Lenora said.

"Yes they have, but this is the first time you've ever been here," Connor said.

"You caught me. I met with Ashley on one of the supply runs at the compound two weeks ago," Lenora said.

Connor arched an eyebrow. "You were looking for Noah," he said.

"You bet I was. I swear the little squirrel can hide with the best of them."

"I see," Connor said.

Lenora gave him a challenging look. "It's easy to say no on a vid, but get him in person . . ."

"And he melts. I get it," Connor said.

"You got it. This is really quite a setup you got here. You still haven't taken me up on that offer to come out and see the ruins we found," Lenora said.

She looked at him with those beautiful eyes of hers, and Connor almost found himself agreeing to go.

"I'd like to, but we've got something big planned for them this week," Connor said.

"I bet they wouldn't mind if you gave them the week off," Lenora said. Cupping her hands around her mouth, she shouted, "Do you guys want a week's vacation?"

Connor's mouth hung open as he heard Ramirez shout to the others about getting time off.

Lenora laughed.

"You're unbelievable! I can't believe you just did that," Connor said and snorted.

Lenora patted him on the arm. "Live a little, will you?"

Connor chuckled. "I will. When things calm down here, I'll come out to your base and see what all the fuss is about."

Lenora held him in her gaze. "I'll hold you to that."

Connor had little doubt that she would. "Since you're here, have there been any increased sightings of the local predators? We've seen reports of heightened berwolf activity around the compound and some of the research bases."

"I saw that, but there's been no berwolf activity out by us. We've seen the new species that you spotted—the ryklars, four arms and two legs. Looks mean as hell. Leopard spots on its back," Lenora said.

"Have they attacked anyone?"

Lenora shook her head. "No, they just make their presence known. I've only seen them at a distance. Rogers has seen them much closer, like across-this-camp kind of close. He kept saying that the creature seemed more intelligent than he thought it should be."

Connor nodded. "I know what he means. Be careful. I know they're smaller than the berwolfs, but I think they're more dangerous."

Lenora smiled and leaned in as if she wanted to whisper something, so Connor met her halfway and she gave him a kiss on the cheek.

"That's for being sweet," Lenora said.

Connor felt his cheeks redden. He couldn't get a bead on this woman. One moment she acted like one of the guys and the next . . . He didn't know what to think.

"It's about time. I haven't got all day," Lenora said, looking past Connor.

"I had to get my stuff," Noah replied. "I can't do an analysis of the alien tech you found without my equipment."

"Great, and now you're armed too," Lenora said.

Noah carried his AR-71 rifle along with his utility bag in his other hand.

"I see all this physical training suits you. Got some muscles now," Lenora said.

Noah smiled, made a show of flexing his biceps, and climbed into the ship.

Lenora turned back to Connor. "It seems like the moment I get to talk to you I have to leave a few minutes later. I'll take care of Noah for you. He's one of the good ones, and I like to make sure he's doing okay."

"He's lucky to have you looking out for him," Connor said.

Noah was alone in the colony—one of the colonists from the Ark program who didn't come with any family or significant others. Noah had explained that his family sacrificed a lot to get him qualified to even come on the Ark. Connor was positive that Noah's aptitude and high intelligence had determined his candidacy for the Ark program rather than the lottery randomly awarding him a spot.

"I'll see you around, and don't forget about that invitation," Lenora said.

She headed back to the ship and waved over at Diaz, who was on his way over to Connor.

Connor glanced at Diaz. "We should probably back up. I don't know if her takeoffs are any better than her landings."

They backed up, and the transport ship's engines burst to life. The ship rose steadily into the air and Connor could see Lenora and Noah sitting in the cockpit. He waved, and the ship sped away.

Diaz snapped his fingers in front of Connor's face. "Snap out of it. We've got work to do. I mean, I know she's a rare beauty, that one, but come on. Focus, sir."

"Stop," Connor said. "It's really not like that."

Diaz gave him a pointed look. "You mean to tell me you couldn't tell she was flirting with you?"

Connor frowned. "Give me a break. She's just being friendly."

"Well, she can be friendly like that with me anytime then, or with half the guys here or anywhere else," Diaz said.

Connor glanced at Diaz with a disapproving frown.

"Yes, sir, I'm Connor Gates. I can't afford any personal attachments," Diaz said.

Connor shook his head. "Let's get back to work."

"We got a minute. Let's explore this a bit," Diaz pressed.

"There's nothing to explore, and there's nothing going on with Lenora," Connor insisted.

Diaz nodded. "Lenora, you say. You mean Dr. Bishop? The world-class archaeologist? What's the problem? I'm not telling you to get married, but you know . . ." he said and shrugged.

"It's not appropriate," Connor said.

"What's not appropriate? You're a man. She's a woman. You're nature's designated mating pair."

"It's not that simple. I've left—"

"People behind. We all did, and you told me you hadn't spoken to your wife in over five years. You said there was always another mission," Diaz said.

Connor glared at him, losing his patience. "Are you done?"

Diaz smoothed his features, feigning disinterest. "I'm done. Let's get back to work."

Connor glanced in the direction the ship had gone and spied a creature beyond the fence near the forest line. He stopped moving and peered in that direction, trying to decide whether it was just a trick of the light or something else. The forest line was a mass of overgrowth, with thorny vines and large leaves, but mixed in with all the foliage were the thick, bloody red protrusions on the elongated head of a ryklar. Within the thick, muscular folds were dark slits for the creature's eyes.

"Diaz, follow my line of sight toward those trees over there beyond the fence. About seven feet off the ground mixed in with that thorny mess. Do you see anything?" Connor asked.

Diaz peered in the direction. "I don't see anything, but I haven't got eyes like yours."

Connor used his implants to recall the nearest drone and sent it toward the target location. "I think it's a ryklar, but I only see one of them."

He headed toward the fencing and Diaz walked beside him. Connor heard the drone zooming over the camp and looked back to the creature, but it was gone, so he brought up the drone's feeds on his internal heads-up display and set it to pursue. The drone plunged into the forest, and Connor had a bird's-eye view of the ground. He saw the swaying of plants that marked the creature's passing and he had the drone move forward around the corner of a large tree, but there was nothing there. He engaged the drone's other cameras, giving him a three-hundred-sixty-degree visual of the area, but there was nothing there. Switching the view to infrared, he looked for a heat signature.

"Did you find it?" Diaz said.

Connor shook his head and released his control of the drone, setting it on patrol mode. "No. Let's grab some gear and go check it out."

"Are you sure? We have to debrief the recruits in fifteen minutes," Diaz said.

"I just want to go out into that area and see if there are any tracks," Connor said.

Connor went over to their armor depot and retrieved his AR-71. Donna Marten caught sight of them and jogged over. She was already carrying her weapon.

"Need some help, sir?" Marten asked.

Connor waved her over and they headed toward the gate. "Yeah, I thought I saw a ryklar across the way over there. I just want to see if there are any tracks."

Nate Poe and the other recruits saw them leaving and raced over to them, wondering what was happening.

"We're just going to check something out. Poe, why don't you and Bling get up on the observation platform with your Vipers. The rest of you man the gates," Connor said.

The recruits deployed, following his orders without question. Sean Quinn and Nate Poe retrieved their M-Viper sniper rifles and were climbing the observation platform soon after Connor and the others left the gate.

Connor focused on the way ahead of them while Diaz and Marten divided their attention between the sides and the front. As Connor closed in on the area, he wondered how the creature would have been able to climb up the dense thorny mess just to take a look at them.

Connor made a circling gesture, and they moved around the thicket. The drones hadn't detected anything and there didn't seem to be anything around.

They went a short distance beyond the tree line, and Connor looked on the ground for some evidence of clawed footprints.

"Sir, I think I found something," Marten said.

Connor turned around and headed toward Marten, who was looking at the area behind the thicket. She squatted down and gestured toward a shallow slash in the soft ground. It was just a single slash, with only the shallow impressions of two prongs from the creature's other foot.

"I don't get it. Why is there only one track?" Diaz asked.

"Because this is where it could have leaped down from up there," Marten said and gestured toward the overgrowth that Connor could now see covered the remnant of a log. "It wouldn't be all that comfortable, but it would give a nice view into our camp while providing excellent coverage."

Connor glanced at the area where the creature had been and then down at the shallow track, trying to determine where it had gone and why there were no other tracks. The recent rainfall had the plants swelling with water, so there would be nothing broken to mark the creature's passing.

"Could you track it?" Connor asked.

Marten stood up and took an appraising look around. "I could search the area for more tracks and maybe I could track it then."

Connor nodded, considering.

"What do you want to do, sir?" Diaz asked.

"Let's go back. If the drones pick it up, we'll investigate," Connor said.

They headed back to camp, Connor deep in contemplation. Since ryklars were ambush hunters, why would a single one come near the camp? A scout perhaps, but even scouts didn't venture far from the pack. Maybe he hadn't seen what he thought he had after all.

They reentered the camp, and Diaz announced it had been a false alarm. Poe and Sean hadn't seen anything from the observation platform. As the recruits gathered in the assembly area for debriefing and classroom instruction, Connor and Diaz moved to the front.

Connor took a moment to look at all of them, and his eyes lingered on Blake, a.k.a. Babyface. She now carried herself with a sense of confidence that he'd only seen her exhibit when doing medical examinations before, and he saw the same confidence gleaming from the other recruits. At this point in their training, they had a better idea of their capabilities and knew where their weaknesses were.

"Welcome to the final week of training. You've all worked very hard and have come a long way from where you were just six short weeks ago," Connor said.

There were several chuckles from them and Connor knew that none of them had thought any part of their training had been short or easy. They'd taken the brunt of breaking in a new training program, and they were the first class of what he hoped would be many. And as with many of life's circumstances, the first was always most memorable.

"This final week is a make-or-break moment for you, a culmination of all you've learned. To prove that you've mastered what's required of you and that you can function as effective teams, you'll be divided into two groups and flown out to two remote locations. You'll need to work your way to a different location for extraction, and you'll have four days to complete this exercise," Connor said.

Amy Owens raised her hand. "Why four days, sir?"

"If you can survive out there for four days, there's no reason to believe you couldn't survive together for longer periods of time. Other climates may require different skill sets, but the basics are the same—water, shelter, food. Those are priorities. You'll be required to function as a team and use the skills you've learned here, putting them to practical application. Let me be clear on one thing. You either pass this exercise as a group or you fail it as a group. This survival training exercise is not a graded exercise. It's strictly pass or fail and is required to earn your badges," Connor said.

Ramirez raised his hand.

"Go ahead, Bones."

"What happens if we fail, sir?" Ramirez asked.

Connor fixed them all with a hard stare. "Then you would have failed basic Search and Rescue training."

Ramirez swallowed hard. "Sir—"

"One second, Bones—and this is for the rest of you as well—Sergeant Diaz and I will be monitoring your progress, and if you fail to reach your objective, your performance will be evaluated as a group," Connor said.

There were no other questions, so Connor continued. "You'll also be required to locate several victims in your area. Somewhere between your drop-off point and the extraction point, you'll receive a distress call and you'll investigate. Could be more than one. You'll need to determine how best to proceed," Connor said and gave them a knowing smile, something the recruits had come to dread. "The purpose of this is to give you a taste of what we'll be called upon to do. Sergeant Diaz and I have reviewed the records for rescues that Field Operations has on file. They range from minor injuries to vehicle breakdowns, people getting lost, and serious injury. It will be up to you and your team leader as to how best to deal with it. I've selected two team leaders for this exercise, but before I tell you who they are, I want to make a few more points. One, any one of you may be called upon to step into the role of team leader. Two, this isn't a popularity contest. And three, you will respect the chain of command. For the purposes of this exercise, the team leaders have operational authority. Is that understood?"

"Yes, sir," the recruits replied in unison.

"Okay, since Noah had to leave, the teams will be split evenly. Team Alpha will be the following: Owens, Winters, Deacon, Poe, Jackson, and Compton. Your team leader will be Winters," Connor said.

Those recruits glanced at each other and gave an acknowledging nod.

"Team Bravo will be the following: Ramirez, Allison, Marten, Cooper, Randle, and Quinn. Your team leader will be Randle," Connor said and gave them a moment. "You're all aware of the dangers waiting for you out on the frontier, and this entire planet is the frontier. I expect daily reports to be sent back to camp from the team leaders."

Randle raised his hand. The big man appeared extremely uncomfortable. "Sir, what do we do with the victims we find?"

"What do you think, recruit?" Diaz said. "We're Search and Rescue. Treat this exercise as a live simulation."

Randle shook his head and quickly apologized.

"As I said before, Sergeant Diaz and I will be observing your progress and will not be far. We'll also function as COMCENT for this exercise. The team that finishes first gets the honor of setting the camp record," Connor said.

Winters narrowed her gaze. "Will you be out in the field with us, sir?"

"Perhaps, recruit," Connor said. "The official kickoff for this exercise is at oh six hundred. Dismissed."

The recruits stood up and snapped a salute. The remainder of the day was spent with the recruits gathering the equipment they'd need for deployment. Connor shared a knowing look with Diaz. They'd spent much of the last six weeks doing everything in their power to keep the recruits on their toes, and this would be no different.

When Connor noticed Sean Quinn watching him, the recruit went inside his tent to get some rack time.

20

CONNOR MET Diaz outside the command center at oh one hundred hours. They wore full combat gear and green camouflage uniforms.

"Almost go time," Connor said.

"If they thought we were going to let them have a full night's sleep, we may not have done our jobs," Diaz said.

"I think some of them suspect something," Connor said and glanced toward the observation tower where Randle and Jackson were on watch.

Connor and Diaz received an updated ETA for the two transport ships coming from the compound.

"They're twenty minutes out," Diaz said and gave Connor a sidelong look. "You're looking forward to this, aren't you?"

Connor nodded enthusiastically. "This is the fun part—deployment out in the field, where we can observe them and put a few obstacles in their way. I ran a check on the distress beacons and they're all ready."

"Then it's time to sound the alarm," Diaz said with a hearty laugh.

Klaxon alarms blared and the exterior lights for the camp came on simultaneously. Connor and Diaz went into the recruits' tents, yelling for them to wake up.

A few minutes later the recruits were lined up in full combat gear with their weapons ready for inspection. Connor and Diaz walked among them, checking that their equipment was ready. None of them failed the inspection, and they shouldn't because Connor had drilled them for this.

"In the next few minutes, troop carrier ships will be here to take you away and this exercise will officially have begun. The mission for Team Alpha: An expedition exploring mineral deposits has become overdue, and their last known position will be transmitted to your PDA. Your job is to sweep the area and look for any survivors. Time is of the essence since we've already received two distress beacons," Connor said, transferring the mission brief to Elyse Winters.

"Sir, I've received mission details," Winters acknowledged.

"Fall out, Team Alpha. Your ride is here. Make us proud," Connor said.

Winters led her team over to the landing area, where a troop transport was coming in for a landing. Diaz followed at a short distance behind to observe.

"Team Bravo: A downed survey ship is reported in zeta quadrant. There were four members of the survey team on that ship. Your job is to find out what happened to them," Connor said and transferred the mission brief to Wayne Randle.

"Sir, I've received mission details," Randle said and read the information on his PDA.

The second troop carrier ship was approaching the landing area, and Randle called for his team to head over to the landing zone.

Sean Quinn lagged behind for a moment. "Sir, are you coming with us?" he asked.

"You're focusing on the wrong thing, recruit. You have a job to do. Now go do it," Connor replied.

Sean Quinn sprinted over to the rest of Team Bravo and Connor walked over. He watched as Randle ordered his group to double-check their equipment, particularly their ammunition, food and water rations, and their medical supplies. He assigned individuals specific jobs. Randle looked at Sean Quinn's equipment and noted that he had the M-Viper with him.

"There's no need for two people on the team to have that rifle for this mission. Go get the AR-71 and put a scope on it. You can multipurpose with that setup, alright, Bling?" Randle said.

Sean Quinn saluted the Team Bravo leader and ran off to exchange his weapon. Connor made a note on his tablet computer regarding Randle's forethought into how his team was equipped before embarking on the four-day mission. It played to the recruits' strengths.

Connor headed over to Diaz. Team Alpha was climbing aboard the troop carrier. Winters stood at attention and saluted Connor, then followed her team into the ship.

"Everything checks out for Team Alpha, sir," Diaz said.

Connor nodded. "Good. I expect Winters will do a good job leading them."

"That she will," Diaz said and frowned.

"You have doubts?" Connor asked.

Diaz shook his head quickly. "No, I have no doubts about what any of the recruits can do. It's just that . . ."

Connor smiled. Diaz had never trained a platoon before. "I see. We train them and teach them as best we can. Now it's up to them to put it to use."

"I'd be lying if I said I didn't want to be out there with them."

"Me too. Soon. This is for them to prove themselves, and there will come a time when neither you nor I will be there for them to lean on," Connor said.

The first troop carrier ship rose into the air and headed off into the northeast. The second ship took off soon after that, heading in a different direction. The sounds of the engines faded and all was quiet but for the nightly hum of New Earth. Connor glanced over at the Hellcat. Their gear was already on board, but they wouldn't be flying out just yet. He and Diaz would be monitoring the two teams from the command center for a time and then head out after that. None of the recruits knew for sure whether Connor or Diaz would be out in the field with them, but Connor suspected they knew there'd be a good chance they would be.

They walked back to the command center and Connor brought up a map on the main holoscreen, then launched a secondary window to run a check through the automated protocols Noah had set up for him. He'd dispatched a trio of drones to monitor the two quadrants where his recruits would be. As part of the standard deployment, Connor had equipped both teams with a drone of their own to use as they saw fit, but the tactical drones the teams were using were smaller and didn't have the range that Connor's patrol drones had.

Diaz poured them both a cup of coffee that they drank while watching the progress the two troop carriers made as they approached their destinations. Connor uploaded a report back to Field Operations so the monitoring division was aware that the scheduled training mission had begun. They monitored each of the troop carrier's comlinks, and Team Alpha had just reached their drop-off location. The drop feed showed each of the recruits' heat signatures on the ground. Their names appeared on screen as their locators transmitted their position to the GPS satellites in orbit. Winters had Compton and Jackson on point, and Connor brought up the output from Winter's PDA. She already had the location of the expedition marked on their map, and a few minutes later they started heading toward it. The second distress beacon call was also designated in the vicinity of the last known location of the expedition.

"There they go," Diaz said.

"We've run enough nighttime exercises for them to function in those conditions," Connor said.

Team Bravo reached their location at the edge of a canyon. They would need to find a way into the canyon to reach the survey ship.

"I wonder how long it will take Randle to find a path down into the canyon at night," Diaz said.

"If it were me, I'd check in with Command Central for a survey map of the area, and if I didn't have that, I'd split into two groups to scout for a way down into the canyon," Connor said.

A few minutes later Randle called in, asking for a topographical map of the quadrant he was in, and Connor transferred the information back to them. There was more than one way to achieve the objective, but time was always of the essence.

The hours went by quickly as they monitored each team's steady progress. They moved quicker once it was daytime. Team Bravo would reach their first victim soon. As part of the exercise, Connor and Diaz had built in tripwires that would create different situations, depending on when the teams reached them. The distress beacon that Team Alpha was moving toward went offline. They quickened their pace, and Winters sent an update back to them.

"Almost time for us to take this show on the road," Diaz said. Working from his own holoscreen, he frowned. "What the hell is that?"

Connor glanced over but didn't see anything on the screen. "Play back the drone feed from thirty seconds ago."

Several hundred meters away, the infrared spectrum of the feed revealed several creatures following the recruits on Team Bravo. Then they disappeared, as if the creatures were suddenly cloaked in a shroud of cold that prevented them from being detected.

They had the drone focus in on the area but couldn't find anything.

"I'm not sure what they were. Could be they've got something following them," Diaz said.

"We can do a flyover with the Hellcat once they call in a pickup for the first victim," Connor said.

"Is that the broken leg?"

"That's the one," Connor said.

A few minutes later, Randle called in to Command Central for a pickup. They'd found the first person from the survey ship.

"Where are the other survivors?" Connor asked.

"The victim has lost consciousness due to the pain of his injuries and is not responsive, sir," Randle replied.

"Understood. Hellcat is being deployed and will be at your position within the next thirty minutes," Connor said.

They set the camp systems to follow passive protocols, including the fence remaining electrified to deter any curious creatures, and left the command center. Connor and Diaz walked over to the Hellcat troop carrier that had been assigned to Search and Rescue. Connor used his implants to send his authorization, and the side entrance door opened. He climbed aboard and headed to the cockpit. The Hellcat's systems came online, and he established a connection to the camp's computer system. All data feeds would funnel through there. Diaz joined him in the cockpit and sat down in the copilot's seat.

Diaz checked the ship's systems. "All systems ready."

Connor engaged the engines and the Hellcat rose into the air. His heads-up display showed Team Bravo's location through the retrieval beacon they'd set up. Connor punched the coordinates into the navigation system and pushed the throttle. Their velocity took Diaz by surprise.

"A little warning would have been nice," Diaz said.

Connor had spiked the velocity, which caused a delay in compensation by the inertia dampeners. He'd been expecting it, so he was ready when the brief gravitational forces pressed him into the seat. Diaz wasn't.

"This is payback for all those comments about Lenora, isn't it?" Diaz said.

"I don't know what you're talking about. We have an unconscious victim who requires medical attention, so I maximized the speed," Connor replied innocently.

Diaz snorted. "Right," he said, sounding unconvinced.

The Hellcat sped across the skies, and fifteen minutes later they were closing in on Team Bravo's position. Randle waved at them. The Hellcat was a highly maneuverable carrier ship that could navigate the small spaces inside the canyon if required, but Team Bravo had harnessed the victim and brought him up to the top of the canyon to expedite the rescue operation. Connor set the Hellcat down and opened the rear doors. He and Diaz raced to the back of the ship. Recruit Blake was there, along with Ramirez and Quinn. They carried the ballistics-gel form of a one-hundred-and-eighty-pound man.

"Sir, the victim's injuries were sustained from a fall while climbing down the canyon wall. Bruising and basic med scans indicate several bone fractures on the victim's right leg, including the femur. There is no evidence of internal bleeding, but the victim should be put into a medical capsule immediately and treated by the doctors at the main compound," Blake said.

Diaz had a stretcher ready to go, and Ramirez and Quinn helped transfer the victim onto it.

"Confirmed transfer of the victim. We'll get him the help he needs. Was he alone?" Connor asked.

"Sir, we believe the victim was going for help when the accident occurred. No distress beacons have been detected, but we've found evidence of the trail the victim was following. We intend to follow it and hopefully find the other members of the survey team," Randle said.

"Understood. We'll update Command Central with the status and alert the hospital at the main compound," Connor replied.

He and Diaz were playing the part of the emergency response team. Randle left the Hellcat and joined the rest of his team that was following Marten, who'd found the victim's trail.

He and Diaz secured the victim and updated Team Bravo's performance ratings for the exercise.

"They did a good job," Diaz said when they were back in the cockpit.

Connor lifted off. "They did everything by the book. The next one won't be so easy."

Some of the victims had timers counting down, and the more time it took the rescue team to find them, the worse their injuries would become until the victim eventually died. As with any search and rescue operation, they were always running against the clock. Team Bravo had handled themselves professionally and stuck to established protocols. Connor couldn't be prouder of them.

"Let's do a sweep of the area," Connor said.

Diaz cleared the view on the heads-up display, and the onboard cameras piped in a live video feed. In a few moments, they were over where Diaz had spotted the creatures that might have been stalking Team Bravo.

"I got nothing," Diaz said. He cycled the feeds through several visual spectrums, and while there were some forms of wildlife, they weren't what they'd seen before.

"Maybe whatever it was has moved on," Connor said.

He glanced at one of the feeds and saw a herd of landrunners moving south. Their long legs propelled them at great speeds that people could only match using machines.

"Sean says they can maintain that speed all day," Diaz said.

Connor nodded. The landrunner herds hadn't gone anywhere near the main compound, which was why it was such a shock for Connor when he'd first encountered them while scouting for an area to establish the training camp.

"Let's see what Team Alpha's doing," Connor said and brought up the map.

"She split the team. I was wondering how she'd handle the second beacon," Diaz said.

Elyse Winters had split her six-person team into two groups of three. Preferring not to waste fuel, Connor set the Hellcat down while they watched Team Alpha's progress. The first group closed in on the distress beacon and later reported that they'd found a colonist who'd gotten separated from the expedition and was now traveling with the team.

"They found the hologram of the lost colonist," Connor said.

The small team was now working their way toward Winters and the others. Winters opened a comlink to Command Central.

"This is COMCENT. Go ahead, Team Alpha," Connor said.

"Winters reporting in. We've located the second distress beacon, but there are no colonists nearby. We'll continue to do a sweep of the area and look for signs of where they may have gone. We've found berwolf tracks near the beacon and suspect the colonist left the area to take refuge on higher ground."

"Acknowledged, Team Alpha. Proceed with caution," Connor replied.

He closed the connection.

"I thought the tracks were a nice touch," Diaz said.

A warning of inclement weather broadcasted from the main compound.

"Looks like we're gonna get some storms moving through the area," Connor said. He brought up the weather feed, which showed projections for high winds and thunderstorms.

Diaz peered at the feed. "They might have to hunker down until it passes."

Connor forwarded the weather alert to the two teams, along with the standard recommendation for taking shelter. Over the next hour, the skies became dark with storm clouds and distant thunder boomed across the sky. If the wind got bad enough, he'd have to send the patrol drones to a safe area until the storm passed. The storm system moving in looked like it was going to be around for a few hours, and with the onset of nightfall, both teams would be searching in the dark. Team Bravo had found an overhang under which to weather the storm, but Team Alpha was still moving.

"She should have found shelter by now," Diaz said.

"She's determined to find the rest of the expedition," Connor said.

"Yeah, but they're in a flood plain, and if there are flash floods, this could become a real rescue mission," Diaz said.

The drone feed showed Team Alpha navigating across a rocky terrain, angling upward. Connor had the drone pan the camera up and saw a cave.

"Shit," Connor said in surprise. He'd been so distracted by the storm that he hadn't paid attention to where Team Alpha was.

"Is that the entrance to the cave where you put the rest of the expedition?" Diaz asked.

"Yeah, but Winters found a faster way to it. We assumed she'd follow the path over it and have to rappel down to the entrance once they'd found it," Connor said.

That was the original plan. Winters must have done her own area surveys and narrowed down the potential locations the expedition would have used for shelter.

The storm blew in and lasted for most of the night. Both teams had checked in, and Winters reported the successful rescue of the expedition that had become lost while scouting for potential mineral deposits. The members of the expedition suffered from dehydration and exposure because they didn't have their survival packs with them. Winters completed the rescue simulation and, in actuality, retrieved the holograms Connor had placed in the cave.

"Winters is doing a great job. She could lead her own team," Diaz said.

They were standing outside the cockpit, stretching their legs and taking advantage of the downtime to rest while the storm blew through the area. Diaz's snoring had echoed from the cargo area most of the night. Connor only needed a few hours' sleep, so he'd spent the time monitoring the teams and writing up his own evaluation of their simulated survival mission mixed with a search and rescue exercise.

"She's doing well. I reviewed the drones I had assigned to Team Alpha and saw that she took a gamble by leading the team through a ravine to reach that cave. In this case, it paid off, but that may not work the next time," Connor said.

"Maybe. She made a decision and took a risk based on the information she had. What would you have done differently?" Diaz asked.

"I would have stayed with the high ground as long as I could before committing to going to the cave. We'll need to account for that when we train the next group," Connor said.

Diaz rolled his shoulders and cracked his neck. The sound of it sent a shudder through Connor. He couldn't even stand the sound of someone cracking their knuckles.

"Think there'll be another group?" Diaz asked.

"You bet. This class is good. Most of them came to us with *some* training, with the obvious exception, but even Sean Quinn has shown a level of commitment I hadn't expected," Connor said.

"That kid looks up to you. I think you're the first person to really challenge him," Diaz said.

They had a quick breakfast of some tasty field rations, and Diaz grumbled about the lack of coffee. They'd returned to the Hellcat's cockpit when a comlink from Team Bravo reached them.

"This is COMCENT. Go ahead," Connor said.

"This is Team Bravo. We've found the survey ship and three remaining members of the survey team—one survivor and two casualties," Randle said.

"Confirm one survivor and two casualties. What was the cause of death for the two casualties?" Connor asked.

"One person died from injuries sustained during an emergency landing. The second person survived the emergency landing but bled out from her injuries after eighteen hours," Randle said.

Connor heard the bitter tone of failure in Randle's voice. This was a hard lesson for them to learn. Had the storm not come in, they might have saved the second person. This was one of the reasons Connor used adaptive simulations so the outcomes would change as the exercise progressed.

"Understood, Team Bravo. Rescue simulation complete. Updated mission parameters being transmitted to you now. You have forty-eight hours to reach the extraction point," Connor said.

There was a long pause and Connor knew Randle was blaming himself, but Connor knew better than to break protocol. Team Bravo hadn't failed this exercise. How Randle handled himself would be a clear indication of what kind of soldier he'd be. The same went for the rest of the team.

"Acknowledged. Received updated coordinates. Team Bravo, out," Randle said.

The comlink closed. Connor had decided last night to change the extraction point for each team and had more updates for them as they closed in on their destinations.

"Sir, are we asking too much from the recruits with all these changes?" Diaz asked.

"They need to be challenged and be able to deal with unanticipated events. If we just gave them a set of coordinates and said get there at a predetermined time, that might challenge them, but I'm aiming to keep them off balance. They need to be able to adapt," Connor said.

He glanced at one of the video feeds that showed the area ahead of the ship. A shadow passed beyond the view of the camera, and Connor adjusted it. They were in a small clearing surrounded by forest. Grassy plains stretched out before them until the forest started back up again. Connor brought the video feed to the main holoscreen.

"What is it?" Diaz asked.

"I thought I saw something—" Connor began and stopped.

Ahead of them Connor saw the spotted back of a ryklar standing up and glancing toward their ship. If it hadn't moved, he might have missed it. The red-colored protrusions around the creature's mouth made it look as if it had recently killed something.

"Crap! Where'd that thing come from?" Diaz said.

"There've got to be more of them," Connor said.

"What's it doing just standing there?" Diaz said and blew out a breath. "That thing is creepy."

The ryklar's muscular chest heaved and it backed up toward the forest.

"I think it wanted to be seen," Connor said.

"Seriously? What the hell for?"

"I bet it wants us to follow it," Connor said.

Diaz's eyes widened. He accessed the video feed interface, and a row of feeds appeared, showing the area surrounding the ship.

"I wonder . . ." Connor said.

"Please tell me you're not going out there," Diaz said.

Connor shook his head. "No, but let's see if it responds."

Connor activated the searchlight on the nose of the ship. He powered it off and on three times before leaving it off. The ryklar jumped back, startled by the light. Then the creature let out a shrill scream and charged forward a few steps before pounding its clawed fists on the ground.

"I think you just made it angry," Diaz said.

"Nah, I think it's just trying to prove it's not afraid of us," Connor said.

Diaz looked at the sub-screens below the main holoscreen and gasped. "They're all around us."

Ryklars stood up, revealing themselves. There were at least ten of them. Connor frowned and brought up the different sensor spectrums. He stopped on infrared and detected the body heat from the creatures. Their dark red figures stood in sharp contrast to the surrounding area. Then, one by one, they disappeared. The ryklars hadn't moved. It was as if they'd stopped producing body heat.

"Where the hell did they go?" Diaz asked.

Connor's hand brought up a secondary interface. "I think they're still there," he said and brought up the sonic wave detector. The ship's computers quickly analyzed the ambient sounds and Connor applied the filter to detect the rhythmic sounds of breathing. The holodisplay background changed to a pale blue screen and showed faint outlines of anything that made noise. Dark outlines of the ryklars showed up again.

"How'd you do that?" Diaz asked.

"Sonic detectors show the sources of any noises in the area, and I applied a filter to focus in on a creature's breathing," Connor said.

Diaz's mouth hung open. "I didn't know it could be fine-tuned like that."

"Most combat suits trap body heat to reduce the risk of being detected, so we had to rely on sound to find out where our enemies were hiding," Connor said.

Diaz nodded. "One day you're going to have to tell me more about your old unit."

Connor snorted and then his stomach clenched. If the ryklars were here, there could be more of them in the area. Diaz must have had the same thought.

"We have to warn them," Diaz said.

Connor made a swiping motion with his hand, and the video feeds all minimized to the lower right corner of the main holoscreen. He brought up the drone feeds, and two of his six drones were offline. Connor maximized the limited sonic abilities of the drones.

There was a loud bang on the side of the ship, followed by more on top. The local video feeds show the ryklars trying to get inside. One of the creatures slammed its claws repeatedly into the same spot. The harsh clang echoed throughout the ship, accompanied by loud stomping on the roof. Connor started the engines, and the sound of it startled the creatures. All banging on the hull ceased. He did a quick preflight check and engaged the engines. The Hellcat rose into the air and Connor set it to auto-hover a hundred feet off the ground. The video feeds showed the ryklars scurrying away.

Connor brought the drone interface back up, and he still only had four drones to work with. They were flying low, marking the progress of the two teams of recruits. He had the drones make a sweep of the area using the creature-recognition software to alert on ryklars.

He opened a comlink to Team Alpha. "Winters, have your team find a defensible position and await further instruction—"

The comlink was severed, and they heard the sound of metal being torn from the hull. Connor engaged the thrusters and banked hard to the right. He circled around and saw a ryklar falling to its death.

"Communications offline. That thing must have torn off the array," Diaz said.

Connor swore. With their communications offline, they didn't have access to the drone feeds. "I'm calling it. This exercise is canceled."

"Are you sure? We can head back to camp and get the drone feeds there," Diaz said.

Connor shook his head. "It'll take too much time. If we go back there only to find out there are more ryklar hunting both teams, we might lose them. They're armed, so they should be able to hold out, but they don't know that those things can camouflage themselves from detection."

Connor brought up the map, and the last known locations of each team appeared. Their ship was right in the middle between the two. He couldn't recall which two drones were offline. Could the ryklars have taken them out?

"Okay, this is what we're going to do. You're going to drop me off at this point here, north of Team Alpha's position. I'll cut across and flank them. I want you to take the Hellcat and extract Team Bravo. They're on a more open plain, so even if the ryklars decided to ambush Randle and the others, they should see them coming," Connor said.

"I don't like just leaving you in the middle of nowhere. You're breaking your own rule about solo missions," Diaz said.

"I know. We need to adapt, and I can move faster alone than we can together," Connor said.

Connor left the cockpit and slipped into his Nexar combat suit armor. The combat suit was designed to be donned quickly, and he used his implants to send the command for the power armor to open. Connor stepped inside and the armored sections closed in rapid succession. The suit was military grade and part of their arsenal of equipment, most of which remained on the Ark. Connor pulled the helmet on, and the power armor computer systems came online. His implants immediately connected to the internal systems. Connor grabbed his AR-71 assault rifle with grenade launcher and loaded the high-density nano-robotic ammunition. His helmet's internal heads-up display showed the ammunition count in the upper right corner.

Connor walked to the back of the ship and opened a comms channel to the cockpit.

"Maintain speed and heading," Connor said.

"I can slow down and give you a softer landing."

"No. Do not slow down. The suit jets are enough for me to make a hard landing and move on. Speed is our most important asset. Since comms is down, we have no way to warn them. Retrieve Team Bravo and then come pick us up. You're cleared to use the Hellcat's weapons at your discretion," Connor said.

Connor was still patched into the Hellcat's flight systems and saw that they were rapidly approaching the drop zone. He grabbed onto the handle and engaged his mag boots so he wouldn't be sucked out of the ship when he hit the button to open the rear doors. The treetop canopy zipped past below him in one green blur. After the initial blast of air that threatened to pull him off the ship, Connor disengaged the mag boots and released his hold on the handle. With two hands on the AR-71, he made a running leap from the ship.

The combat suit's systems sensed the drop in altitude and deployed flaps to help slow his descent, and Connor pulsed the suit's jets to further slow himself down. He clutched his legs together, his armored body becoming a missile, and sank below the treetop canopy. He used his suit jets to maneuver past thick tree branches as best he could, but it wasn't enough to avoid them all. He bounced between two thick trees and gritted his teeth as he crashed to the ground. The combat suit kept his body protected, but the bone-jarring landing left his brain addled for a few moments.

Connor regained his feet and swung around to face in the direction of Team Alpha's last known position. He set the combat suit's systems to scan everywhere he looked. The software would run real-time analyses of the different spectrums, noting any anomalies and immediately alerting Connor. He was ten kilometers from where Team Alpha had last been, and he darted off in a southerly direction.

As he ran through the forest, he tried to keep watch for any ryklars in the area. Their sudden appearance now—and even at the camp two days ago—made him wonder just how intelligent these creatures actually were. The compound didn't have a population count because the ryklars were so hard to find. After his first encounter with the creatures, Connor had searched the Ark database on the known predators and their hunting habits. Most hunted for food, but the ryklars' behavior toward the Hellcat denoted a higher intelligence akin to that of humans.

He set the ammo configuration of the AR-71 for incendiary rounds. He'd have fewer shots than a standard round, but he aimed to intimidate the ryklars by the sheer force of the weapon's capability and hoped the creatures would react like any other animal and run from a stronger foe.

The recruits had their weapons, but they didn't have the military-grade combat suit Connor wore. They hadn't been trained in its use and didn't have the upgraded implants to interface with the advanced computer systems of the suit. The combat suit also assisted Connor with moving much faster than he would be able to without it, but the recruits wore the standard body armor issued by Field Operations and Security.

Connor slowed his pace when he crossed the two-kilometer threshold from Team Alpha's last known position, then stopped and listened. He used the limited communications systems of the suit to try to connect with any drones nearby, but he couldn't find any. Connor started moving again at a slower pace and a few minutes later heard the sharp sound of an M-Viper sniper rifle being fired. He quickened his pace toward the sound and found a large tree he could climb. He slung his rifle on his back and quickly gained a panoramic view.

The forest floor sloped downward toward a nearby stream. Connor peered across to the other side of the small valley, and the way was clear, so he dropped down from the tree and raced across the depression. The sounds of a semiautomatic AR-71 set for three-round bursts echoed above him. Connor crossed the shallow stream and ran up to the top of the hill, where he came to a halt and squatted down to stay under cover. A short distance to his left he caught his first sight of Team Alpha being set upon by twelve ryklars. His combat suit's targeting computer showed six more trying to circle around and flank the recruits. The ryklars used the trees for cover but steadily moved forward. The bodies of several creatures lay unmoving nearby. Connor saw Winters bring her M-Viper up and take a shot. The ryklars dove for cover.

Connor opened a comlink to Winters. "I'm northwest of your position. There are six bogies trying to circle around you to your left."

Connor saw her turn to the left and signal Compton to lay down suppressing fire.

"I can hardly see them, sir," Winters said.

"They've taken cover," Connor replied.

"Sir, they came out of nowhere. Our drone didn't pick them up and our equipment doesn't register them. We tried to reach COMCENT, but we've been cut off."

"Understood. You're doing fine. Keep them pinned down. I want you to start falling back to a more defensible position," Connor said.

He saw Winters glance over toward him, and Connor flashed his IR tag.

"There's a rock wall about half a klick from your position. You should be able to climb it and hold that position," Connor said.

"Sir, these things are smart and they're hard to kill. They'll figure out what we're doing," Winters said.

"They don't know I'm here. They'll follow you, which is what I want, and when they bunch together, I have something special in mind for them," Connor said.

He heard Winters relay his orders.

"Sir, we're ready, but once you reveal yourself they'll pounce on you. If you coordinate with me, I can have the team provide covering fire for you," Winters said.

Connor smiled. "Good job, Winters. This is why I put you in charge of the team."

Connor watched as Team Alpha began an orderly withdrawal from the ryklars. Winters and two others retreated, then provided covering fire for the others' retreat. The ryklars pressed forward. Several climbed the trees and jumped to the next tree, using their claws to propel them along at incredible speeds. Connor saw a ryklar get hit, but it hardly slowed down. He couldn't tell whether the shot had penetrated the skin.

Connor stayed parallel with his recruits, anticipating that the ryklars' hunting instincts would drive them to push forward. Connor clutched the AR-71 and readied the grenade launcher. He glanced at Team Alpha's progress and saw that they were nearing the rock wall.

The pack of ryklars roared as they pushed forward. A small group broke away and tried to circle around the retreating recruits. Connor fired two grenades at the main pack and then another at the smaller group. The grenades landed right in the middle of the creatures and detonated. A small explosion killed the ryklars closest to the grenades and wounded several others. The remaining creatures scrambled back and Connor opened fire. Incendiary rounds streaked into the ryklars, penetrating their toughened skin. The remaining creatures dove for cover, using the base of trees. The recruits also fired their weapons, pinning the ryklars down.

"Good, now run away," Connor muttered.

He moved closer to the recruits and came to the rock wall. The ryklars hadn't come out of cover, and the recruits began scaling the wall, each taking a turn to watch for an attack.

Connor heard rapid foot stomps behind him a split second before he was slammed into the wall. He struggled to regain his feet and then dove to the side. A ryklar slammed into the wall and spun around to face him. The creature's heavy breathing was a mix of grating growls. It held all four of its arms wide, and the clawed, elongated fingers were curled menacingly. The creature charged and Connor swung the butt of his rifle up, catching it in the face. The ryklar shook its head. Connor fired his rifle and the incendiary rounds burned a hole right through the creature's chest.

Another ryklar started to charge, but a loud shot from the M-Viper sniper rifle snapped the creature's powerful head back. Connor engaged the combat suit's jets and jumped ten feet into the air. His armored hands gripped the rock wall and he began to climb. The recruits were near the top, and Winters was providing covering fire. Connor quickly caught up to the recruits and crested the ridge. He spun around and fired his weapon at any ryklar that dared approach the wall. The rest of the recruits reached the top.

"Extraction point is this way," Connor said.

The weeks of conditioning kicked in as the recruits followed his orders and moved away from the edge. Compton stayed by his side.

"It's good to see you, sir," the big man said, keeping his weapon aimed at the cliff's edge.

The area near the cliff was open. Connor activated his IR tag, and the recruits did the same. A few ryklars attempted to come over the cliff, and they fired their weapons at them, convincing them of the futility of that approach.

The Hellcat streaked across the sky and quickly came to their position. Diaz swung the nose of the ship around so the rear doors were closer to them and the doors opened. Team Bravo helped them climb aboard, Connor getting in last. He turned around and faced the edge of the cliff where a lone ryklar stood with its arms hanging loosely. The creature cocked its head to the side.

Compton aimed his weapon.

"Lower that weapon," Connor said.

"But, sir, it's right there," Compton said and lowered his weapon.

More ryklars climbed over the edge, but they didn't charge. Several of them cocked their heads to the side and turned away from the Hellcat. The creatures then began running toward the west with hardly a backwards glance.

Connor frowned and brought up the sonic detector interface for his combat suit. He scanned the higher frequencies.

"I don't understand those creatures," Compton said.

"Sir, any idea why they attacked us?" Winters asked.

"I'm not sure, but check this out," Connor said. He sent the data feed to the nearby wallscreen in the Hellcat.

Diaz set the Hellcat to auto-hover and joined them.

"What are we looking at?" Diaz asked.

"I don't know. It's some kind of high-frequency signal," Connor said.

"Sir, this is beyond human hearing, but perhaps those creatures can hear it," Deacon said.

"That's crazy," Compton said.

"Not necessarily," Blake said. "Their skull is pretty big, particularly near their ears. I bet they can detect this frequency. Think of it as a dog whistle."

"Who's blowing the whistle?" Connor asked.

The more they learned about the ryklars, the stranger those creatures became.

"Were you guys attacked too?" Compton asked.

"They tried to ambush us," Randle said. "We were fighting them off when Sergeant Diaz came and picked us up."

Connor did a quick headcount and all recruits were accounted for. "Sergeant, get us back to camp."

Diaz headed for the cockpit. The rest of the recruits sat down, but they were all looking at Connor, waiting for some kind of explanation.

"They attacked the Hellcat, too, and disabled our communications. That, and two of the surveillance drones are offline. My guess is that the ryklars somehow coordinated this attack," Connor said.

The recruits took a moment to absorb this information. No one wanted to talk about it anymore, but the questions kept coming to Connor. He'd never heard of any creature besides humans launching such a wide-scale attack.

"We'll debrief when we get back to camp," Connor said.

The recruits settled back into their seats.

"You guys did well today," Connor said.

"But we didn't make the extraction point," Deacon said.

"The exercise was a test of your search and rescue capabilities, as well as your abilities to adapt to new situations. For the record, you all passed this exercise," Connor said.

The recruits let out a hearty cheer except for Randle and other members of Team Bravo.

"Sir, we didn't successfully rescue our targets. Two people were dead," Randle said.

"I'm aware of that, but you did manage to save two of them. Things are going to happen. Things like that storm—that's going to impact any operation. There are times to take risks and there are times to hunker down. It's the mark of a good leader to know when to do which," Connor said.

"Yes, sir," Randle said. He leaned back, rested his head against the seat cushion, and closed his eyes.

21

—————

THEY RETURNED to camp and Connor had the recruits get checked out by Deacon and Allison. The two medics made quick work of assessing any injuries. Blake approached Connor with all the authority of the ranking medical officer and told him in no uncertain terms that he couldn't simply order her away by insisting he was fine. But except for a few bumps and bruises, Connor *was* fine. The combat suit armor had held up well against the ryklar attacks.

Connor stood outside the Hellcat. The recruits were getting cleaned up and hitting the showers. He had Sean Quinn manning the monitoring station.

"Commander, you should see this," Diaz called down from the roof of the Hellcat.

Connor stepped back inside the ship and climbed the ladder to the roof. Diaz and Compton stood over a jagged hole where the ship's communications array had been housed.

"Those things are freaking strong. It's as if the bunch of us bashed the crap out of this thing with pry bars, except the ryklars did it with their bare hands," Diaz said.

Connor squatted down and took a closer look. "We just need to patch it up until we get back to the compound for repairs."

"You think we'll be recalled?" Diaz asked.

Connor glanced at Compton. "Why don't you go get cleaned up."

Compton left them.

"How long do you think it will be before you'll have this ready?" Connor asked.

"It's just a patch job, so not long at all," Diaz said.

Connor nodded. "To answer your question . . ."

Sean Quinn shouted for Connor from the command tent.

"I think that answers your question. I need to go report this. I'll send Owens up here to help you," Connor said.

He entered the command tent and saw Franklin Mallory's face on the main holoscreen.

"Hello, Franklin, we've got some new intel on the ryklars," Connor said and proceeded to bring Mallory up to speed.

Franklin took a sip from his black coffee mug. "Sounds like you trained them well."

"Considering what they were up against, they've more than satisfied the requirements to graduate to the next level of training. I'd say they've been field-tested and are ready to be put to use," Connor said.

"Good, then it's not a surprise that you're being recalled to the compound. In preparation for this, we've designated part of Field Ops Headquarters for your use, as well as a permanent parking space on the airfield. You'll even have designated barracks while on duty," Franklin said, his eyes gleaming.

"A permanent parking spot. I bet Mills loved that. We'll start breaking down the camp then," Connor said.

"Just make sure the equipment is secure and stowed for now. I'm sure it's only a matter of time before the next class of recruits will start the training. We'll see you tomorrow," Franklin said.

The comlink closed.

News of their imminent departure soon spread among the recruits, which added a spring to their steps. The recruits spent the remainder of the day packing up all the equipment that needed to be secured. Connor had to write up a report of the events that had transpired during the exercise. He recalled many of his fellow officers complaining about the endless reports they had to file, but Connor had never minded all that much. He looked forward to the quiet time to reflect on the performance of his team—the objectives they'd achieved, or failed to achieve. It was how they improved.

The next morning, the first Search and Rescue team of New Earth boarded the Hellcat. Utility bags were stuffed with personal belongings. Weapons crates and ammunition were stored as well. Connor took one last look at the camp and then closed the rear doors, joining Diaz in the cockpit.

Connor engaged the flight controls and the Hellcat rose into the air. Less than thirty minutes later they were landing at the main compound.

"Civilization," Diaz said.

The recruits lined up just outside the Hellcat.

"There will be a graduation ceremony later today. Fresh uniforms are located in the barracks. Report to Field Operations Headquarters in two hours. Dismissed," Connor said.

The recruits snapped a salute and then headed off the airfield. Diaz also left him, and Connor waited for the maintenance crew to arrive. He hadn't spent that much time at the compound, and the training camp felt more like home to him than this did. He noticed a team of Field Operations personnel equipped for an excursion beyond the confines of the compound across the airfield.

Damon Mills was with the team, and Connor walked over. Mills was issuing orders to his team and they climbed aboard the troop carrier ship.

"I heard you were coming back into town," Mills said.

His tone was neutral, borderline professional, which was enough to pique Connor's curiosity.

"Where you heading?" Connor asked.

"One of the FORBs went dark last night. We're heading out there to see what their status is," Mills said.

"Have there been a lot of problems with the research bases?"

"Can't afford to take chances. Since you showed up, Mallory has had me updating our protocols, which includes that if a FORB goes dark for six hours or more, we have to go investigate," Mills said. There was still some bitterness in his tone but none of the hatred that had been there before.

"I'm not your enemy, Mills."

Mills snorted. "No, you're just a pain in my ass," he said and frowned. "But some of your suggestions did help. I better get to it."

Connor walked back to the Hellcat. There were times when he wanted to choke the life out of Damon Mills and other times when the man wasn't too bad to be around. Connor had no illusions that they'd ever be friends, but it would help if they could work together.

THE GRADUATION CEREMONY was a small affair attended by friends and family of the former Search and Rescue recruits. There were no dress uniforms for any division of Field Operations and Security, so they wore the green jumpsuit with the golden sunburst patch on one shoulder and a white shield with a black lightning bolt across the middle on the other.

Connor stood at a podium, delivering a commencement address to the new Search and Rescue Squad.

"You're the very first class to graduate from the new Search and Rescue Division of Field Operations. I can confidently say that you've set the bar high for the next class," Connor said.

The squad of former recruits rose to their feet and snapped a crisp salute, each with a hungry, confident gleam in their eyes. Connor brought his heels together and returned the salute. His gaze lingered on each of them.

Juan Diaz stepped forward, shoulders back and chest puffed out. "Lightning Platoon, dismissed."

There were cheers from those in attendance. Connor glanced over at Tobias and Ashley Quinn, each of whom wore proud expressions for their son. Allison Blake was alone, and she walked over to Connor.

"We're missing Noah," Blake said.

"Agreed. No one here at the compound for you?" Connor asked.

Allison shook her head. "My brother is still on the Ark."

"Oh, I had no idea," Connor said.

Nate Poe came over and asked if he could borrow Blake for a few minutes, so

Connor was left standing alone. He saw Diaz was with his on-again-off-again girlfriend, Victoria. Connor never knew what to do with himself at these types of formal functions. He'd stay here for his new team because they deserved that much, but he wouldn't like it. He'd been on the colony for just over two months and he still felt completely out of place.

Ashley Quinn spotted him and came over. "Boy, if you don't look like a fish out of water, I don't know who does."

"Have you heard from Noah?" Connor asked.

Ashley shook her head. "He's still at Lenora's research base. So what are you going to do now?"

"Do you have a job for me already?"

"Not my department. Speaking of which," Ashley said as Franklin Mallory joined them.

"The man of the hour," Mallory said.

"Not me. Them. Have you reviewed the mission report for their final exercise?" Connor asked.

"Yes, and I've circulated your comments about the ryklars to our field biologists. They're very excited," Mallory said.

"I wouldn't get too excited. Those things are dangerous and hellish to put down if they attack," Connor said.

"Toughened skin that's resistant to the standard round and the ability to conceal their body heat," Mallory said.

Connor pressed his lips together. "They want to study them?"

"Of course," Mallory said.

Connor glanced at Ashley. "I understand wanting to learn about them, but where are the ethical lines here? This is a highly advanced species with almost humanlike intelligence."

"Calm down, Connor. We're not going to start bagging and tagging them. We did, however, retrieve a few of the deceased specimens to study," Ashley said.

"They respond to a high-frequency sound, and I wonder if we can trace it to the source. When is Noah getting back?" Connor asked.

Mallory frowned. "I thought you knew. Forward Operating Research Base number 97 has gone offline. I sent Damon out there this morning. They should be arriving at the base soon."

"Mills mentioned going to investigate an offline base, but I didn't know it was that one," Connor said.

He kept thinking that the coordinated attacks by the ryklars and their abrupt withdraw from the area were connected somehow.

"What's the matter?" Mallory asked.

"Something doesn't seem right to me. I'm suspicious that the attacks and now this offline research base are connected somehow," Connor said.

"That base is over two hundred kilometers from your camp. That would be a fair distance for any animal on foot, even a quadruped," Mallory said.

"They hunt those landrunners and they're fast. I need to check into this," Connor said.

"It's okay to take a day off," Ashley said. "There's a team already en route to the base."

"There *are* no days off. You know that," Connor said.

Mallory sighed. "Alright, let's head to the command center and see what we can find out."

Connor and Franklin slipped away from the celebration and entered the command center, where the watch commander greeted them.

"I just need to borrow one of your techs," Connor said.

"Of course. Use Bailey," the watch commander said.

Bailey sat at a workstation nearby and Connor headed over to him. Bailey had a pouch gut and long shaggy hair. He saw Connor and Franklin and immediately straightened up.

"What can I do for you, sir?"

"I want you to scan for this frequency," Connor said and used his implants to upload the data to Bailey's terminal.

Bailey examined the data dump. "Ultra-high-frequency sound. Hmm . . . Okay, let's task some of our drones on this," he said.

The tech worked through the options for the drone-control network.

"Now we just need to amplify the signal and . . . Here we go," Bailey said.

The graphic output appeared on the screen.

"Can you trace it to the source?" Connor asked.

Bailey frowned. "Not right now. I'd need to task ten percent of our drones for this, but they're needed to support the teams we have in the field. I can, however, tell you which direction the signal gets stronger."

"What good will that do?" Franklin asked.

"We can map out the path of the signal and see what's in its path," Connor said.

Bailey nodded. "Exactly. One sec and I'll put it on the main screen."

Connor looked up from Bailey's workstation and faced the main wallscreen. A map of the area had a quadrant overlay superimposed over the main compound. The signal for the high-frequency sound became stronger in a westerly direction.

"Show the research bases along that path," Connor said.

The doors to the command center opened and Tobias Quinn walked in. He headed over to them.

"What's going on?" Tobias asked.

"Chasing a hunch," Franklin said.

Connor hadn't spoken to the governor since his son had joined Search and Rescue. Franklin quickly filled Tobias in on what they were doing.

"Bailey," Connor said, "show the research bases on the map."

"Sorry," Bailey said and tapped a few commands into the interface.

The output on the map updated.

"There!" Connor said.

Forward Operating Research Base number 97 was a short distance off from the line.

"This doesn't prove anything. We don't have a location for the source of the signal. We just know the general direction, and that happens to be in the direction of the base," Tobias said.

"You're right," Connor said, "but we should investigate. Has Mills checked in?"

Tobias frowned. "Franklin," the governor said and conveyed his opinion on the matter.

"Connor, 97 has had communications issues at least a half a dozen times. It's one of the things Noah keeps having to fix," Mallory said.

Every instinct in Connor's gut shouted that there was trouble at that base. "Lenora said they'd found more alien ruins near the base. What if the signal is from something they've found?"

"That's a hell of a leap, even for you," Tobias said.

"You didn't see how the ryklars reacted to the signal," Connor said.

"How do you know they reacted to the signal at all? We don't know when it began," Tobias said.

"Let me take my team and go investigate," Connor said.

Tobias's eyes widened.

"Mills took a team out there to assess the situation. If they have an issue or observe any ryklars in the area, he'll report it," Franklin said.

Connor glanced at the two men. Neither looked as if they were inclined to listen to him. "Can you at least send a warning to Mills?"

"I know you and Damon got off on the wrong foot, but he's really quite capable. I'll have the watch commander send him a message," Franklin said.

The Director of Fields Ops walked away, and Tobias regarded Connor for a moment.

"I was against Sean joining Search and Rescue, but I've seen some real changes in him. I need to level with you. Sean is meant for more than a glorified soldier. I hope you realize that," Tobias said.

"You should speak to your son about what he wants instead of telling me about your plans for him," Connor said.

Tobias's nostrils flared as he tried to control his temper. Connor left the governor and took a closer look at the information on the main wallscreen.

Franklin met up with Connor. "The watch commander will keep us apprised of the situation," he said and guided Connor from the command center.

Connor felt that they were making a mistake, but his arguments for sending his team had fallen short. Even he acknowledged that his reasoning had a number of flaws to it and that any chain of command would have done as Franklin Mallory was doing right now. Connor established a network connection to the command center so he'd have a firsthand look at any new developments. If Mills missed a check-in, he'd take his own squad to investigate, with or without permission.

22

CONNOR SPENT the rest of the day noting equipment locations and visiting the munitions depot to confirm that his access still worked. He didn't have reason to believe otherwise, but it didn't hurt to check. While there, he put in a requisition for a shipment of high-density nano-robotic ammunition to be delivered to the Hellcat. The desk sergeant reviewed the requisition and gave Connor a hard look.

"This is for that new squad?"

Connor nodded. "That's right. Is there a problem?"

The desk sergeant shook his head. "Not at all, Colonel. My name is Williams, sir, and I just wanted you to know that I appreciate everything you've done for Field Ops."

Williams stuck his hand out and Connor shook it.

"Have we met?" Connor asked.

"Not exactly, sir, but my wife was with the security detail you assisted a few months ago. I'll have the boys deliver this to your ship right away. Regarding your ship . . ." Williams said.

"What about it?"

"I noticed the Hellcat isn't outfitted with the main gun."

"That's right. It was supposed to follow in a different container," Connor replied.

Williams nodded. "We've got it here. Just say the word and I can have it mounted."

Connor's eyes widened. "That would be great. If I had any, I'd give you a bottle of Kentucky's finest bourbon."

Williams held up his hand and shook his head. "No need. I'm a scotch man myself and a group of us have a batch of Canadian whiskey that'll be ready soon. You join us for a drink some time and we'll call it even."

Connor said he would and left the munitions depot, heading for the armory. He spotted Sean Quinn following him and waved him over.

"Shouldn't you be out celebrating?" Connor asked.

"I was, but a friend of mine overheard you in the command center. Do you think there's trouble in one of the research bases, sir?" Sean asked.

Connor glanced around to be sure they weren't being overheard. "Who talked?"

"Sir?"

Connor gave him a hard look and the denial fled Sean's face.

"Lars Mallory told me," Sean said.

Connor nodded, remembering that Lars, Sean, and Noah were all friends.

"It could be nothing. Mills took a team out to a research base that went offline," Connor said.

Sean looked unconvinced. "Permission to speak freely, sir."

"Go ahead."

"Respectfully, sir, that's a load of garbage. If you really thought there wasn't going to be any trouble, you wouldn't be moving supplies to the Hellcat. 'Hope for the best but prepare for the worst' is how you put it, sir," Sean said.

Connor met the kid's challenging stare. "You're right. I think there's a problem at the research base."

"Are we going on a mission?" Sean asked excitedly.

"Keep your voice down," Connor said.

"Sorry, sir. Which base is it? Where is it?"

Connor walked away from the armory doors and Sean followed him. "It's 97."

Sean frowned and then his eyes lit with sudden comprehension. "Oh my god! Noah's there!"

"I know," Connor said.

"We need to do something! We should take the Hellcat and go right now," Sean said.

"We need do nothing. You should be on your way. If it comes time that Lightning Platoon is needed, you'll be alerted with the rest," Connor said.

"But, sir—" Sean began.

"That's an order, Private. Now get out of here."

Sean's lips became thin. "Yes, sir," he said and turned around.

Connor started heading toward the Armory door.

"Sir, if you plan to acquire something along the lines of Field Ops combat suits, you might be in for a surprise," Sean said.

Connor's shoulders stiffened and he turned around.

"The desk sergeant is a real hard-ass and is loyal to Damon Mills," Sean said and shrugged.

"Shouldn't matter," Connor said and turned toward the door.

"You're right, it shouldn't, but he could bury your request in red tape, and if something really *is* wrong at 97, we'd be delayed getting there," Sean said.

Connor clenched his teeth together, considering.

"And you think you can help out with that," Connor said.

Sean smiled and nodded. "Governor's son."

Connor knew he shouldn't encourage this sort of ploy, but he didn't have time to wait for a desk jockey on a power trip to thwart his efforts. Connor jerked his head toward the door, and Sean entered first.

Sean Quinn stuck by Connor's side after that and made himself useful. Once they were back at the Hellcat, they checked that the communications systems had been properly repaired and that Williams' team had mounted the main gun below the nose of the ship.

"What kind of gun is that?" Sean asked.

"It's not a gun. It's an M-180 gauss cannon and can shoot projectiles up to thirty millimeters in size," Connor said.

Sean's mouth rounded in surprise. "Too bad we couldn't mount something like that to the armored ATV we've got in the Hellcat's cargo area."

"Could never handle the recoil. This cannon is bolted into the Hellcat's frame," Connor said.

"What are we going to do now, sir?" Sean asked.

"Nothing. We've done everything we can for now," Connor replied.

Night had settled over the compound, and they hadn't heard from Damon Mills' team since they were at the halfway point to the research base.

"Shouldn't we recall the others? You know, to be on standby?" Sean asked.

Connor shut down the diagnostics he was running using the Hellcat's computer systems. Everything checked out.

"No," Connor said. "There're protocols in place for a reason. Damon still has time to check in before they're overdue. I'll send out an update and recall the team if something develops. Otherwise, you're dismissed."

Sean looked as if he wanted to make another argument but let it go. "Yes, sir."

Sean left him, and Connor went to the barracks that were set aside for Search and Rescue. He opened the metallic door and walked inside. Elyse Winters was lying on one of the beds and Wayne Randle was on another.

"I thought you guys would be with your significant others," Connor said.

They both sat up.

"Sean contacted us earlier, so we thought we'd stick around," Winters said.

"Guys, I appreciate it, but you can go home. I'll call you if I need you," Connor said.

"If it's all the same to you, we'll stay here," Randle said.

"Suit yourselves," Connor said and headed for the officer's quarters. He couldn't help but feel a little bit of pride in their dedication.

There were two officers' quarters in these barracks, and Juan Diaz slept inside one of them. Deciding not to wake his second in command, Connor went inside his own quarters and lay down. He had every intention of sleeping for the little bit his body required, but he couldn't seem to get settled. After half an hour he gave it up, got out of bed, and activated the terminal in his room. A large holoscreen flickered on. He brought up a map of the quadrant they were in and then put in a flight path to FORB 97. A fully loaded Hellcat would make the journey in about three hours. He checked his connection to the command center at Field Operations Headquarters. There still hadn't been a check-in from FORB 97 or Damon Mills.

Connor went over to the sink and splashed some cold water on his face, looking at himself in the mirror.

"It's *not* nothing," he said and strode to the door.

Once outside, he heard Diaz shuffle to his feet from the other room and hastily opened the door.

Connor looked toward the bunks and Lightning Platoon was on their feet, waiting for him.

"What the hell?" Connor said.

Diaz cleared his throat. "We know you, sir. If you think there's something wrong at that base, we're with you."

Connor walked toward the bunks with Diaz at his side. All of Lightning Platoon stood at attention.

"Alright," Connor said. "Let's get to it. Be on the Hellcat in five minutes."

Diaz clapped his hands together. "Yeah, let's go get her."

Connor looked at Diaz and frowned.

"Lenora. 97 is her base," Diaz said.

Connor shook his head. "There is no . . . There are lives at stake."

"I know," Diaz said quickly. "And Lenora's there," he said and grinned.

Connor's brows pushed forward. "Just get on the damn Hellcat, will you?"

It was still the middle of the night, so the airfield was quiet. Connor and the others made it to the Hellcat without being seen. They opened the doors and Connor called Amy Owens to the cockpit.

"We might need your help with something," Connor said.

"What do you need, sir?" Owens asked.

"I need you to block our transponder for the next hour. Until then, they can lock us out of the ship," Connor said.

"No problem," Owens said and returned to the back.

Connor went through the preflight checks while Diaz did his own checks.

"At some point we're going to need a pilot of our own," Diaz said.

"I'll place an order at the pilot store," Connor replied.

They were green across the board and Connor engaged the engines. The Hellcat was located on one of the secondary fields for smaller ships used by Field Operations and Connor had noted the hole in security for this field. He ran a quick sweep with his scanners and there were no drones and no Field Ops security in the area. That would probably change after today. He raised the thrusters and they left the compound behind.

Connor had Owens activate their transponder, which would automatically check in at the compound command center. It was a half hour later that Franklin Mallory raised them on a comlink channel.

"This is Gates," Connor said.

He activated the holoscreen and Mallory's face appeared. His gunmetal hair was ruffled as if he'd just gotten out of bed.

"I should have known you were going to be a thorn in my side," Franklin said.

"It's not intentional," Connor replied and checked their heading.

They'd been scanning for any comlink signals from FORB 97 or distress calls from Mills' team and had come up empty.

"I know what you're going to say and I know Tobias is going to have a fit about this. Worst-case scenario, we waste a trip out there," Connor said.

Franklin shook his head and bit his lower lip. "That's not the worst-case scenario. If you're wrong, it's both our asses on the line. I stuck my neck out for you."

"I'll tell him it was all me," Connor said.

"And that you ordered your team without authorization—" Franklin began.

"Cut the crap. Tobias is a governor. He's not an overlord. We started down this path because of what was happening near the compound. We're Search and Rescue. Let us do our jobs," Connor said.

"Okay, we'll do this your way, but I want regular check-ins," Franklin said.

"Will do. I have one more request," Connor said.

"When don't you?"

"Stop worrying. This is the price we pay for being able to live with ourselves," Connor said.

The comlink closed and Diaz shook his head. "Did you bump heads with your superiors back home?"

"Sometimes, but we had a lot of latitude because we conducted operations out of contact with COMCENT," Connor said.

He tried not to think about the last time he'd trusted his gut in his hunt for the Syndicate on Chronos Station. Millions of people had died. He'd spent a lot of nights thinking about it since he'd awakened aboard the Ark, about what he could have done differently.

He brushed those thoughts aside. He was on a planet that was over sixty light-years from Earth. As strange and somewhat familiar as this planet was, it was a place for new beginnings, and he'd committed himself to being a shield for these colonists. Part of him hoped he was wrong and the research station was just experiencing communication issues. If so, Mills would lord it over him for a while. But if Connor was right, at least what they were doing now would count for something.

23

CONNOR LEFT Diaz in the cockpit and went to check on the squad. Their gray metallic combat suits gleamed under the overhead lights. Their helmets were on, but the visors weren't engaged, so he could see all of their faces. Most were armed with the AR-71s, but Winters had an M-Viper sniper rifle and the M11-Hornet SMG holstered on her side. Connor glanced over at Sean Quinn and saw that he had the same equipment. He moved on and stood in the middle of the squad.

"We've had no reply from the research base, so we'll assume the worst. We'll be doing a flyover of the base to assess the situation. Be prepared for a low altitude combat drop deployment," Connor said.

He looked at each of them and they all acknowledged his command. "We'll break out as we did before for your final exercise—same teams as before except either Sergeant Diaz or myself will be with you. Winters and Randle, you'll be our seconds. Is that clear?"

"Yes, sir," the squad said.

"Remember your training. Stay focused," Connor said.

He headed back up to the cockpit and glanced at the broadcast signal. Connor took back control of the Hellcat and sent a canned check-in message to the compound.

The research base was nestled in the foothills of a vast mountain range. Connor had the scanner array activated, but there were no signals of any kind being detected.

"Not the best sign," Diaz said.

Connor focused on the heads-up display as the Hellcat sped along. He'd kept their approach at an elevated altitude so they'd have a bird's-eye view of the research base, and he finally caught a glimpse of a glistening metallic structure in the distance. They were flying over thick forests, so they didn't have a clear view of the ground. Connor switched on the ultrasonic high-frequency detector and the signal was orders of magnitude stronger than back at the compound.

"The source of that signal has to be close by," Connor said.

They closed in on the research base and the scanners detected an energy signature.

"At least the lights are on," Diaz said.

As the Hellcat sped closer, the grounds near the research base appeared to be moving. Connor tightened his grip on the thruster controls.

"They're under attack," Connor said.

There was a large perimeter fence surrounding the standard prefab habitat structures, and there were bright flashes of light all along the fence. Connor magnified the view and saw hordes of ryklars storming the base.

"Look," Connor said, "there are survivors."

They saw weapons being fired into the ryklars, but more kept coming. Connor knew the electrified fence was meant to be a deterrent but couldn't sustain an ongoing assault.

Diaz peered at the screen intensely. "They're only armed with CAR-74s."

"You'd better get back with the others," Connor said.

Diaz pulled himself out of the copilot's seat. "And here I thought I was going to have to talk you into staying," he said and gave his armor a quick check. "You're the better pilot."

Connor glanced at the heads-up display. There were hundreds of ryklars scrambling around and some were making a run on the base. He saw a few make it over the fence.

"Use the incendiary rounds. And scrounge up every weapon we've got on the ship and take them down with you. I'll make passes, cutting into their lines with the main gun. Conserve your ammo as much as you can," Connor said.

"I'll see you down there, sir," Diaz said and left.

Connor glanced at the door to the rear of the ship. He wanted to be on the ground with his team. He was almost of a mind to call Diaz back in so he could fight with the group, but the sergeant was right. Connor was the better pilot, and with the main cannon he could do much more damage from the Hellcat.

The Hellcat flew toward the besieged research base, which was just a collection of standard habitat buildings arranged like a small compound. ATV tracks had worn dirt paths leading away from two gates in the perimeter fence. Connor flew to the FORBs interior and pressed the button that changed the jump indicator in the back of the ship to green. The onboard video feed showed Lightning Platoon in two lines, dropping twenty meters down to the ground. Diaz and Compton pushed an armored, high-impact storage crate out of the back of the ship and then followed.

Connor closed the rear doors and pushed the accelerator. The Hellcat lurched forward and Connor gained some altitude. He armed the main cannon and set it to full auto, then leveled off his approach. The ryklars were concentrating their efforts at the two main gates. They had the research base surrounded, but they moved around so fast that it was hard to get an accurate count. Connor swooped down to make his first attack run, grabbing the stick and squeezing the trigger.

The Hellcat's main gun unleashed the M-180 gauss cannon in an onslaught of thirty-millimeter projectiles. The slugs tore a line through the ryklars, cutting them to pieces.

Connor made another pass and this time he saw the red blaze of AR-71 assault rifles cutting into the ryklars from the observation platforms around the research base.

Connor swung the Hellcat around and continued to mow down the ryklars, but they kept trying to get into the base. He made three more passes before the ryklars retreated into the forest, leaving the land outside the base covered with their dead. Connor circled around the base and saw that there were quite a few dead ryklars inside the perimeter fence as well.

He hovered in the air, running a scan of the area. The ryklars must have retreated deep into the forest. He couldn't detect them at all, and the Hellcat's engines were too loud for any kind of sonic detection. Connor made one more pass, circling the perimeter of the research base. He saw the troop carrier Mills had taken from the compound the day before. It looked charred, as if it had been in a battle. There were large gouges in the hull.

Connor brought the Hellcat in for a landing in the middle of the research base, cut the engines, and left the cockpit, taking his rifle with him. The cargo bay doors opened and Connor walked down the ramp, hearing the cries of the wounded. There were research base personnel running around, most looking haggard and scared. They looked at him as if they couldn't quite believe he was really there.

There were two women clutching each other in a firm embrace. One of the women gave him a determined look.

"Where's Damon Mills?" Connor asked.

"We need to get out of here. They're gonna come back. They always come back," one of the women said.

The more levelheaded of the two held the other closer. "Shhh, we're going to get out of here now. The ships from the compound will be here any minute now, you'll see."

Connor's mouth went dry. They thought they were being evacuated.

"This is Carol. She's just scared. I'm Lori."

"I know you've been through a lot, but can you tell me where Damon Mills is? He came on that troop carrier yesterday," Connor said.

"We can't all fit on that ship," Carol said, her gaze fixed on the Hellcat.

"If he's still alive, he was at the gate where the fighting was worst," Lori said.

Connor nodded. "We're going to get you out. Are you alright here?"

Lori sucked in her bottom lip and nodded.

Connor left them and walked toward the front gates. There were several Field Ops personnel gathered around a man who was lying on the ground. Blake hovered over him. Connor went closer and saw that the man was Damon Mills. He had a deep gash down his thigh from a ryklar claw, and Blake was treating the wound with medipaste to bind it.

Damon Mills looked up at him with bloodshot eyes. "Never thought I'd be happy to see you."

"What happened here?" Connor asked.

Damon winced as Blake prodded the wound, and he sucked in a shaky breath. "Where are the other ships?"

"There are no other ships. It's just us," Connor said.

Mills gritted his teeth and tried to get to his feet. Blake tried to stop him and he scowled at her.

"Somebody, help me up," Mills said and looked back at Blake. "Go help someone who needs it."

Blake glanced at Connor and he nodded for her to go.

"I called in an evacuation shortly after we arrived yesterday. Are you saying the compound has no idea we're in trouble?" Mills asked.

Connor glanced around at the people at the base. They looked exhausted and almost dead on their feet. They kept looking past the perimeter fences as if the ryklars would return at any moment. "Mallory has no idea."

24

Mills sagged on his feet and Connor helped him down to a sitting position.

"Just rest for a second," Connor said and opened up a comlink to Diaz. "What's your status?"

"We've got a lot of wounded people here. Deacon is helping. I had Blake on the other side of the base. The fence is in really bad shape. I don't know how it's still standing," Diaz said.

"Have Randle secure that area. Get Ramirez to assess the fence and then meet me at the Control Center," Connor said.

One of Mills' team members helped the commander to his feet.

"What happened to your ship?" Connor asked.

"Those damn creatures happened. The landing zone for this base is outside the fence. They attacked it sometime yesterday. We cut a path to the ship and managed to move it over there, but it's taken heavy damage. It can't fly," Mills said.

Winters headed toward them with Owens, Poe, Jackson, and Compton.

Connor waved them over. "Compton and Jackson, I want eyes on this gate at all times. If the ryklars so much as poke a claw beyond the forest line, I want to know about it. Poe, I want you up in the observation tower right there."

The three men left for their assignments.

"Winters and Owens, I need you to get the troop carrier flight-ready if you can," Connor ordered.

They left, and Connor followed Mills as he limped to the command center.

The holoscreens inside showed systems offline and multiple errors.

"Charlie," Mills said, "we need that power generator online."

Charlie wore a dirty blue jumpsuit and looked as if he hadn't slept in days.

"We took it offline to make repairs to the fence," Charlie said.

Mills turned toward Connor. "How many people can you fit on that ship of yours?"

Connor glanced around. "Not enough. Why are communications down?"

"Some kind of interference. That kid Noah was working on it," Mills said.

"Where is he?" Connor asked.

"He was with the archaeological team that went to the ruins yesterday, led by Dr. Bishop. They left before we got out here," Mills said.

Connor's insides went cold. "Yesterday? Did you send anyone to look for them?"

"The ryklars started gathering shortly after they left and stayed in the area, with more coming all the time. They started attacking the fences last night. There was no way we could get anyone through. The team took the only armored ATV," Mills said and gave Connor a sympathetic look. "There's no way they could have held out this long. I'm sorry. They're dead."

An image of Noah joking with him at the training camp's command center immediately came to mind and was quickly followed by a vision of Lenora with her quick wit and long auburn hair. He remembered the brush of her lips on his cheek.

"I'm not abandoning them," Connor said.

"What about the people here?" Mills asked. "They need your help too."

"I have an armored ATV in the Hellcat. I'll take a small team to assess the status of the archaeological group," Connor said.

Mills limped over to him. "Connor, there's no way they survived the night."

Connor glared at him. "Some would call it a miracle that *you* survived the night here. With comlink signals severely limited, I'm not counting anyone out. On the off chance that they *did* survive, they'll need help. They'll never make it here on foot with all the ryklars in the area."

"We need to contact the compound." Mills frowned in thought and checked the wall clock. "You're early. We're not considered overdue until right now."

"I had my suspicions that something was wrong when you failed to check in," Connor said.

Mills shook his head. "Shit, knowing you, I bet you disobeyed orders to be here," he said and sighed. "I guess I owe you my life, but I still think you're a pain in the ass."

"Likewise," Connor said. "We had communications with the compound until we were within fifty kilometers of this base. I'm going to leave some of my team here to assist in the base's defense. We'll also take the Hellcat out of range of the interference and let the compound know we need a base-wide evacuation."

"Going to the archaeological site is suicide," Mills said.

"Then you can return the favor and come rescue us," Connor said and started walking toward the exit. "Oh, one more thing. My team is very good at their jobs. If they have a suggestion, I strongly urge you to listen to them."

Connor left the command center and recalled his team to the Hellcat. Diaz had armed the surviving Fields Operations security detail with the weapons they'd brought. They were now standing watch.

The team assembled outside the Hellcat, with the exception of Deacon and

Blake, who were still attending the wounded, and Winters and Owens, who were working to get the troop carrier ship flight-ready.

Connor explained the situation to his team. "Diaz, I want you to take the Hellcat out about fifty kilometers and send an emergency broadcast back to the compound and the other research bases. If there're Field Ops people there with a ship, they're to come here and help evacuate this base on my authority."

"Yes, sir. Where will you be, sir?" Diaz asked.

"There's an archaeological team unaccounted for. They left before the attack yesterday. The last drone surveillance had ryklars heading toward the site," Connor said.

"Is Noah with them, sir?" Sean Quinn asked, his brows drawn up in concern.

Connor nodded. "Listen up. This base needs to be defended. If the ryklars are anything, they're determined to get in here. My guess is they're regrouping for another attack."

"Regrouping," Donna Marten said. "Sir, animals don't regroup like a fighting force."

"The ryklars are smarter than your average predator," Connor said.

"What about the research team, sir?" Sean asked.

"I'm going to take the armored ATV to investigate what happened to them," Connor said. Several people started to speak, and Connor held up his hand so they'd quiet down. "I'll take three volunteers with me, but I won't order any of you to come. None of you have to go, but we're the only chance they have."

"I volunteer, sir," Sean said without hesitation. "We're Search and Rescue, sir. We go where no one else will go."

Sean was echoed by all the rest. All of them were willing to put their lives on the line for this. Connor had trained many soldiers in his career, but all the training in the world couldn't predict how a person would react when they found themselves in the thick of it.

"This sucks," Diaz said, drawing the team's gazes toward him. "I can't volunteer because no one else can fly the Hellcat," he said and glared at Connor. "I told you we needed a damn pilot."

"I have one on order for when we get back," Connor said and looked at the rest of the team. "Thank you. All of you. I'm sure if the others were here, they'd do the very same thing. I've only seen that kind of courage in one other team I've worked with, and they were the best."

The Lightning Platoon's faces gleamed with pride. Connor had told them of the Ghosts on more than one occasion—how they were the most effective team he'd ever served with. He still wished they were here with him, but looking at his new squad, he saw echoes of what the Ghosts had been in each one of them, and it made Connor proud to be their commander.

"Compton and Jackson, you're with me," Connor said.

Sean Quinn gave him a hard look and Connor regarded him for a moment.

"I'm coming with you, sir," Sean said in a determined voice that was reminiscent of his mother.

Maybe it was the fact that Connor had once had a son named Sean, or perhaps it was the fact that Ashley Quinn had been one of the first people on the

Ark to be kind to him—a mother figure for all—but he felt responsible for Sean Quinn. He'd even bumped heads with Tobias about Sean and the man he was becoming. But Connor couldn't allow himself to view Sean as a boy anymore. It just wasn't fair.

"Alright, you can come," Connor said.

Compton's deep voice let out a hungry laugh. "You're running with the big boys now, Bling," he said.

Sean smiled widely for a moment and then was back to business.

"You all have your assignments. Protect this base until help arrives. Stay focused. The ryklars like to try to overwhelm their prey. Marten and Poe, you can do more damage up high with your rifles than fighting in the thick of it," Connor said.

Diaz ran to the Hellcat and returned with a small black case, handing it to Sean. "Flare gun. Fire it into the air and I'll come get you with the Hellcat."

"Excellent work, Sergeant," Connor said.

There was still an angry glint to Diaz's gaze, and Connor knew he hated that he couldn't go with him.

"These people need you here. Keep them safe," Connor said.

Diaz snapped a salute and headed back to the ship, muttering about pilots.

Connor glanced at Compton. "Let's get this ATV offloaded."

25

THE ARMORED ATV left the research base at sixteen hundred hours. Connor saw an unnamed mountain range in the distance, its high peaks wreathed in clouds. Jackson drove and kept them moving at a steady pace. He kept a sharp lookout ahead as he drove down the worn path. Compton held his weapon and kept a close watch out of one side of the ATV while Sean Quinn kept watch out of the other side. Connor wished there were a turret on the roof. It would have given them a good view of everything around them.

Connor tried to open a comlink to the archaeological team, but there was no reply. The ultra-high-frequency sonic detector still showed a strong signal up ahead, and Connor was certain the alien ruins were tied to the ryklar attack. What he didn't understand was why the ryklars were so focused on the base.

The forest was quiet but for the steady grind of the ATV's tires on the ground.

Connor ordered Jackson to go faster and looked at Compton. "Standard protocol for remote security is a two-person Field Ops team as escorts?"

"Affirmative, unless there were predators spotted in the area. Then they might have taken two more with them. They'll only be armed with the CAR-74s, and the others will only have sonic hand blasters," Compton said.

"Noah would have brought his own rifle with him," Connor said.

Compton nodded. "I'd forgotten about that."

Connor glanced over at Sean. He cradled his M-Viper with one hand and had his other hand on his SMG. He peered out the window of the ATV, keeping careful watch outside.

"Sir, we're picking up another vehicle's beacon ahead. It's really close," Jackson said.

Connor returned to the front of the ATV and looked at the small heads-up display that appeared over the dashboard. The other ATV was less than half a kilometer away. If the ryklars had broken off from the main group, would the team be holed up in the ATV, or would they have gone somewhere else? He should have asked someone at the base what they knew about the ruins. Any information would have given them an advantage. Instead, they were blazing their own trail. Hopefully, Lenora and her team left enough evidence that they could follow them.

Ahead of them the ground sloped upward, and as they drove over the edge, Connor caught a glimpse of the other ATV. The heavy vehicle was turned over on its side. One of the tan doors was bent outward as if something had used brute strength to tear it open. Jackson slowed down and pulled the vehicle over to the side of the path.

Sean Quinn made a move to open the side door.

"Wait a minute," Connor said.

They waited a full two minutes before Connor opened the door and exited the vehicle. He switched his helmet view to infrared, and the overturned ATV appeared in cool blues, the only warm spots being where the sunlight hit the vehicle. Connor circled around and saw that the windshield had been kicked out. The interior was shredded, but there wasn't any blood.

"I don't think anyone was inside when this damage was done," Sean said, looking relieved.

Connor engaged the sonic detectors and scanned the immediate area. No ryklars were detected. He switched his helmet back to normal combat-assist view, which had a HUD overlay. His suit computer would help identify any threats that came into view.

"Let's follow the path. Compton, I want you to bring up the rear," Connor said.

"You got it, sir," the big man said.

Connor took point with Sean right behind him. Jackson and Compton followed. The path took them through the brush to a large fissure in the ground. Connor glanced up and saw a bright blue sky overhead, but this place would be hard to detect if they were flying. Connor walked to the edge and saw a fifty-foot drop to the bottom. Thick vines with wide, pale yellow leaves grew across the narrow fissure, and Connor could only just make out the bottom.

"There's an elevator," Sean said.

Connor saw the winch system with cables that went over the edge. "See if you can raise the platform."

Sean went over to the winch and pressed one of the buttons. The winch motors started retracting the cables, and Compton and Jackson kept their AR-71s aimed at the area where the platform would appear.

There was a loud snapping sound and then the top of the platform appeared. Connor peered over the edge and then stepped onto the platform. The others joined him and Connor pressed the button to descend.

They moved downward at a steady pace, all of them keeping a watchful eye on the surrounding area.

"I've got nothing in IR," Compton said.

"I'm not tracking any movement either," Jackson said.

Connor tried to reach Noah with the comlink, but there was no answer to his broadcast signal.

They reached the bottom, where a shallow stream trickled by. Piles of dark stone and dirt were off to the side. A flickering light lit the tunnel across from them. Connor gestured for the team to be quiet as they headed toward the tunnel. The rounded entrance was eight feet across and gave them more than enough headroom. Overturned lights littered the ground, but the few that were still working cast a soft yellow light. Connor's helmet display automatically compensated for the dim lighting. The smooth walls had uniform scuff marks from an industrial digger. Connor's heads-up display registered the end of the tunnel at twenty-five feet, and they cautiously approached to find that it opened into an enormous underground cavern. They emerged onto a ledge that overlooked a small underground city. Over a hundred light-stands were positioned on the rooftops throughout the cavern, which gave it an artificial glow. Flat square rooftops stretched out before them with deep shadows down below the rooflines. Faint glowing lines surrounded some of the rooftops, adding more light to the dim cavern.

"I knew they'd found ruins, but this is amazing," Sean whispered.

They were high up above the grounds, and Connor glanced around, looking for a way down.

"Contact!" Sean hissed. He brought up his M-Viper sniper rifle and peered through the scope.

"Easy," Connor said. "Tell me what you see."

"Twelve hundred meters that way," Sean said and gestured toward the left side of the cavern.

Connor looked in that direction and enhanced the view so he could see better. Scurrying from rooftop to rooftop was the spotted back of a ryklar. Connor panned his view but didn't see any more in the area.

"Should I take the shot?" Sean asked.

"No," Connor said.

Sean looked up from his scope. "I can get him."

"I know you can, but I don't want the other ryklars in the area to know we're here," Connor said.

Sean nodded. "Understood, sir."

Connor continued looking for a way to get down and saw a few anchor bolts drilled into the rock wall with a nylon rope attached. They used the rope to lower themselves from the outcropping, and Connor found himself wondering how Lenora had discovered all this in the first place.

They ended up on top of a flat roof that butted against the cavern wall. There were small metallic bridges that connected the buildings, and Connor squatted down to feel the smooth surface. Certain parts of the substance glistened in the light from his combat suit.

Connor led them toward the middle of the cavern. The buildings had octagonal shapes carved into them and he wasn't sure whether they were doors or windows. They were much larger than any standardized door he'd ever seen. Connor opened a comlink and set it to broadcast.

"Archaeological team, this is Connor Gates from Search and Rescue. Acknowledge."

Connor waited fifteen seconds before repeating himself.

The comlink status on his helmet display showed a red circle with a line drawn through it, and Connor was about to repeat himself when the status changed to green.

"Commander, this is Noah Barker. Thank god you're here. We read your signal."

"Good to hear your voice, Noah. What's your status?" Connor asked.

"The ryklars tracked us in here and we lost some people when they attacked. We tried to reach the base, but our signal couldn't get through," Noah said.

Connor could hear the tension in Noah's voice. "How many people are with you?"

"There are seven of us now. We came here with ten, sir."

"Understood. We came in through the tunnel and are near the middle of the cavern. Can you tell me your location?" Connor asked.

He heard Noah repeat the question and it sounded like the comlink was handed off to someone else.

"Connor, Lenora here. Noah said you were in the middle of the cavern. We're—"

A loud screech echoed through the cavern, making Connor jump. He spun around, checking the area. The others were doing the same.

"We've been made, sir," Compton said, pointing his rifle.

Standing on the rooftop a hundred meters away was a ryklar, each of its four arms held out, its muscular chest heaving as it drew breath. Another one climbed up next to it and let out an ear-piercing cry. Several more ryklars climbed on top of nearby buildings within a hundred meters of their position.

"Could really use that location," Connor said.

They slowly moved off the roof they were on and retreated from the ryklars.

Jackson cursed and brought up his weapon. Before Connor could tell him to hold his fire, an incendiary round burst forth from the chamber and streaked a line of red, taking a ryklar in the chest.

The ryklars charged.

"Don't shoot them! We weren't attacked until we fired the first shot," Lenora said.

Connor fired his weapon as they retreated to the next rooftop.

"A little late for that. Where are you?" Connor asked.

Compton and Jackson provided covering fire while Connor and Sean moved to the adjacent building. Sean aimed his rifle, and the M-Viper unleashed with such force that the projectile took out two ryklars that were charging toward them.

"We're inside one of the buildings. Noah said he's painting our location for you," Lenora said.

Connor scanned the area and saw an IR laser moving in side-to-side motions.

"I've got 'em. Fall back," Connor said.

They made steady progress toward Noah's IR signal. The ryklars weren't charging them in a blind rage like they had been at the research base, but there were more coming and the cavern echoed with the sounds of their calls. Connor and the others dropped off the roof and sprinted toward Noah's signal. When they reached the building, a thick octagonal door opened and they rushed inside. It took all of them to push it closed. Connor listened by the door and heard several ryklars growling as they ran by.

Connor blew out a breath and pressed his hand against the door. The smooth cold surface seemed sturdy enough, but he couldn't be sure it would withstand ryklar claws.

"It's made out of some kind of alloy," Noah said.

Connor patted him on the back. "Thanks for showing us the way. I'm glad you're alright," he said and looked at the others in the room.

"Any injuries?" Connor asked.

Lenora stood with her arms crossed and her eyes blazing with anger. "The ryklars had just settled down enough that we were going to try to get out of here, but now we'll have to wait even longer, thanks to you."

Connor frowned. "My team risked their lives to get here. A little appreciation would go a long way."

"I'm sorry if you're feeling underappreciated, but the creatures were scattered until you barged in. I was trying to tell you not to shoot them. What is it with you soldier types? You think the only way to solve problems is with a gun in your hands," Lenora said.

"They were closing in on us," Compton said and clenched his teeth.

"Yeah, and you panicked," Lenora said.

"Compton," Connor said, "stay on that door."

Compton blew out a frustrated breath and walked over to the door. Connor regarded Lenora for a moment, and underneath her show of anger was fear. They were all shaken up and lashing out.

"Let's just calm down for a minute. We've got some field rations and water. When was the last time any of you ate?" Connor asked.

At the mention of food and water, the archaeological team perked up and came over. A man in a blue Field Ops uniform approached him. He had blond hair that was shaved on the sides.

"I'm James Brennan, sir. Me and my partner, Craig, are the security detail for this group. I just wanted to say that if your man Noah hadn't been with us, there would be even fewer of us left," Brennan said.

Connor glanced over at Noah, who was off to the side speaking with Sean.

"I'm glad he could help," Connor said.

"Emmerson, Craig, sir," said a man who looked barely eighteen years of age. "Brennan and I would like to join your platoon," Emmerson said and looked away. "If we make it out of here."

"We'll talk about it *when* we get out of here. Just stay focused and be smart, and we'll all get out of here." Connor glanced at Lenora and she looked away. "Give me a moment. Go check in with Compton."

The two Field Ops agents nodded and went toward the door, where Compton leaned against the wall.

Connor stepped closer to Lenora. "Team here looks kind of young."

Lenora shook her head and sighed. "I'm sorry about before. It's just that we've been running around here for over a day and those two won't listen to me," she said, nodding toward the two Field Ops guys. "The ryklars showed up and they just fired their weapons at them. Then the ryklars attacked and two of us were down almost before we had a chance to react. We lost Ellena this morning." There was a catch in her throat. "She was—damn it—" Lenora looked away, her shoulders shaking. Connor reached out and rubbed her shoulders soothingly.

"Sounds like you've been through a lot. It's okay to take a moment," Connor said.

Lenora jerked away and her blue-eyed gaze became stormy. "Don't you try that psychological crap with me, Gates."

"Okay, I won't," Connor said and held up his hands in front of his chest. He then reached inside his pack and pulled out a container of water, offering it to her.

Lenora's gaze softened. "Thanks," she said and drank from the container.

"The ryklars have attacked the research base. Hundreds of them. They even attacked my team back at our camp a few days ago, which is hundreds of kilometers away. I can assure you it was unprovoked."

"The base? Is it . . . Is everyone okay?" Lenora asked.

"There are a lot of people hurt. Mills and his team were defending the base until we showed up. Most of my team is back there helping. They've called for an evacuation by now," Connor said.

"We can't leave here now."

Connor frowned. "It's too dangerous to stay. We've got to focus on getting out of here and figure out why communications are blocked. It's going to be dangerous out there. The ryklars were moments from attacking us, and I won't fault Jackson for defending himself."

Lenora sighed. "How would we even know what provokes them? Our presence here could be enough of a provocation. You react with violence and you'll receive the same in kind. Before the attack they seemed agitated, but I'm not sure by what," Lenora said.

"You want to make friends with them?" Connor said and immediately wished he hadn't.

Lenora thrust the container back at him. "What is it with you? Not everything is black and white, friend or foe. We need to figure out why they're attacking in the first place."

"We need to get out of here, alive. That's my first priority, not doing a study on a creature that wants to kill us," Connor said.

"You don't realize what we've found here. An alien civilization built this place," Lenora said.

"Where did they all go then?" Connor asked.

"Haven't figured that out yet," Lenora said.

Connor glanced toward the door, his gaze taking in the octagonal shape. "You're not going to say the ryklars built all this?"

Lenora shook her head and laughed. "No. De-evolution is the most absurd theory there is. An intelligent species will not suddenly become stupid because of evolution. Cultures and societal practices lead to the downfall of intelligent species, not evolution."

"Okay, so not the ryklars," Connor said.

"Also, we found several statue fragments and none of them look like a ryklar," Lenora said.

Connor pressed his lips together. "So that whole speech about evolution . . ."

"Was just so I could impress you, and it helps me calm down," Lenora said.

Connor felt the edges of his lips pulling upward. "How much of this place have you explored?"

He took a quick glance at the others in the room and tried to gauge their chances of going out the way they'd come in—navigating the cavern and climbing the ropes with the ryklars dogging their every step. Their chances weren't very good.

"We were in here quite a long time before the ryklars showed up. We first discovered this place about a week ago, came across some technology here, and sent for Noah to come help with the analysis," Lenora said.

Connor looked at the sparse room. While it served their purposes, he couldn't figure out what it was originally meant for. "What kind of technology are we talking about here? Advanced tech like what we have? Better? Worse? The same?"

Lenora's brows drew up together in thought. "Not more advanced than us, at least not that I can tell. We didn't find any spaceships or anything like that. We need more time to study this place. Take the material this building is made of— some type of alloy. We need a chemical analysis of its composition, but there are things we can learn from this place that will help with the colony."

"Like a new element. Could be useful."

"Not my area. We've been making new alloys from the elements on Earth for thousands of years. Perhaps this species has a new compound or way of mixing things together. Stuff like that," Lenora said.

Connor nodded. "I understand that this find is important, but my first priority is to get everyone here to safety. I can't do that if we stay in this building. Do you know of another way out?"

Lenora regarded him for a moment. "There's the main entrance."

"Good, let's go there and get out of here. We can make a path and keep the ryklars at bay while we escape. We have an armored ATV that we can squeeze everyone into," Connor said.

Lenora shook her head. "The ryklars are at the main entrance."

"How do you know?"

"I had a small surveillance drone mapping the cavern. The last video feed I saw from it showed the entrance with a lot of ryklars already there," Lenora said.

"What were they doing?"

"I'm not sure. Looked like they were guarding it. They'd go to the interior and then return to the entrance."

"Is it still online? I scanned the area and didn't detect any drones," Connor said.

Lenora shook her head. "No, we lost contact when we entered a chamber deeper inside the cavern."

Noah walked over. "We didn't touch anything. Things just sorta turned on by themselves when we came inside this place."

"What was inside?" Connor asked.

Noah glanced at Lenora for a moment. "It was like a double pyramid. You know, like someone stuck the bottoms of two pyramids together. The middle of it started glowing. That's when the comms went out."

"By the next day, the ryklars started showing up," Lenora said.

"When did this happen?"

"Two days ago," Lenora answered.

"Did anything else start coming on when you guys started poking around down here?"

"Several places had power to them, which I thought was interesting. Why do you ask?"

"Because during a training exercise, my team was attacked by three packs of ryklars that seemed to be coordinating with each other. Then they suddenly ran off and we detected an ultra-high-frequency transmission. The source of it wasn't far from where we're standing," Connor said.

Lenora glanced at the others excitedly. "Some of us thought that perhaps the ryklars were some kind of guard dog for this place. If what you say is true, a lot more of them are heading this way."

Connor's mind raced but kept coming back to the same thing. "We need to get out of here. We can't wait for them to calm down."

"The main entrance is guarded, but there might be a back door if we go deeper into the ruins," Lenora said.

Compton turned around. "Did someone say go deeper into the ruins?"

Connor nodded. "It might be our only way out of here."

"Great," Compton said dejectedly.

"That's why you have the biggest gun," Connor said and then ran his hands over his face. "Okay, we can't stay here. I need to know who's armed and any supplies or equipment you have with you—anything we can use to help us stay alive."

26

For the next twenty minutes, Connor spoke with Lenora's team about the layout of the ruins here. The one thing they had going for them was that the alien race that built this place planned it out like a large grid and used all the space. All the buildings were square, and even the walkways between them had a consistency in measurement that was equal to any of the planned cities back on Earth. If the ryklars hadn't been out there waiting to kill them, Connor could have appreciated that. As it was, he had to pull the useful information he needed from them while asking that they keep their conjecture to a minimum. But these were scientists, a breed of humans that was conditioned to being long-winded.

Connor went to the door. He would be taking point. There weren't enough guns for everyone. Sean had handed Lenora his SMG and she assured Connor that she knew how to use it. Lenora was standing behind him, and at first, Connor had been worried she'd shoot him in the back. Accidentally, of course. But whenever he looked back, she was holding the SMG as if she'd been handling firearms her whole life.

Noah came over to his side. "I just wanted to let you know that I've made some progress with that other project."

"You were finally able to decode it?" Connor asked.

Noah shrugged. "I had some help. I stored my findings so far on my personal data storage device. You're gonna wanna see it. There's been a lot more going on back home than anyone realizes."

"Some people already know," Connor said.

Noah bobbed his head. "Yeah, some people."

Connor had been extremely curious about Noah's side project decoding the data burst from the deep space buoys that bolstered data communication signals from Earth, but he needed to push all that aside.

The two teams were clustered near the door. Connor had assigned them their places and interspersed his squad among them while having Compton cover their six.

"Once we're outside this room, we need to be as quiet as possible. If you spot something, don't shout or scream. Instead, inform the nearest member of my squad or Field Ops security. No one will fire their weapon without my say so unless a ryklar is bearing down on you. We want to avoid a confrontation with them. Is that understood?"

Everyone acknowledged their understanding.

"Lenora and Noah, you're with me at the front," Connor said.

They opened the octagonal door. While the door was heavier than it looked, it made hardly any noise. Connor took a quick look outside and there were no ryklars in sight, so he stepped out and stayed near the wall of the building. He glanced above and didn't see any creatures. Connor frowned, not trusting that the ryklars had just given up on them.

He waved over to the others and they quietly left the building. Connor peeked around the corner of the building and saw that the way was clear. Lightning Platoon's helmets enabled them to see well in the low-light conditions, but the archaeological team didn't have that luxury and had to stick close to the people who could see.

They made steady progress deeper into the cavern. Several ryklars screeched a call that sounded as if they were on the other side of the cavern, but because of the echoes Connor couldn't be sure. They reached the end of the cavern and there was a clear path that went off in either direction. Connor glanced at Lenora, who gestured toward the right. There were rows of squat buildings and the cavern ceiling was lower there.

Noah whispered Connor's name and he looked back. Down the line of people, Compton gestured with his rifle up toward one of the buildings. Connor nodded and held his finger up to the face of his helmet. He brought his rifle up and waited.

Don't be there.

Connor gestured to the others to stay where they were and pointed at Noah to follow him. They crossed the narrow pathway and circled around one of the buildings, then Connor stopped and listened for a moment. He heard the sounds of a clawed foot scuffling nearby, then a blast of the breath sounds the ryklars made. Connor craned his neck around the corner of the building and saw a group of ryklars in the distance, heading toward them. He stepped back into cover and he and Noah went back to the others. Connor gestured to his team that the ryklars were closing in on them. Compton bobbed his head that he understood and focused his attention behind them.

Connor motioned for the others to follow and he set off at a quicker pace than before. The cavern floor became uneven and sloped toward the wall, but the wall curved around to a passageway that led them away from the cavern. He glanced back at Lenora and she gave him an encouraging nod. There was a light toward the end of the tunnel, and as they got closer, Connor realized it came from outside. They jogged the rest of the way to the end of the tunnel and stopped. To the right, the sounds of rushing water came from a nearby waterfall. They left the tunnel and emerged into a forested valley that was surrounded by mountains. Amidst the trees were alien ruins that closely resembled what they'd seen inside. The pathways were carved from a pale stone, which was also used to form the base of the buildings. In the middle of the valley was a tall spire.

"They're in the tunnel," Compton said, trying to keep his voice down.

Connor looked at Lenora. "Have you been here before?"

"Only briefly."

"We need higher ground so we can see where we are," Connor said.

He tried to open a comlink back to the research base, but there was no response. That would have been too easy.

The tallest thing in the valley was the spire, and Connor led them toward it.

Lenora grabbed his arm. "Not directly toward it. The ryklars like to occupy the middle. We should circle around and then go inwards."

Connor changed direction and they skirted the edges of the ruins. The forest had swallowed up some areas of the city. A loud screech pierced the air, echoing off the mountains, and more ryklars responded from inside the valley. Connor quickened the pace, taking the group along the edge. He caught a few glimpses of the interior of the ruins and the spotted backs of the ryklars. They were hunting for them, and Connor quickly started looking for a place they could use to hide.

There were several more screeches, followed by snarling. Connor looked back toward where he'd seen the ryklars and saw two groups of them fighting. They'd charge each other, attacking with their claws, and then they'd break apart.

"Commander," Noah said in a low voice. "I've detected the source of the ultra-high-frequency waves coming from that tower. If we—"

Noah was cut off as gunfire erupted from the end of the line, and Connor's attention snapped toward the sound. There were three ryklars charging toward them. Compton and Jackson fired their weapons with precision. Sean Quinn aimed his M-Viper and took out the third ryklar with a shot to the chest. Connor called for them to follow him. Abandoning all pretense of sneaking around, Connor led them from the trees into the ruins.

They ran near the remnant buildings and Connor looked at Noah. "If I can get you into that spire, do you think you can shut down the signal?" Connor asked.

Noah's eyes widened. "I'll do my best, sir."

Lenora's mouth slackened. "The two of you can't go off by yourselves."

Connor gestured for the others to come closer. The ryklars were searching the forest but hadn't detected them in the ruins yet.

"We're going to split up," Connor said. "Compton, I want you, Jackson, and Quinn to take these people and hide in that building over there. Noah and I are going to take out the signal coming from that spire. Once it's down, call for backup."

"Sir, you need more than just the two of you if you're going up to the spire," Sean said.

"I'm going with you," Lenora said. "I'm the most familiar with the ruins."

"Bling is right, sir," Compton said. "Take him with you."

Connor didn't like it, but he knew they were right. Their odds of success were higher if they had a few more people with them.

"I hope you guys can run fast," Connor said. "We'll draw the ryklars away."

Connor sprinted away, with Noah, Sean, and Lenora following close behind. He screamed and fired a few shots into the air. The ryklars responded almost immediately, as howling and snarling sounded nearby. Connor weaved his way through the ruins, pushing toward the spire. He glanced behind him and saw a ryklar galloping on all fours, closing in on Sean Quinn. Connor raised his weapon and Sean darted to the side. Connor squeezed the trigger and an incendiary round shot out, hitting the creature in the chest. The ryklar roared and kept coming. Connor shot several more times before it stumbled and fell.

Noah and Lenora passed him, and Sean thanked him when he caught up.

They had reached the bottom of the bronze-colored spire, and Connor saw glowing lights on the inside. He glanced behind him and saw more ryklars running toward them in a frenzy.

"Go on. We'll hold them off," Connor said.

An octagonal entrance lay open before them, and Noah and Lenora ran inside while he and Sean positioned themselves on either side of the entrance. Connor squatted down, using the wall for cover, and Sean did the same thing. A horde of ryklars came toward them down the main thoroughfare. Connor applied the high-density nano-robotic ammunition to his grenade launcher and fired grenades one after another into the horde. As the grenade timers expired, he and Sean took cover. Several loud explosions shook the ground at his feet. Connor came out from cover and ryklar corpses littered the road. Some ryklars crawled away, their roars becoming whimpers. Ryklars beyond the blast radius shifted their clawed feet, rocking from side to side. Some of the ryklars started shoving others, and a vicious battle broke out among them.

Connor heard Sean load a high-density ammo pack into his M-Viper. More ryklars showed up and Connor noted that several large alphas were driving the others forward. The ryklars' growls came from within their mass of thick red tentacles, and with so many of them, Connor felt that he was looking at a horde of bloody beards bringing the promise of death.

Connor heard shots being fired from somewhere within the spire.

"The others are in trouble," Connor said.

He looked for a way to barricade the doorway, but there was nothing. What he wouldn't give for some heavy explosives.

"Fall back into the spire," Connor said.

They left the entrance and headed into the spire's interior. The inside of the spire was an empty space with a hollow shaft running toward the top. There weren't any stairs, but a wide ramp ran along the wall. Connor glanced up and saw that a platform extended from the wall about fifty feet above them.

Connor and Sean ran toward the ramp. They'd just completed their third time around when Connor heard more shots being fired, but he couldn't see what the others were shooting at. He glanced downward, expecting ryklars to come inside at any moment.

Sean Quinn had turned out to be among the strongest of all the recruits, and it was no surprise to Connor that he could keep up with him. They quickly closed in on the platform. There was a pedestal in the middle, and hovering above it was a twin-sided pyramid with a glowing light emanating from the two bottoms. The bottom point of the pyramid hovered between two small columns. There were workstation panels near the pedestal, and one of them glowed red. Five ryklars dropped down from above. Connor brought his rifle up to shoot but waited to see if the ryklars would attack. They seemed enthralled by the twin pyramids. Connor heard a strange hum and the floor began to vibrate. The ryklars turned toward Connor and Sean, then charged. They fired their weapons, tearing the ryklars apart at such a short range. Even in the creatures' final death throes, they tried to claw their way toward them. It was as if they were hyped up on some kind of stimulant.

Connor and Sean ran over to the others. Noah was hunched over the wide glowing panel, which was made out of a curved translucent material.

"Is this the source of the signal?" Connor asked.

"It is, but I can't figure out how to turn it off. I don't know what any of these symbols mean," Noah said.

Connor looked for some kind of power source but couldn't find anything.

"It's held up there by a magnetic field," Lenora said.

The sound of ryklar screeches came from the bottom of the spire. Noah slammed his fist down and growled, then looked back at Connor and held up his hands in silent resignation.

"Stand back," Connor said.

Noah glanced at him and then pulled Lenora away. Connor raised his weapon and fired it at the floating pyramid, but the high-grade incendiary ammunition ricocheted off, making a loud gong-like noise that reverberated off the walls. The ryklars howled in response, almost as if they were in agony. Seeing that his shots had no effect, Connor stopped shooting.

He had another grenade but didn't want to waste it. The ryklars resumed their snarling, which became louder as they got closer to the platform. Sean went to the other side and knelt down. He aimed his weapon and started shooting.

"There's nothing I can do. I'm going to go help him out," Noah said.

Connor looked at Lenora. "Any bright ideas?"

"Well, shooting it was a waste of time," Lenora said and started circling around it. "The ryklars are clearly conditioned to have a response to this thing, and they don't want anyone . . ."

Lenora's voice trailed off. She walked over to the pedestal where the bottom point of the twin pyramid hovered about a foot above the top. She looked back at Connor and belted out a loud whoop. Lenora's voice echoed off the walls of the spire.

Her eyes widened. "Come here!" she said, waving him over.

Connor rushed to her side.

"Does your helmet have a speaker? Can it amplify the sound of your voice?" Lenora asked.

"Yeah, but what good is that gonna do us?"

Lenora whipped out her PDA and brought up the small holodisplay. "This place is one big acoustic resonance chamber. It's designed to amplify sound waves. If we can match the frequency coming from this thing, the acoustics in this chamber will amplify it and cancel out the original signal."

Connor's heart raced. "What do you need from me?"

"Just leave your helmet here," Lenora said and glanced over at Sean and Noah. "And get their helmets and place them on two opposite sides of the platform."

Connor ran over to the others. The ryklars were quickly coming up toward them. He brought his weapon up and fired his last grenade into the ryklars storming up the ramp. Connor ducked down, and Sean and Noah did the same.

Boom!

Connor winced at the sound, the brunt of which he bore without the protection of his helmet.

"I need your helmets," Connor said.

Sean and Noah snatched off their helmets and handed them to him. "Keep slowing them down. Lenora might have a way to stop them."

Connor ran and placed the helmets on opposite ends of the platform and used his implants to connect the output from his helmet to the other two helmets.

He went back to Lenora, who was busy working.

"How long is this going to take?" Connor asked.

Lenora glanced up at him. "I need to record one complete sequence of the original frequency. Then we'll see. Should only be a few minutes."

The ryklars were getting closer.

"We may not have a few minutes. Do we have to stay in here to transmit the broadcast?"

Lenora jumped at the sound of the ryklars. "No. No, we don't."

Connor grabbed her arm and pulled her along with him. He called for the others and they went back out onto the ramp. They headed upward, and as they curved around the spire, they saw the ryklars from across the way.

Connor glanced at Lenora and she shook her head. The ryklars noticed them and quickened their pace up the ramp.

"Getting low on ammo," Noah said.

Sean echoed the same.

Connor already knew he was low. "Hold your fire. We just need to keep them from doing an all-out charge."

The ramp came to an end and the top of the spire was still high above them. The ryklars came around the ramp. The redness of their stubby tentacles extended upward so their entire faces looked inflamed. There were hundreds of them on the ramp.

"I've got it. Signal broadcasting!" Lenora said.

Connor glanced around, looking for something to happen. The ryklars came to a stop, their heads making jerking movements.

Connor and the others bunched together at the end of the ramp. The ryklars' growling gave way to a high-pitched whining, and the reddish color of their tentacles began to fade. One creature pushed its way through the others and let out a vicious roar.

Connor took a few steps away from the others and howled in response. The ryklar beat its claws on the ground and came closer.

Connor strode forward. "Is that all you've got?"

He heard Lenora say something and Noah urged her to stay back. "The commander knows what he's doing," Noah said.

Connor hoped he knew what he was doing. He glanced down at his AR-71 and the ammo meter showed that he was nearly empty.

When the ryklars reared up, they were easily six feet tall and thickly muscled, but they spent most of their time hunched over.

Connor watched as the ryklar's claws twitched, and he ventured even closer, screaming and waving his weapon back and forth. The ryklar jerked its head to the side and looked as if it were wincing in pain. Then it collapsed to the ground. Other ryklars did the same, but there were still hundreds of ryklars between them and the exit.

"It's working," Lenora said.

Connor slowly moved back toward the others. With the ryklars quieting down, Connor was able to hear the loud groans of metallic supports protesting under too much weight.

Shit.

The others looked around in alarm. The floor shook beneath their feet and there was a loud crashing sound beneath them.

Connor grabbed hold of Lenora. "Hold on to me," he said and pulled her into a firm embrace.

"We've got to get down. Use your suit jets to slow down your descent," Connor said.

"I'm almost out of propellant," Noah said, his eyes wide with terror. "I had to use some—"

"I've got you," Sean said. "And if you tell anyone about this, I'll kick your ass."

The loud snap of a cable ripping echoed throughout the spire.

"No time," Connor said.

Holding on to Lenora, he leaped away from the ramp, using a burst from his suit jets to push them out into the middle of the shaft. They quickly closed in on the central platform. The twin pyramids tumbled to the side, falling off the pedestal, and then the platform crashed down to the side. Lenora cried out. They were free-falling down the spire. Connor gritted his teeth. Without his helmet, he had no readout that told him how far away the ground was, so he had to judge based on what he saw. He fired his suit jets in a long burst. Holding on to Lenora threw off his center of gravity, and they sailed toward a ramp filled with ryklars, but the creatures hardly noticed them. They were still disoriented from the signal going offline. Connor leaned toward the left, angling the suit jets, and they moved away from the ramp.

Sean and Noah flew past them. Connor saw that Sean was trying to slow down using his jets, but the two of them weren't aligned. There was nothing

Connor could do. He could hardly keep himself and Lenora stable as they barreled toward the ground. He saw the two young men slam against the side of the ramp and bounce off, hitting the ground hard.

Connor fired his suit jets at full blast and they landed roughly. He clutched Lenora's body to him while holding her head to his armored chest. His feet got tangled and they both went down. Above them the ramp supports were coming apart faster and soon the whole thing was going to come crashing down. Connor quickly regained his feet and helped Lenora up.

"I'm fine. Go check on the others," Lenora said.

Noah and Sean were sprawled nearby, and neither of them was moving. Connor ran over to them. Without bothering to check whether Noah and Sean were alive or dead, he grabbed hold of each of them and started pulling them toward the exit. Lenora came to his side to help. Connor heaved and pulled, and they dragged the two boys through the exit.

Sean Quinn cried out in pain. There was blood coming through the arm of his combat suit. Connor could hardly breathe as he kept pulling, and he heard Lenora gasping as she did the same. He glanced up at the spire towering above them, and it looked as if it were swaying.

"Come on, damn it," Connor said through gritted teeth.

He wasn't going to let those two boys die here. He made his burning muscles move through sheer force of will, and Lenora grunted with effort. Connor's foot slipped and he fell back. Then he heard the pounding boots of people approaching from behind.

"We've got this, sir," Compton said.

Connor looked up in surprise. Compton and Jackson, along with the two other Field Ops agents, picked up Noah and Sean.

Connor pushed himself to his feet and helped Lenora get up.

"Sir, we have to move," Compton said.

"Don't wait for me," Connor said.

Lenora stumbled, favoring one foot. The spire started coming down. Connor scooped Lenora up and ran.

"To the side!" Lenora said.

Connor bolted to the side, following the others into the forest. Loud cracking sounds came from behind him, and a blast of air pushed him onward. Connor tried to go faster, but he had almost no strength left. Lenora told him to put her down. Connor glanced behind them as the spire crashed down right where they had been.

Connor gasped for breath. "How are they?"

Sean and Noah had been placed on the ground. Sean was awake, wincing if he tried to move, and Noah was unconscious.

"This one has a broken arm and the suit computer says a few cracked ribs," Compton said, gesturing toward Sean Quinn. "I'm not sure about Noah. He got banged up pretty bad."

Lenora hobbled over to Noah and began assessing his injuries.

Connor glanced around. "Where are the ryklars?"

"They hardly chased us. Most of them followed you into the spire. There're still some in the ruins, but they're acting strange," Compton said.

"Sir," Sean said, his voice hitched higher in pain.

Connor went over to him. "Just lay there."

"In my pack . . . flares, sir," Sean said.

Connor rooted through Sean's pack and found the flare gun just as a comlink registered with Connor's suit computer. With the spire down, communications had been restored. Time enough to figure that piece out later.

"This is Search and Rescue," Connor said.

"Search and Rescue team, this is the Hellcat. What's your position? Over," Diaz's voice said over the link.

Connor held the flare gun above his head and fired. He waited a few moments and fired again.

"I have your position. Will be there in a few minutes. Hellcat out," Diaz said.

Connor sat down because he couldn't stand up anymore. He was spent. Compton told him that he'd found a safe place for the archaeological team to stay while they made their way to the spire. Compton offered him some water and Connor drank it. Not wanting to get too stiff to move, he got back on his feet and looked out toward the ruins. The ryklars swayed on their feet as if they were too exhausted even to stand. Some of them collapsed to the ground. A few of the creatures glanced toward them when Diaz came with the Hellcat, but none came any closer. They carried Sean and Noah on board.

"Evacuation of the base has started," Diaz said and paused to take a good look at him. "What the hell did you do in there?"

Connor coughed and felt a sharp pain in his side, which made him wonder if he'd broken a few ribs, too. "Oh, you know. Jumped down off a tall building after Lenora fixed our communications problem and saved our asses."

Lenora glanced over at him. She'd just secured Noah to the stretcher in the Hellcat. "You need to sit down. Diaz, make him sit down. He's got injuries. I know it."

"So do you," Connor replied.

Diaz shook his head. "You guys are a pair, I tell you," he snorted.

They finished getting everyone on board and Diaz flew the Hellcat out of the alien ruins. Connor sat down and leaned his head back, took a deep breath and blew it out. He'd thought colony living was supposed to be easier than this. He hadn't been this exhausted in a long time.

He activated the wallscreen nearby. There were hundreds of ryklars among the ruins, but they were hardly moving at all.

"I don't think I've ever seen them so calm," Connor said.

Lenora watched the wallscreen. "Are you recording this?"

"I am now," Connor replied.

He looked over at Sean and Noah. Both were strapped to a stretcher. They'd be at the research base in a few minutes. Connor closed his eyes.

27

CONNOR WAS JERKED awake by the Hellcat's rough landing. He looked around the cargo area as the others were jostled from their thoughts. Connor sucked in a deep breath and rubbed his face with his hands. His nanites gave him a distinct advantage over others in that he needed less rest to fully recover his strength, but the fifteen minutes it had taken to fly from the ruins back to the research base hadn't been enough.

The rear cargo doors opened and Allison Blake ran up the ramp, heading directly to the two stretchers where Noah and Sean lay. She knelt down and immediately started assessing their injuries.

Connor walked down the ramp and saw Damon Mills in the distance, coming toward the ship. He walked with a limp and was using a stick as a makeshift crutch. There were multiple troop carrier ships setting down and lifting off as the base was evacuated. Lenora came out of the Hellcat and stood by Connor's side. She glanced at all the damage—from the ruined perimeter fences to ryklar bodies outside the fence and inside the base.

Mills stopped in his tracks when he saw Lenora and the rest of the archaeological team step out of the Hellcat, and Lenora asked Connor what was wrong.

"He thought your team was all dead," Connor said.

Lenora frowned. "Given the state of this place, I can hardly blame him, but I'm glad you didn't share his opinion," she said and looked back at her team. "Looks like we're evacuating. Take a few minutes to gather your personal belongings and come back here."

Diaz came out of the Hellcat. "Sir, Blake reports that Noah and Sean are stable, but we need to get them back to the main compound for treatment."

"Understood," Connor said.

Lenora glanced at Connor. "I assumed that since you've gotten us this far we'd catch a ride with you back to the compound."

"I wasn't going to just up and leave you by the side of the road. I'm not that heartless. I'd at least make sure you had a ride home first," Connor said.

Lenora's mouth rounded in surprise and then she narrowed her gaze. "If you leave without me, I'll hunt you down."

Connor laughed.

"Dr. Bishop," Mills said as he approached. "I'm happy to see that you and your team are alive. We've initiated the system shutdown of the research base, and the data backups are already en route to the compound."

Lenora thanked him and then headed over to the command center.

Mills walked over to Connor. "You have this habit of proving me wrong. I'm thankful you and your team were here. They were critical to our survival even after you left."

"How bad was the attack?" Connor asked.

"They came at us hard like they did before. Thanks to Diaz in the Hellcat and the weapons you brought, we managed to hold them off. There were some casualties. It seemed that the ryklars became even more ferocious before they suddenly broke off their attack and headed your way," Mills said.

"We might have had something to do with that," Connor said.

"Judging by how you look, it must have been quite an ordeal. There'll be more of a debriefing when we get back. I wanted you to know that you're still a pain in the ass, but if you ever need anything . . . let's just say I owe you a few," Mills said.

"I'll hold you to that. And one more thing before we get out of here. I know there's something going on with the colony and how we came to be here, and I'm not the only one. I know you and Mallory probably know more about our situation here than most," Connor said.

The frown on Mills' face became grim. "You're right. We'll talk more when we get back," he said and walked away.

Connor watched him go. Mills hadn't even tried to deny it, which bothered Connor more than he cared to admit. The rest of Lightning Platoon returned to the Hellcat, and Connor greeted them. He was relieved they'd all made it, although not entirely unscathed. Some of them had a few wounds requiring treatment.

Diaz shook his head. "You never let up. No sooner does one crisis end than you want to jump into the next one."

"I understand the need for secrecy, but if what Noah found is really as bad as it sounds, everyone has a right to know," Connor said.

"Right to know what?" Lenora asked. She carried a large backpack stuffed to the max.

"I'll ready the Hellcat for takeoff, sir," Diaz said and fled.

They went back to the ship. "One of Noah's side projects. Something we were working on together," Connor said.

Lenora arched an eyebrow. "Oh, you're the other person. I knew he was working on something, but he wouldn't say what it was."

She stored her pack in one of the compartments, and Connor glanced at the cockpit.

"We've got a few hours' flight back to the compound. You can fill me in on the way," Lenora said.

She leveled her gaze at him as if daring him to tell her that he couldn't talk about it.

"Why don't you join us up front and we can talk," Connor said.

"Oh boy, I get to sit up front with the big boys," Lenora joked.

28

It had been barely two days since the evacuation of Forward Operating Research Base number 97. Connor had shared the information Noah had found with Lenora, and she was as perplexed as the rest of them despite her close friendship with Ashley Quinn. She advised him to take his concerns directly to Franklin Mallory and Tobias Quinn. There would be a debriefing at Field Ops and he'd use that opportunity to kick over some rocks and see what turned up.

Since Connor still didn't have a permanent residence at the compound, he stayed at the barracks near Field Ops where he'd just returned to get cleaned up. There was hardly anywhere he could go in Field Ops without someone expressing an interest in joining Search and Rescue. Between answering questions about ryklar behavior for representatives from the field biologists' office and checking on Sean and Noah at the hospital, Connor had very little time to himself. Sean and Noah had suffered some broken bones and Noah had a concussion, but otherwise they would make a full recovery. Quick healing treatments would have them back on their feet in no time. He'd also met with the rest of his platoon to go over the events that had transpired at the research base. They would be returning to the alien ruins to retrieve the armored ATV they'd left behind.

There was a knock on his door.

Connor had just finished dressing in a Field Ops green jumpsuit with the Search and Rescue shield on his arm. He opened the door to Sean and Noah.

"Shouldn't you two still be at the hospital?" Connor asked.

"My leg has healing strips around it and I can walk on it now," Sean said.

Connor looked at Noah with a raised brow. "You had a head injury. I know you're not cleared to be here."

"Oh come on, you don't think I'm going to stay in bed while you confront Tobias and the others alone," Noah said.

Connor considered having Noah escorted back to the hospital.

"Sir, I checked the readouts for the halo Noah's been wearing. The numbers over the last twenty-four hours show that the swelling has gone down almost all the way," Sean said.

"So you're a doctor now?" Connor replied.

"No, sir, but you know my mother. Some of that stuff rubs off, and I've worked a rotation through the hospital."

Connor speared a look at Noah. "Alright, but if you feel the slightest headache, dizzy spell, or anything like that, I want your word that you'll speak up."

"Yes, sir," Noah said, his eyes shining with excitement.

They left the barracks.

"Haven't they given you a permanent apartment yet?" Noah asked.

"I'm holding out for a place with a waterfront view and a boat," Connor replied.

They walked to Field Ops Headquarters and headed to the upper levels. Diaz met them along the way and had Lenora with him.

"They moved the meeting to the conference room across from the command center," Diaz said.

"Any idea why?" Connor asked.

"Above my pay grade."

Connor smiled a greeting at Lenora.

"I figured I'd be here too, since you told me about Noah's side project," Lenora said and looked at Noah. "Shouldn't you be resting?"

"I already told him," Connor said.

They walked past Franklin Mallory's office, and his son, Lars, was just coming out of the command center.

Lars' eyebrows rose. "What's going on?"

"Time to get some information about that thing I told you about," Noah said.

Connor heard Lenora snort. "So much for secrets," she murmured.

Diaz opened the doors to the conference room and they walked in.

Tobias and Ashley Quinn sat at the far end of the table with Franklin Mallory and Damon Mills. There were a couple of other people Connor didn't recognize.

Ashley stood up and stared pointedly at her son. "I don't recall inviting the two of you to this meeting. Or you, Lars."

"They already know pieces of it, so whether they find out the complete picture now or I tell them later is up to you," Connor said.

Tobias narrowed his gaze. "I'm surprised. I would have thought you of all people would be familiar with the concept of the need to know."

"There's a time and place for it," Connor said. "I can vouch for Sean and Noah's character since I've worked with them. And if Lars is anything like his father, that's good enough for me. It's not that far of a stretch that Noah discovered something he didn't completely understand and asked his two closest friends for advice on how to handle it."

"Indeed, the three of them are inseparable at times," Tobias said and looked at the young men, considering.

"I suggest we let them put that youthful energy into something constructive," Connor said.

Tobias glanced at his wife.

"Oh for heaven's sake, sit down then," Ashley said. "But fair warning to you three. You may wish you only knew the half of it by the time we're done here."

Connor sat down in the nearest chair, and Lenora sat next to him. Noah and the others filled the seats nearby.

Tobias cleared his throat. "I guess we'll begin. To my right is Dr. Eric Zabat, astrophysicist, and next to him is Dr. Marie Parks, planetary scientist."

Dr. Zabat was a small man whose facial features looked to have Asian ancestry. His beady eyes showed an active intelligence that Connor had come to recognize in the colonists. Parks was a plump woman who gave Connor and the others a friendly smile in greeting.

"Why don't you tell us what you know first, and then we'll fill in the gaps as we go," Tobias said.

"Sounds fair," Connor said. "While at the training camp, Noah reached out to me about a data burst he'd stumbled upon from the deep space buoy network. I thought he was trying to play a joke on me at first, but the more he showed me, the more interested I became. Noah, why don't you put what you found on the holoscreen so everyone can see."

Noah used his PDA to activate the holoscreen in the middle of the conference table. Two holoscreens appeared so everyone around the table could see the data.

"The data header had this reference: EOD-Extinction Critical Alpha. What followed was a set of programming instructions for the Ark. There was also mention of M. Wilkinson, but I'm not sure who he is," Noah said.

Connor's gaze slid to Tobias. "Admiral Mitch Wilkinson, flag officer of the Battleship Carrier *Indianapolis*. I'd say that's one hell of a coincidence."

Tobias met his gaze and nodded.

"Before the attack on the research base," Noah continued, "I was able to decode the remaining parts of the partial data fragment."

"That's a bold claim," Dr. Zabat said. "How did you decode the message?"

"I had help," Noah said.

Zabat looked over at Tobias.

Connor looked at Noah and pressed his lips together. "He had help from someone on the Ark. Now he's got the entire thing decoded and I'm pretty sure he can find the rest of it. Now tell us what's going on. Why was the Ark mission changed and what happened on Earth?"

Tobias sighed. "Why didn't you come to us when you found the data burst?"

Noah stiffened. "I don't know."

Tobias regarded him for a moment and then looked at Connor. "Only the first group of us who were awakened know what I'm about to tell you. This won't be easy for you to hear."

Connor leaned forward and clasped his hands in front of him.

"When we first woke up we discovered that we were sixty light-years from Earth, according to the Ark's nav computer. The journey had taken us over two hundred years. We only had fragmented records from Earth, which I'll go into shortly. We knew that a Dr. Lucia Stone headed up the effort to override the Ark mission and that she was working with your friend, Admiral Wilkinson. You see, they'd found something in Earth's oceans, some type of parasitic organism or virus. Marie, you're better at explaining this than I am," Tobias said.

"Of course," Dr. Marie Parks said. "Dr. Stone doesn't go into a lot of details about the origins of the virus other than to say that it came from the oceans and eventually spread to humans."

"There has to be more than that. What does this virus do, exactly?" Connor asked.

"It's hard to explain because in some respects it behaves like a virus and in others like a living entity. For example, viruses rarely cross from one species to another. This one does and on a wide scale, particularly among mammals. This virus can affect the DNA of the infected host and causes dormant genes within our genetic makeup to express themselves. This causes the infected hosts to die. Dr. Stone said there were theories that the virus was going through a growth stage as it perfected itself. Nothing was immune to it. They tried to find a cure using every means at their disposal, but the virus had found a rich genetic diversity in one of the most populous species on Earth," Parks said.

"Humans," Connor said, his voice sounding grim.

"Exactly. Scientists attempted to alter the virus since it couldn't be cured," Parks said.

"What'd they do?" Connor asked.

"We're not exactly sure, but Dr. Stone said they made it worse. Instead of weakening the virus, they made it stronger somehow. This was all in the summary, which includes references for more detailed information, but the data is gone. Even parts of the summary don't make sense," Parks said.

Connor glanced at Tobias. "What do you mean the information is gone? Where is it?"

"Oh my God," Noah said.

Connor looked at Noah, but he was watching Tobias, waiting for the governor to confirm what he was thinking.

"The deep space buoy network was designed to transfer data transmissions from Earth to our ship. The buoys bolstered the signal, among other things," Tobias said.

"Right, so why don't we have all the data this Dr. Stone sent?" Connor asked.

"The Ark didn't arrive here entirely free from damage. We've had some system failures. The data was expunged by the Ark's maintenance systems for managing data storage," Tobias said.

Connor scratched the stubble of his beard and his eyes widened. "Are you saying some data janitor program deleted the transmissions from Earth?"

Tobias's eyebrows pulled together. "Yes. There's a fixed amount of data storage available. The updated mission program that included our amended destination took up a significant amount of space. The Ark's systems rightfully determined that the lives of three hundred thousand colonists outweighed the updated information from Earth. The system had been designed for an eighty-five-year journey."

Connor glanced at Lenora, and her mouth was hanging open in shock.

"Can't we contact Earth to find out what happened?" Connor asked.

Tobias slumped in his chair. "We sent a response back, but you must remember that a small data burst will take over sixty years just to reach Earth and then we'd have to wait just as long for a response."

Connor's heart sank. "Can't we recover the data somehow?"

"All attempts have yielded only fragments," Tobias said.

Dr. Zabat cleared his throat. "We're limited to the speed of light, but we don't need to wait that long to see what happened to Earth."

"Show them the model," Tobias said.

Dr. Zabat opened the holoscreens, which showed a distant image of a star with nine planetary bodies highlighted.

"This was our home. The telescopes on the Ark took pictures of our solar system during the first leg of its journey. Here's the image from farther away. I'm going to speed up the orbits of the planets and the simulation is going to emphasize the wobble in the light coming from our sun. This is normal," Dr. Zabat said.

The image moved to the side so it only took up half the space. "This is the current image of Earth's solar system. And remember, anything we see now is from sixty years ago."

Connor watched as a secondary distant image of the solar system appeared on the second holoscreen. The image was from much farther away, but the wobble occurred more often than on the other screen.

"We think the increased wobble is from a massive debris field," Dr. Zabat said.

Connor's mind raced as he tried to think of all the space stations that had been built over hundreds of years—colonies established at places like Mars and Ganymede Station.

"Destruction on an unimaginable scale," Tobias said.

Bile crept up Connor's throat and he forced it back down. "This has to be some sort of mistake. What you're saying doesn't make any sense. How did the virus lead to that?" Connor rose from the chair and started pacing. His thoughts were scattering to oblivion and he kept shaking his head.

"There are references in the data we received that talk about a massive war fought between Earth and the colonies. The virus altered human beings, making them into something else. There was more from Wilkinson. He was adamant about an unstoppable fleet," Tobias said.

Connor wanted to hit something, anything, to distract him from what he was hearing.

"Connor," Lenora called out to him.

Connor looked at her, not knowing what to say. Noah and the others had somber and pale expressions.

"This is a lot to take in. We'll make all the data available for you to look at," Ashley said.

"What was that about a fleet? Is this why they changed where the Ark was going?" Connor asked.

"That's what we think. Now we have a decision to make. This is something those of us in the room have been struggling with ever since we arrived on this planet," Tobias said.

Connor's hands came to rest on his hips.

"We have to decide whether to abandon this world," Tobias said.

Leave! Where could they go?

"Are you crazy?" Lenora said and looked at Ashley. "Please tell me this isn't true."

"Why would we have to leave?" Noah asked.

Tobias cleared his throat. "We think there's a fleet of these things heading here right now."

Connor's hands dropped to his sides.

"We didn't have credible evidence of it until recently," Tobias said.

"Help me understand something," Connor said. "The Ark program took the combined resources of the solar system to build and equip the ship for an interstellar journey. It was the only one of its kind. So how could a fleet of ships that aren't even designed for interstellar travel be coming here?" Connor asked.

Tobias shrugged. "I have no idea how, but the technology is there and we have evidence of something coming."

Connor sucked in a deep breath and looked at the others in the room. "What have you found?"

"Dr. Zabat, if you please," Tobias said.

"The buoys in the deep space buoy network can operate with a bit of autonomy, but they only keep track of the nearest buoys. They report the locations of each buoy in the chain to be sure it remains intact," Zabat said and began updating the image on the holoscreen. "Based on the reports from the *Galileo*, there were thousands of buoys deposited on our way here from Earth. Are you with me?" Dr. Zabat asked.

Connor and the others nodded.

"We would expect to find a number close to the number of buoys deployed when the nearest one checks in, but the number of buoys remaining is less than a few hundred," Zabat said.

Connor frowned in thought. "You think something is using the buoys to find out where we are?"

Tobias regarded him for a moment. "You have good instincts for gauging a situation. Given the evidence, what do you think?"

Connor looked away as he searched for some reasonable explanation that could account for what Tobias and the others were saying.

"You know what? Take a few minutes to consider it," Tobias said.

The governor got up and left the conference room with Mallory and the two scientists. Ashley stayed behind and went over to her son.

"You knew about this?" Sean asked.

Ashley nodded. "We didn't know how to tell you."

Connor glanced at Noah, who looked extremely pale.

Noah noticed him watching. "I'd hoped it had all been a mistake, some misunderstanding. What do you think?"

"I don't know what to think," Connor said.

"We look at the evidence," Lenora said. "We look at the data they have and validate the claim."

"What if they're right? Let's assume for a moment that it's just as they say and we are the last . . ." Noah's voice trailed off.

Connor's shoulders slumped and he used the chair to hold himself up. "Damn it!" he cried and pulled the chair away from the table, flinging it into the wall. He began pacing and shaking his head, then looked at Ashley for a moment and turned back around.

Lenora stood up and looked at him with concern.

Connor spun around. "You know, when you first pulled me out of that stasis pod and I got down here, I told myself that he'd had a good life. Wilkinson was a man of his word and would look after him." Sorrow closed Connor's throat and he swallowed hard. "It was the only saving grace for coming to terms with the fact that I would never see my son again, and now that's been taken away."

"Oh, Connor, I'm so sorry," Lenora said.

All the assumptions he'd had about his son having a good life melted away and the inside of his eyelids felt hot. Instead, he was filled with the certainty that his son had died a horrible death along with everyone else he'd ever known. He took several deep breaths to steady himself and something cold took over inside him—that part of him that showed up when he'd fought battles with his old platoon. It swept the pain to the side so he could think and function. He had no other choice. To give in to everything he felt would unravel him, and that was something he couldn't do. Not now.

Tobias and the others returned to the conference room. Damon Mills looked at Connor and gave him an understanding nod.

Lenora came over to him and placed her hand on his arm. Her touch was soothing. "Are you alright?" she asked softly.

Connor shook his head. "No, but I'd rather know the truth than believe a lie."

He bent over and righted the overturned chair, bringing it back to the table. Tobias sat down and waited.

"We'll want to see the data, but given the loss of so many buoys . . . In any other circumstance, I'd say it was a hostile force following a trail of breadcrumbs right to our door," Connor said.

"You mentioned before that you were considering whether we should leave?" Lenora asked.

"This isn't my decision to make," Tobias said. "But it might be our best option."

Connor shook his head. "No, it's not."

"We've deployed a few telescopes and have them mapping the nearby stars for habitable worlds. We could pack everyone here back on the Ark and head to one of those worlds," Tobias said.

"That's a terrible idea," Connor said.

Tobias frowned. "We've had months to consider this and you've only just found out. You should know that there are more than a few of us who think this might be the best option."

"Well then, I'd tell them the same thing I'm telling you. Leaving is the last thing we should do," Connor said.

"Why don't you tell us what you're thinking?" Ashley interjected before her husband could reply.

"You've worked hard to build a colony here. There are things in this world we simply didn't have back home," Connor said.

"You mean the alien civilization that died out here?" Tobias said.

"For one. Lenora says there's a lot we can learn from them. Perhaps there's something we can use. If we pack everything up and try to run to some other star, there's no way to know what we'll encounter once we get there. And there's also no guarantee that whatever is on its way here wouldn't find us wherever we go," Connor said.

"Statistically, we have a much better chance of survival if we were to move the colony to another place without leaving a trail of breadcrumbs for those things to follow," Zabat said.

"Oh, really? Tell me, how fast are they coming? Do you know when they'll get here?" Connor asked.

"It's hard to say. We don't have an accurate date for the last transmission from Earth. It could be ten months from now or ten years," Zabat said.

"Do we really want to risk our lives on another few hundred years' journey on a ship that's already out of design specifications and hope for the best?" Connor asked.

"When you put it in those terms, no, but we've been checking the Ark, system by system," Tobias said.

"We can dig in right here. Make this place our home. We've already expended a tremendous amount of resources to set up what we have here," Connor said.

"How can we succeed where billions of people have failed?" Tobias said.

"I don't know," Connor said.

"We know hardly anything about them. We don't know how many there are, whether it's one big ship or a fleet, not to mention the specifics of the virus," Tobias said.

"We know they're coming, which is more than the people of Earth knew. That's what this Dr. Stone gave us: a warning. Not to mention three hundred thousand of humanity's best who are still asleep on the Ark. We have intelligence and a new world. Let's leverage our assets. I, for one, would rather spend the next few years preparing to face an enemy I know is coming than take my chances on another journey where I have no control over my own fate," Connor said.

Tobias leaned back in his chair and breathed deeply.

"I agree with him," Mills said, speaking up for the first time.

"Really? *You* agree with him. I think you're feeling appreciative that he saved your life," Tobias said.

"Maybe, but Connor has demonstrated skill sets we're lacking," Mills said.

"Tobias," Connor said, "I know you and the others conceived this whole idea of a colony with the intention of distancing yourself from people like me—the military, that is. Your instincts are telling you to run. Mine are telling me that we stay and fight. Most of you left Earth for your own reasons—the sense of adventure, pioneering to the unknown, a fresh start. I bet not one of you expected to be the last humans in the universe. But we may have to accept the fact that everyone and everything we left behind is gone, killed by an enemy we can't even begin to understand. The mission was altered for a purpose, and that purpose was to give us a fighting chance.

"Someone back home kept sending us messages about the enemy because they thought we would need it, that we'd be here to receive them. We owe it to those brave souls to make a stand here. You said we couldn't make this decision on our own. Then let's wake everyone else up and decide. Perhaps there's someone who'll have some key piece of knowledge we'll need."

Tobias rubbed his forehead in thought.

"I agree with Connor," Franklin Mallory said.

Lenora did the same.

"I do as well," Ashley said.

Tobias glanced at his wife with his mouth open wide.

"You're the smartest man I know and you've done a great job getting this colony started, but in this, Connor's right," Ashley said.

"Once we wake everyone up, there's no going back onto the Ark," Tobias said.

Ashley nodded. "I know," she said.

Tobias sighed and swung his gaze to Connor. "You know, when you first showed up I didn't know what to expect from you, but it definitely wasn't something like this. Even if I was against waking everyone up, I'd be outnumbered by the votes of those already awake."

Connor nodded, not feeling the slightest bit satisfied. He'd already moved on to the next task. A small part of him demanded that the grief he was locking up inside must have its due, but he wouldn't let it. He'd spent more years as a soldier than not, and those instincts drove him onward. This colony was only just beginning, and he would see to it that they had a fighting chance to survive.

29

SEVERAL DAYS after learning about the fate of Earth, Connor found himself on the Ark once again. He hadn't even thought of returning to the behemoth-sized ship that had carried all the colonists to this planet, but Ashley Quinn had been insistent that he come at once. He'd brought Sean with him on the shuttle.

"Your mother can be . . ." Connor said.

"You have no idea," Sean said.

They docked the shuttle and left the hangar bay. Ashley had given them instructions to come straight to the medical wing. It was a bit strange for Connor to be back there. The last time he was there, he'd thought he'd been taken prisoner by the Syndicate and this was some elaborate way to test out their interrogation techniques. Boy, was he way off the mark on that one.

Sean knew the interior of the ship better than Connor, so he led the way. They went to the medical wing where he remembered first coming awake. They passed Dr. Baker, who did a double take when he saw Connor and then scowled. Connor ignored the doctor and headed to the administration area. A duty nurse was sitting at the desk. She looked up and smiled, recognizing Sean.

"Oh good, you're here. She's been expecting you. She's down the hall in room twenty-three," the nurse said.

Sean thanked her and led Connor down the hall. They reached room twenty-three and knocked on the door.

Ashley Quinn opened the door and smiled at both of them. "You brought my son with you. What a nice surprise."

"I had a mother once, too. I know what you guys like," Connor replied.

Ashley gave her son a quick hug and then beckoned them inside the room.

There were two stasis pods across the room and Connor glanced at Ashley. "What's this about?"

Ashley walked over and stood between the two pods. "Remember when you wanted to know if there was anyone else here we weren't expecting? Well, take a look for yourself."

Connor walked over and peered inside the pods. A wide grin escaped his lips and his eyes gleamed.

Sean walked over and looked inside. "Who are they?"

Connor put his hand on one of the pods. "This is Major Kasey Douglass and that is Wil Reisman. They were part of the Ghosts."

Sean's eyes widened. After hearing Connor talk so much about his old platoon, they'd become legends among Search and Rescue.

"We're not finished going through everyone yet, but if this Admiral Wilkinson got the three of you on board the Ark, there's a good chance he got the rest of you on as well," Ashley said.

Connor laughed and couldn't keep the smile from his face. Finding the Ghosts would help immeasurably with training more troops. He narrowed his gaze at Ashley playfully. "You brought me here to help wake them up."

"Of course. Can't have another one of you military types running around the ship, acting crazy. Sit tight. This is where things get interesting," Ashley said.

Connor kept looking at the stasis pods as if he wasn't quite sure whether this was a dream. He'd wondered what the admiral had done with the other Ghosts. It would be tough on them, but at least they would have their unit to support them. It was a cold comfort, but sometimes the men and women who served with you were what got you through the day.

NEMESIS

FIRST COLONY - BOOK 2

1

GENERAL CONNOR GATES leaned against the railing on the observation deck of the Montgomery III construction platform and watched the spectacle unfolding before him with flinty eyes. Clutched within the platform's massive robotic arms was the last major section of the *Ark*, the interstellar ship that brought the three hundred thousand colonists living on New Earth to this star system. Bright flashes of light ignited along the partially finished hull of the Colonial Defense Force's first battleship carrier.

"Glaring won't make them work any faster," Reisman said.

Connor arched an eyebrow at Wil Reisman. The man was part of the original Ghost Platoon that Connor had commanded before being "volunteered" into the *Ark* program. At Connor's age, being drugged, stuck in a stasis pod, and then snuck aboard Earth's first interstellar colony ship couldn't exactly be called a kidnapping; "shanghaied" was the nautical term for what happened to Connor and the surviving members of Ghost Platoon. Though it had been seven years since he'd come out of stasis only to learn that he was now part of the colony, it was still sometimes a bitter pill to swallow. But the actions of Admiral Mitch Wilkinson had ultimately been for their benefit. If he hadn't done what he'd done, it was likely that he and his old platoon would have rotted in a military prison—that is, until they perished when all the people back home mysteriously died.

"We're a year behind schedule for this ship," Connor said.

"Priorities," Reisman said. "Titan Space Station came first and is our first line of defense against an attack force."

Connor speared a look at his friend.

"Kasey advised that I was to remind you of the obvious things from time to time," Reisman said.

Connor remembered when Reisman had been just a fresh-faced intelligence officer. His talent for intelligence gathering had made him a valuable asset back then, and now, with the Colonial Defense Force being so small, former Ghosts were nearly irreplaceable. They were among the few who had actual combat experience in the new colony.

A chime sounded from the nearby speakers. "General Gates, please report to the hangar bay for immediate departure," the monotone voice of the computer systems said.

"That's our cue to leave," Connor said.

They left the observation deck and started making their way to the hangar bay, where Connor's shuttle waited for him.

"You wouldn't think it would take a congressional hearing to get resources for the defense of the colony," Connor said.

Reisman shrugged. "Gone are the days of big budgets and a unified effort for a common purpose."

Connor snorted. "Budgets—as if money had anything to do with it."

"Allocation of resources then. There's only so much to go around."

"I guess I should feel lucky that Titan Space Station is at least mostly completed. Now, if we only had enough power stations to operate all the weapons systems at the same time," Connor said dryly.

Reisman pressed his lips together and shrugged, unable to think up a reply.

Connor nodded. "Exactly."

The new governor, Stanton Parish, wasn't their staunchest supporter these days. When they'd first put the CDF together, Connor had the backing of most colonists, but as more people were brought out of stasis over the years, support had begun to wane. Now it was an almost endless debate to get the resources they needed to finish the defense initiatives they'd already begun.

They entered the hangar bay, and Connor shoved the inner doors open. Thinking about meeting with Governor Parish was enough to ruin his mood.

There were fewer than a hundred people stationed on the platform, along with a fleet of robotic workers. Work on the final piece of the *Ark* had only just resumed after the project had been put on hold due to resource constraints.

They crossed the hangar bay to the dull gray shuttle with a golden sunburst painted on the side, the CDF emblem now faded from extensive use. They walked up the loading ramp and entered the transport. Connor's protective detail was waiting for him.

Sean Quinn stuck his head out from the cockpit. "We're cleared to leave."

"Okay, let's get going then," Connor said and sat down near a window. He'd rather be meeting with Tobias Quinn, Sean's father, who had been governor of the colony until the election last year. At least Tobias had given much more than provisional support to the CDF.

One of the perks that came with Connor's rank was that he rarely had to fly himself anywhere. But the thing was, he missed flying. Reisman sat next to him, opened up his PDA, and brought up Connor's schedule.

Connor glanced at the screen. "I'll be right back."

He climbed to his feet and headed for the cockpit, where he opened the door.

There were two seats in front of the instrument control panel and an empty seat off to the side.

"Is this seat taken?" Connor asked and sat down.

The copilot's eyes widened.

"All yours, General," Sean said. "Flight check, Lieutenant."

The copilot swung his gaze back to his station. "Cleared for takeoff, sir."

"Acknowledged," Sean said and informed the flight officer that they were ready for launch.

The shuttle lifted off, and the landing gear withdrew into the hull. Connor watched as Sean swung the nose about and took them out of the hangar.

"Let's do a quick flyby," Connor said.

"But, sir, we're already pressed to reach Sierra in time."

Connor looked at the copilot, and his identification appeared on his internal HUD—Lieutenant Anthony Frook, pilot assigned to the protector's division of the Colonial Defense Force.

"They'll wait," Connor said.

Making the congressional committee wait wouldn't increase his chances of getting what he needed, but Connor knew that even if he was on time he was unlikely to get what he needed.

Sean updated their heading and brought the construction site into view. Since they were using part of the *Ark* for the battleship carrier's construction, the interior was already mostly laid out. There were some adjustments to the design that needed to happen to make her a military ship, but it was much quicker than starting from scratch.

"She's coming along. Looks like they've already got some of the heavy cannons installed," Sean said.

Connor glanced up and, indeed, saw the cannons. "Impressive looking but not worth anything without the ammunition tracks to arm the thing or the depot ready to even store the ammunition. I would much rather have had the missile tubes finished than the rail-cannons installed."

Sean didn't reply.

"Alright, take us to Sierra," Connor said.

Sierra was the capital city of the colony on New Earth. Thinking of the colony led Connor to reflect on the humble beginnings of the compound that had been there before. As Sean changed the shuttle's course and started heading toward the planet, the light from the sun illuminated the planetary rings that surrounded New Earth. Connor had long gotten used to seeing them, but they were still a stunningly brilliant display as well as a reminder that no matter what they called this planet, it was a very different place than what they'd left back home.

"Sir, we're being hailed from the *Vigilant*," Sean said.

Connor turned toward the main heads-up display. "Put him through."

Captain Ian Howe appeared on screen. "General, I wanted to let you know that we'll be ready for departure tomorrow. Captain Benson of the cargo ship is waiting for final approval to depart."

"I delayed approval in hopes that there would be some extra things to be added to his manifest," Connor replied.

Howe nodded. "That's what I told him. CDF destroyers *Banshee* and *Wyatt* are on standby for escort duty."

"This is the fun part," Connor said.

Sean glanced at Connor but didn't say anything.

"Since you have the extra time, make sure the *Vigilant* is fully stocked," Connor said.

The sides of Howe's face lifted upward. "Understood, sir. *Vigilant* out."

Connor glanced at Sean. "Yes?"

Sean checked the shuttle's approach to the planet. "Nothing, sir. I was just remembering when I first heard you say those words. The fun part, I mean."

Connor nodded. Sean had been in the first class for Search and Rescue before he transferred to the CDF. He now led his own platoon, which was currently assigned directly to Connor.

"Then I'm sure you can guess what comes next," Connor said.

"Wouldn't be good at my job if I couldn't at least anticipate your orders, sir," Sean said.

Connor left the cockpit and returned to his seat. They were still another forty minutes out. To the casual onlooker, it appeared that Connor was taking a nap, but what he was really doing was using his implants to check that the plans he'd set up were in motion. Since there were so few people in the Colonial Defense Force with actual military experience, Connor went to great lengths to ensure that drills were as realistic as possible. He knew that all the training in the world could only go so far until a soldier was in the thick of it, but he aimed to get their soldiers as ready for action as he could. If that meant an excessive amount of training and mock execution of tactics, then so be it.

2

THE SHUTTLE MADE its final approach to the CDF airfield located at Sierra. The sprawling city and expansion projects were enough to keep most of the predators at bay. They didn't live behind electrified fences anymore, thanks to the countermeasures they'd developed to dissuade predators from getting too close. There were also deterrent systems in place that helped defend Sierra's denizens until Field Operations and Security could arrive.

The shuttle landed, and Connor climbed out of his seat. Reisman went ahead of him to make sure ground transportation was ready. The shuttle door opened and a breath of warm, humid air blew inside the cabin. Connor preferred the settlements farther away, where the climate was significantly drier than it was here, but this was the cradle of civilization here on New Earth.

"Sir," Sean called out to him, "there's been another ancient city discovered farther inland. I was wondering if you'd heard about it."

Connor frowned. "Any ryklars in the area?" The last time they'd found a city built by the alien civilization that used to live on this planet, they'd triggered a silent alarm. The local apex predators, known as ryklars, had begun hunting humans as a result. Once they'd disabled the alarm, the ryklars migrated to another area, and it had been years since any had been seen near Sierra.

Sean shook his head. "No, and no defense mechanism to call them in either."

Connor walked down the ramp and saw that there was no ground transport waiting for them.

"They're requesting that an aerial scan of the alien city be performed," Sean said and then glanced away to speak to someone through his comlink.

Connor checked the time.

"Should be here in a few minutes," Reisman said.

Connor started walking and the other men followed. He glanced at Sean. "Why are you telling me this?"

"I thought you'd be interested," Sean said and looked away guiltily.

Connor quickened his pace. He knew what Sean was implying. He hadn't seen Lenora in months.

"And the things the archaeological team discovered could have—"

"That's enough, Captain," Connor warned. "I don't have time to placate the people who spend all their time digging in the dirt—not when there's a colony to defend. If they're in trouble, the request should go through Search and Rescue. If they want a survey done, that request goes through Field Ops and not the Colonial Defense Force."

Connor didn't wait for a reply. A ground vehicle that had been barreling its way toward them came to a stop. Connor opened the door and climbed inside. "What the hell took you so long? I hope you can find the congressional building faster than you picked me up."

The driver apologized, and Wil Reisman took the front seat.

Connor opened the window and looked at Sean. "Make sure the shuttle's refueled and ready to leave. I don't plan on being planet-side for long."

The vehicle pulled away, and Reisman turned around with a question on his lips.

Connor held up his index finger. "Don't!"

Reisman frowned and turned back around. Connor was tired of people prying into his personal life. With the safety of New Earth resting squarely on his shoulders, he didn't have much time for relationships, despite the colonial mandate that encouraged procreation among the colonists. Family units in the colony were very different from what they'd been back on Earth. There were children and their immediate parents, but families were also reinforced by extended families and support groups that greatly eased the colonists' burdens of raising children. Education programs were geared toward learning about New Earth, and most things that had comprised Connor's life until seven years ago were referred to as Old Earth history.

While he had a strong connection with Lenora Bishop, she had no interest in having children. She was dedicated to learning all she could about the alien civilization that had thrived here. Most archeologists believed that intelligent life had flourished here from a few hundred to a thousand years before humans arrived. The debate was still ongoing about what had happened to them. But Connor was more concerned with the impact of what that civilization had done to the ecosystem of the planet. Predators like the ryklars and berwolves had been genetically modified, which made them highly intelligent and quite dangerous. The ryklars had abandoned this part of the continent and migrated away once the alien signal that triggered some latent protection protocol within them had been removed. At that point, ryklars had ceased attacking humans. Berwolf hunting packs required more persuasion, but there were some groups living far away from the cities that sought to tame the predators.

The vehicle drove along the paved streets of Sierra. The shimmering, bronze-colored buildings were constructed of a refined alloy they'd discovered among the alien ruins. It was light and strong. The resulting city looked familiar—since the architecture was similar to what they'd had back on Earth—but also alien as well, due in part to the materials used in the construction of the buildings.

They drove toward a large dome-shaped building where the golden sunburst flag draped unmoving in a windless sky. The vehicle pulled to a stop and Connor opened his own door. He and Reisman climbed the stairs and entered the building. Connor sent his credentials along the network, and they quickly passed through the security checkpoint.

A handsome older woman waited for him. She had her arms crossed in front of her chest and her thick brown hair was pulled back.

"Trying to make an entrance by arriving late?" Dr. Ashley Quinn asked and made a show of looking behind Connor. "And you didn't even bring Sean with you."

"No, Mother, I didn't bring him up," Connor replied.

"Mother?" Ashley snorted and arched an eyebrow at him. "I'm certainly not your mother, but I would accept the role of big sister."

Connor leaned in and kissed Ashley on the cheek as she patted his arms. "Well, in that case, I think we're fine then."

Ashley eyed him for a moment. "I know you only need two hours of sleep, but you're looking a bit worse for the wear."

"Why is it that whenever I have to come to one of these things it's you who gets to walk me inside?" Connor asked.

"I figured you'd want to see a friendly face before you get fed to the lions," Ashley said.

They walked through the wide-open atrium, and echoes of conversations gathered above them like a storm.

"At least Tobias believed in the threat we're facing, unlike the current governor," Connor said.

"Parish was the one voted in," Ashley replied.

"By telling people what they wanted to hear," Connor said with a grumble.

They reached the large metallic doors that led to the congressional chambers.

"Well, make them listen, just like you made all of us listen seven years ago," Ashley said.

She entered the chamber first.

"At least you guys were reasonable," Connor called out after her.

She didn't turn around, but Connor knew she'd heard him. His mouth drew downward and he glared at the doorway, waiting for his queue to be allowed inside. Franklin Mallory had insisted that Connor come to this meeting to make the request. Many colonists didn't want to listen to conversation about the proposed danger coming from Earth; they'd prefer to pretend the threat didn't exist. It hadn't always been this way, but the faction that questioned the threat from Earth had gained more and more support over the years.

They called his name. Connor blew out a breath and waited an extra few seconds before going inside.

3

CONNOR ENTERED the chamber to the quiet murmurings of those inside. All the seats in the vast chamber were taken, and there were even people standing in the back. Connor squared his shoulders and strode down the center aisle. The far wall showed an image of the *Ark* with the Earth in the background and then changed to the *Ark* with New Earth in the background. New Earth was similar in size and composition to Earth, but where there were several large continents on Earth, New Earth boasted a singular large landmass that occupied nearly a quarter of the planet. Vast oceans covered the rest. The most striking difference between the two planets was the rings that surrounded New Earth. They made for a beautiful sight from any perspective.

Connor walked through the gated threshold and stopped at the central podium, where he looked at the trio of people who led the colony. In the center was a thin man who, though not a particularly imposing person, had managed to convince a majority of the colony to give him the job of governor —Stanton Parish. To his right was the former governor, Tobias Quinn, who was now serving as the head of the judicial committee. To Stanton's left was a dark-skinned woman with long black hair and intense eyes, Selena Brown, who was head of the legislative committee in charge of proposing the laws of the colony.

A woman came through the gates behind Connor and went to stand at another podium nearby. Connor had no idea who she was, and she seemed to regard him as someone she'd rather not have in her presence. Connor thought she must be a Parish loyalist.

Governor Parish started the meeting, and the people in attendance immediately quieted down.

"Thank you for joining us, General Gates," Parish said.

Connor cleared his throat. "I appreciate you taking the time for this request."

"For the sake of this session, can you please touch on the high points of this request for the record," Parish said.

Connor cleared his throat. "Space Station Titan has been completed for over a year and is currently running at half capacity because we haven't been given approval for the resources to bring up the secondary power generator," Connor said.

Governor Parish examined a small holoscreen in front of him. "Yes, I've seen this request come across my desk before. We delayed this in favor of expanding the power grid supplying New Delphia."

Connor mused that this was good for the colonists living in that growing city but bad for the Colonial Defense Force's state of readiness.

"Given the members of this appropriations committee, I didn't think I needed to remind you of the threat we face. Titan Space Station represents our first line of defense," Connor said.

Governor Parish narrowed his beady eyes. "Potential threat, General."

Connor's brows pulled together and he glared at the man.

Parish held up his hand. "I know you don't agree, but, if anything, the last election has proven that not all the people on New Earth agree that the messages received from Earth imply that we're in any danger. They are quite disturbing, I'll grant you that, but there are simply too many unknowns to commit the resources of the entire colony toward efforts that don't best serve the problems we're facing today," Parish said.

Connor leveled his gaze at the governor. "You and I have vastly different opinions on how the colony would be best served, but what you're doing is negligent."

There was a sharp intake of breath by the people nearby.

The woman at the nearby podium looked at him. "We've refuted the standing argument that the offline deep-space buoy network is an indication of an invading force making its way toward this star system."

Connor frowned. "I'm sorry, who are you?"

"Dr. Gabriela Mendoza, astrophysicist."

"Dr. Zabat had a different opinion," Connor said.

"I'm well aware of what my predecessor thought. I'm afraid that the partial message, coupled with the data we've received, influenced his judgment," Dr. Mendoza said.

Connor looked back at the governor. "I thought I was here to address my request for Titan Space Station, not to debate the last message from Earth."

Governor Parish regarded Connor for a moment. "I think it's important to revisit it since what you're requesting represents a significant investment of resources that could be better utilized elsewhere. Dr. Mendoza, please."

"Thank you, Governor. As General Gates has stated, the long-held belief is that because the comms buoys supporting the deep-space network were going offline, it meant that some kind of invasion fleet was making its way to this star system, following a trail of breadcrumbs right to us. However, many astrophysicists agree that the reason for the buoys going offline is simply that they reached the end of their lifecycle," Dr. Mendoza said.

Connor glanced at Tobias, who gave a slight shake of his head.

"So we'll ignore the warning message from Earth and their last act, which was to alter the *Ark's* mission and bring us here instead of the intended destination. I'm sure you're a fine astrophysicist and you could be right about the buoys. They could be failing because they're beyond their life cycle, but even engineers know that the likelihood of these buoys failing sequentially is almost nil," Connor said.

"The only thing we know for sure is that something significant happened to Earth, nothing more than that. A reference to some super virus doesn't mean they're crossing interstellar space to reach us here," Dr. Mendoza said.

"Are you willing to bet your life on that?" Connor asked and swung his gaze toward Parish. "Are you, Governor? Are you willing to bet the lives of the entire colony on that?"

Parish leaned back. "I may be the governor, but this is a decision shared by all colonists."

"You're acting as if your decisions won't have any bearing on whether or not we survive. The decisions you make affect lives. When you have people like Dr. Mendoza spreading doubt about the very real danger we're in, it sends the message that you don't believe the colony is in any danger despite the evidence that supports the claim," Connor said.

"Everyone agrees that the initial message that changed the *Ark's* mission was sent out between ten and twenty years after we left." Dr. Mendoza said. "So, in essence, if there *was* some kind of fleet heading for us, we potentially have thirteen more years before they arrive. That's even if they know exactly where we are in the first place. Even if we err on the side of caution, we still have three years, which leaves a substantial amount of time to address the defense of the colony."

"You're assuming that their speed and method of travel is the same as the *Ark*. You know what the root of the word 'assumption' makes you, right?" Connor asked.

Dr. Mendoza sneered. "I don't have to listen to this."

"General Gates," Parish warned.

"My job is to defend the colony, which means I need the resources to do so without leaving our first line of defense at half capacity. I don't want an invasion. In fact, I hope people like Dr. Mendoza and you, Governor, are right and that we're observing the sequential failure of the deep-space buoy network. But, if you're wrong, wouldn't you sleep a bit better knowing that we're doing everything we can to keep this colony safe?" Connor asked.

Governor Parish leaned forward, and his hands formed a bridge in front of him. "Not every request from the Colonial Defense Force can be pitted against the survival of the colony. Over the past seven years, we've devoted enormous resources to the defense of the colony—from missile-defense platforms to using a large chunk of the *Ark* that went toward the construction of Titan Space Station and the battleship cruiser. So when it comes to our defense capability and the efforts of people like you, General, I sleep *very* well at night."

"So will you approve the request this time?" Connor asked.

"We've approved the creation of the additional supplies you've requested, but in regards to the secondary power system for the space station, that request will be denied. We'll review it again in the next twelve months," Governor Parish said.

Connor pressed his lips together. He wanted to tell them they were going to become victims of their own shortsightedness and make them all cower in the face of their reckless decisions. Something was coming for them—something that none of them really understood. Connor might have had more doubts if Admiral Wilkinson hadn't been involved. The aged war veteran of the NA Alliance Navy had been nearing the end of his career when he'd snuck Connor and the rest of the Ghosts aboard the *Ark*. Connor wholeheartedly believed that Wilkinson had included his own name in the mission summary brief that changed the *Ark's* destination in order to lend credibility to the content of the brief. It had been a message for Connor, and it was meant as a direct instruction to prepare the colony for invasion.

Connor looked at the governor, and his gaze strayed over to Tobias. He tried to think of something to say that might change their minds but couldn't think of anything that hadn't already been said. Connor didn't want to spread panic across the colony, so he had to work within the current confines, and this wouldn't be the last request he ever made. If anything, the last seven years had taught him that a little bit of tact went a long way.

The session ended, and despite Connor's outwardly calm demeanor, he was seething. He'd thought they'd at least grant the request in a few months' time, and to be put off for an entire year was ridiculous. If only they'd been able to successfully extract more information from the deep-space buoys, but they weren't designed to hold vast amounts of information. They had a specific job to do, which was to relay the data, not store it. After the data had passed through the buoy network, the operating systems expunged it. Connor glanced around the chamber, thinking that there were a few government officials he'd like to expunge.

4

CONNOR THREADED his way out of the congressional chambers. A few people tried to stop him by asking questions, but he put them off, having no interest in glad-handing anyone. He saw Ashley making her way toward him and then getting stopped by a small group of people. Connor used the opportunity to slip away. These requisition-type committees were usually attended by Franklin Mallory, Director of the CDF. Connor couldn't bear attending them, and after getting his request denied again, he had no wish to stand around complaining about it.

Wil Reisman was waiting for him outside the congressional building. Reisman took one look at him and frowned. "Went that well, did it?"

Connor quickly went down the stairs, and Wil walked next to him. "Oh, you know, same old crap. 'This isn't a priority. Come back in a year and perhaps you'll get what you need then.'"

"This administration isn't like the last one," Reisman said.

"At least Tobias listened to reason. Parish flat out refuses to believe there's even a threat to the colony," Connor said.

"What's our next move? Return to the shuttle?"

Connor glanced at the line of electric cars outside the building and couldn't find the one with the CDF designation on the door.

"Yeah, if we can even find the damn car," Connor said.

A high-priority message appeared on his internal heads-up display.

::*Sorry to hear that the request was denied again*,:: F. Mallory said.

::*Maybe the fourth time's the charm*,:: C. Gates replied.

::*I want to meet with you before you leave. I'm working out of Field Ops today*,:: F. Mallory said.

Connor sighed. He just wanted to get going. He had enough to do without spending the afternoon stuck in Field Ops.

::*Do I need to make it an order?*:: F. Mallory asked.

::*On my way,*:: C. Gates replied.

The chat window closed.

"Change of plans," Connor said.

He walked to the nearest car that had the golden sunburst colony emblem. The driver stood outside and glanced at them.

"I need a ride to Field Ops headquarters," Connor said.

The driver frowned at them. "This is Governor Parish's transport."

"Excellent. I'm on official business for the governor, and it's vital that I get to Field Ops as soon as possible," Connor said.

Reisman snorted and had the grace to look away. Connor grabbed the passenger side door handle. The driver glanced up at the congressional building, conflicted.

"Look, it's either you or me driving the car. What's it gonna be?" Connor asked.

"Fine," the driver said and walked around to the other side of the car.

Reisman leaned toward Connor. "He denies your request so you commandeer his ride?"

Connor smirked. "Sometimes it's the little things that get you through the day."

Reisman chuckled and climbed into the back of the car. The driver pulled away, and Connor had him send out the priority signal so they'd move through traffic quickly. Fifteen minutes later they were in front of Field Operations Headquarters. Connor and Reisman climbed out of the car just as a comlink connection came to the driver.

"Hey, wait a minute. You lied to me. The governor is outside the congressional building right now," the driver said.

"Tell him General Gates appreciates the ride," Connor said and walked over to the security checkpoint.

"Couldn't resist rubbing it in his face," Reisman said.

Connor shrugged. He didn't care. The governor had caused him no end of frustration this past year, and he felt a small tinge of satisfaction at taking the man's ride.

The Field Ops security detail snapped a salute toward Connor. "General Gates, Director Mallory said to inform you that he's at his office near command central."

Connor thanked them and headed inside. Field Ops Headquarters had grown significantly from the prefabricated structure that was there when he'd first arrived. The new building was all angles the color of dark bronze that drank in the sunshine.

His rank granted him priority treatment throughout the building. Before he'd been promoted to general—a rank he'd had no illusions of achieving in the NA Alliance military back on Earth—he'd sometimes found it annoying that the higher-ranked officers received preferential treatment, but as he'd been promoted through the ranks his opinion had changed. With the rank came a significant increase in workload. So, yeah, moving to the head of the line was a perk, but the tradeoff was more work. The Colonial Defense Force wasn't much different from the NA Alliance military in that respect. The one major difference in the two militaries was that the NA Alliance was an actual military force and the CDF was just starting to get its bearings. Connor was a general because there was no one else senior enough in rank who had actual combat experience. More than once he'd experienced fleeting moments when he'd wished there were someone up the chain of command who could take over the defense of the colony. But there wasn't anyone else, so he committed himself to doing the best he could and hoped it would be enough.

The Field Ops Command Center was akin to the mission controls of old. There were several Field Ops centers throughout Sierra and among the smaller settlements on New Earth.

A red-haired man with an almost permanent scowl on his face stuck his head out of an office and waved to Connor. "Why, General Gates, I'm so glad you could come by Field Operations," Damon Mills said.

Connor grinned. "If you keep that up, I'm gonna start calling you Director Mills."

Connor and Damon had gotten off to a rocky start when Connor had first come to the colony, and they'd nearly come to blows on more than one occasion, but all that was ancient history.

"Okay, enough with that nonsense. I'm glad you're here," Mills said and beckoned them to his office. "Franklin is on his way down."

They walked into Mills' office and sat down.

"Why do I get the feeling you're about to ask me to do something for you?" Connor asked.

Mills smiled. "Give and take, and I believe this time *you* owe *me*."

Connor arched an eyebrow. "To be honest, I've lost count."

"Trust me, you do."

"You know I don't trust anyone," Connor said.

Reisman glanced at him.

"Present company excluded, of course," Connor said. "Alright, what is it you need?"

"I have a group of engineers who need a ride to an archaeological dig site past the new frontier boundary," Mills said.

Connor's brows pulled together. "Are you seriously asking me to provide transport for a group of engineers?"

The door to Mills' office opened and Franklin Mallory walked in.

"Good, you're here," Mallory said and looked at Mills. "Did you tell him?"

Mills shook his head. "I was about to."

Connor glanced at Mallory. "The only thing he told me was to ferry a team of engineers to a dig site past the frontier boundary. Are you in on this too?"

Mallory looked confused. "What do you mean?"

"When we landed, Sean kept bringing up Lenora and some find at her new dig site. I assumed—" Connor stopped speaking, suddenly feeling foolish.

"As interesting as you think your personal life is to the rest of us, I can assure you it has no bearing on this request," Mallory said.

Connor looked away and shook his head. Sometimes he walked right into trouble. "Alright, I'm done being an idiot. What's so special about this site?"

"Oh, you mean beyond Dr. Bishop being there? I so wish you guys had stuck together," Mills said, his voice going high.

Reisman snorted, unable to keep it in anymore.

"Look, I have a shuttle waiting for me. Seriously, what's this all about?" Connor asked.

"Lenora may have found another city," Mallory said.

Connor frowned. The last time Lenora had found the ruins of a city, they'd set off some kind of auto-protect protocol that signaled the ryklars to attack them. The ryklars had demonstrated intelligence beyond that of normal predators and many people had died.

"She said this city appears to be larger than what they found seven years ago, but the real find that applies directly to you is an intact power station in the ruins. Lenora knows better than to tinker with what she found. Her team took some preliminary readings, and they look quite promising," Mallory said.

"I still don't see where I figure into all of this," Connor said.

"Oh, it's not you personally; it's just the combat shuttle you're flying around in. It's much faster than our troop transport vehicles. You can drop the engineering team off at the site in half the time it would take one of my carriers," Mills said.

"Well, that's good for you. What's in it for me?" Connor asked.

"How about some gratitude?" Mills said.

"Now who's a pain in the ass?" Connor said.

"Connor," Mallory said. "I want you to take a quick look before you head off to Titan Space Station. Our engineers learned quite a bit from the alloy they found at the last ruined city. They've perfected it since then and we've obviously used it in the construction of Sierra. What if we find something similar in terms of the power station? New fuel for our reactors that has a higher energy output. Can you think of nowhere that would be useful?"

Connor drew in a breath and nodded. "I get it. Definitely worth a look."

"I'm glad you agree," Mallory said.

"I guess I'm the pain in the ass now," Connor said.

"What's this about you stealing the governor's car?" Mallory asked.

Connor's eyes widened. "I didn't steal his car. I had the driver give us a ride here."

Mills palmed his face and shook his head.

"He'd already denied my request for Titan for a year," Connor said.

Mallory's PDA chimed an incoming message. He glanced at it and the edges of his lips pulled upward.

"What is it?" Connor asked.

"Kallie's with the doctor. I'm going to be a father again," Mallory said with a wide grin.

Connor shot out of the chair and shook Franklin's hand, offering congratulations.

"I guess Lars will be an older brother. Where is Lars stationed these days?" Connor asked.

"He's heading up the remote Field Ops centers in the other settlement. He's due to be a father soon, too," Mallory said.

Connor couldn't remember the last time he'd seen Lars Mallory, who was nearly twenty-five years old by now.

"Doing your part for procreation, I see. You're making the rest of us look bad," Mills said.

There was a general colony campaign promoting the importance of having children and how crucial it was to the colony's survival beyond a few generations. Connor felt something cold in the pit of his stomach. He'd left a son behind on Earth. He's always intended to reconnect with his son, but never had the chance.

"I'm sure all three of you will do your part," Mallory said while pointedly looking at each of them.

A wave of fear stole across Reisman's features.

"I'm a bit old—" Mills began.

"Don't talk to me about age. I'm over a hundred years old. Prolong treatments more than double a person's lifespan. There's no excuse for any of you not to start families of your own," Mallory said.

Mills cleared his throat. "About that ride for the engineering team."

"Right, just send them to the shuttle and we'll get them there," Connor said.

Mallory grinned. "You guys are a pair, I tell you."

"I'm happy for you. I really am. But we all know something's coming and the buoys are not just going offline because they're at the end of their lifecycle," Connor said.

Suddenly, the warmth felt like it was being sucked out of the room and the smile fled from Mallory's face.

"I'll leave you to it," Mallory said and left.

Connor made as if to leave but Mills asked him to stay a moment longer. Reisman, sensing the dismissal, left to wait for Connor outside.

"Sometimes you really don't know when to keep that mouth of yours shut. We're all aware of the danger, and we don't need you to keep shoving it in our faces," Mills said.

Connor felt a pang of guilt warm his cheeks, but his iron will choked the life out of it. "I know, but we can't afford to get distracted."

"Distracted! The man just found out he was going to be a father again and you couldn't let him enjoy it for five minutes without bringing up that damn crap from Earth."

Mills was right. Connor *was* being a jerk.

Mills held his hand in front of his chest. "I know you're not doing it to be malicious or cruel, but even you've got to remember that the men and women serving under you have their own personal reasons to fight. Let people like Mallory have his few moments of happiness, even if you won't allow it for yourself."

Connor chewed on the inside of his lip. "You're right. I'll go apologize."

Mills frowned. "Honestly, the best thing you can do right now is just go.

Franklin is going to be with Kallie today. In layman's terms, he's taking the day off," Mills said and leaned toward him. "Remember what those were? Now get out of here. And thank you for taking the engineering team."

Connor left Mills' office grim-faced and feeling more foolish than ever. He walked in silence for a few minutes, then glanced at Reisman. "Do you think I drive you guys too hard?"

Reisman's eyes widened in shock and then he laughed almost uncontrollably.

Connor shook his head and quickened his pace. "Forget I asked."

5

A SHORT WHILE LATER, Connor was back at the CDF airfield. He sent a message to Mallory, congratulating him on becoming a father again and apologizing for being such a killjoy. The message would be waiting for Mallory whenever he checked his inbox. After he'd sent it, he pushed all thoughts of Mallory's blossoming family out of his mind.

They entered the CDF hangar, and Connor saw Sean supervising the loading of equipment onto the combat shuttle. Seven passengers were waiting to board, one of whom he immediately recognized.

"Coming out of retirement, Bones?" Connor asked.

A ripcord-thin man with black hair turned around and saluted Connor.

"I'm still with Search and Rescue, sir. Let me introduce you to the team," Joe Ramirez said and presented the team of engineers that was traveling to the archaeological dig site. The engineers seemed friendly enough, but they were quite reserved with him, as if they weren't sure how to act around Connor.

"Those of us with engineering backgrounds also consult on projects," Ramirez said.

Ramirez had been part of the alpha class to go through Connor's first Search and Rescue training program. Some of the graduates of that first class had stayed in Field Ops, while others, like Sean Quinn, joined the Colonial Defense Force as soon as it was ratified.

Connor looked at Sean. "How much longer until we can be under way?"

"This is the last of it, so just a few more minutes, General," Sean said.

The engineering team walked up the loading ramp and checked their equipment containers.

Connor saw Ramirez checking the seats and Connor grinned. "I won't be dumping you out mid-flight this time."

An engineer named Dave Rogers became pale and his gaze darted to Ramirez. "Please tell me that was a joke."

Connor kept walking.

"He only does that to the people under his command," Ramirez said.

"He's the general of the CDF. Doesn't that mean you're still under his command?" Rogers asked.

"That's right," Connor called over his shoulder. "Rarely do I dump people out of my ships twice, but in Ramirez's case I might make an exception."

Never one for riding as a passenger when he didn't have to, he headed up to the cockpit as Ramirez coaxed Rogers back into his seat.

Sean joined him in the cockpit and sat in the copilot's seat.

"Do they really think I'm going to just toss them off the ship?" Connor asked.

Sean pressed his lips together in thought. "Let's just say you've developed quite a reputation over the years. Go for preflight, sir."

Connor sat in the pilot's seat and set about going through the preflight checklist. Lieutenant Frook entered the cockpit and sat in one of the rear seats. Connor engaged the engines and withdrew the landing gear. He eased the combat shuttle out of the hangar and thrust the stick. The main engine's power output spiked and the shuttle sped forward. He set a heading for the coordinates of the dig site.

Connor opened a comlink to the rear of the shuttle. "Attention, all non-CDF passengers. We'll reach the dig site beyond the frontier border in a little over an hour. Please remain in your seats with your seat belts securely fastened at all times. In the event of a sudden loss of pressure in the shuttle, I will click the eject button and jettison all of you to safety," Connor said and brought up a video feed of the passengers. "Unless you're sitting next to Joe Ramirez. In that case, you might not survive."

Connor grinned as he watched Dave Rogers check his seat belt and then decide to change seats. He heard Ramirez's hearty laughter coming from the rear of the shuttle.

Connor glanced at Sean. "What? I'm just lightening the mood."

"Whose mood would that be?" Sean asked.

Connor opened the comlink again. "Pay no attention to that last bit. This combat shuttle is a Falcon III and survived a two-hundred-year journey through space to get here. She's been flight tested and approved for flight by top Colonial Defense Engineers. Pilot out," Connor said but left the comlink open. "There, see, I took it back. Everything's fine. Oh, did you make sure the power coupling for the mid-tier inertia dampeners was replaced?"

Sean glanced at him, his mouth hanging open. He glanced at the open comlink and smirked. "I submitted the request to the repair technician when we landed. Let me just check their comments . . . hmm, that's strange."

"What's that, Captain?" Connor asked.

They heard Ramirez shouting from the passenger area that they could hear them.

Sean could barely contain himself. "They were replaced, but the diagnostic is showing they're defective. Sir, we're going to have to make an emergency landing or anyone sitting in the middle of the shuttle could fly out of their seats . . . Oh no, sir. That's the master alarm."

"You're right. That inertia dampener is throwing out all kinds of errors in the logs. That's strange. They all have Ramirez's name on them," Connor said.

"It makes for a much more interesting ride," Ramirez shouted.

Connor grinned.

"In all seriousness," Sean said, "the ship is fine. Relax and enjoy the flight."

"Aw crap. I'm showing all kinds of cargo failures now," Connor said. "They could be cut loose at any moment. Do you think that team knows their chief engineer is so incompetent he hardly made it through graduate school? It's no wonder he was kicked out of Search and Rescue. Wait a minute, is that a coolant leak being reported?" Connor said.

Sean closed the comlink and they all burst out laughing, including Lieutenant Frook, who'd never seen his general act this way.

Connor blew out a breath. "God, that was so much fun. I haven't laughed like that in a long time. Remind me to have Reisman tell you what we did to Colonel Douglass after one of our missions."

Connor glanced at the video feed from the back of the shuttle and saw that Wil Reisman was fast asleep. Typical. That man could sleep anywhere, any time.

Less than an hour later the nav computer displayed an alert that they were nearing their destination. They'd been flying over a large grassland area for the past fifteen minutes. Connor magnified the view and saw the research base up ahead.

"How does Dr. Bishop even find these places?" Sean asked.

Connor peered at the heads-up display. "She hardly sits still for more than a few minutes, for one. Plus, she's really good at her job."

Connor watched as they closed in on the research base, which butted up against a vast dig site.

"Sir, would you like me to land the ship?" Sean asked.

"No, I've got it," Connor said.

There was an area of flattened grassland that looked to be the designated landing area for supply runs. Connor set the combat shuttle down there. He shut down the engines and set the shuttle's computer systems to standby, then climbed out of his seat and left the cockpit. Connor didn't get to fly all that often, but when he did, he always experienced a longing to return to the pilot's seat again. Generals weren't supposed to fly their own ships, but oh how he missed flying sometimes.

Ramirez grinned when he saw Connor.

"That was quite the show," Ramirez said.

Connor gave him a playful slap on the shoulder. "All in good fun. It was really good to see you again, Joe."

Most of the engineering team was much more at ease now that they were on the ground. Dave Rogers gave him a friendly nod.

They lowered the loading ramp and were met by a woman with short brown hair.

"General Gates, I'm Martha Campbell."

Connor shook her hand and stepped off the loading ramp. His internal heads-up display showed that the temperature was a comfortable seventy degrees with ten percent humidity. There wasn't a cloud in the sky. Only the pale rings that surrounded the planet were visible along the southern horizon.

The engineering team began offloading their equipment, and Martha directed them to where they should go. Sean and other members of Connor's protective detail began securing the area.

"At ease, gentlemen. There are no predators around here except for the ones with guns," a familiar voice said.

Connor turned around and saw Lenora, and he felt his lips pull upwards into a smile. Lenora's eyes widened for a moment and she started to smile, but then her eyes narrowed in annoyance. Her long auburn hair hung freely and the soft breeze toyed with the ends.

"It's good to see you, Sean," Lenora said, her gaze softening when she looked over at the young man.

Lenora looked back at Connor. "Do you still have Noah way out on the outskirts of the star system at that space station?"

Connor frowned. "Nice to see you too."

Martha, who'd been standing quietly nearby, gave Lenora a meaningful look.

"I'm sorry," Lenora said. "Thanks for coming out here. Franklin was insistent that you see what we've found."

Lenora gestured for Connor to follow her. He noticed that everyone else seemed to give them some space.

"How did you find a city way out here?" Connor asked.

"Survey flights, and I noticed several structures less than half a mile from where we're standing. Ground-penetrating scans revealed a lot of vast structures under the ground. I assembled a team and we came back out here. We started to survey the area, marking places to dig. That was when we detected the power station," Lenora said.

"Mallory was pretty impressed with your initial report," Connor replied.

Lenora frowned. "That's what I don't get. Why would the CDF be interested in a thousand-year-old power station?"

"Is that how old it is?"

"Tough to say. There's some radiation in the area, which can throw off some of our equipment. And before you ask, the radiation is within acceptable levels," Lenora said, clipping her words as if she were swatting an annoying fly.

"Alright then, why don't you show me what you've found?" Connor said.

"Of course, right this way, General," Lenora said, her voice dripping with sarcasm.

Connor stiffened. She walked ahead of him and he supposed it could have been worse, but not by much. The last time they'd spoken to each other they'd ended up doing more shouting than talking. They hadn't spoken since.

Lenora led them toward a pair of all-terrain vehicles. A large brown ball of fur came from around one of the vehicles and howled. Connor drew his pistol and charged in front of Lenora.

"Don't shoot!" Lenora shouted and ran in front of him.

The berwolf ran gleefully into Lenora's outstretched arms. A large pink tongue lolled out of the blocky head with a mouth full of impressive teeth. The berwolf had a muscular body, but judging by the size, this one was a juvenile. Its black claws could still rend through steel, however. The berwolf nuzzled its head into Lenora's middle and she used both her hands to scratch his thick brown coat.

Lenora glanced up at him. "This is Bull. I found him as a cub."

Connor holstered his weapon and Lenora gestured for him to squat down.

Bull pulled away from Lenora and swung his head toward Connor. The berwolf cub took a few steps toward him but kept his hindquarters leaning against Lenora. Gobs of drool hung from its chops as it peered at Connor.

If this thing charged him, Connor had little chance of deflecting it before getting mauled.

Connor met its gaze and stuck out his hand. "You could have warned me about your new friend," he said.

Lenora grinned. "And miss the look on your face?"

Bull charged. The movement was so sudden that Connor didn't have time to react before the berwolf had him pinned to the ground under two giant paws. The berwolf closed its mouth and lowered its snout to sniff him. Connor heard the shuffling of feet behind him and hoped Sean and the rest of the protective detail didn't do anything stupid to set the creature off.

Connor looked into the berwolf's gaze. "Alright, what now, buddy?"

He reached up and gave the creature a light scratch under its chin. A deep growl rumbled from its massive chest, and Connor slowly moved his hands away.

"I'd like to be friends, but if you don't get off me one of us is going to get hurt," Connor said in a calm voice and started reaching for his sidearm.

Lenora came to Bull's side and nudged him. The berwolf decided to allow Connor to live and pushed himself off. Lenora helped him to his feet.

"Is this how he greets everyone?" Connor asked and dusted himself off.

"He mostly ignores people. That's the first time I've seen him do something like that. Must be your animal magnetism," Lenora said.

"Berwolfs aren't pets," Connor said.

"I don't keep him locked up. He leaves and comes back on his own," Lenora said.

She climbed into one of the ATVs, and Connor got in on the other side. The engineering team, as well as his security forces, divided up and rode in the passenger compartments. Lenora drove away and Connor watched as Bull trotted along beside them, easily keeping up with the ATVs.

"Bull isn't the first berwolf cub to be found. I'm sure he'll wander off when he's ready. I checked with the field biologists' office and they confirmed that since I'd found him so young he'd probably developed an attachment to me," Lenora said.

Not the first male to fall under her spell but definitely the first berwolf ever to do so.

"So, he just follows you to whatever dig site you happen to be on out here?" Connor asked.

"Pretty much. He actually helped us find the power station—the general area at least," Lenora answered.

She drove them toward a series of alien structures. The rounded architecture had twisted metallic pieces on the top. There were ramps that went up the sides of each building. For some strange reason the ancient aliens that built this place hadn't built stairs and instead constructed wide ramps to get to the upper levels.

Lenora stopped the vehicle and they climbed out. Bull came to a stop a few feet outside Connor's door, and he thought about waiting inside the vehicle for the berwolf to move. The creature looked at him as if he was waiting to see what Connor was going to do. Connor opened the door and stepped out of the vehicle. He knew that making eye contact with certain pack animals was the equal of challenging them, so he met the berwolf's gaze and then continued toward Lenora. Hopefully, the berwolf cub wouldn't take it as a sign of submission on Connor's part.

Lenora walked ahead and Bull trotted to her side.

"Looks like you've been replaced," Sean said.

"Seems that way," Connor said.

The path toward the building angled downward, revealing a complex of buildings that had been hidden under the dirt. The parts of the buildings that were exposed all had ramps to the upper levels.

Connor walked over to Lenora, who was directing the engineering team down into the site so they could check the power source.

"Doesn't look like they believed in making stairs," Connor said.

Lenora shook her head. "Just like the other city, though this site seems to predate that one."

Connor frowned. "How can you tell?"

"Well, the other one was built underground and then extended out into the valley. The architectural design was sparse, as if they didn't have time for all the ornamentation we have with these buildings," Lenora said.

Connor glanced around and could see her point. He'd always been fascinated by the things Lenora was able to find.

"Do you want me to take you down inside?" Lenora asked.

"Maybe. I'd like to hear what Ramirez and the others have to say first," Connor replied.

He used his implants to connect to the research base's computer systems and pulled the survey data for the site. The data compiled and an overlay appeared on his internal heads-up display, showing him the vast alien city with only a few buildings aboveground. Connor gasped and took a few steps away from Lenora as he peeked through a synthetic window to another time. The aliens that lived here had constructed almost everything into a smooth, curved surface without any seams so the appearance was of one continuous piece. Multilevel pathways ran to and fro in an elaborate framework that connected all the buildings in the city.

Lenora peered at him curiously. "You see it, don't you?"

"It's amazing," Connor said in awe.

He almost hated to turn off the overlay on his HUD, but it wasn't something he could have on and safely walk around.

"So Mallory thinks you can use what we learn here as an alternative power source?" Lenora asked.

Connor told Lenora about his request for additional resources being denied for the space station.

"I see their point," Lenora said.

"Don't tell me you doubt the warning now, too," Connor replied.

"Something bad did happen to Earth. I don't doubt that, but why would it come all the way here? What kind of living entity does that?"

Connor shrugged. "Understanding is not a prerequisite for us to take action to defend the colony."

"Yeah, but at what cost? Do we stop building medical facilities in favor of outfitting a space station or whatever war machine the CDF can come up with for a threat that might never manifest? There has to be a balance."

Connor shook his head, not believing what she was saying.

"Look at yourself. I can see it written all over your face. Anyone who doesn't agree with you is dooming the colony and everyone in it," Lenora said.

Connor took a steadying breath. "You don't understand. Whatever this thing is wiped out all the militaries back home. Wilkinson sent us that warning so we could prepare ourselves to face what's coming."

"And you have. For the past seven years you've worked yourself and everyone around you mercilessly. We have defense platforms, some godawful monstrosity of a space station equipped to fight off an armada, and the last chunk of the *Ark* is devoted to building another ship for the CDF to use. You've never once stopped and thought about what would happen if those things never showed up. What if they don't come for another forty or fifty years? How long can you keep this up?" Lenora asked.

"For as long as I have to until the job is done and you're safe," Connor replied.

Lenora pointed her finger at him like a knife. "Don't you dare say you're doing this for me. I didn't ask you to give up your life in order to work tirelessly for something that might never happen. You're doing this because you love the challenge. It's right up your alley—an intangible obstacle that you have to figure out how to overcome. *That's* why you're doing this."

"So defending the colony isn't a good enough reason?"

"Who are you fighting for?" Lenora shot back, holding her arms out wide. "Who is it? I want to know. You don't have me; you have the soldiers who report to you. So who is it that you fight for? What is it that drives you so hard?"

Connor snarled and turned away from her. Bull twisted his head to the side, looking at him curiously. Lenora came around to his other side so he had to face her.

"The mere thought of this threat not being real scares you more than anything else because it would mean you might have to move forward with your life without a war to fight. We're sixty light years from Earth and the pattern is just the same. You devoted yourself to stopping the Syndicate and you were willing to put everyone else aside, and you're doing the same thing again here," Lenora said.

"No, I'm not," Connor replied.

Lenora drew back in mock surprise. "Is that so? Then give up the Colonial Defense Force. Let someone else take command and stay here and explore these ruins with me. Right here. Right now. Do it."

Connor's heart pounded in his chest. His thoughts couldn't keep up with his emotions. "No one else can—" he began to say.

"Do what? Oversee the armed space station or train soldiers? Yes, they can. Your old platoon was on the *Ark* too, and Kasey Douglass is quite capable, as you've said on more than one occasion," Lenora said.

Her gaze bored mercilessly into his. Connor clenched his hands into fists. "I can't," he said, his voice sounding raw. "I can't sit by and let others fight, knowing there's something I could have done to help."

"You *can* help. You can stay here," Lenora said.

Connor glared at her. "You don't want me here."

"No, I never said that. You walked away from me. Remember?"

Connor swallowed hard and his throat felt thick. "There was too much to do."

"You've done enough. Let it go," Lenora said, and Connor heard the pleading in her tone.

She wasn't one for showing much of her feelings, but he could see it in her eyes. She must have been thinking of these things for a long time.

Connor glanced around and was thankful they were far enough away from other people that they couldn't be overheard. Then he saw Sean, who was pointedly looking away. The security detail assigned to Connor had to stay near him.

Suddenly, there were shouts coming up from inside the dig site, and Ramirez came running over to them.

"Sir, this place is amazing! There's a significant power source here," Ramirez said.

"Is there anything we can take with us?" Connor asked, his voice sounding husky.

Ramirez shook his head. "We need to run some extensive analyses of the systems before we start figuring out how to take it apart. We might be able to use the materials here and convert them as a base for our own power stations, but I'll need more than this small team to figure that out." Ramirez looked at Lenora with excitement. "This is an unbelievable find. My heartiest congratulations to you, Dr. Bishop."

Lenora thanked him.

Ramirez headed back to the research base, saying he needed to send a preliminary report back to Sierra.

Connor stepped closer to Lenora, and she stiffened. "I have to go," he said, hating the words.

Lenora narrowed her gaze. "Go then. Be with your squads, your platoons, your fleets, where you're in charge and can quell any argument anyone makes. Run away, Connor, just like you've always done. Run away from living a life worth remembering," Lenora said and stalked away from him.

Connor watched her go, at a complete loss for words. Bull walked next to her, following her into the dig site. Part of him wanted to lash out at her and scream how she was wrong about everything, especially him, but the words wouldn't come. Deep in the pit of his stomach a gnawing fear uncoiled inside him, whispering that Lenora's words were truer than he was willing to admit.

6

CONNOR SAT ALONE, brooding in the back of the combat shuttle. The CDF soldiers occupying the area closer to the cockpit spoke in hushed tones. They'd just left the archaeological dig site. He glared at the blank console in front of him. The harder he tried to push everything Lenora had said from his mind, the more he dwelled on it. He could hear echoes of his arguments with his ex-wife, though Lenora had done a much better job at getting to the point.

Reisman left his seat near the front of the shuttle and walked toward him. The former Ghost eyed him with an arched brow. "So, what'd you do this time?"

Reisman had known him too long to stand on ceremony, and he sat down in the seat next to him.

Connor sighed. "I work too much and I have control issues."

Reisman nodded.

Each of the former members of the Ghosts had experienced varied reactions when they were brought out of stasis aboard the *Ark*, but most of them had reacted much better than Connor.

"Do you ever think about everyone you left behind?" Connor asked.

"Of course, all the time," Reisman said. "Did I ever tell you about what my brother Jamie and I did camping one summer?"

Connor shook his head.

"There were eight of us, but since me and Jamie were so close in age, we stuck together. Strength in numbers. Anyway, one night we kept finding all these frogs roaming around the campground. It was like someone sent out a signal and frogs were everywhere. So we got one of those big five-gallon buckets and started tossing them in. No plan. We just kept catching them and tossing them in the bucket. Eventually, we caught so many frogs we had to drape a towel over the top to keep them from escaping. The bucket became so overloaded we could hardly carry it anymore, so we put it down. Some people walked by, coming from the communal showers. It was nighttime," Reisman said, frowning. "Not sure if I mentioned that or not. Me and Jamie looked up at the bathrooms and then back at our bucket of frogs at the same time." Reisman started laughing. "We knew better than to head directly toward it, so we circled around, using the woods for cover, and ended up on the women's side of the bathroom. We waited until the coast was clear and bolted to the door. We could hear the girls in the stalls and showers, but no one saw us in the doorway. We each took a side of the bucket and heaved it back like a battering ram. My little brother Jamie pulled the towel off at the last second and we must have sent hundreds of frogs into the bathroom," Reisman said, breaking off in fits of laughter, and Connor joined in.

"We hauled ass out of there so fast I think we lost the bucket. Within a minute or two we heard shrieking from the women's bathroom and then the park ranger came driving up to investigate. God, that was so much fun," Reisman said and sighed.

"Did they ever figure out it was you guys?" Connor asked.

Reisman shook his head. "Well, the next morning my dad asked us about the bucket that had gone missing, but before Jamie or I could make something up, he said something about hearing raccoons coming through the campsite the night before. He winked at us and kept whipping up some eggs for breakfast. We got some extra bacon that morning."

Connor snorted.

"So that's what I think of when I think about home," Reisman said, and he became somber. "It beats thinking about that other stuff . . . you know, the virus."

Connor nodded. He'd obsessed over that mysterious message Tobias had shown them all those years ago. They'd hoped that perhaps there were remnant pieces of the detailed data that was alluded to in the message on one of the buoys. They were wrong. Despite their resident tech genius, Noah Barker, and a number of other engineers' valiant attempts to extract data, it turned out to be simply and irrevocably gone.

"What about you? Do you ever think about home?" Reisman asked.

"Sometimes, but as the time goes by it gets harder to remember any of their faces, and it's not like the *Ark* had any of our personal files, since we weren't supposed to be here in the first place," Connor replied.

Not all the Ghosts had adapted well to colony life. Eventually, they'd joined the CDF, and at the time Connor was just happy to have their help. He should have realized that their willingness to devote themselves to this fight went hand in hand with their unwillingness to let go of everything they'd been forced to leave behind. Could he ever walk away from the CDF and leave its fate to someone else?

"General, we're starting our final approach to board the *Vigilant*," Sean's voice said over the speakers.

"Acknowledged," Connor replied, letting his own musings dissipate.

"Time to get back to work," Reisman said. All evidence of former mirth was erased.

"When we get aboard the ship, can you check that the updated targeting protocols for the missile-defense platforms have been pushed out across the system?" Connor asked.

"Yes, sir," Reisman said.

The *Vigilant* was their only heavy cruiser and was orbiting New Earth. Connor had no idea how the NA Alliance military had been convinced to give up a heavy cruiser and two Starwolf-class destroyers for the *Ark's* mission, but he was glad they had or their defense of New Earth would have been primarily near the planet itself.

An immediate sense of familiarity came over Connor as he made his way from the *Vigilant's* main hangar to the bridge. The stark gray battle-steel walls were a reminder of Connor's time in the Alliance military, although the uniforms were different. The colony's selection committee recruitment process did ensure that the people recruited had the skill sets to fly these ships, but they had the bare minimum experience to make them proficient at their jobs. The Colonial Defense Force was an amalgamation of the NA Alliance military branches since their numbers barely scraped above ten thousand soldiers, and even then the actual infantry was only a small portion of the CDF as a whole. They were relying heavily on automated defense platforms and drones. When putting the CDF together, Connor had tried to leverage every asset the colony had available, which made them significantly different than the militaries of old. He hoped it would be enough.

He entered the bridge and the ship's computer announced his presence. Colonel Ian Howe rose from the commander's chair on the raised platform central to the bridge. Like most of the higher-ranked officers in the CDF, he had the rank because he was the most experienced. However, Connor wasn't fooled. No matter how you sliced it, he commanded the most inexperienced military forces in the history of humankind.

"Welcome aboard the *Vigilant*, General," Colonel Howe said.

The colonel was a trim man whose mostly bald head sported close-cropped hair barely beginning to show a color closely matching that of the nearby bulkhead walls.

"Thank you, Colonel. What's the status of the *Banshee* and the *Wyatt*?" Connor asked.

"They're escorting the cargo carrier *Chmiel* to Titan Space Station. They departed ten hours ago," Colonel Howe said.

Connor nodded. "I think we've given them enough of a head start."

"We're ready to depart at your command, sir," Colonel Howe said.

"Make it so," Connor said.

Colonel Howe began issuing orders. The *Vigilant's* fusion reactor core increased its output to the main engines and the ship began moving away from New Earth.

"Comm, send a message to COMCENT that we've gone command blackout and will no longer be sending automated transponder updates for our ship's location," Colonel Howe said and gave Connor a nod once the communication was away.

Connor used his implants to activate a ship-wide broadcast. "Crew of the

Vigilant, we're about to begin our combat operations drill. Our target will have no advance warning of our intentions and will act accordingly. This is as much a test of Major Corwin and Major Cross's reactions to us as it is to see how well you perform the orders you've been given. Combat drills are nothing new and we will continue to do them long after today. This is our time to prove ourselves and conduct ourselves with the highest orders of excellence. And if that doesn't motivate you, then how about a reminder being given to our two destroyer crews as to why a heavy cruiser is not to be underestimated in this star system."

Connor closed the broadcast and saw the hungry gleam in the eyes of the bridge crew. He looked over at Colonel Howe.

"I've invited senior staff to go over the plan, as well as a few ideas that have cropped up that I thought you might like to hear," Colonel Howe said.

Connor gestured for the colonel to lead the way.

7

OVER THE NEXT SEVERAL DAYS, Connor observed the crew of the *Vigilant* as they stalked their prey. The Starwolf-class destroyers were restricted to the cargo carrier's best speed. The *Banshee* and the *Wyatt* traded scouting sweeps, patrolling the area ahead of their escort. Their course headings took them near the missile-defense platforms, and Connor noted that they had applied the software updates for the onboard AI cyber warfare suite.

Major Savannah Cross of the destroyer *Banshee* proved to be the more dangerous player in the cat-and-mouse game Connor was executing. Since this was their home system, Major Cross did a fair number of active scans while on scout patrols and had nearly detected the *Vigilant*.

Major Alec Corwin of the destroyer *Wyatt* was a bit more conservative with active scans while on scout patrol and he didn't take his ship as far away from the ship he was escorting as Major Cross had. Both destroyers executed their orders as they saw fit, and there were risks to both of their approaches. Major Corwin liked to stay closer to the cargo carrier and would quickly be able to respond should the carrier run into trouble. Major Cross made wider patrol sweeps and so had more of an insight into the surrounding area but would take longer to respond if the cargo ship got in trouble. Connor preferred Major Cross's approach and noted that in his report. Those reports and analyses would be made available to the destroyer commanders after the training exercise.

Connor also kept an ongoing report on how Colonel Howe and the crew of the *Vigilant* performed. There were times when the colonel had all the subtlety of a blunt instrument. The *Banshee* had almost detected them while Colonel Howe had been on duty and thought that running a scheduled scan of the system was acceptable. Colonel Howe was a good man, but he needed to break free of running his command by adhering to a checklist. Connor glanced over at

Reisman, who was sitting across from him, working on his own terminal. They were in a strategy room near the bridge. Connor had taken over the room during his stay on the *Vigilant*.

Reisman was studying a data readout from last night's logs. His green eyes slipped into calculation, and he seemed to reach some sort of conclusion. He noticed Connor watching him. "They can't all be Kasey Douglass," Reisman said.

"No, they can't," Connor replied. "That's the thing I always noticed about ship commanders who've spent too much time on a certain type of vessel. They tend to think only in terms of the vessel's well-established practices and aren't willing to push the limits. Colonel Howe is a good commander. He can get things done, but he lacks a certain finesse when it comes to all this sneaking around."

"Well he does have quite a large ship with great big guns and what not," Reisman said.

Connor glanced over at Sean, who sat at a different terminal. "What do you think?"

Sean twisted his mouth into a thoughtful frown. "He's not a hunter. He commands the ship, firm in the knowledge that he has the tactical weapons advantage in any engagement."

Reisman looked at Connor. "*Colonist.*" He snorted. "You've corrupted this young man."

"Corrupted or not, he's exactly right. The question is what to do about it," Connor said.

"You could shift the ship commanders around, but then you'd need to account for a learning curve. I would suggest taking the straightforward approach —telling him what he's doing wrong," Reisman said.

Connor had already made up his mind but was curious to see what Sean and Reisman would suggest. Sean had great instincts for engagement and had grown into an excellent leader.

"We're due to be on the bridge, sir," Sean said and closed his terminal session.

Reisman did the same and rose from his seat.

"Time to scare the crap out of a few people," Connor said.

They entered the bridge and Connor went over to the command area where Colonel Howe sat. Connor sat in the seat next to him.

"Tactical, confirm the position of the decoys and put it up on the main holoscreen," Colonel Howe said.

The output on the main holoscreen updated to show the current position of the cargo carrier, along with its destroyer escorts. Then fourteen red dots appeared for each of the decoys they'd deployed. When their transponders went active, they would do so with different classes of warship identifications, and the decoys could also generate the drive signature of vessels both large and small.

Connor used his implants to check a few data feeds and saw something that gave him pause. "Tactical, don't activate the decoys yet. We just need them to check in on the passive channels. It will take longer because of the distance, but it won't give away their position just yet."

The tactical officer paled. "Yes, General. I'm sorry. I was just looking to get the quickest response possible."

Colonel Howe glanced at Connor. "Pre-mission jitters."

"We're playing poker, and once this thing begins we'll see how well Corwin and Cross can play," Connor said.

8

MAJOR ALEC CORWIN slouched in the commander's chair on the bridge of the *Wyatt*. They'd been at this combat patrol for nearly a week and it was extremely tedious work. However, the work seemed to suit Savannah Cross just fine; she loved this stuff. Corwin would have preferred to see a bit more action. Weapons training on nearby asteroids was more fulfilling than running escort duty. It was thrilling to fire the rail-guns and missiles, giving the destroyer's weapons system a chance to clear its throat.

There was nothing out here that hadn't been placed here by the CDF. He glanced at his terminal, and it was the same as before. All the weapons platforms in the system were active and their onboard diagnostics indicated that they were functioning normally. Perhaps on one of the next scouting missions he'd push the engines a little more as a way to break up the monotony. The crew always appreciated that. There was only so much a person could learn running training drills anyway.

"Major, I've detected an anomaly with the last passive scan," Lieutenant Green said.

"On screen," Corwin ordered.

The main screen showed the scan data from the most recent passive scan. There were two anomalous detections, and Corwin glanced at his tactical officer.

"The second one was just detected, Major. The computer matches the drive signature to that of a Raptor-class cruiser," Lieutenant Green said.

"Comms, are we being hailed?" Corwin asked.

"No, Major," Lieutenant Kordek replied.

Corwin pressed his lips together in a thoughtful frown. "Can you confirm these are actual ships and not decoys?"

"Running diagnostics on the system. It checks out," Lieutenant Green replied.

"Run an active scan of the area," Corwin said.

"Major," Kordek said, "Captain Benson of the *Chmiel* is asking for a status update. He says that the two ships are appearing on his sensors as well."

Corwin sat up in his chair. If those ships were being detected on a cargo carrier's sensors, they must be closer than initially thought.

"Comms, open a channel back to COMCENT," Corwin said.

"Sir, the time lapse is over an hour," Lieutenant Kordek said.

"Okay, never mind that—"

"Sir, one of the ships is on an intercept course," Lieutenant Green said. "Make that both of them."

Corwin sat in the command chair with an ugly twisting feeling churning in his gut. If those ships weren't decoys, could they be part of the alien fleet that had rampaged Earth? Could they have made it here already? And how would they have gotten this far into the system without being detected? Surely the automated defenses for the turrets and missile-defense platforms would have detected them.

"They're heading right for us, Major," Lieutenant Green said. "What are your orders?"

Corwin's mouth became dry and he couldn't tear his eyes off the main screen.

"Three more ships detected, sir."

"Orders, Major."

Corwin sat in the chair, unable to move or think. This couldn't be happening. This must be some kind of drill, but what if it wasn't? He was out here with just one other destroyer. There was no way they could stand against Raptor-class cruisers. The armament differential was too great, and they already knew the *Wyatt* was here.

"What are your orders, Major?" Lieutenant Green's voice went up an octave.

The breath caught in Corwin's throat as he tried to think of something they could do.

"Any response to our hails?" Major Savannah Cross asked.

"No, Major," Lieutenant Daniels said.

"Okay, they had their chance. Action stations, set Condition One," Major Cross said. "Helm, move us ahead of the *Chmiel*. Operations, I want the anomalies designated by groups, beginning with alpha. Tactical, I want firing solutions ready to go, both long and short range, if any of them decide to close in."

Her orders were confirmed and carried out. Savannah peered at the main screen, which showed that the *Wyatt* hadn't changed course.

"Comms, link up the ship's systems to any defense platforms in the area. Tactical, I want you to account for missile platforms' capabilities in your firing solution. If these really are hostiles, I want to be able to return fire as soon as possible," Savannah said.

"Yes, Major," Lieutenant Daniels said.

Captain John Elder, who sat next to her, leaned over. "Major, with so many potential hostiles in the area, should we necessarily wait for them to fire their weapons first before we engage?"

Savannah eyed him for a moment. "You know the rules of engagement. We're away from COMCENT, and until they make their intentions known, I don't want to be the one to fire first. We'll tag them so they know we mean business but won't fire our weapons just yet."

Captain Elder nodded, but he still looked pale. Savannah understood his concern. With five potential hostiles, three of them cruiser-class or above, they might not survive the first salvo.

"Comms, any word from the *Wyatt*?" Savannah asked and was unable to keep a tinge of annoyance from her voice.

"No, Major. I've tried to reach them multiple times, but they won't respond," Lieutenant Daniels replied.

"Open a comlink to the *Chmiel*," Savannah said.

A successful connection to the cargo carrier registered on the main screen.

"Captain Benson, I need you to update your course to the space station with the one we're sending you now," Savannah said.

"Course received," Captain Benson said, his voice sounding relieved. "We tried to reach Major Corwin but haven't had a reply."

"They could be having an issue with their communications array," Savannah said.

John Elder glanced at her, making his opinion of Major Corwin known with just a passing look.

Savannah shrugged.

"Use best speed available and we'll cover you," Savannah said.

"Understood, Major, and thank you," Benson replied.

The comlink was severed and she looked at her comms officer.

"Still no reply from the *Wyatt*, Major."

Savannah nodded. She hoped he was having a communications issue and just couldn't respond. "Computer, record the following," she said, and the status on the main holoscreen showed that the computer was ready. "Major Corwin, I've sent the *Chmiel* an updated navigation course for Titan Space Station. Our current firing solution will cover their escape for a time. We've been unsuccessful in opening a comlink to the *Wyatt*. If you're receiving this, can you go on an intercept course to the cargo carrier to protect them in the event that these anomalies do prove to be hostiles? End recording. Send message."

"Message sent, Major," Lieutenant Daniels said.

"Contact!" Lieutenant Brennan said. "Incoming missiles detected."

Savannah swung her gaze to the main screen. The missiles were almost on top of them. They shouldn't have been able to get this close and avoid detection. "Launch countermeasures. Evasive maneuvers," Savannah said.

Since they were already at battle stations, the bridge crew was strapped to their chairs.

"Tactical, launch firing solutions alpha, bravo, and charlie groups," Savannah said.

Savannah noted the time and waited for the confirmation that their weapons had successfully fired. She watched as the main screen showed missiles closing in on the *Banshee*. They each had an unknown designation, so she didn't even know who the hell was firing on them. There had been no communication from the hostile ships.

"Still waiting on that confirmation, tactical," Savannah snapped.

"I'm sorry, Major. I authorized the firing solutions as you ordered. The system won't respond," Lieutenant Brennan said.

"Major, we're being hailed by General Gates on the *Vigilant*. Transponder codes and authorization clearance are a match," Lieutenant Daniels said.

Savannah's brows pulled together and she narrowed her gaze. "On screen," she said.

General Gates' face appeared on the main screen. "Major Cross, stand down. This is a training exercise designed to test your actions against a surprise attack force."

Savannah clenched her teeth. General Gates had a reputation for being opportunistic with his training exercises. She felt her racing heartbeat slow down but only slightly. "Acknowledged, General. *Banshee* will stand down."

General Gates' hard gaze softened for a moment. "Major Cross, please congratulate your crew on their exemplary performance. They did well, but there's a lot of room for improvement, as I'm sure you're aware. I want you to review the data from this encounter and in the next twenty-four hours I want you to present to me ten alternative actions you could have taken. *Vigilant* out."

General Gates' face disappeared as the comlink was severed. Savannah blew out a breath and John Elder did the same.

"Alright, you heard the general. This was a training exercise. Set action stations to condition three. I want the entire dataset from this encounter, beginning with the first onset of the anomaly detection, put up in the simulators so we can start running combat scenarios against them," Savannah said.

"How does he already know that we could have done better, Major?" John asked.

"Because General Gates designed this whole encounter. Do you think he didn't already have more than a few tactical solutions on how best to deal with this scenario ready to go?" Savannah asked.

"I see your point, Major," John replied.

She got up from her seat and walked over to Lieutenant Brennan. Her tactical officer's hands shook as he tried to work through the menu options on his terminal.

"You didn't do anything wrong. You followed my orders, which is exactly what you were supposed to do," Savannah said.

Lieutenant Brennan sucked in a deep breath and glanced up at her. "It all happened so fast. I don't know what I could have done differently, Major."

"That's the whole point of this exercise. The secrecy of its execution was the best way to test us. I know once we all calm down and put our heads together we'll improve our performance. Let's get to work, shall we?" Savannah said.

"Yes, Major, and thank you," Brennan replied.

Savannah went back to her command chair.

"What the hell happened to the *Wyatt*?" John asked.

Savannah nodded. "An excellent question and one I'm keen to know the answer to myself," she said and pressed her lips together. "One of the first scenarios I'd like to run is a coordinated response that includes the *Wyatt*."

"But they weren't available during the encounter," John said.

"Doesn't matter. We know the capabilities of our own ship, and that's a resource we have available. The fact of the matter is that if this had been a true encounter, we would have died. Don't get me wrong, we would have bloodied the enemy, but we would have died or come close to it. We need to devise a way to respond to that scenario where we don't lose our capacity to fight, and we only have twenty-four hours to do it," Savannah said.

"Understood, Major."

Savannah nodded. "Call in your reserves to the bridge. We'll need all hands working on this for the time being. I want ideas and solutions for the current engagement, and don't be afraid to stretch the encounter with a couple of 'what if'-type scenarios."

The call went out and Savannah sent her orders to the rest of the crew, bringing them up to speed. She knew there was a better way to respond to the threat they'd just faced. Now she needed to set her mind to finding the best solution so the next time General Gates wanted to test them, the *Banshee*, at least, would be ready for the encounter.

9

CONNOR COULD SCARCELY KEEP the scowl from his face. The comlink to the destroyer *Wyatt* had just been closed. Throughout his military career he'd seen all manner of people who'd frozen up at the first real sign of danger, but this was the first time he'd seen the commander of a damn destroyer do so. Had this been the NA Alliance military, Major Alec Corwin would have been relieved of duty and replaced with a more capable commander.

He sat in the officers' conference room near the bridge with Reisman and Sean across from him, and they were joined by Colonel Howe and Major Nathan Hayes.

"The shit hit the fan," Connor said. "I can't have a destroyer commander freezing up like that. By all accounts, it was Corwin who failed to even execute a rudimentary response to the hostile forces in this exercise. Where was his XO?"

"She was performing an inspection in Engineering when the attack occurred," Major Nathan Hayes, XO of the *Vigilant*, answered.

Colonel Howe leaned forward. "Captain Mattison hightailed it to the bridge shortly after the attack began, but by then the damage had already been done. That crew has suffered a major blow to their morale that I'm not sure they can recover from."

"So that's one for replacing Alec Corwin as the commanding officer of the *Wyatt*," Connor said and looked at Major Hayes.

"There's a pool of candidates we can draw from if we go that route, and I agree with the colonel. Major Corwin should be relieved of command," Major Hayes said.

"General, meaning no disrespect to anyone here, but I disagree," Sean said.

Connor glanced at him, considering. "Care to elaborate, Captain?"

"The training drills are designed to expose weaknesses so they can be addressed. Simply yanking Corwin off that ship won't help us in the long run," Sean said.

Connor narrowed his eyes thoughtfully. "There are some things you don't get a second chance on. The lives of the hundred and fifty crewmembers aboard the *Wyatt* depend on their chain of command not faltering at the first sign of danger. I'd initially thought his approach to escort duty was on the conservative side, but now I'm thinking Major Corwin was just being lazy."

Reisman brought up some data on his personal holoscreen. "General, there's nothing in his performance history that indicates a dereliction of duty. If you're taking votes, sir, mine is to allow the major to complete the escort duty and return to New Earth. Then we can decide what to do with him."

Connor sighed and looked at all of them. "Two of you think I should yank him out of the chair and two of you think I should give him another shot. You guys are no help."

Reisman chuckled. "One other thing to consider is the amount of time that went into training Major Corwin. I know Captain Mattison. She's a topnotch officer, and I'm sure things would have been different had she actually been on the bridge."

"That's not good enough," Connor said.

Colonel Howe cleared his throat and drummed his fingers on the table. "I may have been hasty with my recommendation. I'd like to see what Major Corwin and his crew can come up with in terms of solutions to the combat drill. To me, that will be very telling as to whether he should be left in command."

Connor nodded. "I agree. Okay, let's move on to the *Banshee*. Wil, put the simulation up on the main screen."

Reisman tapped a few commands into his personal terminal and the main holoscreen came on.

Connor leaned back in his chair and watched the simulation play out. This gave an accurate representation of how Major Savannah Cross had handled the combat drill.

"She's a scrapper," Connor said. "She tried to hail the unknowns, and when they didn't respond she had her tactical team formulate multiple firing solutions. Those firing solutions provided the maximum coverage for the cargo carrier, and she even sent an updated course to Captain Benson of the *Chmiel*, which was accounted for in her plans. Pause the simulation," Connor said. "She followed the rules of engagement and even tried to leverage use of the missile-defense platforms nearby. If I had another heavy cruiser, I'd give it to her right now. Alright, resume the simulation and let's see how this plays out."

The combat simulation sped forward, and the destroyer was able to extract a heavy toll from the enemy forces, but there was still a ninety percent certainty that the *Banshee* would have been destroyed.

"Look at that. The computer shows an eighty percent estimate that the *Chmiel* would have escaped the encounter unscathed," Sean said.

"That's right. So now, a test for *you* guys. What could Major Cross have done differently that would have allowed her ship to survive the encounter?" Connor said and looked squarely at Colonel Howe.

"I see this is for me," Colonel Howe said and narrowed his gaze thoughtfully. "Assuming the raiders or enemy forces were only after the cargo carrier, she could have leveraged that to her advantage, using them as bait to draw them farther inside the envelope of the missile-defense platforms. That would have given her more cover and provided protection for the cargo carrier."

"That's not bad. Wil, can you input Ian's changes into the simulation and see how that plays out?" Connor said.

Reisman nodded and began updating the parameters for the simulation. "Okay, playing back at one-half speed."

They watched as the simulation played out. The *Banshee* did survive the encounter but still sustained significant damage.

"I think that, given the situation, drawing the enemy forces toward the missile-defense envelope is a good way to go. The one thing that's missing is the other destroyer," Connor said, and Colonel Howe's eyes lit up in understanding. "If Corwin and Cross had coordinated their efforts, they would not only have survived the attack but inflicted significant damage on the enemy. This represents one of my primary concerns." Connor glanced at the *Vigilant's* commander and XO. "We're too siloed in our approach to enemy engagement. I take partial responsibility for that. We need to come up with some combat drills of our own that necessitate the coordinated use of our resources."

Colonel Howe nodded. "I see what you're saying. I don't think I would have seen it if it hadn't been thrown in my face."

"That's why we train. I want you to have a private word with Major Corwin and lay it out for him. His job is on the line if he can't convince me that he deserves to be in the commander's chair. I also want Major Cross informed that she's promoted to squadron commander," Connor said.

"Yes, General," Colonel Howe said.

"I know you have a ship to run, Colonel, but I want the tactical officers rotated through here to undergo these simulations and propose changes of their own. The best ones become the standard for the CDF Fleet."

10

Major Savannah Cross splashed cold water on her face and then patted her cheeks and neck down with a towel. The commanding officer's room had its own private bathroom. She would have loved to have a shower, but short on time, she'd elected to get some chow instead. If she were being particularly wishful, a swim in one of the lakes near Sierra would have drained the tension right out of her. She wondered if she could convince the engineers who designed the next class of starships to include a lap pool.

She deposited the towel into the reclamation canister that would separate the water from the towel for recycling, then ran a brush through her short blonde hair and put on a fresh uniform. She and her crew had been working for twelve hours straight, poring over the recorded events from the last combat drill. They'd come up with some clever alternative actions that she was sure would meet General Gates' criteria for success. While the various teams worked in shifts, Savannah and John Elder had taken turns working with them all to come up with acceptable alternatives that would change the outcome of the combat training exercise. Between that and the fact that she'd already been awake for a long time before the "attack," she hadn't slept for almost thirty hours, but she'd managed to get four hours' rack time and was preparing to meet with her XO to finalize their simulations on alternative ways they could have handled General Gates' surprise training exercise.

Her personal terminal alerted an incoming call, voice only.

"Yes," Savannah said.

"Major, I have a comlink from Major Corwin, who'd like to speak with you privately, ma'am," Lieutenant Kordek said.

Savannah frowned. Had the shift changed already? She glanced at the ship's clock.

"Alright, put him through," Savannah said.

Major Corwin's thin face appeared on her terminal. He looked haggard, as if he hadn't slept much. He was speaking to her from his own quarters on the *Wyatt*.

"What can I do for you, Alec?" Savannah asked.

"Thank you for speaking with me," Major Corwin said.

Savannah nodded. "I'm due to meet with my team in a few minutes."

"That's what I wanted to speak with you about—the presentation to General Gates."

Savannah watched as Corwin's brown eyes slipped into calculation while he considered what he was going to say.

"Savannah, I messed up big time," Corwin said and sighed.

Savannah felt the skin around her eyes tighten for a moment and then she sat down. "What happened to you?"

Corwin shook his head. "I froze. When those ships started to appear, I panicked. I knew what I was supposed to do, the ROE and protocols we were to follow. I even remembered all the training drills we'd done as a crew, but when it came down to it, I just couldn't . . ."

Savannah leaned toward the holoscreen. "You screwed up. You can't change that, but the fact that they haven't taken your command away means you're getting a chance to convince them you belong in the commander's chair."

Corwin nodded and swallowed hard. "I know, it's just . . . I saw how you responded to them. How'd you even do that? You were ready to lay it all on the line."

"I hit back, but there were things we could have done much better. As for how I knew what to do," Savannah said and speared a look at the floundering destroyer commander, "we're here to protect the colony against any threat that comes our way. I stuck to our mission parameters—protect the cargo carrier. If you think you can't do that, it's your responsibility to take yourself out of that chair and let your XO finish the mission. The way I see it, you can try to pull the pieces together and learn from your mistakes because General Gates is never going to let up. He's relentless in the training of the CDF because he believes there's a threat coming for all of us from Earth. It's what drives him, and it's what drives me. Why are you here?" Savannah asked.

Corwin's eyebrows pulled together. "Same as you. To protect the colony."

"Well then, get back to work instead of talking to me," Savannah said.

Corwin regarded her for a moment and nodded. "Thank you, Major Cross."

The holoscreen went blank as the call ended, and Savannah shook her head. She hoped Corwin could pull himself together both for himself and the sake of his crew. He wasn't a bad person, but he lacked motivation. Had Corwin been under her command, she'd have ridden him until he either broke or rose up and confirmed his right to wear the uniform. The *Banshee's* crew was no stranger to her no-nonsense attitude.

She rose from the chair and left her quarters. They had a few hours until their meeting with General Gates, and she aimed to squeeze every ounce of productivity from her crew during the time they had left.

She headed to the bridge, and the ship's computer announced her presence as she approached the commander's chair, currently occupied by Captain Elder.

"What have you got?" Savannah asked.

Elder's face lit up and he glanced over at Lieutenant Green, who worked at his tactical station. "I think you're going to be impressed with what we've come up with."

"We'll see about that. Dazzle me," Savannah said.

The crew of the *Banshee* had come together during this exercise and Savannah felt her chest swell with pride for her crew. She knew Alec Corwin had a much harder road to travel to get the same from his crew and hoped he rose to the task. If not, she might have to replace her XO because he was a prime candidate to take command of the *Wyatt*.

11

GENERAL GATES TO INFIRMARY TWO.

The announcement resonated along the corridor Connor was in since the ship's computer would only send the message to his location. He'd been speaking with the *Vigilant's* lead engineer, who had an idea about updating the cooling systems for the rail-cannons.

"Increasing the rail-cannons' rate of fire is extremely important. Run the numbers for your proposal, and if they check out, we can try it," Connor said.

"Will do, General," Major James Hatly said.

They left the forward aft gunnery area, where Connor had been making good on his promise to personally visit different sections of the ship.

He glanced at Reisman. "Where's Howe?" Connor asked.

The *Vigilant's* commanding officer was overdue to meet with them.

"According to his locator, he's already at the infirmary," Reisman said.

Connor frowned and pulled up the ship's layout on his internal heads-up display. The *Vigilant* had two medical bays on the ship, each located mid-ship toward either the bow or the stern. They made their way through the ship, soldiers giving way to Connor. As they closed in on the medical bay, there was a line of pale-looking soldiers waiting to be seen.

Connor quickened his pace and walked into the bay. There were beds along the far wall, and all of them were occupied. Doctors and nurses were rushing around, all of them with face masks on to block contagions. Connor glanced to the side where a desk clerk sat. Multiple people surrounded the desk, all asking questions at once. There was a clear plastic container that had more face masks, and Connor reached in and grabbed two of them. He tossed one to Reisman and put the other one on.

The desk clerk glanced at him, noting the gold collars of his uniform.

"Dr. Allen is down over there, sir," the clerk said.

Connor thanked her and headed in the direction the clerk had gestured. They came to an area of the medical bay that was sealed off from everyone else, and he saw several medical personnel surrounding two beds that were just beyond the barrier. Connor peered inside and his eyes widened. Lying on the bed closest to him was Colonel Ian Howe, and right next to him was his XO, Major Nathan Hayes. They were both intubated.

"This doesn't look good," Reisman said.

"No, it doesn't," Connor replied grimly.

Connor pressed the button on the comlink for the quarantine area. "Is Dr. Allen in there?"

One of the doctors leaned away from the others, who were still huddled around the two patients. Dr. Allen waved to Connor and then quickly spoke to his colleagues before going through the airlock separating the two areas. The medical officer waited in the airlock, going through decontamination protocols, and then came out.

"General, thank you for coming so quickly," Dr. Allen said.

"What's going on, doctor?" Connor asked.

"The colonel and major are experiencing symptoms of an acute allergic reaction and we're trying to identify the source," Dr. Allen said.

Connor glanced over at Ian Howe. "That looks like more than an allergic reaction to something."

"We intubated them to force the airway to stay clear and induced a medical coma," Dr. Allen said.

"You have them quarantined. What's the risk to the rest of the crew?" Connor asked.

Epidemics on a ship could be catastrophic if the crew couldn't perform their jobs.

"Only a precaution in case we've missed something," Dr. Allen said.

"We saw a line of soldiers waiting to get in here. Has this thing already spread?"

"Too soon to tell. What I know so far is that the colonel and the major ate at the same mess hall, and there have been several allergic reactions experienced by other soldiers who ate there—anything from upset stomach to severe vomiting. In extreme cases, the soldiers in question have reported problems breathing," Dr. Allen said.

Connor pulled off his face mask. "So if it's something they ingested, I don't need to wear this mask."

"Correct, General. As the ranking officer on this ship, I must inform you that you are now the commanding officer of the *Vigilant*. I will send you status updates every hour unless something changes, but I expect you'll be wanting to go to the bridge," Dr. Allen said.

Connor took another look at the bedridden colonel and major. He pulled up each of their files on his internal heads-up display, and neither of them had any known allergies.

"Very well. If you need anything to get them back on their feet, you let me know," Connor said.

"Yes, of course, General," Dr. Allen said.

Connor and Reisman left the medical bay. He opened a comlink to the bridge.

"Who has the con?" Connor asked.

"I do, General. Lieutenant Vladimir LaCroix."

"I want three security teams to make a sweep of the mess halls, looking for any signs of tampering or spoilage, and I want it done with the cooperation of the officer in charge," Connor said.

"Do you suspect foul play, General?" Lieutenant LaCroix asked.

"I'm not sure, Sergeant. I'm on my way to the bridge," Connor said and switched off the comlink.

"It's a good question," Reisman said.

"I don't think anyone deliberately sabotaged our food storage, but we need to rule it out. I *am* concerned that the senior officers were more affected than the others so far," Connor said.

"I guess it was luck that we're here," Reisman said.

"If we were lucky, no one would be getting sick. The question is: what changed? The *Vigilant* has made multiple trips to the Titan Space Station," Connor said and pressed his lips together. He opened a comlink to Sean Quinn. "Listen, I need you and your team to review the change logs for critical ship systems, particularly things like food and water, but expand it to filtration systems and our air supply. And we need a list of soldiers who've accessed those systems within the last forty-eight hours."

"At once, General," Sean answered.

Once the comlink went dark, Reisman cleared his throat. "Your protégé is coming along nicely."

Connor arched a brow. "Sean is quite capable."

"Yes, he is, and he goes to great lengths to serve at your side," Reisman said.

Connor shrugged. "I'll admit I do like him. He gets things done and has good instincts. Remind me to tell you how he came to be under my command."

Reisman grinned. "Diaz already told me about that. The kid stored himself in a high-impact storage crate you promptly dumped out of the troop carrier for a low-altitude drop-off at that first training camp. Kid's lucky to be alive."

"You can say that again. Fortunate for him, he stored himself with some delicate equipment so there was adequate padding. Sean has proven to be quite a soldier. If we were back home, I'd have recruited him to be part of the Ghosts," Connor said.

Reisman's eyes widened. "Now that *is* high praise. Too bad Diaz prefers to stay planet-side these days he would have made a good addition to the Ghosts as well."

Connor nodded. Juan Diaz was part of the Colonial Defense Force but was on leave now for the birth of his second child. Diaz had requested a post that allowed him to train infantry troops, which would keep him planet-side and much closer to home. Diaz was his first friend in the colony, and Connor made a mental note to check in on him when he returned to New Earth.

They entered the bridge and Lieutenant LaCroix surrendered the commander's chair to him.

Connor sat in the chair and opened a broadcast channel to the entire ship. "Crew of the *Vigilant*, this is General Gates. A short while ago I was informed that both Colonel Howe and Major Hayes are in the medical bay due to a severe allergic reaction and are being carefully watched over by the chief medical officer, Major Richard Allen. Therefore, I'm assuming command of this ship. We will continue with our mission, which is to escort the cargo vessel *Chmiel* to Titan Space Station, as well as make our own delivery of supplies. Stay focused on your assignments and continue to execute your duties with the absolute excellence I've come to expect from this crew. Gates out."

Reisman sat in the XO's chair next to his.

"Comms," Connor said, "there will be a medical briefing circulated throughout the ship. I want to be informed the moment it's sent out."

"Yes, General," Sergeant Boers said. "Oh, General, I have Major Cross and Major Corwin standing by."

Connor glanced over at Reisman.

"We're scheduled to review their proposed solutions for the combat drill," Reisman reminded him.

"Ah yes. Lost track of time. Put them through," Connor said.

A few seconds later both Major Cross and Major Corwin appeared on the main screen.

"I apologize for the delay," Connor said and told the two destroyer commanders what had happened. "Major Cross, as squad commander for the destroyer group, you'll present first, but before you begin I have a few things I'd like to say to you both."

Savannah Cross gave him a firm nod and Alec Corwin looked as if he expected to be yelled at.

"No doubt you and your crews have spent the last twenty-four hours going over the combat scenario that was part of the drill. You were tasked with providing multiple solutions to the engagement, and given the circumstances, I expect there to be some overlap in your approach, so don't be alarmed if that happens. Is that understood?" Connor asked.

Both of them said yes.

Connor swung his gaze toward Major Corwin. "Let's get the elephant out of the room, shall we, Major?"

Corwin looked startled to be spoken to and Connor felt his temper rising.

"Major Corwin, I expect nothing but complete professionalism for the duration of this meeting," Connor said.

Corwin directed his gaze into the camera. "Yes, General."

Connor glanced over at Major Cross. "I think we're ready to begin."

Over the next few hours, both majors presented their solutions to the combat drill engagement. As Connor expected, Major Savannah Cross had done her homework and improved on even his own plans for how the combat scenario should have been addressed. Alec Corwin did come up with acceptable solutions to the combat drill, but there was still a lingering doubt in Connor's mind as to whether Corwin should remain in command of that ship.

"I think everyone here has learned a great deal. Savannah, I particularly enjoyed the solution whereby you used the *Chmiel* as bait to entice the enemy forces to come within the missile-defense platform's envelope. It was a bold move, and I concur with the line of thinking that the cargo ship was already at risk and could, therefore, be leveraged as an asset while not increasing the risk to it," Connor said.

"Thank you, General," Major Cross said.

Connor gave her an approving smile. "We'll use some of these solutions as the training standard."

Connor swung his gaze to Major Corwin and pressed his lips together.

"Major Corwin," Connor said sternly.

"Yes, General."

"Is Captain Mattison with you?" Connor asked.

Major Corwin frowned for a moment. "No, sir . . . I . . . she's on the bridge."

Connor glanced over at Sergeant Boers at the comms station. "Open a comlink to the *Wyatt's* bridge."

A third window opened, showing a young dark-skinned woman. She was standing near the command chair and gave Connor a determined look.

"Captain Delta Mattison, I'm ordering you to assume command of the destroyer *Wyatt* as the ranking officer on the ship," Connor said and looked over at Major Corwin. "Major, you are hereby relieved of duty as commander of the *Wyatt*. You are confined to your quarters until we reach Titan Space Station, and arrangements will be made to take you back to New Earth. Your performance in command of the *Wyatt* was reprehensible, and no amount of pathetic looks is going to convince me to give you a second chance. The soldiers serving aboard that ship would not get a second chance if they all died because you froze up at the first sign of battle. This next part is for all of you," Connor said and glanced at the rest of them. "I know it's become a popular notion to question whether there really is an attack force heading to this star system. Our job in the Colonial Defense Force isn't to agree one way or another, but I think you know what I believe. Regardless, every one of us has to be prepared for the unexpected. We don't have a fleet of ships at our disposal. We're all we've got for the time being. It will be years before we build enough ships to defend the colony. Major Corwin, I want you to think long and hard about your performance and the road that led you to where you are today. You're not commanding officer material, but perhaps there's some other way you can contribute to the CDF. As commanding officers, we set the standard, and it would be outright negligence on my part to leave you in command of that ship."

Major Corwin's shoulders slumped and a flush swept across his face. A moment later he stood up straight and gave a salute. "Yes, sir," Corwin said, and the video feed cut out.

Connor softened his gaze and looked over at Delta Mattison. "Captain, are you equipped to carry out the orders I've given you?"

Captain Mattison stood ramrod straight. "Yes, sir."

Connor bobbed his head. "Okay then. I'll need a list of candidates who can serve as your XO, at least until we return to New Earth."

"Yes, General," Captain Mattison said.

Connor looked at Reisman. "Send the data burst to them now."

Reisman opened a menu on his terminal and, after a few moments, said, "Encrypted orders sent, sir."

Connor turned back to the main screen. "Alright, ladies, time for the real fun to begin. What Colonel Reisman has sent over is an updated mission plan for Titan Space Station. At the *Chmiel's* best speed, we're still several days out from Titan Space Station. However, we can and will go much faster than that. I expect you to review the plans with your crew. If you have any suggestions, I want to hear about it."

"General, may I ask a question?" Major Cross asked.

"Yes, Major."

"Colonel Douglass is in command of the Space Station. Won't he expect something like this?"

"I know I've developed something of a reputation for springing training missions when you least expect them, and I'd hate to disappoint Colonel Douglass. He and I have served together for a long time. If anything, these surprise drills teach us how we will react in tough situations," Connor said.

"Grace under pressure, sir," Major Cross said.

"Yes, and if we succeed, you have my permission to lord it over Colonel Douglass whenever you see him," Connor said.

"I'll do my best, General," Major Cross said.

Connor dismissed the two of them so they would have time to review the details of his planned assault on the space station.

"She's right. Kasey is expecting something like this," Reisman said.

"He better be or I'll bust him down to private," Connor said.

"I have a question, if you don't mind," Reisman said.

"Go ahead, Wil."

"Major Corwin. Had you already decided to relieve him of command, or did you decide during the presentation?" Reisman asked.

"I meant everything I said before. If I wasn't convinced he should be in command, then he was done. The thing I'm debating now is whether to send you over to the *Wyatt* to take command," Connor said.

"Wouldn't be my first tour of duty on a destroyer. If you give the order, I'll go over there and whip that ship into shape, but you might miss me," Reisman said with a wry grin.

"Watch it or you'll draw that short straw to be the pregnant woman this time," Connor said.

Reisman's eyes lit up. "Samson Denton! God, he hated when that happened to him. Too bad we don't have any of those Ghost combat suits here. I could have a lot of fun with that."

Connor laughed. "Let's go over our assault plan with the rest of this crew. I really want to catch Kasey off guard."

"If you really want to catch him off guard, you should send Sean in with a small team to temporarily disable some key systems," Reisman said.

Connor's eyebrows rose. "That's not a bad idea. Too bad we don't have any stealth combat shuttles."

"Therein lies the fun," Reisman said.

Connor shook his head. "We're not modifying our shuttles. The heat stabilizers are there for a reason and I won't risk a shuttle for the sake of a training mission."

"Fine," Reisman said, feigning disappointment. "I'll come up with another way."

"I'm sure you will," Connor said and glanced at the main holoscreen, which now showed a star map and their trajectory to the space station.

Connor studied the area beyond the space station and sighed. For everything they'd accomplished in the past seven years, they still didn't know what was beyond the nearest buoy. Noah Barker had thrown himself at the problem, trying a multitude of ways to glean more intelligence from them. They'd even debated sending a deep-space probe out there as an early warning device. At least then they'd have some confirmation that an attack force was coming for them. But this was around the time Stanton Parish had been voted into office, and the proposal was denied. So Connor had devoted time and resources to Titan Space Station instead. The station was their first line of defense and he hoped it was enough. He'd much rather be the fool who was wrong than be right and have everyone else pay the price if the CDF failed.

12

NOAH RAN his fingers through his short-cropped hair as he waited for the latest diagnostic to finish for the modified HADES IV missile system. He'd ditched his long hair years ago when he joined the Colonial Defense Force. Sometimes he missed it, though having long hair wasn't the most practical of things to maintain. In truth, he liked not having to deal with it when he got up in the morning.

He was in a cramped engineering work area on Titan Space Station and had been for eight months, which was longer than he'd originally been assigned, but the work he was doing here was important. The bulk of Titan Space Station's infrastructure had been taken from the original *Ark*. On more than one occasion Noah'd had trouble imagining that the space station was once part of the massive colony ship that ferried over three hundred thousand humans to this star system. The original intention for the *Ark* had been to be broken up and taken to the surface of New Earth to be used by the colony. Those goals had changed. The colony needed this outpost to monitor and scan for any threats that meant the colony harm. Titan Space Station was the first line of defense for the entire star system. They maintained their position relative to the nearest deep-space buoy. Over the years, Noah had come to appreciate the engineering marvel of the deep-space buoy network that was put in place as a means to bolster communication signals from Earth. He was also well aware of their shortcomings. For years he'd worked on trying to glean any piece of data off of the deep-space buoys that would give them some insight into what catastrophe had befallen Earth and whether there was an invasion force coming for the colony. He'd failed on both counts.

The powered door to the Engineering lab hissed open and Noah glanced behind him.

Kara walked in, carrying two cups of glorious, steaming coffee.

Noah perked up in his seat. "You're a saint. Thank you."

The edges of Kara's lips curved upward into a smile that exposed an adorable dimple on the side of her cheek. She handed him his coffee and set hers down.

"Where we at?" Kara asked.

Noah took a sip of his coffee and relished the taste of the creamy brew. "Oh, attempt number eight hundred and thirty-six . . . maybe thirty-seven," he said, bringing up the simulation iterance number and frowning.

"Only slightly off there, genius. You're at eight hundred and forty-seven. What did you change this time?" Kara asked.

She rested her hand on his shoulder and peered at the holoscreen in front of them.

Noah turned toward her and caught the sweet scent of the lavender shampoo she'd used.

Kara glanced at him and smiled, then gave him a quick peck on the lips and sat down.

"When I stopped thinking of these things as missiles and thought of them as small spacecraft, I had the idea of adding additional systems. Primarily I added a secondary targeting array and had the shielding for it pop off during its flight. I even added a third, which will enable the guidance system to stay on target and not get blinded by other detonations or point defense systems," Noah said.

Kara frowned and had the computer highlight the systems that were modified. "I can see that it's longer, but show me—" She stopped speaking and took control of the interface. The simulation showed that the HADES IV long-range missile had reconfigured itself during its flight toward its intended target. "I can see why Colonel Douglass was so excited by this."

"He just said that no matter what I changed, the missile still had to fit in the tube. But once it leaves the ship it doesn't need to retain its shape, which gives us some flexibility. It's not like there's any aerodynamics in the near vacuum of space," Noah said.

Kara frowned. "Yeah, but there *is* always a cost. The engines still need to push the added weight along. See, the range is cut down by twenty percent."

"Yeah, but it's more accurate. What's more important—that we hit our target or how far away we can miss them?" Noah asked. He'd known the additional equipment would impact the range, but he'd rather stand a better chance of hitting his mark.

"Depends, and it's not up to us, regardless," Kara said.

"The range of the missile isn't fixed, so couldn't we modify that to get the twenty percent back?" Noah asked.

"We could. It just depends on how far away the targets are and it also depends on the warhead on it. Let's run a few more simulations and then take it to the colonel," Kara said.

Noah nodded and took another sip of his coffee. Kara was the lead engineer when it came to the defense systems of Titan Space Station. Noah had learned that with any weapons of war it was a game of give and take. Higher accuracy required more sophisticated systems, which impacted other things like weight and yield. There was always a price to pay.

"I'm not saying the colonel won't like the idea, but we need to be upfront about the system's limitations. However, given that we're constantly being expected to accomplish more with less leads me to believe he'll approve these changes," Kara said.

Noah nodded and stood up. He stretched his arms overhead and worked out some of the stiffness in his shoulders.

"He'll probably want to know how many HADES IVs we can modify," Noah said.

Kara grinned and shook her head. "You're learning, but it won't be you and me modifying all these missiles. We'll need to come up with a process so we can task my team with it."

Noah pressed his lips together. "I'm not sure—"

"You just worry about the technical steps and I'll worry about how to get it done once I make sure you won't blow us up," Kara said. "I was kidding," she followed up quickly.

"That was a long time ago," Noah said, getting a bit defensive.

He'd made a quick update of the power relay systems when he'd first arrived and nearly destroyed one of the subsections of the space station. He'd only been trying to help, but he'd thought Colonel Douglass was going to ship him back to New Earth before the cargo carrier left. Noah hadn't been particularly enthused to be assigned to the space station, but Connor insisted that they could use his help. It was only supposed to be for one six-month rotation, but he'd requested to stay when his six months were up, which was in no small part due to the work being done and meeting Kara. He'd even sent a vid to Lenora telling her about Titan's lead engineer. Though they weren't related, Lenora Bishop was like a big sister to him and she was as close to family as he had here on the colony. He looked forward to introducing Kara to Lenora one day.

Noah spent the next few hours finalizing the process required to modify the HADES IV missiles. The best thing about his proposed process was that it required very little in the way of fabrication. They could feasibly get away with the supplies they had on hand. When it came to work, Kara Roberts was all business, and just because she happened to be in a relationship with Noah didn't mean she took it easy on him in the slightest. She went over his proposed process with a fine-toothed comb and refined the areas where it was lacking.

"This should be good enough to present to Colonel Douglass, but we'll likely adjust it more as we have more people analyze it," Kara said.

"Only if they want to break what I've done," Noah replied.

He'd had some engineer jockeys go through his work for other projects and try to improve on them, only to break the system entirely. If they'd just followed his process, things would've worked out fine.

"We'll see," Kara said and climbed out of her chair.

She arched her back, and Noah couldn't help it as his gaze took in the sight of her.

"Eyes up. We don't have time for that now," Kara said.

As Noah complied and turned toward the door, he felt Kara's hand squeeze his shoulder and her breath tickle his neck.

"Perhaps tonight, if you're lucky," she said in a breathy tone.

Oh god. If she kept that up, he'd have trouble walking down the hallway. Kara darted ahead of him and Noah had to run to catch up to her. One thing he definitely didn't like about the space station was that the corridors were so small.

He wondered if he could convince Kara to come back to New Earth with him, not that he'd have much time on the planet. He had a feeling that Connor would send him to help work on the battleship carrier being constructed with the last section of the *Ark*, but he should be able to make a decent argument that his next assignment be planet-side instead of in space. He missed the good old days when he was simply dispatched to different parts of the colony to set up systems and fix things. Once Connor Gates showed up, that all changed. The CDF founder and general had snatched him up and would only share him with Lenora, at least for a time. Lenora and Connor hardly spoke to each other anymore, which was a shame because he liked them both and thought they were a good pair.

They waited for the elevator that would take them up to the Command Center level. He checked the elevator's location and noted its steady descent. A cluster of CDF personnel approached and waited to get on the same elevator. Suddenly, the lighting in the area went out and the emergency lighting came on.

The station's AI chimed and then spoke: "Power consumption exceeds the usage designated for this area of Titan Space Station. Mandatory power rationing is in effect."

Noah looked at Kara and rolled his eyes.

"Apologies, folks on E deck. We're testing the failover system for the power relay between the upper and lower decks. The power should be restored momentarily," a man's voice said over the nearby speaker.

Noah glanced at Kara. "Next, we'll hear Butters screwed up the assembly again and what should be a five-minute fix turns into a five-day nightmare for the rest of us."

"You really don't like that guy," Kara said.

"I'm sure he's a great guy who works awfully hard to make stupid mistakes. Makes me wonder if he was sent out here as some kind of punishment," Noah replied.

Kara grabbed his arm and guided him toward the ladder shafts they could use to climb to the upper levels. She started climbing first and Noah followed.

"Too bad they didn't put in stairs," Noah said as he climbed.

"Wouldn't work well here," Kara answered.

"Why not? Certainly would be easier than climbing a ladder," Noah said.

"Stairs are fine when there's gravity, but when there isn't, you'd be glad for the ladder instead of the stairs, trust me," Kara replied.

"Great. Maybe they can get Butters to work on the artificial gravity fields next," Noah said.

Kara didn't reply and they continued to climb. Noah glanced down and wished he hadn't. Beneath him was a dizzying view of a ladder shaft that was eight decks long. He swung his gaze in front of him and squeezed his eyes shut for a moment. He should have waited for the elevator.

They got out of the ladder shaft a few levels above and took the elevator the rest of the way. The Command Center for Titan Space Station was a large open space with many workstations that rivaled the bridge of most ships. Titan was more of a space port than merely a station, given the size of the place. Most of it had been converted and retrofitted with missile tubes and various types of heavy cannons. There were plans for another hangar bay to be added to support a squadron or two of small attack spacecraft.

Command Center had a large observation area with a clear view into the great expanse of space. Noah glanced over and, even from this distance, still saw an ocean of stars beyond the station. He often took some time to go and take in the view from the observation decks on the station. They weren't constructed specifically for the station but had, in fact, been repurposed from the *Ark*. The view was spectacular and humbling at the same time.

They found Colonel Kasey Douglass standing amidst a throng of CDF personnel. He was speaking to them and gave Noah and Kara an acknowledging nod as they closed in. Then the colonel dismissed the people around them.

"Good, I was wondering if you two were going to make it on time. Walk with me," Colonel Douglass said.

The colonel was a tall man, trim and extremely professional. Kasey Douglass had been part of Connor's infamous Ghosts special ops team that had been shanghaied onto the *Ark* by Admiral Mitch Wilkinson. The soldiers of the Colonial Defense Force had their roots in the NA Alliance military and aspired to the same level of professionalism that people like Connor and Kasey exuded. Once given an objective or committed to an objective, they worked toward it, leveraging all the resources at their disposal. Noah had found it interesting that the old Ghost Platoon still supported Connor in his belief that an extinction-level event had happened in Earth's solar system. Noah still believed as well and didn't care for the wavering loyalty that the current political climate fostered in Sierra.

"I think we've got it, Colonel," Noah said.

"You've increased the accuracy of the HADES IV?" Colonel Douglass asked.

"Yes, with modifications to the existing missiles we were able to increase their accuracy substantially," Noah said.

"But," Kara interjected, "there's a potential impact to the range of up to twenty percent, Colonel."

Colonel Douglass's gaze darted back to Noah.

"That's right, but based on the simulation variables for an engagement, you get a fifty percent gain in accuracy over what you had before," Noah said.

Colonel Douglass pressed his lips together in thought. "How do these changes affect the field envelope for potential targets? Is the fifty percent gain persistent regardless of the distance, or does it waver the farther out we go?"

Noah took a moment to think about it. "It really depends, and I know you hate that answer, so please bear with me for a second."

They headed to Titan's Central Command cradle, which was the heart of all the space station's activities.

"It's better if I show you," Noah said and went over to a vacant terminal. He powered it on and expanded a blank canvas so he could draw freestyle. "Let's say that this circle here is us and these guys way over here are the enemy," Noah said and pointed to his rough drawing of a ship. "Right now, we launch our missiles and update their targeting systems while the missile is traveling at near relativistic speeds. If the enemy detects the incoming missile, they'll launch countermeasures and decoys that can effectively blind our missile so it will most likely miss its intended target. This is why a barrage of missiles is sent—in the hopes that at least one of them will detonate its warhead in proximity to the intended target." Noah drew multiple lines from the space station to the enemy fleet.

Colonel Douglass arched an eyebrow. "Get to the point. Tell me how you increased the accuracy."

Noah swiped his hands to the side, clearing what he'd just drawn. "What I did was modify the missiles with secondary and tertiary targeting systems that are shielded respectively. The missiles are launched in groups and are networked together so they can receive a signal from us, as well as communicate with each other. As each sensor array is blinded by countermeasures, the secondary systems are engaged and so forth for the entire group. So, if we sent twenty missiles to target a battleship cruiser, or anything really, the missiles would get new eyes on the target and adjust their trajectory accordingly and then communicate the most up-to-date information within the group; thus, giving you a higher chance of hitting your target," Noah said and finished his drawing with the decimation of the enemy fleet. He added a smiley face for good measure.

Colonel Douglass rubbed his chin in thought and then glanced at Kara. "What are your thoughts on this, Major?"

"We've run the numbers and all the simulations support it, Colonel," Kara replied.

"How long would it take to modify the HADES IV missiles for proof of concept and"—Colonel Douglass elevated his tone before Noah could quickly answer—"will this work on smaller, mid-range missiles like the HORNET IIs?"

"We could work on that," Noah answered. "My first thought for the smaller missiles is to only have a secondary targeting system and lose the tertiary. That way, even if our sensors were blinded for some reason, they could still target an enemy ship."

Colonel Douglass nodded. "Okay, you're cleared for the second phase of this project. Since you're using existing technology, the test bed can be larger than we normally would try. How long would it take you to modify a hundred HADES IVs?"

Noah's eyes widened and he glanced over at Kara.

"If I assign a few teams to it, it should only take about six hours for the group. We have a process written out. We just need to go over it with the teams; otherwise, the timeline would be much shorter," Kara said.

Colonel Douglass smiled. "Excellent work, you two. I'm really quite impressed, or I will be if it works as well as you say it will. So, I guess I'm hopeful."

Noah swallowed hard. "Thank you, sir."

"Colonel, has there been any word from New Earth regarding the additional power generator?" Kara asked.

The lines of Colonel Douglass's face became grim. "Our request was denied for a further twelve months."

Noah's mouth hung open. "Twelve months!"

"I can assure you that General Gates had quite a few more colorful metaphors to describe what he thought of that decision," Colonel Douglass said.

"I bet, knowing Connor," Noah said.

"Oh, that reminds me," Colonel Douglass said, looking at Noah. "You're being recalled back to New Earth. You'll be shipping out in a few days."

Noah felt Kara stiffen at his side. "Back to New Earth? Did they say why?"

Colonel Douglass speared him a look. "Yes, of course, every bit of the general's thinking was explained to me in detail. No! You go where you're ordered to go."

Noah straightened his shoulders. "I'm sorry, Colonel, I just thought I'd be here for another six months."

Colonel Douglass's face softened. "I certainly don't want to lose you and I doubt others are ecstatic with the decision, but that's the way it is."

Noah nodded. While he didn't exactly love life on the space station, he had reasons for wanting to stay. He glanced at Kara and her face might have been carved from stone for all the information it yielded to him.

Colonel Douglass dismissed them and they left the Command Center, hardly uttering a word to each other. Kara walked behind him and Noah resisted the urge to turn around since the corridor was hardly the appropriate place for what he wanted to say. CDF personnel were walking to and from the Command Center in a steady stream. Noah felt as if someone had punched him in the stomach. They reached a set of elevators that for once weren't crowded with people waiting for them, and he pressed the button to summon the car with only a slight shake in his hands. He risked a glance at Kara. Her honey-brown eyes were staring at a fixed point in front of her and her normally full lips formed a thin line.

Noah glared at the progress indicator that showed the elevator taking about two hundred years to reach them. Eventually the speaker above the elevator doors chimed and they opened. Noah stepped inside and he allowed his shoulders to slump. Kara stood next to him and glared out the open doors. There were a couple of CDF personnel who approached the elevator doors, but upon seeing Kara's expression they decided to wait for the next elevator.

The doors closed and Noah felt the elevator begin its slow descent.

"So, I guess I have to leave in a few days," Noah said while staring at the floor.

He glanced at Kara and saw that her shoulders were drawn up near her ears. He reached out and placed a hand on her shoulder and she winced. She turned toward him, her eyes intense.

"Shut up," Kara said and grabbed his shirt, pushing him against the wall and proceeding to kiss him until he forgot he was in an elevator.

A few minutes later they reached the engineering level and the elevator doors opened. Kara pulled away from him. "This isn't over, Barker," she said and stormed out.

Noah stepped away from the wall and saw more than a few people grinning at him from outside the elevator. He left them behind and had to run to catch up to Kara. If he'd had any doubts about whether she wanted to return to New Earth with him, they were now gone. All that stood in their way was whether she'd be allowed to come with him.

13

THE NEXT SEVEN hours were packed with so much work that Noah had hardly any time to see Kara. The engineering deck was flooded with teams tasked with learning the process to modify the HADES IV missiles. The actual modifications only occurred after the engineering teams went through and provided their input on Noah's process. A few of them made some good points, which Noah had to concede. He even got a head start with the modification proposal for the HORNET II missiles, which was going pretty much as he suspected. Due to the size and sophistication of the missile, he was limited in what he could get away with. He could add only one additional sensor array and targeting computer core for the missile. It would help, but they wouldn't see the improvements they expected to see with the HADES IV.

Noah was on his way back to the Command Center. They were going to test five HADES IV missiles for a live proof-of-concept test. The high-yield payloads were removed so they wouldn't be wasted. The purpose of the test was to prove that the modified missiles could retarget an objective after standard countermeasures and point defense protocols were used. Noah knew all eyes would be on him since he'd boldly made the claim that it was not only possible to improve the accuracy of long-range missiles but that he could have it done in a matter of a few weeks. This fed the reputation he had of being a loudmouth and a show-off, but if this worked, it would shut a few of those doubters up.

Noah sucked in a deep breath as he strode toward the Command Center doors. They seemed larger than they'd been before. He should have gotten something to drink before coming up here. Had they applied the guidance software patch before loading the missile into the tubes? He needed to check that.

Noah glanced around. He was supposed to meet Kara. She'd been supervising the teams doing the modifications, so they hadn't had much of a chance to talk. He stood right outside the Command Center doors. It was quiet here, and he knew once those doors opened there would be no turning back. He'd either prove that he was worth the reputation he'd earned over the past seven years, or he'd be a laughing stock who was amusing to those in power for a time.

The metal doors split open as someone left the Command Center, and the peaceful quietness of the corridor vanished. Noah walked inside with a determined stride and saw that the Command Center was fully staffed, with all teams being brought on deck for this test.

Noah went straight toward the cradle. Colonel Douglass was pacing with his hands clasped behind him. The colonel gave him a grim nod as he approached.

"Still confident this will work?" Colonel Douglass asked.

No.

Noah met the colonel's gaze. "Yes, sir. Get ready to be wowed."

Colonel Douglass blinked a few times. "Connor warned me you were a bit unorthodox. Alright, take that workstation right over there and let's see if you're as good as you think you are."

Noah went over to the work area nearest the colonel and collapsed into the chair, although he preferred to stand while he was working. He used his implants to authenticate to the workstation and the holoscreen came on.

"Colonel, we're go for Icarus test at your command," Noah said.

"Acknowledged," Colonel Douglass said. "Tactical, is our target in place?"

"Yes, Colonel. The broadcast beacon has been checking in for the last half hour."

Noah looked over to see who was working the tactical workstation and saw Caleb Thorne.

Noah glanced back at the colonel.

"Go ahead, Captain."

"Yes, sir," Noah said. "Tactical, I'm showing HADES IV-B missiles are in tubes one through five. Can you confirm?"

"Confirmed. Ready for launch," Thorne said.

"You're go for launch," Colonel Douglass said.

"Yes, sir, HADES away," Thorne said.

Noah watched the data output as the five missiles successfully launched from the tubes—not surprising because all they'd done was add a few more systems on top of the existing missile structure.

"Targeting package has been beamed to the missile group alpha. Target reference is zeta," Thorne said.

Noah waited for the status update to be sent back from the missiles. "Showing that all five missiles have good connections."

Confirming the successful network connections between the missiles was the first step. The real test would come after the first waves of countermeasures were launched.

"Missiles locked on target, Colonel," Thorne said.

Colonel Douglass stood next to Noah, watching the holoscreen. "Deploy countermeasure package bravo and have zeta move to coordinates beta."

Thorne confirmed the command and executed. There was nothing for them to see other than the data on screen, but Noah tried to imagine the missiles barreling toward their target and the bright flashes of countermeasures being fired to thwart their targeting systems. This, of course, was completely inaccurate as to what was truly taking place. Standard ship countermeasures were for blinding sensor arrays, with broad-stream lasers designed to sweep the area the missiles were coming in from.

"Missiles still on target," Thorne said.

"Launch second set of countermeasures and have zeta move to the next series of coordinates. Proceed on automation, initial time interval fifteen seconds," Colonel Douglass said.

Noah watched as the missiles continued to close in on zeta, but after the third set of countermeasures, they failed to update their trajectory to align with zeta's new position.

"Confirm the secondary targeting computer has been brought online," Noah said.

The missiles were moving at a fraction of the speed that was possible, which made it possible for them to manually execute the test and monitor the engagement. Otherwise, the engagement would be over in only a few seconds or less at this distance.

Noah hardly dared to breathe. This was a crucial step in the test and would happen almost simultaneously. The missile track showed a change in course toward zeta, but Noah knew the countermeasures would be fired more frequently, attempting to blind the missile systems. The duration between updates became shorter, and those in the cradle watched the mock battle unfold on the large main holoscreen.

Noah pressed his fist to his lips as he watched. The targeting updates showed the zeta darting to a predetermined set of coordinates and the missiles course-correcting as they closed in. The blips seemed to spontaneously move about the screen until the zeta ceased to report its position, followed by the confirmed detonation signal sent from the missiles.

Noah felt a wide smile spread. There were cheers from those CDF personnel working in the cradle, and Noah turned toward Colonel Douglass.

"I see the general's confidence in you is not misplaced in the slightest. Amazing thing you've done," Colonel Douglass said and looked at Lieutenant Colonel Donnelly. "I want all the HADES IV missiles modified as soon as possible."

"I'll put four teams on it, sir," Lieutenant Colonel Donnelly said.

Colonel Douglass turned back toward Noah. "I don't think you fully realize what you've accomplished."

"But the impact to range. There's got to be a way to maximize that deficit," Noah said.

"Oh I'm sure there is, and I know Major Roberts is more than up to the task. I'm sorry to see you go," Colonel Douglass said.

Noah felt a mix of pride and a growing lump in his throat. He wanted to request that Kara return to New Earth with him, but he knew that not only was it not appropriate for him to make the request but when Kara found out she'd be livid with him. Noah believed she wanted to come with him, but her sense of duty would win over and she'd remain here on the station.

Noah glanced around, trying to find Kara, but she was nowhere to be seen. More than a few people came over to congratulate him. Noah returned to Caleb Thorne, who had his hand pressed against his ear so he could hear someone else on his comlink.

Caleb glanced over at him and jutted his chin up in greeting.

"I think you owe me a beer, or three of them," Noah said.

"You're the man of the hour. In thirty minutes, I'm buying," Caleb replied and then frowned as he looked away from Noah. "Seriously. I'll put it on screen."

Caleb made a quick swiping gesture toward the holoscreen and all the data was swept away. Noah watched as a live feed from the PRADIS console came on. The console showed multiple groups of unknown ship signatures.

"Multiple contacts, Colonel," Thorne announced.

Colonel Douglass turned from the conversation he was having and glanced at the screen. A hush swept over the CDF personnel in the cradle.

"Action stations. Set Condition One throughout the station," Colonel said.

Months of training drills kicked into gear. Noah went back to his workstation and waited for orders. Klaxon alarms sounded in the Command Center and Noah knew they could be heard throughout the station. CDF personnel ran to their posts.

"Colonel, we have multiple contacts showing in delta quadrant. At this range they could be fleet groups bunched together to hide their true numbers," Thorne said.

Noah brought up a PRADIS feed on his own console. At least the unknown contacts weren't coming from gamma quadrant, which was the direction of the deep-space buoy network.

"Ops, run a diagnostic on PRADIS. I want to know if the system is malfunctioning," Colonel Douglass said. "Comms, prepare to beam open hails on my command."

Lieutenant Colonel Donnelly came over to Noah's side. Not sure what else he should do, Noah started to surrender his workstation.

"You're fine right where you are, Captain," Lieutenant Colonel Donnelly said.

"Colonel, PRADIS is functioning normally. Signals are good," Lieutenant Gabriel said from the Ops work area.

"Acknowledged. Start recording the engagement," Colonel Douglass responded. "Comms, send our standard hails to them in the open channels. See if we can get a response."

Noah swallowed hard. He kept watching PRADIS, hoping that there was some kind of glitch in the system and those ships . . . contacts . . . would disappear. Contacts didn't become ships until they were confirmed.

"Comms, what's the status of our hails?" Colonel Douglass asked.

"No response, Colonel," Lieutenant Foster said.

Colonel Douglass rubbed his chin in thought and glanced at Lieutenant Colonel Donnelly.

"Wrong quadrant," Lieutenant Colonel Donnelly said.

Colonel Douglass nodded. "Comms, authorize first-contact communications package."

Noah's mouth hung open. First-contact protocols were only used if they suspected they were encountering an alien species—something that had never occurred on Earth, but they had nonetheless established a standard protocol for the situation.

"Colonel, they're still heading right for us," Thorne said.

"Acknowledged," Colonel Douglass said. "Comms, still waiting on that first-contact communications package."

Noah watched as Lieutenant Colonel Donnelly walked over to Lieutenant Foster's workstation. The frazzled lieutenant was having trouble finding what she was looking for and Lieutenant Colonel Donnelly leaned down to help her find it.

"First-contact communications package has been sent, Colonel," Lieutenant Foster said.

"Now, we wait," Colonel Douglass said.

Noah's heart thumped in his chest. He didn't know how the colonel could be so focused. Who or what was heading for them? What did they want? Did they know they were here?

"Colonel," Lieutenant Foster said, "judging by the distance, the unknown contacts should have received our first-contact communications package."

"Acknowledged," Colonel Douglass said. "Tactical, I want firing solutions on unknown contacts ready to go."

"Colonel, do you want to give them a warning shot or an all-out assault?" Thorne asked.

"I want solutions for both, Captain. Authorize HADES IV in available tubes. I want half of those tubes loaded with the HADES IV-Bs," Colonel Douglass said.

"Yes, sir. I'll have firing solutions for you in sixty seconds," Captain Thorne said.

Noah glanced back at the colonel.

"We might get to do more than test the modified missiles," Colonel Douglass said.

Not knowing how to respond, Noah merely nodded and his mouth went dry.

"Computer, open a broadcast channel to the entire station," Colonel Douglass said. "Titan Space Station, we have unknown contacts showing up on PRADIS. We've attempted to communicate with them using open hails and I've authorized the use of first-contact protocols. If we don't get a reply, we'll fire our weapons at them. Our mandate for this station is quite clear. We're the first line of defense for the colony. If these are hostiles, they'll know we're not an easy target. If we're wrong and this is an unknown alien species coming to make first contact, the responsibility is mine. Given the status of the deep-space buoy network and the fact that there was a catastrophic event on Earth, I'm not inclined to let any species just waltz their way here unopposed. Douglass, out."

Colonel Douglass closed the broadcast channel. "Comms, send a data burst back to New Earth with our current status."

Noah glanced at the PRADIS console. The unknown contacts were now well within their long-range missiles.

Colonel Douglass looked at the main holoscreen.

"HADES IV and HADES IV-Bs loaded in all available missile tubes, Colonel," Captain Thorne said.

Noah couldn't believe this was happening. Just a short while ago they'd been running a proof-of-concept test and now they were about to open fire on an unknown enemy.

"Fire alpha salvo, and I want bravo ready to go," Colonel Douglass said.

Silence dragged throughout the normally lively Command Center for Titan Space Station.

"Confirm missile launch, Captain," Colonel Douglass said.

Noah swung his gaze toward Caleb Thorne, who was frowning at his output. "Colonel, I don't understand. I submitted the command as you ordered, but the system won't take it."

The edges of Colonel Douglass's lips pulled upward. "Stand down, Captain. Comms, open a channel on CDF-encrypted ship channels." The colonel waited a few moments for the channel to connect. "General Gates, did we pass your test?"

There were a few moments of silence.

"With flying colors, Colonel Douglass. Please extend my congratulations to the CDF personnel on Titan Space Station."

"As you wish, General."

"Did I get you worried even a little bit?"

"You had us worried there for a few minutes, and then we were going to unleash holy hell on you," Colonel Douglass said.

"I can see that. What are HADES IV-B missiles?"

"I'll tell you about it when you come aboard, General," Colonel Douglass said.

Noah blew out the breath he'd been holding.

"Understood," Connor replied. "For the record, Wil wanted me to authorize a covert ops team to take the Command Center."

Colonel Douglass chuckled. "You tell that slippery little twerp that any time he wants to receive a good ass-kicking he should go ahead and try to sneak aboard my station."

Noah heard muffled laughter on the comlink. The unknown ships on PRADIS disappeared and were replaced by CDF transponder codes along with the cargo carrier.

"Colonel, I have the cargo carrier *Chmiel* requesting to dock with the station," Lieutenant Foster said.

"Permission granted," Colonel Douglass said.

Noah felt the tension leave his shoulders. He could use a hot shower and something to eat. He wondered where Kara was since she hadn't shown up for the missile test. He thought about reaching out to her through his comlink, but she likely just wanted some space, so he resisted the urge. Noah logged off the console and stepped away from the workstation. A comlink wouldn't do for what he wanted to ask Kara anyway. Knowing Connor Gates, he wouldn't be at Titan

Station for very long before returning to New Earth, which meant that Noah had twelve hours max to find Kara and personally ask her to come back to New Earth with him. She might say no. She could be stubborn at times . . . well, most times. He smiled. He just knew that asking her to change her life for him was better handled in person than on a comlink.

Noah was about to leave the cradle when he heard Caleb Thorne call out to Colonel Douglass again.

"Colonel, I have multiple unknown contacts again, this time on the fringes of PRADIS," Thorne said.

Noah looked at the PRADIS output, which was still on the main holoscreen. This grouping was in a different quadrant than before. Noah's gaze slid down to the quadrant's designation, and his brows pulled together as he read.

"It's gamma quadrant, Colonel," Thorne said.

Noah went cold and then pressed his lips together. "Is this another drill?" He'd voiced his question aloud without thinking about it.

"Open a comlink to the *Vigilant*," Colonel Douglass ordered.

"Comlink ready, Colonel," Lieutenant Foster said.

"*Vigilant*, this is Titan Space Station. PRADIS is showing us multiple unknown contact groups at the edge of its range coming from the gamma quadrant. Can you confirm the drill is over?" Colonel Douglass asked.

Noah hardly moved while they waited for a response.

"The drill is over. Those contacts are real," Connor replied.

Colonel Douglass frowned. "Shit," he said.

"You got that right," Connor said.

A grim silence took hold of the CDF crew at the Command Center. The drill had been gut-wrenching, and it hadn't even been real. Noah felt something cold seize his stomach. The contacts were real, and they were heading right for them.

14

CONNOR STOOD on the bridge of the *Vigilant*. Several bridge officers turned in his direction, awaiting his orders. He had no more training drills planned and they all knew that whatever was being detected on PRADIS was a true anomaly.

"Tactical, can you confirm anomalous detection on PRADIS?" Connor asked.

"Negative, General. They were there and now whatever it was is gone," Lieutenant LaCroix said.

Connor pressed his lips together in a tight frown. He activated the comlink to Titan Space Station. "Titan, the anomaly has disappeared from our PRADIS. Can you confirm whether it still appears on yours?"

"Confirm, the anomaly is gone from our PRADIS. We're running a diagnostic on the PRADIS system," Kasey said.

Connor gave Vladimir LaCroix a meaningful look and the tactical officer began running diagnostics on the *Vigilant's* PRADIS system. After a few moments, he looked over at Connor and shook his head.

"Go to a private channel, Colonel," Connor said.

He used his implants to authorize a separate encrypted communications link with Titan Space Station.

"Ain't this a pickle," Kasey said.

"I don't like this at all," Connor said.

"Agreed, and I don't believe this is just some system glitch," Kasey replied.

"Suggestions?" Connor asked.

"Monitor and see if it shows up again. At that range, it could be nothing," Kasey replied.

Connor muted the line. "Nav, I want a course plotted to put us in better range of the anomaly so we can get a better PRADIS detection. Just send the plot to my terminal."

Connor walked over to his terminal and unmuted the line to Kasey. "I was going to come aboard and pay you a visit, but I think I'll stay right where I am."

"I could send a shuttle out to get you," Kasey offered.

"It's not that. We've got a bit of a situation here on the *Vigilant*," Connor said and told Kasey about Colonel Howe and Major Hayes.

"Are they the only ones who got sick?" Kasey asked.

"No, there are some others. So I need to stay because I don't want to run the risk of spreading whatever this is to the space station," Connor said and rubbed the tips of his fingers together. If he had an actual fleet of ships, he'd send a taskforce to investigate. "Let's continue to monitor and alert me if you detect anything. I'll have the crew of the *Vigilant* do the same."

"I do have an update for you that you're going to like," Kasey said.

"I'm always ready for some good news," Connor said.

Kasey told him about Noah's upgrade procedure for the HADES IV missile and how it vastly increased the missile's targeting systems.

"I told you that kid was something. That's why I snatched him up when I first got here," Connor said.

"There's no shortage of bright spots in the colony, but I'll admit Noah is brighter than most, just a bit rough around the edges on some things. Speaking of which, he didn't seem particularly keen on leaving here," Kasey replied.

Connor felt his eyebrows rise. "He wasn't excited to go to Titan either."

"I'm sure it has nothing to do with Major Kara Roberts, a lead engineer here," Kasey said.

"What is it with these guys? Someone turns their head and suddenly they won't do what we need them to do," Connor replied.

"They've been very professional. Honestly, situations like this in the CDF are becoming more frequent. It's not like the Alliance," Kasey said.

Connor shook his head. "No, that it's not," he agreed. "Don't tell me you're another one."

He heard Kasey snort.

"No way. If we live another ten years, then maybe," Kasey said.

A message from Dr. Allen appeared on Connor's terminal.

::*General, Colonel Howe's condition has taken a turn for the worse. I've had him moved to the main medical bay. Please come at your earliest convenience,*:: Dr. R. Allen said.

::*Understood. I'll be there shortly,*:: Gen. C. Gates said.

Connor closed the chat window.

"Kasey, I need to report to the medical bay. I'll follow up with you later. Also, send over the upgrade procedure you have for the HADES IV. We don't have nearly as many of them as you do, but that advantage is too good to pass up," Connor said.

"Yes, sir, I'll see to it that a data burst gets sent to the *Vigilant* in a few minutes. One more thing, though. The odds of a commanding officer and his XO getting sick at the same time are minuscule," Kasey said.

Connor rubbed his eyes. "Yeah, I know. So far nothing has turned up."

He closed the comlink and rose from his seat. "Colonel, you have the con.

Titan Space Station is going to be sending an upgrade procedure for the HADES IV missiles. I want them immediately sent down to Engineering to be worked on as their top priority."

"Yes, General," Reisman said.

"If you need me, I'll be down at the main medical bay with Dr. Allen," Connor said.

Reisman went to the command chair. "I'll inform you if that anomaly returns."

Connor left the bridge. Just outside, he saw Sean speaking with a few members of his CDF Squad. Upon seeing Connor they stopped what they were doing and saluted him.

Connor looked at Sean. "Walk with me."

Sean walked next to Connor while the rest of his squad followed them at a distance.

"What did you find?" Connor asked.

"We've looked into all the change logs since we left New Earth. I even cross-referenced them with the lead officers responsible for the specific ship systems. Everything checks out. The security team that checked all the equipment in the mess hall didn't find any signs of tampering," Sean said.

"Did you check?" Connor asked.

Sean frowned. "No, sir, I didn't. There's nothing suspicious going on that I could find. I can make a sweep of the mess hall now if you'd like me to, but it's been put back into operation."

Connor shook his head. "That won't be necessary."

"You still believe there's foul play involved?" Sean asked.

Connor regarded the young man for a moment. He was extremely intelligent in most respects and still young enough to be naive in others. "You used to be a sniper. A hunter. If you had a target you needed to hit and you couldn't use your firearm, how would you do it?"

Sean's gaze narrowed and he glanced around to be sure they weren't being overheard by anyone. "You think this was an assassination attempt?"

"I can't afford to rule anything out at this point," Connor said.

Sean pressed his lips together and then blew out a breath, shaking his head. "I can't imagine anyone in the colony, let alone the CDF, doing something like this."

"I'm heading to see Dr. Allen and I want you to come with me," Connor said.

"Of course. What do you need me to do?" Sean asked.

"Keep a lookout for anything that doesn't seem right," Connor replied.

"You can count on me, sir," Sean said.

They reached the *Vigilant's* main medical bay a few minutes later. The door opened and Connor walked through. The medical bay was quiet and not at all like the infirmary he and Reisman had been to a few days ago.

Dr. Allen walked over to them. "Thank you for coming so quickly, General."

"What's Ian's status?" Connor asked.

Dr. Allen's expression became grim. "His organs are shutting down."

"What!" Connor exclaimed. "I thought this was just an allergic reaction."

Dr. Allen nodded. "That's what I thought too. Those were his symptoms. I had him brought here so I could get him into a medical capsule."

Dr. Allen led them over to the quarantined area of the medical bay. "We'll need to go into decontamination one at a time and then I'll show you."

One by one they each went through the decontamination and entered the chamber where the *Vigilant's* commanding officer and his executive officer clung to life. Connor approached the medical capsule and looked at Colonel Ian Howe. He was deathly pale, and if not for the steady rise and fall of his chest because of the breathing tube, Connor would have believed the man was already dead.

Connor glanced over at Nathan Hayes. The *Vigilant's* XO rested in a bed, and though he was also intubated, he didn't look anywhere near as sick as Howe.

Dr. Allen went over to the control panel for the medical capsule.

"I need to know what happened, doctor," Connor said.

Dr. Allen looked up from the control console. "This isn't a contagion. His organs are shutting down. I looked up his symptoms in the medical database on the ship and the artificial intelligence keeps coming up with the same answer."

Connor glanced at Howe again and then looked back at Dr. Allen.

"He's suffering from acute radiation poisoning," Dr. Allen said.

Connor's brows pulled together tightly. "Radiation poisoning? There were no leaks reported. How could he be suffering from that?"

"I know. I checked with Engineering to see if there were any leaks or anything else that could have done this. There was nothing," Dr. Allen said.

"Then how could he be dying of radiation poisoning?" Sean asked.

Dr. Allen swallowed hard and looked worried. "I found lethal levels of Polonium-210. I haven't filed the report yet because I thought you'd want to hear this first, but the colonel was poisoned."

"Hold on a minute," Connor said. "We were in the aft gunnery area of the ship and Ian was at the munitions station. There could have been a containment leak there but on a small enough scale that it wasn't detected by onboard systems."

Dr. Allen shook his head. "I researched Polonium-210's usage and we haven't used it in any great capacity in over a hundred and fifty years."

Connor shook his head. "This is rich. You're telling me that Ian is dying of radiation sickness from some kind of element we don't even use anymore. How the hell did he get exposed to it then?"

"He was in the mess hall, so he must have ingested it somehow," Dr. Allen said.

Connor sighed heavily. "Still doesn't explain where it came from," he said, rubbing his chin and then glancing over at Hayes. "Was he exposed?"

"Yes, but he'll make a full recovery. His exposure must have been much less than Colonel Howe's," Dr. Allen said.

"And the rest of the people at the infirmary?" Connor asked.

"Mixed. Some had allergic reactions and others had various other symptoms," Dr. Allen said.

"I need them tested to see if they were exposed, too," Connor said and looked at Sean. "I want you and your team to go to the munitions center and look for trace detections of any radioactive material. If anyone asks, you're doing a spot inspection at my request."

"Yes, sir," Sean said and left.

Connor looked at Dr. Allen. "You said Major Hayes is going to make a full recovery. When is he going to wake up?"

"It won't be for a few more hours. The treatment is helping his cells rebuild and it's working so far," Dr. Allen said.

"Okay, I want to be informed the moment he's awake," Connor said.

"Understood, General," Dr. Allen said.

"I'm going to assign a security detail to the medical bay," Connor said and looked over at Ian Howe inside the medical capsule. "Can you wake him up? There might be something he could tell us."

"I could, but I won't do that to him," Dr. Allen said.

"Why not?" Connor asked in a hard tone.

"If I were to wake him up, he'd be in so much pain that I doubt he'd be coherent. I wouldn't put anyone in that kind of pain. The only thing we can do now is make him as comfortable as possible," Dr. Allen said.

"You're wrong, Doctor. That's not the only thing we can do for him," Connor said and walked toward the door. "We can find the son of a bitch who did this. I'll have that security detail here soon and I want you to file your report under DSP protocol."

Dr. Allen frowned. "I'm not familiar with DSP protocol."

"Enter it in the type field for your report and the interface will handle all the rest. Basically it'll seal the records so only you and I can review the contents," Connor replied.

"What if something happens to either of us?" Dr. Allen asked.

"I'll authorize a few others, including Captain Quinn, who you just met, and Colonel Reisman. That's it. In the event that we all die—unlikely, I know—but in that event, only senior bridge officers or COMCENT can open those records. You're part of this investigation now. If you think of anything else, I want you to contact either myself, Captain Quinn, or Colonel Reisman."

"Understood, General," Dr. Allen said.

Connor paused at the door. "One more thing. Keep them in here. I don't want the guilty parties to know we're onto them yet."

Dr. Allen bobbed his head once.

Connor left the medical bay and stormed down the corridor. There was a potentially hostile force on the edge of PRADIS and now a murder on his hands. One of these things he was better prepared to face and the other just made him sick. Why would anyone want to murder Ian Howe? His mind refused to come up with any reason that made sense. His brows pushed forward and Connor clenched his teeth. Attempting to kill the leader of the CDF, however...That would make sense. There were no murders at the colony and now there was an assassination attempt? Nothing was ever easy.

A FEW HOURS later Connor was still on the bridge. The bridge crew had changed shifts and he was reviewing the latest progress reports on his terminal at the command chair when he noticed someone walking toward him. The man was tall and thickly muscled. He came to a stop near Connor and snapped a salute.

"May I have a word with you in private, General?" the man asked, and Connor looked up to meet intense dark eyes.

Connor glanced at the PRADIS status screen, which was still empty. Whatever the anomaly had been, it hadn't returned.

"And you are?" Connor asked.

"Captain Toro, Head of Security, sir."

Connor knew that Sean was making steady progress with his investigation, so Connor should have expected a visit like this. He stood up. "LaCroix, you have the con."

"Yes, sir," Lieutenant LaCroix responded.

"Right this way, Captain," Connor said.

They left the bridge and entered the nearby ready room. It was sparsely furnished with a curved desk that had wooden accents along the edges. A wallscreen activated when he walked in and showed a view of the stars. Next to the desk was a cylindrical aquarium with an impressive coral reef growing through the middle. Several species of fish swam in the churning water. The interior lights of the aquarium sent small bands of reflected light onto the walls. It was soothing. Connor hadn't realized that Colonel Howe had created such a space on his ship and he was left to wonder how much he really knew about the people who were serving under him.

He went over to the cubby and selected the option for black coffee. He asked Captain Toro if he wanted some, but the captain refused.

Connor sat down on the cushioned chair behind the desk and gestured for Captain Toro to have a seat on either of the padded chairs on the other side of the desk.

The captain took a moment to appreciate the aquarium and then swung his gaze toward Connor.

"General, I'd like to know if I'm suspected of a crime," Captain Toro said.

"No, you're not, Captain," Connor answered.

"Then why is there an investigation being conducted without my knowledge? I'm the head of security on this ship and those issues should have been raised through my department, sir," Captain Toro said.

"Why don't you tell me what you know, Captain," Connor said.

"Just that Captain Quinn is performing spot inspections near the munitions centers, which may fool the average officer but not me. I'd wager a guess that he's looking for something dangerous, something radioactive. The question is why," Captain Toro said.

Connor nodded. "We have reason to suspect that Colonel Howe was poisoned."

Captain Toro's eyes widened and he frowned.

"Dr. Allen informed me that Howe was exposed to lethal levels of a radioactive substance," Connor said.

Captain Toro's brows furrowed and his lips twisted into a partial sneer. "This doesn't make any sense. You said lethal levels. Are you saying Ian is going to die?"

"Yes," Connor confirmed.

Captain Toro looked away.

"How well do you know Colonel Howe?" Connor asked.

"He's godfather to my daughter, sir."

Connor drew in a deep breath.

"Put me to work, sir. Tell me what you know and I can find out who did this," Captain Toro said.

Connor pressed his lips together. "I'm not sure that's such a good idea."

"Not good enough. I can't sit by while this is happening. The safety of the *Vigilant's* crew is my responsibility, so if you don't suspect me, I should be involved in this investigation. There were more than a few people sick and we thought there was some kind of new virus spreading, but when no one else got sick I decided to do some checking of my own," Captain Toro said.

"Captain Quinn is already investigating this," Connor said.

"Yes, but he doesn't know this ship like I do," Captain Toro said.

Connor bridged his fingers in front of his chest.

"Please, sir."

"Alright, I'll inform Captain Quinn that you're now part of this investigation, but I want to make this perfectly clear to you. Quinn is on point and you will take your direction from him. The sophistication and nature of this crime means there are a limited number of people with the skills capable of pulling it off," Connor said. He glanced at his coffee, trying to decide if he still wanted it.

"Thank you, sir. I'll report to Captain Quinn immediately and offer my services," Captain Toro said.

Connor rose from his seat and came around the desk. "We'll find who did this, I promise," he said.

Captain Toro came to his feet as well. A chime came from the speaker near the door.

"General, I have Colonel Douglass on a comlink to speak with you. Shall I patch it to your ready room, sir?" Sergeant Boers asked.

"No, I'm returning to the bridge," Connor said and headed for the door.

"Sir," Captain Toro said.

Connor turned back toward him.

"Your coffee," Captain Toro said and handed him the mug.

Connor took it and thanked him. Toro headed away from the bridge. The big man's foot stomps could be heard as he left.

Connor entered the bridge and glanced down at the coffee, deciding he didn't want it after all. The corporal at the door glanced at him.

"Sir, I can take care of that for you if you want," the corporal said.

"Thanks," Connor said and handed him the mug.

Connor headed toward the command chair and sat down. "Comms, put Colonel Douglass on screen."

The main holoscreen flickered as the comlink was connected and Kasey Douglass's bearded face came on.

"After multiple diagnostics on our PRADIS and connected systems, my engineers assure me that the systems are functioning properly," Kasey said.

Connor had expected as much. "Same here. I don't like leaving this to chance. That's why I'm ordering the *Vigilant*, along with the *Banshee* and the *Wyatt*, to make a scouting run to see if we can find this anomaly if we extend PRADIS's range."

Kasey nodded. "I suspected you would, which is why I must advise against it, sir."

"Noted, Colonel," Connor replied.

"Sir, I'm not disputing the need to investigate. What I'm protesting is whether you should be the one doing the investigating," Kasey said.

Connor considered what Kasey said and he was right. This was something he *should* delegate. "Ordinarily you'd be correct, but with the possibility of an unknown virus on this ship, I can't risk the exposure to Titan," he lied.

Kasey narrowed his gaze. Connor knew there was no argument Kasey could make that wouldn't bring more suspicion to what was really happening on the *Vigilant*.

"Understood, sir. We'll relay your preliminary reports back to New Earth," Kasey said as a soft reminder that Connor needed to keep the government of the colony informed.

"Thank you. We'll get underway and I'll be in touch. In the meantime, keep a ready status," Connor said.

"Yes, General," Kasey replied.

Connor severed the comlink. "Nav, plot us a course into gamma quadrant. Let's see if anything's lurking in the void that we should know about."

15

CONNOR SAT in the ready room just off from the bridge. It was one of the few places he could be alone to get his head straight. It had been thirty-six hours since they'd left Titan Space Station behind. There were regular check-ins with Major Cross of the *Banshee* and acting commander, Captain Mattison, of the *Wyatt*. Connor had considered leaving the *Wyatt* at the space station, but if there was trouble brewing out beyond the fringes of known space, he needed firepower. This was a scouting mission, but if they found something, it could just as easily become a first-strike mission.

The chime sounded at his door.

"Come in," Connor said.

The door opened and Major Hayes hovered in the doorway. He was back in CDF-standard blues with the golden sunburst displaying proudly on his shoulder.

"Nathan, come inside," Connor said, rising from his seat. "I was glad to hear about your recovery."

Major Hayes stepped inside. He still looked a bit pale, like he could use several healthy meals and more sleep.

"Sir, I'm no good to you lying in bed," Major Hayes said.

Connor glanced at the man's hands. They were sometimes fidgety and then sometimes clenched.

"You've been through a lot," Connor said.

"I got to walk away. I'm ready to resume my duties as XO, sir," Major Hayes said.

"Alright, I'll bring you up to speed, but there's something I need to know first," Connor said.

"I told Dr. Allen everything I could remember. Colonel Howe and I were just finishing up our meal and he collapsed to the floor," Major Hayes said.

"I'm aware of that, but what I want to know is if you know of anyone who has voiced an opinion that makes you question whether they should be on this ship," Connor said.

Major Hayes looked away, taking a second to think about it. "Nothing comes to mind. Some people become frustrated from time to time, but there've been no red flags that indicate anyone is unfit for duty, sir."

Connor nodded. "I keep hearing the same thing from other officers, but I wanted to confirm with you."

"The *Vigilant* has a good crew. How's the investigation going?" Major Hayes asked.

"Ongoing, I'm afraid. We've started questioning crewmen about their whereabouts on that day and we've been scanning the interior of the ship for trace amounts of radioactive material," Connor said.

"And this scouting mission? Is there anything I need to know about that, sir?"

Connor told Major Hayes about the anomaly that had been detected by the PRADIS system on Titan Space Station and how they'd confirmed it on their own system, but the anomaly hadn't shown up again.

"So that's why we're traveling at such a slow speed," Major Hayes said.

"I just want to take a look," Connor replied.

"And when will we reach the end of the envelope for this scouting mission?"

"In eight hours. At that time, if nothing's been detected, we'll turn around and head back to Titan Space Station," Connor said.

Major Hayes traced the stubble of his mustache and beard. "I saw in the logs that you've ordered engineering crews to modify the HADES IV missiles."

"Yes, but we can only modify twenty percent of our arsenal. Engineer Hatly came up with an alternative. It's not as good as the actual upgrades, but it helps," Connor said.

He brought up a holoscreen and opened a high-level schematic of the HADES IV. "See, the proposed upgrades add systems to the existing missiles. What we're doing with the missiles we can't upgrade is updating the command-and-control software so it will accept updates to targeting from the HADES IV-B missiles," Connor said.

Major Hayes read the information on screen. "This is really something. You're making the unmodified HADES IVs slaves to the HADES IV-Bs. Too bad we can't increase the range of PRADIS. Don't you think we should have detected something by now?"

"I expected us to detect something several hours away from Titan, but that wasn't the case," Connor said and rubbed his eyes. He didn't need much sleep but he couldn't remember the last time he'd had some rack time.

"So in eight hours we turn around and go back home," Major Hayes said.

"That's correct. We know that PRADIS is less accurate at extreme distances," Connor said.

"I understand now, sir."

Connor powered off the holoscreen and stood up. "I'm due to relieve Colonel Reisman for the next watch."

Major Hayes came to his feet. "Do you mind if I take this watch, sir?"

Connor glanced at the major for a moment. "Are you sure you're feeling up to it?"

"Yes, sir."

"Alright, you take this shift. I'll be along in a few hours to take over," Connor said.

"Understood, sir," Major Hayes said and headed for the bridge.

Connor stood up and thought about going to his quarters. "Dim the lights," he said.

He sat on the long couch and then lay down. After setting an alarm to wake him in two hours' time, Connor closed his eyes and went to sleep.

THE ALARM gently pulled Connor from a deep sleep, but years of training kicked in and he was fully awake in moments. He swung his legs off the couch and stood up, walked to the head, and waved his hand in front of the faucet to activate it. He splashed cool water on his face and rinsed his mouth out.

Connor used his implants to reconnect to the *Vigilant's* computer systems and narrowed his gaze at the ship's status. He quickly dried his hands and face and left the ready room. He strode onto the bridge and saw Major Hayes speaking with Lieutenant LaCroix.

"Sir, I'm not following. PRADIS should already be able to detect what you're asking me to do," Lieutenant LaCroix said.

Major Hayes glanced over at Connor for a moment and then looked back at LaCroix. "Just get it ready, Lieutenant," Major Hayes said.

"Yes, sir," LaCroix said and went back to the tactical workstation.

Connor approached the command area. "Why are we stopping?"

"Playing a hunch. If you'll allow it, I can explain," Major Hayes said.

Connor's brows pulled together angrily. He had very little patience for his orders being countermanded. "This had better be some hunch," Connor warned.

The door to the bridge opened and Wil Reisman raced in.

"General," Colonel Reisman said, "Major Hayes checked with me before making any changes."

Connor smoothed his features and nodded at Major Hayes. "Alright, give it to me straight."

"Prior to this mission, Colonel Howe and I were working on fine-tuning the PRADIS detection system. We were actually talking about it when . . . we got sick. This anomaly disappeared once we detected it on our PRADIS systems. We know that the accuracy of PRADIS is significantly reduced when hitting the fringes of its range. It got me thinking: what if the anomaly we first detected is able to cloak itself somehow and become invisible to PRADIS?" Major Hayes said.

"You can't cloak a fleet of ships. The NA Alliance military spent stupendous amounts of resources trying to achieve what you're saying and failed to do so," Connor replied.

"You're right, we can't, but perhaps someone else could," Major Hayes said.

Connor felt his stomach clench at the thought. "You've got my attention, Major."

Major Hayes nodded, clearly relieved that Connor was going to hear him out. "You had us moving at a slower speed already as a precautionary measure. What I ordered our taskforce to do was to slow us down even further so we're now moving at a fraction of our former speed. You see, our forward motion can interfere with PRADIS detections."

"This is the first I'm hearing of this," Connor said.

Colonel Reisman raised his hands in front of his chest. "Give him a chance to explain."

Connor nodded for Hayes to continue.

"PRADIS looks for a hard return in order to register a contact; then our cyber warfare suite attempts to catalog the detection with known vessels. This didn't work before and we didn't get enough of a signature to be of any use. So, instead of using PRADIS to scan for active contacts, I have LaCroix updating the parameters to look for evidence of ship wakes instead," Major Hayes said.

Connor frowned as he thought about it. "So you think that if there *is* a fleet of enemy ships out there that can avoid contact with PRADIS, they'll be unable to mask the effects of their ships flying through space?"

"Precisely," Major Hayes said.

Connor glanced at Reisman, who gave him an I-told-you-so look. "Alright, let's see what we've got."

He wasn't going to start congratulating anyone just yet, but Connor had to admit that it seemed like a clever tactic.

"Tactical, what's the status of PRADIS?" Major Hayes asked.

"The PRADIS system has accepted the updated parameters, sir," LaCroix answered.

"Put the output on the main wallscreen," Major Hayes said.

The PRADIS output showed a three-dimensional field out away from the *Vigilant*. Nothing showed up in the scanning field. Connor and the rest of the bridge crew watched for a few minutes. He glanced at Reisman and arched an eyebrow, but then there was an audible chime. Connor's gaze snapped toward the main holoscreen, which showed the first contact. Another contact quickly followed, until the chimes for additional contacts detected became almost one continuous stream. Each chime was like a shot to the gut, describing what could only be the wake of a massive fleet coming right toward them.

The PRADIS output continued to show the wake fields of starship engines. Connor darted his gaze to the data output on the PRADIS system.

"They're not going very fast," Colonel Reisman said.

Connor went to the command chair. "They don't need to if they think we can't see them," he said and brought up the ship command interface. "Action stations, action stations. Set Condition One throughout the ship. This is not a drill."

Connor heard Sergeant Boers repeat the ship alert as she transmitted to the battle group.

"Tactical, I want a firing solution for that group nearest us and the main group," Connor said.

"Sir, it's going to take a few minutes because PRADIS is just finding the engine wakes and not the actual ships themselves," Lieutenant LaCroix said.

"Understood, Lieutenant. I need those solutions as soon as you have them. Major Hayes, please double-check the firing solutions once they're ready," Connor said.

"General, may I have a word?" Colonel Reisman asked.

Connor gestured for him to come closer. "Comms, I need our targeting data sent to both the *Banshee* and the *Wyatt*."

"Yes, sir," Sergeant Boers said.

Reisman leaned in and spoke softly. "Sir, should we spend more time learning about the potential hostiles?"

Connor frowned. "Potential hostiles," he repeated. "The fact that they're trying to sneak up on us pretty much states their intent."

"Understood, sir, but we're not exactly sure what we're dealing with. I'm just trying to say that we should take a few moments and see if we can learn more about them," Colonel Reisman said.

Connor pursed his lips in thought. "We have an opportunity here. If we start sending probes to take a closer look, we'll give away the fact that we know their positions. I'd much rather send a stronger message."

Connor watched as his long-time friend tried to come up with another argument for delaying the inevitable.

"I know what you're saying, Wil, but the criteria for engagement have been met. Hails have already been sent from Titan Space Station, and if this force intended to answer, they would have done so by now," Connor said.

Reisman swallowed hard. "Yes, General."

"Tactical, I need that firing solution," Connor said.

Connor watched as Major Hayes and Lieutenant LaCroix worked. After a few moments Major Hayes looked over at Connor. "We have a solution, sir, but it's not pretty."

"Let's have it," Connor said.

"We send the first wave of HORNETs into the area we expect the enemy ships are and hold the HADES IVs in reserve until we can confirm targeting," Major Hayes said.

Connor brought up LaCroix's console on his own screen. "Negative, Major, lead with the HORNETs, then hit them immediately after with the HADES IVs. No delay. Relay the firing solution to the rest of the battle group."

"Yes, sir," Major Hayes said.

Less than a minute later, he heard, "Weapons systems ready, sir."

"Fire," Connor said.

The Panther-class heavy cruisers were similar in construction to most of the other warships humans fielded. The hull was roughly cigar shaped, though flattened to provide a narrower side profile and a wider top and bottom upon which to mount the super structure and the mag-cannon turrets. Between the turrets were the missile tubes, which at this moment were launching the first salvo of HORNETs. The mid-range missiles were being used to paint the targets.

Connor watched the countdown for the HADES IVs.

"Targeting profile uploaded to the HADES IVs to track the HORNETs, sir," Lieutenant LaCroix said.

"Very well," Connor said.

The timer chewed down to zero and then the HADES IV missiles launched. Connor looked at the statuses for the two destroyers. They were ready to fire but were waiting.

"Helm, plot a course back to Titan Space Station," Connor said and looked back at the plot as the missiles fully engaged their engines. Missile systems were delayed from main engine burst to make it harder for the enemy to determine where they'd been fired from.

"Comms, send a data burst back to Titan Space Station with our current status," Connor said.

"Yes, sir, sending now," Sergeant Boers said.

Connor looked at Reisman. "Now, we wait."

"You don't want the *Banshee* and the *Wyatt* to fire their missiles?" Colonel Reisman asked.

Connor shook his head. "No, I want them to fire theirs on the second wave after the enemy has given away their position."

Connor noted the time after the missiles began their initial burn. "Ops, begin visual scans of the enemy force with the high-power optics."

"Sir, I'm not able to get confirmation that Titan Space Station has received our data burst," Sergeant Boers said.

Connor peered at the main screen. "Request current status of the *Banshee* and the *Wyatt*."

Connor watched as Sergeant Boers did as he asked. She looked back at him helplessly.

"Sir, it's the same thing. We're sending the data, but we're unable to get confirmation."

Connor glanced at Reisman and saw the same grim acknowledgment on his face that he was feeling.

"Sir, the *Banshee* has just gone offline—make that the *Wyatt,* too. Both destroyers are no longer reporting," Sergeant Boers said with rising panic in her voice.

"We're being jammed," Connor said.

Reisman's eyes widened.

"Helm, all ahead one half. Go evasive," Connor said.

"Confirmed, all ahead one half, evasive," Sergeant Edwards said.

"Contact!" Lieutenant LaCroix said.

Connor's eyes darted to the main screen. For an instant, the screen showed a looming, irregularly shaped mass that Connor thought could be an asteroid or other natural formation.

"Sir, target is maneuvering," Lieutenant LaCroix reported.

"Engage point defense systems. Target that ship," Connor ordered.

"Sir, the target is appearing on PRADIS now," Lieutenant LaCroix said.

"They must have realized we can see them. What's the status of our missiles?" Connor asked.

"No confirmed status sent back to us," Ops reported.

"Sergeant Boers, prepare a comms drone for quick launch back to Titan Space Station. We need to inform COMCENT that we've encountered a new enemy," Connor said.

"Yes, sir," the normally unflappable Sela Boers said in a trembling voice. "Drone is ready."

"Launch it. Now!" Connor said.

The drone launch registered on the main screen and then the alert immediately minimized.

"Sir, I have sensors back," LaCroix said.

"Reload the tubes and target that ship," Connor said.

"Sir, I have confirmed detonation of missiles," Ops reported.

"Put it on screen," Connor said.

The main screen showed multiple detonations along the front of the main enemy forces. They must have moved beyond the enemy ship's jamming signal or they wouldn't be seeing anything. The PRADIS contact was intermittent, so it was clear they were trying to get another lock on them.

More missiles appeared on the main screen, fired from the *Banshee* and the *Wyatt*. Connor watched the seemingly pathetically slow tracks creep across the main display as the computer opened another window to show the *Vigilant* in relation to the enemy ships.

"Ops, do we have another visual?" Connor asked.

"Negative, sir. With the detonation of our missiles, it's going to take some time to filter it out," Ops replied.

"Multiple targets are on the move. They're tracking toward us," LaCroix said.

"They're moving pretty fast. Are the missiles updating their targeting profile?"

"Yes, sir," Tactical reported. "Tubes one through eight are reloaded."

"Target the ship tracking us," Connor said.

"Missiles away, sir," LaCroix said.

The enemy ship didn't try and dodge or intercept the missiles bearing down on it. The hardened nose cones of the HADES IVs slammed into the organic-looking hull of the target. The engines would fire one more time to maximize penetration before detonating the warhead. A bright flash swamped the main screen as multiple missiles bombarded the target. Once the flash cleared, the *Vigilant's* optical sensors showed the enemy ship's hull peeled back where the missiles had hit it.

"Sir, I'm getting intermittent transmissions from the *Wyatt*," Sergeant Boers said with a hand held to her earpiece and her brows pulled together in concentration. "It's messy, sir. Something about . . . repelling boarders."

Connor's gaze darted to Reisman. "That's why they haven't returned fire yet."

"Maybe, or they could just be seeing what we throw at them," Colonel Reisman said.

"Sir, the *Wyatt* is offline," Ops reported.

"Could they be jamming us again?" Colonel Reisman asked.

"Negative, sir. The signal is clear. One moment they were there and now only the enemy ship is there," Tactical said.

"Helm, can you plot an intercept course?" Connor asked.

"Negative, sir, not with that enemy behemoth bearing down on us," Edwards replied.

Connor clenched his teeth. "What about the *Banshee*? Do we have their location?"

While he suspected the answer wouldn't be what he wanted to hear, he needed to ask anyway.

"Negative, sir. The last transmission from them was confirmation that they fired their weapons," Tactical said.

"Helm, push our nose to port by six degrees and punch it," Connor said. "All ahead full."

"Ahead full. Yes, sir," the helmsman reported.

The ship began to shake as the engines came to full power and the *Vigilant* surged toward their target.

"Sir, our window of engagement just narrowed with the velocity change," Tactical warned.

"Then don't miss," Connor said. "Nav, once we pass the target I need a course best speed to Titan Space Station."

"We're running away?" Reisman asked.

"We're collecting invaluable data," Connor replied. "Slugging it out with a fleet we hardly know won't help anyone. We make this pass and see what damage we can deliver."

"If we survive the pass," Reisman said.

"Right, if we survive," Connor agreed.

The bridge crew of the *Vigilant* watched the main holoscreen tensely as the nearest ship resolved in greater detail. The high-resolution optics showed the asymmetrical hull, the profile of which tugged at the back of Connor's memory, but he couldn't make sense of it.

"Point defense engaged. Firing proton beams!" Lieutenant LaCroix called out, startling anyone who hadn't been watching the range countdown. Several nonessential systems dropped out so the power draw for the proton beams could be met. Connor watched as the projectors heated up under the continuous fire, but he saw parts of the damaged enemy hull get sloughed away by the powerful beams.

"We've got a thermal buildup along the target's starboard side," Lieutenant LaCroix said.

"Let's get a—" Connor's command was cut off as a brilliant flash lanced out from the enemy ship and slammed into the *Vigilant* full on the nose of the ship. The main display winked out and all other sensor feeds were cut in an instant. Klaxon alarms were blaring on the bridge and the terminals that were still working were scrolling a seemingly endless list of warnings.

"Some sort of high energy thermal blast. Most of the sensors are out!" Colonel Reisman said.

"Switch to backups," Connor said and tried to access his own terminal, but it was down. "Get damage control teams to the affected areas and get me a casualty report."

Secondary sensor systems came online as the armored hatches opened along the forward edge of the *Vigilant's* hull. Soon the main holodisplay popped back up. The enemy ship was venting a substance into space but didn't show any signs of slowing down.

"Helm, once we're on course, cut the engines. Tactical, go to passive scans," Connor said.

Reisman frowned at him. "We're not leaving?"

Connor shook his head. "No. We still have more we can do here."

"Sir, we can't make a stand against so many. We don't have the firepower for that. You've seen how many there are," Reisman said.

"I know that, Colonel!" Connor shouted and clenched his teeth for a moment. "Listen up, and this goes for the rest of the crew. Nothing we're about to do is going to follow the established procedures for facing an enemy force. Those procedures would have us either tuck tail and run or stand our ground and die, neither of which appeals to me. We still have more damage we can do to the enemy so there'll be that many fewer Titan Space Station has to face. We know they're out there. The fact that they now show up on PRADIS means Titan Space Station knows as well. We're not going anywhere. The *Banshee* is still out there and likely went silent to avoid enemy detection."

Reisman arched a brow and nodded. "The *Wyatt's* last transmission had to do with repelling boarders. Whoever they are might be seeking to capture us rather than destroy us."

"Let's work the problem. Tactical, bring up the last known position of enemy ships," Connor said.

The holoscreen flicked on and showed a populated tactical readout of the engagement.

"There it is. This is what we couldn't see before. They sent out a smaller group for this engagement," Connor said.

Major Hayes stood near the tactical workstation. "Why are we able to see this now, sir?"

"The cyber warfare AI is still going through the captured tactical data and is now filling in some of the gaps we couldn't see before," Connor said.

"Then there's still more of the enemy in the area and we can't use active scans or we'll give away our position," Reisman said.

Connor nodded. "Major Hayes, you are to be commended. If it hadn't been for your actions, we wouldn't have known the enemy fleet was there until it was much too late."

Major Hayes looked uncomfortable for a moment. "Thank you, sir."

Connor looked over at Reisman, who was working on something on his own terminal. "We hit their main fleet," Reisman said.

"How can you tell?" Major Hayes asked.

"We can't track where the HADES IVs detonated. We can only see the aftermath from the fission warheads. It's likely their main fleet is as blinded as we are right now," Reisman said.

Major Hayes glanced at Connor. "Who are they?"

Connor noticed that most of the crew on the bridge craned their necks in his direction. They knew who it was but needed to hear it from him. They needed their commanding officer to confirm it for them.

"You all know who they are. These are the forces we were warned about over seven years ago. A last warning from Earth," Connor said.

"But these aren't Earth ships, and their firepower is beyond anything I've ever seen before," Major Hayes said.

Connor glanced around at all the CDF crew on the bridge. Most looked pale, as if they were walking over their own graves. "The question of whether a malevolent attack force is coming to New Earth has been answered. Humanity's enemy is right out there. They've traveled across the void to get here, to get to you and your families. This is why we formed the Colonial Defense Force. We don't cave in to fear. Only the best of us came onto the *Ark* all those years ago.

"Now, there are a lot of unanswered questions and we have our work cut out for us getting those answers. Accept that there is nowhere we can run or hide. They wouldn't have come as they did if they sought an alliance with us. We need to settle down and focus on our jobs. We have a lot of data to go through and we need to keep a sharp eye out because they're hunting for us. They have the advantage both in numbers and in knowing the capabilities of our ships. What they haven't counted on is us, people like Major Hayes, who had the insight to configure PRADIS to scan for ship wakes through space. This is where we pull together and face our enemy."

Determination burned from the eyes of the bridge crew and they went back to their assigned tasks with renewed vigor. Connor gestured for Reisman and Hayes to come closer so they could speak.

Reisman gave him a hungry look. "It's been a long time since we've been in the thick of it. What's our next move?"

Major Hayes frowned. "I sometimes forget that you two served together before becoming part of the colony."

Connor felt the edges of his lips curve just a tad. "You're doing fine. I want you on damage assessment. You've spent more time on this ship than either Wil or me. I need to know what systems were damaged and what we have in terms of weapons capability."

"Sir, I have to admit . . . when I heard you order us to make a head-on pass, I froze up," Major Hayes said.

"So did I, for a moment," Connor said. "We do the best we can with the information we have."

"You'll get used to it, Major. I've learned to trust the general's instincts over the years." Reisman shrugged.

"We haven't used the mag-cannons yet. I could have the engineering team check the accelerator rails in each gun and recalibrate the turret actuators to be sure they're fully operational," Major Hayes said.

Connor shared a look with Reisman. "Good thinking. Feel free to share any more gems like that."

"I'll get to it," Major Hayes said and left the bridge.

Connor turned toward the main holoscreen. Nothing on the passive scans indicated a change in any of the known enemy contacts.

"This isn't going to last long," Reisman said.

"I know. We need to come up with a plan now that we have more of an idea of what we're dealing with," Connor said and brought up the first visual they had of the enemy ship. The image had been refined and compiled against the closer scans from their engagement.

"That hull looks like it's carved out of an asteroid," Reisman said.

Connor rubbed his chin and squinted. "There's something familiar about its shape. Computer, can you put a spectral analysis on the ship's interior?"

An error message appeared on the screen, indicating insufficient data.

"Not like an asteroid," Reisman said and zoomed in on a smooth section that curved as if it were blanketed over something else. "That kind of shape doesn't occur naturally."

Like lightning, a thought blazed across his mind. "I've got it!" Connor said. He opened another window on the main holoscreen and brought up a schematic diagram of a Barracuda-class battleship carrier. "Computer, scale the schematic diagram so it's of the same dimensions as the enemy vessel."

The image resized to the parameters Connor had given. "Overlay schematics on top of the enemy ship. Angle the plane so it matches the approach vector."

The two images came together and Connor blew out a breath.

Reisman's eyes widened and he stepped closer to the image. "I don't believe it," he said.

"Can't be a coincidence," Connor replied. "Computer, run an analysis of the dynamic planes and their alignment relative to the enemy ship."

Ninety percent match.

Connor's mouth went dry. They'd just traded blows with a ship that out-massed them by more than twenty times their tonnage.

"What the hell happened to the ship?" Reisman asked.

"The substructure is that of a Barracuda-class battleship carrier. I have no idea what that hull is made of, but you can be damn sure it's not an asteroid," Connor said.

He glanced at Reisman, who seemed to have had a thought and then shook his head.

"Spit it out, Wil. I'll take anything at this point," Connor said.

"It's like someone put an exoskeleton over the existing ship. Like a clam that grows its own shell one layer at a time," Reisman said.

Connor pinched his lips together. "In space?"

Reisman shrugged. "It's the first thing I thought of. I didn't say it made any sense."

"Let's see if we have images of the damage we caused. Maybe there's a clue in there that will indicate what it is," Connor said.

"If these are old alliance military ships encased in some kind of living exoskeleton, that could be the reason they're so hard to detect on PRADIS," Reisman said.

Connor sighed. "I hope the mag-cannons are operational."

Reisman frowned. "Why is that?"

"Because proton beams and perhaps even the HADES IVs aren't going to be enough to penetrate the armored hull, whatever that material is. Maybe a good old-fashioned slug shot can cause more damage and pave the way for a more powerful warhead," Connor said.

Reisman grunted.

"Let's get this organized. Piecemeal out the analysis," Connor said.

"And just hope they don't detect us before we can detect them," Reisman replied.

Connor didn't respond. He didn't have to. They were on borrowed time. Hopefully the intelligence they gleaned from their encounter would pay dividends going forward.

16

NOAH GLANCED at the time in the upper right corner of his terminal session's display. It was oh three hundred hours and he'd slept only a handful of hours since the battle group had left to investigate the anomaly that appeared on PRADIS. Since then, Colonel Douglass had set the status for Titan Space Station at Condition Two for the existence of a probable threat that wasn't present yet. Noah had worked almost around the clock to upgrade the HADES IV missiles. And it wasn't just him. Colonel Douglass had ordered every able-bodied person to help with that effort, as well as getting additional weapons systems online.

A message appeared on his holoscreen.

::*Report to the Command Center a.s.a.p,*:: Col. K. Douglass said.

Noah acknowledged the message and closed down his session. He was alone in the Engineering lab, where he'd been checking the calibrations for the subsystems of the HADES IV-B. If he'd had more time, he might have worked out a way to add some kind of point defense systems to the highly accurate missiles, but he couldn't make it work and fit them into the launch tubes they had available.

Noah glanced around at the Engineering lab. He'd hoped to see Kara before he was due to leave but that had been all but impossible with what was happening. She could have been avoiding him, but he wasn't sure of that. He couldn't be sure of anything given how tired he was.

Noah double-timed it to the Command Center and headed right toward the cradle, where he knew Colonel Douglass would be. The heart of the Command Center was fully staffed, with each workstation occupied by CDF personnel.

Noah glanced at the PRADIS screen that showed the CDF attack group. They were nearing the predetermined range where they'd turn around and head back to the station.

"Comms, open a link to the *Chmiel* and find out why Captain Benson is sticking around. He was cleared to disembark hours ago," Colonel Douglass said.

"Sir, you requested to see me," Noah said and stood at attention just outside the cradle.

Colonel Douglass glanced at him.

"Colonel, Captain Benson is requesting to speak to you," Lieutenant Jason Lew said.

Colonel Douglass raised his finger for Noah to wait. "Put him through," Douglass said. "This is Titan actual."

"Colonel, I thought I'd stick around in case you needed further assistance," Captain Benson said.

"I appreciate the gesture, Captain, but the best thing you can do is disembark and head directly back to New Earth," Colonel Douglass said.

"I'd be happy to extend an invitation to any noncombatants you need off the station," Captain Benson said.

The cargo ship captain wasn't part of the Colonial Defense Forces and wasn't required to stick around to offer assistance.

"Thank you, Captain. All personnel on Titan Space Station are essential to its operation," Colonel Douglass replied.

"Understood, Colonel. The *Chmiel* will shove off within the hour. Captain Benson out."

The cargo ship captain sounded disappointed that he couldn't help in some way.

Colonel Douglass turned toward Noah. "Just the engineer I wanted to see."

"I'm at your disposal, sir," Noah replied.

"We received a partial data burst from the *Vigilant* and I'd like you to take a look. We've tried the known reassembly protocols, but they're not working, and I know you have extensive experience with this type of work," Colonel Douglass said.

Noah had spent years trying to get data from the deep-space buoy network in order to glean more information about what had happened to Earth and why the buoy network was failing. Despite all his efforts, he'd only been able to get precious little information from the colony's only link to Earth, but he had developed a talent for deciphering partial data dumps.

"Absolutely, sir," Noah said.

"Excellent. Take over the aux work area over there and report to me when you have something," Colonel Douglass said.

The aux work area was at the edge of the cradle. Noah went over to it, sat down, opened up a terminal session, and went to work. The signal appeared to be intermittent, as if part of the burst had been cut out at different intervals. Noah quickly coded an algorithm to isolate the data burst into individual chunks that the system could interpret. That should make the comms system cooperate and become useful rather than throwing up errors. Noah then started reviewing the data, and in an instant, his exhaustion evaporated in a rush of adrenaline. He stood up.

"Multiple PRADIS contacts!" Captain Thorne said.

Noah glanced up at PRADIS and frowned. The *Vigilant* disappeared from PRADIS, only to reappear a few moments later. The same went for the *Banshee* and the *Wyatt*.

"Keep tracking," Colonel Douglass said and glanced over at him. "What have you got?"

"I broke down the data burst. They modified how PRADIS scans and had it focus on ship wakes through space," Noah said.

Colonel Douglass became somber. "Put what you found on the main screen."

Noah used his fingers to snatch the image on his terminal, and he flicked it toward the main screen. A PRADIS output showed a massive force that was almost atop the scout force.

A hush came over the Command Center at the image on display. Noah glanced at Colonel Douglass, who was studying the display intently.

"Tactical, configure our PRADIS to alternate scanning intervals for active contacts and ship wakes," Colonel Douglass said.

"Sir, I'm not sure—" Captain Thorne began.

"I can help him, sir," Noah said and darted over to Caleb's workstation.

He showed Caleb where the settings were hidden amongst the options.

"Comms, set Condition One," Colonel Douglass said.

Throughout Titan Space Station for the second time in its history, they readied for imminent attack.

Noah stepped away from Caleb's workstation once it was clear that it was ready. An updated PRADIS feed showed on the main screen.

"Multiple warhead detonations detected," Captain Thorne reported.

Noah searched through the crowded PRADIS screen. "Where's the *Vigilant*?"

"Connor is likely masking the ship's presence from the enemy," Colonel Douglass said.

Noah's face twisted into a confused frown, but he remained quiet.

"Tactical, I want a firing solution on the main attack group," Colonel Douglass said.

"Sir, the intermittent returns on PRADIS will make precise targeting a problem," Captain Thorne replied.

"Understood. Ready the HADES IV-Bs. I want them in the tubes, ready to go," Colonel Douglass said.

Since Noah wasn't assigned to a particular workstation, he went to the colonel's side.

"Sir, if we launch the missiles, isn't there a chance we'll hit the CDF scout force?" Noah asked.

Colonel Douglass regarded Noah for a moment and he had the distinct impression he'd overstepped his bounds.

"I'm sorry, sir," Noah said quickly.

"Listen up," Colonel Douglass bellowed. "There are very few of you who've actually fought in a war. This is the day where that all changes. The CDF scout group has engaged the enemy fleets. From here on out, that is how we will refer

to them. General Gates is commanding the *Vigilant*. We'll work like hell not to
hurt one of our own, but it may not be helped. War is messy. Our job is to
defend the colony from attack. We suspected that this enemy fleet from whatever
damn hell they crawled out of was coming for us. The colony is depending on us
to do our jobs, and we will."

The CDF soldiers in the Command Center went back to work. Noah looked
at Colonel Douglass. "What do you need me to do?"

"Help me figure out how to stop that fleet. Is there anything else in the data
burst?" Colonel Douglass asked.

"Just the PRADIS configuration update to detect ship wakes and that they
were engaging the enemy. The rest doesn't make much sense. If we get more
information, I can try and parse it into what we already have," Noah replied.

"Understood. I want you to stick around. Sit with Captain Thorne at the
Tactical work area and lend assistance as needed," Colonel Douglass said.

"Yes, sir," Noah replied.

Noah walked over and sat down in the seat next to Caleb. "The colonel wants
me to give you a hand," Noah said.

"Thanks for the assist earlier. I didn't know PRADIS could be configured to
scan like that," Caleb replied.

"How do you decide what to target?" Noah asked.

Caleb pinched his lips together. "It's all about establishing priority targets. We
have some time because they're still pretty far out."

"How much time do we really have? Couldn't they have already fired their
weapons . . . you know, missiles of their own?" Noah asked.

"They could, but we would have detected them," Caleb said.

Noah frowned at the tactical display. "Why haven't they fired on us yet?"

"I have no idea. What I have here is a long-range firing solution. It's pretty
run of the mill, designed to strike at the heart of this main attack force. Since
we're targeting ship wakes, we have to guess where the ships actually are," Caleb
replied.

"If you launched the missiles in groups, wouldn't the targeting systems
update?" Noah asked.

"Yes, but that's assuming a strong PRADIS contact. What we have is
essentially a passive scan," Caleb said.

"Tactical, still waiting on that firing solution," Colonel Douglass said.

"Alpha, bravo, and charlie packages uploaded and awaiting your approval,
sir," Caleb said.

Noah glanced over at Colonel Douglass, wondering what the man was
thinking. Noah didn't know what he would do if he were in the colonel's shoes.
At this range, even if they launched their missiles, it would still be hours before
they reached their targets.

"Approved. Launch the first salvo now," Colonel Douglass said.

Noah watched as Caleb authorized the launch. Armored hatches opened as
the HADES IV-B missiles launched from their tubes. The automated loaders
were already loading more missiles.

"This is the first of many salvos," Caleb said.

Noah nodded. What would they do after all their birds were in the air? Noah wondered if he should say a prayer. He wanted to know why the enemy fleet hadn't attacked them yet. He looked at the PRADIS screen and hoped his friends serving aboard the *Vigilant* were okay.

17

CONNOR SAT in the command chair on the *Vigilant's* bridge. Several hours had passed since their initial encounter with the enemy fleet. Major Hayes had just reported in.

"That's four of the main projectors that are simply gone," Reisman said.

"Could have been a lot worse. A few degrees lower and the entire bulkhead for that section might have been gone," Connor replied.

Reisman's brow furrowed as he read through the damage report.

"Excuse me, sir," Sergeant Boers said, standing at attention outside the command area.

Connor waved her over. "Yes, what is it, Sergeant?"

"I've been going back through the recorded signals during the encounter and I was able to make something out. I've isolated some transmissions from the *Wyatt* and I thought you'd like to hear it," Sergeant Boers said.

"Sure thing. Anything we can learn about them will help," Connor said.

Sergeant Boers held up her tablet computer and replayed the signal she'd recorded.

The sounds stemmed from a partial transmission from the *Wyatt*.

". . . They're right on top of us. . . prepare to repel boarders. They're coming through the hangar bay . . ." The person speaking faded away to static. Then another voice spoke in a deep rasp. "Vemus . . ."

The recorded signal finished and Sergeant Boers closed the tablet interface.

"Vemus? Is that all there is?" Connor asked.

"I've heard that word spoken a few other times, but it always sounds the same. Shortly after this recording was when the *Wyatt* went offline. I cross-referenced it in our systems and came up empty," Sergeant Boers said.

"Thank you, Sergeant," Connor said.

The comms officer returned to her workstation and Reisman came over. "We should consider posting security teams at the hangar bay and the airlocks," Reisman said.

"Agreed. I wish I knew why they would try to board a ship in the first place. They clearly have ample firepower," Connor said.

"Vemus. Not sure what that even means," Reisman said.

"Could be a war cry of some sort. The fact that we can't find any remains of the *Wyatt* means they might have been captured instead of destroyed. Two hundred CDF soldiers unaccounted for," Connor said.

"We haven't heard from the *Banshee* either. Do you think they've been captured as well?" Reisman asked.

Connor shook his head. "No. Our scans show there were no enemy ships near them. I suspect Savannah went comms silent to protect their position and she's waiting for our cue on how to proceed. Her greatest weapon is the fact that she's able to sneak around."

Reisman tilted his head, considering. "That's a hell of a gamble."

"And one we'll need to account for in our plans," Connor said.

Reisman blew out a breath. "Good, so you have a plan," he said with mock severity.

Connor was momentarily taken aback and then snorted. "You'd think after all these years I'd be expecting that kind of crap."

The doors to the bridge opened and Sean walked in, leading two other men from his team. He turned back and gave them some orders, and they began using handheld scanners to make a sweep of the bridge.

Connor had received a message from Dr. Allen that Colonel Ian Howe had died a short while ago. The body had been preserved. He needed the perpetrators found, but this was a distraction he couldn't afford right now.

Sean came over. "Sir, we're making a sweep of the bridge."

"Do you really expect to find traces of radioactivity here?" Connor asked.

"Leave no stone unturned, sir," Captain Quinn replied. "We've narrowed it down to a specific type of radiation and have found trace amounts of it in the mess hall and in common areas of the ship. We searched through crewman quarters, but that didn't yield anything."

Connor glanced over at the two CDF soldiers scanning the bridge. They earned themselves more than one annoyed glance from the busy bridge crew.

"We've questioned soldiers who had access to equipment that would extract the substance used to poison Colonel Howe, but they all check out. They all had alibis and a reputation for being loyal to Howe," Sean said.

The soldiers waited just outside the command area, and Connor gestured for them to come do what they needed to do. The soldiers hastened inside.

"Has Captain Toro turned up anything?" Connor asked.

"He's chasing down a few leads but nothing so far. We've been widening our search beyond the most direct places. Engineer Hatly has been helpful in showing the bare minimum we would need to extract polonium. Unfortunately, a crude setup can be hidden almost anywhere," Sean said and glanced over at the soldiers who were scanning the area. They'd stopped around the command chair.

"Do you have something, Lieutenant?" Sean asked.

The soldier nodded. "I have trace readings on the arms of the chair and on the terminal interface."

Connor walked over and looked at the data on the scanner. There was just enough to show that someone who'd been in the command chair had come into contact with the polonium.

"Trace readings though, so not an immediate danger," Reisman said.

The soldier with the scanner pointed it at Reisman and then at Connor. "You're fine," the lieutenant said.

"This narrows things down," Connor said, glancing at his hands.

Throughout his career as a soldier, people had tried to kill him, but it had always been more direct, such as with a gun in hand.

"Sir, I need your authorization for the command logs to the bridge, as well as your personal quarters and anywhere else you've been for the past week," Sean said.

Reisman's brows pulled together in surprise and he looked at Connor. "You're the target?"

Connor clenched his teeth for a moment. "You can have whatever you need. Catch the bastard."

"Sir, in light of this recent development, I need to assign you a security detail for your own protection. They'll be with you at all times until this is resolved," Sean said.

Connor shook his head in disgust. They needed to focus their attention on the enemy, not be suspicious of one another. "Comms, give me a ship-wide broadcast channel," he said and waited for Sergeant Boers to open the channel. Connor stepped toward the railing that separated the command area from the rest of the bridge. With teeth clenched, he grabbed the metallic bar and squeezed as if he could choke the life from it. "Crew of the *Vigilant*, this is General Gates," Connor said, his voice sounding harsh. "I have disturbing news to share with you beyond the enemies nipping at our heels. Colonel Ian Howe has died. He's been murdered. I realize this comes as a shock to most of you. By all reports, Colonel Howe was highly respected by his crew, and he will be deeply missed. The fact that he was murdered by a despicable act of cowardice leaves little doubt in my mind that we have a traitor in our midst. Colonel Howe was poisoned, and the guilty parties are still at large. Dr. Allen informed me that Colonel Howe succumbed to radiation poisoning. Though Dr. Allen made him as comfortable as possible, it was not gentle. He died in pain and he suffered. Crew of the *Vigilant*, rest assured that I will do everything in my power to find the people responsible for this and they will be dealt with decisively." Connor paused with a sneer and glared upwards. "And to the people responsible for this, I know you're out there, listening on this ship-wide broadcast, wondering what you're going to do next. Don't bother. I'm going to find your traitorous ass and I'm going to nail it to the wall. You may be hiding now, scurrying in the shadows, but there is nowhere you can hide from me!"

Connor cut the broadcast. Of all the things they should be focusing on right now, a traitor among them wasn't at the top of his list. That slippery son of a bitch was going to pay. The one thing above all others that couldn't be tolerated in any military was a betrayal of one's own.

Connor swung his gaze toward Sean. "Find who did this."

Sean leveled his gaze in return. "You have my word, sir. I will find them."

Connor nodded and turned his gaze back to the main holoscreen. Sean left the bridge and sent in two security officers, posting them just outside the command area.

Reisman came to stand beside him. "You think your speech will smoke out our assassin?"

"I hope so. I have a very short list of people I absolutely trust. You and Sean are on the top of that list," Connor said.

"It's going to take more than two of us to survive this," Reisman said.

"Now we have more than two of us. Howe was loved by his crew. It was a cruel twist of fate that he got caught in the crossfire, but this also proves something else," Connor said.

"What's that?"

"This would-be assassin didn't act alone. Someone told him to do this," Connor said.

Reisman frowned while he thought about it. "Governor Parish?"

Connor shrugged. "Or one of his supporters. He's been the most vocal about his thoughts on the CDF. Even if he didn't give the actual order, someone in his administration did. If we live through what we're doing out here, I hope we find out who."

"I'll make sure the next comms drone we send back has an extra package for Frank Mallory," Reisman said.

Connor smiled grimly. "Time to move forward with the plan," he said.

Connor scowled at the command chair. He couldn't use it until it had been decontaminated. He stood in the middle of the command area with his hands clasped behind him. "Ops, I want a scanner drone deployed. Use only CDF encrypted channels. I want anything remotely related to the old NA Alliance protocols isolated from the system. Lock out those options unless I give my express permission."

"Yes, sir, initiating lockout of Alliance protocols from the system," Sergeant Browning said.

"Tactical, can you isolate the enemy ship that took the *Wyatt*?" Connor asked.

"I have its position at the time of the engagement. We've been drawing steadily toward Titan Space Station," Lieutenant LaCroix said.

"Sir, scanner drone has been deployed. Configured to go active on your command," Sergeant Browning said.

"Acknowledged," Connor responded.

"Once we activate that drone, they'll know we're scanning the area," Reisman said.

"I'm counting on it. We'll need to move quickly once we get targeting data," Connor said.

"What about using the *Banshee*? I think I have a way to send specific instructions to Major Cross," Reisman said.

"Now that we know the enemy fleet is made up of NA Alliance military ships, we do have an insight into their capabilities. You find a way to reach the *Banshee*, and if you succeed, I want her to send her missiles at the main fleet while continuing on toward Titan Space Station," Connor said.

"We should be within long-range missiles. Kasey will likely have already launched them," Reisman said.

"Yup, which means our window to find which of these ships has the *Wyatt* is closing. I'll leave you to it. I need to speak to LaCroix," Connor said.

He walked over to the Tactical response work area of the bridge. "Lieutenant, I need you to do a couple of things for me. Some of them will seem unorthodox," Connor said.

Lieutenant Vladimir LaCroix looked up at Connor. "Ready when you are, sir."

"First, I want you to bring up the schematics of a Barracuda-class battleship carrier. Mark all the enemy ships identified as having that ship design and give them the designation Vemus," Connor said.

Lieutenant LaCroix updated the output on the main holoscreen. There were over a hundred ships of the Vemus fleet that had that designation, but there were still many ships that didn't meet that criteria, and Connor wasn't sure what they were.

"We'll need to do this with the known ship types and try to align them with Vemus ships. Allow for a ten percent tolerance to account for that additional exoskeleton the ships seem to have," Connor said.

"Understood, sir. I have a suggestion," LaCroix said.

"Go ahead," Connor replied.

"We do have the ability to deploy mines using a cold launch so they won't be detected. I'm thinking that littering the battlefield with them and just setting an old-fashioned timer to detonate when the bulk of the enemy fleet is on them would have some lasting results," LaCroix said.

"That could work and does get around the fact that they can block our communications. I'm just not sure how effective they'll be," Connor said.

"Just something to consider, sir," LaCroix said.

"We'll hold off on it for now. Once we activate the scanner drone, I'll need firing solutions fairly rapidly," Connor said.

"What's the targeting priority, sir?"

"The way their fleet is deployed makes me think they expect to take their hits at the very front—the line of battle, if you will. I want to bypass them and have our birds hit them in the middle. The HADES IV-B should be able to handle that. How the ships on the line react will reveal which one of them has the *Wyatt*. They likely latched onto the ship somehow, which would make that ship oddly shaped, unless they try to fit it in the middle hangar. It would be a tight fit, and I expect that ship would be the least likely to react," Connor said.

"That's the one you want me to isolate when the scanners go live?" LaCroix asked.

"Yes, and I'll need a solution for disabling that ship," Connor said.

"What's this about disabling a ship?" Reisman asked as he walked over.

Connor glanced over at the colonel. "We'll need a boarding party of our own, unless we get confirmation that the *Wyatt* has been destroyed and all her crew lost. Otherwise we go get them back and try to learn more about the enemy," Connor said.

Reisman's mouth hung open. "That's likely to be a one-way trip."

Connor leveled a look at him. "With as many ships as we've snuck aboard, is this any different?"

"Very much so. We don't even know who's flying those ships," Reisman said.

"Exactly. We need more intelligence," Connor said.

"Let me guess. You want to lead the team over there," Reisman said.

Connor frowned and leaned back.

"It's not appropriate for a general to be on the away team," Reisman said.

"Fine, I'll promote you to general and demote myself. Either way it's gonna happen. There's no one more qualified to lead a team for that," Connor replied.

"We'll see about that," Reisman said.

Lieutenant LaCroix glanced at both of them, looking extremely uncomfortable. "I don't want to get in the middle of this," he muttered.

Connor looked back at LaCroix. "Carry on, and remember what I said about those firing solutions. Do you need additional support?"

"That won't be necessary, sir," LaCroix said.

Connor headed back to the command area and Reisman followed him.

"It's neither here nor there unless we can find them. Otherwise, we're going to keep picking away at the Vemus. They're not searching that hard for us given that they just keep heading toward Titan Space Station. Have you found a way to contact the *Banshee*?" Connor asked.

Reisman gave him a bored expression. "Of course. Just need the final word on the plan and the coordination involved."

"I'm thinking fire and run," Connor said.

"Major Cross won't like that. She likes to fight," Reisman said.

"She'll get her chance. Let's go over the message. Are you sure it won't be detected?" Connor asked.

"Oh, it'll be detected, but they won't be able to read it," Reisman said.

Connor gave him a look.

"Shouldn't be able to read it."

Connor nodded. "Alright, let's not give the enemy abilities we can't confirm they have."

18

"MAJOR, we have an encrypted-channel, one-way communication from the *Vigilant*," Lieutenant Daniels said.

The bridge of the Destroyer *Banshee* became quiet. Major Savannah Cross looked up from her terminal.

"Send it to my screen," Savannah said.

They'd gone into stealth mode, or as stealthy as any ship of the wall could go. At least the *Banshee* was designed to loiter in enemy territory.

Savannah waved her XO over.

John Elder returned to the command area and looked at Savannah's screen.

"Message header looks authentic," John said.

"I concur," Savannah said and opened the message.

She read through her orders twice and allowed John to take a look.

"They want us to strike out and then retreat to Titan Space Station," John said.

"Evidently, General Gates would like to use us as a distraction and as bait. We're to get the enemy forces to commit their forces to the space station," Savannah said and sat back in her chair.

She hated those orders but agreed with them at the same time. The preliminary scans they'd managed to salvage from PRADIS showed a huge fleet of ships heading right toward New Earth.

Savannah opened a broadcast channel to her ship. "Crew of the *Banshee*, this is Major Cross. We've just received our orders from the *Vigilant*. Our enemy is called the Vemus. It's the only word that could be deciphered from recorded transmissions. Our orders are to strike at the Vemus's frontlines and draw their attack in toward Titan Space Station, at which time we are to report in to Colonel Douglass on Titan. Stand by for additional orders. We stay at Condition One. Cross out."

Savannah closed the broadcast comms channel. "Tactical, in a few minutes' time we're going to get targeting data from a scanner drone. We'll enable PRADIS for a short burst. Then you'll have a small window in which to formulate a firing solution," Savannah said.

"Ready, willing, and able, Major," Sergeant Brennan said.

"Helm, plot a course to Titan. Best speed," Savannah said.

"Yes, ma'am, best speed to Titan," the helmsman replied.

Savannah glanced at John Elder. "You'll want to strap yourself in."

"Thank you, ma'am," Captain Elder said and hastened to his seat.

Savannah kept her eyes on the main holoscreen, waiting for all hell to break loose.

"Drone activation in one minute, General," Sergeant Browning said.

"Acknowledged," Connor replied.

A timer appeared in the upper right corner of the main holoscreen. The onboard computer systems were about to get a heap of much-needed targeting data. Six rail-cannons reported "status ready." HADES IV missiles were loaded in the remaining tubes. Engineer Hatly had assured him that since they kept the reactors hot the engines could be quickly brought online. Connor didn't dare give the order before the scanner drone started broadcasting.

The timer dwindled down to zero and a connection status of "waiting for data" appeared on the main screen. Connor counted off in his mind. They were about to get a peek into the battlefield as it was in real time.

Vemus contacts began populating the tactical screen.

"You have thirty seconds, Lieutenant LaCroix," Connor said.

Connor put up another timer on screen. As the enemy contacts continued to show up on screen, he knew LaCroix was working up a firing solution.

"Fifteen seconds, Lieutenant," Connor said.

The tactical officer's fingers flew through the interface as he kept updating the targeting parameters with more Vemus ships.

"Ready for launch," Lieutenant LaCroix said as the timer reached zero.

"Fire!" Connor said.

HADES IV-B missiles shot from their tubes. No sooner had the order been given than another countdown timer appeared. LaCroix was already hard at work identifying additional targets for the next wave of missiles.

"Ops, you're going to bring PRADIS back online. Active scans," Connor said.

PRADIS came back online and the *Vigilant's* computer system fed the data from the scanner drone into it.

"Scanner drone has gone offline," Sergeant Browning reported.

That hadn't taken the Vemus long. Connor watched the PRADIS output and didn't know if it was an act of providence that had spared them from having any Vemus ships around them or if they were just lucky, but they were alone for the time being.

A second wave of HADES IV-Bs fired from their tubes.

"Helm, bring us about, toward the Vemus fleet," Connor said.

"Yes, sir, bringing us about," Sergeant Edwards replied.

"Sir, I'm showing HADES IV missiles have been launched from Titan Space Station," Sergeant Browning said.

"Acknowledged," Connor said, thankful Kasey hadn't wasted any time engaging the Vemus. "Tactical, account for the incoming HADES IVs from Titan into your targeting solutions."

"Yes, sir," LaCroix answered.

"General, one of the Vemus ships has broken away from the front and is on an intercept course for us," Reisman said.

"Ops, target that ship with the rail-cannon. It's big enough for us to hit it even at this distance," Connor said.

The rail-cannons were bolted into the superstructure of the ship. It was the only way they could be fired without tearing the ship apart.

"Colonel, any sign of the *Wyatt*?" Connor asked.

Reisman peered intently at his own holoscreen. He looked up at Connor. "Negative, sir."

"Understood. Helm, hold this position for twenty seconds and then plot a course toward Titan Space Station, best speed," Connor said.

Sergeant Edwards echoed his command. Connor watched as the Vemus battleship carrier drew steadily closer.

"Confirm hits with rail-cannon, sir," Sergeant Browning said.

"Good, keep pelting it. Tactical, what's our missile status?" Connor asked.

"All our birds are in the air, sir," LaCroix said.

They'd gone through their HADES IVs already? Connor glanced at the main holoscreen. There were still so many enemy ships. They had to get out of there before they were caught in the crossfire of their own weapons.

"Sir, I'm detecting a faint comms channel from the *Wyatt*," Sergeant Boers said.

"Can you lock onto their signal?" Connor asked.

"Yes, sir. Ship has been identified," Sergeant Boers said.

Connor looked back at the main screen. On the other side of the Vemus line, drawing steadily toward Titan Space Station, was a signal from the *Wyatt*. "Helm, plot a course to that signal, best speed. Tactical, make use of the Hornets as we go but keep twenty percent in reserve," Connor said.

This mission could go to hell at any moment. The Vemus ships were scrambling to find them. Connor had no illusions that this was a battle he could win. He was just determined to take down as many of the enemy as he could.

"Enemy missiles detected! Danger close! Brace for impact!" Reisman shouted.

Connor checked his seat straps to be sure they were securely fastened. It had been only a matter of time before the Vemus fired back at them. Now it was a matter of how long their luck would hold.

Connor felt a violent shudder spread across the bridge and then his body jerked hard against his restraints. He watched helplessly as Sergeant Browning crashed into his workstation panel and then slumped over in his chair. Connor gritted his teeth and held on. As the ship stabilized, Sergeant Boers and several others went over to help Sergeant Browning.

A massive overload registered on Connor's terminal. He opened a comlink to Engineering. "Damage report," Connor said.

"Sir, we lost two of our main drive pods. The system is completely overloaded. Main engine power down to twenty-five percent," Engineer Hatly replied.

Connor's mouth went dry. "What about the other two drive pods?"

"One is fully operational and we're attempting to reroute power to the other one. Pods three and four are completely gone, sir," Engineer Hatly said.

"Understood. Get me that other drive pod ASAP," Connor said.

He cut the connection to Engineering and looked over at the Ops station. Sergeant Browning was awake and back in his chair.

"Ops, I need a damage report," Connor said.

"Looks like they concentrated fire on our stern engines. Missile tubes six through fifteen are offline," Sergeant Browning said.

"Understood," Connor replied and looked at Reisman. "They're trying to disable us, and they knew where to hit us."

"Agreed. I think it must be what they did to the *Wyatt*," Reisman said.

Connor looked at the PRADIS readout. The ship that had the com signal from the *Wyatt* had disappeared.

"Comms, are we still receiving a signal from the *Wyatt*?" Connor asked.

Sergeant Boers worked with a frantic frown. "Negative, sir. They're no longer broadcasting any signal," Boers said with a shaky voice.

The *Wyatt* was gone. Two hundred CDF souls aboard.

"Sir, I'm showing waves of HADES IV missiles making their final approach. We need to get out of here to achieve minimum safe distance," Lieutenant LaCroix said.

"He's right, sir. With the *Wyatt* gone, we should head back toward Titan Space Station," Reisman said.

Connor clenched his teeth. They were still just inside the Vemus front lines, and the enemy fleet hadn't increased their speed. "Helm, plot a course for Titan Space Station. Best speed. Execute as soon as you have it."

"Yes, sir," Sergeant Edwards said.

Connor ran the numbers on his terminal. With only one drive pod, even at best speed they only stood a slim chance of clearing the detonations of the HADES IV missiles.

"Come on, Hatly, get me that other drive pod," Connor said softly.

Reisman heard him and gave a grim nod. They needed that engine or they were going to die.

"Sir, I'm showing drive pod two is now active!" Sergeant Edwards said.

"Punch it!" Connor said.

The *Vigilant* lurched forward as the magneto-plasma drive pods sucked in power from their remaining reactors. Connor felt a shudder under his feet and he watched the plot as the *Vigilant* slowly moved ahead of the Vemus fleet.

19

Noah had remained in the command center and continued to assist Caleb at the tactical workstation. He glanced at the time on one of the main tactical holoscreens that were tracking the missiles they'd launched at the enemy fleet. When Noah first joined the CDF, he'd assumed that missile deployments were effectively straightforward affairs. Nothing could be further from the truth. Even with the increased accuracy he'd been able to achieve for the HADES IV-Bs, they still had to reach their relative positions. Colonel Douglass hadn't gone for the simple and direct approach, which would have been to fire all the missiles in their arsenal. Each wave of missiles had an effective targeting location and they flew at different speeds in order to hit the enemy fleets all at once. There was a delicate balance of timing and precision that Noah had come to appreciate.

He glanced at the PRADIS screen, and none of the enemy fleet had broken formation.

"Colonel, I'm showing a CDF responder coming just ahead of the enemy fleet's front line. It's the *Vigilant*," Caleb Thorne said.

Noah's eyes widened in excitement. They hadn't heard from the *Vigilant* since the attack first began.

"Sir, I have a comms channel from the *Vigilant*. It's General Gates," Lieutenant Foster said.

"Put them through," Colonel Douglass said. The comms channel registered as active. "I was beginning to think you were going to miss the party."

"We had a few shake-ups of our own. The *Wyatt* is gone. I sent the *Banshee* to you, but we've taken significant damage and I don't know if she made it," Connor said.

"Major Cross has checked in and I told her to stay close to the station. She'll get to see some more action before this day is done," Colonel Douglass said.

Noah's brows drew upward and he looked over at the colonel. Surely all the

HADES IV missiles armed with their nuclear warheads would be enough to severely damage the approaching fleet?

"What's the status of the *Vigilant*?" Colonel Douglass said.

"The Vemus started to return fire on us. They targeted our engines and we're down to only two main engine pods left. Our analysis is that they were just trying to disable the ship so they could take us alive. One of the last broadcasts from the *Wyatt* was that they were repelling boarders. There's a good chance they're going to try the same thing on the space station," Connor said.

"Understood. We'll be ready," Colonel Douglass said.

There was a long moment of garbled static before the channel was cleared by the comms AI that automatically aligned communications signals for optimum performance.

"How long do we have, Kasey?" Connor asked.

Noah frowned at the somberness of the tone. He'd rarely heard Connor break protocol on an official CDF channel before. He looked over at Colonel Douglass and saw that the former Ghost's mouth formed a thin grim line.

"Not long," Colonel Douglass said, his voice sounding thick.

"I thought so. Our PRADIS array has taken some damage, so not all the scanner fields are working anymore," Connor said.

Colonel Douglass muted the comms channel so Connor wouldn't hear him. "Tactical, will the *Vigilant* reach minimum safe distance?"

"Hold a moment, we're picking up something on our sensors," Connor said.

Within moments, multiple contacts showed on PRADIS.

Colonel Douglass took the comms channel off mute. "We see them."

Captain Thorne worked through the blast radius from the HADES IV missile envelope whose detonation timing was closing in on the *Vigilant*. "It's going to be real close, sir."

Colonel Douglass nodded. "General, you're almost at a minimum safe distance. You're still in this. The noose is closing in standard V deployment."

"Understood. The new contacts are moving much faster than anything else we've seen so far. They're smaller vessels. Can't do the analysis here, but I suspect they're some form of Talon 5 assault crafts," Connor said.

Noah brought up a search on his terminal. Titan's computer systems held a data repository of all known NA Alliance navy vessels in existence when the *Ark* left Earth's solar system. He entered Talon 5 into the search field and his mouth went dry. Talon assault crafts were specifically designed to puncture a hole through bulkheads and deliver troops onto enemy vessels. They were also designed for speed and were highly maneuverable. Soldiers were strapped into place and administered a special cocktail to help them withstand forces that were beyond the inertia dampeners' ability to compensate.

"Ops, I need you to confirm that," Colonel Douglass said.

"Yes, sir. We're tracking," Sergeant Moors said.

"We'll attack them from the rear, but you're going to need to unleash the fury and initiate Jade protocol," Connor said.

Noah glanced at Colonel Douglass. He'd never heard of Jade protocol and had no idea what that meant.

"Understood, General. I'll be in contact," Colonel Douglass said.

"Good luck, Titan," Connor said.

Noah watched as Colonel Douglass went over to his terminal.

"Colonel, the Talon 5s will be here within thirty minutes," Sergeant Moors said.

Colonel Douglass broke focus on his terminal session and glanced up. "Understood. Go to Condition One. Imminent attack on the station. Defense protocols authorized."

Noah heard the operations officer send a broadcast throughout the station. A new notification appeared on Noah's terminal with orders for him to report to the main hangar. He glanced at Colonel Douglass and noticed that several CDF personnel began leaving the Command Center. Other CDF personnel sprinted in to fill the vacant posts. Noah closed his terminal session, stood up, and went over to Colonel Douglass.

"Colonel, is this accurate?" Noah asked and flipped the screen of his PDA toward the Colonel.

Colonel Douglass stood up. "Donnelly, take over. I'll only be a few minutes."

Lieutenant Colonel Donnelly went to the command chair.

Colonel Douglass looked at Noah. "Walk with me, Noah."

Noah frowned. The colonel addressing him by his name rather than rank didn't make him feel at ease in the slightest, but he followed his commanding officer away from the Command Center. They went toward the lifts.

"Your orders are correct. You are to report to the main hangar and board the Frigate *Abacus*," Colonel Douglass said.

Noah's eyes widened. "I'm not sure I understand, sir."

Colonel Douglass glanced around to be sure they weren't overheard. "You're returning to New Earth."

"But why, sir? I can help you," Noah said.

He knew he was overstepping his boundaries by questioning his superior officer, but he didn't want to leave.

Colonel Douglass placed his hand on Noah's shoulder. "Listen to me. Jade protocol was put in place so we could ensure that key personnel would be transported back to New Earth in case this station fell into enemy hands. This is not a slight on your abilities. Quite the contrary. You're one of the good ones and essential for the defense of New Earth."

Noah swallowed hard. He didn't know what to say. He didn't want to leave. He wanted to stay and fight.

"Now, can I count on you to get to the frigate, or do I need to assign a security detail to take you there?" Colonel Douglass said.

Noah glared at the man. "Yes, sir."

Colonel Douglass gave him a firm squeeze on his shoulder and then headed back toward the Command Center.

"Colonel," Noah called out, and Douglass turned around. Noah stood up straight and snapped a salute. "Good luck, sir."

Colonel Douglass saluted in kind. "Good luck to us all."

As Noah ran toward the lifts, he brought up his PDA and looked for Kara's signal. Her personal locator showed that she was several levels up from the main hangar, in Engineering. Noah went inside the elevator and selected the Engineering level. A group of soldiers ran toward the elevator as the doors started to shut and Noah thrust his hand out to stop them from closing.

The CDF soldiers piled inside, easily filling the space. One of the soldiers glanced at him. "Captain, you should be armed. The order was just given. Where are you heading?"

Noah hadn't heard the order. "Engineering. I'll stop at the nearest weapons locker."

"Phelps, give him a weapon."

The soldier named Phelps turned toward Noah and handed him an M11-Hornet. Noah took the SMG and thanked him.

"Are you familiar with that weapon, sir?" the sergeant asked.

"Yes, I've used one of these before," Noah answered. He'd kept up with his weapons training after his introduction to them when Connor had recruited him to Search and Rescue and then later to the Colonial Defense Force.

The elevator stopped and the CDF soldiers ran out. Noah hadn't even gotten the sergeant's name before the doors shut and the elevator resumed its descent to Engineering. As Noah checked the Hornet, the elevator came to a sudden halt. The lights flickered and Noah glanced at them in alarm. There was a muffled boom and he gasped. He went over to the doors and tried to pry them open, but they wouldn't budge. He opened the control panel and tried to override the door, cursing when it failed.

"Think, Noah!"

He glanced around and then looked up at the ceiling panel. He'd have to climb. He went to the side of the elevator and opened the service panel to metal rungs that led upward. Noah climbed up the ladder and reached the service hatch, which he unlocked and thrust upward. The hatch swung open and he climbed out of the elevator.

The long gray elevator shaft stretched out above him. The shaft shuddered as if something massive had slammed into the space station, and the elevator car jerked downward. Noah stumbled toward the wall. He was stuck between floors. Emergency lighting shined on the yellow rungs of a ladder built into the shaft. Noah ran over and began climbing. He reached the next floor and pulled on the emergency release for the door. The metal doors slid open and Noah yelled for help. He heard someone yelling, but they sounded as if they were far away. With one firm hand on the ladder, Noah reached across and grabbed the edge. He let go of the ladder and shuffled across, using his hands to hold him. The elevator car was only ten feet beneath him, so he wouldn't die if he fell, but he didn't relish the thought. Noah pulled himself up and swung his foot to the side, climbing out the rest of the way and pushing himself to his feet.

"Alert! Vemus forces have entered the station."

Noah's mouth hung open. They were already here! That must have been the loud booming sound he'd heard—the sound of those Talon 5 assault ships slamming into the station. Noah glanced over at the emergency container fastened to the side of the wall. Those containers were spaced throughout all the floors of the station. He raced over and opened it, pulling out a rebreather mask and then grabbing a few more, which he stuffed into the sack that hung inside. He slung the sack over his shoulder and tied it off. Since there were ships dive-bombing the station, there could be a sudden loss of atmospheric pressure. The one thing Connor Gates had drilled into him was the value of being prepared so he could adapt to new situations as they unfolded.

Noah ran down the corridor, worming his way among people as they scrambled to get where they needed to be. He opened a comlink and tried to reach Kara. He was one level above where she was, but there was no answer. Noah came to the end of the corridor and turned right.

There was a squad of CDF soldiers heading toward him. Their commanding officer scanned Noah's PDA and frowned. "Sir, you're supposed to be at the main hangar bay. Jade protocol."

"I'm heading there right now," Noah said and tried to worm his way past.

The soldier stopped him. He glanced at the collar of her uniform. T. Reynolds was stenciled on the shoulder.

"Not going that way you're not," Sergeant Reynolds said.

Noah pressed his lips together. "I'm going to Engineering to make sure my friend gets to the hangar too."

Sergeant Reynolds frowned. "Is this friend also part of Jade protocol?"

Noah had no idea if Kara was on this special list. "I think so," he said.

"Then they should already be making their way toward the main hangar. We'll escort you there," Sergeant Reynolds said.

The soldiers began ushering him back the way he'd come. "Stop!" Noah shouted. "I'm not going anywhere until I go to Engineering first, which is one floor below this one."

Sergeant Reynolds shook her head. "My orders are clear," she said.

"I'm giving you new orders then, Sergeant," Noah said. Technically he held the rank of captain in the CDF, but he'd never leveraged his rank before. "You can escort me to Engineering and then we can all go to the hangar."

Sergeant Reynolds' brows pulled together. "Yes, sir, but we can't go that way. The area at the end of the corridor has been depressurized."

"Okay, there's a maintenance shaft this way," Noah said.

He led the group of CDF soldiers back the way he'd come and stopped at the maintenance shaft.

Noah took a quick look down. "It's clear."

He moved to step inside the shaft, but Sergeant Reynolds stopped him. "Let one of my squad go first. Butch, you're up."

One of the CDF soldiers came forward and entered the maintenance shaft first. Another followed. Noah went next, and they quickly climbed down the shaft. Butch waved for him to come through and then told him to wait for the others.

Noah looked impatiently down the corridor. The Engineering tech lab was only a short distance away. He took a few tentative steps in that direction and tried to raise Kara on her comlink, then clenched his teeth together in frustration when she didn't answer. She was notorious for casting her comlink to the side when she buried herself in her work.

The rest of the CDF squad came down the shaft and they headed toward the Engineering lab. They heard sounds of weapons fire and Noah quickened his pace.

"Any security squads on deck J? Report," Sergeant Reynolds said on an open channel.

The light flickered overhead and Noah could hear the sounds of the station's defensive batteries firing into the approaching enemy fleet. They came to the end of the corridor and turned left. The entrance to the tech lab was a short distance away. A group of strange figures stood toward the far end of the corridor.

Noah frowned. Something appeared off about the shape of the figures. He brought up his M11-Hornet and aimed it. The end of the corridor was dark and he could only make out faint silhouettes.

"Sir, I get no transponders at the end of the hallway," Butch said.

The squad of CDF soldiers readied their weapons. There was a loud screeching noise and a white energy bolt came toward them. Noah scrambled toward the wall and squeezed the trigger. Shots spat out of the M11-Hornet in rapid succession. Noah heard the other CDF soldiers fire their weapons. More white energy bolts came toward them, and one struck Butch in the chest. He crumpled down. The CDF squad kept firing their weapons and Noah saw the dark shapes at the end of the long corridor drop from view.

"Sir, Butch has been stunned," a soldier said.

"Pick him up," Sergeant Reynolds said.

Noah raced forward to the tech lab doors and banged his fists on them, then hastily entered his authorization code. The door opened. Kara Roberts sat at a workbench, frantically working at a terminal.

Noah shouted her name. "I've been trying to reach you."

Kara looked over as if surprised to see him. "What are you doing here?"

"I've come to get you. We need to get out of here. The station is under attack," Noah said.

"I know. I just need to finish this first," Kara said.

Noah ran over and tried to grab her arm. "We don't have time for this. They're on the station."

Kara evaded him and went back to her terminal. "I know. I've been picking up their transmissions."

Noah glanced at the bench and saw the transceiver. He opened one of the overhead cabinets, looking for the portable power supply. He found it and connected it to the transceiver.

"Come on, we've got to get to the hangar," Noah said and grabbed the transceiver.

"Alright, I'm coming," Kara said and reached out for a few other devices, stuffing them into her pockets.

They left the tech lab, and the CDF squad was waiting outside for them.

"Major Roberts, I have to get you out of here. Jade protocol is in effect," Sergeant Reynolds said.

Kara frowned, but before she could say anything, Noah said they were ready to go. They went back the way they'd come. Kara glanced around in surprise at the flickering lights and the sound of weapons fire. Sergeant Reynolds led them in a different direction.

"The maintenance shafts are this way," Noah said.

"I know but the quicker way to the hangar is this way," Sergeant Reynolds said.

Noah followed the CDF soldiers.

"Titan Station, this is Colonel Douglass. Vemus forces have entered the station and managed to get a foothold on the lower sections. Security forces have established a perimeter. I'm ordering a general evacuation of the base."

The message ended. Looks like they all needed a way off the station. Sergeant Reynolds quickened her pace and led them into a maintenance tunnel. Once inside, they ran up a ramp and came to the hangar entrance. Noah looked inside the hangar through the window in the door. There was no freighter. CDF personnel were racing toward the shuttles.

"We can't get out that way. They'll fill up the shuttles before we can get near them," Noah said.

Kara held up her PDA and opened a technical readout of the area they were in. "There are escape pods this way, near the end of the hangar."

"Good enough for me. Let's go," Sergeant Reynolds said.

Noah opened the door and heard shouts from the people storming the shuttles. Several shuttles lifted off and sped out of the hangar. They ran along an elevated walkway. The end of the hangar was over two hundred meters away and Noah was breathing heavily by the time they reached it. They entered a maintenance lift, which lowered them to the ground level. Kara ran to an escape pod and began entering her credentials. There was a series of explosions coming from across the hangar. Tall, dark shapes poured out of a smoking hole in the bulkhead. They moved so fast that they seemed to streak toward the mass of CDF personnel clamoring to get on the remaining shuttles.

Noah raised his SMG and fired at the dark shapes. Several of the CDF soldiers with him fired their weapons as well. A couple of the dark shapes went down and then rolled back onto their feet. Noah heard a loud snarling, and several of the Vemus fighters broke away, heading right for him.

Someone grabbed Noah from behind and shoved him into the escape pod. Kara was already inside. Sergeant Reynolds gestured for two of her squad to get inside.

"Not without you, sir," one soldier said.

Sergeant Reynolds looked at Noah and Kara. "We got this," she said.

Before Noah could protest, the sergeant slammed her fist on the controls for the escape pod. The doors hissed shut and the pod launched from the station. Noah cried out, but all he could see was a rapidly retreating view of the main hangar. Off to the side was a cigar-shaped ship that had crash-landed near the hangar. There was no way the small CDF squad could hold off that many.

Noah growled and slammed his fist against the reinforced door. He looked over at Kara, whose eyes were wide with terror. "Why didn't they come with us? They could have just come inside."

Kara glanced at him. "I knew the enemy was coming, but I had no idea. I didn't know."

An alert appeared on the central control panel. Kara opened the interface. "It's a broadcast," she said.

"Escape pods of the Titan Space Station. This is Captain Benson of the cargo ship *Chmiel*. I've included our coordinates in this message. We're not far from your position. Please input the coordinates into the pod's guidance systems and you should be able to reach us."

The message repeated. Noah watched as Kara updated the coordinates. He sat down next to her and strapped himself in. The pod's engines engaged, and Noah felt a small bit of force as the pod took them to the cargo carrier.

"Thank you for coming to get me," Kara said.

Noah was snapped out of his thoughts. "You weren't answering your comlink."

Kara glanced away guiltily. "I know. It's a terrible habit."

"What was so important that you ignored the fact that the station was under attack?" Noah asked.

"The transmissions are under a protocol we don't use. I was recording them so they could be deciphered. We'll need them," Kara said.

Noah looked away. He wanted to ask her why she'd been avoiding him but couldn't bring himself to do so. He kept seeing those dark shapes on the hangar deck. It was like they were made up of a swirling mass.

Kara opened the holo-interface of her PDA and went to work with the recorded signals. Noah looked at it and then joined her. If he couldn't be fighting the Vemus on the station, at least he could do this.

20

Connor sat in the command chair on the bridge of the *Vigilant*. The visco-elastic used in the seat back and cushion contoured perfectly to his body, but there was no getting comfortable for any of them. Engineer Hatly had created a miracle in record time when he and his team managed to reroute power to the main drive pods, restoring their engine capability to half strength. They'd managed to stay ahead of the Vemus fleet for a short while until the enemy fleet as a whole seemed to wake up.

Even with the limited capability of PRADIS, they were able to see that the HADES IV-B missiles had extracted a heavy toll on the Vemus fleet. Kasey Douglass, Connor's longtime friend, had done his job well. The timed execution of the massive launch of their most powerful missiles, carrying multiple types of warheads, had partially decimated the enemy. They tore into the Vemus fleet, creating a powerful envelope that closed in on them from all sides, squeezing them together. It was a good plan, but it wasn't enough. There were simply too many Vemus ships, and their armored hulls had proven to be highly resistant to nuclear blasts in the vastness of space. Smaller ships hadn't had a chance, but the larger ones that were concentrated toward the middle of the Vemus fleet formations had managed to survive. They'd estimated that the Vemus fleet was down at least forty percent.

After the storm of HADES IVs had done their utmost to destroy the enemy fleet, their Talon 5 assault crafts sped toward Titan Space Station. There was no mistaking the enemy's intentions. The Vemus wanted to take Titan Space Station intact. Connor tried using the *Vigilant's* remaining mag-cannons to take out the Talon 5s as they flew by, but they were moving so fast and there were so many of them that they hardly made a dent in their numbers.

Connor shook his head. If the CDF had a hundred heavy cruisers of their own then perhaps they could have mounted a better defense. As it was, he'd lost a large chunk of his crew through damage to the *Vigilant* alone.

The main holoscreen showed bright flashes as Titan Space Station fought to keep the enemy at bay. The station's point defense systems, including auto-cannons and particle beams, tore into oncoming Vemus ships.

Connor's guts were twisted up in knots. He knew better than to order "all ahead" and help the CDF's first line of defense, but it was hard not to. The soldiers he'd trained were giving their all so the colony could survive, and he couldn't have been prouder.

He stopped himself from displaying any sign of weakness. He had to remain strong for his crew, but he felt a deep, roiling anger that, if left unchecked, would cause him to make more mistakes.

He should have fought harder for the secondary power station Titan needed. The space station even now was exceeding projected capabilities, and Connor attributed that to the CDF soldiers serving on it alongside Kasey Douglass. Connor thought about Governor Parish and the growing political movement that called into question the validity of an attack ever taking place. They'd had seven years to prepare for this, and there were thousands of lives on Titan Space Station that would pay the price. Connor kept thinking of all the things he could have done differently, given what he now knew—how he could have shifted priorities. It was a brutal rabbit hole to get sucked into, even if it was only in his mind, and Connor fought to pull himself out of it. He needed to stay focused.

He opened up the comms interface on his terminal. At least Titan Space Station still had their communications array working.

"*Vigilant*, this is Titan actual," Kasey Douglass said. His voice sounded strange and mildly distracted.

The former Ghost's face appeared on the screen and Connor stood up. The Command Center was a buzz of activity. Most of the CDF personnel Connor could see were armed. There was a shallow gash on the side of Kasey's head.

"Situation report," Connor said.

Kasey leveled his gaze at the camera. "I've ordered an evacuation of the station. Those of us who remain are fighting as long as we can."

Reisman came to stand at Connor's side.

Kasey saw him. "Hey there, you slippery bastard. You watch out for our CO."

"I will," Reisman said, his voice sounding thick.

Connor wanted to tell his friend to run, to get out of there, but the soldier in him knew it was impossible. He knew what Kasey was doing and would have done the same thing himself if he'd been in that position.

Kasey looked over at Connor. "At least it's not as bad as the Sandy Springs Op."

"But we got to walk away from that one," Connor said.

A sad smile appeared on Kasey's face. "I remember when Malarkey got stuck in the compactor. For a medic, he could curse with the best of them. I'll say hello when I see him."

Connor clenched his teeth together. "We both will."

"Going soft on me, General? I know you're not religious at all and don't believe in all that stuff. In fact, I believe you kept calling it superstitious nonsense," Kasey said.

"I changed my mind. I've seen the error of my ways. All is forgiven, right?" Connor said and felt the skin around his eyes tighten. "I wish I could be there with you."

Kasey glanced away from the camera and Connor heard shouting. "If we had ever developed a transporter, I would gladly teleport myself and my crew over to your ship. Regardless, we beamed the intelligence we gathered to COMCENT on New Earth."

A wave of bitterness stiffened Connor's muscles.

"It won't be long now. Vemus forces are fighting toward the bridge. They're vulnerable to our weapons, but they're more interested in capturing us than killing us. Several battleship carriers have continued onward. Do you think you can take care of those for me?" Kasey asked.

"We'll come up with something," Connor answered.

"Sir," Lieutenant LaCroix said, and Connor glanced over at him. "I'm detecting a thermal mass building at the station's main reactor core."

Connor looked back at Kasey and stood up straight. "I'll take it from here, Colonel. You've done more than anyone could have asked of you."

Kasey was about to reply when shouting erupted all around. There were flashes of light. Connor heard the distinct sound of weapons fire before the comms channel was severed.

"Sir, the thermal mass is reaching critical levels. We need to make best speed possible to escape the blast," Lieutenant LaCroix said.

"Helm, get us out of here," Connor said bitterly.

The main holoscreen showed a massive swarm of Vemus ships surrounding the station, trading blows. Connor wondered why their forces were putting so much effort into capturing the station rather than destroying it and moving on to New Earth. The tactics they were using proved that they still fought an enemy they didn't fully understand. In some respects, the Vemus were extremely slow to respond, and in others, like Titan Space Station, they used an overwhelming show of force, as if their ships didn't matter. Connor frowned and felt like there was something he was missing.

"Ops, I want to know where those Vemus battleship carriers are—"

Connor stopped speaking. A bright flash came from Titan Space Station, and the feed to the main holoscreen cut out. The sensors were blinded. Connor balled his fists and glared at the empty feed, thinking about all those people who had just died.

"Get me their locations," Connor said, his voice sounding raspy and strained. "Wil, take the con."

He left the bridge and the two CDF soldiers assigned to be his security detail followed him.

Connor looked back. "I need a few minutes," he said and gestured to his ready room. The two soldiers stopped just outside the bridge.

Connor opened the door to his room and stepped inside, letting the door shut. The steady hum of the large aquarium cast a warm glow in the dim room.

"Lights," Connor said.

As the lighting in the room became brighter, Connor saw Sean lying on the floor. Connor gasped and ran over to him. He glanced down at Sean's hands and saw that they were bound together at the wrists.

"He's alive," a cold voice said from behind Connor.

Connor spun and was struck in the head by something hard. He instantly went sprawling face-first to the ground. Pain blossomed on the side of his head where he'd been struck. He moved his hands under his chest and pushed himself over. Standing in front of the aquarium, holding a hand-cannon on him, was Captain Alec Toro.

Toro locked the door.

Connor glanced at Sean and then up at the *Vigilant's* head of security.

"It was *you*," Connor said and started to rise.

"Stay down, General," Captain Toro warned.

Connor stayed on the floor and leaned back against the wall. He fingered the side of his head and felt a small trickle of blood. "So, what's your plan here? You kill me and then what?"

Toro's eyes became more intense. "I don't know. You screwed everything up."

"I screwed everything up? You poisoned Ian Howe. You were supposed to be his friend."

Toro charged forward and came to a stop. "I *am* his friend."

Connor glanced at the gun. "Oh, really? I'm sure he appreciated suffering from radiation poisoning right before he died. The doctor had him in a medically induced coma so he wouldn't feel the pain, so who knows if he had any last thoughts at all. That's what you did to your friend."

"It was supposed to be you. It should have been you, but you kept changing things. Always changing things. Testing. Constant drills. Updating your schedule. I thought I had you . . . I did have you," Toro said.

"What did you do to Sean?" Connor asked, wondering if the security detail had heard the commotion.

"He found me out. Traced the polonium to me. Here in this room, in fact," Toro said and gave a lazy gesture with his other hand.

"Here? Why would you come back here?"

"To take one more stab at you," Toro said.

Connor leaned against the wall and brought one leg up toward his chest while extending the other.

"We're being attacked by the Vemus and you still want to kill me. What the hell for?"

Toro shook his head. "I had everything thought out. I knew the way investigations were conducted. You were supposed to be at the mess hall after meeting with the engineer. And then Ian and Nathan were there. I tried to stop them, but it was too late. I knew Ian had ingested the poison and it was already too late," he said, glaring at Connor. "I thought I'd gotten you after that."

Connor frowned. He'd only spoken to Toro here in this room. "The coffee," he said, finally remembering. "You laced it with poison."

Toro nodded his beefy head. "Yup, and you took it onto the bridge with you. I thought for sure you would have reported to Dr. Allen, but you didn't."

Connor shuddered. He remembered losing his appetite and handing the coffee off to the soldier. No one else drank it either.

"Who ordered you to kill me?" Connor asked.

"How do you know I'm not working alone?" Toro asked. The head of security lowered his gun to his side, and his hand shook as it held the hand cannon.

"Because you're too damn stupid to have cooked this up for yourself," Connor said.

Toro's nostrils flared and he brought the hand-cannon up, pointing it at Connor's face.

Connor stared up at him grimly. "You're a coward," he sneered.

Toro cried out and lunged forward, his eyes narrowed menacingly.

Connor kicked out with his foot and caught Toro by surprise. The hand-cannon went off but missed him. Connor sprang to his feet and grabbed onto Toro. The head of security was so strong that Connor might as well have been wrestling a tree. He slammed his fist into Toro's head and tried to hold onto the wrist holding the gun, but his grip slipped. After several long seconds during which Toro didn't take the shot, Connor tore his eyes away from the hand-cannon. Sweat poured from Toro and his face was pale.

"You're dying. You've exposed yourself to too much polonium," Connor said.

Toro seemed to weaken right where he stood and then stumbled backward. He fell, landing near the unconscious Sean. Connor stepped toward Sean, but Toro pointed his gun at Sean's head.

"Haven't you caused enough death? We have an enemy that wants to kill us and we're here killing each other. It's over," Connor said.

"They weren't supposed to find us. The experts made such compelling arguments. Parish said it was impossible. No one was supposed to find us here," Toro said.

"Was it Parish? Is that who ordered you to kill me?" Connor asked.

He didn't glance at the door but he heard the two CDF soldiers outside. Any second now, they were going to open that door. He had to keep Toro's attention on him or Sean would get shot.

"You changed things again. Instead of keeping the investigation quiet, you broadcast it to the whole damn ship. Everyone knew Colonel Howe had been murdered," Toro said.

The door to Connor's ready room burst open. Connor held up his hand. "Hold!"

The two soldiers glanced at him and then down at Alec Toro, who was pointing a gun at Sean's head.

Toro glanced at the soldiers, his eyes seeming to linger on their uniforms.

"Look at me," Connor said.

Toro swung his gaze toward Connor. "I know this kid is your friend. He's good. Really good. I can see why you keep him around. If I hadn't blindsided him, he would have caught me."

Toro pressed the hand cannon against Sean's head.

"You don't have to do this. It's over," Connor said.

"You're right; it *is* over. I'm dying. Either you or those soldiers are going to kill me—all because we wanted to believe a lie, that there was no invading force coming to the colony and that everyone we left behind on Earth was okay. None of this was supposed to happen," Toro said, and his lips pressed together.

"Don't. He's a good kid and deserves a chance to die fighting for something he believes in," Connor said.

Toro looked at him with red-rimmed eyes and winced in pain. "That's all *I* wanted," he said and then raised the hand-cannon to the side of his own head and squeezed the trigger. Blood and brain matter splattered onto the wall as Toro's dead body slumped into its final rest.

Connor went over to Sean and glanced up at one of the soldiers. "Get a medic in here, now!"

The other soldier went over to Toro's body.

"Get a decontamination team here. He had radiation poisoning and I can't be sure he doesn't have the substance on him," Connor said.

"Sir, you need to step away from him then," the CDF soldier said.

They cut the bonds that held Sean's wrists together and carried him over to the couch. A medic came and started to examine Sean. A few moments later he used smelling salts and Sean woke up.

Connor blew out a breath and rubbed his face. Toro had been right: he did care for Sean like a son—like the son he'd left behind on Earth who bore the same name. He wouldn't have been able to forgive himself if something had happened to Sean.

"Sir, are you alright?" the medic asked him.

"I'm fine," Connor said in a strained voice.

Sean looked over at Toro's body and then looked at Connor. "We found traces of polonium in his quarters and his locker. After I found traces of it on the bridge, I checked everywhere you'd been. It was on your desk, so I knew someone who'd met with you had to be the killer. He must have figured out that I was on his trail. I caught up with him here and he got me."

Connor nodded. "Don't beat yourself up about it. We should be hunting the Vemus, not each other."

Sean sat up but stayed on the couch. "Did he tell you who else was involved?"

"Not directly, but I have a strong suspicion," Connor said.

Sean frowned. "Who?"

"Let's say his orders came from the top, or at least someone close to Parish," Connor said.

Sean shook his head slowly. "What do we do now? We can't let them get away with this."

"Stanton Parish is the least of our concerns. We can worry about it if we make it back to the colony," Connor said.

"What about Titan Space Station?" Sean asked.

Connor's throat became thick. "It's gone."

Sean's eyes widened in shock.

"They called for an evacuation and then Colonel Douglass ordered the self-destruct," Connor said.

Sean swallowed hard. "Did it . . . stop them?"

"I don't know. I'm going back to the bridge. Want to join me?" Connor asked.

"Always, sir. You know that."

Connor did know that and was thankful Sean hadn't been killed, but how many more would he fail to save? He had to get back to the bridge. The self-destruction of Titan Space Station might have struck a crippling blow, but this battle was far from over. They had to activate the missile-defense platforms they had positioned throughout the star system. Perhaps they would be enough to weaken the remaining Vemus ships even further.

21

THE ESCAPE PODS CARRYING Noah and other survivors from Titan Space Station were actually part of the *Ark*, humanity's first interstellar ship that had ferried three hundred thousand men, women, and children out among the stars. Although anything but comfortable, the pods were equipped so that the people inside could survive for weeks.

Noah glanced at the holoscreen that showed them closing in on the *Chmiel*. The cargo carrier had become a lifeboat to hundreds of personnel aboard the life pods that were lucky enough to escape from Titan Space Station before the Vemus made that all but impossible. They'd used the pod's limited thrust capabilities to take them to the cargo ship, reserving just enough fuel so they could perform emergency maneuvers to slow down. Kara had reminded him of that little necessity when he'd suggested they reach the *Chmiel* as quickly as possible.

"The drone is almost here," Noah said.

Kara bobbed her blonde head once and remained focused on her personal holoscreen. Noah had disabled the distress beacon for their life pod. He wasn't sure whether the Vemus could track them, but he felt safer without the broadcast signal going out. The pod's short-range communications worked, so they could speak to other survivors, as well as Captain Benson of the *Chmiel*. The cargo carrier was equipped with a small army of drones that were designed to retrieve smaller asteroids but were now guiding the life pods into the main cargo bay. They would keep as many of the life pods as they could. One thing that had been drilled into the colonists of New Earth was the need to not waste anything that could be useful. In this case, the life pods themselves were made from high-grade materials. Noah had even done some calculations and determined that the cargo vessel should have just enough room to store them all.

Noah brought up the video feed on his own holoscreen. The *Chmiel* was a short distance away, and if there had been any windows on the pod, the only thing they'd have seen was the cargo carrier. There were several lines of circular objects heading toward the ship in steady succession. Although there were hundreds of escape pods, Noah knew that many CDF personnel had stayed behind to fight the Vemus.

He heard a clang as a drone made contact with their pod and propelled them toward the ship. Noah noticed that they were being guided to one of the shorter lines of pods.

He glanced at Kara, considering.

Kara noticed him looking at her. "What's the matter?" she asked and looked briefly at his holoscreen.

"Nothing. They're just lining us up, is all," Noah said.

"Oh, good. We're lucky Captain Benson decided to stick around," Kara said.

"It would have been a much longer trip home," Noah replied.

He felt foolish. Titan Space Station had been attacked. They'd evacuated and here they were talking about how lucky they were. He was immensely grateful to be alive and ashamed all at the same time.

"Before all this happened, I was going to ask you something," Noah said.

Kara closed down her holoscreen and stretched her hands out in front of her before bringing them to rest in her lap. "About what?"

"I was reassigned back to New Earth, and I was going to ask if you wanted to come back with me," Noah said.

There, he'd finally said it.

Kara stiffened next to him. "I knew you were going to ask," she said quietly.

Noah's eyes widened. "You did? Is that why you've been avoiding me? Because you didn't want to come?"

Kara looked away from him and Noah felt a flush of embarrassment redden his face. He shouldn't have brought this up here in this cramped life pod. Of course she didn't want to come back with him. This thing between them was just a fling, something to pass the time during a particularly long rotation at the station.

"No," Kara said softly. "I was ashamed because I wanted to go with you. More than anything."

Noah looked at her. "You did? Then why did you avoid me?"

Kara swallowed hard. "Because I thought I'd be abandoning my post, shirking my duty. We were handpicked to be assigned to Titan Space Station because we were the best the Colonial Defense Force had to offer for defending the colony against the threat of invasion. I loved the work I was doing and the people I worked with. It was a close-knit community there. There's very little choice on the space station to be otherwise. Sure, we were way out on the edge of the star system, but we had each other. Then you showed up all those months ago. The legendary Noah Barker, renowned engineer and integral part of the early colonial effort, a personal friend of General Gates."

Noah snorted. He knew he had a reputation but didn't think much of it. Certainly not among his peers. "Being Connor's friend isn't all it's cracked up to be. We often get the most dangerous assignments."

"It was General Gates and Colonel Douglass who approached me to be part of the CDF brigade serving on Titan. It was a tremendous honor even to be asked," Kara said.

Noah's eyebrows pulled together in understanding. "I didn't realize what I was asking you to give up. I'm sorry. We seemed to hit it off. We go together. Knowing the general, he wouldn't have viewed your request to return to New Earth with me as an abandonment of your post. The man may drive himself like a robot, but he understands people."

They were silent for a few moments and Noah heard Kara sigh.

"I would have said yes," Kara said, finally.

Noah smiled widely and he saw Kara doing the same. He took her hand in his and held it, and she gave his hand a gentle squeeze. Noah felt as if a great weight had shifted off of his shoulders, and a renewed determination swept over him. They had to get home. They had to find a way to thwart the Vemus invasion. For the first time since entering the life pod, he felt free despite everything that was going on around him. Then fear threatened to creep back into his thoughts. The Vemus. Why did they come? What did they want? How'd they even get here? But he didn't want to focus on that now and pushed those thoughts out of his mind so he could take this moment with Kara and remember it for however long his life would be.

A comlink opened to the pod. "Life pod 707, execute reverse thrust for final approach," the comms officer of the *Chmiel* said.

Noah looked at the life pod controls and hit the button to slow the pod down.

"Perfect. We'll have you aboard in just a few moments."

"Acknowledged, and thank you," Noah said.

The drone guided their pod to the cargo area, where they were handed off to the robotic loading arms. The arms brought the pod safely inside the cargo bay area. The pod was then shifted to the interior of the ship through a massive airlock. A few minutes later there was a knock on the hatch, and Noah pulled on the release.

"Welcome aboard the *Chmiel*. My name is Jim."

Noah gestured for Kara to go first and followed her out of the pod. Kara told Jim their names and ranks. Noah saw other pods being opened and their occupants coming out.

Jim's eyes widened. "Captain Benson has been waiting for both of you. Please, if you'll follow me to the bridge."

Noah glanced at Kara and then back at Jim. "Of course," he said.

Jim led them out of the cargo area and called out to the deck chief that he was taking them to the bridge. There were a lot of life pods that had made it already, and Noah thought about all those waiting to get on board. He wondered why the captain had seen fit to single out both of them.

"Do you know what this is about?" Noah asked.

Jim looked back at him. "I have no idea, but I have my instructions. We're scooping you guys up and then we're supposed to hightail it out of here as quickly as possible."

The *Chmiel* was a large ship, so it took them almost fifteen minutes to reach the bridge. As they entered the bridge, there was none of the formality Noah had gotten used to on the CDF military ships he'd been on.

Captain Benson was an older, dark-skinned man whose gray hair and beard made him look like a sage. He glanced over at them with a deeply furrowed brow. "Major Roberts and Captain Barker?"

"Yes, sir," Noah said.

Officially, Benson wasn't part of the Colonial Defense Force, but the man was the captain of this ship and had just saved their lives.

Captain Benson eyed him for a moment. "I appreciate the sentiment, son, but though I'm captain of this ship I'm very much at the CDF's service. Regardless, I don't need someone to tell me the right thing to do."

"We appreciate it all the same, Captain," Noah said, and Kara nodded.

"I have orders for you, Captain Barker, and I need your expertise, Major," Captain Benson said.

"How can I help?" Kara said.

"We have to beat the enemy fleet back to New Earth. To do that I need better speed from the engines," Captain Benson said.

"Understood. I can help with that, but I must warn you that there's a significant risk of permanently damaging the engine pods," Kara said.

"I suspected as much," Captain Benson replied.

"I'll head down to Main Engineering and see what we're dealing with," Kara said.

"Look for Marcin. He keeps things running down there," Captain Benson said.

Noah watched Kara leave the bridge and turned back to the captain. "You have orders for me?"

Captain Benson nodded. "I have new encryption protocols you're to use to contact General Gates. You can use my comms station over there."

Noah went over, sat down at the comms station, and put on the headset. Captain Benson enabled the new encryption protocols and then left him. Noah opened a comms channel and waited for it to connect. Once the link was established, Noah saw Connor's face appear on his screen. He was stone-faced, with a burning intensity in his eyes.

"Reporting in, sir. Escape pods are being loaded onto the *Chmiel* as we speak. Captain Benson had me brought to the bridge to contact you," Noah said.

"I'm glad you made it out of there. I have a job for you," Connor replied.

"I'll do whatever you need me to."

"I need you to update the targeting capabilities used on the defense platforms. After that, they must be fully engaged for danger close-fire configuration. Do you understand what I'm telling you to do?" Connor said.

Noah swallowed hard. Danger close-fire configuration would enable the defense platform to prioritize enemy ships regardless of whether there were friendlies in the area. "I do, sir," Noah said, knowing better than to waste time questioning Connor about his own orders.

"Good. We need to prevent as much of the Vemus fleet from getting to New

Earth as we can. I've told Captain Benson he's to head back there using best speed," Connor said.

"Major Roberts is heading to Engineering to try and increase the speed once we get underway," Noah said.

"How long before you're underway?" Connor asked.

Noah had no idea. He glanced over toward Captain Benson and repeated the question.

"They're loading the escape pods now, but it could be another thirty minutes before they're all on board," Noah said.

Connor looked away from the screen for a moment. "Call Captain Benson over to you."

Captain Benson joined Noah at the comms station.

"Captain, the Vemus fleet is reeling from the destruction of Titan Space Station. I appreciate what you're doing, but there's a tough call to be made," Connor said.

Noah's insides went cold.

"I cannot abandon those pods, sir," Captain Benson replied.

"Keep loading as many as you can, but if you receive a signal from us that the Vemus forces are on the move, you're to cut and run. The top priority is for you to make it back to New Earth and for Noah to update the defense platforms. We've had no confirmation that COMCENT even knows the attack has begun. We believe this has to do with the Vemus, but we're not sure. Preparation is key, and the survival of the colony is at stake," Connor said.

Noah's mouth hung open as he watched Captain Benson struggle with what Connor had just told him. The cargo carrier captain walked away and began shouting orders.

Noah looked back at the screen. "He's gone, sir," he said.

"Sending over the updated parameters for targeting. This includes the PRADIS update in case active scans cannot detect the remaining Vemus fleet," Connor said.

A progress window appeared. "Data received, sir," Noah said.

"Noah, if Captain Benson won't leave, I need you to take control of the ship," Connor said.

"Sir, I have no idea how to fly a cargo carrier. How am I supposed to fly the ship?" Noah asked and glanced around to check if he'd been overheard.

"Calm down. I'm sending you my authorization codes that will give you master control of the *Chmiel's* systems. We checked, and Captain Benson already has a course plotted back to New Earth. All you need to do is execute it. Can I count on you?"

Noah frowned. "What if he overrides it?"

Connor leveled a look at the screen and Noah felt as if he were training with Search and Rescue all those years ago. "Don't let him. This is more important."

The thought of leaving CDF personnel behind made his throat thick. He hated it and glared at the screen.

"Hate me if you need to, but everything is counting on it," Connor said.

"Sir, where are you?" Noah asked.

"Our time is just about up. We're going to try and slow down the enemy as much as we can and get them to chase us right into the kill zone of the defense platforms," Connor said.

At last Noah understood. This could be the last time he ever spoke to his friend, his mentor, and he didn't know what to say.

"Stay focused and get it done," Connor said.

The comms channel was severed, and Noah stared at the blank screen. He sucked in a deep breath and glanced over at Captain Benson. Had the captain heard what Connor told him about taking control of the ship? Noah hoped it wouldn't come to that. In fact, he silently pleaded that it wouldn't come to that.

He opened the data cache and checked the updated PRADIS configuration. He'd have to wait until they were much closer to the defense platforms before uploading the update. It was the only way to confirm that the updates had been accepted by the defense platforms' onboard targeting AI. If he sent the updates out now and they were rejected, the defense platforms' systems could fail to target anything. He'd been part of the team that worked on the original operating code for those defense platforms, so he had a good idea how fragile they could be. Noah started to think about contingency plans if the updates failed to install. The *Chmiel* was a civilian ship and wasn't capable of doing anything but sending transmissions and getting them where they needed to go. There was no cyber warfare suite loaded onto a secondary computer system that was capable of running targeting analyses, and this wasn't something Noah could perform on the fly.

A comms alert from the *Vigilant* appeared on his holoscreen. Noah looked up and saw the same alert appear on the main holoscreen. The Vemus were starting to regroup. Noah's gaze darted to Captain Benson.

The captain returned to the command chair and Noah watched as a video feed from the main cargo doors was brought up. There was still a long line of escape pods from Titan Space Station waiting to board the ship.

Captain Benson looked over at Noah with a pained expression. They had to leave, and they were going to leave people behind.

"Open a comlink to the main cargo area," Captain Benson said.

"Main cargo."

"Deck Officer, you're to close the cargo doors for immediate departure," Captain Benson said.

There was a moment of heavy silence. The bridge crew seemed to huddle at their workstations, hunched as if weathering a terrible storm.

"Captain, there are still a lot of life pods out there. We just need some more time—"

"We're out of time. Close those doors or everyone in the cargo bay will die," Captain Benson said and cut the comlink.

Noah watched as Captain Benson waited a few moments.

"Captain, cargo bay doors are closing," said the ops officer.

"Helm, max thrust for engines one and two. Take us back to New Earth," Captain Benson said.

Noah's eyes became tight—all those pods still outside, their second chance taken from them. He felt hollow inside, as if he wasn't worthy of being one of the people who got to leave while other CDF soldiers were being sacrificed.

"Noah Barker, you need to focus. We all have jobs to do," Captain Benson snapped.

Noah swung his gaze back to his holoscreen. Captain Benson was right. There was work to be done. Deep in Noah's mind he imagined the screams of the CDF personnel still out there in life pods that were being sentenced to death. He was coming to understand the hardened glint that sometimes showed itself in Connor's gaze and he hated it. This was an understanding he didn't want.

A strong hand gripped his shoulder, and Captain Benson leaned down. "Focus, Noah. Make their sacrifice worth something. It will be the only way you'll find peace in the days to come."

Noah wiped his eyes and threw himself at his task, directing his anger and frustration at doing his utmost to destroy their enemy. In that moment, Noah left a much younger version of himself behind, and he began to wonder if he would even recognize himself in the days to come—if they survived.

22

CONNOR CUT the comlink to the *Chmiel*. He felt bile creep up the back of his throat and forced it down, knowing there was nothing he could do. They had a shuttle on board the *Vigilant,* but there was no way it could make the trip from the outer star system to New Earth. The call had to be made. The remains of the Vemus fleet were regrouping, and the escape pods from Titan that hadn't made it onto the cargo carrier would be left behind.

"Sir, the *Chmiel* has started heading back to New Earth," Sergeant Browning said.

"Acknowledged," Connor answered.

Reisman glanced over at him. "Now it's up to Noah. He has to get that targeting package uploaded to the defense platforms to guarantee they'll be able to hit the Vemus ships."

The loss of Titan Space Station exposed a major hole in their defense strategy. The missile-defense platforms could operate autonomously only to a certain degree. Now that Titan Space Station was gone, the platform's targeting computers couldn't be updated without getting into close proximity, something Connor hadn't accounted for in his plans, and now he was mentally kicking himself for the lapse.

Connor looked at the *Chmiel's* location on the main holoscreen and noted the increasing velocity. There were still hundreds of escape pods from Titan and there was nothing he could do for them. The occupants on the pods might survive for a few weeks, at best. Ordinarily a few weeks would be more than enough time to mount a rescue mission, but with the Vemus fleet in proximity, Connor had little doubt that the escape pods would be picked up by them. He didn't know what they would do with the survivors, but it wouldn't be good.

"Sir, I have the two Vemus battleship carriers on the plot now," Sergeant Browning said.

Those were his targets. Somehow he had to soften them up so when they did reach the missile-defense platforms, they could finish the job and destroy them. The *Vigilant* had no more missiles. They had ammunition for their few remaining rail-cannons and grasers that could be used for close-range combat. Range was ever the issue in space warfare. He glanced at the area of the PRADIS output that showed where Titan Space Station had been. The *Vigilant's* systems were still trying to make sense of the data in order to put it into some type of output he could use. They didn't know how many of the Vemus fleet had been destroyed by the Titan Space Station self-destruct sequence, but Connor knew it hadn't been all of them.

"Helm, plot an intercept course for the two battleship carriers. Keep our approach slow. I want ample time to react if they change course," Connor said.

"Yes, General, laying in course now," Sergeant Edwards said.

Major Hayes came onto the bridge and walked over to the command area. He'd been working with the damaged areas of the ship. News of Alec Toro's assassination attempt had spread throughout the ship. Reisman had raised the question of whether Toro had been working alone. In the end, Connor didn't know, and given their list of objectives, it wasn't something he could worry about at the moment. If someone else was trying to kill him while they were fighting the Vemus, then so be it. Sean stood off to the side and listened in.

"By all accounts, Toro completely lost it at the end," Reisman said.

Connor nodded. "He was becoming desperate because he was dying. I'm not sure it really registered with him that his main reason for killing me was null and void now that the Vemus are here."

"He cracked under the pressure, and the whole thing could have been avoided if we'd looked for the signs earlier," Major Hayes said.

"Toro was the one who would have been reporting in on stuff like that. Regardless, we need to focus on the bigger enemy," Connor said

Major Hayes glanced at their two targets. "How do we destroy something that big?"

Reisman shrugged. "It's not a matter of whether we can; it's how we want to go about it."

"Well, missiles are out. No more HADES IVs. They'd destroy us well before we could destroy them if we used our remaining rail-cannons. That's even if we had enough ammunition to take the ships out," Connor said.

"What about the *Banshee*? That ship had a purely offensive armament," Major Hayes said.

"Whereabouts are unknown. What we need to do is get aboard those ships and take them out from the inside," Reisman said.

Major Hayes's eyes widened. "You can't be serious," he said.

"Oh, he's serious," Connor replied. "And he's right; that's exactly what we need to do. Given our current resources, the only way we're going to stop them is from the inside. They're in relatively close proximity to each other, so that could work to our advantage."

Reisman nodded. "I was thinking the same thing—two for one, or at least seriously damaging the second one."

"All we need are some tactical nukes and a team to take them aboard," Connor said.

Major Hayes frowned. "We don't have any tactical nukes. All of our nuclear warheads went out with our missiles."

Connor was about to answer when his comms officer spoke.

"Sir, I'm picking up a faint transmission. It's from the *Banshee*. It sounds like a status loop," Sergeant Boers said.

"Put it on speakers," Connor said.

"This is Major Savannah Cross of the Destroyer Banshee. The Vemus have severely damaged our engines. They're closing in on our ship. I've deployed all available weapons to the crew and we're preparing to make our final stand . . ."

"I'm sorry, General. The message becomes garbled after that. I'll try to clean it up," Sergeant Boers said.

"What's the timestamp for the message?" Connor asked.

Sergeant Boers checked her terminal. "Sixty minutes ago."

Connor arched an eyebrow and looked at Reisman. "Tactical, can you trace the source of the transmission?"

"I'll try to isolate the signal, sir," Lieutenant LaCroix said.

"I'm not following. What's significant about the time of the message?" Major Hayes said.

"The message was sent out at about the same time self-destruct protocols were initiated on Titan Space Station, which might have affected the Vemus ship stalking the *Banshee*," Connor said.

He watched the PRADIS output and waited.

"I have it, sir. It's a weak signal, but it appears to be coming from one of the battleship carriers. The AI is basing its trace on the highest probability because the signal is so faint," Lieutenant LaCroix said.

One of the battleship carriers became highlighted on PRADIS.

"I think we have our target, gentlemen," Connor said.

"You want to catch up to that ship and do what exactly?" Major Hayes asked.

"Determine if the *Banshee* is still intact, for one thing, and whether the crew is still alive. The primary mission is to take out that ship. The secondary objective is to attempt to rescue the crew that's been taken by the enemy. Since we don't have any tactical nukes, we might find some on the *Banshee*. Either way, we're going on that ship," Connor said.

Reisman arched a brow at Connor. "For the record, as your second in command I must advise against you being on the away mission."

Connor pressed his lips together. "Noted, for the record."

Major Hayes frowned. "Does that mean you'll send a team?"

"You bet I will, and I'm going to lead it," Connor replied.

"Sir, we need you," Major Hayes said.

"Don't bother," Reisman said. "You'll never talk him out of going."

Major Hayes frowned.

"We need to get some intelligence on what we're dealing with. The only way that's going to happen is if we get down and dirty on that ship. That means a heavily armed away team," Connor said.

Major Hayes turned toward Reisman. "Colonel, please, I can't be the only one with these objections."

"I agree with the objections, and at the same time it will be both of us on the away team," Reisman said.

Major Hayes's mouth hung open in surprise. "Why?"

"Because we're among the few who were actually part of the NA Alliance military. Those ships look different, but underneath, whatever the hell the Vemus have done to those ships, the underlying system is Alliance military. I still have the access protocols in my implants. The same for the colonel," Connor said.

"And you think that access will still work?" Major Hayes asked.

"Won't know until we get there. Certain access protocols are contained within the implants themselves. They only come online with the correct challenge protocol. I'm not even aware of what they are, but I know they're in there. If Wil and I had officially retired from active duty, our implants would have been removed, but since that didn't happen, it's a potential advantage that we can't afford to pass up," Connor said.

"I hadn't realized that," Major Hayes said.

"It's not common knowledge. Plus, if there's a chance we can rescue the crew of the *Banshee*, I'm going to take that chance. I think we've left enough of our people behind," Connor said, thinking about the *Wyatt* and all of the destroyer's crew, and now the CDF soldiers who'd served aboard Titan Space Station.

"What about the risk of being exposed to the virus that was mentioned in the last transmission from Earth? I know the combat suits can protect the wearer from biological contagions, but what about the crew of the *Banshee*?" Major Hayes asked.

Reisman glanced at Connor. "He's right, General."

Connor nodded. "I know he is. We'll need to bring a doctor with us who can help with the assessment. I'm sure Dr. Allen could make a recommendation."

"Okay, it's clear you've thought this out, so I won't get in the way. Is it safe to assume you were planning to leave me in command of the *Vigilant*?" Major Hayes asked.

"I am," Connor said.

"What do you need us to do while you're aboard the ship?"

"I'd initially thought of taking the shuttle and finding a place to sneak aboard, but I don't think that's a viable option now," Connor said.

"Why not?" Reisman asked.

"We need to catch up to them first and figure out what we're dealing with. We thought the *Wyatt* was attached to the outside of the ship, and there's really no reason to believe the *Banshee* isn't in the same position. The Vemus so far have sought to disable our ships and take them intact. They targeted our engines as well. There's still a lot of interference out there, but I'm willing to bet that those two ships have already sustained some damage. I say we approach them and try to dock with their ship," Connor said.

Reisman smiled. "Even better. If the *Banshee* is outside, we send a team onto the ship and split up, with one team going aboard the main battleship carrier."

Connor nodded. "I like that. This way, if one team can't find warheads in the

Banshee's armory, we still have the other team that's going on the main ship …"
Connor's lips twisted into a frown. "To disable that ship, we'd need to cause the main reactor to fail. Overload would be better."

"Yeah, but a ship that big is bound to have more than one reactor powering it," Major Hayes said.

"Oh, it does for sure, and there are contingencies in place that prevent a chain reaction to the overload of a single reactor," Connor said.

"Okay, so what's the plan then?" Major Hayes asked.

"We're speculating and we have some good ideas, but until we actually get on board that ship, a lot of what we come up with will remain hypothetical. We know what kind of ships they were, but they've clearly been modified and have survived a two-hundred-year journey to get here," Connor said.

"That alone presents a multitude of questions, but the foundation for the ship's design is the same. It's a warship, but it all goes back to the same action. We need to get inside that ship," Reisman said.

Connor looked at Major Hayes. "You'll monitor the mission from here. Hopefully, we'll bring back some extra passengers. Assuming we do, we'll need areas established as quarantine zones. We know next to nothing about this virus, so we need a completely isolated system for quarantine. I want you to work with Dr. Allen on that."

Major Hayes nodded and then looked at Connor grimly.

"If it comes to it, you need to blow the ship up before we reach New Earth. If Noah does his job, the missile-defense platforms will be targeting the main Vemus forces. After that I told him to get to New Earth to update the orbital defenses," Connor said.

"Do you think they'll reach New Earth?" Major Hayes asked.

Connor glanced at the PRADIS readout. There was still a substantial fighting force intact. It would be a close thing. "We can only do the best we can. Our single highest priority is to prevent the Vemus from reaching New Earth. If we fail that, we've lost everything."

Connor hated all the assumptions they were making. Taken as a whole, they were stacking up, but they had little choice. The Vemus obviously had hostile intentions and they still didn't have a clear understanding of what the Vemus actually were. Sometimes one had to go into the monster's lair to see how much of a monster they really were.

Connor looked over at Sean, who'd been listening quietly.

"My team is ready, General," Sean said.

"Good. Tell them to assemble on the main hangar deck," Connor said and then snorted. "She's never going to forgive me for this."

Sean smiled. "I think she'll understand in this case."

Major Hayes looked confused. "I'm not following."

"Captain Quinn's mother is none other than the legendary Ashley Quinn—a force to be reckoned with," Connor said.

Major Hayes shook his head with a tired smile. "I hadn't realized."

Connor glanced at Sean. "See, it's working. No more special treatment," he said and looked back at Major Hayes. "When Ashley found out that her son had joined me in Search and Rescue, she punched me in the stomach."

Sean laughed. "She never admitted that."

"How do you think she reacted when the Colonial Defense Force was formed?" Connor said.

"What did she do?" Major Hayes asked.

"Let's just say I'm glad I'm a quick healer," Connor said.

Sean shrugged. "She always said you reminded her of her younger brother."

It was a momentary reprieve from what they were about to face, and Connor appreciated it. They all did, but after a few seconds a somber silence settled over them.

"The Vemus forces have been reactionary for the most part. Not sure why, so I think as we approach, if we don't show any aggression, they might just let us get near enough to board the ship," Connor said.

"By no aggression, you mean . . .?" Major Hayes asked.

"I mean we don't scan them or have our weapons pointed at them. Let's just fly right up to them and see what they do. Earlier, they took a shot at us because we were firing at them; otherwise, I'm not sure they would have bothered with us at all," Connor said.

"That's the part that bothers me," Reisman said.

"You're not the only one," Major Hayes agreed.

"It's worth a shot. We can get our weapons online and hope they don't hit us," Reisman said.

"A shot in the dark is better than no shot at all," Connor said.

He aimed to shine a bright light on the enemy. There were too many unanswered questions. Allegedly, these Vemus had defeated the combined military forces of Earth and had then come here with a large fighting force. Connor couldn't help but think there was so much more they needed to learn about their enemy. Gaining more intelligence was worth dying for if it yielded knowledge that gave them a fighting chance.

"Helm, plot a course for the Vemus battleship carrier. Best speed possible," Connor said.

23

IN THE HOURS THAT FOLLOWED, Connor grudgingly agreed that he wasn't to be on the first away team. He had to concede that Sean's cold logic left little to be argued with. Let Sean and his team secure the initial area, and when the all clear was given, the VIPs could come aboard. Reisman was amused to no end, and Major Hayes approved. So Connor remained on the bridge for the moment. Being outthought by his protégé should have made him proud. It didn't.

Reisman glanced at him. "Still reeling from the upset? It's always the quiet ones you need to watch out for."

"You'll be saluting him before long," Connor replied.

"Maybe. I was thinking of retiring after all this is done," Reisman replied.

Connor arched an eyebrow at him. "You'd go crazy inside a few months."

Reisman nodded. "Ordinarily yes, but I'm sure I can think of a better way to spend my time than being stuck on a warship for the rest of my life."

They were still on the bridge and were speaking quietly.

"I know better than to ask what *you'll* do," Reisman said.

Connor frowned. "You mean after we survive annihilation? I hadn't thought of it. I guess I'm too busy with the whole 'staying alive' part."

"Overrated. We all need reasons to fight, sir," Reisman said and walked over to speak with Major Hayes.

Connor wouldn't allow himself to think beyond the next few objectives. It helped him focus on what needed to be done. During his career, he'd noticed that some people liked to think about what they would do in the future and make plans. It was a coping mechanism—that he understood. A person needed to believe there was a light at the end of the tunnel even if, in truth, there was just more darkness waiting for them. When he was younger, Connor hardly ever thought about dying on any of the missions he was part of. Death was always present, but as a young man, he'd felt invincible. However, those were a much younger man's thoughts. Connor didn't feel invincible anymore. Far from it. Most recently he focused on what he could accomplish now and how that work could be carried on in the event that he did die. These past seven years he'd been so focused on protecting the colony that he'd never really thought about what he'd do if the danger passed. He'd always assumed he'd figure it out later, but seeing Lenora again a few weeks ago had him questioning whether that approach was best for him moving forward.

"Sir, I have the images from the high-res tactical array ready," Sergeant Browning said from the operations workstation.

Connor returned to the command chair. "Put it on the main holoscreen."

Using the high-res array, which was a system of high-powered optical imagers that weren't used during normal operations, was a calculated risk. Preferring not to push his luck, Connor ordered that the high-res array be retracted after they were done.

The rough outer hull of the Vemus ship appeared on screen. There were large gashes in the exoskeleton that surrounded the Alliance Navy vessel. Connor zoomed in on one of the damaged areas.

"Can you augment the darker areas inside that damaged section?" Connor asked.

Sergeant Browning tapped a few commands and the designated area of the image was rendered, but there wasn't much clarity with the updated image.

"I don't think we can improve on what we've already got, sir," Sergeant Browning said.

Connor zoomed out from that section of the image and noticed a metallic protrusion that didn't match the rest of the ship. On the starboard lower half of the ship was the cigar-shaped, gleaming hull of the *Banshee*. The destroyer appeared to be tethered to the ship by the same living exoskeleton that was part of the hull.

Reisman sat down in the chair next to Connor. "The ship looks intact."

"Yes, and it looks like several maintenance hatches are still available," Connor said.

"I'm not sure landing directly on the hull of the Vemus ship is a good idea. It could grab hold of the *Vigilant* and not let go," Reisman advised.

"Agreed. We'll use our own emergency docking clamps and attach them to the *Banshee*. Then the team can go through one of the maintenance hatches, make our way through the ship, and take it from there," Connor said.

"Sir," Sergeant Boers said, "should I try hailing the *Banshee*?"

"No, let's maintain radio silence for now. Continue to monitor for any communications," Connor said.

"Yes, sir."

They made their final approach to the Vemus ship and there was no indication that there was anything amiss. He wondered why the ship was traveling well below an ordinary battleship carrier's capability. Ships of the wall weren't designed for speed, per se; they were designed to deliver and take significant damage. The bulk of the remaining Vemus fleet was behind them. They'd seen the fleet increase their velocity for the assault on Titan Space Station.

Connor and Wil had run some comparison analyses against what they knew of NA Alliance ships' capabilities, and so far they had been comparable to what the Vemus ships had shown.

"Sergeant Edwards, take us in," Connor said.

"Yes, sir," Sergeant Edwards said.

Aaron Edwards was part of the primary bridge crew for the *Vigilant*. His performance scores for piloting the ship edged him over his alternate on the secondary bridge crew. Connor knew the *Vigilant* was in good hands.

A wave of tension-filled silence settled over the bridge, with most people's eyes glued to their own terminals or on the main holoscreen.

"Tactical, any change in the Vemus ship?" Connor asked.

"None, sir. It's like they don't care that we're here," Lieutenant LaCroix answered.

Reisman shrugged. "You know the saying about looking a gift horse in the mouth."

"Yeah, but I'd rather not get kicked by that same gift horse," Connor said.

What kind of invasion fleet would let an enemy ship just fly right up to it like they were doing? Connor watched the active plot on the main holoscreen showing their position relative to the battleship cruiser. They moved into position next to the *Banshee's* stern maintenance hatch. This would put them close to the primary ammunition depot.

Connor looked at Major Hayes. "Depending on what we find over there, we should consider adding additional teams to offload any ammunition we could use."

"The *Banshee's* computer system appears to be offline, but if we can get that up, we might be able to use the automated systems for munitions offloading," Major Hayes said.

Connor nodded. "We'll check the ship's systems once we get over there."

Connor stood up and Reisman did as well.

"Sir, we've matched velocity with the Vemus ship. Holding steady," Sergeant Edwards said.

"Ops, commence emergency docking procedure," Connor said.

"Emergency docking procedure being executed, sir," Sergeant Browning replied.

Connor looked at Major Hayes. "You have the con. Good luck, Major."

"I have the con. Good luck to you as well, General," Major Hayes replied.

Connor headed for the door, with Reisman and their CDF escort following. He opened a comlink to Sean. "We're all lined up. You're a go once we're docked."

"Acknowledged, sir. We'll do a quick sweep and give the okay for the second team," Sean replied.

Connor closed the comlink and frowned.

Reisman snorted. "Feels strange not to be the first ones through the door this time."

"I was thinking the same thing. Too bad more of the old team wasn't here,"

Connor said, thinking of Samson and Hank, who were training CDF Infantry on New Earth.

"Could have used Woods or Tiegen on this," Reisman said.

"Would have been nice, but they're working on the orbital defense system we have around home," Connor said.

Reisman glanced at him with a bemused expression. "I think that's the first time I've ever heard you refer to the colony as home instead of Earth."

"I'm evolving," Connor said and quickened his pace.

They went to the main hangar, where their combat suits would be waiting. He used his implants to check the status of the Away Team. They were making their way across the emergency airlock tube that connected the two ships. There were two combat suits waiting for them.

Sergeant Hoffer waved them over. "Right this way, General and Colonel."

He couldn't see Hoffer's face because he was already in his combat suit, but the soldier's name appeared on Connor's internal heads-up display, as did the names of the other soldiers on the secondary team. His Nexstar combat suit was split down the middle, with the chest plate opened. Connor climbed inside and activated the suite. His implants registered with the Nexstar's computer systems. The power armor closed itself up and the suite status showed on his helmet's HUD. He was green across the board. Connor felt the familiar adrenaline burst from being in combat armor once again. These combat suits were modified series eights, designed for space combat. They carried enough oxygen to last them for days, and the onboard medical systems could administer treatment depending on the type of injuries. The Nexstars were as tough as they came. He picked up an AR-71 assault rifle with grenade launcher attachment, Connor's preferred weapon these days.

Connor and Reisman moved toward the front where Captain Lee waited. Saluting with a combat suit wasn't practical, so Captain Lee simply greeted Connor.

"Captain Quinn is at the maintenance hatch now," Captain Lee said.

Connor nodded, and his armored head bobbed up and down. Time to find out what the hell these Vemus really were.

24

Connor waited near the emergency airlock. Within ten minutes of Sean's platoon entering the *Banshee*, he opened a comlink saying they were clear to come aboard. They walked across the emergency docking tube and Connor stepped inside the *Banshee* first.

"No contacts at all?" Connor asked Sean over a comlink.

"That's affirmative, sir. It's like the crew of the *Banshee* all left. There are no life signs on the ship," Sean said.

The interior of the ship was sparsely lit from the emergency lighting along the ceiling. Connor scanned for any active comms channels, but there were none.

"Sir, we just got to the bridge. The systems here appear to be on standby. According to the logs, the crew left the ship," Sean said.

"Does it say where they went?" Connor asked.

"It was a quick entry from Major Cross. She just says the ship isn't safe and that they went inside the enemy ship to try to secure another ship to escape with," Sean said.

"That doesn't sound right. Major Cross wouldn't endanger her entire crew on a whim. There has to be more to it than that," Reisman said.

"See if you can restore emergency systems," Connor told Sean. "Captain Lee, I want you to take half the team and see what can be salvaged from the ship. We need to know if there are any intact warheads we can use."

"On it, General," Captain Lee said and began issuing orders.

Connor and the rest of the platoon headed toward the bridge. The Destroyer-class vessels were much smaller than the heavy cruiser. The scans they had of the ship from the outside showed that it had been heavily damaged before the Vemus disabled it. Savannah Cross hadn't given the ship up without a fight.

More emergency lighting came on as they made it to the bridge. Sean had

CDF troops stationed outside. Connor and Reisman went inside and found Sean standing at the tactical workstation, where he had a holoscreen active.

"They used the forward hatch to get aboard the Vemus ship, sir," Sean said.

Connor used his implants to access the *Banshee's* systems. He skimmed the logs quickly. "They did repel boarders, but they suffered severe casualties. I still would have expected a small group to have been left behind."

"Wouldn't want to draw that short straw," Reisman said.

Connor glanced at him. "Come again?"

"Think about it. You've lost a bunch of your crew fighting this enemy and then the few that remain have a choice. Stay holed up in here and make the enemy come to you or head out on their ship and make them chase you," Reisman said.

Sean brought his hand up to his ear. "Go ahead, Anders."

"Sir, we've found some of the living exoskeleton stuff near the hatch. It's on the walls too," Anders said.

"Let's go check it out. I doubt we'll find anything of further use here," Connor said.

They left the bridge and headed along the corridor to the forward port hatch, where they met a three-man team. Along the walls was a glistening, thick film of brown sludge.

"Wynn, report. What is this stuff?" Sean asked.

Sergeant Nick Wynn was the medic with a background in biology.

"Seems to be coming from the Vemus ship. It doesn't react to stimuli, but it will stick to whatever it comes in contact with, so I wouldn't touch it," Sergeant Wynn said.

Connor looked at the closed hatch and saw that the brown sludge was coming through the door, which wasn't airtight anymore. At least it hadn't reached the door controls.

"Open the hatch," Connor said.

Sergeant Wynn stepped back while two soldiers went over to the hatch. Connor looked at Wynn. "Did you collect samples?"

Wynn's eyes widened and he shook his head.

"We'll need some samples to study," Connor said.

"I'm sorry, sir. I have a sample kit. I'll start collecting some immediately," Sergeant Wynn said.

The CDF soldiers at the hatch stopped while Wynn went over to the wall. He opened a metallic container and withdrew a thin plastic rod with a small scoop on the tip. He dipped it into the brown sludge and deposited a dollop into the container. Sergeant Wynn closed everything up and gave them a nod.

"If you see something you think is important, let us know and we'll make sure you have an opportunity to check it out," Connor said.

"Understood, General," Sergeant Wynn said.

"Open the hatch," Sean ordered his men.

A soldier activated the manual release and checked that the team was ready. Four more CDF soldiers held their weapons in covering formation. If there was anything on the other side of that hatch, it would be dead before it knew what hit it. The soldier pulled the hatch open. There was a slight hiss and the atmosphere equalized with that of the Vemus ship.

Connor's combat suit scanned the air for any contaminants. His internal heads-up display showed the analyses of the atmosphere, all of which indicated a breathable atmosphere that was standard for a spacefaring vessel.

"My scanners are showing that the air is good," Reisman said.

"Same," Connor replied.

Beyond the hatch was a dimly lit corridor. Connor's helmet compensated for the low light so he could see clearly. The dark gray walls had a purplish tint to them, as if there was a small electric charge running through the material, and appeared to have been created from a similar substance to that which they'd observed on the outer hull.

They slowly entered the enemy ship. Connor kept waiting for some kind of alarm to sound, but there was nothing. He used the butt of his AR-71 to test the sturdiness of the corridor walls. They were hardened and, upon closer inspection, Connor saw that there were multiple layers, as if they'd been grown.

"There's a lot of humidity. Could be why the walls have that glistening sheen to them," Sean said.

They delved deeper into the ship and still didn't see anyone else. Connor checked for open comlinks again, but there weren't any. They came to an open area where multiple deck levels were exposed. It was only then that Connor saw exposed pieces of material that were definitely manmade. There were angled edges of the metallic alloy used in NA Alliance ships.

"There has to be some kind of crew aboard this ship. There's no way it could be flown otherwise," Reisman said.

"I think the mere fact that this ship is here is miracle enough," Connor said.

"What do you mean?" Reisman said.

Connor walked to the edge of the deck and gestured over at the far wall.

Reisman gasped.

The black-and-gold lettering had once gleamed a proud name that was familiar to any NA Alliance soldier. The lettering was so faded that there was only the vague impression of their shapes, but they were clear enough to read.

Sean came to Connor's side and peered at the far wall. "*Indianapolis*! *The Indianapolis*? The battleship carrier you were last on before being shanghaied onto the *Ark*?"

Connor glanced at Reisman, who for once was clearly at a loss for words. He glanced around, unable to believe that over two hundred years ago he'd stood upon the very decks of this ship—a Barracuda-class battleship carrier, the pinnacle warship in the NA Alliance Navy.

"I can't believe it," Connor said at last.

He used his neural implants to find an open network connection using an encrypted Alliance protocol. Connor's eyes widened when the ship's systems replied to his request.

"There's an active computer system here that responds to Alliance protocols," Connor said, looking at Reisman.

Reisman's eyebrows pulled together in concentration as he used his own implants. A moment later he nodded. "This is too frigging weird. How the hell is this ship even here? It's like some cruel joke."

"What do you mean?" Sean asked.

Reisman gestured to Connor and then back at himself. "We were both on this ship. All the Ghosts were. This ship intercepted us after the Chronos Space Station was destroyed."

Connor kept looking around, trying to peer past the strange material that covered the walls. Knowing it was the *Indianapolis* gave him a strange feeling of déjà vu. Connor probed beyond the initial network connection, seeking to get the status of the ship's systems.

"I'm only seeing systems that are locked out. It's like there was a system-wide lockout," Connor said.

"If that's the case, how are you even able to access the system for it to tell you that everything is locked out?" Sean asked.

"Because our credentials must still be in the system somehow," Connor replied.

"How is this ship flying without computer systems? We saw it use weapons and navigation. Those systems have to be working," Reisman said.

Connor's thoughts kept racing with all the possibilities. "I know where we can find the answers."

Reisman nodded. "The core systems. I can try to bypass the lockout there."

"Do either of you know where it is?" Sean asked.

"Of course. It's near the bridge," Connor said at the same time Reisman said, "near Main Engineering."

Sean glanced at both of them. "Which one is it? By the bridge or Main Engineering?"

Connor glanced at Reisman, who gave him a challenging look. "They'd never put the system core by the bridge," Reisman said.

"You're wrong. The system core is by the primary bridge in the forward section near the middle decks, where it has the most protection," Connor said.

Reisman shook his head. "I'm not wrong. You're thinking of the secondary bridge just behind midship near Main Engineering."

Connor frowned in thought, considering. Was he wrong? He'd only served aboard naval warships early in his career, which was required for any active combat soldier regardless of the military branch they served in.

Sean pressed his lips together. "Could there be more than one computing core?"

Reisman shook his head. "No, there was a primary computing core with the ability to isolate different systems in case the cyber warfare suite failed."

Sean glanced at Connor. "We need a decision here. I'd rather not divide our team to chase two leads."

"Sir, come on, this is me," Reisman said. "I was the operations and intelligence officer in our old platoon. It was my job to know how to take down systems so if the shit hit the fan you could say to me, 'Wil, I need this broken ASAP,' and I'd be able to do it."

Connor shook his head. "Not quite like that," said Connor, giving his friend a pointed look. "We're in the aft section or just beyond it, so midship is this way. We can check it out on the way."

"When we get there, you'll be saying how sorry you are for ever doubting me," Reisman said.

Connor grinned and then blew out a breath. Sean had six of his team take point while Connor and Reisman stayed in the middle. Connor kept thinking about Admiral Mitch Wilkinson, who, to the best of Connor's knowledge, had remained the flag officer of the battleship carrier *Indianapolis*. Wilkinson had been referred to by Dr. Stone in the summary message that was part of a major update to the original *Ark* mission.

What virus or parasitic life form does this? Connor wondered. He glanced at the hardened substance on the walls.

A comlink from the *Vigilant* registered on his internal heads-up display and Connor called for a stop.

"General," Major Hayes said, "the two battleship carriers have increased their velocity. The remaining Vemus fleet has also caught up with us. We've run the numbers and I'm sending a timer out to you to show how much time we have before we reach the defense platforms and New Earth's orbital defenses."

A countdown timer appeared on Connor's heads-up display and the others around him confirmed they were seeing the same thing.

"Understood. We have it now. Captain Lee is still on the *Banshee*, looking to salvage materials," Connor said.

"He's already contacted us and we're starting the offload. There were only two warheads left intact, so they're removing those and configuring a detonator for them. We've also done some analysis of the remaining Vemus fleet. We've noticed that many of the ships don't match up with the NA Alliance Navy or any navy. Lieutenant LaCroix believes the Vemus fleet is made up of multiple ships merging together somehow. We're not sure of the reason, but some of the ships have features of civilian ships, particularly freighters. Anything with a lot of mass," Major Hayes reported.

"Still no reaction to our presence here?" Connor asked.

"None that we can detect. We've run passive scans, which they don't seem to mind. In the event that they attack us, I have a comms buoy set to deploy to COMCENT," Major Hayes said.

"Understood. We're checking the computing core to see if we can learn more about the enemy," Connor said.

The comlink closed.

"Merging ships," Reisman said thoughtfully. "The only reason I can think to do that is to address resource needs."

Connor nodded. "So that brown sludge is absorbing the *Banshee*, and if we stay here long enough, it will start absorbing the *Vigilant* as well."

"Into the belly of the beast, as it were," Reisman said.

Connor sent a quick message to Major Hayes to monitor the living exoskeleton material and not let it near the *Vigilant*. Then they quickened their pace as much as they could. They didn't have schematics of the interior of the ship, so they were reliant on the faded maps on the parts of the walls that weren't covered by foreign materials, as well as Connor's and Reisman's memories. Not the most reliable way to navigate through an enemy ship, but it was what they had to work with. They stayed near the center of the corridors and had to occasionally backtrack because the way forward was blocked by a crag-laden wall of the hardened brown sludge.

As they neared the Main Engineering section of the ship, the hardened material was restricted to a bulging mass along the middle of the wall instead of covering the walls and the ceiling. The mass was rounded, with glowing material moving inside it.

"The system core should be up ahead on the right," Reisman said.

The way forward widened by several meters and there were two massive rooms on either side.

Sean was in front of Connor. He looked over to the left. There were multiple large tubes of the exoskeleton material going into the room. The room itself was a vast network of the same material, as if a host of vines had taken over the area.

"What is this place?" Sean asked.

"That's supposed to be Main Engineering, which includes the main reactor that powers the ship," Connor said.

"And over to our right, just where I said it was," Reisman said, smiling triumphantly.

"I can admit when I'm wrong, but there *is* a computing core near the main bridge," Connor said.

Reisman nodded. "The secondary one."

Connor looked over to the right. The computing core was largely intact. The workstations were grouped together before a vast array of high-end server farms that were the brains of the warship. Glowing green lights came from the data storage arrays as electrical arcs walked their way through the vast array in rapid succession, only to be lost from view.

Connor walked over to the main workstation. An amber holoscreen showed that a system-wide lockdown protocol had been initiated. He glanced at the date and time stamp for when the lockdown had happened.

"Look at that," Connor said. "The lockdown was initiated twenty years after we left."

"That's around the time the *Ark's* mission was updated," Reisman replied.

Connor watched as his friend sat down at the workstation. He brought up several submenus and initiated login attempts. After a few minutes of failing to initiate a bypass, a single screen appeared and Reisman snatched his hands away from the interface.

"What the hell is this!" Reisman shouted.

::*Col. Gates protocol. Input required.*::

Connor stared at the prompt, his mouth agape.

"This thing just asked for you by name with your old Alliance rank," Reisman said.

"Well, I did try to access it before," Connor replied.

One of the CDF soldiers keeping watch in the corridor called out for Sean.

Reisman stood up and gestured for Connor to sit in the chair. Connor sat down and tried inputting his date of birth and military identification number. The prompt just reset back to the same challenge. He tried to think of other things that would satisfy the challenge, but nothing worked.

"How about the date you enlisted?" Reisman suggested.

Connor tried it and that didn't work. He narrowed his gaze and concentrated hard. Suddenly, a thought blazed like a beacon in his brain and he entered a specific date and time that would appear random to anyone else but him.

::*Input accepted. Initiating data dump. Please specify destination.*::

Connor glanced at Reisman questioningly.

"One second," Reisman said and opened the holo-interface on the arm of his combat suit. "I've opened a secure channel to the *Vigilant*," Reisman said and made a passing motion of the channel to Connor.

A new data storage connection appeared on Connor's internal heads-up display and he mounted it to the session.

::*Success. Dump in progress . . .* ::

Connor stood up.

"What was that date you entered?" Reisman asked.

"The date my father died. He was close friends with Admiral Wilkinson," Connor replied.

"Why is that date important to Wilkinson?"

"My father was KIA and saved Wilkinson's life," Connor said.

Reisman glanced at the holoscreen. "This could take a while," he said, noting the progress. He brought up another window and started checking a few things.

Connor glanced over at Sean and noticed him speaking with his men. He walked over to them. "What's going on?"

"We think we've found the *Banshee* crew," Sean said.

"Where?" Connor asked.

Sean frowned. "That's the thing. Sergeant Anders picked up a partial link detection when they scouted down the corridor going toward the bridge."

Connor glanced back at Reisman, who was busy working away at the workstation. "Let's leave three men to guard Wil's back and the rest of us will go check out the bridge," he said.

Reisman said he was going to try to learn all he could about the ship before they had to leave. The countdown timer for when they would enter the defense platform's missile range was steadily drawing downward.

They headed toward the secondary bridge. Connor kept thinking about the system access challenge meant for him. Admiral Wilkinson must have set all this up, but how? If they were losing a war with the Vemus, why would he choose to single Connor out from any number of people who might have come onto this ship? What if no one had ever come aboard? Would that data have been lost forever? It was quite a gamble. What had happened to Earth during the final stages of the war? Wilkinson was a brilliant strategist, so it wasn't unlike him to have many pans in the fire at once, working toward the same goal.

"Your friend was really counting on you to be here," Sean said.

"I was just thinking the same thing," Connor replied.

"Noah is always going on about how there are ways to code subroutines that only become active if certain conditions are met. Same thing could have happened here," Sean said.

Connor scanned for comlink traffic, but they were still flat-lined.

"How far ahead did Anders' group scout?" Connor asked. They were approaching the secondary bridge.

"It's just over here," Sergeant Anders said.

Connor pushed ahead with Sean at his side.

The bridge doors were shut. One of the CDF soldiers palmed the access panel, and after a few moments, the doors squeaked opened. The secondary bridge was designed to take over the operation of a warship in the event that the primary bridge became compromised during a conflict. The workstations and command area were largely intact but for the scorch marks that dotted some of the workstations. There were long, faded, dark stains on the floor and behind some of the workstations. The onboard sensors must have detected their presence because some of the less damaged workstations sparked to life.

Dust swirled through the partial lighting, giving the bridge a ghostly flare. Connor headed toward the command area.

"What do you think happened here?" Sergeant Anders asked.

"These are calcium deposits," Sergeant Wynn said while squatting down. "These were bodies. People died here."

Connor stood in front of the command chair. There were no dark splotches on it from a battle that must have been fought here over two hundred years ago —more than enough time for a body to decompose, assuming the Vemus maintained even a partial atmosphere throughout the ship. Connor sat in the command chair and activated the terminal. He used his implants to provide his Alliance credentials. A long list of failed system statuses scrolled through the screen as if the computer systems were relieved to finally offload their burden. Then a lone active alert appeared. Connor frowned and selected the alert, which highlighted the main hangar bay.

The main holoscreen flickered on. Part of the imager was damaged, so they could only see a small part of the screen. There were flashes of light but no sound. Connor peered at the screen and saw several people moving. They were wearing CDF uniforms.

25

CONNOR SPRANG FROM THE CHAIR. "I know where the crew of the *Banshee* went. They're at the main hangar."

"They're fighting something. That could be why no one has detected our presence here," Sean said.

The imager died with a fizzle as the aged circuitry finally gave its last breath and the main holoscreen powered off.

"Come on, we're heading to the hangar," Connor said.

He opened up a comlink to Reisman. "How's the data dump going?"

"About halfway through," Reisman said.

"We've found the crew of the *Banshee*. They're fighting Vemus forces in the main hangar. We're heading there now," Connor said.

"Acknowledged. Captain Lee has just arrived with the modified warheads. They're going to deploy them in Main Engineering," Reisman said.

"How are they getting inside it?" Connor asked, remembering the overgrowth of hardened materials throughout the area.

"They brought plasma torches and are cutting that stuff away. I'll send an update once we're all set to go here," Reisman said.

"Understood," Connor said.

"One more thing," Reisman said. "I've been poking around the ship's systems. It's like the entire thing has been through a major overhaul. Nothing is where it should be as far as systems go. There's some kind of broadcast signal coming through the main communications array, but it's using a protocol I've never seen before."

"Is it active?" Connor asked.

"Yes," Reisman answered.

"Can you shut it down?"

"I'm not able to. The only thing I can tell is that there's an active connection

—a pretty powerful one—but I'm not clear on where it's coming from," Reisman said.

"Keep working on it. Send what you have so far to Major Hayes. Perhaps the *Vigilant* can detect the signal as well," Connor said.

The comlink closed and Connor bit his lower lip in thought. If these signals were consistently present among the Vemus fleet, it might be something he could use against them.

As they closed in on the main hangar bay, Connor and the others heard weapons being fired. He scanned the comms network and was able to find Major Cross's signal. He didn't open a link yet, preferring to get a better sense of what he was dealing with. Connor looked back at Sean and held up two fingers, then made a circular motion.

Sean signaled to one of the CDF soldiers and he nodded. The soldier reached into the storage compartment of his Nexstar combat suit, pulled out two reconnaissance drones, and tossed them into the air.

Connor used his implants to access the drone feeds. They flew into the hangar and separated, making a general sweep of the area. There were smaller attack craft lined up on the far side of the hangar, and the crew of the *Banshee* was clustered around a combat shuttle. They were firing their weapons at a group of large dark figures that stalked their way toward them. White bolts were being fired at the remainder of the *Banshee* crew, who scrambled behind cover. Connor zoomed in on the Vemus forces. They were massive, with some of them easily twice as tall as he was. Their skin was a deep, dark purple that glistened in the light. Their rounded heads angled to a pointed snout. Lighter-toned oval shapes could have been eyes, but Connor wasn't sure. They had thick legs, with rippling muscles that ended in clawed feet. They staggered their approach and another group was working their way toward the *Banshee* crew's flank. Between the dark shapes and how they kept on the move, it was hard to get an accurate count, even with the help of his combat suit's computer systems.

A series of high-pitched whistles and clicks came from the Vemus forces. They moved fast and seemed to be able to move as quickly on two legs as they could when hunched over like a quadruped.

The crew of the *Banshee* was mixed, with some wearing combat armor while others wore a breather. Their hands and other parts of their bodies were exposed to the atmosphere. They fired their weapons in controlled bursts, halting the Vemus advance while conserving their ammunition.

Connor opened a comlink to Major Cross.

"General! They can detect active comlinks. Go to short-wave IR," Major Cross said.

Just after she spoke there was an uptick in the whistles and clicks coming from the Vemus forces. Connor immediately deactivated the comlink and did as she asked.

"What's your status, Major?" Connor asked.

"I saw the drones. As you can see, we're pinned down. Every time we try to move, they press the attack. We were trying to use one of these shuttles to get out of here," Major Cross said.

"Is the shuttle operational?" Connor asked.

He saw Sean gesturing to the CDF soldiers. They were moving into position just inside the main hangar behind a barricade to provide covering fire. The drone feeds cut out at the same time. They'd been shot down.

"Negative, sir. None of shuttles are operational. I guess sitting in the hangar for two hundred years depleted their power cells," Major Cross said.

"We can provide covering fire. Can you make it to us?" Connor asked and shot an IR laser, marking their location.

There was bellowing from the Vemus forces. Connor peered past the wall and saw several of the enemy scrambling toward them.

"Take them down!" Connor shouted.

The CDF soldiers unleashed the might of their weapons, cutting into the Vemus as they charged toward them. The *Banshee* crew fired their weapons at the Vemus force's exposed flank, and the colossal giants started to fall. Dark liquid burst from their bodies. Connor and the rest of the team fired their weapons, scattering the Vemus forces, who scrambled to cover, where they returned fire. A CDF soldier next to Connor took a white bolt to the chest. His armor absorbed the blow and the soldier knelt back into cover. In a short span of time, they'd cut the Vemus forces in half.

Connor opened a short-range IR channel to Major Cross. "Now's your chance. Come on."

"You don't understand. Those things aren't dead—"

A loud ringing tone sounded and Connor was forced to cut the connection.

"Why aren't they coming?" Sean asked.

Connor glanced over the wall, looking at the fallen Vemus. "She said they aren't dead."

Sean frowned and looked over the wall. His eyes widened. "Some of them are starting to move again!"

Connor fired his weapon at a rising Vemus, but the standard round for the AR-71 had little effect. He accessed his weapons systems and changed it to fire incendiary rounds. When the nano-robotic ammunition had changed over, Connor aimed his weapon and fired. Flashes of superheated rounds burst from the barrel, and he caught the Vemus soldier in the chest. The scorching rounds burned a massive hole in the creature's chest. The Vemus soldier didn't so much as cry out in pain as it flew back onto the ground. Connor took several more shots, cutting up the remains. The rest of the CDF soldiers nearby updated their nano-robotic ammunition for their weapons to incendiary rounds.

"Lay it on them," Connor said.

He opened a comlink to Major Cross. The Vemus already knew they were there, so there was little risk at this point. "This is your chance. We'll provide covering fire and you make your way toward us. That's an order, Major."

Connor fired a grenade into a cluster of Vemus forces, blowing them apart. The crew of the *Banshee* burst from cover and Connor and the others provided covering fire. The Vemus forces whipped up into a frenzy. They charged out after the fleeing crew, heedless of the weapons being fired at them. They snatched a few stragglers, taking the CDF crew down to the ground. They hovered over them, tearing off masks and helmets. The Vemus opened their wide mouths and spat thick black liquid onto the CDF soldiers' faces.

Connor aimed for a Vemus soldier's head and fired. He watched as a struggling *Banshee* crewmember's body went into convulsions, their entire face covered in blackish goo.

Fallen Vemus soldiers began to rise again.

"What the hell is it going to take to kill these things?" Sean said while firing his weapon.

The *Banshee* crew was being picked off by the emboldened Vemus forces. Connor fired several more grenades, figuring the explosive impacts would slow them down.

"Bringing down the hammer!" Sergeant Woods cried.

The heavy weapons soldier fired a tactical missile, and the hangar floor behind the fleeing *Banshee* crew was engulfed in flames.

As the fire diminished, Connor heard the strange, high-pitched whistle coming from the Vemus forces caught in the blast, and the call was taken up by the remaining Vemus that were beyond the blast zone. Several flaming figures crawled away, only to collapse and stop moving. The remaining *Banshee* crew sprinted toward them. There was only a fraction of them left. Several CDF soldiers kept firing their weapons at the Vemus forces. The ones on the far side of the hangar started to regroup. They barreled into the flames, heedless of the heat, and their long strides carried them across the hangar despite Connor's efforts to stop them.

Major Savannah Cross came around the wall. Connor could hear her gasping.

"How did you hold out for so long?" Connor asked.

"We had to keep changing the type of ammunition we were using. Only when they're blown completely apart do they stay down," Major Cross said, gritting her teeth. "They don't ever stop. They just keep coming."

Connor heard shouting from down the line of soldiers. Sergeant Wynn was down. Blue bolts were arcing through his combat suit. The sergeant screamed, and nearby CDF soldiers tried to take his armor off. The power armor was unresponsive and Sean used the manual release to pop the chest cavity. Connor peered at Sergeant Wynn's blackened chest as the man writhed in pain. Wynn looked as if he were struggling to say something, and then the dying soldier let out a gurgling gasp.

More blue energy bolts fired toward them and one hit Sergeant Anders. The CDF soldier screamed as he went down.

"Take cover!" Connor shouted and dove behind a barrier.

The Vemus forces had changed their tactics. They had weapons that could disable their power armor and kill the person inside. They had to get out of there, quickly.

"Sergeant Woods, do you have anything to cover our escape?" Connor asked.

"You bet, sir. I have a portable MS-Hydra," Sergeant Woods said.

The MS-Hydra was a robotic mini-turret capable of firing millions of high-velocity darts a minute, devastating to an ordinary attack force. They would soon find out how effective it was against the Vemus.

"Take it to the end of the corridor and get ready. We'll buy you some time," Connor said.

Sergeant Woods called one of the other CDF soldiers over and they ran down the corridor.

The rest of them continued to fire on the Vemus. There was a mix of ammunition being used, from blistering incendiary rounds to armor-piercing rounds and small grenades. Connor ordered them to fall back, and the CDF soldiers began to quickly move into the corridor. The Vemus forces detected the decreased rate of weapons fire and began to press forward.

"Time to go, sir," Sean said.

Connor backed away from the wall, and they shuffled down the corridor, firing their weapons in controlled bursts as they went. Soon after, they turned around and ran as fast as they could.

Connor reached the end of the corridor where the MS-Hydra sat on a tripod of thick legs that were drilled into the ground. The Hydra mount was a metallic, rectangular box and inside were thousands of high-velocity darts capable of piercing armor and destroying flesh.

"The Hydra is ready," Sean said.

"Good. Enable the sensors to fire on the targets when they're within two meters," Connor said.

He glanced down the corridor at the hangar beyond. The dark, colossal shapes of the Vemus forces started gathering at the corridor entrance.

Connor went toward the front and began leading his team back the way they'd come. High-pitched whistles and clicks seemed to echo all along the corridor.

Connor opened a comlink to Reisman. "Wil, what's your status?"

Reisman grunted. "Ah, data upload is complete."

Reisman sounded as if he were straining with something. "What's wrong?" Connor asked.

"Captain Lee planted the bomb, but something happened to them inside Main Engineering. They've been cut off," Reisman said.

Connor urged the soldiers in front of him to move faster.

"Are you hurt?" Connor asked.

"No—uh, just get back here. Watch out for that brown sludge on the walls. It's creeping into the computing core," Reisman said.

The CDF soldiers ahead of him checked the corners and then cleared them to proceed. Connor was about to tell Reisman to get out of there when an ear-splitting shriek sounded from behind them. The MS-Hydra had fired its payload.

Connor and the others quickened their pace. They had to make it back to the *Vigilant* or they were all going to pay the price.

They reached the atrium where the name *Indianapolis* in all its faded glory adorned the wall. Vemus forces appeared on the decks across from them. Connor and the others took turns firing their weapons to hold them off. These forces were much shorter than what they'd encountered in the main hangar bay, and they tracked from the other decks like a pack of rabid wolves. Shooting at them only seemed to ignite their ferocity. The Vemus weapons fire was a mix between the white stunner bolts and the armor-disabling blue bolts. Connor and the others made it to the corridor that would take them out of the vast atrium. He took one last glance at the Vemus forces. Some were attempting to jump across the distance to the deck he stood on. Several dark-skinned bodies missed and plunged down.

The Vemus stopped and clustered across the way.

"General, we have to go," Sean called out to him.

Connor took a step back but couldn't tear his eyes away. The Vemus forces were huddled together in a mass, their bodies quivering. Finally, one of them emerged and leaped onto the railing of the upper deck, stretching its arms wide. Connecting the creature's wrist to its feet was a thick layer of leathery skin.

"General!" Sean called again.

Connor aimed his AR-71 as the Vemus soldier leaped from the upper railings. The creature glided across the atrium, flying straight toward him. Connor fired his weapon, aiming for the creature's head, and then adjusted his aim and tore through the wings. More of the Vemus emerged from the mass that huddled together. They vaulted from the upper deck.

At last Connor turned around and ran, catching up with Sean.

"What did you see back there?" Sean asked.

"They changed forms," Connor said.

Sean glanced behind him for a moment while they ran. "Shape-shifting?"

"No . . . well. Not quite. Only partially. It's like they can rapidly adapt. I've never seen anything like it," Connor said.

The weapons the former *Banshee* crew carried were depleted of ammunition. CDF soldiers from Sean's platoon shared their spare ammunition, but it was tough going while they were on the run.

Connor glanced behind him. He could hear the Vemus, but they hadn't come down the corridor yet. The team ahead of them stopped outside the computing core. Connor saw a webbing of hardened vines that stretched across the ceiling from Main Engineering to the computing core. He looked over at the workstations where Reisman was working and gasped. Hanging from the ceiling to the floor was a wall of the brown sludge that had hardened into an exoskeleton.

"Connor?" Reisman called out, and his voice was coming from the other side of the pillar.

Connor took a step into the room. "I'm here," he said and circled around the workstations, careful not to get too close. Reisman's combat suit looked as if it were partially submerged into the exoskeleton. Connor could see his friend's face through his helmet. He took a step closer, but Sean held him back.

"Probably a good idea," Reisman said in a mild attempt at humor.

"What the hell happened?" Connor asked and glanced around. "There were some plasma cutters around here. Go find them."

Sean repeated the order.

"There's no time for that. It's inside my suit. I can feel it working its way up my legs," Reisman said, and his face crumpled in pain.

Connor glared at the other CDF soldiers. "Damn it! Where are those cutters?" He looked back at his friend. "We're gonna get you out of there."

Reisman shook his head and gave him a solemn look. "Not this time, sir. You have to listen to me."

Connor glared over at the CDF soldiers who were scrambling to find something that would help, but they couldn't find anything.

"Fine," Connor said and checked his AR-71.

Deep in the corridors, the high-pitched whistling sound of Vemus soldiers could be heard. Connor saw several CDF soldiers take up positions on either side of the corridor, keeping a watchful eye on the way they'd come.

Connor set his ammunition to high-heat incendiary and aimed his rifle.

"No, you can't!" Reisman cried.

Connor paused with his finger on the trigger. If he could just cut a line on the edges of the base, Reisman could get free. "This will work," Connor insisted.

"It won't work. It's in my suit," Reisman said.

"Sir, perhaps we should listen to him," Sean said.

Connor clenched his teeth. The sounds of the Vemus forces came steadily closer. He opened a link to Reisman's suit computer, which quickly provided the current status of the suit. The last line of code felt like a punch in the stomach.

::*CAUTION: Foreign contaminant present.*::

Connor eased his hand off the trigger and lowered his rifle. "Damn it, Wil."

Reisman winced in pain. "I know. I know. I really stepped in it this time—" He cut off, crying out in pain. "I can feel it crawling along inside me."

Connor took a step forward. He wanted to crack open the combat suit and pull his friend out.

"You have to leave me behind," Reisman said.

Sorrow closed Connor's throat and he gritted his teeth. The sounds of the Vemus forces were becoming louder. The CDF soldiers called out.

"Sir," Sean said.

Connor knew what he was going to say, and he hated him for it. Sean called out to him again.

"Take them back to the ship," Connor said, scowling.

"Not without you, sir," Sean replied.

"That's an order, Captain," Connor said.

"With all due respect, sir, if I have to knock you out and order my men to drag you, I *will* do it," Sean replied stubbornly.

Reisman laughed. It sounded harsh and laden with pain, and it tapered off into a fit of coughing. "You trained him too well."

Connor looked at Sean. "Order them to fall back. I'm right behind you."

Sean narrowed his gaze and then turned around and began ordering them to fall back to the ship.

"You have to do something for me," Reisman said.

Connor looked back at his friend. His face had become pasty white. The AR-71 Connor carried suddenly felt heavy in his arms.

"I'm still in their systems. There's a signal the Vemus use. I'm still tracing it," Reisman said.

"Never mind that," Connor said.

"It's important. I've linked our suits so the data that comes to mine will flow freely to yours. You have to get off this ship and ensure that I'm not dying for nothing. You hear me?" Reisman said.

Connor glanced at the CDF soldiers in the corridor. They were focused. They'd hold the area as long as they could, but it wouldn't be enough.

"Hey!" Reisman called out to him.

Connor looked back at him. "I can't leave like this. First Kasey and now you, Wil. I won't do it."

Reisman's eyes softened. "Yes, you will. These people don't stand a chance without you. It's our time, not yours. Save as many as you can."

An alarm appeared on Connor's heads-up display and he looked at Reisman.

"I'll hold out as long as I can. Remember that case of scotch we liberated from that senator's office? What was his name?" Reisman asked.

Connor frowned. "It was bourbon."

"You're going to argue with me now? You . . . What was his name?"

Connor's brows pulled together. "Senator Wellington."

A countdown appeared on Connor's HUD.

"You need to run. In a hundred and twenty seconds I'm going to blow this area to kingdom come," Reisman said.

Connor knew he was right. Wil had engaged the self-destruct protocol of his combat suite. It would easily take out this entire room.

"Run!" Reisman said.

Connor clenched his teeth and took one last look at his friend. Wil gave him a firm nod. Connor turned around and called for the CDF soldiers to retreat.

They ran down the corridor, away from the approaching Vemus forces. Connor glanced at the data connection to Reisman on his heads-up display. As long as it was active, his friend was still alive. As Connor ran he felt a weariness take him, making his feet feel weighed down. Part of him just wanted to stop. Stop fighting. Stop trying. A primal part of him seemed to take control and he wanted to strike out at his enemies, make one last stand right here in the corridor, but he knew it was foolish. He'd be struck down and then it would fall to someone else to lead the Colonial Defense Force against the Vemus.

Blue bolts struck the wall near him, and Connor scrambled out of the way. The Vemus had caught up with them. Connor spun around and returned fire, as did several of the CDF soldiers near him. A loud pop sounded and the corridor that had been filled with Vemus became engulfed in flames. The data connection to Reisman's combat suit severed and Connor knew his friend was dead.

Connor cried out a rage-filled scream. Sean grabbed him and pulled him around while urging the others to run. They made it back to the *Banshee,* and a comlink opened to him from Major Hayes.

"We're the last ones aboard. Do you have the detonation signal from Captain Lee?" Connor asked.

"We have it but have been unable to reach Captain Lee for some time now, sir," Major Hayes said.

They ran through the CDF destroyer. Emergency lighting was still on.

Connor could still hear the Vemus following behind them. Some of them must have survived the blast or had been out of proximity.

There was a cluster of soldiers waiting to get through the emergency docking tube to the *Vigilant*. There was nothing they could do but wait for everyone else to get aboard.

"Major, once we're all aboard, we need to get out of here quickly," Connor said.

"Understood, General. We'll be ready," Major Hayes said.

Connor kept his weapon pointed back the way they'd come. The Vemus were likely on the *Banshee* by now. Sean didn't say anything as he came to stand by Connor's side and readied his own weapon.

They heard the Vemus, faint at first but quickly becoming louder.

"Here they come," Connor said grimly.

He and Sean drew steadily backward, closer to the emergency dock. Connor kept his gaze fixed on the darkened corridor, waiting, anticipating the enemy's approach.

"I have an idea," Sean said.

Connor kept his attention on the end of the narrow ship corridor. "What?"

The emergency lighting cut out, plunging the already dimly lit corridor into darkness. The heads-up display in his helmet had already compensated for the lack of lighting.

"I don't think they're afraid of the dark," Connor said.

"No, but if they can see in the dark, they can be blinded by the light," Sean said.

Connor gave a mental nod to Sean. The young man was a fighter. He'd fight with everything he had.

Several Vemus soldiers came into the corridor and Connor and Sean engaged their helmets' lights. Bright searchlights cut a swath through the darkness, blinding the Vemus soldiers. Then they opened fire on them, catching the Vemus completely by surprise, and their bodies started littering the corridor. Connor had no idea whether they'd done enough damage to put them down permanently or not.

Major Cross called out to them, and Connor and Sean beat a hasty retreat to the emergency docking tube. They went inside and Connor closed the airlock doors. As they headed toward the *Vigilant*, Connor saw several white energy bolts hit the door. They had to move. The docking tube was pressurized, and if the Vemus weapons pierced the walls, they'd be sucked out into space.

"Go. Go!" Connor shouted.

First Major Cross made it onto the *Vigilant* and then Sean. Connor grabbed the handle and pulled himself over the threshold. He turned around and saw Vemus soldiers stepping into the tube. Connor pushed the doors closed and disengaged the tube.

"Get us out of here!" Connor shouted.

The *Vigilant* engaged its maneuvering thrusters and lurched away from the ship. Connor watched through the airlock windows as the Vemus soldiers were sucked into the vacuum of space. Their dark bodies still moved, even in the frigid temperatures.

The *Vigilant* moved away from the former battleship cruiser *Indianapolis*. Connor seized the detonation signal with his implants and sent it to the waiting nukes aboard the ship.

Nothing happened.

Connor tried again but the ship was still there. He slammed his fist against the wall, then opened a comlink to the bridge.

"Major, send the detonation signal," Connor said.

"Sir, we've tried . . ." Major Hayes replied.

"They're blocking the signal. We can't get through the interference," Sean said.

Connor clenched his teeth and then a message appeared on his internal heads-up display.

::Vemus signal analysis complete.::

Connor frowned. This signal was the one Wil had found. The price he'd paid had better be worth it.

Major Hayes had sectioned off the ship so they could follow decontamination protocols. Connor made his way through the waiting line of CDF soldiers, who stepped aside so he could pass. His Nexstar combat suit would need to be checked for breaches and decontaminated. Then Connor would need to be checked. The surviving members of the *Banshee* crew without combat suits were cordoned off to isolation and observation since they posed the greatest risk, having been directly exposed to the Vemus ship.

"General," Major Cross called out behind him.

"Yes," Connor said.

"If it's alright with you, sir, I need to see to my people," Major Cross said.

"Of course," Connor replied. "And Savannah, you did everything you could for them. The fact that you're still here is a testament to what kind of commanding officer you are."

Major Cross's eyes became hard. "The only reason we're still alive is because you and your team came looking for us. The combat shuttles were our last-ditch effort. We even brought improvised nukes of our own, adapted from a HADES IV warhead. The soldiers carrying them were among the first to die."

"Major," Connor said sternly, "you kept your people alive. Making a run to the hangar was a good decision. I would have done the same thing if I'd been in your shoes. Remember that."

Savannah Cross lifted her steady gaze up toward his. "Yes, sir."

She turned around and headed toward her crew. Though she was wearing combat armor, Connor doubted she'd leave her crew to their fate. She'd wait until they were all cleared through decontamination protocols.

An image of Wil Reisman trapped in a Vemus exoskeleton came to mind and he felt an ache in his chest. First Kasey and now Wil. How many more of them were going to have to die? A flash of Lenora Bishop's blue eyes blazed through his thoughts. The last time they'd spoken she'd been furious with him. He wished he could change that. He wanted to hear the sound of her voice, even if she just yelled at him. He glanced around at all the soldiers waiting to be processed through decontamination, but all he saw were the missing faces. So few of them had made it back. There were hardly any wounded. The Vemus had tried to take them alive until they'd realized they fought CDF soldiers in combat armor. Then their tactics had changed, becoming deadlier.

"Sir, they need you on the bridge," Sean said.

Connor glanced over at the young captain. He'd done a job that far exceeded what was required of his rank. Connor would need to rectify that.

"We're not done yet," Connor said.

"No, we're not, sir. Not until all the Vemus have been stopped," Sean replied.

As they headed toward the front of the decontamination processing area, Connor looked at the CDF men and women who'd gone into the belly of the beast and survived to tell the tale. There was no loathing or betrayal in their gazes, which was what Connor felt he deserved despite all they'd learned about the enemy. The fact that so many had died weighed heavily on him, the responsibility resting firmly on his shoulders. Going onto that ship had been the right call, but it was one he'd have to learn to live with. How long would it be before he could stop seeing one of his closest friends give his all so they had a fighting chance? Wil, Kasey, and so many other CDF soldiers had died to protect the colony. Connor promised himself that their sacrifices wouldn't be for nothing. He'd keep going. He'd keep fighting because that was who he was. Quitting wasn't something he'd ever thought about in his entire military career. There had always been the mission. He was weary, but he needed to be strong for his fallen comrades, to fight so the colony on New Earth could survive. They were all that was left of humanity. A few hundred thousand souls were a mere flicker in comparison to the billions of people they'd left behind on Earth and the colonies throughout the solar system. Those billions must be dead, fallen to an enemy they were still trying to understand. Their recent skirmish was just a taste of what they'd face if the remains of the Vemus fleet reached New Earth, and Connor would do everything in his power to prevent that. No matter the cost, it was his duty. For a brief moment, he saw Lenora's beautiful face in his mind. He made another promise to himself knowing the odds were stacked against his keeping such a promise, but he had to make it.

Connor marched forward with determination. This battle was far from over.

26

The holoscreen in front of him blurred, and Noah rubbed his eyes.

Stay focused and get it done.

Noah kept Connor's last words at the forefront of his mind when he noticed the slightest bit of tiredness threatening to distract him. He felt like his face had formed a permanent scowl from concentrating so hard. He glanced over at Kara. They sat together on the bridge of the *Chmiel* and had taken over the auxiliary workstation.

"Thirtieth time's the charm?" Noah asked and sighed.

"It only has to work once," Kara reminded him.

"Who knew reprogramming the targeting computer on the defense platforms would be so darn difficult," Noah said.

If there was a finickier computer system, Noah hadn't encountered it. He guessed this was the price he had to pay for precision, trying only to hit enemy targets instead of every ship in the vicinity. When they'd first tried to apply the update to the targeting systems of the defense platforms, they failed so spectacularly that the system became unresponsive. The frozen targeting systems had nearly given him a panic attack until the system fail-safes automatically rolled back the update. The update had been intended to enable the targeting computer to alternate between scanning for active ship signatures and ship wakes from fusion-powered engines. Noah had become much more cautious since then because he didn't want to single-handedly leave the colony defenseless. If he didn't get the defense platforms fixed, they would be nothing but useless piles of junk that would let the Vemus just waltz right into the inner system of planets unchallenged.

Noah glared at the screen. The uncooperative nature of the defense platform systems still made them piles of junk, in his opinion, but he was trying to squeeze every ounce of usefulness out of them he could while he still had the chance. The navigation system of the missile-defense platforms was much more reliable. Since his initial update to the targeting systems had failed, he'd had to move all the defense platforms farther into the system. This gave him time to come up with a fix and hopefully keep the platforms they'd already passed in range for when the update eventually worked. If it didn't, they were in serious trouble.

There were downsides to moving the missile-defense platforms, the primary one being that the maneuvering engines of each platform were limited, and they had to be sure there was enough fuel in reserve to allow them to stop. Even with those considerations, the platforms weren't meant for extensive space travel, so they moved frustratingly slowly.

Another downside was the fact that Noah wasn't authorized to move the defense platforms. He authenticated to the defense platforms' flight systems by using Connor's identification. He didn't have time to explain the situation to the people at COMCENT, who were still unable to reach the *Vigilant*, and then wait for their reply. Noah pressed his lips together. He didn't think Connor would mind, and he hoped the CDF general wasn't incorporating the missile-defense platforms into whatever he was doing. Noah's stomach twisted in knots and he glanced at the comms workstation. They'd sent several messages to New Earth, apprising COMCENT of the situation, but hadn't heard back from them yet. He had to tell them something; otherwise, COMCENT could override his orders to move the defense platforms.

"What are you waiting for?" Kara asked.

"I'm just trying to think if there's anything we haven't thought about yet. The targeting system really doesn't like the updates to PRADIS. Its entire design is predicated on the fact that it can precisely identify a target before it engages. We're essentially telling the computer, 'Nah, that's okay, don't worry about it. A vague impression of engine thrust is as good as a precise location. Fire your weapons,'" Noah said.

They'd fallen into hundreds of pitfalls due to the security protocols designed into the targeting system that was doing its utmost to prevent what they'd been trying to do. If something went wrong, the useless piles of junk *could* determine that the *Chmiel* was the enemy and needed to be destroyed.

"We went over it with a fine-toothed comb. Everything is going to be fine," Kara said.

Noah frowned. "A fine-toothed what?"

Kara smiled. "It's an old saying."

Noah snorted. Kara's family had originally lived in what had been known as the mid-western United States before the country was dissolved when the North American Union was formed. Kara had explained that the area was still known as the Midwest, and Noah had come to learn that there was no shortage of sayings from that part of the world.

"You betcha," Noah said in an attempt to allay his angst by using the only Midwest saying he could remember. He reached his hand out to launch the updated version thirty-point-one and stopped. "If this works, will you promise to make those fried ravioli things you talked about?"

Kara speared her gaze at him. "Stop stalling and send it out already," she said.

Noah pressed the digitized button and the update started to upload to the defense platforms. He watched the screen intently, willing it to finally work.

Kara leaned over and placed her hand on his arm, giving him a slight squeeze.

"Captain Benson, I have a comlink from General Mallory," the comms officer said.

Captain Benson glanced over at Noah. "Put him through."

Noah watched as Captain Benson spoke quietly on the comlink.

"No, General Gates is not on this ship . . . Oh, he's right here. I'll connect you. One moment please, General," Captain Benson said and jutted his chin in Noah's direction.

Noah put on his headset and waited for the comlink to transfer over to him. "Hello, General."

"Cut the 'Hello, General' crap, Barker, and tell me what the hell is going on out there," General Franklin Mallory said, his voice sounding strained.

"The short version is that we've been attacked. Titan Space Station has been destroyed," Noah said.

"We know about Titan," General Mallory said in a calmer voice. "We received a data burst from them, but none of our replies made it back to them. Then we got the self-destruction communication from the station. What I need to know from you is why you're redeploying the missile-defense platforms . . . and where is Connor?"

Noah glanced at his holoscreen and the update he'd coded was still being pushed to the missile-defense platforms. "Sir, this is going to require a bit of explaining, so please bear with me for a few minutes."

Noah told the CDF general everything he knew about the attack on Titan Space Station and that Jade protocol had been initiated by Connor. Noah went on to tell him about the escape pods they'd left behind, and his info dump to General Mallory became a sort of confession for him, as if he was finally able to unload the burden he'd been carrying. The last thing he mentioned was Connor's orders for him to update the targeting protocols of the defense platforms.

"What's the status of the update?" General Mallory asked.

"We just started pushing it out, so we're waiting on final confirmation that the defense platform systems have taken it," Noah replied.

"Acknowledged. Did Connor specify whether the updates should be applied to the orbital defenses?" General Mallory said.

"No, sir, he didn't. Are they online?"

"As soon as we got the first alert from Titan," General Mallory answered.

Noah blew out a breath. They'd been so isolated that it felt good to hear from someone else. "Sir, about the people we left behind . . ."

"We won't abandon them. Do you know the status of the Vemus fleet?" General Mallory asked.

"The *Chmiel* is only a cargo vessel, so it doesn't have PRADIS. We were relying on the missile-defense platform detections for that information," Noah said.

"Understood," General Mallory said and then covered his microphone to speak with someone else.

"We know Connor first engaged the Vemus fleet and then Titan Space Station took out a lot of the ships, but we're not sure how many are left," Noah continued.

Kara grabbed his arm. "Look," she said, gesturing to the holoscreen.

Noah looked at the status of the holoscreen and felt the edges of his lips pulling upward. The thirtieth time *was* the charm!

"Sir, the defense platforms are reporting in. The update worked. The targeting systems are coming back online and we should have telemetry in a few minutes," Noah said.

Kara clutched his arm and he leaned in toward her.

"Copy that. Good work," General Mallory said.

"I had a lot of help," Noah said, his eyes beaming.

The missile-defense platforms began to check in with their targeting updates and the plot on his screen filled with enemy ship signatures. The smile drained from his face and he heard several members of the bridge crew gasp. Vemus ships were gaining on them, nipping at their heels.

"Noah," General Mallory said in a knowing voice.

"Sir, the Vemus are almost here. I need to authorize the defense platforms to engage."

"Not yet," General Mallory said sternly.

The PRADIS systems on the missile-defense platforms were still discovering Vemus ships.

"Sir, they're out there. We have to open fire," Noah said.

"Listen to me," General Mallory replied. "We have to wait, draw them farther inside the funnel."

Noah frowned, wondering why the CDF general would be reasoning with him, and then his eyes widened in understanding. With Connor's credentials, he could order the defense platforms to engage any time he wanted. They were closer to the defense platform on the *Chmiel* than COMCENT was back on New Earth, which also meant an account lockout wouldn't work. Noah glanced at the screen. There were over three hundred Vemus ships heading toward them.

Noah placed his hand on the edge of the workstation. "What do you need me to do?"

"The defense platforms aren't enough to take out that many ships. We need to wait until they're within range of our orbital defenses," General Mallory said, clearly relieved that Noah wasn't going to take matters into his own hands.

"Sir, if the enemy determines the nature of the defense platforms, there's a risk of them being taken out before they can deliver their payload," Noah said.

"That's right, there is. And that's also why I need you to have Captain Benson slow his ship down," General Mallory said.

"Slow the ship down? Why?" Noah asked.

Captain Benson walked over to him and waited.

"Latency," General Mallory replied.

Once again, Noah's eyes widened in understanding. They were closer to the defense platforms and could start firing earlier than if those orders came from COMCENT.

"In this, every second counts," General Mallory said.

"I understand, sir," Noah replied and explained to Captain Benson why he needed to slow the ship down. The added bonus was that they would be bait to draw the Vemus where they wanted them to go.

Noah looked at the plot on the holoscreen and then shot to his feet. He turned toward the main holoscreen, which was much larger than the one at the workstation, and peered at the ships lining the edges.

"Sir, the *Vigilant* has just appeared on the plot," Noah said, his voice rising in excitement.

They were still alive, at least for the time being.

27

Once cleared through decontamination, Connor headed for the *Vigilant's* primary bridge. Sean followed along, with several CDF soldiers as an escort. They entered the bridge and Connor caught himself looking for Reisman in the *Vigilant's* command chair. It was a habit that had formed during the weeks they'd been aboard the ship.

Wil is gone, Connor reminded himself.

"General," Major Hayes acknowledged.

Connor approached the command area. "Sitrep."

"The Vemus forces are regrouping and the former battleship carrier *Indianapolis* has moved away from our ship," Major Hayes said.

Connor looked at the main holoscreen and noticed their current position on the plot, then glanced back at Major Hayes. "What happened? We were at the head of the vanguard when we went aboard the *Indianapolis*."

"That's correct. The remaining Vemus fleet caught up to us and now we're right in the middle of what's left," Major Hayes said.

Connor turned toward the main holoscreen. "Tactical, any response from the Vemus ships?"

"Negative, General," Lieutenant LaCroix said.

"It's almost as if . . ." Connor's voice trailed off and he glanced at Sean.

"We're not enough of a threat for them to deal with," Sean said.

"We were before. What's changed?" Major Hayes asked.

"They've been slow to respond throughout this whole engagement. They're reliant on superior numbers to achieve their objective," Connor said.

The Vemus fleet had focused on Titan Space Station with an almost singular purpose and now they were heading directly toward New Earth. He looked for the *Indianapolis*. Why had they moved away from them? Did the Vemus know they'd planted bombs on board?

"Why haven't the defense platforms engaged them?" Connor asked.

Those platforms should have delivered their missile payloads to the enemy by now. Connor looked at the system counts for enemy ships and there were still hundreds left.

Too many, Connor thought.

"Sir, the defense platforms have been moved. We only just discovered this a few minutes before you arrived," Major Hayes said.

Connor pressed his lips together. Noah must have moved the defense platforms, which meant something had gone wrong with the update for the targeting computers. They couldn't access the platforms because it might draw the Vemus fleet's attention. He had to assume Noah was working on the problem and was nearing a solution. Noah hadn't disappointed him yet, and he knew the stakes. Connor studied the plot and the enemy ship positions. He needed to get them bunched together so that when the defense platforms did engage, they could do maximum damage.

"The *Chmiel* must still be in front of the vanguard. Tactical, highlight the orbital defense range around New Earth," Connor said.

A few moments later New Earth was highlighted in yellow and the orbital defense range was shown in a paler shade of orange.

"They're drawing them in before they open fire on them," Sean said.

Connor nodded. "Noah wouldn't know to do that on his own. He's not a strategist. He must be in contact with COMCENT. Are we able to contact them?"

"Negative, General. We still have limited communications capabilities while we're so close to the Vemus fleet," Sergeant Boers said.

Connor looked over at the comms officer, considering. Moving away from the Vemus fleet would be a waste of time and opportunity. "How long would it take you to input a new signal protocol for the comms array?"

"Shouldn't take that long. Send over what you have, sir," Sergeant Boers said.

Connor used his implants to send over the Vemus signal Reisman had found. He'd taken a quick look at the analysis and couldn't make sense of it. There were limits to what could be done within an internal heads-up display.

Major Hayes glanced at him questioningly.

"While Colonel Reisman was in the Vemus ship systems, he found this protocol that he thought was linked to all their ships," Connor said.

"I was very sorry to hear about Wil. He was a good man," Major Hayes said.

Connor clenched his teeth for a moment and kept his gaze on the main holoscreen. He looked back at Hayes and nodded.

"General," Sergeant Boers said, looking worried. "I'm not sure what I can do with that signal. It's really complex."

"Excuse me, sir," Sean said. "Sela, can you put what you have on the main holoscreen?"

Sergeant Boers looked at Connor.

"Go ahead," Connor said.

An image of the signal spectrum appeared on the main holoscreen.

Multicolored peaks and valleys represented the many layers of the signal. Connor rubbed the bottom of his chin.

"I've seen something like this before," Sean said.

"What do you think it is?" Connor asked.

Sean stepped closer to the large holoscreen. He took control of the image and swiped it to the side. Then he brought up another communications signal. The wave pattern was similar to the Vemus signal but much less complex.

"This is a signal we use for encrypted CDF communications, which is based on the NA Alliance military protocols," Sean said and then brought up another image and juxtaposed it with the CDF signal. The pitches in the second signal hardly peaked at all but were a constant stream.

"What's that other one?" Major Hayes asked.

"It's the command and control signal for drones," Sean said.

Connor's eyes widened, and Sean brought up the Vemus protocol. They weren't identical, but they were a close enough match to show they were at least similar.

"This is why they're seemingly slow to respond. What if most of the fleet is being controlled by one ship?" Connor said. "Can you upload the protocol to the comms array as is and see what we get?"

"Yes, sir," Sergeant Boers said.

No sooner had the comms officer uploaded the protocols than a high-pitched feedback loop sounded from all the comms speakers on the bridge. Connor brought his hands to his ears and winced at the sound.

Sergeant Boers tore off her headset and adjusted some of the settings. The sound stopped.

"I'm sorry, General. The signal is too strong to listen to. It's overwhelming some of our sensors," Sergeant Boers said.

"Can you put the Vemus signal on the main holoscreen?" Connor asked.

The signal power was off the charts, above and beyond anything the CDF was using. The power requirements for maintaining that kind of a signal must have been immense.

"We don't have the capacity to jam that kind of signal," Major Hayes said.

"We don't have to jam it," Sean said.

Connor shared a knowing glance with the young officer and gave him a nod. This was something they'd both picked up from Lenora.

"We just need to disrupt it," Sean said.

Major Hayes frowned and he looked at Connor. "I'm not following."

"We disrupt the signal by broadcasting one of our own," Connor said.

"We do that and whatever ships are within the vicinity of our signal will be cut off from wherever the broadcast is coming from," Sean said.

"Can we trace the signal?" Major Hayes asked.

Sergeant Boers shook her head. "No, sir, it's too strong. We'd have to move far away from the Vemus fleet."

"What good will disrupting the signal to a few of their ships do?" Major Hayes asked.

Connor watched the signal output on the main holoscreen and then turned back toward the major. "It will get them to follow us," Connor said.

Major Hayes nodded in understanding.

Connor went to the command chair and sat down. Major Hayes sat next to him in the XO's chair.

"Action stations. Set Condition One throughout the ship," Connor said.

His orders were repeated by Sergeant Browning, who sent a broadcast throughout the ship. All crews would be reporting to their combat posts, and bulkhead doors were closing and sealing in case of decompression.

"Helm, plot a course right through the middle of the Vemus fleet. Close quarters. When they start shooting at us, I want their ships as likely to be hit as we are. Then stand by," Connor said.

"Yes, sir, plotting course and standing by," Sergeant Edwards said.

The course appeared on the plot that showed on the main holoscreen. Connor engaged the straps on his chair and they came over his shoulders, securing him in place. He heard the same as the rest of the bridge crew strapped themselves in.

"General, Vemus ship on approach vector," Lieutenant LaCroix said.

"Looks like they finally noticed us," Connor said. "Comms, start broadcasting the Vemus signal, max capacity."

"Yes, sir, broadcasting now," Sergeant Boers said.

"Helm, you're a go," Connor said.

He felt a slight shudder through the bridge as their two remaining engines engaged and the *Vigilant* lurched forward.

"Tactical, stand by countermeasures and short-range weapons," Connor said.

"Yes, sir, standing by countermeasures and short-range weapons," Lieutenant LaCroix said.

Connor watched the plot. The tonnage of the Vemus ship heading toward them was similar to theirs, which led Connor to believe it was a heavy-cruiser class vessel.

"Helm, push our nose to starboard by three degrees and punch it," Connor said. "All ahead full."

"Ahead full, yes, sir," the helmsman reported.

The ship began to shake as the engines came to full power and the *Vigilant* surged forward.

"Enemy ship hasn't altered course," Lieutenant LaCroix said.

Connor watched the plot. They were closing in on the ship. "Tactical, tag that target as alpha until we pass it. I need a firing solution for our remaining rail-cannons on that ship."

"Yes, sir. Firing solution ready," Lieutenant LaCroix said.

"Ops, any change with the enemy ship?" Connor asked.

"No, sir. Same heading and speed, sir," Sergeant Browning said.

Connor was playing a hunch. He glanced at the countdown timer to intercept with the enemy ship. They were closing in.

"Fire, Lieutenant," Connor said.

The rail-cannons on top of the ship began firing at the Vemus ship in rapid succession. The rail-cannon was a crude weapon that had been kept in service to appease a certain nostalgia of a bygone age where two ships would slug it out.

"Confirm multiple hits, sir," Sergeant Browning reported.

The rail-cannons peppered the hull of the Vemus ship and then became silent as the two ships passed each other.

"Ops, monitor that ship and let me know when it alters course," Connor said.

"That would be our effective range for broadcasting the Vemus signal," Major Hayes said.

"Yes. Now the cat and mouse game begins," Connor replied.

The Vemus fleet continued on toward New Earth, and the *Vigilant* was firing on another ship in the fleet before the alpha finally changed course.

"Can we boost the broadcast signal?" Connor asked.

"We'd need to divert more power to the array, sir," Major Hayes said.

"Get someone from Engineering on it," Connor said.

Major Hayes went to his own comlink and started speaking to someone from Engineering.

"General, multiple Vemus ships are altering their courses. It's like they can't get a lock on where they want to go," Lieutenant LaCroix said.

Connor surveyed the plot with grim satisfaction. The Vemus ships on PRADIS appeared to be tracking toward multiple trajectories, none of which were where the *Vigilant* actually was.

"Sir, Engineering says they can route more power to the array but would need us to stop broadcasting in order to do it," Major Hayes said.

"For how long?" Connor asked.

"More power to the comms array requires higher-capacity cabling to the power assembly for the array. They can lay out everything they need beforehand and perform the switch in fifteen minutes," Major Hayes said.

Connor sighed. "Tell them to get started. Once everything's in place, I'll order the broadcast stopped."

They needed to find a way to survive for fifteen minutes while utterly exposed to the Vemus fleet. Connor glanced over at the plot. Their current heading had them crossing the Vemus fleet formation in tighter quarters, making steady progress toward the front. There was no easy way out of this. If they retreated to a safe distance, the Vemus fleet would regroup and quickly recover, but if they stayed and stopped disrupting the Vemus control signal, they ran the risk of being destroyed while they were trying to increase the broadcast range. The Vemus knew they were here even if they couldn't locate the *Vigilant* at this time.

There was no other way. Increasing the broadcast range of the Vemus signal was essential if they were going to protect New Earth.

"Sir, Engineering is ready for the cut over," Major Hayes said.

Connor looked at the plot and their current position. "Helm, try to keep us near the center of the enemy fleet formation."

He glanced around the bridge. They all knew that the odds of surviving what they were about to do were stacked against them. Even if they miraculously stayed alive for the fifteen minutes required to reroute more power to their comms array, they were well within range of the defense platforms. Either the Vemus ships or missiles from the CDF defense platforms would destroy them. They couldn't even abandon ship. Their escape pods weren't equipped to repel the harsh radiation from nuclear warheads and couldn't get far enough away to escape. Only by remaining on board the *Vigilant* did they stand the slightest chance of survival, but more importantly, they'd stand a much better chance of delivering a crippling blow to the enemy.

28

THE CARGO CARRIER had slowed its velocity to a crawl to allow the Vemus fleet to catch up to it. Noah watched the plot, which the frustratingly slow ship's computers had to update based on the data feeds sent back from the missile-defense platforms. There was probably at least a twenty-minute delay because the processing power of the *Chmiel's* computing systems was nowhere near that of an actual warship. On a ship like the *Vigilant*, the data feeding the plot would be processed in almost real time.

"I still can't figure out how he's doing it," Noah said, probably for the third time.

Kara stood next to him. "It's like they can't see him for some reason. General Gates likely found a way to throw off their sensors, but the range is limited."

The Vemus forces held their formation along the edges of their approach, but the ships toward the interior were breaking formation as they pursued the *Vigilant*—at least they had been as of twenty minutes ago.

Noah glanced at the timer for the next data refresh and sighed heavily.

Captain Benson came over and stood beside them. "General Mallory just informed me that the three orbital defense platforms have been moved into position."

"That took a while," Noah said.

"They reside at the Lagrange points so the distance they had to cover was pretty great," Captain Benson said with a shrug.

Noah shook his head. "Did you know they're only partially outfitted?"

Kara glanced at him sharply. "What do you mean?"

Noah bobbed his head up and down. "There's supposed to be a full complement of HADES IV missiles on those platforms. They have the anti-ship missile tubes but not the missiles. Resources were diverted elsewhere since we'd already completed the missile-defense platforms."

"Governor Parish?" Captain Benson asked.

"The one and only. So the orbital defense platforms have a couple of rail-cannons each and one plasma-cannon each," Noah said.

"What about the moon base where the shipyard is?" Captain Benson asked.

"There's a CDF battleship carrier being constructed using the remaining resources from the *Ark*, but it's nowhere near ready. Any defenses on New Earth's moon will be on the wrong side of the planet by the time we get near it," Noah said.

The timer on the main holoscreen dwindled down and the main plot started to update with new information. As the information refreshed, Noah's eyes widened at the snapshot from twenty minutes ago that finally appeared on their screens. He stepped closer. The Vemus ships seemed to be converging on a single point of contact with rigid clarity.

"Whatever they were doing isn't working anymore. You have to authorize the launch," Kara said.

The remains of the Vemus fleet were well within range of the missile-defense platforms. If he authorized them to fire now they could destroy the *Vigilant*. Connor's ship was in trouble.

"Even if we did fire on them now, it wouldn't mean they'd be in time to make a difference," Noah said.

Though Kara outranked him, he had operational authority over the defense platforms, so it was on him to execute the launch commands.

"You don't know that. All the calculations in the world can't tell you that. If you launch them now, at least they might have a fighting chance," Kara said.

Noah walked back over to his terminal. He felt like he was on autopilot, as if someone else were moving his body and he was just along for the ride. He brought up the command module for the missile-defense platforms and hesitated. His mouth went dry and he glanced up at the plot.

Captain Benson walked over to him. "Your friends are on that ship?" he asked gently.

Noah's throat became thick. "Yes," he answered, his voice sounding husky. "They're my family," he said, thinking of Connor and Sean. He had other friends in the colony, but from their earliest days together a powerful connection had been forged among all of them, even Dr. Bishop, who had looked after him like an older sister. How could he face Lenora if he did this?

"What would they do in your place?" Captain Benson asked. His deep voice was soothing, but there was an edge to it.

Noah pressed his lips together tightly. He knew exactly what they would do. They'd push the damn button. They'd hate themselves, but they would do it. Noah glared at his terminal and authorized the missile-defense platforms to finally engage the enemy. He closed his eyes for a moment and whispered a prayer, pleading that his friends . . . his family . . . would somehow survive what he'd done. A rush of adrenaline surged through his veins and a deep-seated anger stretched throughout his chest. He wanted to scream and shake his fists above him, but he knew neither of those things would help.

"It's done," Noah said.

Now, they'd wait.

"MULTIPLE BOGIES INBOUND, SIR," Lieutenant LaCroix said.

Connor cursed. "Helm, keep us in tight near that ship."

When they'd stopped broadcasting the Vemus signal, their ships had quickly regrouped and targeted the *Vigilant*.

The Vemus ships used a powerful particle-beam cannon that melted deeply through their hull. The *Vigilant* was belching atmosphere from hundreds of hull breaches. Their only saving grace was being able to stay nearby a Vemus ship that had suffered tremendous damage from friendly fire. They peppered the hull with shots from their remaining rail-cannons and narrowly avoided the harrowing particle beams from their main batteries. They couldn't stay anywhere long, and if an opportunity came for them to move to another Vemus ship, they took it.

Connor looked at the status of the comms array. It was still red. The area near the comms array had taken damage and there were engineering teams trying to fix it. They were well beyond the envelope for piloting a heavy cruiser. Sergeant Edwards' skills as a helmsman were one of the reasons they were still alive.

"Sir, I'm seeing missile launches on PRADIS," Lieutenant LaCroix said.

That was it; they were out of time. The missile-defense platforms had been engaged. They either stayed where they were and got destroyed or made a run for it and likely got torn apart by Vemus particle beams. Those weapons had been new when Connor was part of the NA Alliance military. There must have been developments in the years since the *Ark* left the Sol System.

He kept thinking about the beings they'd encountered on board the *Indianapolis*. Some were human-like but so much more. It was known that they were some type of virus or parasitic organism that came from Earth's oceans and was able to target multiple species of mammals. The scientists had tried to stop the virus from spreading and made it worse. They had records they'd downloaded from the *Indianapolis*, but they hadn't had time to analyze them. Connor had ordered the data stored on multiple comms drones that hadn't been launched yet.

"How long until the missiles reach us?" Connor asked.

Lieutenant LaCroix updated the information on the main holoscreen. Not much time. The defense platforms were in close proximity. Given the capabilities of the NA Alliance military, Connor thought the Vemus would have made use of other weapons of war. This fleet relied on sheer numbers and large weapons like the particle-cannon. They didn't use combat drones or short-range fighters, and Connor didn't understand why that was the case.

"Sir, the comms array is coming back online," Sergeant Boers said, her voice high with hope.

Connor swung his gaze to Major Hayes, who was already on a comlink with the engineering teams in the area.

"The system's charging. Full power will be available in sixty seconds," Major Hayes said.

Connor nodded. "Ops, confirm the range of the broadcast with the higher-yield energy available once we start boosting the signal."

Connor waited for the capacitors to finish charging. "Comms, begin broadcast."

The battered communications array on the *Vigilant* started pumping out the complex signal.

"Broadcast has started at known levels, increasing incrementally," Sergeant Boers said.

"Helm, take us away from their shadow and stand by for evasive maneuvers," Connor said.

"Taking us out, sir," Sergeant Edwards said.

The *Vigilant* moved away from the Vemus ship. Scans had indicated that it was a cruiser class, but there was evidence of smaller vessels that had been absorbed into the main hull.

"Vemus ships in the area are firing their weapons!" Lieutenant LaCroix said.

Connor felt a gasp catch in his throat.

"Sir, they're firing blindly," Sean said, frowning at the tactical screen.

"Put it on screen," Connor said.

Bright flashes of charged particles being fired in rapid succession appeared on screen as if there were a lightning storm in space. Sean was right; the Vemus were firing blindly, banking on the off chance they might hit them, which meant they'd updated their tactics.

"Comms, boost the signal to maximum," Connor said.

"Boosting signal to maximum, sir," Sergeant Boers said.

"Tactical, focus our high-res optics on the ships farthest away. I want to know if they start firing their weapons," Connor said.

Their current trajectory didn't put them in the path of the Vemus weapons, but that could change at any moment. Connor watched the range of their broadcast leap across the plot as the more powerful signal doubled its range.

"Confirm additional ships firing their weapons. They're hitting each other, sir," Lieutenant LaCroix said.

"Helm, plot a course back to New Earth, best speed, but wait to execute," Connor said.

"Yes, sir. Plotting course back to New Earth," Sergeant Edwards said.

Connor waited.

Major Hayes glanced over at him. "Firing blindly isn't going to cut it."

"No, it won't—" Connor began.

"Sir, Vemus ships within range of the broadcast are altering course," Lieutenant LaCroix said.

Connor frowned at the PRADIS output. The CDF missiles were closing in on them. If they were going to live, they had to move.

"They've realized they're getting cut off from each other and are trying to find us," Connor said.

There was a bright flash as one Vemus ship's particle beam cut into another. More of the same continued to appear on the screen. It was chaos.

"Helm, execute course, emergency!" Connor said.

The lighting on the bridge dimmed and Connor felt a shimmy move through the weakened hull of their ship. Their two remaining drive pods gleamed as they were brought to maximum capacity. The *Vigilant* lurched forward with the maneuvering thrusters firing at the behest of the navigation computers that kept the ship on course. The energy drain on their main reactor was enormous, and Connor ordered all available power to the engines and the comms array. They had to keep that signal up for as long as they could.

The *Vigilant* flew through a nightmarish maze of charged particle beams in the heart of the Vemus fleet. Connor watched the PRADIS screen, knowing that a maelstrom of HADES IV missiles was about to tear the Vemus fleet apart.

"Detonation detected, sir," Lieutenant LaCroix said.

Connor looked at the main holoscreen and saw that the first wave of HADES IV missiles was striking at the rearmost forces of the Vemus fleet. They would drive the Vemus forces forward into the orbital defense platforms that were stationed at the Lagrange points around the planet.

Klaxon alarms blared on the bridge as a particle beam lanced through the forward section of the ship. There was nothing he could do for the CDF soldiers serving there. Bulkhead doors would automatically shut and there were damage-control teams moving to the area. The casualty count kept rising. How many more of them would need to die in order to stop this enemy fleet?

A rough shimmy worked its way through the ship and Connor gritted his teeth. He didn't need LaCroix to confirm that they were now within the shockwaves of multiple HADES IV missiles that had delivered their warheads.

The optical sensors went offline and the holoscreen blanked out. They still had PRADIS, but for how long?

29

THE *CHMIEL* HAD PASSED the orbital defense platforms and Captain Benson had his ship on an approach to New Earth. It seemed strange to Noah to be offloading people from the ship when there was an attack force on its way to the planet. HADES IV missiles had been launched from the defense platforms and the monitoring systems running on those platforms reported updates for as long as they could. Once the warheads started to detonate, they lost their visibility into what was happening to the enemy and, more importantly, what the fate of the *Vigilant* was to be. In the lengthy time between updates, the snapshots showed the Vemus ships in the interior of the attack force going into complete disarray and the ships on the edge converging in a feeble attempt to restore order.

The chaotic mass of enemy ships moved closer to them.

"Orbital defense platforms have begun firing their weapons," Kara said.

"How do they even know what they're firing at?" Noah asked.

"They're using the rail-guns to paint the targets, then the plasma-cannon to finish the job," Kara said.

Shuttles were inbound from New Sierra and would be arriving soon. Offloading the CDF personnel from Titan Space Station would begin as soon as they arrived. Noah felt completely drained and useless. They'd succeeded in updating the targeting systems of the missile-defense platforms, but this constant waiting was wearing on his nerves. Even now, those missiles were tearing apart the remains of the Vemus fleet, but there was no way for them to know exactly how much damage they were inflicting on the enemy. Were the orbital defense platforms enough to finish the job?

Thirty minutes later the shuttles arrived. They still hadn't gotten usable data from the missile-defense platforms. Most of them were now offline, which wasn't a surprise given how much interference there was from all the detonations in the area.

"COMCENT has sent a request for you to be in the first group to return to the planet," Captain Benson said.

Noah's brows pulled together. Jade protocol—protect the best and the brightest. "I'm not going," he said harshly.

Kara looked at him in concern.

"I may not officially be in the Colonial Defense Force, but refusing direct orders isn't tolerated, as far as I know," Captain Benson said.

Noah clenched his teeth. "You've done as they asked and delivered the message. I'm not going anywhere, not until I know what happened to the *Vigilant*."

Captain Benson regarded him for a moment. "I understand, and I'll have them informed."

Noah looked away and focused on the main holoscreen. He didn't want to believe the *Vigilant* was gone. They must have survived but were unable to contact them.

Stay focused, Noah thought to himself.

Captain Benson had given them full access to the ship's systems, so he went over to his terminal and opened the communications interface for the *Chmiel*. He started scanning different broadcast signals, hoping for some sign that the *Vigilant* was still intact.

The *Chmiel* was a cargo ship and wasn't equipped with military-grade sensor arrays or high-res optics. They had standard avoidance protocols, which could identify if a ship was in the vicinity of a communications array. The data that fed the plot on the main holoscreen was hours old, so Noah removed the plot in favor of using the limited optics on the ship. They could see flashes of bright red from the orbital defense platforms, but the targets the onboard computers were firing at were too far away to see. He rubbed his eyes, giving them a momentary respite. He couldn't remember the last time he'd slept and he was sure he could use a shower.

He snorted as a thought came to mind. Kara glanced at him questioningly.

"I just thought of something. Don't know why it hasn't occurred to me before," Noah said.

He opened a comms channel to the orbital defense platforms and connected to their onboard computer systems. Since the *Chmiel* had the slowest data processing capabilities imaginable, Noah stopped what he was doing to consider how best to access the data he wanted.

"I got this. We just need to see what it's firing at," Kara said and took over the comms session. She quickly coded a query to pull only the targeting data from the system and then had it output to the plot they'd used before.

The software suite took the new data and added it to the plot.

"Thanks," Noah said tiredly.

They watched as ships emerged from the area where their last payload of HADES IV missiles had torn into the Vemus fleets. The targeting systems first scoured the area for something to shoot and then fired their weapons. If the *Vigilant* was there, it would have to broadcast its unique identifier so the orbital defense platforms wouldn't fire at it. They couldn't tell what the condition the few ships appearing on the plot were in, only that they were there.

A bright flash shone from the sub-holoscreen, followed by an explosion as one of the orbital defense platforms went offline. The weapons systems on the remaining two platforms targeted another blip on the plot. The ship was still far away. There was another bright flash that lanced across their video feeds.

Noah's screen began filling with errors as the orbital defense platforms' systems became unresponsive.

"That has to be a main weapon from a battleship carrier," Kara said.

Noah was about to reply when he noticed another ship appearing on the plot, but then it just as quickly disappeared. Noah leaned in, peering at the holoscreen.

"What did you see?" Kara asked.

"I thought I saw the *Vigilant*," Noah said.

The CDF ship signatures appeared as green on the plot so they could easily identify friendly ships. Noah glanced at the terminal session he had open to the orbital defense platforms. The data connection for one of them was still alive. He did a quick rundown of the critical systems.

"We have to help them," Noah said.

"What can we do? This isn't a warship," Captain Benson said.

"I know what I saw. The *Vigilant* is still out there, fighting," Noah said.

He turned back to his workstation, his eyes taking in all the holoscreens with renewed vigor. "The plasma-cannon from that platform is still online. It can still fire," Noah said.

He pulled up the targeting systems and they were online as well. Noah frowned, trying to think of why the weapon wasn't firing, and glanced at one of the error messages on the screen.

::*Turret field out of alignment.*::

Noah pointed to the error message and looked at Kara. "Do you know what this means? What turret field?"

Kara peered at the error. "It means the actual turret is damaged and the system can't point the weapon in the right direction."

Noah rubbed the top of his head and pulled his hair. "We have to get out there," he said, rising out of his chair.

Captain Benson shook his head. "There are thousands of lives on this ship. We can't just stop offloading people to the surface."

Several members of the *Chmiel's* bridge crew turned in their direction and glanced at both of them.

Noah clenched his teeth. He suspected the bridge crew would overwhelm him if the captain ordered it. Regardless, the cargo ship captain was right. "What about a shuttle? Something. You must have something you use to do visual inspections of the ship."

Captain Benson's mouth hung open, then he swallowed hard. "We do have a shuttle."

"Fine. I'm taking the shuttle. Where is it?" Noah asked and started walking toward the doors.

"Mid-ship hangar. I'll tell them you're coming down," Captain Benson said.

Noah fled the bridge and Kara followed him.

"You didn't think I was going to let you go off by yourself," Kara said.

Noah knew better than to ask her to stay behind. Truth be told, he'd need the help. He didn't know how to fix a turret, but he had to do something. He had to find a way to get that plasma-cannon to fire its weapons again.

They ran to the small mid-ship hangar. The shuttle was strictly used on maintenance runs for the ship. Noah had learned to fly years ago because Lenora Bishop had questionable flying skills, and he preferred softer landings.

They climbed aboard and headed for the cockpit. After a quick check of the flight systems, they flew the shuttle away from the cargo ship. Noah punched in the coordinates for the orbital defense platforms. The distance to the Lagrange point from New Earth wasn't that far. There hadn't been any more weapons fire from the battleship carrier. The Vemus must have thought the platforms were no longer a threat. While the shuttle was en route, he and Kara slipped into EVA suits. They didn't engage their helmets, which were collapsed into a tight compartment near the base of the necks.

There was a debris field from the remains of the other platforms, and Noah piloted the shuttle through it, heading toward one of the larger sections that was intact. The shuttle was highly maneuverable and they quickly wove their way through. Noah engaged the searchlights.

"The cannon looks intact," Kara said.

It appeared that the orbital defense platform had been sheared in half and the section that housed the rail-cannon was nowhere to be found. Noah circled around the large plasma-cannon. There was a damaged section that was blackened from when it had been hit, but the cannon itself looked intact. Most of the damage was restricted to the base of the cannon where the rollers were that swung it in the direction it was to fire.

Noah patched into the platform's systems. Power levels were slowly falling, but there was enough to fire a few more shots. Now all they had to worry about was aiming the plasma-cannon, and he had no idea how they were going to do it.

30

Connor didn't know how the *Vigilant* was still holding together. It might have been their relatively central position when the HADES IV missiles had hit the remains of the Vemus fleet. Or perhaps it was the Vemus signal they'd been disrupting that prevented them from launching countermeasures or taking evasive maneuvers. What he *did* know was that the enemy ships had formed a temporary cocoon that protected them from destruction.

Connor glanced through his helmet at the others on the bridge. He'd ordered the surviving crew to go to life support. There were large sections near the central part of the ship where the interior atmosphere was intact, including the bridge, but places like the forward rail-gun batteries were completely exposed.

"Ops, what's the status of 01?" Connor asked.

They'd been having problems getting ammunition to their only remaining rail-cannon due to extensive damage to the ship. Engineering teams were connecting a workaround to take the ammunition from other rail-gun batteries that were damaged beyond repair.

"They're still working on it. A few minutes more, sir," Sergeant Browning said.

Connor glared at the blank PRADIS output. They were still flying blind. There was another Vemus battleship carrier that had been hidden away in the rear of the fleet, and there had been a handful of smaller vessels that survived the onslaught of HADES IVs, but they'd been picked off by the orbital defense platforms.

The PRADIS screen became active and showed a Barracuda-class battleship carrier nearby. It was heavily damaged and Connor narrowed his gaze at the onscreen designation. *Indianapolis.* The battleship carrier had fired its main particle-cannon, which had chewed through the orbital defense platforms in short order.

They tracked the battleship carrier visually since their sensor array was offline. The damage-assessment teams couldn't make it to where the sensors were housed and the armored hatches that protected the secondary sensor array had been damaged. If it weren't for the optical array, they'd be flying completely blind.

New Earth appeared as a bright blue orb in the distance, but the Vemus battleship carrier was much closer to them. The exoskeletal hull had been burnt away by the fusion warheads of the HADES IVs, and there were large sections of the original battle-steel hull once again exposed to space.

"Do I have to go down to the forward sections and load the damn gun myself? I need that weapon now!" Connor growled.

If they couldn't get the rail-cannon back online, Connor would order the remaining crew to abandon ship and he'd take out the engines of the battleship cruiser himself.

"Sir, they're really close," Sergeant Browning said.

Major Hayes had left the bridge to organize the engineering crews. Connor knew the man was doing everything he could, but it just might not be enough. The Vemus appeared hell-bent on getting at least one of their ships to the planet that the last of humanity called home. But no trace of the Vemus could be allowed to reach New Earth, which might include the *Vigilant's* crew since some of them had been exposed.

Connor could barely discern where the orbital defense platforms had been. All that was left of them was debris. All their preparation for the past seven years had led to this. That enemy ship must be stopped.

Connor opened a comms channel to broadcast to the entire ship. "All hands—"

"Sir, rail-cannon is back online!" Sergeant Browning said.

Connor glanced at the operations officer and gave him a nod. "We're about to make our final attack run on the enemy. We're all that stands between them and our home. Should this attack run fail to disable that ship, I will sacrifice this ship in order to stop the enemy from reaching New Earth."

Connor closed the comms channel. "Tactical, one more firing solution. Concentrate fire behind the MPDs. Helm, keep us in position as long as you can."

Connor's orders were confirmed. He heard some of his officers muttering a prayer. The die was about to be cast, and sometimes one had to roll the hard six.

NOAH AND KARA left the shuttle, each of them carrying a plasma cutter. He thought that if he could remove some of the damaged sections, he could free the turret enough so they could align it for a shot, but they had to move fast. The plasma-cannon was the size of a large building. They quickly circled around the base and closed in on the damaged sections. Noah peered at the area and there were several large pieces of twisted metal jutting out from the base. They looked to have been pieces from another platform.

He'd been poised, ready to use the plasma cutters, but when he saw the extent of the damage, he glanced down helplessly at the tool. If he had a week and a crew of fifty, he might have been able to do something.

"This isn't going to work," Noah said.

Kara had been standing off to the side and had an access panel open. "Come over here."

Noah walked over to her, his mag-boots keeping him firmly attached to the metallic surface.

"What did you find?" Noah asked.

"Look here. There are still some thrusters active," Kara said.

Noah peered at the maintenance terminal and his eyes widened. "You're a genius! Come on. We need to get back to the shuttle," he said, a plan forming in his mind.

He'd been so focused on trying to fix the turret that he'd overlooked the main problem of just aiming the weapon. The orbital platforms were large space vehicles designed to be stabilized while the weapons were active. Stability came with the use of gravity fields, along with redundant power stations.

"I should have caught this," Noah said as they went through the hatch and back onto the shuttle.

"We both missed it. I didn't even think of it until we saw the extent of the damage," Kara replied.

Noah sat in the pilot's seat and engaged the shuttle's controls, easing away from the base of the plasma-cannon.

"I have thruster control online," Kara said.

Noah swung the shuttle around so they could see the approach of the enemy warship. There were several bright flashes of light and he felt his mouth go dry. Kara gasped. If that ship fired on them, they had no chance of getting away.

Noah squinted, trying to extract every bit of detail from the tele-view on the shuttle's heads-up display. There were more flashes of light, but it was gleaming sections of the battleship carrier as it tumbled toward them, out of control. The flashing was from the ship's magneto-drive pods, half of which were disabled.

Noah brought up the platform's control systems. "I'm ready to disable the gravity field."

"Go," Kara replied.

Noah disabled the field and Kara engaged the platform's thrusters. The plasma-cannon swung around and Noah began priming the shot. Kara frantically tried to control the platform's thrusters, but she couldn't keep it stable enough. Noah tried to engage the gravity field, but it wasn't responding. Without it, they'd only get a few shots because there was nothing to keep the cannon in place.

The massive ship came barreling toward them and Noah waited for the remains of the orbital defense platform to come around again.

"Hold on," Noah said.

Gritting his teeth, he waited for the plasma-cannon to align on the target at point-blank range. At the last possible second, he fired the weapon. The plasma-cannon unleashed molten fury in a hail of magnetic bolts with superheated centers. The bolts tore into the hull of the battleship carrier while Noah maximized the shuttle's engines. He angled away from the ship and sped away. As they cleared the ship, Noah saw that the plasma-cannon was still active, which meant it was still firing. He swung the nose of the shuttle around and could see the battleship carrier being ripped apart. The barrel of the plasma-cannon was lodged in the belly of the ship. Noah glanced over to the side and saw two streams of white bolts coming from a heavy cruiser. It was the *Vigilant!* Sections of the ship had been shorn away, but its remaining rail-cannon fired mercilessly on the enemy ship. He watched as the large behemoth expanded and then the exoskeleton split apart the fusion warheads, rending the ship to shreds.

"Noah, get us out of here or we'll be caught up in it!" Kara shouted.

Noah got on the controls and maximized the thrusters. The shuttle raced away and Noah saw the *Vigilant* try to do the same, but the shockwave sent the severely damaged CDF heavy cruiser tumbling. The gleam from the remaining drive pods went offline as the ship slowly rolled over on its axis. The shuttle's power systems shut down because the destruction of the battleship carrier sent out an electromagnetic pulse. Noah knew they'd come back online because the shutdown was part of the emergency response built into the system fail-safes for smaller spacecraft.

Noah glanced over at Kara. "Are you alright?"

Kara looked around. "I think so. The shuttle's intact."

The power systems came back online, along with their heads-up displays. A massive debris field stretched out before them, filled with huge sections of the Vemus ship. Telemetry of the field showed that they wouldn't be coming near the planet. New Earth was safe.

They'd lost track of the *Vigilant* when they lost power, and the shuttle's limited scanning capability couldn't distinguish the *Vigilant* from the space debris in the area. Noah sent out automated ship hails on all comms channels. After getting no response, he flew the shuttle into the field and began looking for the *Vigilant*.

"If they abandoned ship, we should at least be getting beacons from the escape pods," Kara said.

They caught up to the dead CDF ship a few minutes later. Noah tried opening a comms channel to the ship, but there was no response. The *Vigilant* looked more like a ship under construction than a vessel that had just come from a battle. Noah kept trying to get a response from anyone alive on the ship and felt a tinge of desperation creeping into his voice.

Finally, a comlink registered on the shuttle's heads-up display.

"We're here," Connor replied, his voice sounding strained. "We're still here. Did we destroy it?"

"It's good to hear your voice, sir. No Vemus ships in the area. We have a lock on you. We'll transmit your position back to COMCENT and get rescue operations going," Noah said.

"That sounds good. Better tell them to use quarantine protocols," Connor said.

Noah frowned and glanced at Kara. "I don't understand. Quarantine protocols for what?" he asked.

"It's a long story. Better patch in COMCENT if you can. We need emergency medical supplies as well. What's your location?" Connor asked.

"We're on a shuttle near the remains of the orbital defense platform," Noah said.

"So you're the ones who got off that final shot. Good work. You saved us all," Connor said.

"I had help," Noah replied and Kara spoke up.

"Thanks to you, too, Major," Connor said.

"COMCENT is ready . . ." Noah said.

31

A WEEK HAD PASSED since the attack. It had taken several days to get the survivors organized and make sure that there were no more ships in the Vemus fleet. The *Vigilant* was towed to the space docks near the lunar base. Unless they rebuilt the entire ship, Connor doubted it would fly again anytime soon, if ever. Given what they'd faced, he wasn't sure investing in a fleet was their best option at this time. Officially, he and the rest of the *Vigilant* and the *Banshee* crews were still under quarantine. He was supposed to stay at the hastily constructed quarantine sections of the lunar space docks where they'd been building their own battleship carrier, but Dr. Ashley Quinn had cleared him and a small task force to leave. Connor had asked her to keep his clearance under wraps for the time being. None of the crew that had been directly exposed to the Vemus ship's atmosphere showed any indication of infection, which was both a very good sign and a troubling one because they were no closer to understanding how humanity had fallen.

Once news of the attack had spread throughout the colony, the populace celebrated the Colonial Defense Force. The attack they'd all feared had come and they'd survived. All their preparation and sacrifice had paid off. But Connor had trouble thinking of it as a victory. They'd survived only by the skin of their teeth. Their defenses were virtually gone, and he was haunted by thoughts of the soldiers they'd left behind.

The CDF had commandeered the *Chmiel* and were heading back out to where Titan Space Station had been, looking for CDF soldiers still alive in the escape pods. Connor wished that was the only reason the *Chmiel* had returned to that area of space. The cargo carrier was also tasked with setting up a high-powered sensor array taken off the battleship carrier they'd been building.

Only a few people knew Connor had returned to the planet and he aimed to keep it that way for now. He had Noah going through the data Reisman had taken from the *Indianapolis*, which was hitting the "mother lode," as Noah liked to put it, in terms of learning about their enemy. One of the first orders of business Connor initiated from quarantine was to reposition their deep-space sensor array. At the same time, he'd ordered salvage crews to extract the Vemus communication protocols from the *Vigilant's* comms systems.

"I think our bird has finally come home, sir," Sean said.

Connor waited in a darkened office in the governor's residence. They'd easily disabled the security forces stationed at the governor's home, and Stanton Parish was on his way home. There had been celebrations of their "victory" over the Vemus, and Governor Parish had no end of speeches to give commemorating the occasion. Connor had brought a team of special CDF forces with him that was led by the newly promoted Major Sean Quinn. He deserved the promotion and was smart enough to know there was a lot more work coming his way.

"Target has entered the premises," Sean said.

Connor leaned against the wall in the shadows. The governor's desk was on the far side of the room. Connor had been to this office often over the years when Tobias Quinn had been governor but not so much since Stanton Parish had been elected. Connor heard Stanton's voice outside the office doors and then they opened.

Parish walked into the office and the interior lighting slowly illuminated to a casual brilliance. He walked over to his bar and poured himself a glass of scotch. Connor heard the ice hit the glass and then cleared his throat.

Parish spun around, spilling some of his drink. "Who's there?"

Connor stepped from the shadowy confines of the dark corner. "Hello, Governor."

"General Gates. I'm surprised to see you here," Parish said, blanching.

Connor didn't answer right away. Instead, he slowly crossed the room.

"I thought you and I needed to have a private chat. Why don't you have a seat?" Connor said.

Parish glanced at the door.

"Don't worry, we won't be disturbed. My men have your security forces detained for the moment," Connor said and sat down.

Parish swallowed hard and walked over to sit at his desk. "When did you get out of quarantine?"

Connor narrowed his gaze for a moment. "You'd be better served to just listen for the moment while I put the cards out on the table. Wouldn't you agree?"

Parish drained his scotch and set the glass on his desk with shaking hands. There was no question in Connor's mind that the man was afraid of him, as he should be. He'd thought long and hard about being in Parish's presence again.

"You tried to kill me," Connor said.

Parish's eyes widened. "That's absurd. I would never do such a thing. You're a hero. You saved us from the Vemus—"

Connor slammed his fist on the desk and Parish jumped. "You don't get to call me a hero. Not now. Not ever. I may not have the evidence to prove what you tried to have done to me, but I know it was you who put the pieces in motion."

Parish began to protest and Connor leaped from his chair and launched himself across the desk. He grabbed Parish by his shirt and slammed the man against the wall. "Colonel Ian Howe died a horrible death because of you, because your man screwed up while following your orders. Do you have any idea how painful it is to die of radiation poisoning? The utter collapse of your entire body? Here, have a look," Connor growled.

He slammed Parish down onto his desk and held him in place. Connor used his implants and sent a video feed to the nearest wallscreen. A deathly pale man lay on a bed in the *Vigilant's* infirmary.

"Look at it," Connor said and grabbed Parish's head, making him look at the screen. "We kept Ian in a coma because he was in so much pain. We had fifteen more soldiers suffering from milder cases of radiation poisoning, including Major Nathan Hayes. With one fell swoop, your efforts to have me killed almost took out the senior officers serving on the *Vigilant* right before the Vemus attacked."

Parish gasped for breath. "I didn't know. You have to believe me. I didn't know that was going to happen. I'm sorry."

Connor stepped back from the governor and sneered. "You're sorry. The enemy we were warned about has come and you're playing a petty scheme?"

Parish pushed himself up and staggered back against the wall. "I was wrong. I didn't know how wrong I was."

"Who else was working with you?" Connor asked while unholstering his sidearm.

"No one else!" Parish cried. "I swear, it was just Toro. That's it; he was my contact."

Connor glanced at his sidearm as if considering whether or not he was going to shoot the governor. Then he holstered his weapon. "I'm not going to kill you. While it would be immensely satisfying to me, it would set us back. This war isn't over."

Parish blinked and he opened his mouth. "What do you mean it isn't over? You stopped the Vemus fleet. Nothing has been detected from our sensors."

Connor sucked in a breath and sighed. "This wasn't the main fleet. They were being controlled."

Parish's eyes widened. "Not the main fleet? Over a thousand ships came. How many more could there be?"

"We don't know. They sent a scout force to soften our defenses, learn what we're capable of. When they come at us again, they'll bring the full measure of their attack force," Connor said.

Parish was silent for a moment and licked his lips. "How do you know this?"

"We found their control signal. It was how we stopped them. We interfered with the signal, which sent their fleet into disarray. Otherwise, they would have gotten past all our defenses," Connor said.

"My God," Parish said and swallowed hard. "What do we do?"

Connor glared at the man. There were so few of them left that Connor knew they needed every able-bodied person if they were going to have a chance of survival.

"Why is it that men like you make your speeches and look at soldiers like me as a necessary evil, but when your life's in danger, you look to me to save it for you," Connor said with a sneer.

He took a few steps away, not trusting himself to be near the governor.

"I was wrong. Is that what you want to hear? I was wrong. Now tell me how we can survive what's coming," Parish said.

Connor shook his head. "That's just it. I don't know if we can survive."

Parish stepped around the desk. "You must have something in mind, some kind of plan. We wouldn't even be here if it weren't for you."

"Not me," Connor said. "Thousands of CDF soldiers gave their lives so you could talk about victories at public events."

Parish held his hands in front his chest in a placating gesture. "What do you want me to say? The public has a right to know. They need to celebrate those victories. It gives them hope."

"You're just making up for all the doubt you've sown for the past year you've been in office. I can't fight an enemy with my men conflicted about what they're fighting for," Connor said.

"All that is done now. You'll have whatever you need," Parish said.

Bile crept up Connor's throat. The governor stank of fear and was now trying to barter away everything he could to ensure his survival.

"I know I'll get whatever I need now. I may not be able to prove in a court of law that you tried to have me killed and worked to manipulate the Colonial Defense Force in such a way as to sow dissent among our ranks, but you represent a sickness, a cancer that needs to be removed," Connor said.

Parish stepped back. "You said you wouldn't kill me."

Connor nodded. "You're right; I'm not going to kill you. You'll always know where you stand with me. I have a question for you."

Parish pressed his lips together. "What?"

"How badly do you want to survive? Would you give anything so the colony can survive?" Connor asked.

"Yes, of course I would," Parish said.

"Are you sure? Because that's what it's going to take. Setting aside our differences and coming together is what I think is going to give us our best chance."

"You're one hundred percent right."

"I'm glad you think that way. So you won't have any objections to stepping down as governor then?" Connor asked.

Parish's face twisted into a confused frown. "What . . . stepping down? I'm not sure I understood you correctly."

"I think you understood me perfectly. You've spent the last year running the CDF around in circles, denying critical requests. I think the only way forward is for you to step down as governor of the colony," Connor said.

"Who would take my place? You?" Parish asked.

Connor's lips lifted into a smile that didn't reach his eyes. "Not me."

"Who then?"

"There's a fascinating bit under emergency powers in the articles of the colony from subsection thirty-six. It talks about an elected official who's called upon to deal with a situation he's not equipped to deal with," Connor said.

Parish looked away.

"This is your chance to atone. Step down and restore Tobias Quinn as governor of the colony. He understands the threat we face," Connor said.

Parish turned away and brought his hands to his hips, his head hung low. "Alright, you win. I'll do it. I'll call a press conference in the morning and announce my resignation."

"There *will* be a press conference called tomorrow, but not by you," Connor said.

Parish turned back toward him in alarm.

"Governor Quinn, did you get that?" Connor asked while showing the comms channel he'd had active since Parish had entered the office. The wallscreen changed to show Tobias Quinn's face.

"Yes, I did," Tobias said and looked at Parish. "We have it on record, and I would strongly caution you against making the argument that you're abdicating the governor's seat under duress. We'll handle the formal transfer tomorrow, but effective immediately, the powers of the governor are transferred to me. Do you concur?"

Parish glanced at Connor for a moment. "Yes," he said in a tight voice.

"Good," Connor said. "I'll leave you to it."

"Thank you," Tobias said. "Franklin is waiting for you at CDF headquarters with a full staff."

Connor left the office. Tobias would handle the legality of what had just transpired and then they would all regroup in the morning. In the hall, CDF soldiers stood over the governor's security personnel, who were lined up against the wall.

Connor walked over to Sean. "Leave a team here to secure the residence and make sure Parish doesn't try anything. You and the rest of the team will be coming with me to CDF headquarters."

"Yes, sir," Sean said and issued orders to the men who were staying behind.

Sean caught up to Connor. "I'd say the hard part is over, but that would be a lie."

They headed to the troop carrier that was standing by. "You're right. The hard part is just beginning, but we have an idea of what to expect now."

They climbed aboard the troop carrier, which left the governor's residence. It was in these quiet moments that he felt the loss of his old friends and those from the colony. He still felt that Kasey and Wil were just a simple comlink away. He'd come to rely on them as trusted confidants. He wanted their counsel now more than ever as people looked to him to come up with a way to defend them against the Vemus.

The door to the cockpit opened and Connor heard the heavy thuds of combat boots trudging along. He glanced up and saw Juan Diaz staring down at him.

Diaz gave a playful punch to Sean's arm. "He's got that look again, that look that says the world is riding on his shoulders. Don't worry, General, we got your back. Always have. Always will."

Connor felt his face lift into his first genuine smile in a long time. "It's good to see you."

Diaz plopped down in the seat next to Connor. "I have to admit, I almost hoped we were wrong."

Connor nodded. "So did I," he said and sighed.

Diaz glanced over at him. "Focus, Connor, we've got a lot of work to do."

AUTHOR NOTE

Hello,

I hope you're enjoying the First Colony series. There is a small part of this book that is based on actual events. The event in question involves the collection of a lot of frogs, a five-gallon bucket, and the women's bathroom at an undisclosed campground. The incident unfolded pretty much as Wil Reisman describes for Connor. There wasn't a whole lot of thought that went into the actions of my ten-year-old self and the others who were there that night. If you're a member of the opposite sex who happens to be reading this, then the forty-something that is me apologizes but the ten-year-old cannot stop grinning. Boys will be boys.

There is another book (Legacy - First Colony - Book 3) that immediately follows this note, but while you're here...

Please consider leaving a review for this book.

Comments and reviews allow readers to discover authors, so if you'd like others to enjoy this series, please leave a short note.

If you're reading the ebook then click the link below to review the book before continuing the series.

Click Here to Review

Paperback readers please review the book where you bought it.

LEGACY

FIRST COLONY - BOOK 3

1

(Two hundred years before the Ark reached New Earth)

FLEET ADMIRAL MITCH WILKINSON's stooped form walked the bridge of the battleship carrier *Indianapolis*. Once, this vessel had been the flagship of the NA Alliance Navy, but now it was a solitary life raft for the precious few survivors remaining in the birthplace of humanity. The Vemus had changed everything, spreading across the planet like an untamed plague. But even considering all the destruction wrought by the enemy, humans hadn't been able to overcome certain behaviors of their own that had been consistent throughout their existence—the burning desire for power. Greed and corruption had doomed the human race on Earth.

Twenty years earlier, when he'd smuggled Connor Gates and the rest of the Ghost Platoon aboard the *Ark*, he never would have guessed that mankind's first interstellar colony would be the key to the survival of their entire species. Mitch had been an old man even then. After the *Ark* was on its way, he'd planned on a quiet retirement while keeping his promise to watch over the son Connor had left behind. It had been a good plan.

Mitch glanced over at the young man who was speaking with Dr. Stone. There were times when the light caught his facial features in such a way that he reminded Mitch of Connor. Mitch had plucked Sean Gates from Earth before the Vemus had really begun to spread. He'd brought the boy aboard the *Indianapolis* as part of an internship awarded to survivors of fallen veterans. While Mitch knew Connor was very much alive, he'd leveraged his "death" as a means of keeping Sean Gates close to him.

Sean looked over at him. "We're ready to execute our final broadcast, Admiral."

Wilkinson turned his slate-blue eyes toward Sean. "Acknowledged," he replied.

The Vemus had developed an insatiable appetite for humans, and now there was evidence that they would even venture out beyond the solar system in pursuit of the last of them. In a final effort to give the colonists a chance of survival, Dr. Stone was running some last-minute checks of their most ambitious undertaking to date.

"Elizabeth," Mitch said, "going back through it for the thousandth time isn't going to change anything."

Dr. Stone turned her gray-haired head toward him and then closed down the holoscreen she'd been working from. After speaking softly to her assistant, she walked over to Mitch.

"It's ready. I just wish . . ." Elizabeth said.

Mitch nodded knowingly. "We all do."

The *Indianapolis* may have been a ship of the wall, but it was now only a shell of what it had been. The vast stockpiles of armament once kept there had long been used up and the weapons they'd managed to keep online were based on energy beams. They had no missiles and there had been no resupply missions in the past ten years—not since the governments of Earth had all collapsed and the militaries had splintered into groups that focused on gathering the remaining resources for themselves.

Earth had been lost to them. For a while they'd scraped together an existence on space stations and solar colonies, but those were gone now, too. It had taken thousands of years for mankind to rise from its meager beginnings and—for a brief stint that began during the twenty-first century—had seemed to achieve a golden age of technological wonders. But humanity's fall into barbarism had been swift when the Vemus spread to the solar colonies, taking on a form that none of the survivors had been prepared to face. Mitch had banded together with a faction of the old NA Alliance Navy to try and secure a future, but the Vemus were too strong. They adapted too quickly and there simply weren't enough humans left to fight them. None of those who'd fought the Vemus had even the appearance of being human anymore.

Mitch glanced over at Dr. Stone. She'd found him five years ago, bringing refugees to a space station that orbited Ganymede. Jupiter's largest moon had become a haven. It was there that the brilliant Dr. Stone had eventually convinced him they only had one chance at survival and that all the people in the solar system were already dead, including the two of them; it was just a matter of time.

Mitch had denied the claim at first, believing her to be yet another brilliant scientist who couldn't cope with one of the darkest moments in human history. But shortly after that, remnants of Earth's space navies had begun fighting each other. Men and women Mitch had been friends with had either been killed or given in to despair and made a mad grab for power so their last days could have some semblance of comfort. Then the first Vemus ships from Earth had shown up at the colonies, preying on the survivors. Mitch had taken his most trusted tacticians and tried to come up with a way to survive, but the fact of the matter was that all their projections proved there was absolutely no chance. They could only succeed in delaying the inevitable. The Vemus had adapted and hunted only humans. Mitch didn't understand how a parasitic organism discovered deep in Earth's oceans could have decimated mammalian life on Earth, but that's exactly what had happened. Then it started targeting humans exclusively, and the real fight had begun.

Once he'd exhausted all his options, Mitch sought out Dr. Elizabeth Stone again, wanting to learn more about her far-fetched plan. He'd mistakenly believed that perhaps she had a way to actually help *them* survive. She didn't. What Dr. Stone had in mind was for the survival of those aboard the *Ark*—to update its mission and send it even farther away than they'd originally planned while gathering up whatever resources and people they could and heading out to the fringes of the solar system. It was a death sentence and also one of the biggest leaps of faith Mitch had taken in his entire life.

Dr. Stone had the appearance of a sweet little old lady who had somehow managed to survive, but Mitch had learned that she was one of the smartest and shrewdest people he'd ever met. He and Elizabeth had become mother and father to the survivors they'd taken with them.

Elizabeth had given him a timetable to work with. Updating the *Ark* mission wasn't simply a matter of sending a transmission; they had to enhance their communications array to handle a sustained data burst beyond anything they'd ever done before. And doing so would alert the Vemus to their presence.

Mitch's job was to gather the supplies they needed for the mission. They scavenged anything they could from decimated space stations and unmanned satellites that were the last vestiges of an age now gone. Even though he'd agreed to help Dr. Stone, he hadn't become a true believer in their mission until years later when, on a scavenging mission, they'd found an intact satellite uplink and seen an image of Earth. The bright blue planet was still there but with a cloud cover that could only come from a holocaust the likes of which had only been hinted at during a much earlier nuclear age. Communications from the last space stations had gone dark, but there were plenty of ships still in the system—ships that were patched together and would attack without provocation. Those ships and the people serving aboard them had been absorbed into the Vemus Fleet. Mitch had tried to avoid the Vemus, but they'd become aware of the *Indianapolis* and hunted it. The Vemus had grown in intelligence and complexity in the years since Mitch had first seen their existence appear on mission reports. Some were vaguely humanlike, but there were others that were beyond anything he could have imagined.

Their final mission was such a mundanely obvious thing that Mitch couldn't believe he hadn't thought of it before, but Elizabeth had known. Mitch suspected she'd always known. It was the last piece to the puzzle and it was the thing that would bring the Vemus down on them in full force.

Sean walked the length of the bridge and stood in front of Mitch.

"Credentials to override the *Ark's* mission parameters have been uploaded, Admiral," Sean said.

"Good. What about my other request of you?" Mitch asked.

Sean scowled. "I don't know what you expect me to say. I hardly remember him at all."

Mitch arched an eyebrow. "But you do remember him at least a little bit."

Sean looked away for a moment. "My father left when I was three years old. Then you smuggled him aboard the *Ark*. I have nothing to say to the man."

Mitch regarded the young man. He was beyond his years in so many ways and yet managed to be so young in others. "I doubt that. Your father had no choice. I've told you he had decided to go back to you, to be your father."

"Yeah? Well, he didn't!" Sean snapped, then grimaced. "I'm sorry. You don't deserve that. You've been more of a father to me than he ever was."

"Circumstances made it this way. You don't have to say much. Just tell him who you are. That's all he'll want to know," Mitch said.

There was a quiet buzz on the bridge as the various teams made their final preparations. Mitch watched as Sean glanced at the PRADIS output on the main holoscreen. The Vemus fleet had almost caught up to them.

"Why are you pushing for this? None of it will matter in a few hours," Sean said.

Mitch's gaze hardened. "It matters. Your father didn't deserve what happened to him, just like you don't deserve what's happening to you. We're all in the same boat, but you have a chance to send one final message to someone who cares about you. The rest of us here don't have any family left. We only have each other, and not for much longer."

Sean clenched his teeth. Doing what they'd set out to do wasn't easy for them, knowing that their last efforts would ultimately be for someone else's benefit. Mitch chose to look at it as an investment in a dark future, but there was a lot of bitterness among the survivors on the *Indianapolis* because they knew there would be no escape from the Vemus. They'd exhausted all their resources and this would be their final stand.

Mitch looked at Sean, who returned his gaze. Stubbornness was a Gates' family stock-in-trade. With a slight shrug of his shoulders, the young man finally walked over to one of the consoles and sat down.

"Tactical, put the countdown on the main screen," Mitch said.

He glanced over at the command couch. He was tired of sitting and planning, but most of all he was tired of failing. He wished he could have come up with a way to stop the Vemus, and he supposed that if they'd had more time perhaps they could have found a way together. But that wasn't the case. He was going to die today. They all were. Since these were going to be his last moments alive, he chose to meet his end on his feet.

Elizabeth's hand grasped his. "Thank you," she said softly.

Mitch gave her hand a gentle squeeze. "You were right."

"I know, but it's good to hear you say it," Elizabeth said.

Mitch watched the countdown timer drain away. The main reactor was charging the power relays at the communications array in preparation for the broadcast signal. The signal would reach the nearest deep space buoy and then continue until it reached the *Ark*. Once the colony ship received the data burst, the onboard computers would set upon the task of changing the ship's trajectory and hopefully that of the last humans in the galaxy.

A klaxon alarm sounded, and Mitch glanced over to the woman serving as his tactical officer.

She silenced the alarm. "Vemus forces are aboard the ship, sir."

Mitch swallowed hard. He'd been prepared for this, but when it came down to it, all men fear death when it's their time to go. "Understood," he said and used his implants to begin the powerful broadcast.

The Vemus would be able to follow the broadcast. There had already been evidence that they were amassing ships together for a long journey, and the race for humanity's survival was about to begin.

As the signal went out, the survivors aboard the *Indianapolis* fought a foe that dead scientists back on Earth had determined was of their own making. Those scientists had failed to stop a sickness they hadn't fully comprehended, but the survivors valiantly fought them once more to the last man, woman, and child until they closed upon the bridge. Some of the people there had chosen to take their own lives. Their bodies wouldn't be contaminated by the Vemus, but there were others who fought with weapons in hand until the bitter end—an end for the crew of the *Indianapolis* but the promise of a new beginning for the rest of mankind.

(Sierra – New Earth Colony)

CONNOR STOOD IN HIS QUARTERS, his gaze lingering on a video file he'd selected from the long list on his screen. He wasn't sure whether he could watch it again, but something deep inside him urged him to do it one more time. He pressed his lips together in determination and then pressed play.

"You don't know me at all. In fact, I can hardly remember you. The admiral believes I should record this stupid thing and send it along. Said I should tell you who I am. So who am I? I'm the guy it sucks to be. Hell, I'd have settled for the short end of the stick. Any of us would have settled for *any* part of the stick, but we don't get that. I've fought in a long war with little hope of survival, let alone a victory. Yet *you* get to live. You're the lucky one. By the time you see this message, you'll be alive on some colony world, living your life. Maybe you'll even have a family and be someone else's father—"

Connor stopped the video, his throat thick with emotion at the bitter catch in his son's voice, which came across perfectly preserved. Connor leaned on the small shelf before the holoscreen, momentarily overcome by the weight of regret, but then he reached out and restarted the video so it could disgorge its ancient message into the darkened room.

"I don't know what to say to you. Even though I know what happened, I'm mad at you for leaving. I'm still mad. I'm mad because you left in the first place and I'll never know why. Not really." His son looked away from the camera for a moment. "If my mother knew, she never told me. She died, you know. She was among the first to become ill with what became the Vemus infection. The funny thing is that Vemus isn't . . ." His son's voice trailed off. "The admiral tried to help me find her. We didn't know at the time that it was the beginning of the end for us. Yet it's upon our blood and sacrifice that *you* get to live. *You*, who left . . . left us all behind."

Connor knew what he meant. *You left me behind.* He imagined his son saying it, and it stung like a slap across the face.

"I don't have anything nice to say. I'm not going to say something that will make you feel better about leaving. I don't think you deserve it. If you were here, I might be screaming at you. Maybe we'd even fight," Sean said, glaring at the screen. "I'm good at fighting. Maybe I get that from you. Heh. I can't even imagine you sitting there getting this message. What you must be thinking. Do you even feel anything? The admiral said I should tell you who I am. I'm a soldier, and it sucks. I didn't choose to be a soldier. It chose me. I hate it almost as much as I hate you. That's who I am. I don't think any of this is going to make you feel better. I know I don't feel . . . and I'm long past caring about . . . anything." Sean glanced away from the camera at something off-screen. "They're almost here. I'm surrounded by dead bodies, along with those of us who won't take our own lives. This is all that's left. This is our legacy. We are to make sure that the broadcast signal stays on as long as possible. For you. So you get to live. Who am I? Science says you're my biological father, but I have no father. I'm a soldier fighting on the losing side. It sucks being me. I have nothing left but fury and hate."

The video message from Connor's son had been part of the data cache Reisman had stolen before he died, and the message was over two hundred years old. Connor hadn't known what to expect when he first watched it, but every time he watched his throat became thick with sorrow and regret. He must have watched this video hundreds of times. The bitter man his son had become left Connor smothered with guilt. He should have been there. He'd give anything to change the past, to stay behind and raise his son. Protect him, even knowing what he knew about the Vemus. At least he could have been there to fight at his son's side. Then Sean would have known how much Connor loved him.

He'd thought long and hard about what must have been going through his son's mind in those final moments. The crushing pain he felt at finally seeing Sean and knowing what had become of him struck him like a blow every time he watched the video, but he had to keep watching it. He owed his son that much at least.

With the pain came a sense of pride that his son had fought to the very end. It was a measure of who he'd been. Connor couldn't imagine what Sean had had to endure, the kind of life he'd led. Connor would never forgive himself for not being there. He'd hated Wilkinson for putting him aboard the *Ark*, but those feelings had long since faded away. Connor's choices many years before that event were what had made him leave his family, which had nothing to do with Admiral Mitch Wilkinson. The old admiral knew that, and even Connor's son knew it.

He powered off the holoscreen and rubbed his face. His eyes were puffy and tired. He made himself watch the video of his son as a kind of penance, as if subjecting himself to all the pain would somehow ease Connor's most profound regret. He clenched his teeth and slammed his fist down on the shelf. He hated that video and hated himself for what it represented—a life of regret and a reminder of what he'd left behind.

2

———

NOAH WAS SURROUNDED BY HOLOSCREENS. Each had data feeds being piped into them that fed several regression-analysis queries he had running. The work he was doing could only be done at CDF headquarters in Sierra. It had been two months since the Vemus attack, and Noah was tasked with data mining everything the late Colonel Wil Reisman had been able to steal from the Vemus warship. More than a few times Noah wished he had Reisman's help. The colonel had been extremely clever and could glean useable intelligence from anything he set his attention on. Noah missed Reisman and had thrown himself at his current project to ensure that Reisman's last action hadn't been for naught.

He was in a large work area where his team was carrying out smaller projects serving the same goal: find anything they could use against the Vemus forces coming for them. Working with scientists for so long had taught Noah that often the best results of a large project came from collaboration with others, so when Connor asked him what he needed to get the job done, Noah had told him he needed a team, a large room, and priority access to one of the CDF's supercomputers. He'd been given all of that, and Noah and his team worked tirelessly. As a result of those efforts, they'd made quite a few discoveries that were being closely examined by subject-matter experts.

As the days passed, Noah kept looking at the clock. They all did. He felt like they were working on borrowed time and at any moment the rest of the Vemus attack force would show up to finish what they'd started.

Someone cleared their throat behind him.

"So this is where they've been keeping you."

Noah turned around and swiped the holoscreen to the side. "Allison, it's so good to see you. Or should I call you Dr. Blake now?" he asked with a smile. The former medic for Search and Rescue had recently become a medical doctor.

Allison gave him a quick hug. She was tall, with long auburn hair and cupid's-bow lips. She peered at him. "You're not getting enough sleep."

Noah snorted. "No one is."

Allison glanced around. "I've heard a lot about what you've been doing. You're an official hero, but I'd love to meet your wife."

Noah felt the skin tighten around his eyes. He and Kara had decided to get married shortly after they returned to New Earth. It had been a quiet ceremony, which was what they'd wanted. "I'd love for her to meet you, but she's at Lunar Base working on . . . I'm sure you can guess."

Allison's eyes drew down in empathy. "I'm sorry. It must be hard being apart like that."

Noah nodded. "I'm sure you're not here to reminisce about our old Search and Rescue days."

"No, I'm not," Allison said.

"What can I do for you?" Noah asked.

"You remember my specialization?" Allison asked.

"Of course. Field biology."

"I've branched out into—" Allison began to say.

One of Noah's analyses finished running and flashed on the holoscreen next to him. He glanced at it, noting the returns.

"What's that?" Allison asked.

"The data cache we got from the Vemus ship. It's over two hundred years old and I'm trying a new regression analysis on the video files. It seems that video logs were the preferred method of recording one's experiences, which makes it difficult to glean useful information," Noah said.

Allison frowned as she read the screen. "What are you trying to find out?"

Noah blew out a breath. "How much time do you have?" he asked with a half-smile. "We needed a quicker way to analyze the information people were recording that didn't require us to watch every video. If we tried to do that, it would take years to get through them all."

"Why wouldn't you focus on the research information and such?" Allison asked.

"That's what we did initially, and I've given that to Connor, but I think there's more to be found," Noah answered.

"Like what?"

Noah pressed his lips together in thought. "Have you ever heard the phrase 'missing the forest because of the trees'?"

Allison nodded.

"I think we're so focused on the facts about the Vemus and what happened to Earth that we're missing key insights from the people who were actually there," Noah said.

"Now you've lost me."

"They fought the Vemus for years, but there was a time *before* the Vemus became as we know them now. I think that's how we can find something in the records we can use against them. Despite everything we've done for the past seven years, we've only really had one encounter with the Vemus, and that was about two months ago. The people back on Earth had years to contend with them. So I'm after those people who had a thought or theory they recorded but didn't have time to fully explore," Noah said.

"I understand. You're looking for a needle in a haystack."

"That about sums it up, but I know you didn't come all this way to hear about what I was doing," Noah said.

"I'm doing something similar—" Allison began.

A comlink came to prominence on one of the holoscreens, drawing their attention. It was a priority message with CDF General Connor Gates' identification on it. Noah opened the channel and Connor's face came on screen.

Connor looked at Noah and then noticed Allison.

"It's good to see you, sir," Allison said, moving to stand next to Noah.

"You as well, Dr. Blake," Connor replied and then looked at Noah. "I need a status update from you."

Before the Vemus attack, Noah had thought of Connor as a friend—albeit a friend who tolerated very little in the way of nonsense—but after their encounter with the Vemus, Noah had noticed his friend becoming increasingly bitter as time went on. He understood why, but he missed the old Connor just the same.

Noah brought up another window on the holoscreen. "I have it right here. I've sent all I found to Sanctuary."

"I'm aware of that, but you were supposed to be looking for more information about the power requirements," Connor said.

"The colossus cannon was theoretical to begin with. I'm not even sure they actually built it back on Earth . . ." Noah's voice trailed off when Connor speared a look at him.

"Let me guess. You're still mining those video logs," Connor said.

Noah looked away guiltily. "There's good information in there. Things we can use."

"The only thing in those recordings is how the people of Earth were defeated by the Vemus. Wilkinson found plans for an atmospheric weapon, but we haven't been able to produce the power required," Connor said.

Noah felt a flush warm his face. He'd spent a lot of time watching those videos. At first, he'd convinced himself it was just curiosity, but now he couldn't stop thinking about them. Some of them were horrifying, but he found comfort in knowing there were others who had faced what the colony was now facing.

"Noah," Connor called. "All those people are dead. They can't help us, but you can."

"I'm doing my best, sir," Noah replied.

"I know, and I need more from you. I want you to go to Sanctuary and see it for yourself," Connor said.

"I'm not sure I can help them. There are plenty of engineers there who are trying to adapt the power station from the alien city to use with the colossus cannon," Noah said.

"Do I need to make it an order?"

Noah glared at the screen. He wanted Kara with him. She was on the lunar base and the Vemus could attack at any moment. "No," he said and sighed.

Connor's gaze softened. "Thank you," he said.

"Sir, I have a request I'd like to run by you. It will only take a minute," Allison said.

"Make it quick," Connor replied.

"We've been studying the data about the Vemus and its origins, but in order to figure out how it will affect us here on this planet, we need samples. Living samples, that is," Allison said.

Connor frowned. "We've provided living samples to the research laboratory at the lunar base."

Allison shook her head. "That was the remnant virus. What we're looking for is the parasite. They work together. All the samples contain only the dead virus."

"What is it you're asking for? I won't authorize any of the samples to be brought down to the planet surface," Connor said.

Allison shook her head. "No, that's not what I'm asking. We have a team on the lunar base. They've been requesting permission to try and gather live samples from the larger pieces of wreckage of the Vemus ships in the debris fields before they get too far away."

"I'm not sure that's a good idea—"

"Sir, this is as important as any weapon system we currently have. Perhaps even more so. This thing spread like wildfire across Earth and we're not sure if the same thing is going to happen here on New Earth," Allison said.

Connor pressed his lips together in thought. "Explain it to me then, but keep it brief. I have to give a report to the colonial congress about our readiness status."

"I'll be brief. We're different because we've been living on this planet and making it our home, and it's changed us. Our immune system is different because we've been exposed to this planet. There are mammals of a sort here. We've sent samples of parasites and viruses we've collected to the lab station on the lunar base, but we can't see how they'll interact with the Vemus unless we have live samples to work with," Allison said.

"I thought you've been running simulations," Connor said.

"We have, but they'll only get us so far. What we could learn from a live sample is whether some kind of organism here would make us resistant to the Vemus. The data from Dr. Stone that was found on the Vemus ship said the Vemus exclusively targeted humans *after* Earth scientists failed to find a cure. We suspect that the scientists were trying to modify it so it wouldn't target humans, but, instead, it had the opposite effect," Allison said.

Connor glanced over at someone who was speaking to him off-screen for a moment. "That's a hell of a theory, Blake."

"It's the only one that makes any sense. We know there are viruses on Earth that can rewrite their DNA, but the Vemus represents a much more complex system than a simple parasite and virus pair. This is our chance to gain a better understanding of what we're dealing with," Allison said.

"Okay, you convinced me. I'll authorize a scouting mission. Send me the team leader you want on the mission, and we'll make it happen," Connor said.

"Thank you, sir," Allison said, sounding relieved.

Connor shifted his gaze to Noah. "There will be a transport going to Sanctuary tomorrow morning and I want you on it. Gates out."

The comlink closed and Noah stared at the blank screen for a few seconds before looking away. He rested his hands on his hips.

"He seemed kind of harsh toward you," Allison said.

Noah shrugged. "They've placed the survival of the colony in his hands. How would you be?"

Allison pursed her lips in thought. "All this wasn't real to me until two months ago. Earth and everything about it seemed so far away."

"Trust me, it's real," Noah said. He powered off the holoscreens he'd been working from. "I'm worried about him."

"What do you mean?" Allison asked.

"Some of the things we found in the data cache were for Connor specifically. There was at least one video log," Noah said.

Allison's eyes widened. "Oh god."

"I have no idea what was in the video log or who it was from. The only thing I do know is that after I sent it to Connor, something seemed to break inside him. At first I thought it was because of everyone we'd lost, but this seems different," Noah said.

"Have you told anyone about this?"

"Who would I tell? I'm not sure what good it would do. If it's personal, then shouldn't it remain personal?" Noah asked.

Allison gave him a look that somehow made him feel foolish. "He's grieving, and whatever was on that video log certainly didn't help. Why didn't you look at it before you sent it to him?"

"It wasn't meant for me," Noah said.

Allison arched an eyebrow.

"Fine, I couldn't access it to see what it was. So I sent it to him."

"There must be someone he can talk to about this," Allison said.

The first people Noah thought of were Wil Reisman and Kasey Douglass, but they were both dead. "Diaz might be able to help."

"Maybe. What about that archaeologist, Dr. Bishop?" Allison said.

"Lenora! I'm not sure whether that would help at all. They're not exactly on speaking terms," Noah said.

"I'd try to talk to him, but I don't think he'd listen to me. Frankly, I'm surprised he agreed to my request," Allison said.

Noah nodded, thinking the same thing. Should he contact Lenora and see if she would speak to Connor?

"I have to go," Allison said.

Noah frowned. "You never did tell me what you came to me for."

"Oh, I got what I wanted. I was going to ask if you'd found more information about the Vemus and then I was going to run my request to Connor by you to see if you thought he'd listen," Allison said.

"Glad I could help," Noah said.

Allison left him, and Noah glanced around the room. There were glowing holoscreens active, with several teams of two or three people working together.

Noah brought up a smaller, personal holoscreen and sighed. He really wanted to talk to Kara, but there were comms restrictions to the lunar base. He pressed his lips together, then sat down in a chair nearby. The holoscreen sank down with him. He sent a comlink out, which was immediately answered. He'd almost hoped it wouldn't be.

"Hello, Lenora. Do you have a few minutes to talk? I need your advice about something. It's about Connor."

3

CONNOR STEPPED off the personnel carrier onto the landing pad on the roof of the congressional building. His security detail followed him, and Connor glanced over at the rooftops of the tall buildings nearby. Rail-cannons were mounted on them for Sierra's defense. CDF soldiers were stationed throughout the city and were on alert. With the imminent threat of invasion, some people were reluctant to leave their homes, but a familiar face met him at the rooftop entrance to the building.

"Major Quinn. I was expecting to encounter a different Quinn before the meeting," Connor said.

"She's already inside, so you're stuck with me, sir," Sean answered.

They went inside and entered the stairwell.

"Not a huge group of people in the congressional committee, but they're all expecting you to give them an update on the state of our defenses," Sean said.

"They want much more than that," Connor said and quickened his pace.

They left the stairwell and quickly made their way through the building to the main hall. Sean stopped just outside the meeting room. "Director Mallory wanted me to inform you that Parish is part of the committee," Sean said.

Connor's chest tightened. Stanton Parish had tried to have Connor killed before the Vemus attacked them, but he couldn't prove it. Connor and Tobias had managed to remove Parish from the office of governor, but they couldn't be completely rid of him. Like it or not, Parish was an elected official, but he was unfit to deal with the current threat to the colony. There had been a push from Parish's supporters for him to remain in an advisory role on the defense committee, and in the interest of a smooth transition of power, Tobias had agreed. Connor hated the man. Parish had reallocated resources away from the defense of the colony and denied multiple requests to finish the defensive projects they'd begun, and the result was that the CDF had had to face their enemy at half their fighting capacity. Too many lives had been lost due to the actions of Stanton Parish. Removing Parish from office seemed like a slap on the wrists compared to all the CDF soldiers who had died defending New Earth.

"Alright, I've been informed," Connor replied.

Sean eyed him for a moment and then opened the door. The interior chambers were mostly empty except for the committee that sat at the meeting table. Defense of the colony was everyone's priority now that the Vemus had finally shown up.

Tobias Quinn was speaking, and Connor went to the empty seat next to Frank Mallory. Sean stood off to the side. Sitting across from Connor was Dr. Ashley Quinn, who had retained her post as chief of staff for all things medical in the colony. She regarded Connor knowingly. He knew that, being the gifted doctor she was, she could just glance at him and know he hadn't been taking care of himself. Connor looked away and glanced around at the others on the committee. Like himself, they were all lacking sleep and working long hours. Thanks to Connor's implants, he only needed two hours' sleep. It had taken the scientists here years to reverse-engineer Connor's NA Alliance military-grade implants that had been cutting edge when the *Ark* left Earth space. The CDF, given the nature of their work, were given top priority for the new implants. Colonial scientists had managed to improve on the design so that a person was less likely to reject them, but they were in short supply, and they could only outfit about five percent of the colony, or fifteen thousand people.

More than one committee member shifted their focus to Connor while Tobias was speaking. Many of them had doubted Earth had been lost, thanks to the efforts of Stanton Parish. Now they looked to Connor to protect them, and the fact that he couldn't weighed heavily on him.

"I've asked General Gates to come to this meeting to provide a status update on our readiness for the Vemus threat," Tobias said.

"Excuse me, Governor, I'd like to raise a question for General Gates that I believe those of us on this committee would like to hear his opinion on."

"Dr. Mendoza, why don't we hold all questions until General Gates has provided his update," Tobias said.

Connor looked at the woman who had spoken. She was tall, even when seated, and had long features. Her bony shoulders drew up toward her ears, giving her the appearance of a hawk's wings right before it was about to fly. Dr. Gabriela Mendoza was a staunch supporter of Parish and had been his scientific advisor.

"What is it you'd like to know?" Connor asked the astrophysicist.

"The Vemus signal you discovered during the battle two months ago—has it been detected since the battle?" Dr. Mendoza asked.

"No, it has not," Connor answered.

"Are you certain, then, that the Vemus have another attack force coming here?"

"Yes, I am," Connor said and addressed the rest of the committee. "You've all read the reports from that attack. The source of the signal was away from the attack force and we have no idea where it was actually coming from. The signal went dark after the attack."

"Isn't it possible that the source of the signal could have been from one of the ships that was destroyed?" Dr. Mendoza asked.

Connor shook his head and reminded himself that they were scared. "Look, we've been down this road before. You doubted the attack was coming in the first place and that didn't work out so well. Now you're wondering: if there *is* another attack force out there, why haven't they come yet?"

There were several head-bobs around the conference table.

"I don't have a good answer for you. I just know they're out there. The fact of the matter is the Vemus learned as much about us as we did about them during our encounter. They quickly adapted their tactics during our battle with them. We know from the data cache taken from one of their ships that when the Vemus left Earth, they had a massive fleet of ships—more than what we've faced. Our engineers believe the Vemus signal was coming from outside this star system. That's all we know. We've scanned the area where we thought the signal was coming from and haven't detected anything, but it could be that we don't have the ability to detect them with our scanners. What I believe is that the second Vemus attack force changed their tactics and will enter this star system from a different point of entry," Connor said.

"Why?" Dr. Mendoza asked.

"Because we're dangerous. We've proven that much. They'll be cautious on their second attempt, but make no mistake; they're coming here because this is where *we* are."

"We can't possibly scan all vectors of the sky," Dr. Mendoza said.

"You're right, we can't. We're doing the best we can. It's been two months since the attack. Every hour we get is a gift. More time to prepare. The Vemus aren't going to blunder into the star system again. Every able-bodied person is going to be called upon to fight, and it still might not be enough. Our orbital defenses aren't going to be able to stop another attack force like what we faced before," Connor said.

"What do you need then?" Dr. Mendoza asked.

"Five more years and the full effort of the colony to build our own fleet of ships and orbital defenses. That's what I need, but it won't be what we'll get. We'll be lucky if we get another five days," Connor said.

There were several gasps.

"What the general is saying," Mallory said, speaking up for the first time since Connor entered the room, "is that there's no way we can know when the Vemus will attack again. It could be at any moment. We have bunkers set up and we've been identifying archaeological sites that could be used as shelters," Mallory said and inclined his head toward Connor.

"Yes, we've done all that," Connor said. "The fact of the matter is that when the Vemus attack us, we're not going to be able to stop them in space. There's a high probability that an invasion force will land on this planet."

There was a long silence in the meeting room. If the Vemus were able to land an attack force, they could also spread themselves to mammalian life on New Earth.

Stanton Parish cleared his throat, and Connor swung his powerful gaze at the man.

"What about the colossus cannon?" Parish asked.

"We're reviewing the schematics for it," Connor said.

"But with all the resources being devoted to Sanctuary—"

"As I said before, we're reviewing the schematics for it," Connor said. Not wishing to disclose the current status of the cannon, he looked over at the other committee members. "We're doing everything we can, and it still might not be enough."

Many of the committee members focused on the area in front of them. They'd wanted Connor to come in here and give them hope, but there very well might not be any hope for them to survive. He instinctually believed the Vemus attack was imminent, but even he was at a loss as to what they were waiting for, and the anticipation of attack was wearing away at all of them.

"We still don't know why they're coming," Dr. Mendoza said.

"That's not entirely accurate," a man said, and Connor's internal heads-up display showed that the man's name was Dr. Fritz Kramer.

"We know from the data cache and the video logs that the Vemus spread themselves across mammalian life on Earth. This is unprecedented in any organism that has come before. The Vemus started infecting sea mammals— whales and dolphins—before it started spreading on land," Dr. Kramer said.

Connor remembered the Vemus soldiers they'd fought on the *Indianapolis*. They had thick, dark skin, were massive in size, and were extremely strong.

"The Vemus are, in fact, two separate organisms that have formed a symbiotic circle. They depend on each other to thrive. Many scientists believed that the Vemus didn't show up until they were exposed," Dr. Kramer said.

"Exposed?" Tobias asked.

"Disturbed is perhaps a better word. Earth scientists weren't sure, but they couldn't find a credible theory as to how the Vemus spread so rapidly. This leaves us with two or three possibilities. First is that the Vemus are a biological weapon that was created in a lab and simply grew out of the control of its creators. The second is that chance brought the two organisms together and it spread itself through the food chain to the point that by the time people became aware of its existence, it was already too late," Dr. Kramer said.

"And the third?" Connor asked.

"The third is the most far-fetched. One or both of the organisms are not Terran based. A meteor crashed into the Pacific Ocean and brought one or both of the organisms to Earth," Dr. Kramer said.

"And we can never be sure," Connor said.

"No, we can't," Dr. Kramer said.

"Even if we knew the origins of the Vemus, why would they come all this way for us? That's a tall order for a disease," Dr. Mendoza said.

"We modified it," Connor said.

"No, that can't be right," Dr. Kramer said.

"It *is* right," Connor said, pressing on. "When the Vemus started spreading to animals on land, there was a tremendous loss of life. In a panic, our scientists tried to modify a strain of the virus so it would avoid humans. I have no idea what they did, but I do know that after they modified the virus, it seemed to seek out humans exclusively."

"You're oversimplifying what happened," Dr. Kramer said.

"Am I? I don't think so, because that's what the records say happened. You said it yourself. The two organisms depended on one another. One of those organisms was a virus that was capable of rewriting its DNA, but after the scientists got through with it, they had augmented its ability. Instead of simply being able to rewrite its DNA, it could store DNA from any infected host. I can give you a firsthand account of how the Vemus are highly adaptive to situations. I saw them change forms to get us as we left their ship," Connor said.

Ashley cleared her throat. "The basis for any living organism is to reproduce as part of its life cycle. When the Vemus started targeting humans to the exclusion of all else, it found a species of more than twenty billion throughout the solar system."

"This doesn't explain how the Vemus were able to track us over sixty light-years. How does an organism fly spaceships, use weapons, and plan attacks?" Dr. Mendoza asked.

There was a heavy silence throughout the meeting room.

"Like I said, we modified it. Made it stronger," Connor said.

More than one committee member's face became ashen.

"Stronger, yes," Franklin Mallory said, "but some of their tactics denote a lack of imagination. They can execute basic attacks, but they haven't done anything complex as far as strategy goes. That's why we were able to stop them before."

Mallory gave Connor a pointed look, and Tobias steered the discussion to the preparations being made. Connor had already drafted what he thought was the best strategy for when the Vemus invaded, and it hadn't been well received. He felt as if Wil and Kasey were standing behind him, judging everything he said and did, and he didn't think they approved either.

4

AFTER THE MEETING ENDED, Tobias asked Connor and Frank to stay behind for a few minutes. Connor glanced at the clock on the wall. He just wanted to get out of there. He'd had enough of being around these people for the time being.

When the room cleared, Tobias regarded him for a moment. "When I asked you about the state of our readiness, I didn't think you'd dash all hope of our survival."

Connor sighed. "That's reality. I can't spread false hope."

"I wasn't asking you to, but we need everyone to keep working. We're barely holding together as it is, but if you take away all hope, they'll just give up . . ." Tobias paused for a second. "What's going on with you? You don't need me to tell you all this."

Connor looked away. The image of his dead son came to his mind and he could hear his son's bitter words in his mind, twisting him up in knots. "It's been a rough few days."

"I'm sorry, did you say days? How about months or years? We need you focused," Tobias said.

"I'll be fine. I just need to get out of here and get some air," Connor said.

He hastened toward the door and was out of the meeting room before anyone could reply. He hardly saw the faces of the people he passed as he fled down the hall. There were too many faces, all looking to him to protect them. Everywhere he went people looked to him to give them hope, but deep inside he was hollow. He felt he had nothing left to give. He would fail them all and then his life would be over.

Connor rounded a corner and nearly collided with another person. The exit to the building was within sight and he hastened toward it, muttering an apology.

He knew his security detail was likely closing in on him, but he just wanted to be alone for a while.

Connor shoved his way through the side exit of the congressional building and took several deep breaths of fresh air. He was greeted by the scent of freshly mown lawns, sliced by paved paths that led throughout the campus. The sun gleamed and the blue sky overhead had hints of green to it that were unique to New Earth. He jogged down a path through the gardens.

He was well away from the building when he heard his name being called, and something in the voice penetrated his angst. Connor spun around and saw Lenora running toward him, her long, thick hair trailing behind her. The sight of her made his pulse quicken, but the respite was short-lived. Connor glanced in the direction she'd come from and saw the personal transport ship she must have used to fly here.

"Is that your ship?" Connor asked.

Lenora frowned. "Yes," she said.

"I need to get out of here. Can you take us somewhere?" Connor asked.

Lenora eyed him for a moment.

"Please, I just need to get away from here," Connor said.

"Yeah, sure. Let's go," Lenora answered.

They hurried toward Lenora's ship and climbed aboard. Connor glanced out the window and saw Sean Quinn, along with Connor's security detail, racing toward them.

"Should we wait for them?" Lenora asked.

Connor shook his head. "No. Just take off," he said, his voice sounding strained.

Lenora engaged the thrusters and the ship lifted off the ground. Once they were above the buildings, she flew them away from the city. Connor used his implants to shut down the transponder inside the craft.

An alert appeared on the heads-up display, and Lenora glanced at him. "What's going on?"

"They'll track us through the transponder. I just need to get away for a while," Connor said.

"It's not going to fool Sean," Lenora said.

"I know," Connor replied.

He'd trained Sean well, and he had the makings of a great leader. Too bad he might not get the chance.

Lenora took them away from Sierra, and after a few minutes she set them down in an open clearing surrounded by trees. A hundred kilometers away from Sierra and New Earth looked as if it had never been inhabited by humans.

Connor's heart was racing as he hastily climbed out of the seat. He opened the hatch and his shoulders brushed against the sides as he went out before it fully opened.

"Where are you going?" Lenora asked, following him.

Connor stepped out onto the grassy field, and the soft ground yielded to his heavy footfalls. His breath came in gasps. He kept thinking about how they were all going to die and it was all his fault. He hadn't fought hard enough for what they needed. Perhaps *he* had even started to doubt that the Vemus were coming for them, and he'd bought into what Stanton Parish had been saying. He felt so small and insignificant compared to the vastness of everything around him. They were still so new to this world that there would be nothing to mark their passing if everyone in the colony died.

Lenora's brows drew up in worry. "You need to calm down."

Connor swallowed hard. "I can't."

Lenora placed her hands on his shoulders. "Look at me. Look into my eyes."

Connor did as she asked.

"Good. Now just take slow, deep breaths. Do it with me."

Lenora took a deep breath and Connor tried to follow along, but he couldn't feel his hands and he was becoming dizzy. His chest tightened and he pushed away from Lenora. He backed away, his gaze darting back and forth as if he were about to be attacked.

"It's okay. You're fine. It's just the two of us here," Lenora said soothingly.

Connor just wanted to run. He needed to run. He spun around but felt something jab into his back. There was intense heat, the strength went out of his muscles, and he collapsed to the ground. Lenora caught him and eased him down. His vision faded and he blacked out.

He heard Lenora speaking as he began to wake up. There was something soft under his head. He opened his eyes and found that he was lying on the ground in the same field she had taken him to. He drew in a deep breath and blew it out. His heart was no longer racing.

Lenora put her comlink away and came over to him.

"What did you do to me?" Connor asked.

"I used my stunner on you. You were having a panic attack and weren't thinking straight," Lenora said.

"A panic attack?" Connor repeated, frowning. "That can't be right."

"Why? Because you're the great Connor Gates? The CDF general who singlehandedly defeated the Vemus?"

Connor didn't reply. He knew she was baiting him. Instead, he sat up. "How long was I out?"

"A few hours. I called Ashley and she told Sean I took you somewhere to rest," Lenora said.

Connor stood up and rolled his shoulders. "You stunned me?"

"You were about to go running off. So it was either stun you or chase you through the forest and *then* stun you."

"And you left me on the ground?"

"You needed the rest," Lenora said.

He could think more clearly, but he still felt tired. "How'd you even know where to find me?"

"Noah called me. He's worried about you."

"I'm fi—"

"Don't you dare tell me you're fine! You're not fine. Having panic attacks and telling everyone they're going to die is not fine," Lenora snapped.

Connor clenched his teeth and sighed. "I don't want to fight with you."

"That's because you know I'm right. Everything that's happened is exacting a toll on you. You can't compartmentalize everything no matter how hard you try," Lenora said.

"What's that supposed to mean?" Connor asked.

"Wil and Kasey. They were your closest friends. You have to grieve."

"They're dead. There's nothing I can do about that."

Lenora's gaze hardened. "They deserve better than that."

Connor threw his hands in the air. "What do you want from me?"

"All you're stating is facts—they're dead. What you're refusing to admit is that they mattered to you. That their loss means so much to you that you can hardly stand it," Lenora said.

"I'm sorry. Roaming around Sierra weeping isn't going to help anyone," Connor replied.

"God, you can be such an ass. You could teach a rock about being stubborn, and when it graduated from the Connor School of Stubbornness, you'd still have more to teach it. Why is everything black and white with you? It's either hot or cold. I'm not telling you to run around crying uncontrollably, you idiot. I'm telling you to acknowledge their loss. Accept that they're gone. You don't have to be okay with it. In fact, you shouldn't be," Lenora said.

Connor looked away from her. He knew he was keeping everything locked up inside. He felt it all pushing against the walls he'd built, but he was afraid that if he let it out, there would be nothing left.

"Wil was right there in front of me. I should have been able to save him. If I hadn't left him in the computing core . . ." Connor's voice trailed off.

Lenora came over to his side and stood next to him, rubbing his shoulder with one of her hands.

"He was dying and he was still concerned with the data he'd found on the ship," Connor said.

"He knew it was important," Lenora replied.

Connor's shoulders slumped.

"What's the video log you keep watching?" Lenora asked.

Connor's shoulders stiffened, and he wheeled away from her.

"Noah told me you keep watching something that was retrieved from the *Indianapolis*," Lenora said, leaning toward him.

A wave of fury washed over Connor. How dare that little shit pry into his personal logs! "Did he say what it was?"

Lenora shook her head. "No, just that you watch the same ten-minute video multiple times a day and have been doing so since he gave you the files. What's on it?"

Connor balled his hands into fists, thinking how he'd like to pummel Noah for poking around where he shouldn't. But that would be stupid because it was those same instincts in Noah that Connor had come to count on over the years.

"What's on it?" Lenora asked again.

A long moment passed before Connor spoke. "It's my son," he said softly and looked away from her.

"Your son?" Lenora muttered in disbelief. She walked in front of him.

"He died on the *Indianapolis*. Our team made it to the bridge of the *Indianapolis* two months ago and there were signs of a battle having been fought there before. I think that's where he—" Connor said, his voice cracking.

Lenora looked at him, her brows drawn up in concern. "That's awful, Connor. I'm so sorry. Why didn't you tell anyone?"

Connor felt as if he were standing on the edge of a cliff and all it would take was a slight breeze to push him over it.

"Who would I tell? You? The last time we spoke we ended up screaming at one another," Connor said.

Lenora's face reddened. "I would have listened," she said. After a few moments, she continued. "What was he like?"

Connor swallowed hard as sorrow tried to close up his throat. "Young. He looked strong and bitter, with eyes that had seen too much. He didn't want to record anything. Wilkinson asked him to do it. He was more of a father to him than I was."

"You can't do this to yourself."

"What? Admit the truth?"

"That's not fair and you know it. You didn't leave him behind. You were forced onto the *Ark* against your will. You didn't leave your son behind. He was left behind because of what Wilkinson did. You want to punish someone, punish him," Lenora said.

"Wilkinson was just trying to protect me."

"Fine, then just accept that none of this was fair and there's nothing you can do to change anything," Lenora said.

Connor's eyes became misty. "My son hated me, blamed me for leaving him."

"You're not to blame—"

"Aren't I? I was the one who volunteered to lead the Ghosts, to do my duty."

"Why does anyone have to be blamed? It doesn't make any sense. His memory of you is that of a small boy who missed his father," Lenora said.

"That's right. A father who should have protected him."

"You can't do this to yourself. This guilt you've been carrying around is eating you up inside. It's not right. It happened. You made your decisions and then life happened. You can dwell on it and keep punishing yourself for everything that's out of your control or you can move on," Lenora said.

"Move on," Connor sneered. "Just like that. Brush it to the side and pretend it didn't happen?"

"That's not what I meant and you know it."

Connor looked away from her and shook his head. "I have to take responsibility—"

"That's crap. You're trying to make yourself feel better because you regret how everything turned out. You're not doing this for your son. You're doing this as a way to atone for leaving. You're feeding your regrets. That's not how it works.

Give yourself a break. You can't live your life based on hindsight. No one can," Lenora said.

Connor pressed his lips together. "It's not right," he said.

"There *is* no right and wrong. He was about to die. He must have been angry and scared. Did you even consider that?"

"Of course I did, but . . ." Connor said, his voice dying off. The words just wouldn't form in his mind.

"Mitch Wilkinson was a manipulative son of a bitch. You have this unshakable perspective that everything he did was to protect you, right?" Lenora asked.

Connor jutted his chin out and then nodded.

"In that case, he didn't have your son record a message so he could yell at you. Wilkinson knew it would cause you pain, but if you're right about him, I think he just wanted you to *see* your son. See the man he grew up to be. He wanted you to know that he did look after your son just like he promised you. He didn't send the message so you could torture yourself. So stop it. You can't fight the Vemus if you're weighed down by guilt," Lenora said.

Connor stood there, allowing himself to come to grips with what Lenora was saying. His brows pushed forward and he felt his body sag. He was so tired.

"Stop pretending you're in this fight alone."

Connor was about to deny it, but she was right. How had he come to be so lost?

"I don't know if we can survive," Connor said at last.

"Then we'll die, but it won't be because we didn't fight. If Wil and Kasey were here, they'd be telling you the same thing," Lenora said.

Connor felt his mouth hang open. There was so much he wanted to say. He wished he could be the person Lenora deserved, but he wasn't.

He heard the high-pitched whine of a combat shuttle's engines flying toward them, and a data link came to prominence on his internal heads-up display, identifying the CDF shuttle.

5

THE HANGAR BAY of Lunar Base was a buzz of activity, and Captain Jon Walker glared at the power conduit he'd been struggling to replace on his ship for the past few hours. Being stationed on the Colonial Defense Force moon base was a new post for him. He'd only been there for six months. What had started out as a tech platform for building missile defense platforms and ships had become a full-blown military base. Since the Vemus attack, personnel had been working tirelessly to conceal the base. Aboveground installations were either hidden away or relocated to belowground facilities per General Gates' orders. There was so much work going on that he couldn't wait on a flight engineer to fix the power conduit on the combat shuttle.

The connectors for the conduit wouldn't meet. He grabbed one end of the connector and pulled. Straining to get the pieces closer together, his hand slipped off and he banged it against the sidewall.

"Piece of shit!" Jon shouted, about to kick the damn thing.

"That ought to do it," someone said from behind him.

Jon spun around to see his brother, Brian, laughing at him. Brian glanced at what Jon had been working on.

"What the hell did you do to this thing?" Brian asked.

"Not me. Something from that damn debris field out there tore into the rear of my ship," Jon said. He noticed that his younger brother had a pale orange EVA suit on. "What's going on? I didn't think they let you scientists come topside, where the real work's done."

"Salvage run in the debris field," Brian replied.

Jon frowned. "Salvage for what?"

Brian regarded him for a moment. "We're looking for an undamaged section of a Vemus ship."

Jon frowned. "You've got to be kidding me. Why would they have you do that?"

"They're not having me do that. I volunteered," Brian said.

While Jon had chosen to join the Colonial Defense Force and become a soldier, his younger brother had gone in a different direction. Brian worked at a level of intelligence that was a cut above the norm. It was for this reason that Jon and Brian had gotten to come on the *Ark*. Jon's aptitude scores were high, but Brian's were definitely pretty far to the right of the bell curve that measured such things.

"What are you doing?" Jon asked.

"I told you, I'm—"

"I don't mean that. This is a field mission. Aren't you supposed to be in a lab somewhere trying to figure out a way to stop the Vemus?"

Brian jutted out his chin. "We need samples, living samples, in order to figure out how this thing works."

Jon eyed him for a moment. "Can you wait a couple of hours? I'll take you out there myself."

Brian was about to reply when someone came around the rear of the shuttle.

"What's going on here?" Colonel Hayes asked.

Jon immediately stood straight and snapped a salute. "Nothing, sir."

Colonel Hayes looked at Brian. "Walker, you and your team are to report in on *Explorer II*."

"Sir," Jon said, "permission to go on the salvage mission."

Colonel Hayes frowned and then looked at the state of Jon's ship. "Your ship isn't flight-ready."

"Sir, I can have it fixed and ready in an hour," Jon said.

Colonel Hayes glanced at the power conduit Jon was trying to get installed. "Those conduits are always a pain in the ass. After that, you've got to get the couplings on the right or the actuators won't pivot the pad properly. You've got more than an hour's work here, Captain."

Jon tried to think of a reply, but everything the colonel had just said was right. Damn it! If he'd just left it alone he could have flown Brian and his team out there. *Explorer II* was piloted by Davis, who wasn't the best pilot for the job.

"Dr. Walker, get on over to *Explorer II*. They're waiting for you, son," Colonel Hayes said.

"Yes, sir," Brian said.

Jon watched as his brother left. "Stay sharp, kid," Jon called out.

Brian turned around and gave him a wave.

"He'll be alright," Colonel Hayes said.

"I'm sorry, sir."

"I know he's your brother," Colonel Hayes said.

"Yes, sir."

Colonel Hayes called over a flight engineer and ordered him to get Jon's ship ready.

"Where am I going, sir?" Jon asked.

"Another run to the *Phoenix*. We've got HADES IV-Bs fresh off the line that need to be delivered ASAP," Colonel Hayes said.

Jon sighed inwardly. Delivery runs were about the only thing they got to do these days. He understood the necessity of it, but that didn't make it any less boring.

"We'll get it done, sir," Jon said.

"Carry on, Captain," Colonel Hayes said.

The flight engineer examined Jon's work and then called a couple of his crew over while Jon set about helping them repair his ship. They couldn't afford not to have all of their birds flight-ready. He glanced over at *Explorer II* as it flew out of the hangar. He'd promised his parents he'd watch out for Brian, which hadn't been so easy since they normally weren't at the same place. The Vemus were dangerous. He'd heard stories from the survivors of the *Vigilant* and the *Banshee*. What they'd faced on the Vemus ship was enough to give anyone nightmares, but he knew Brian didn't see them that way. He was too analytical. He thought of the Vemus only in scientific terms and not as an enemy to be destroyed. If his ship hadn't had a damaged engine pod, he could have flown Brian out there. Now his brother was out there with Davis, who wasn't the worst pilot on the lunar base, but he wasn't the best one either. He'd seen the debris field full of the remnants of Vemus ships. It was dangerous space to fly through, and with only one ship that could be spared for Brian's mission, a rescue if things went wrong would be long in coming.

Brian had wanted a mission of his own and now he'd gotten it. Jon just hoped it wasn't too exciting for him.

6

NOAH HAD SPENT the remainder of his day prepping his team before he left for Sanctuary. He knew Lenora had spoken to Connor, but he hadn't heard anything else since then. He hadn't seen Connor either. He thought of opening a comlink to Sean, but since Sean was always within earshot of Connor, he didn't think that was his brightest idea.

Lars Mallory waited for Noah to power off the holoscreens. "Why are they sending you to Sanctuary?"

Noah left his work area, and he and Lars walked out into the hallway.

"They want me to look at the alien power station there," Noah said.

"Last I heard about that was that they weren't able to get it to generate a significant amount of energy," Lars said.

"Yeah, the preliminary report I saw was that it's early fusion tech. Looks like the alien species that lived here was developing their own fusion reactor," Noah said.

"They said it was a few hundred years old," Lars said.

"Yup, and no one knows where the species that built it actually went."

"That's probably a blessing," Lars replied.

"Why do you say that?" Noah asked.

"Because they also genetically altered some of the species here."

"Like the ryklars and the berwolves?"

"Precisely. They're way more intelligent than we expected from a predator," Lars said.

"Maybe we should convince them to fight with us when the Vemus get here," Noah said.

Lars stopped walking and pursed his lips. "That's not a bad idea, you know."

"I was kidding," Noah said quickly.

"I know, but it really isn't that bad an idea," Lars said and started walking in the opposite direction.

"Where are you going?" Noah asked.

"I'm going to talk to my father. Have fun in Sanctuary, and try not to blow the place up," Lars called back as he hastened down the hall.

Great, Noah thought. He'd just become responsible for the CDF putting animals in their war against the Vemus. He'd better get to Sanctuary quickly before he accidentally gave anyone else ideas of questionable moral implications.

7

The combat shuttle flew toward Phoenix Station, and Connor brought up the optical feed onto his personal holoscreen. Sean shifted in his seat next to him, and Connor noticed him looking at the holoscreen.

"She would have made a beautiful ship," Connor said.

"It would have been something to see her fly, sir," Sean said.

The *Phoenix* was supposed to be the Colonial Defense Force's first battleship carrier, but Connor had scrapped that plan after the Vemus attack. Instead, he'd challenged his engineers to come up with something the CDF could use in defense of New Earth, and this was their answer. They'd presented Connor with the option of having a battleship carrier that could be combat ready in six to eight months or a slower-moving space station with a comparable combat arsenal in just two months. Thus, the *Phoenix* became Phoenix Station, whose combat readiness increased with each passing day. On the surface, it was an easy decision to make, but it had meant forgoing any type of mobile combat units beyond New Earth's immediate vicinity.

"There are only a few sections I recognize from the *Ark*," Sean said.

Connor nodded.

Phoenix Station was an elongated cylinder with a massive section of it covered by the Montgomery III construction platform. Instead of a grouping of massive magnetic drive pods in the rear of the ship, they'd put smaller MDPs in subsections of the station.

Connor watched as Sean brought up his own holoscreen and zoomed in on one of the subsections.

"Looks like they've completed sections seven and eight," Sean said.

Phoenix Station was like a heavily armed mobile wall positioned at a point in space where the gravitational pull from New Earth and the star in this system were equalized. Positioning Phoenix Station here made maintaining its orbit relatively easy, but the downside to the smaller MDPs was that the behemoth combat station was slow to reposition.

"Two more sections to be brought online," Connor said.

They'd had to cut some corners to get Phoenix Station operational, which meant that not all the sections were equal in their capabilities. Each section had a wide array of weapons capabilities, but not all sections had the same complement of sensor arrays. The sections without sensors were dependent on those that had them. Sections that were comprised primarily of missile tubes just needed targeting data, which could be uploaded from any sensor array. Connor knew the ingenuity that had gone into Phoenix Station was enough to make any NA Alliance general proud, and since he was the CDF's only general, he was quite pleased with what they'd been able to accomplish in a short span of time.

"We only need ten or twenty more just like it," Connor said.

"Well, if we're wishing for something, how about a universal override for Vemus ship navigation systems so they fly right into the star and we don't have to worry about 'em." Sean said with a snort.

Connor nodded. He'd noticed that Sean and others who served close to him were paying more attention to Connor's own readiness. He couldn't blame them. He'd let himself go. He didn't take care of himself, and his performance suffered severely for it. Sleep helped. Ashley had prescribed him meds to help him sleep. He still felt compelled to watch the video log of his son though. He could recall every moment of it with startling clarity. He hadn't watched it today, but he couldn't promise himself that he wouldn't watch it later on, believing that once he made the promise he would soon break it.

"Sir, Noah has reported in. He's arrived at Sanctuary," Sean said.

Connor glanced over at Sean, arching an eyebrow. "Planning to apprise me of each CDF's individual location, Major?"

"No, sir, I just thought you'd want to know about this particular instance," Sean replied.

"I guess this is where I could tell you to lock it up and command you to silence," Connor said.

Sean calmly met Connor's gaze.

"I'm not angry with Noah," Connor said. *At least not as much,* he thought to himself.

"Yes, sir," Sean said.

"Is that a 'yes, sir' or an 'if you say so, sir'?"

A small smirk snuck onto Sean's face. "Yes, sir," he replied mildly.

The smirk reminded Connor of Ashley. "Well played, Major. Your mother would be proud."

"I've learned from the best, sir."

Connor looked back at his holoscreen. They were on final approach to the main hangar. He was overdue to inspect Phoenix Station, and Connor suspected the reason for Tobias and Franklin suggesting it was due in part to the lengthy travel time out to the station. Mandatory downtime, as it were.

"Colonel Cross will meet us in the hangar, sir," Sean said.

Connor nodded and closed down the holoscreen. His stomach tightened as the combat shuttle entered Phoenix Station's gravity field. The main hangar was designed to be in a permanent vacuum, which conserved resources by not requiring the hangar to be depressurized every time a ship needed to land. The pilot flew the shuttle to the landing pad, and the auto-dock extended to the rear hatch. There were several knocks as the auto-dock sealed against the hatch and the indicator light went from red to green.

Connor exited the shuttle first. CDF personnel in full dress uniforms lined the way forward to where Colonel Savannah Cross waited to greet him. The lines of soldiers saluted Connor as he took his first steps onto Phoenix Station. Connor returned their salutes.

"Welcome to Phoenix Station, General," Colonel Cross said.

She stood ramrod straight and had a burning intensity to her gaze. Savannah was like Connor in that they were both workhorses. Shortly after the Vemus attack, he'd assigned the *Banshee's* commanding officer to Phoenix, and she hadn't disappointed him in the slightest.

"Thank you, Colonel," Connor replied.

Connor glanced at the CDF officers near Colonel Cross and noted that her XO was nowhere in sight. He made a mental nod of approval. No doubt Colonel Cross had kept Major Elder on the main bridge of the station. Though they were at Condition Three, maintaining combat readiness was paramount to their survival. Connor had browsed the station's records on the way here and knew that Colonel Cross dedicated a significant amount of time to combat drills. She was determined to be as prepared as humanly possible for the next engagement with the Vemus.

"General, if you will follow me, I'm prepared to give you a tour of our primary systems for the main section of the station," Colonel Cross said.

"Excellent, Colonel. I'm looking forward to it," Connor said.

They kept to the main section of the station because it would have been impractical to tour the other eight subsections. He was here to check that operations of the station were running smoothly, not to visit every nook and cranny of the station, which would have taken him weeks.

For the next several hours, Savannah led Connor through Phoenix Station, meeting the crew. Some of them had served on Titan Station and, having survived, pushed to be part of this station. The former Titan Station soldiers knew what was at stake. They'd faced the Vemus before. In all Connor's years in the military, he found that the CDF soldier showed a level of dedication normally reserved for an elite few he had observed in his military career.

He was reminded of Wil and Kasey throughout the tour. He remembered doing a similar inspection of Titan, and while Wil and Kasey had been completely professional, there'd been an underlying camaraderie that Connor missed. Kasey had been his second in command since his days with the Ghosts. Wil had been an outstanding intelligence officer who had a singular talent for finding his way around almost any obstacle. Connor was at home around people in uniform, be it the NA Alliance Military or, as now, the Colonial Defense Force, but there were so many missing faces that he would have liked to see.

Colonel Savannah Cross was an exemplary military officer. Given that there were only about three hundred thousand colonists, Connor hadn't been sure what caliber of military personnel he'd be able to find among them, especially since one of the driving forces for the *Ark* program had been to limit any military presence in the colony. Circumstances had changed all that, and Connor was struck by how well the colonists had risen to protect their future. A strong will to survive was embedded in human nature, along with the tenacity to overcome obstacles and become what they needed for survival. It was both awe-inspiring and concerning how quickly humans could go from being civilized to adapting to war in a short span of time.

"We dedicate this part of the station to weapons engineering and development," Colonel Cross said.

Most of Phoenix Station's mass was to support weapons systems, so when they went into the open area, Connor was surprised at the extensive amount of activity.

Connor looked at Colonel Cross. "What's going on here?"

"We had a number of soldiers who had ideas for our current weapons systems to simply repurpose what we've already got. It started out as a small group of soldiers collaborating in their off-duty hours," Colonel Cross said, and there was no mistaking the pride in her voice.

The CDF soldiers began to notice they had an audience, and one of them detached himself from the group. He was a bull of a man, which had inspired the designation Connor had given him when he'd been part of Search and Rescue.

"Captain Randle," Connor said and glanced around at the all the construction bots that were in various states of retrofit.

"General," Captain Wayne Randle said. "I'm glad you made it here."

"What are you doing to the construction bots?" Connor asked.

A hungry gleam appeared in Randle's eyes. "We had a surplus of machines that were part of the drone workforce, so I thought I'd make use of them. These construction bots were built for salvage, and since we're not doing much of that anymore, I'm fitting them with a one-meter storage bay," Captain Randle said.

Connor took a closer look at one of the bots. The storage bay extended from the back and the robotic arms were tucked away for extra storage. Realizing the potential of what Randle had created, Connor smiled.

"They can penetrate the hull of a ship and deliver their payload. They're not reusable, but they can get into some pretty tight places that would be hard to detect," Captain Randle said.

"What's their range?" Connor asked.

"Two hundred thousand kilometers. As long as we paint the target, they can do the rest," Captain Randle said.

Connor glanced at Colonel Cross. "You authorized this?"

"Yes, General," Colonel Cross said.

"How many more projects like these have you got going on?" Connor asked.

"We have a few others like this. Mostly, the crew is dedicated to the established weapons systems, but for these rare gems I thought it prudent to allow some good old-fashioned ingenuity, sir," Colonel Cross said.

Connor nodded. "Excellent work."

Captain Randle looked relieved.

"I mean it. It's efforts like this that will help us the most in the long run," Connor said.

He heard a chime from the nearby speakers.

"Colonel Cross, please report to the bridge," a computerized voice said.

Colonel Cross frowned and then sent her acknowledgment. "General, we were going to end our tour at the bridge, but something must have come up."

"Indeed, Colonel. Let's get to the bridge," Connor said.

Colonel Cross's face suddenly became ashen, and she pressed her lips together.

"Are you feeling alright?" Connor asked.

Colonel Cross's cheeks reddened for a moment. "I'm fine. Just felt a bit of nausea for a second."

They proceeded to the bridge of the main section of Phoenix Station. Though Phoenix Station was comprised of the last major section of the *Ark*, the bridge was entirely new construction. Workstations were being manned for all the major systems that would be found on a ship. Major John Elder stood in the command area that was slightly elevated above the workstations.

Connor glanced at the main holoscreen and saw a PRADIS scope on the screen. On the edge of the star system was a detected anomaly. The anomaly was in a quadrant far away from where Titan Station had been.

"Situation report," Colonel Cross said.

"The anomaly just appeared, ma'am. PRADIS indicates that it's over twenty kilometers across. We're repositioning tactical drones to get a better reading of it," Major Elder said.

"Could this just be a large asteroid?" Connor asked.

He didn't believe it was but needed to ask the question just to be sure.

"We're not sure, General. We're double-checking this anomaly against the known large asteroids already mapped in the system," Major Elder said.

"It's not an asteroid," Major Quinn said.

Connor looked over at Sean.

"It just changed course as of the last PRADIS sweep, so either it hit something large that forced it to change course or someone is flying it," Major Quinn said.

Connor glanced back at the main holoscreen. Sean was right. Connor felt his stomach sink to his feet. Their time was just about out.

8

Colonel Nathan Hayes sat in his office at Lunar Base and glanced over at the cylindrical aquarium that used to belong to his commanding officer on the *Vigilant*. Ian Howe had loved the aquarium, which was home to several species of brightly colored fish, and Nathan kept the aquarium as a tribute to his friend and mentor who had died aboard ship. To help him unwind at the end of a long day, Nathan would turn out the lights in his office and leave on the interior lights of the aquarium. The small bands of reflected light and soft sounds of churning water provided a taste of being planet-side, and it helped keep him anchored.

Nathan left his office and began to make his way toward the residential modules at Lunar Base. New Earth had one moon that was in orbit three hundred and twenty thousand kilometers away from the planet. They'd been able to tunnel into the softer sections of the crust and currently housed over two thousand people on base. They'd already been expanding the base before the Vemus attack, but since then Nathan had been tasked with minimizing base operations on the surface.

He came to the elevator that would take him to the residential modules, where a shower and a warm meal would be waiting for him, but he had a thought that caused him to hesitate before pushing the button. Instead, he used his neural implants to check the duty roster for the Command Center and saw that Major Shelton was on duty. Nathan sighed. Major Shelton was new to Lunar Base and Nathan wanted to see how she was settling in. He also liked to observe all his officers on duty. Nathan retreated from the elevators and started to make his way to the Command Center.

As Nathan entered the room, Major Vanessa Shelton acknowledged his presence by standing up from the command chair. She glanced at her workstation, and Nathan noted that her worried expression had nothing to do with him being there but with the alert on her screen.

"Sir, I was about to contact you. Blackout protocol has been authorized. We're to cease all surface activities immediately and restrict communications to direct laser communications only," Major Shelton said.

Nathan frowned. DLC was old technology that could be used over long and short distances but was highly susceptible to being intercepted and spoofed. Nathan wasn't sure whether the Vemus could detect a DLC beam, but the concept was simple and they needed to be very careful. He leaned in so he could see Major Shelton's screen, quickly using his implants to confirm that the message from CDF COMCENT was authentic. DLC would limit their comms capabilities, but it also minimized the risk of their base being detected by the Vemus since they weren't broadcasting a communication signal.

"Set Condition Two, Major," Nathan ordered.

Nathan looked at the main holoscreen while Major Shelton sent out a base-wide alert. There was an incoming data dump from Phoenix Station.

"Colonel, Dark-Star status will be achieved in twelve hours," Major Shelton said.

"Understood," Nathan replied.

In twelve hours, they would have virtually no presence on the lunar surface, which was a vast improvement when compared with the drills he'd run when he'd first assumed command of the base. Coming from a warship command, twelve hours seemed like a lifetime, but Lunar Base was comprised of more than just CDF personnel. They were essentially a small conclave of soldiers mixed with scientists and construction workers in their munitions factory. They were stocked with supplies that would last for six months.

"Major, we need the current status of all teams deployed. And start checking them off as they report in," Nathan ordered.

Orders for blackout protocol could only come from CDF command, and Nathan knew General Gates would not give the command unless he had credible evidence of an imminent threat to New Earth.

Major Shelton went to the auxiliary workstation so Nathan could take command. It seemed that he and Major Shelton would become better acquainted over the next few hours after all.

Lunar Base was vitally important to New Earth's defenses, and General Gates had changed their mandate to a purely passive presence until they were authorized to engage. Rules of engagement for Lunar Base could be given from COMCENT or, in the absence of the chain of command, by the commanding officer. Connor had gone over his strategy for how Lunar Base would be used when the Vemus arrived. They would lend support to Phoenix Station if called upon or, in the worst-case scenario, as a secret base from which to engage the enemy. They were to keep their presence hidden for as long as possible.

"Colonel, we have an overdue salvage team. It appears they were on a deep salvage mission in the debris field," Major Shelton said.

Nathan brought the specs to his personal workstation. Captain Davis's team had missed their check-in. They were escorting Dr. Brian Walker's science team, who was trying to capture living samples of the Vemus.

"What are your orders, Colonel?" Major Shelton asked.

"That's a high-priority mission. We're going to send in a second team," Nathan said.

"Colonel, once we're in Dark-Star status, if the second team runs into trouble we won't be authorized to respond."

"Understood, Major," Nathan said, knowing Major Shelton was just doing her job. "I want Captain Walker's squad on point for the second team. They're authorized to assess the current status of the first team and assist with their mission. If there's evidence of Vemus infection, then they're to use containment protocols."

"Yes, Colonel," Major Shelton replied.

Nathan hoped Davis's team was just experiencing some kind of communications issue due to the fact they were in the debris field rather than having encountered any trouble. Captain Jon Walker was an exemplary pilot and could effect a rescue mission if it came down to it. Besides that, if Nathan had a brother, he knew he'd be out there looking for him if he could.

"Tactical, keep our PRADIS updated with the data dump from Phoenix Station and continuously update it for as long as they send their feeds to us," Nathan said.

"Yes, Colonel," the tactical officer replied.

Lunar Base going dark meant that any active scanning of the star system must stop and they would become reliant upon sensor feeds from Phoenix Station. As their PRADIS was updated, Nathan began to understand why General Gates had put him in command of Lunar Base. He'd seen combat and knew that it would be a waiting game. The real test of Nathan's resolve would come when the first shots were fired and those at the base could only watch the engagement from afar. Even if Phoenix Station were to become compromised, Nathan could not reveal their presence unless they could decisively destroy the Vemus invasion force. And as of this moment, they still didn't know what was coming for them.

9

ALMOST TWENTY-FOUR HOURS had passed since they'd first detected the anomaly, and Connor was returning to the Command Center on Phoenix Station. He'd just finished briefing the defense council, and the cities of New Earth were on high alert. There had been no further course changes from the anomaly, and after careful analysis of its apparent change of course, Phoenix Station's operations team was almost evenly divided on whether the anomaly had, in fact, changed course. The change had been so slight that there were credible arguments to be made that this was just a natural occurrence for objects in deep space. Connor had decided to err on the side of caution and ordered Phoenix Station to Condition Two, which set a series of actions into motion, including Lunar Base going dark. Lunar Base was their failsafe if Phoenix Station was destroyed, and it would not be an easy thing for Colonel Hayes to carry out his orders should the worst happen, but Connor had the utmost faith in him.

"Sir, Dr. Allen is requesting to speak with you at your earliest convenience," Sean said.

Connor checked the time. "Tell him I'll follow up with him in a few hours."

Dr. Allen had been the *Vigilant's* chief medical officer and Connor knew Allen wouldn't reach out to him if it wasn't important. On the other hand, if Dr. Allen had an urgent matter, he would have said so.

They reached the corridor to the Command Center.

"Sir, there's something I need to bring to your awareness," Sean said.

Connor stopped walking and glanced at his security detail. "Give us a minute."

The armed soldiers walked farther down the corridor, giving them some privacy.

"What is it?" Connor asked.

Sean frowned. "This may be nothing, but it's just something I've noticed. I think Colonel Cross is hiding something."

Connor's eyebrows rose. Even in the CDF, it was no small thing to accuse a superior officer of hiding something, but Connor knew Sean Quinn had good instincts.

"Go on," Connor said.

"I'm not sure, exactly. She seemed a bit distracted, like she had something else on her mind. Don't get me wrong. Colonel Cross is good at her job and I don't think she's being negligent in her duties, but there's something on her mind," Sean said.

Connor frowned. "We're all under a lot of pressure. If this anomaly is the Vemus, it's enough to unsettle anyone."

"That's just it, sir. I noticed it while she was giving us the tour before the anomaly appeared on PRADIS. I just wanted to make you aware. Perhaps she'll . . . I don't know . . . tell you about it," Sean said.

Connor pressed his lips together. "Alright, I'll keep an eye out for it, but if you notice something while we're in there," Connor said, jabbing his thumb in the direction of the Command Center, "you need to either let me know or ask Colonel Cross about it."

"Yes, sir," Sean said.

Connor suppressed a frustrated sigh. It wasn't Sean's fault. Connor blamed the former governor, Stanton Parish, for this development. In addition to facing their next encounter with the Vemus, his officers were keeping a close eye on everyone Connor came into contact with. It was Captain Alec Toro's failed attempt to assassinate Connor aboard the *Vigilant* that had prompted this response. While Connor didn't doubt Colonel Cross's loyalty, the fact that Sean had raised the concern was a symptom of the repercussions of their dreadful experience aboard the *Vigilant,* which had cost the life of the ship's commanding officer.

They entered the Command Center, and Connor looked over at Colonel Cross, who had her blonde hair pulled back into a tight bun. She spoke to her operations officer and looked as Connor expected—completely focused on her duties.

Colonel Cross looked over at him as he approached.

"Phoenix Station will be in the direct path of the anomaly in the next six hours, General," Colonel Cross said.

Phoenix Station was big and moved as slow as molasses, not having been built for speed. They'd thought that anything detected would be far enough out to give them ample opportunity to reposition.

"Understood. What's the status of Lunar Base?" Connor asked.

"Dark-Star status. They have one overdue salvage mission. Colonel Hayes has dispatched a second team to investigate, sir," Colonel Cross replied.

"Any change from the anomaly?" Connor asked.

"Slow and steady as she goes, General," Colonel Cross replied.

They couldn't afford to sit there and wait for whatever the hell this thing was to show its teeth, so Connor had ordered that stealth recon drones—or as they were commonly referred to, SRDs—be deployed. Stealth was a bit of a misnomer because the drones worked by using a tremendous burst of speed that put them on an intercept course. The engines would then cut out and the drone would only make slight course adjustments. What they got was a very fast flyby of the anomaly, and the drones would transmit scan results and high-res images.

Connor looked at the PRADIS scope and saw that the SRDs were on a staggered approach from different vectors. They were moving at the ultra-high speeds that could only be achieved by unmanned spacecraft. Only a human presence aboard a ship necessitated that the ship slow down so people didn't die.

"The SRDs' preliminary scans don't reveal much," Sean said.

"That's why we equip them with high-res optics so we can get actual eyes on the target," Connor replied.

"If that *is* the Vemus, they could have their fleet flying in a tight formation to fool PRADIS into thinking it's one large astronomical body. Either way, we'll know in a few minutes," Colonel Cross said.

She stepped away as a call came to her personal comlink. Connor glanced over and noticed she was speaking in hushed tones.

"Is everything alright, Colonel?" Connor asked when she came back over to him.

"It's fine. Just a report in from one of our weapons R&D engineers, sir," Colonel Cross said.

Connor nodded and looked back at the main holoscreen. Sean was right. Colonel Cross was definitely hiding something. R&D engineers normally didn't have a direct line to the commanding officer. They would go through proper communications channels. The question remained: what was Colonel Cross hiding, and would it impact her ability to carry out her duties?

Connor decided to wait. They were about to receive an update from the first SRD to pass the anomaly. The remaining four SRDs would be close behind.

"We have an incoming transmission from the SRDs," Lieutenant Daniels said.

Connor turned toward the comms officer. "Put what you've got on the main screen."

They waited while the incoming transmission completed and then images began to appear on the main holoscreen. The first series of images showed a circular object the lead SRD had photographed from farther out on its approach. The cyber warfare suite then analyzed and grouped the images together from all the drones they'd sent. As the SRDs came closer to the anomaly, the images had the appearance of a large asteroid over twenty kilometers across. Connor peered at the images, looking for some indication that the celestial body was something other than a naturally occurring piece of space rock.

As the SRDs drew closer to the anomaly, the computer system grouped images by the drone designation. SRD-1 was the first to fly and provide images of the rear of the anomaly. The back of the asteroid seemed to have been cut off, and it appeared as if they were looking into a deep, dark cave. There was no light, so they couldn't see inside.

"Which SRD had the full scanner array?" Connor asked.

"SRD-3, sir," Colonel Cross answered.

"Prioritize the SRD-3 feed, Lieutenant," Connor said.

Lieutenant Daniels entered a few commands and the SRD-3 feed came to prominence.

Connor kept his eyes on the main holoscreen. Everything in his gut told him that this was the Vemus, but he wouldn't do anything until he had undeniable proof. They were resource-stricken as it was, and he couldn't afford to send any missiles out there until he was sure it was the enemy.

The SRD-3 feed cut out. Rather than start barking out orders, Connor waited for Phoenix Station's crew to do their jobs.

"SRD-3 is no longer transmitting. Putting the partial transmission up on the screen, sir," Lieutenant Daniels said.

SRD-3's sensor sweep had been about to give them a view of the dark side of the anomaly when it suddenly cut out, but there was no indication that the SRD had been fired upon.

"Tactical, show me where our remaining SRDs are in relation to number three. Is there any overlap so we can see what happened to it?" Connor asked.

He knew there was no chance to change the SRDs' approach because there was already a significant delay in the data transfer from the edge of the star system, not to mention the speeds with which the SRDs were moving away from them. No, they were essentially looking at a window into the past. Whatever had happened to the SRDs had already happened.

"I believe I have something, General," Lieutenant Daniels said and showed them the feed from SRD-4. "It's in the upper left quadrant of the feed."

The feed showed a close-up view of the rocky asteroid surface, and Connor could barely see something small flying through the edge of the camera feed. Lieutenant Daniels replayed it and zoomed in on the spot. Connor watched the grainy image of something flying past that seemed to slam into something invisible. There was no flash. The SRD simply broke apart.

"What happened to it?" Sean asked.

"Were there any spikes detected in the scanner array?" Colonel Cross asked.

"No, ma'am," Lieutenant Daniels said.

"There wouldn't be," Connor said, drawing their attention back to him. "It was destroyed before the array could have detected anything in the first place."

"How do you know that, sir?" Sean asked.

"It's the Vemus. They used some type of X-ray laser to take out the SRD. The drone didn't actually hit anything, but a focused shot could easily disable the drone," Connor said.

Colonel Cross frowned. "If that's true, why wait for the SRD to get so close? Why not take it out sooner?"

"They didn't want to show their hand. A short high-power pulse is all it would take. It likely didn't target the other SRDs because they were just taking pictures. Number three was actively scanning it when it passed," Connor said.

"So when the drone got to something the Vemus didn't want us to see, it had to take action," Sean said.

"Correct. We forced their hand. Now we know they're coming," Connor said.

"How do you think they'll react, sir?" Colonel Cross asked.

Connor drew in a deep breath. "They're still pretty far out in the system, but my bet is they're going to speed up."

"Look at the size of that thing. Twenty kilometers across. How many of them could there be?" Sean asked.

"Work with tactical. I want to find out all we can about them. We run the numbers and devise firing solutions based on what we get. Remember, we've got to be smart about this. There's not a single weapon that can take out something of that size. We need to wear them down layer by layer until there's nothing left," Connor said and then looked at Colonel Cross. "Call in your reserves. We need all hands for this."

"Yes, General," Colonel Cross said.

"Comms, send a preliminary report to COMCENT, along with all SRD data," Connor said.

Connor swung his gaze back toward the main holoscreen. The Vemus had tracked them to this star system, sent in an invasion force, and collected data about the colony. Now they were coming. He hesitated to even think of what they'd seen on the images as a ship, but he didn't know what else to call it. The Vemus ship was larger than any city they had on New Earth, and it was heading right for them.

10

CAPTAIN JON WALKER had only just returned from a Phoenix Station supply run when he got the call from Major Shelton. The deep-salvage team led by Daniels had missed two check-ins. His brother was part of that team and was now among the missing CDF crew. Colonel Hayes had specified that Jon was to lead the rescue team and go in search of the overdue salvage team. Jon wasted no time calling in key members of his squad to be part of the away team. The combat shuttle was stocked with the extra supplies required for a rescue mission and headed out almost immediately.

Six hours later, they still hadn't found a trace of the missing salvage team.

"Nothing on our scope, not that it would do much good here," Lieutenant Chester said.

Daron Chester had been assigned to Jon's squad shortly after Jon arrived on Lunar Base. The two of them had become fast friends.

"We're following the path Daniels took," Jon replied.

"Yeah, but why don't we just head to their last known check-in point and start searching there?" Lieutenant Chester asked.

He gave Daron a sideways glance. "You really don't know?"

"No, I just love the sound of your voice. Just brightens my day," Lieutenant Chester said mockingly. "No, I don't know. That's why I asked . . . sir."

Jon snorted. The tacked-on formality was a nice touch. "We follow the path they took. If we skip around, we run the risk of missing something vitally important."

"Like what?" Lieutenant Chester asked.

"What if they were returning to Lunar Base and had an issue? Or their ship was damaged somehow? Or anything else you can think they'd encounter in the middle of a debris field like this? We'd miss them while we just skipped ahead," Jon replied.

Daron thought about it for a minute. "I guess you're right."

"I am right, and if I'm not, we can continue moving forward with our search knowing for a fact that we didn't miss them rather than just hoping we didn't," Jon replied.

They'd been following the path Daniels had taken through the debris field, and there was so much enemy-ship wreckage that Jon wondered how Brian could hope to find anything. They flew amidst the ruins of battleship carriers and heavy cruisers, which were on a slow but steady course away from New Earth in a field of space known as no-man's-land. The salvage team had staggered their flight path through this wreckage.

"Explain to me again what they were doing out here," Lieutenant Chester said.

"They were looking for live Vemus samples. My brother's a field biologist, and the team that's studying the Vemus needs live samples for analysis," Jon answered.

Lieutenant Chester shivered. "The whole situation gives me the creeps. This thing took out all the people back home and then traveled sixty light-years to get to us here. And your brother wants to get up close and personal with one?"

"I wouldn't say that. He just needs a sample. They want to understand how the Vemus work so we can protect ourselves," Jon said.

"Really think we can do that? Protect ourselves, I mean," Lieutenant Chester asked.

"No idea. I don't know how any of that stuff works, but I hope there's something our scientists can find that was missed," Jon answered, craning his neck back. "Sims!"

A few moments passed and Corporal Sims came to the cockpit.

"You wanted me, sir?" Corporal Sims said.

"Yes," Jon said. "Chester is wondering whether we can really protect ourselves from the Vemus."

Sims' narrow eyes peered at him for a moment. "You mean the infection that leads to becoming the Vemus?"

"That's the one," Jon said.

"Sir, I'm not sure—"

"I'm not asking you to answer me definitively. I know you're not a biologist, but you *are* a medic. So what's your opinion?" Jon asked.

Corporal Sims swallowed. "I really don't know. The write-ups they sent out about it say the Vemus is a parasite that uses a virus to spread itself. You have to come into direct contact with a parasite to be affected by it."

Lieutenant Chester frowned. "What does the virus do?"

"No idea. My suggestion is not to let it touch you if we find ourselves in the presence of any Vemus forces," Corporal Sims said.

Daron swung around in his chair to look at the medic. "Don't let it touch you," Daron said with a hint of sarcasm. "You're a big help."

Jon snorted and Sims shrugged.

Chester grumbled. They were all worried about the Vemus. Sims's advice was as good as any. A few minutes later, an active response to their scans appeared on the combat shuttle's heads-up display.

Jon adjusted their course and headed for it. They flew toward a large piece of wreckage that was the size of a CDF heavy cruiser like the *Vigilant*. As he studied it, he couldn't begin to guess what part of a ship the wreckage could belong to, but it must have been from a battleship carrier.

They found the salvage team's shuttle attached to the hull.

Jon decreased their velocity.

"Looks like they found an exterior hatch left intact," Lieutenant Chester said.

The salvage team's shuttle was located near an airlock. Jon tried to open a comlink to the shuttle, but he didn't get a response. He switched over to the personal comlink channel and still didn't get a response.

"This is the place. Now, do we go inside or do we fly around this thing and see if there's anything more to learn?" Jon wondered aloud.

Sergeant Roger Lee came to the cockpit and looked at the heads-up display. "I'm not sure if flying around the outside will tell us that much, but you never know. It shouldn't take long to make a quick sweep."

Jon nodded in agreement. He decided to play this by the book and do a bit of recon by flying around the outside of the Vemus ship wreckage. Specialist Hank Horan attempted to reach the salvage team as they went, but there was no response.

Their previous approach had showed that the wreckage was the size of a heavy cruiser, but as they circled it they learned it was significantly larger. The broken innards of a battleship carrier came into view on the HUD. Glowing lights were strewn from the twisted metal framework where the ship had been ripped apart.

"They still have power," Sergeant Lee said.

"And judging by the size, there should be several intact layers to explore," Jon said.

"You say that like it's a good thing," Lieutenant Chester said.

Jon frowned at him.

"Not to worry, Captain. That's what the big guns are for," Lieutenant Chester said.

"Alright. Suit up. We're going inside," Jon said.

They finished their circuit around the wreck and still couldn't raise the salvage team.

"Sir," Specialist Thoran said, "since there's still power in the wreckage, whatever the Vemus are using to suppress communications must also be active."

"Understood, Specialist," Jon said.

What the specialist didn't say was that there might not be a reply because the salvage team members were all dead. He glanced at Daron, who bobbed his head. Jon wasn't going to leave until he found out.

He flew the shuttle back to the salvage team's ship and engaged the landing gear. Metallic spikes drilled from the metal skids, holding the shuttle in place. Jon set the shuttle's systems to standby and climbed out of the pilot's chair, then walked to the back of the shuttle and stepped into his Nexstar Series Three combat suit. He slipped his arms into the open sleeves, which closed upon feeling his presence. Jon activated the combat suit's systems, bringing them online, and the rest of the suit closed up, sealing him inside.

"Final gear check!" Jon called. "Check yourself and the person in front of you." There was a flurry of activity as they all did one final check on all the joints and fittings of their equipment, along with those of the people around them.

Jon depressurized the shuttle, and the hatch popped open and swung down into position. They all quickly moved to the edge and hopped off. They engaged their magboots, which kept them attached to the hull of the ship. At least this section of the exposed hull was original and not that Vemus exoskeleton crap.

Jon led the five-man team toward the airlock and saw that the salvage team had used the manual override to gain access to the ship.

"Once we're inside, we go slow and steady. Check your corners," Jon said.

He opened the airlock. They stepped inside and closed the outer door.

Lieutenant Chester stepped to the inner door, and Jon stood ready with his AR-71. There was a faint flickering of light beyond the small round window. Lieutenant Chester hit the door controls and stepped to the side. Jon went through first and entered a dark corridor. His HUD compensated for the low light, so he could easily see the features of the corridor.

Jon shuffled a few steps away from the door to allow the others to come through.

"No comms chatter, sir. Shall I try to reach the salvage team?" Specialist Thoran asked.

"Not yet. They have to be somewhere inside here. No need to draw unwanted attention until we have more of an idea of what we're dealing with," Jon replied.

"What we're dealing with . . ." Lieutenant Chester muttered.

Jon spun around. "Do we have a problem, Lieutenant?"

Daron Chester sucked in a harsh breath. "Sorry, Captain. Won't happen again."

"Alright. Stay to the back and guard our flank," Jon said.

Daron was a good man, but there was no way to know how someone would react to imminent danger until they found themselves in harm's way. Jon needed his whole team.

Sergeant Lee moved up to take Chester's place. Jon kept a slow pace as they made their way down the deserted corridor. Emergency systems lit the way, but the rooms they passed were all dark and abandoned.

Jon's suit sensors indicated there was minimal atmosphere being maintained. It had been over two months since the battle, and Jon was confident that the section they were in was as well sealed as they could have hoped.

As they moved forward, they hit a few dead ends and had to backtrack, but they soon settled into a routine as they delved further into the wreckage. They checked all the rooms they came across and then moved on.

"I think we're in one of the aft sections of the ship," Sergeant Lee said.

"How do you know?" Jon asked.

"This part of the ship would have been reinforced to compensate for the main engines. It's likely the missile that took this ship out hit near the forward sections. This area is relatively intact," Sergeant Lee replied.

"Intact and a strong possibility for contact with the enemy," Jon said.

He activated the comlink in his combat suit and began sending out a series of pings, waiting for a reply. None came.

"Captain," Lieutenant Chester said, "the IR spectrum shows an increase in temperature down the corridor to the right."

Jon peered down the corridor. "Any idea what's down this way?"

"Hard to say. If Lee is right, this could be part of the munitions factory they had on board the ship," Lieutenant Chester said.

"Makes sense. That area of the ship would be heavily shielded," Jon said.

They headed down the corridor, and Jon felt a shudder coming through the floor. It quickly stopped and then there was a loud chafing of metal grinding along. Each of them moved to the side and braced themselves against the wall.

"Impacts along the outside of this thing," Sergeant Lee said.

Jon nodded. The wreckage they were in, while large, was still in the middle of a vast debris field. He wondered what they could have hit that would be felt throughout the area they were in.

They continued but Jon brought the team to a halt when he heard a knocking sound echo through the corridor. The repeated cadence was too regular to be a simple impact from wreckage outside the ship. This came from within. Jon motioned to the rest of the team that he'd heard something.

Jon pressed onward, thinking about how much he'd like to have the layout of this place. The farther they went down the corridor, the louder the knocking became. The emergency lighting became brighter as they came to a wide doorway. There was a long window that had years of dust along the edges, and there was also the periodic flashing of light from inside. This must be the munitions factory, but why would the equipment be operating?

Jon crept toward the window and eased himself up to get a better look. Beyond the wide doors was a vast space with long pieces of machinery.

"What do you see?" Lieutenant Chester asked.

"I'm not sure. This has got to be the munitions factory, but I don't—"

Jon ducked back down, and the others backed away in response to his sudden movement. He'd seen something and it had caught him by surprise. Jon slowly rose again and peered through the window. He adjusted the visual spectrum of his helmet and zoomed in on the far end. There was a dimly lit room where he saw several objects moving in the shadows.

Jon swallowed hard and sank back down below the window. "We found them."

"Good. Let's get them and get out of here," Lieutenant Chester said.

"We can't," Jon said and looked back at his squad. "There are Vemus forces inside. They're clustered around a particular area."

Damn it, Brian. Why did you have to volunteer for this? Jon thought. The salvage team was in serious trouble, and Jon wasn't sure if he could get them out.

Sergeant Lee crept by and peeked through the window, then came back to him. "I saw the salvage team. They're pinned down in a room on the far end, but . . ."

Jon shook his head. "There are a lot of Vemus soldiers."

At least that's what he thought they were. Even with the enhanced display, it was difficult to make out the details from this distance.

Daron looked at him pointedly. "There are only five of us," he said.

"I know. I just need a minute to think," Jon replied.

His brother was trapped and there was no way he was going to walk away. He just needed to figure out how to get him free.

11

CONNOR WASN'T sure if the initial shock of what they were going to contend with could ever wear off, but they got to work nonetheless. The SRDs had long since stopped sending transmissions. By their best estimate, only two of the SRDs had made it past the massive Vemus ship. The remaining three all went offline while they were sending their data back to Phoenix Station. All three SRDs going offline in virtually the same fashion was a strong indication that they had been shot down. They had images of one of them being destroyed, which was evidence enough of hostile intent.

Connor had called in his tactical officers and separated them into groups. Each of the groups was tasked with coming up with a firing solution that would destroy the enemy. They were clustered together in nearby work areas while Connor remained in the command area.

Colonel Cross came to stand at his side. "We were expecting another fleet," she said.

"So was I. Instead we got . . . *that*," Connor said while gesturing toward the main holoscreen. "Even if we'd been able to resupply the missile defense platforms, I'm not sure it would've been enough to destroy it."

"The tactical groups are divided as to when we should fire the weapons we've got," Sean said.

Connor pressed his lips together in thought. "If we fire now, they'll know we see them coming and it'll give them ample time to take out the incoming missiles."

"What if we waited until they were close to our relative position?" Sean asked.

"How close? Give me a distance," Connor said.

"Within Sagan's orbit," Sean said.

Connor frowned in concentration while weighing the possibilities. Sean hadn't just now come up with this idea. He was pitching his own agenda. Sagan was the fifth planet in this star system and relatively close to New Earth.

"You think we should wait until they're within Sagan's orbit before we fire our missiles? Why would we wait that long?" Colonel Cross asked.

"Our previous engagements with the Vemus showed that they limit themselves to basic strategy, but if we send out our missiles now, they stand a greater chance of taking them out. Even though the HADES IV-Bs with Noah's enhancements were designed to overcome fleet ship-point defenses, we don't have to deal with that here. What we need is to maximize the effect our weapons have on them, and I think if we wait until they're much closer to us, we'll stand a better chance of doing the most damage," Sean said.

"But if we attack now, we could soften them up before they come in range of our short-range weapons," Colonel Cross said.

"I don't think that's going to be enough," Connor said and realized he agreed with Sean's proposal. "We'd do some damage, but they could just slow down and repair their ships before coming the rest of the way. If we wait, they're committed."

Colonel Cross glanced at Sean as if seeing him in a new light. "I can see why you keep Major Quinn close at hand."

"He still surprises me sometimes. Remind me to tell you how he first came to be in my service," Connor said.

Colonel Cross laughed. "No need. I've heard the story before. He snuck into a storage crate not knowing you intended to do a low-altitude drop."

Sean grinned. "The general dumped everyone out of that Hellcat as a welcome-to-basic-training gift."

It had been seven years since that first Search and Rescue platoon was formed, and Connor had become as fond of those recruits as he had of the Ghosts. Most had moved on to join the CDF, but some had chosen other pursuits. Those had been much simpler times, when only a few thousand colonists had been brought out of stasis.

Connor glanced at the image of the Vemus ship on the main holoscreen. "They're not very imaginative, are they?" he said.

Sean frowned. "I'm not sure what you mean."

"The Vemus. They fight and move toward an objective with an almost singular purpose. Throughout our entire engagement with them aboard the *Vigilant* they never once slowed down or retreated. They hunted us, but only because we kept coming at them. We kept attacking," Connor said.

"We blocked their signal so they couldn't coordinate their efforts," Sean said.

"True, but even when we went aboard the *Indianapolis,* there were only a few hundred Vemus aboard," Connor said. He had to keep referring to them this way because he didn't want to think of them as having been human before they were infected. "So we wondered where the rest of them were."

Sean's eyes widened. "They held the bulk of their troops in reserve for this attack. At twenty-two kilometers across, there would be room enough for millions of them aboard that ship."

"But why send a fleet of ships ahead? Wouldn't they have kept some in reserve? Now we can just focus our efforts on the one ship," Colonel Cross said.

"Like I said, not very imaginative. They could have ships hidden away. We didn't get a good look at the back of their ship," Connor said.

"We can send in more recon drones and see if they can sneak up behind them, sir," Colonel Cross said.

"I think they'll just shoot them down before we can get any usable intelligence. Instead of sending the drones, let's position our recon drones out near Sagan's orbit," Connor said.

"If we're going to do that, why not a minefield?" Sean said.

Connor nodded. "We keep them dormant with a periodic check-in so they're powered off while the Vemus ship approaches. Then, during their periodic check-ins, we broadcast the signal for the mines to go active."

"We can coordinate that with our missiles then," Colonel Cross said.

"Why don't you go inform the tactical teams that we've decided on a direction and see what else they can come up with," Connor said.

"Yes, sir," Colonel Cross said.

After Cross walked away, Connor looked at Sean. "Any more bright ideas you'd like to share?"

Sean scratched the stubble of his beard. "I need to shave this thing. It itches something fierce."

"Now you sound like Diaz," Connor said.

Sean smiled but then it slipped away. "I wish I could think of something I knew would blow that ship out of the sky."

"You and me both. I know we can do some serious damage to it, but I'm not sure we can stop it," Connor said.

He quickly glanced around. He hadn't meant to say so much, but Sean had been with him for a long time. The kid was smart enough to be a true general one day, not like Connor, who had the position because there was no one else with enough combat experience to effectively do the job.

"I don't think anyone heard you, but I agree. Have you considered adding Lunar Base as part of our resources for facing the Vemus?" Sean asked.

The question alone spoke volumes about Sean's natural leadership ability. Most officers were siloed into their specific area, whereas Sean saw the whole playing board.

"I have, but I'm not convinced it will change things," Connor said.

"Why not?"

"Well, we could use their resources and weapons and list them among our assets. But we don't know what else the Vemus are capable of. I'm trying to account for things we haven't thought of yet. If the Vemus defeat us here, Lunar Base is our last line of defense in space. They'll be that much more of a threat to the Vemus if they don't know we have a base there," Connor said.

Sean nodded in understanding. "It's a gamble either way. If the Vemus detect Lunar Base somehow, Colonel Hayes will engage them. Otherwise, he'll stay there and continue to do a tactical assessment."

"Those were his orders. Nathan wasn't thrilled about them, but he's the best man for the job," Connor said.

"I know *I* wouldn't like watching someone else fighting while I just sat on the sidelines," Sean said.

"Yeah, but you'd do it if it meant saving everyone back home. We need to grind the Vemus down," Connor said.

Sean glanced at his PDA. "Dr. Allen is still waiting to speak with you."

Connor frowned regretfully. "I know, but he'll just have to wait."

12

Nathan waited for PRADIS to update on the main holoscreen. They were about to get another data dump from Phoenix Station. He glanced at the series number for the incoming data and felt a weariness creep into the small of his back. The Lunar Base Command Center had settled into a routine since achieving Dark-Star status. Every two hours they received a new data dump from Phoenix Station and had been doing so for the past twenty-four hours.

Major Shelton joined him in the command area, and they watched the PRADIS screen in silent anticipation. It had been over twelve hours since General Gates had given the anomaly heading for them the designation Alpha with a subheading of Vemus. The data points on PRADIS refreshed, showing the Alpha moving significantly closer to New Earth and increasing its speed by thirteen percent.

"They still haven't fired any of their missiles," Major Shelton said.

The Vemus Alpha was still quite far out in the star system, only now coming within range of the sixth planet's orbit. Gigantor was a gas giant that had blue bands and out-massed Jupiter by more than eighteen percent. Nathan had only seen pictures of it. For over seven years, the colony had been devoted to settling on New Earth and preparing for a threat that turned out to be the Vemus. They simply hadn't had much time to explore their surroundings. They were aware of similarities with the Sol System, which was part of the reason New Earth was similar in size and composition to their former home. Nathan would have liked to explore their new planetary system more, but as he watched the Vemus Alpha on the screen, he wasn't sure he'd ever get the chance.

"Colonel," Major Shelton said, her tone tight with tension, "the Alpha is within range of the HADES IV-B missiles. Why hasn't General Gates fired any of them yet?"

"One minute, Major," Nathan replied.

He walked toward the main holoscreen and studied the details of the PRADIS output, pressing his lips together while considering his response. He turned back to Major Shelton and noticed his tactical officer, Lieutenant LaCroix, waiting for his response as well. Other CDF soldiers craned their necks toward him as if sensing something.

"Some of you are wondering at the lack of response toward the Vemus Alpha heading toward us," Nathan began and waited a moment. "Why hasn't Phoenix Station taken any offensive action against our enemy?"

There were several head-bobs from the CDF soldiers in the command area.

"This will be among our greatest challenges because of our orders. We're in a communications blackout, with our only updates coming through the PRADIS system. This is necessary to conceal our presence from the enemy. There's no way to know for sure what strategy General Gates and his staff at Phoenix Station have decided on to address the Vemus threat. We've been expecting another fleet and suspected it would be bigger than what we faced over two months ago," Nathan said and flung his arm back toward the main holoscreen. "That is something different, something we *didn't* anticipate, and we're in the dark as to how Phoenix Station plans to engage the enemy. The fact that they haven't opened communications with us indicates that our orders haven't changed. We remain in communications blackout and observation status," he said and allowed his gaze to take in his staff. "It's a shit job, and it's ours. We're the last line of defense for New Earth. We're the Trojan horse if Phoenix Station fails. Our forces *will* engage the enemy and you can be sure that General Gates will do his utmost to stop the Vemus. So, instead of wondering why Phoenix Station hasn't fired their missiles, we'll be working on our own plan for engaging the enemy. I want teams divided up and focused on separate theaters for engagement. The first will be based on how we can assist Phoenix Station with the attack on the Vemus Alpha. The second will be how we'll engage the Vemus Alpha should Phoenix Station be destroyed."

The CDF soldiers became grim-faced and determined.

"We focus on what we *can* do, and don't be afraid to think of the worst scenarios you can come up with as long as you concentrate on the solution to those scenarios. The Vemus are bringing an invasion force. Given the sheer size of the enemy ship, we have to find the weak spots. We have to be smarter than our enemy. That's the only way we're going to survive," Nathan said. He waited a few moments. "Now get back to work. The colony and our fellow CDF soldiers are depending on us. We will not let them down."

The soldiers in the command area returned to their posts, and Major Shelton came over to stand by his side.

"Sir, I must apologize. If you want to relieve me of command I will understand," Major Shelton said.

"I'm not relieving you, Major. We have a job to do. All of us. As commanding officers, the burden is on us to remain steadfast and hold to our orders even when we don't have all the information," Nathan said.

"I won't let you down again, Colonel," Major Shelton said.

Nathan leaned toward her so no one else could hear him. "I'm just as scared as you are," he admitted.

A small smile appeared on Major Shelton's face. "I'm glad you're here, Colonel. With your permission, I'd like to broadcast what you've said to the rest of the base. I think it will be good for them to hear it."

Nathan considered the request for a few moments. "Permission granted."

Major Shelton left him and went over to the ops station.

"Colonel, I've just received a message from Captain Walker," Sergeant Boers said.

Nathan walked over to the comms workstation. "What have you got, Sergeant?"

"They've found the salvage team, but there are Vemus forces keeping them pinned down. Captain Walker is requesting backup-team deployment, sir," Sergeant Boers said.

Nathan's eyes widened. The fact that they'd found the salvage team in all that wreckage was a monumental feat, but Vemus soldiers being aboard one of the wrecks was a sobering thought. He'd thought they'd all be dead by now.

"Sir?" Sergeant Boers asked.

"Acknowledged receipt of the message, Sergeant. Do not send a reply," Nathan said and hated having to say it.

"Yes, sir," Sergeant Boers said, her voice sounding thick and constrained. "Sir, can't we send Captain Walker backup?"

Nathan's mouth went dry. "No," he replied solemnly.

Sergeant Boers opened her mouth to speak.

"You have your orders, Sergeant," Nathan replied sternly.

"Yes, sir," Sergeant Boers muttered and turned back to her workstation.

Even though Nathan was following orders, he still couldn't escape the feeling that he was abandoning soldiers under his command. It would be such an easy thing for him to order another combat shuttle with reinforcements. There would be no shortage of volunteers should he ask for them. Nathan glanced over at the operations work area with an almost wistful urge to do just that, but he squelched the urge almost as suddenly as he felt it. He would not disobey his orders. Captain Walker and his crew were on their own. He hated it, but given what they were about to face, he had to believe it was the right call.

13

THE CDF SOLDIERS on Phoenix Station worked at an accelerated rate, preparing for the Vemus Alpha. Authorization for the use of stimulants had been given, but it was a narrow line to walk. Connor had sent out an advisory to all officers reminding them to rotate their crews, allowing a soldier to work only two extra shifts before rotation was mandatory. It was difficult for any of them to rest, even when off duty.

Connor entered a small conference room where Colonel Cross and Major Elder were already sitting. Connor went to one of the unoccupied chairs and sat down with Major Quinn, who came to sit at Connor's side.

A holoscreen was powered on in the middle of the conference table, and a comms channel was opened that connected them to CDF headquarters in Sierra. They were greeted with a view of a small conference room occupied by Governor Tobias Quinn, Director of CDF Operations Franklin Mallory, Director of Field Operations Damon Mills, and Captain Juan Diaz of the CDF Infantry Division.

Connor was glad Tobias hadn't brought the rest of the colonial defense committee into this meeting.

"Just so we're on the same page," Connor began, "this will be our final meeting before we engage with the Vemus Alpha ship. From here on out we'll send data bursts that will contain any intelligence gathered about the enemy, as well as our own analysis of our engagements with the enemy."

"That's clear, Connor. Just one question. Why isn't Colonel Hayes patched into this meeting?" Tobias asked.

"Lunar Base remains in comms blackout," Connor replied.

"But shouldn't—" Tobias began and then stopped himself. Franklin Mallory leaned over and spoke into Tobias's ear, and the governor nodded. "Never mind. Franklin has just reminded me. Please continue."

Over the next hour, Connor laid out the plan they'd come up with for engaging the Vemus Alpha. Connor couldn't remember planning a more complex operation in his entire career, nor could he remember learning about one in history. The militaries of Earth hadn't had to face a singular enemy like what the colony was about to.

Connor watched the holoscreen and saw Tobias take a sip of his coffee before responding. "I just want to make sure I understand this on a high level. Once this Vemus Alpha crosses Sagan's line, you'll begin firing our missiles at them?"

"This is not a simple point-and-shoot exercise. That's only one facet of the plan—"

"I trust you, Connor," Tobias said. "I know you've picked over this plan of yours eight ways till midnight . . . or is it Sunday?" Tobias frowned. "I can't remember. What I want you to know is that we're not going to pick apart your plan. You have our support and gratitude."

"On behalf of Phoenix Station, we appreciate it," Connor said. They'd traveled a long road to get here, and on the eve of what would ultimately become the defining moment in human existence, they had to trust each other.

"I would like a few moments to speak with you alone," Tobias said.

Connor nodded and looked over at the others, but they had already risen from their seats and were starting to leave the room. Sean paused to take one last look at the holoscreen. His father gave him a firm nod, and Sean followed the others out.

Connor saw that the committee members had left the conference room on New Earth and Tobias was also alone.

"What's your state of readiness?" Connor asked.

Tobias sighed. "We're still moving people to various bunkers throughout the continent and to Sanctuary. Anyone who can hold a gun has been armed, and we've been training them as best we can."

"But they're not soldiers," Connor said.

Tobias shook his head. "No, they're not, but they have a right to fight for their survival."

"You're right; they do," Connor said and debated in his mind whether to be completely honest with Tobias about their chances.

"I need you to do something for me," Tobias said.

"What do you need me to do?" Connor asked.

"Level with me. What are the odds of this plan of yours stopping the Vemus?"

Connor drew in a breath. "We'll hit them hard. We'll make them bleed, but I don't know if we can stop them. That ship is the biggest thing we've ever seen. We're not even sure how it works. In theory, the Vemus are able to absorb other spaceships and this could be the result of that, but without knowing how thick the exoskeletal hull is, we can't be sure exactly how much damage our weapons will do. That's why we hope to hit them by surprise."

Tobias nodded. "With an extremely narrow margin of error."

"Some of the things we're doing here were only theoretical in the NA Alliance military—things like completely replacing how we do secure communications and command-and-control units that make even the thought of targeting missiles flying at point-four c's of light-speed possible. I could keep going, and I know you could do the same," Connor said.

Tobias leaned back in his chair. "The *Ark* was supposed to be our escape from Earth, a way to begin anew without all the historical conflicts dogging our footsteps. We brought the best and the brightest with us. Admiral Wilkinson snuck you and the rest of the Ghosts aboard the *Ark* in order to escape injustice, and I understand his motives for doing so. What I didn't anticipate was how essential you and Wil Reisman and Kasey Douglass would be to our survival. Given what I know now, I believe none of us would even be here if it weren't for you. We'd have fought and cobbled something together for our defense, but it wouldn't have been the Colonial Defense Force. That was your gift to this colony, and no matter how this turns out, I thank you. My son has become his own man in no small part due to your influence. I'm proud of him . . . and of you."

Connor felt a small lump growing in the back of his throat. The path that had led Sean Quinn to join the CDF had always been a point of silent contention between Connor and Tobias.

"Sean earned his place. He's proven himself time and time again," Connor said.

"I know he did," Tobias said knowingly. "I think that's one of the reasons he's stuck by you—the fact that he's my and Ashley's son held no sway with you."

Connor nodded and watched as Tobias seemed to be deciding whether to say something else. It was a question Connor had anticipated and was something any parent had a right to ask, knowing their child was going to be in imminent danger.

The moment passed and Tobias didn't ask Connor anything.

"I'll send Sean in to speak with you," Connor said at last.

Tobias swallowed hard. "Thank you," he said, his voice sounding thick.

"Good luck. Send my love to Ashley," Connor said.

"I will. You take care, Connor."

Connor rose from his seat and headed for the door. Once outside the conference room, he motioned for Sean to go back inside. Connor closed the door, having no desire to hear what father and son had to say to one another. It wasn't that he didn't care; it was that he cared too much. Connor only knew what his own son looked like and had a sense of the man he'd become. But thoughts of his son still brought a deep, powerful pang of guilt. He didn't think he'd ever forgive himself no matter what anyone said. Connor glanced at the conference room door for a moment before walking away.

Colonel Cross and Major Elder walked with him back to the Command Center, where they entered and went to their stations.

"General," Captain Caleb Thorne said, "we're ready to execute operation *Tip of the Spear* on your command."

Connor looked up at the PRADIS screen. The Vemus Alpha was approaching Sagan's line and would cross it within the next few hours. They had to launch now to get their missiles and command-and-control units in place.

"Do it," Connor said and used his neural implants to send his authorization codes.

Phoenix Station had secondary and tertiary computing cores, and the station was designed to be able to maintain operational effectiveness even if the subsections broke apart. Connor watched as Captain Thorne executed Connor's orders. HADES IV-B missiles were launched from missile tubes along Phoenix Station's superstructure. The missiles would cluster into groups, going to their preconfigured coordinates before heading to the main objective.

Connor's mind raced as he thought of all the possible outcomes of his actions. They'd come up with this plan as a team, but Connor was the one who gave the order. The responsibility fell squarely upon his shoulders. He had trouble believing their attack would simply do nothing to the Vemus Alpha, but it was a possibility. The best-case scenario was that they would soften up the Vemus Alpha's outer layers so when it attacked them, the remaining weapons on Phoenix Station would continue to tear apart that ship until there was nothing left.

A countdown timer appeared in the upper right corner of the main holoscreen. The pieces were moving into place and soon the attack would begin. The colony was as ready as it would ever be. Anyone left in the cities was there to fight. Noncombatants had been moved to secure locations.

"Tactical, prep data dump for broadcast," Connor said.

"Yes, sir. Ready to send on your command," Captain Thorne replied.

"Send it, and I want the scheduled dumps to occur more frequently now that our missiles are in the air," Connor ordered.

"Yes, sir," Captain Thorne replied.

At least they could keep Lunar Base in the fold as much as possible. Connor knew Nathan Hayes would follow his orders, but being kept in the dark would wear away on anyone's resolve, and the fact that they were fighting for their very survival would only compound the tension. He'd put Nathan in command of Lunar Base because Nathan believed in the mission. He wouldn't blindly follow orders, and it would take someone with a strong belief in what they were doing to carry out the difficult task Connor had set out for them.

Major Quinn entered the command area and walked toward Connor, coming to a halt at his side.

"Thank you, sir," Sean said.

"You're very welcome, Major," Connor replied.

Together they watched as the CDF soldiers who manned their posts in the various work areas of Phoenix Station executed their duties, all while the Vemus Alpha drew steadily closer, coming toward them like some inescapable leviathan with a purpose none of them really understood. Connor looked around at the CDF soldiers performing their duties. They were rolling the dice. What happened afterward they would deal with, but right now they were committed to a course of action. Connor's gaze came to a stop on the Vemus Alpha image on the PRADIS screen, and he clenched his teeth.

"Sometimes you have to roll the hard six, sir," Major Quinn said, speaking so only Connor heard him.

"You've got that right," Connor said.

There was no turning back now.

14

NOAH HAD ONLY BEEN at Sanctuary for a few days and he hated it. He was supposed to help with the alien power station they had here and somehow adapt its output for the colossus cannon. A short while ago he'd received news that Lunar Base was in comms blackout, which meant he couldn't communicate with his wife. The last he'd heard from her was a prerecorded message that was to be sent down from Lunar Base personnel if Dark-Star status was authorized. Well it was, and now he was out of touch with the most important person in his life. He hated this. Maybe he should steal a ship and head to Lunar Base.

Sanctuary was the largest refugee camp for colonists to hide from the Vemus threat. Its location on the continent put it far more remote than any of the small cities they'd built. Sierra was the only true city, and was the most heavily populated, but Haven and Delphi were a distant second and third. The colony government had put time and resources into building bunkers and temporary housing away from population centers. They'd targeted areas that were naturally fortified against New Earth predators but could also be hidden from an invasion force. Since Sanctuary was a large alien city built mostly underground, it could easily accommodate tens of thousands of people.

He was working in one of the topside temporary work areas the archaeological teams had put there when it was just them way out in the middle of nowhere. It was one of the few quiet places he'd found where he could get some work done. Adapting an alien power source to their equipment was a simple concept, but it wasn't easy to actually do.

The door burst open and Lenora stormed inside, her face contorted with lines of anger.

"What's wrong?" Noah asked.

Lenora swung her gaze toward him, seeming surprised to find him sitting there. The fury in her eyes gained the intensity of one of the tornadoes that used to blaze through this area of the continent until they'd put a couple of storm satellites in the area that used focused microwaves to prevent the tornadoes from even forming.

"All the damn people here, contaminating the site. We had an area cordoned off because we haven't had the chance to catalog the artifacts or really study the area. We just marked their locations. And I just found people moving into a group of habitats because they felt crowded in the designated areas and wanted extra space. Kids were running around, playing with artifacts, if you can believe that. Who lets their kids run around and play with things we barely understand?" Lenora said, her tone shrill.

Noah regarded her for a moment, arching his eyebrow.

Lenora glared at him. "Don't you say it."

"They're scared, Lenora."

Lenora blew out a frustrated breath and shook her head. "I want my dig site back."

"Yeah, well I want my wife back. We should tell the Vemus to stay away because they're inconveniencing our lives," Noah said.

Lenora crossed her arms in front of her and looked away from him. For a few moments, neither said anything.

"I'm sorry. It's just . . ." Lenora said and then growled in frustration. "How can you be so calm?"

Noah's eyes widened. "Calm! Trust me, I'm not calm. I'm just trying to focus on my work."

"That would be nice." Lenora rolled her eyes. "I have a hundred thousand people here interfering with *my* work. Can you tell them to go away?"

"A hundred! I thought they capped it at fifty thousand," Noah said.

"No, we've got a hundred now. One of the major bunkers failed. The area was unsuitable because of seismic activity or some such. Those people were moved here," Lenora said.

"It's only temporary—" Noah began, and Lenora glared at him.

"Don't give me that. And it's not the people being here . . . Well, maybe it is, but it's just . . ." Lenora's voice trailed off.

Noah looked at her. Lenora was like a big sister to him. She'd taken him under her wing when they'd first woken up after being in stasis for two hundred years. But he'd never seen her so agitated. She usually had a tighter rein on her emotions. She was a born leader. Once set upon a task, just get out of her way. It was no wonder she and Connor had had some of the most heated arguments he'd ever seen. In some respects, they were two sides of the same coin, but in others they were polar opposites.

"I can't even figure out where the aliens that built this place went. They're all gone. No remains, nothing. Nothing but these structures to even say they existed, and if the same thing happens to us . . ." Lenora said, her voice becoming thick.

Noah's instinct was to give her a hug and tell her that everything would be alright, but he knew that wasn't something Lenora wanted. "There really is no sign of what happened to the aliens that built this place?" Noah asked instead.

"Nothing but theories. We don't even know what they looked like. We know they manipulated the genetics of some of the species that live here now and that they were quite advanced in some ways and primitive in others," Lenora said.

"So they didn't get on a spaceship and fly away from here?"

"There's no evidence of them being able to fly in the atmosphere, much less in outer space," Lenora answered and pressed her lips together. "Do you think they're alright?" she asked and gestured upward.

Noah swallowed hard. "Right now they are. They haven't engaged the Vemus yet."

"How do you know that?"

"Well, for one, we would have heard about it. Dark-Star status is a protocol that essentially hides the fact that we have a lunar base. It's part of Connor's overall strategy," Noah said.

Lenora looked away. "Connor," she muttered as if the name were a blessing and a curse. Noah heard a tinge of longing in it. "But he wouldn't order that protocol unless they had found the Vemus."

"He wouldn't have done it unless he was absolutely sure," Noah agreed.

Lenora's shoulders drew upward and he watched her body stiffen. "Damn it."

This time Noah did give in to his instincts. He rose out of his chair and hugged Lenora. She was trembling, and after a moment she clung to him, burying her face in his chest. Noah didn't say anything, and after a minute she let him go, quickly wiping her eyes.

"He was never really here. Once we learned about the threat coming from Earth seven years ago, he stopped being here. He threw himself into his work, building the CDF. Then he lost Wil and Kasey . . . and that message from his son. This fight has been more personal for him than it's been for anyone else. I'm worried about him. I'm worried he's going to throw his life away to balance all the loss as if he had no other choice but to sacrifice himself," Lenora said.

Noah's mouth hung open. For as long as he'd known her, she'd never spoken to him about Connor.

"Connor would trade his life for a chance to stop the Vemus from coming here," Noah said.

Lenora shook her head. "I'm sure he thinks he would. It's what he'll convince himself he's doing. But you didn't see him before he left for Phoenix Station. He wants to die. He thinks that if he sacrifices himself, it will make up for all his regrets," Lenora said.

Noah's brows pulled together. "That's not true—"

"Yes, it is. He blames himself for not being there for his son. He blames himself for not being able to save Wil and Kasey and all the other soldiers who've died fighting the Vemus. He refuses to see the fruits of all his efforts and only focuses on what was lost," Lenora said.

"I thought he was doing better. Didn't you speak to him?"

"I did. He seemed like he started to listen, but I'm not sure. You know him; he can teach a boulder about being stubborn," Lenora said.

"Yeah, but—"

"If he really thought he was going to live, don't you think he'd be here fighting or coordinating the attack instead of being on Phoenix Station?" Lenora asked.

"You don't understand just how fast things can change up there. He's right where he needs to be," Noah said.

"Which just happens to be the perfect place for him to perform his heroic sacrifice," Lenora said bitterly.

Noah sighed, becoming irritated. "He may carry all that guilt, as you say. You're probably right about that, but what you don't see is that he wants to protect *you*."

Lenora snorted. "Don't you dare say he's doing this for me."

"It's part of it, whether you want to admit it or not," Noah replied.

Lenora stomped away from him. "If he wanted to protect me, he should have stayed."

Noah's shoulders slumped. "Come on, Lenora. That's not fair."

"No, it's not, and neither is him throwing his life away. Neither is it fair that your wife is holed up on Lunar Base. Nor is it fair that people had to leave their homes so they can hide because otherwise they might die. None of this is fair!" Lenora shouted and stalked out.

Noah took a deep breath and couldn't stop his mind from racing. They were both right, and that worried him more than making Lenora see reason.

He powered off his workstation and went outside. There were makeshift roads worn by all the traffic—be it people on foot or vehicles moving equipment. Work crews were hustling about, relocating into the ruins and off the surface. They needed to mask their presence here as much as possible, but as Noah looked around at all the temporary tents and buildings, he didn't see how that was going to be possible.

Noah glanced around, looking for Lenora, but she was nowhere to be seen. Instead, he heard a high-pitched, piggish voice giving orders while coming closer to him. Noah started walking away but he heard the shrill voice calling after him and turned around.

"Captain Gibson, what can I do for you?" Noah asked.

Captain Raeburn Gibson was a tall man with unusually long arms and torso. His thin dark hair was cropped and his glassy eyes were framed too close together, giving him the appearance of someone who was constantly glaring, although in Raeburn's case that might be true.

"Captain Barker, my PM has informed me that we're behind schedule with the power converter," Gibson said.

Gibson was part of Field Operations and Security and not part of the CDF, so Noah didn't have to report anything to him. Though their ranks were similar, Gibson was in charge of security, but he'd taken it upon himself to meddle in other work that didn't concern him. He was just supposed to keep the peace and run evacuation drills. Noah was convinced that Gibson had been assigned to Sanctuary just to get him out of the hair of whoever sent him here. He had no idea who, but he was sure that was the reason.

Gibson cleared his throat. "Aren't you supposed to be working on that this morning?"

Noah frowned and shook his head. "This doesn't really concern you."

Gibson's sidekick was an imposing man named Barnes. If Gibson was the brains, then Barnes was the muscle. Barnes glared at Noah, and the rest of the security detail waited to take their cue from him. They were all armed with shock sticks.

"You're mistaken, Captain," Gibson insisted.

"Really," Noah replied. "You're not part of the CDF, and Field Ops doesn't have any authority over what I do with my time."

Gibson nodded and pursed his fat lips together as if agreeing with what Noah had said. "Ordinarily you'd be right, but in this state of emergency, Field Operations and Security is granted special authority. Sanctuary is a civilian installation and anyone within its boundaries, including CDF soldiers, are under my jurisdiction," Gibson said.

Noah couldn't believe it. This idiot thought he could actually strong-arm him. "That's crap and you know it. If you think you can stroll around here, throwing your weight around, you're sorely mistaken."

Sergeant Barnes took a step toward him, glaring menacingly, but Gibson placed a hand on his shoulder and pulled him back. Much to Noah's surprise, the large man actually stepped back. What kind of hold did Gibson have on the man to make him so obedient?

"If I find that you're bullying these people, I'll have a squad brought in here so fast you won't know what hit you," Noah said.

Gibson's eyes narrowed dangerously. "Tread carefully. Things won't always be this way. Change is coming, and you'll need friends if you want to survive."

"Go bother someone else," Noah replied.

"Get back to work, Captain Barker. If you don't get the power converters online, Sanctuary is defenseless," Gibson said and walked away, leading his team.

Noah glared at them in disgust. The colony's finest, but fear made people do stupid things. Some people froze and were unable to take action, while others seized the opportunity to grasp at anything to make themselves feel secure.

Noah did need to check with the engineering teams working on the power converters. They couldn't just connect their equipment to the alien power station. They needed a relay to convert the power so it would work with colony equipment, which was easier said than done since the alien power station was prone to overloads and they couldn't figure out why. Noah glanced up at the sky. He bet Kara could have figured it out.

15

CAPTAIN WALKER WAITED for Specialist Thoran and Lieutenant Chester to return. Sending them back to their shuttle to deploy a comms drone had been the right call. Meanwhile, the Vemus soldiers continued to devote all their attention to the trapped salvage team.

"Shouldn't they be back by now?" Corporal Sims asked.

"Let's give them a few minutes more," Jon replied.

Lieutenant Chester had strongly suggested that they send in a request for backup from Lunar Base, and while Jon was anxious to save his brother, he had to concede Lieutenant Chester's point. It should only take an hour to return to the shuttle and deploy a drone. Jon glanced at the time on his heads-up display and saw that they were rapidly approaching the hour mark.

He'd taken the risk that most of the Vemus soldiers were inside the munitions factory area trying to get to the salvage team. Some of the Vemus soldiers continued to slam their fists on the wall, but the bulk of their group waited. Having carefully observed them for the past hour, Jon had the feeling that the Vemus weren't trying to get into the room where the salvage team was trapped so much as keeping an eye on them.

Sergeant Lee squatted down next to Jon. "What do you think of the plan?"

Jon looked over at him. "Once we start, it's not like we get a do-over. They'll know we're here."

They'd been running reconnaissance around the area, looking for a safe way to extract the salvage team. Jon had even considered using the weapons on the combat shuttle to poke a few holes in the area nearby. He'd hoped to draw the Vemus soldiers away, but Sergeant Lee pointed out that it was a terrible idea. Blowing more holes in the wreckage of the ship could make this place even more unstable than it already was. When Jon had pressed Lee to go along with the plan, Lee reminded him that if he persisted with it, they ran a greater risk of killing the salvage team rather than saving it. Instead, they'd placed explosive charges in the adjacent tunnels, hoping that it would draw the Vemus away from the salvage team to investigate.

"Are you sure we can't try opening a comlink to the salvage team?" Corporal Sims asked.

"Too risky. The reports from when the *Banshee* was captured were that the Vemus are able to detect comlink signals, so if we use them, we'll give away our position," Jon answered.

He'd read the reports released by CDF intelligence. They'd disseminated the debriefing from the soldiers involved and sent out useable intelligence throughout the CDF. Jon remembered reading it and thinking it was interesting, but he hadn't expected to use that knowledge. Combat suit-to-suit communications in close proximity didn't require a comlink broadcast, so they were safe from the Vemus detecting them for now. The range wasn't that extensive or else they'd be able to speak with Lieutenant Chester and Specialist Thoran back on the shuttle. Jon wanted to go back to the munitions factory door and look through the window but decided against it. Why tempt fate at this point? They knew what was there. A few combat drones would have come in handy at this point, but they didn't have any.

A few minutes later their overdue team members made it back to them.

"Run into any trouble?" Jon asked.

"No, sir. But we got no response from Lunar Base," Lieutenant Chester said.

Jon frowned. "Not even an acknowledgment?"

"Nothing. We sent out a comms drone and waited for it to get beyond the Vemus jamming signal and return. No response, Captain," Lieutenant Chester said.

Jon looked at Specialist Thoran. "What do you think it means?"

"They should have gotten our transmission. Unless the Vemus can somehow travel at the speed of light and are attacking right now, I think Lunar Base has been ordered to go into communications blackout and couldn't respond even if they wanted to, Captain," Specialist Thoran said.

Jon grimaced. "Dark-Star status. I didn't even think about that."

The other members of the team considered it for a moment.

"It would explain their lack of response," Lieutenant Chester said.

"Yeah, but that means there's another Vemus attack force out there," Corporal Sims said.

"It also means we're on our own. It's safe to assume that they got our transmission but weren't able to respond," Jon said.

"Would they send another team anyway, even if they couldn't respond, sir?" Sergeant Lee asked.

Jon looked at them all and shook his head. "No. Not with another attack force on its way. The priority is New Earth and keeping Lunar Base's location a secret."

Specialist Thoran's face became pale. "We have to get out of here."

"We're not leaving without the salvage team," Jon said firmly. He looked around at all of them. "We can't leave our people behind. They'd do the same for us, and they might have learned something important."

Sergeant Lee nodded grimly.

Lieutenant Chester nodded as well. "We're with you, Captain."

Jon felt the muscles in his chest loosen. "Thank you. You're all heroes. Now let's get this done."

Lieutenant Chester snorted. "Let's just get them so we can get out of here in one piece, sir."

"Alright, enough with the pep talks. Lee and I did some recon while you were gone. We've placed concussive charges . . ." Jon went over the plan he'd laid out with Sergeant Lee. It didn't take long to explain since it was relatively simple. Too bad it wasn't going to be easily executed.

"Were you able to bring what I asked you?" Jon asked.

"We only had one on board," Lieutenant Chester replied and gestured over to the heavy case he'd been carrying.

Jon must have been getting tired because he'd completely missed the fact that Lieutenant Chester had brought the case.

"And the ammunition chest is over there, sir," Lieutenant Chester said and frowned. "Are you sure you're alright, Captain?"

Jon nodded. "I'm fine. I just didn't see that you had the case. We need to place the heavy turret at the far end of this corridor."

He was counting on the Vemus to investigate the concussive blasts, only to walk into the path of their only heavy turret. It should rip them to shreds, giving them time to get the salvage team out of there.

A violent shudder spread from the floors and down the corridor. Power lines inside the walls began to overload, sending showers of sparks until fire control systems cut them off. At least the safety systems were still operational.

"That was another impact," Lieutenant Chester said.

Jon nodded. "We've got no time to waste. Let's get moving."

The five-man rescue team left the area. They'd set up the turret and then observe the Vemus soldiers before executing the plan.

16

CONNOR SAT in his office aboard Phoenix Station. The cup of coffee Corporal Faulkner had brought sat untouched, having long since gone cold. He'd lost the taste for coffee since his time on the *Vigilant* when someone had tried to poison him. While he didn't believe that anyone here would be trying to murder him, he just couldn't look at a cup of coffee the same way anymore. Perhaps he should try tea, but what he really wanted was something a lot stronger.

"General," Dr. Richard Allen said, sitting across from Connor. "I realize the timing of this news is delicate, but with all that's been happening, I wasn't sure when a good time to disclose the information would be."

Connor drew in a breath and sighed. "And you're certain this is accurate?"

"Quite certain, General," Dr. Allen said, meeting Connor's gaze.

"Are there any others in the same condition?" Connor asked.

"Yes, General," Dr. Allen answered, and Connor's eyes widened. "With a crew of ten thousand, there's bound to be more than one. I have a list prepared."

Connor leaned forward in his chair and shook his head. "The ones who're unaware is one thing, but for the people who knew and didn't report it—that's another."

"Sir, these are extraordinary times we live in. We're all coping with the threat the Vemus represent in our own ways—" Dr. Allen said.

"I understand," Connor said and rose from his seat. "I appreciate you bringing this to my attention. Send your list to Major Quinn and we'll get it sorted out. I'm due to return to the Command Center," he said and left his office with Dr. Allen following.

"Good luck, General," Dr. Allen said.

"Good luck to us all," Connor said.

Sean was standing a short distance away with his security detail and walked with Connor on his way back to Phoenix Station's Command Center.

Sean eyed him for a moment. "I take it the news from Dr. Allen was significant, sir?"

Connor nodded. "Let's just say you were right about Colonel Cross."

They walked into the Command Center, where the CDF soldiers on duty were actively working at their stations. The countdown timer on the main holoscreen was mirrored on Connor's own internal heads-up display, but he glanced at it anyway. The first salvo of HADES IV-B missiles would be in target range soon.

Connor headed to the command area where Colonel Cross waited. She met his gaze and something unspoken passed between them. Her eyes narrowed and she glanced away for a moment. Then her shoulders slumped before she squared herself away.

Connor stood next to her with his hands clasped behind him. He could feel the tenseness coming off of her in waves. He glanced at the barely perceptible pooch in her midsection. "You should have told me," Connor said quietly.

Colonel Cross looked at him and was about to reply.

"Alpha missile group closing in on target. Command-and-control units have the target marked," Captain Thorne announced.

Connor looked at the main holoscreen. The alpha missile group was the farthermost away from the Vemus ship. They'd been modified to maximize their speed, reaching forty percent relativistic speeds, which meant that as the Vemus Alpha crossed Sagan's line, the fifty-four-million-kilometer distance would be covered in under eight minutes. Twenty of their modified HADES IV-Bs were carrying fusion warheads.

Connor and the rest of the CDF soldiers on Phoenix Station waited.

"Detonation signal received," Captain Thorne said. "Confirmed detonation of all twenty missiles," he said, unable to keep the excitement from his voice.

Millions of kilometers away from them, the Vemus Alpha ship was blindsided by the CDF missiles. Layers of the exoskeleton sloughed away almost immediately, burning away in chunks. Large gaps began to appear on the hull of the massive ship where the CDF missiles had delivered their powerful payloads.

"Bravo and Charlie missile groups are closing on the target," Captain Thorne announced.

Connor knew those missiles moved much slower. That was why they'd waited to send the alpha group until the other missile groups were in position. A subgroup of Bravo and Charlie were targeted to hit the rear of the Vemus Alpha. Connor's gaze was fixed on the main holoscreen. Those missiles had to reach their target. Since there were no visible engines on the massive ship, they had to be in the rear, hidden away in the cavernous mass. He planned to blindside the behemoth and then continue to hit the ship, chopping away at it and hopefully crippling it in the process.

"Confirm all HADES active," Captain Thorne said.

The breath caught in Connor's chest. The command-and-control units would provide updates for as long as they were active. They didn't have thousands of missiles, so every one of them counted.

The command-and-control units beamed back their updates, but it still took the data over three minutes to make it to Phoenix Station, where the computing core immediately put it into their cyber-warfare suite. The whole process from the time the command-and-control units sent an update to when it appeared on the main holoscreen in Phoenix Station's command area was three-point-two minutes. That didn't sound like a lot of time, but it could make all the difference in a war such as this. There was nothing else for them to do. They were committed to this engagement, just as the Vemus Alpha was.

"Missile groups going offline," Captain Thorne said, his voice rising.

"Can you confirm detonation?" Connor asked.

"I'm trying to . . . negative, General. They must be taking out our missiles," Captain Thorne said.

Connor watched the long list of HADES IV-B missile statuses. Some were getting through the countermeasures the Vemus were using, but not nearly as many as they'd hoped. As more and more missiles went offline without delivering their payload, Connor's gut clenched.

"Sir, command-and-control units are now offline. Switching to PRADIS," Captain Thorne said.

Connor clenched his teeth. Without the command-and-control units, they couldn't know what sort of damage they'd done. He looked away from the main holoscreen, but the officers in the command area still watched with grave expressions.

"PRADIS is online," Captain Thorne said. "Sir, we have three hundred marks on the plot—make that four hundred. Speed and mass readings indicate NA Alliance Condor class heavy missiles."

"Set Condition One," Connor said. "Ready station defenses. We have incoming missiles."

"Action Stations. Action Stations. Set Condition One." Lieutenant Daniel's voice was broadcast throughout Phoenix Station.

"Time to impact—one hour at their current speed, sir," Captain Thorne said.

"Thank you, Captain. Any change in their speed, I want to know about it immediately," Connor said.

"Yes, General," Captain Thorne answered.

"Major Elder, you have the con. Colonel Cross and Major Quinn, follow me," Connor said.

"Yes, General," Major Elder said, giving them a curious glance as they left.

Connor led them to the nearest breakout room and told Sean to wait outside. Colonel Cross went inside, and Connor closed the door.

"What do you have to say for yourself, Colonel?" Connor asked.

"Sir, I was going to tell you—" Colonel Cross began.

"You were *required* to tell me the moment you found out. How far along are you?" Connor asked.

"Not that far—"

"How far along!" Connor shouted.

"Eight weeks. Just over eight weeks, sir," Colonel Cross said finally.

Connor's eyes widened. "Eight weeks," he muttered in disbelief. "You must have known you were pregnant for over a month and didn't report it."

Colonel Cross looked away.

"We have protocols to follow. You were required to report this to me as your commanding officer within seventy-two hours of finding out," Connor said, his voice lowering in volume but no less stern.

Colonel Cross glared at him. "Permission to speak freely, sir."

"Granted."

"I know the damn protocol and the regulations," Colonel Cross said.

"Then why didn't you tell me?"

"Because I wanted to fight! I have a right to fight. My pregnancy doesn't in any way impede my ability to command," Colonel Cross said.

"This is about more than just you, Savannah. 'No pregnant woman shall serve in an active combat zone,'" Connor replied.

"Are you going to arrest me?" Colonel Cross challenged.

"No, I'm not going to arrest you. But I am sending you back to New Earth," Connor said.

"No, don't!" Colonel Cross pleaded. "Let me stay. Let me fight. You need me."

Connor's eyebrows drew together, furrowing over his eyes. "Absolutely not. This isn't just about you anymore. There's another life at stake."

"All of our lives are at stake! What difference does it make whether I stay here and fight or go back to New Earth and fight there?" Colonel Cross said. "Tell me, what difference does it make?"

"All the difference in the world, but you can't see it now. What is the Colonial Defense Force motto?" Connor asked.

Colonel Cross sighed heavily. "Defend the colony and all its people," she said softly.

"Your baby, even at this stage, is part of this colony. The regulations on this are clear," Connor said.

Colonel Cross gritted her teeth, and the edges of her eyes reddened.

"Who is the father? And does he know?" Connor asked.

"Where are you going to send me?" Colonel Cross asked.

"Answer the question, Colonel," Connor said.

"It's Colonel Hayes," she said, and her shoulders slumped.

"Does Nathan know?" Connor asked.

Colonel Cross's lips trembled and she shook her head.

"Understood," Connor said. "For the record, I understand why you did what you did, but I can't condone it. We have these regulations for a reason. You think that fighting here at Phoenix Station is no different than on New Earth, but I say you're wrong. You might hate it, and you might hate me for enforcing the regulations even in times such as these, but I intend to give your and Nathan's baby the best chance at life I can."

Colonel Cross looked away from him.

Connor opened the door. "Major Quinn, have two members of your security detail escort Colonel Cross to the hangar bay. She's been relieved of duty. She, along with several hundred nonessential personnel, are returning to New Earth. See that she's assigned to Sanctuary, then come inside."

"Right away, General," Major Quinn said.

Colonel Cross began to walk out of the breakout room, but stopped before the threshold. She turned around and stood up straight, with her shoulders back. She raised her right hand to her brow and saluted.

Connor brought his heels together and saluted back to her in kind, then gave her a firm nod, and she left.

Connor rested his hands on his hips and sighed heavily. He looked up at the ceiling, still thinking about what Savannah had done. He kept thinking about whether he should inform Nathan that he was going to be a father but decided against it. News like that should come from the mother, but Lunar Base was in a communications blackout. Would it affect Colonel Hayes's ability to command Lunar Base? Would the news of him becoming a father affect his judgment and make him prone to rash decisions? Connor pressed his lips together while he considered. He'd put Nathan in command of Lunar Base because of his commitment to their strategy for fighting the Vemus. While the news of his becoming a father would come as a shock, Connor believed that, of anyone under his command, Nathan could handle that news, but he'd leave it up to Savannah to tell him.

The door to the breakout room opened, and Sean stepped inside, closing the door behind him.

"You wanted to see me, sir," Sean said.

"You were right about Colonel Cross. She's pregnant," Connor said.

Sean nodded. "It makes sense now, sir."

Connor snorted. Savannah and Nathan were hardly the first officers to survive an ordeal like their first engagement with the Vemus and wind up sleeping together. Regardless of the status of their relationship, they both had something to consider.

"Your keen observation skills continue to impress me, Major," Connor said.

"Thank you, sir. I aim to please," Sean said with a smile.

Connor sighed. "You won't like your new orders."

Sean frowned. "New orders, sir?"

"Yes," Connor replied. "I'm sending you back to Sierra. You're to take command of the city's defenses. I'm giving you full authority over all CDF forces on the ground."

"But, sir, I thought I'd be at your side for the duration," Sean said.

"Plans change. You and your entire team will go to Sierra," Connor said.

Sean's mouth hung open. "Is this because . . ."

Connor knew what he was about to ask, and Sean let the question go unfinished. "If you need to ask that, I haven't done a very good job of not giving you special treatment all these years."

Sean clamped his mouth shut. "Permission to speak freely, General."

"Keep it quick." Connor glanced at the clock.

"Why are you sending me back to New Earth? We have soldiers and commanding officers there already," Sean said.

"Let me tell you something. We're not all the same, commanding officers included, but there are some who are born with a certain instinct that either makes them die young or enables them to rise through the ranks. The fact of the matter is, Sean, you're one of the best officers I've ever served with. And that includes Wil and Kasey. They both commented on more than one occasion about your abilities as an officer," Connor said.

Sean swallowed hard. "Thank you, sir. I'm glad you believe in my abilities, but I don't have the rank to take command of Sierra's defenses."

Connor smiled. "A CO once said to me that titles are cheap. People will follow those who do the work. Damon Mills is bullheaded, but he's a good man. He'll listen to you. I'm giving you operational command authority for the CDF ground forces. I'm sending my authorization to your PDA. You're to report to Sierra at once."

"But, sir, I don't know if I can do this."

Connor put his hand on Sean's shoulder. "I know you can. I firmly believe that when the Vemus reach the city, it will stand a much better chance at surviving with you in command. Remember what you've learned and trust your instincts."

"You said *when* the Vemus reach the city. You don't think you can stop them here?" Sean asked.

"You've seen it for yourself. We'll slow them down and do whatever damage we can against them so you'll have fewer to face on the ground. Very little will change that," Connor said. He'd been thinking it for so long that to finally admit it aloud was somewhat freeing.

He watched as a range of emotions crossed Sean's face, but the young man was smart enough to know the answers. Instead, he hardened his gaze. "I'll do my best, General."

"Good luck," Connor said, and his throat became tight.

"You too, sir," Sean said.

They left the breakout room, and Connor watched the young man he had helped shape into a fine young officer walk away from him. He'd always looked at Sean as a son, and he was filled with fatherly pride in the man Sean Quinn had become. He wondered if Admiral Wilkinson had had the same thoughts when he looked at Connor's own son. Connor felt a heavy weight lift from his shoulders. The video recording of his son was painful for him to watch, but he now had a better understanding of why Wilkinson had asked him to record it. Connor had spent a lot of time hating Wilkinson for the actions he'd taken and how Connor had to live with the results. It wasn't a perfect world by a long shot, and if Connor could find it in his heart to forgive Mitch Wilkinson for setting him on this path, then perhaps he could finally forgive himself for his own actions that had put him on this same path.

Connor swallowed those thoughts away. He wished he could tell Lenora that he finally understood what she'd been trying to tell him.

"General, they need you in the command area," a CDF soldier said.

Connor nodded and headed there. This fight was far from over and he intended to make the Vemus bleed as much as he could before the end.

17

NOAH WALKED among the ruins of the alien city the colonists called Sanctuary. He'd been working with a team of engineers to convert the alien power station into something they could use for the colossus cannon. The problem was that the technology was hundreds of years old. The aliens had tapped into geothermal energy deep in the planet's crust. Since the colonists didn't have the resources to build a power plant of their own, they'd taken the option of leveraging what was already there. The plan was simple, just not easy. Noah had finished running a series of tests, and the power output seemed stable enough for further testing. But if the Vemus somehow found this place, he wasn't sure how long the colossus cannon would remain operational.

He'd decided to take a walk to clear his head. He wanted to find Lenora. She'd been pretty upset, and wasn't that what little brothers were supposed to do? A member of the archaeological team had told him she'd gone into an area of the city that was cordoned off from refugees. The soldiers securing that area took one look at his uniform and rank, then let him pass.

The aliens that built this place hadn't constructed anything like stairs. Instead, they preferred ramps that made traversing to the lower levels of the city seem like he was walking along a winding road. It would have been nice if they'd built elevators, but they apparently hadn't had any need for them either. He came to a subterranean level of the city where the only lighting came from some of the temporary light fixtures they'd set up. Noah peered ahead and noticed that the lighting became brighter in the distance. The source of the light came from a building whose large circular door was partially open. Some unseen mechanism must have pulled the door into the wall because there was no way Lenora could have opened it herself.

Noah called out and heard Lenora answer him from inside the building, but her voice echoed and sounded distant. Noah went inside and followed a corridor that circled into a large cavern. There were glowing amber lights along the smooth walls. Noah walked deeper into the cavern and noticed that there were even more levels beneath the one he was on.

He saw Lenora standing a short distance away, in front of a curved screen that showed some type of alien writing scrolling past, going from left to right.

"What is this place?" Noah asked.

"I think it's some kind of archive," Lenora said in hushed tones, as if they were in a church.

"An archive! That's amazing. How'd you find it?" Noah asked.

Lenora gave him a sidelong glance. "A group of refugees wandered down here and said they'd found something. They described this room."

"Maybe having the refugees here isn't such a bad thing after all. You could put them to work," Noah said.

Lenora blew out a breath and looked at him regretfully. "About before. I'm sorry."

"You don't need to apologize. None of this is easy."

"That doesn't mean I didn't mean what I said. I'm just sorry I yelled at you," Lenora said.

Noah glanced at the alien symbols scrolling past on the antiquated screen. It wasn't made of glass but was constructed of some kind of tightly knitted flexible mesh.

"If you really feel that way, then why don't you send Connor a message?" Noah said.

Lenora frowned. "I'm not going to send him some final message professing a bunch of emotional crap. He doesn't need that."

Noah laughed. "No, of course not, but would it hurt for you to tell him you'd like him to come back home?"

"We're not together," Lenora replied firmly.

"I know that, but you still care about him," Noah said, thinking that Lenora could also teach a thing or two about being stubborn.

Lenora regarded him for a moment. "Maybe."

Noah's comlink chimed, and he tapped the receiver near his ear. "This is Noah."

"We need you back topside, sir. Captain Gibson is ordering a test-fire of the colossus cannon," Corporal Johnson said.

Noah jerked back a few steps. *Idiot!* He sucked in his bottom lip in frustration. "I'm coming. You have to stall him. If he fires that weapon, he could overload the entire system."

"Yes, sir," Corporal Johnson said.

The comlink closed.

"God, please save me from idiots like Gibson," Noah said.

"I'll come with you," Lenora said, "in case God is busy."

Noah snorted and, together, they ran out of the alien archive. He contacted members of the engineering team, informing them of what was happening. Three work crews were on their way to the mobile Command Center.

They ran through throngs of refugees, and Noah shouted for them to make a space. Most didn't recognize him, but they did recognize the Colonial Defense Uniform and had come to respect it. A few minutes later they were within sight of the mobile Command Center. There was a crowd gathered, with more than a few work crews. Field Operations and Security personnel had established a perimeter just outside the Command Center, and Captain Gibson was standing just behind the line, red-faced, with a wild look in his eye. His left cheek was swollen. Noah saw Corporal Johnson on his knees. He looked disoriented, as if he'd just had a shock-stick used on him.

Noah pushed his way through the workers, and the line of Field Ops and Security forces held their shock-sticks ready.

"Gibson! What the hell are you doing?" Noah shouted.

Captain Gibson swung his angry gaze toward him and sneered. "Your man attacked me."

Noah looked over at Corporal Johnson and scuttled over to him. "Get away from him," Noah snapped.

The Field Ops agent standing over Corporal Johnson glared at Noah.

"Back off," Lenora said, coming to stand next to Noah.

The Field Ops man glanced back at Gibson.

"This is ridiculous," Lenora said and stepped forward, helping Corporal Johnson back to his feet. Surprisingly, the Field Ops team let her do this.

Corporal Johnson was hunched over, holding his middle.

"Are you alright?" Noah asked quietly.

"You did say to stall him, sir," Corporal Johnson said and grimaced.

Noah motioned to some members of the work crew to take Corporal Johnson, and they led him off to the side.

Noah turned back toward Captain Gibson. "You can't test-fire the colossus cannon. You'll overload the system."

"I had my own people check the latest reports for the power converter. The energy levels are constant. We can test the weapon," Captain Gibson sneered.

Noah took a moment to calm down. He needed to defuse the situation, not exacerbate it. "You don't know what you're doing—"

"I've had about enough of your smug comments. You come here, strutting around, thinking you're so superior. People actually believe you're some kind of hero. The people are scared. They need to know they can be protected here," Captain Gibson said and glanced at a Field Ops person next to him. "Ready the cannon for test-firing."

Noah stepped forward and felt Lenora grab his arm, holding him back. "You're such an idiot. Yes, the power levels are constant, but if you fire that weapon, you'll overload the system and destroy our only means of defense."

"Rubbish," Captain Gibson spat.

The line of Field Ops and Security forces stood ready, almost inviting Noah to try and push his way through.

"I don't know what your tech expert told you, but the power requirements for the colossus cannon are not comparable to the mag-cannons that were installed in Sierra. The power draw is much more taxing on the system and is prone to spikes," Noah said.

Captain Gibson narrowed his gaze. "You would have accounted for that," he said and glanced behind him. "Proceed with the test-fire."

"No," Noah muttered, stepping closer.

One of the Fields Ops and Security agents jabbed the shock-stick into Noah's middle and unleashed its fury. Noah dropped to the ground, crying out in agony.

"Don't do it," Noah screamed.

There was a loud pop, and for a moment Noah thought the colossus cannon had fired, but it hadn't. Captain Gibson glanced up toward the sky in surprise. A few moments later, Noah heard the high-pitched sound of a combat shuttle's engines coming toward them. The colossus cannon hadn't fired. What he'd heard was the sonic boom of a ship reentering New Earth's atmosphere.

Three CDF combat shuttles flew overhead and landed nearby. Noah regained his feet, and Lenora helped to steady him. He glanced over and a slow smile crossed his face. CDF soldiers were pouring out of the shuttle, their dark blue uniforms appearing like a godsend. A group of them were making their way toward them.

Noah straightened and saluted. "Colonel," he said.

Colonel Cross returned his salute. "Sitrep, Captain."

The Field Ops and Security forces lowered their shock-sticks but stayed in formation. Noah was sure this had everything to do with the armed CDF soldiers that stood behind Colonel Cross.

Captain Gibson pushed his way through his men, his piggish eyes glaring. "Captain Raeburn Gibson, ma'am, and I'm in charge here."

Colonel Cross regarded Gibson frostily. "I wasn't speaking to you, but since you're here, are you the one who assaulted men under my command?"

Captain Gibson glanced at the armed CDF soldiers and then back at Colonel Cross. "It was your soldiers who assaulted me first."

"We'll see about that," Colonel Cross said and turned toward Noah. "Captain Barker. Front and center."

"Yes, ma'am," Noah said and noticed Lenora smiling at him in a big-sisterly way. "Field Ops Captain Gibson was trying to test-fire the colossus cannon. We've been adapting the alien power station here. I informed Captain Gibson that this would overload the system, but he decided to use Field Ops to force us to bring the cannon online."

Colonel Cross swung her gaze back to Gibson, who flinched. "Explain yourself, Field Ops Captain."

Colonial Defense Force authority superseded any authority the Field Ops captain had, and he knew it. "The people are scared. I was trying to demonstrate our ability to protect them."

Colonel Cross arched an eyebrow. "Forcibly?" she said, and Gibson stubbornly met her gaze. Colonel Cross glanced to the soldier on her right. "Captain Gleason, take the Field Ops team into custody. Find somewhere to hold them, and I'll deal with them later."

"Excuse me, Colonel," Lenora said, "but I know of a place you can use."

"Thank you—" Colonel Cross said and stopped.

"Dr. Bishop," Lenora said.

Colonel Cross frowned. "Lenora Bishop?"

"You can't do this!" Captain Gibson cried while struggling with a CDF soldier.

"That's about enough of that, Captain," Colonel Cross snapped. "If you don't get yourself under control, I'll order my soldiers to gag you. Is that understood?"

Captain Gibson's face paled.

Colonel Cross leaned forward. "And just because I'm feeling a bit indulgent, I'll tell you another reason why firing that cannon as a way to make everyone feel better for a few fleeting moments is a bad idea. The Vemus are coming. Long-range scanners detected the discharge of orbital defense weapons. In other words, your pitiful attempt to get your gun off would have painted a great big target in the one place we don't want the Vemus to find. Does that clear up any misgivings you might have had?"

Captain Gibson's mouth made a wide circle, but no words came out.

Colonel Cross looked at Captain Gleason. "As you were, Captain."

Noah watched as the Field Operations and Security team was escorted away from the mobile Command Center.

"Dr. Bishop, would you join me inside?" Colonel Cross said. "And you too, Captain Barker."

Noah followed them inside and went to the nearest terminal to make sure the startup power sequence for the colossus cannon had been properly shut down.

"Please, call me Lenora."

Colonel Cross nodded. "And you can call me Savannah."

Noah stepped away from the terminal and looked at Colonel Cross.

"Go ahead and ask, Captain," Colonel Cross said.

"I thought you were in command of Phoenix Station, ma'am," Noah said.

He watched as the colonel pressed her lips together to suppress a sneer.

"Ordinarily, I would dress you down for asking that kind of question of a superior officer, but General Gates and a few others have warned me of some of your eccentricities," Colonel Cross said.

Noah felt his cheeks redden. "Apologies, Colonel."

Colonel Cross glanced at Lenora. "It seems that General Gates is a bit of a stickler for certain rules and regulations."

Lenora snorted. "When it wins him an argument."

Colonel Cross chuckled. "You *are* the Lenora I've heard about."

"I'm not sure what you mean."

"It's not important," Colonel Cross said. "General Gates has sent me to Sanctuary, and I need to know our state of readiness."

Noah still didn't understand why Connor would send someone as capable as Savannah Cross to Sanctuary when the Vemus were coming, but he didn't need to understand to follow his orders. Colonel Cross had a reputation for not tolerating nonsense.

"One hundred thousand refugees are at Sanctuary. The colossus cannon is operational, but we've been experiencing power fluctuations from the alien power station, ma'am," Noah said.

"Can you fix it?" Colonel Cross asked.

"The power station is hundreds of years old. If I had enough time, I'd say it would be better to put our own reactor here, ma'am," Noah said.

"Break it down for me. Can we fire the cannon or not?" Colonel Cross asked.

Noah frowned. "We can, but—and this is a strong but—we can't predict the power fluctuations. The power converter we've installed attempts to manage them, but there's a significant risk that when the colossus cannon is fired in earnest, it could overload the entire system."

"So you're saying we have a gun that we can fire a few times, but if we sustain a high rate of fire the system will fail?" Colonel Cross asked.

"Yes, ma'am."

"What happens if the system fails?"

"It depends. The power converter could burn out, or if there's enough of an overload, we could lose the entire system in an explosion," Noah answered.

Colonel Cross blew out a breath and regarded him for a moment. "You have quite a reputation, so I know you've been working this problem for as long as you've been here."

"Thank you, ma'am," Noah said.

"I can tell you with absolute certainty that the Vemus are on their way here right now. We've engaged them at Sagan's line, and General Gates evacuated all nonessential personnel from Phoenix Station," Colonel Cross said.

Noah swallowed hard. "What happened?"

Colonel Cross leaned back against one of the desks. "We used your modified missile design and sent everything we had against them."

"Did it work?" Noah asked.

"At first. Then the Vemus launched countermeasures and were able to take out a high percentage of the HADES IV-Bs before they could reach their targets," Colonel Cross said, glancing at Lenora. "I'm not sure how much either of you knows."

"We haven't had any news," Lenora said.

"The Vemus are heading here in one massive ship, and the hull is made from the exoskeletal material we faced two months ago," Colonel Cross said.

"How big is the ship, Colonel?" Noah asked.

Colonel Cross looked at them grimly. "Twenty-two kilometers across."

Noah's eyes widened and he gasped. "That's not a ship. That's a flying city."

"We know the Vemus can absorb other ships. We think they've massed together somehow," Colonel Cross said.

"But why would they do that?" Lenora asked.

Colonel Cross shrugged. "This is likely their answer to our defenses. Together in one massive ship, they represent a single overwhelming force."

Noah's mind raced as he did the calculations. "We don't have enough missiles."

"No, we don't," Colonel Cross confirmed.

"What about the rest of the soldiers at Phoenix Station?" Lenora asked.

"They couldn't confirm the amount of damage we'd done. Phoenix Station still has other close-range weapons that will make the Vemus pay for every kilometer closer they get to New Earth," Colonel Cross said.

"What are their chances?" Lenora said, her eyes wide.

Colonel Cross looked at her solemnly and sighed. "I'm going to be honest with you. I'm sorry, but the chances of survival for anyone on Phoenix Station are virtually nonexistent."

Noah watched as Lenora's breath caught in her throat. Then her eyes flashed. "Connor has survived overwhelming odds before."

"I know. I was there. I wish I could tell you something different to give you some hope, but that would be a disservice to you," Colonel Cross said.

Lenora turned away from them. "I need to get some air," she muttered and fled the Command Center.

Noah looked at the colonel, and she nodded for him to speak.

"What do you need me to do, Colonel?" Noah asked.

"You have a little bit of time. I need that cannon operational for as long as you can give me. What we cannot have is blowing ourselves up in the process. You tell me what you need and I'll try and get it for you," Colonel Cross said.

Noah nodded, feeling suddenly lighter because Colonel Cross was there, but then he was dragged back down by the impending invasion. He began with what anyone solving complex problems should do, which was to start by listing their assets. Then they could come up with a plan of action. Noah and Colonel Cross got to work. He didn't know why Connor would have sent her here, but he was glad he had.

18

CAPTAIN WALKER WAITED outside the dull gray doors to the munitions factory aboard a large chunk of Vemus warship wreckage. He'd been watching the Vemus forces through the small window. Their skin was a deep, dark purple that glistened in the light. Their rounded heads angled to a pointed snout with lighter-toned oval shapes where Jon expected the eyes would be. They were clustered at the far end of the room. One of the Vemus towered above the others and pounded against the door while the others tried to beat their fists against the wall.

I'm coming, Brian, Jon thought. He could barely see the salvage team trapped in the room on the far side of the munitions factory floor. He checked his rifle and set the nano-robotic ammunition to incendiary. The high heat rounds worked best at disabling Vemus, according to his combat suit computer. Sergeant Lee and Lieutenant Chester hastened down the corridor. They'd just finished setting up the heavy turret, leaving the ammunition box attached. Jon accessed the heavy turret's camera and controls through his combat suit's systems. All systems were ready.

"Locked and loaded, Captain," Sergeant Lee said.

"Check your weapons," Jon said.

There was a flurry of activity as they all did one final check of their equipment, along with that of the people around them.

"We're ready, Captain," Lieutenant Chester said, giving him a determined look.

"Go ahead, Sergeant Lee, if you please," Jon said.

"Detonating the first group," Sergeant Lee said.

Jon heard the faint pops of the concussive charges and watched to see if the Vemus had heard anything. The Vemus soldiers ceased all activity and became rigidly still.

Sergeant Lee held up two of his fingers. There were more pops even louder than before. The Vemus soldiers began moving off to the side and out of sight—a few at a time at first and then more and more.

"It's working!" Jon said.

All the Vemus had run off, leaving the area. Jon slapped his palm against the door controls and the age-old contraption sputtered as the gears pulled the doors apart. They went inside. Jon kept the heavy turret's camera feed in the upper right corner of his heads-up display. There was still no sign of the Vemus.

"Blow the third group," Jon said.

He didn't wait for Sergeant Lee to respond but kept moving forward. They crouched as they ran, using the munitions factory lines as cover. Tall metal racks stood along the left side of the factory where two-hundred-year-old mag-cannon projectiles were secured in place. There were countless tips of two-meter projectiles perfectly aligned where the NA Alliance Navy had left them. Jon focused in on the room at the far end, and an IR channel opened to his combat suit.

"Jon, is that you?" Brian asked in disbelief.

"We've lured them away. This is your chance to get out. Come on, let's go," Jon said.

Jon heard someone shouting over the comms channel. They were yelling for Brian to open the door.

"What are you waiting for?" Jon asked.

"Jon, please stop," Brian said. "It's not safe for you. Take your team and get out of here."

"What are you talking about?" Jon asked.

He noticed some movement from the video feed of the heavy turret. The Vemus were making a sweep of the area. Jon and the others reached the end of the line of racks and stopped. He held his AR-71 ready and peered around the corner. The Vemus were gone. They hadn't left anyone to guard the prisoners. Jon crossed over to the door where Brian waited. The door control panel was broken and charred.

"Stop. We've been infected. We can't go back with you even if we wanted to," Brian said.

Jon heard more shouting and saw Captain Davis screaming for his brother to open the door.

Brian was pointing a pistol at Captain Davis. "Stay back," Brian said. "I'll shoot."

Another IR channel connected to Jon's combat armor.

"Walker, your brother is crazy. We're not infected. Tell him to let us go," Captain Davis said.

"Brian, you've got to calm down. We can figure this out. Come with me," Jon said.

He heard Lieutenant Chester mention they were running out of time.

Brian turned back toward the window. "Trust me, Jon," Brian said.

Jon felt as if he were hearing an echo of every time Brian had asked him to trust him. They were only a year apart in age, and no matter what they were doing, his younger brother was always there for him. Even after Jon left, Brian was always there when it counted.

Captain Davis screamed for Jon to open the door.

"Sir, the Vemus are at the turret," Sergeant Lee said.

"Activate the turret," Jon ordered.

He looked back through the window, trying to find some sign that the people inside the room were infected.

"You don't look sick," Jon said.

Brian swallowed. "We are. We've all been exposed. First comes the virus and then the parasite, except it works like nothing we've ever seen before. The virus alters the DNA of the host, allowing the parasite in, which takes over the host. It causes genes to express at an astonishing rate—never mind that. We're already dead."

Jon felt his throat become thick. "What if you're wrong?"

Brian glared at him. "Do I tell you how to fly a ship? Shoot a gun? No, because you know what you're doing. I'm *not* wrong."

"How did you even get exposed?" Jon asked.

Brian shook his head. "No time. There's more, much more I learned about them. Things the CDF can use. They're like nothing we've ever seen."

An uplink registered with Jon's combat suit computer using an active comlink. Jon's eyes widened. The Vemus could detect active comlinks.

"What are you doing? You'll bring them right to us!" Jon said.

"It's the only way to transfer the data fast enough. IR bandwidth is too narrow and the transfer will take too long," Brian said.

Jon slammed his fists against the metallic door. "What if you're wrong?"

Brian was watching Davis, who looked as if he were about to charge forward, pistol or not. Jon's gaze narrowed. Where were the salvage team's weapons? How did they only have a pistol? An alarm appeared on his internal heads-up display. The heavy turret was nearly out of ammunition. The video feed showed a corridor littered with the bodies of Vemus soldiers. There was a moving shadow along the ceiling, and the feed cut out. The heavy turret was offline.

"Captain—" Lieutenant Chester cried.

"I know," Jon said and looked back at his brother behind the smudgy window. A series of high-pitched whistles and clicks came from the corridor.

"Contact!" Sergeant Lee shouted.

Jon swung his rifle up and fired his weapon at a Vemus soldier. He took cover by the nearest rack, and the rest of the team did the same. They kept the Vemus pinned in the corridor. Dark liquid burst from their bodies. White bolts flew by as the Vemus returned fire.

Jon heard a startled cry from the IR channel and then heard the pistol go off from inside the room. Jon called out for his brother. The door opened, and Brian stumbled out of the room. Jon went to take a step toward him and then stopped. He couldn't risk it since Brian was infected.

Jon glanced at the grisly mess inside the room. "What have you done?" he said. Brian had killed the surviving members of the salvage team.

"They captured us. Caught us by surprise," Brian said.

Jon looked at the splatter of blood on Brian's EVA suit. He wasn't wearing a helmet, and there was a layer of thick black mucus ringed around his neck.

Brian threw his pistol down. "Give me your rifle. I'll hold them off for as long as I can."

"Captain, we can't stay here. We have to leave. Now!" Lieutenant Chester said.

Jon looked over at his team as they continued to lay suppressing fire toward the Vemus.

Brian rushed toward him and tried to grab his rifle. Jon spun away.

"Go, Jon. Get the data to CDF command. The key to stopping them is in there," Brian said.

Jon gritted his teeth and growled. He turned and fired his weapon at the Vemus. They were clustering in the doorway and were about to charge. A white bolt slammed into the end of the rack and knocked Jon off his feet. Hands grabbed him and he was pulled back. Jon regained his feet and saw that Brian was holding his rifle. Brian roared and then charged the Vemus, firing the AR-71 at full auto.

Jon cried out as his team pulled him away. He heard Brian screaming in rage until he was suddenly cut off.

"He's gone. We have to go, Captain," Lieutenant Chester said and took point, leading them away.

Sergeant Lee pushed him forward and Jon followed Lieutenant Chester, stumbling in a half daze. They reached another door and Jon withdrew his pistol. White bolts slammed into the door as it opened. They returned fire and hastened through the exit. There was movement to the right, and Jon fired his weapon. The Vemus charged toward them. Jon and the rest of the team ran away, firing a few rounds before retreating more. They came to the end of the corridor, and an explosive force slammed him against the wall. This place was coming apart. Jon and the others scrambled to their feet and headed for the ship in an all-out run. High-pitched whistles and clicks from the Vemus followed them. Jon glanced behind him and saw the Vemus closing in on them, propelling themselves on all fours and quickly eating up their small lead.

Jon tripped over something and dove to the ground, sliding down the corridor. He heard someone cry out as he quickly regained his feet. Specialist Thoran was sprawled on the ground behind him. He was climbing to his feet when the Vemus reached him. Jon watched in horror as a Vemus grabbed Specialist Thoran and hauled him back into the mass of soldiers as if he weighed nothing at all.

The big Vemus soldier turned back around, and its pointed snout revealed a line of sharp teeth. Jon fired his weapon, hitting it in the chest and muscled shoulders. The Vemus went down and then struggled to rise.

Sergeant Lee grabbed him. "He's gone. We have to go."

They turned and ran, heading for the airlock. Jon was the last one inside and they quickly shut the door. Jon looked through the window and saw the Vemus soldier he'd just shot rise to his feet and charge toward the airlock doors.

They ran into the combat shuttle.

"Cover that door," Jon said and ran toward the cockpit.

The combat shuttle was on standby and quickly came to full power. He heard something slamming against the shuttle's airlock doors. He disengaged the docking clamps and used the maneuvering thrusters to get away from the wreckage. Outside the shuttle's windows he saw dark shapes pouring out of the airlock into the vacuum. Jon didn't wait around. He engaged the main engines and sped away. Once they reached a safe distance, he fired a pair of hornet missiles, targeting the wreckage. There was a bright flash as the large chunk was blown apart.

"Captain, we have to follow decontamination protocols," Corporal Sims called out.

Jon inputted the coordinates for Lunar Base and set the navigation system on auto. It would be slow going since they were in a debris field, but he wasn't in a rush to go anywhere.

Jon climbed out of the chair and headed to the rear of the shuttle. He heard Sergeant Lee arguing with Corporal Sims.

"Captain, tell him to remain on his own life support. We have to follow emergency decontamination protocols, which now includes the shuttle," Corporal Sims said.

Jon looked over at Sergeant Lee, who was rocking back and forth, not making eye contact with anyone. He kept muttering about needing to get out of his combat suit.

"Roger, look at me," Jon said.

Sergeant Lee looked up at him.

"I need you to stay in that suit just a little longer. Can you do that?" Jon asked. His head was pounding and he felt like everything was trying to push its way out, but he tried to appear as calm as he sounded. "Alright. Just sit tight for a moment. We need to make sure we're not contaminated," Jon said.

Sergeant Lee gave a slight nod and continued to rock back and forth.

Jon looked back at Corporal Sims. "He'll be alright. Remind me again what we need to do."

Corporal Sims swallowed hard. "We need to vent the shuttle for a few minutes. The exposure should take care of anything that might have gotten on our suits."

Jon nodded. "Lieutenant Chester, prepare to vent the shuttle. Once we're vented, we'll open the rear hatch."

"Yes, Captain," Lieutenant Chester said and went to the rear of the shuttle.

There was a loud hiss as their atmosphere was sucked out of the shuttle. Auto-tethers attached to the back of their combat suits. Jon knew it was just a precaution, but he wouldn't want to risk being sucked out of the shuttle without a tether attached.

"Atmosphere vented. Opening the hatch and shutting down the heaters," Lieutenant Chester said.

The rear hatch opened and the debris field spread out before them. They waited the allotted time for the extreme cold to kill any microorganism they'd been exposed to on the Vemus ship.

Corporal Sims scanned them with the bioscanner. "We're clear, Captain."

"Close it up, Lieutenant," Jon said.

The rear hatch closed and they pressurized the shuttle. The heaters quickly brought the shuttle's interior up to acceptable temperatures and they were able to get out of their combat suits.

Sergeant Lee came over to him. "I'm sorry, Captain. Not sure what came over me. It was as if everything was closing in on me."

"It's fine, Sergeant. You stayed in control and followed orders," Jon said.

Jon felt his chest clench. Brian was gone. His brother was dead and they'd lost Specialist Thoran.

"We need to talk about what happened, Captain," Lieutenant Chester said.

Sorrow closed up his throat for a moment and Jon swallowed hard.

"Captain?" Lieutenant Chester asked softly.

"I'm alright. I just need a second, Daron," Jon said and looked away.

He squeezed his eyes shut and rubbed his forehead, feeling the stinging behind his eyes. "Damn it, Brian! Why did you have to go on that mission?" he said and looked at the others. "He should have been in the lab, not out on some salvage recon mission."

Lieutenant Chester regarded him for a moment. "What did he say happened?"

"He said they'd been captured. They were infected," Jon said.

Lieutenant Chester frowned. "I saw the room. He shot all of them."

Jon winced, remembering the sight of the dead salvage team members. "He said they were already dead."

"You knew him best. Could he have just lost it? You know, cracked under the pressure of being captured?" Lieutenant Chester asked.

Jon thought about it and shook his head. "Brian never lost his temper or anything like that. He was strong. He knew what he was doing. He was—"

Jon winced as a wave of grief slammed into him. He forced it back. "He wasn't crazy."

"What do we do now?" Corporal Sims asked.

Jon sighed. "We go back to Lunar Base."

"Empty-handed. We couldn't even rescue them," Sergeant Lee said.

"Not empty-handed. Brian learned something while they were on that wreckage. He said it was something we could use to stop the Vemus. We have to get the data he uploaded to my suit back to Lunar Base," Jon said.

"What's in the data?" Lieutenant Chester asked.

"I don't know, but I think it's time we have a look and see what was worth them dying for, don't you?" Jon replied.

19

CONNOR SAT in the commander's chair at Phoenix Station's main Command Center. Despite taking massive amounts of damage, the Vemus Alpha had increased speed after the Colonial Defense Force's surprise attack. They'd had the high-res optical array focused on the Vemus Alpha ship, and the images showed massive impacts to the colossal ship. Deep chasms were revealed in the exoskeletal hull that hadn't started to regenerate, but the ship hadn't altered course either.

Phoenix Station was directly in its path.

"General," Lieutenant Daniels said. "I have Captains Mason and Saunders from the Bravo and Charlie sub-Command Centers on comms."

"Put them through to my station, Lieutenant," Connor replied.

The holoscreen flickered on, and Captain Wade Mason and Captain Evelyn Saunders appeared on his screen.

"Station separation is just about ready. Can you confirm your status?" Connor asked.

"Bravo station is ready for separation from the main, General," Captain Mason said.

"Charlie station is ready as well, General," Captain Saunders said.

"Very well. We'll stay networked for as long as possible so our attacks can be coordinated, but I'm going to level with both of you. At some point it won't be possible. In that moment, your only mandate is to fire your station's weapons at the enemy for as long as possible. Is that clear?" Connor asked.

"Yes, General," the two captains said.

Connor looked at the station sub-commanders on his holoscreen. Beneath the brave facade were two officers as green as anyone else untested in combat. He'd considered reassigning Major Elder to one of the substations but decided to keep him at Phoenix Station Main with him. One went into battle with the army one had.

"This is what we trained for. Remember your training. We have an objective to achieve. It's as simple as that," Connor said.

"We won't let you down, General," Captain Mason said.

"I know you won't. Now, the second wave of our attack will begin once we reach our target coordinates. Good luck to you both," Connor said.

Both captains repeated the sentiment. They knew the stakes and thought they knew what it was going to be like when the end finally came. But Connor had been in enough dangerous situations to know that when death does finally claim you, it's when you least expect it. He cut the comlink, and the holoscreen powered off.

Phoenix Station was made up of ten large sections. Each of the sections could be self-contained and operate autonomously, though there were only three Command Centers. Connor had decided to break Phoenix Station up into three primary sections, with the central section containing four subsections while the two remaining groups were comprised of three subsections. He thought that the Vemus Alpha having multiple targets would enable the CDF to strike another devastating blow. Over sixty-five percent of the HADES IV-B missiles had reached their target before the Vemus unleashed their countermeasures that took out the command-and-control units. If all the Command Centers were to become inoperable, the burden of engaging the enemy would fall to individual gun-battery commanders.

"At least the wave of Condor missiles is over," Major Elder said. He sat in the executive officer's station next to Connor.

"I think they fired them just to give us something to do," Connor said.

"They fired thousands of missiles at us to occupy us until they could get here to finish the job? I'm not sure I understand those tactics," Major Elder said.

"Condor missiles are the NA Alliance Military's design for long-range engagements. Our HADES IV-Bs have better targeting systems," Connor said.

"Thank god for that," Major Elder said.

Connor agreed. In addition, their point-defense lasers were able to confuse the Condor missiles' guidance systems enough that they could disable them completely. Once compromised, the fact that the Condor missiles didn't retarget reaffirmed Connor's conclusion that those missiles weren't the real attack. It had been a bullying tactic by an enemy that knew the superiority of its position and attack force.

"Ops, has there been any detection of the Vemus control signal?" Connor asked.

"Negative, General," Lieutenant Rawn said.

"Alright," Connor said. He strongly believed that the Vemus had other ships tucked away in that Alpha, but they hadn't detected them. "You're a go to disengage station sections three and eight," Connor said.

"Confirmed, General. Disengaging sections three and eight," Lieutenant Rawn said.

Connor looked at the main holoscreen, which showed a live video feed of the locking clamps that held Phoenix Station together. There was a brief flash that simultaneously appeared on all the video feeds.

"Station sections disengaged, General," Lieutenant Rawn said.

"Acknowledged," Connor said.

He watched as the maneuvering thrusters pushed the two sections away from them. He glanced over to his left and noted the empty space beside him. It had been nearly fifteen hours since he'd sent Colonel Cross and Major Quinn back to New Earth, but he still found himself looking for Sean. He didn't regret his decision to put Sean in charge of the CDF ground forces, but he did miss him.

"General," Major Elder said.

Connor looked up and saw Captain Randle walking toward the command area. Standing at six feet, seven inches tall, Wayne Randle was a giant among men. The working CDF soldiers seemed to part ways, allowing the big man to pass.

"Good of you to join us, Bull," Connor said, using the designation he'd given Captain Randle in Search and Rescue all those years before.

"Wouldn't miss this, General. I've come to inform you that most of the drill-mines have successfully sent in return statuses," Captain Randle said.

"So they made it to the Vemus Alpha," Connor said.

"Yes, they should be drilling beneath that exoskeleton of theirs, sir," Captain Randle said.

"Should? We don't know for sure, Captain Randle?" Major Elder asked.

"No, Major. This is a low-tech solution whereby we can receive only a confirmation that they reached the surface of the Vemus Alpha. The timer starts and they'll detonate the explosive payload at whatever level they reach," Captain Randle said.

"Is there any way to determine how deep those drills will get before they detonate, Captain?" Major Elder asked.

"It depends on how thick that exoskeletal hull is and when those drill heads come into contact with the hardened alloy of the battle-steel hull of a ship. The drill heads can chew through quite a bit before they'll eventually dull. We've staggered the timers so when they *do* detonate, we can maximize the damage to the ship. Worst case is that the drill-heads are only able to penetrate twenty or so meters before they detonate, sir," Captain Randle said.

"Thank you, Captain," Connor said.

"General, with your permission I'd like to stay by your side," Captain Randle said.

Connor arched a brow while considering. "Did Major Quinn happen to put you up to this?"

"I can neither confirm nor deny that Major Quinn sent me any informal instructions upon his departure from Phoenix Station, General," Captain Randle said with only a hint of a smile appearing over his wide jaw.

Connor snorted. "Alright, Captain. You can help Captain Thorne at Tactical."

"Yes, General," Captain Randle said and went over to the tactical work area.

Connor looked over at the PRADIS output on one of the secondary holoscreens. The Vemus Alpha was still coming steadily toward them. It hadn't changed its trajectory and Connor couldn't order Phoenix Station to be moved. They would make their stand here. He opened a broadcast channel.

"This is General Gates. By now you've been informed that we're about to begin our engagement with the enemy. We drew the line here on the doorstep to our home. Thousands of people are depending on us. For the first time in human history, we're fighting for something that's unprecedented—our right to survive as a species. On this day we will stand together and in one voice scream into the void. Our enemy will know what we can do—that we will not be vanquished without a fight. This was to be a colony founded upon peace, moving beyond the hundreds of years of conflicts throughout history. None of you deserve to have to fight in this war. None of our families deserve to die at the hands of our enemies. We few, standing here, looking into the mouth of the dragon and showing our enemy what we're worth, are all that stands between us and them, to stop them from killing us all. We stand together. We fight together. And we'll *die* together if that's what it takes. Many of you know who I am, that I used to serve with an elite special-forces platoon. We were legends. But all of you are part of the Colonial Defense Force and are much more than the Ghosts ever were. You fight for something beyond anything we ever did. The Ghosts had a motto, and I'll give it to you. Remember these words as we face our enemy. 'We are the unsung heroes. We are the quiet protectors. We roam through the darkest nights and through the deepest valleys. We choose to stand the watch. No enemy is beyond our power. We are the Colonial Defense Force!'"

The soldiers in the command area cheered.

"Ten-hut!" Captain Randle's voice boomed.

The cheering CDF soldiers became quiet almost instantly as all of them stood with their arms at their sides and their shoulders back at attention.

"CDF salute!" Captain Randle shouted.

As one, the CDF soldiers saluted Connor. He raised his chin and felt his chest swell with pride as he returned the salute in kind. The soldiers returned to their stations with renewed vigor.

Major Elder leaned toward Connor. "Thank you, sir. They needed that, and, frankly, so did I."

Connor nodded grimly. "Too bad pretty speeches won't stop the Vemus."

"I had no idea that the NA Alliance Special Forces had a motto like that, sir," Major Elder said.

Connor glanced at the major. There was no one on this station who knew the truth.

Major Elder frowned and his eyes widened.

"I'll say whatever I need to so the men and women in the CDF can focus on their jobs," Connor said.

Major Elder nodded. "I understand, sir."

"I know you do. Now, we have a job to do," Connor said.

Connor went back to the command chair. "Tactical, what's the status of the Vemus Alpha?"

"They're within energy weapons range. We were keeping the kinetic weapons in reserve, General," Captain Thorne said.

"I need a firing solution targeting the damaged areas of the enemy ship. Let's see if we can peel back a few more layers and make them bleed some more," Connor said.

"Yes, General," Captain Thorne said. A few minutes passed. "Firing solution ready. Specs are on the main holoscreen, General."

Connor looked up at the screen. "One change to that, Captain. Phoenix Station Main will fire first, then Bravo and Charlie sections."

"Yes, General, updating targeting parameters now," Captain Thorne replied. Connor waited for confirmation from Bravo and Charlie sections.

"Fire!" Connor said.

As the twenty-two-kilometer Vemus Alpha blasted through space, heading for Phoenix Station, a rounded projector swiveled above one of the top sections of the main Phoenix Station group. The magnetic actuators steered the stored-up energy to a wide-open port, and a thick particle beam of protons shot forth in a lance of pale blue light. The proton beam penetrated the Vemus exoskeletal hull before it had to be cycled. Moments later, beams from Bravo and Charlie subsections also cut deeply into the hull of the enemy ship.

"Vemus Alpha taking damage, General," Captain Thorne said.

"Keep firing on them. Ready plasma cannons," Connor said.

They had to keep hitting the enemy ship for as long as they could, and Connor approved the plasma cannon firing solution. Phoenix Station's stabilizing engines went into overdrive to keep them in position. The lights in Phoenix Station's Command Center dimmed as the plasma cannons charged off the main reactor. Next, Connor heard the rapid cadence of magnetically encased plasma bolts being fired into the vacuum. As the bolts traveled, the fusion cores reached a maximum yield in the multi-megaton range. The superheated plasma bolts slammed into the Vemus Alpha. The power draw from Phoenix Station's multiple fusion reactor cores was immense. Connor had the engineers override the safeties so they could run the reactors at critical levels. They needed every ounce of power they could get. Unlike when the Vemus had faced Titan Station, which operated at half the capacity possible, Phoenix Station had an excess of power yield. The reactor cores had been designed for a Barracuda-class battleship carrier and could handle the load.

"Vemus Alpha taking heavy damage, General," Captain Thorne said.

Connor looked at the tactical data feeds. The cyber-warfare AI disseminated and correlated data coming in from all their sensor arrays, giving the CDF the most accurate picture possible of the damage they were doing to the enemy.

"Proton beams are cycling through a down cycle, General," Captain Thorne said.

"Enable Kraken firing solution now," Connor ordered.

Rail-cannons came online. The Vemus Alpha was within kinetic weapons range, which also put Phoenix Station within the known weapons range of the Vemus Alpha. Connor glanced at the latest image of the Alpha. There were immense gashes gouged away from the exoskeletal hull, revealing the dark innards beneath, but it was a blackened section eight kilometers across that seemed to be the soft spot.

"Focus targeting on that dark section off the center," Connor said.

The rail-cannons fired a range of two-to-three-meter projectiles in rapid succession. The long barrels swiveled from side to side, giving the projectiles time to penetrate as deeply as possible before more of them hit. Connor watched as they unloaded Phoenix Station's vast arsenal into the most damaged parts of the Vemus Alpha. He squinted as he tried to make out the details of the visual on the holoscreen.

"Several large pieces of Vemus Alpha's hull have broken away," Captain Thorne announced.

Connor's pulse raced, and Major Elder looked over at him with a hungry gleam in his eyes.

"Don't let up. Keep hitting those spots," Connor said.

"Yes, General," Captain Thorne said.

"General, we're getting multiple reports of weapons overload," Captain Randle said.

"Adjust firing rate down to seventy-five percent and decrease in five percent increments as needed," Connor said.

There were limits to what their weapons could do, but he had to push it. They were breaking the enemy apart.

"Multiple energy signatures being detected on the Vemus Alpha," Captain Thorne announced.

Connor shared a grim glance with Major Elder. Their luck was running out. The Vemus Alpha was about to show them their teeth.

"Incoming enemy fire!" Captain Thorne said.

Connor watched as the tactical holodisplay showed a bright flash of light lancing toward them, and he gripped the sides of his chair as the colossal blast slammed into Phoenix Station with unrelenting force. Connor gritted his teeth, and klaxon alarms blared throughout the Command Center.

"General, we've lost subsection seven. It's showing as completely offline," Captain Thorne said.

Subsection seven held over three hundred CDF soldiers, and their lives had been snuffed out in the blink of an eye.

"Damage report," Connor said.

"Bulkhead doors have sealed off the damaged sections. We've lost twenty percent weapons capability," Captain Thorne said and frowned as new data appeared on his screen.

"What is the status of Bravo and Charlie stations?" Connor asked.

Captain Thorne remained focused on his screen as if he couldn't quite believe what he was seeing.

"Charlie station has been completely destroyed," Captain Randle announced.

Connor gasped and brought up the data feed. Charlie station was completely offline.

"Bravo station is still firing their weapons on the enemy ship," Captain Thorne said.

Connor looked at PRADIS, and the Vemus Alpha was closing in on them. "What the hell are they hitting us with?"

He couldn't think of anything in the NA Alliance arsenal that had such a high yield.

"Tactical, update targeting priority to target their main weapons," Connor ordered.

Connor clenched his teeth. They had to disable those weapons or they were sitting ducks.

"Updates inputted into targeting computers," Captain Thorne said.

The Vemus Alpha fired its main weapon, and a lance of molten plasma blazed toward Bravo Station, burning at two billion degrees Kelvin. The interior of the plasma lance burned hotter than the interior of the sun. The hardened alloy of the battle-steel armor plating didn't stand a chance as the plasma lance sliced through Bravo Station, cutting it down the middle. The Vemus restarted their terrible weapons to finish them off. Plasma lances stemmed from three main batteries on the Vemus Alpha, and they were all pointed at Bravo Station. Phoenix Station Main fired their remaining weapons—which consisted of much less powerful plasma cannons and rail-cannons—at the enemy ship. They pelted the regions around the Vemus Alpha's primary weapons systems. One of them went offline and the plasma lance simply stopped, but it was too late for Bravo Station.

Connor ordered them to go to their own life support. Their battle uniforms were comprised of a thin layer of EVA-suit material, and the thick collars stored an emergency helmet. The Vemus Alpha retargeted their remaining weapons on Phoenix Station Main. Connor could still hear their own weapons firing, for all the good it would do. Multiple systems went offline as the Vemus Alpha's weapon cut them apart. The stabilizing engines were damaged, and Phoenix Station Main rolled onto its back, exposing its belly for the enemy ship to strike. Another blow of unrelenting force struck the station, and the last thing Connor saw was a brilliant flash of light before everything went dark.

20

NATHAN HAD SCHEDULED the watches so he'd be on duty when Phoenix Station finally engaged the Vemus Alpha ship. The bulk of Lunar Base was located more than a kilometer underground. They'd used the lunar crust as a natural barrier that protected them from the dangers of being exposed on the lunar surface. While the moon did have an iron core that provided a weak magnetic field to protect them from cosmic rays and gamma bursts, it couldn't do anything to prevent the level of destruction he saw occurring on Phoenix Station. Despite the Vemus Alpha taking heavy damage, the enemy ship had closed the distance and then unleashed the full force of its weapons. Nathan and the rest of the CDF soldiers on duty in the Command Center had watched the data feeds flood in until Phoenix Station went offline. Ever since, the CDF staff in the Command Center of Lunar Base had taken to quietly working, with a soft buzz of activity that arose from hushed discussions.

Major Vanessa Shelton entered the Command Center and walked toward Nathan, coming to stand by his side.

"I thought I'd lend a hand, Colonel," Major Shelton said.

Nathan nodded. More than one off-duty officer had found their way to the Command Center, looking for something to do. Nathan certainly didn't want to take any downtime lest all the thoughts he'd been holding at bay threatened to overwhelm him.

"I'm glad you came because I can certainly use your help," Nathan said and shared the holoscreens he'd been working from with Major Shelton. "These are the latest projections of the damage Phoenix Station was able to do to the Vemus Alpha."

Major Shelton's eyes slid over the data as she studied it. Above the data was a three-dimensional graphical display of the Vemus Alpha, and it showed that large chunks of it had been destroyed during the attack. "Those sections toward the rear that are breaking away from the Alpha . . . are those . . .?"

"We think they're ships," Nathan said.

Major Shelton's eyes widened in shock for a moment. "Have these feeds been updated into our passive scanner data?"

"Yes. This is the latest iteration," Nathan said.

Several large ships had detached themselves from the Vemus Alpha's main hull.

"What would you do if you were the Vemus?" Nathan asked.

"There would be a lot of assumptions, but if my objective was to invade this world, I'd be keen to find any hidden defenses that might still be in place. Given how this war has been fought, I'd be expecting it," Major Shelton said.

"I agree. That's why I expect one of those ships to be sent here to look for any CDF presence," Nathan said.

"Well, we've evacuated the surface installations and moved people into the interior of the base. So, they could look for us, but they won't find us," Major Shelton said.

"Are you sure about that?" Nathan asked.

Major Shelton regarded Nathan for a moment. "Colonel, if you think the enemy is wise to our presence here and an attack is imminent, shouldn't we be preparing to attack them?"

Nathan pressed his lips together. "That's the rub. We don't know what our enemy knows. Until we have credible evidence that suggests otherwise, we'll operate under the assumption that they don't know we're here."

"How much evidence would you need to order an attack, sir?" Major Shelton asked.

Nathan blew out a breath. "It's a fine line to walk. We'll need to maintain Dark-Star status for the time being, even as they insert their forces into orbit around New Earth."

Major Shelton swallowed hard. "Colonel . . ." she began. "Isn't there anything we can do? Phoenix Station weapons did a lot of damage. If we bring our systems online, we should be able to do as much damage, and perhaps even more."

"If we attack now, the Vemus would be expecting it. We need the element of surprise to maximize the damage we can do," Nathan replied.

"If we do that, the Vemus will be able to land an invasion force on the ground, sir," Major Shelton said.

"I know," Nathan said and then held up one of his hands. "When General Gates and I discussed the strategy for Lunar Base's role in defense of the planet, our best bet was to allow the enemy to be lulled into a false sense of security and then strike. It took me a while to see the wisdom of General Gates' thinking."

"But Colonel, if the Vemus reach the surface of the planet, we'd be risking the exposure of everything living on the planet to this viral parasite organism. What if it finds a way to spread itself among the creatures native to this world?" Major Shelton asked.

"Even our scientific experts believe that risk isn't as high as one would expect.

The creatures of this world followed a very different evolutionary path. They're likely not as susceptible to the Vemus as we originally thought," Nathan replied.

Major Shelton frowned. "You mean because Earth scientists modified the viral strain?"

Nathan could tell that Major Shelton didn't think much of the gamble. "It's a risk. If we strike at the Vemus now, we'd do some damage, but we'd likely not stop them completely. They'd still get an invasion force onto the planet. Take that as a given. And if they defeat us, the Vemus can land as many of their troops on the ground as they want, knowing we have no more orbital defenses available."

"But isn't that their ultimate goal? Land their forces on the ground? They *are* hunting humans after all, sir," Major Shelton said.

"Yes, but it won't happen as fast as you might think," Nathan said. "First they'll need to assess the planet to find our cities, and that will take some time. All planetary broadcasts have been quiet since we first detected the Vemus presence. If the Vemus *did* somehow trace our communications, it would only lead them to communications satellites that have been powered down and put on standby. So it will take them some time to find Sierra and the other cities on the planet."

"I think I understand better now, Colonel," Major Shelton said.

"Also, if we strike at them while they're focused on getting their invasion force to the ground, they'll be even more vulnerable to attack," Nathan said.

"I agree, but . . ." Major Shelton said and stopped.

Nathan understood all too well. His first instinct was to strike out at the enemy and try to stop them in their tracks, but the fact of the matter was that the CDF couldn't prevent the Vemus Alpha from reaching New Earth. That became abundantly clear as the ship bludgeoned its way through Phoenix Station.

"Colonel, we're getting active comms signals," Sergeant Boers said.

Nathan looked over at the comms station. "From where?"

"Escape-pod frequency, Colonel," Sergeant Boers said.

Nathan felt his insides go cold. "How many pods are there?" Nathan asked, fearing the answer.

"Seven hundred in total, Colonel," Sergeant Boers said.

Nathan looked at the main holoscreen with the PRADIS output. It had been populated with the escape-pod broadcast signatures. Considering eight people to a pod, maximum, there could be over five thousand soldiers alive and in need of rescue.

"What are your orders, Colonel?" Lieutenant LaCroix asked from the tactical work area.

"Acknowledged receipt of escape-pod broadcast signatures. Dark-Star status will be maintained. Send no reply," Nathan said.

"But, Colonel—" Lieutenant LaCroix said.

"You've heard Colonel Hayes. You have your orders, Lieutenant," Major Shelton said sternly.

Nathan watched the main holodisplay grimly as the seven hundred escape-pod signatures were grayed out so they hardly had any impression on the display.

Inwardly, Nathan was raging. He wanted to order a rescue mission and get those survivors to safety, but he knew it would be a foolish call.

"Colonel, one of the Vemus ships has broken away from the main group and is on an intercept heading with the escape pods," Lieutenant LaCroix said.

Nathan resisted the urge to rub his hands over his face. "Acknowledged," he said, his voice sounding strained.

A grim silence settled throughout the CDF soldiers serving in the command area. They were being forced to do something that went contrary to basic human nature—abandoning those who needed their help. Though it was in service of the greater objective, that was a cold comfort and Nathan hated himself for it, even if the strategist in him knew it was the right thing to do. If he somehow managed to survive this, would he even be able to look at himself in the mirror?

Over the next few hours, the Vemus Alpha slowly approached New Earth as the news of Phoenix Station's destruction spread throughout the base. Nathan had kept going through the data, hoping to find some indication that there were survivors other than those in the escape pods that had jettisoned. There wasn't any. Phoenix Station was nothing more than a debris field. The escape pods had ceased broadcasting as the Vemus ship came within their vicinity, and Lunar Base couldn't determine whether the Vemus had captured the seven hundred escape pods or simply destroyed them all. The only thing they knew for sure was that they had stopped broadcasting a signal.

Two ships broke away from the Vemus Alpha, heading toward New Earth's moon.

"Passive scans show the ships are Cruiser-class vessels, Colonel," Lieutenant LaCroix said.

Lunar Base was still getting data feeds from robotic scanning platforms they had in orbit around the planet, and they'd been tracking the Vemus Alpha since it crossed Sagan's line and then engaged Phoenix Station at the Lagrange point. The Vemus Alpha had decreased its acceleration, slowing its approach to the planet, while the Vemus cruisers were heading for the moon. The cruisers inserted themselves into a lunar synchronous orbit and were actively scanning the surface where the construction platforms had been.

"Colonel, they're charging their weapons," Lieutenant LaCroix said.

"Acknowledged," Nathan said. "Ops, confirm that those surface installations have been evacuated."

"Zero life-signs, Colonel--," Sergeant Martinez began. "Sir! I'm seeing activity at one of the smaller research and development facilities in sector twenty-seven."

Nathan frowned. "Comms, are their systems still attached to the internal network?"

Sergeant Boers worked through her terminal and nodded. "Yes, Colonel. Comms channel is available."

"Put me through," Nathan said.

"R&D outpost eight. This is Dr. Kendra Robinson."

"Dr. Robinson, you need to power down that outpost and head to your evacuation point immediately. We have two Vemus cruisers inbound," Nathan said.

"Negative, Colonel. We've received a data communication from Dr. Walker's salvage run that claims they've found critical information about the Vemus," Dr. Robinson said, her voice sounding spotty from the low-powered comms channel.

Nathan watched the scope as it showed the Vemus cruisers inbound to the R&D outpost. They only stopped to fire their weapons at the surface installations. "Doctor, you need to listen to me and get your people out of there. The Vemus ships are doing a reconnaissance flyover. They're taking out all surface installations."

Nathan was waiting for a reply when Lieutenant LaCroix suddenly shifted in his seat. "Colonel, I have a surface gun battery being brought online."

Nathan swore. "Find out who it is," he said and then switched back to the R&D outpost comms channel. "Dr. Robinson, confirm that you've heard me."

"We hear you, Colonel. Shutting down the outpost now," Dr. Robinson said.

Nathan closed the channel and glanced at Major Shelton. "Can they make it to the nearby shelter?"

"If they hurry, they can, Colonel," Major Shelton said.

Nathan swung his gaze toward Lieutenant LaCroix. "What's the status of the gun battery?"

"Colonel, they're refusing to shut it down. There's a Lieutenant Robinson who won't comply with your commands. He's switched on the manual override," Lieutenant LaCroix said.

Nathan frowned. "Robinson," he repeated and then his eyes widened. "Ops, get a security detail over there ASAP."

Nathan heard Sergeant Martinez begin speaking to a security detail in the area. He looked up at the screen. "Damn it, there's no time. LaCroix, can you cut the power to that gun battery?"

Lieutenant LaCroix's face became pale. "Sir, he's defending his wife."

"I know that, Lieutenant!" Nathan snapped. "It's them or all of us. Now cut the damn power to that gun battery. Shut it down!"

Lieutenant LaCroix swung his flustered gaze toward his console, and his hands flew through the interface. "Power has been cut off to the gun battery. I've locked out the override and closed the doors."

There was a bright flash on the main holoscreen video feed of the R&D outpost. One moment it was there and the next it was gone. Nathan's mouth went dry and he checked the surface scanners. No one from the R&D outpost had escaped. They were all dead.

"Ops, any change in the cruiser's flight pattern?" Nathan asked.

"Negative, Colonel. They're maintaining speed and heading," Sergeant Martinez said.

That was something at least.

"Ops, let me know when the security detail has Robinson in custody," Nathan said.

There were several surprised glances from the CDF soldiers in the command area. Nathan's brows pulled together sternly. "Listen up. We're at war. Anyone who fails to follow orders will be relieved of duty, brought up on charges of treason, and shot. Is that clear?"

"Yes, Colonel," the CDF soldiers in the area answered.

Nathan nodded grimly and felt a sneer lift his upper lip. But what surprised him was that he would carry out his threat. This was what it meant to survive, and the thought sickened him to no end.

21

MAJOR SEAN QUINN stood on the rooftop of the Colonial Defense Force Headquarters in Sierra. The sun shone brightly over the cradle of New Earth's first colonial city as it stretched out around him. Over a hundred and fifty thousand people had lived here. What had started out as an encampment for a few thousand colonists was well on its way to becoming a full-blown metropolis. He glanced upward, remembering the *Ark* as it had been when it was orbiting their new home. One of humanity's most ambitious efforts, the *Ark* had been the biggest ship he'd ever seen—so large, in fact, that it had been easily visible in New Earth's night sky even with the planetary rings that surrounded the planet.

He'd been among the first to be awakened after their two-hundred-year journey, and those early days of the colony seemed like a lifetime ago. So much had changed. Sean's gaze sank back to the city. The Vemus Alpha dwarfed even the *Ark*. A shiver traveled up Sean's spine, snapping him out of his reverie. He narrowed his gaze as he took in the city through the eyes of a defender. He saw the CDF soldiers setting up multiple defense installations in preparation for an invasion that was difficult for them to comprehend. Mostly, the installations were outfitted with RF mag-cannons whose mobile platforms not only allowed them to track targets in the sky but on the ground as well.

Connor had sent him back to New Earth with orders to defend Sierra. After reviewing their defenses and knowing the Vemus Alpha was on its way here, he wasn't sure how long the city *could* be defended.

To say that his presence was a surprise was an understatement, but when he'd informed the colonial government of his orders, they were met with little enthusiasm. He'd expected as much.

The door to the rooftop opened and Sean glanced over. Captain Juan Diaz strode over to him and saluted.

"We've received news from Phoenix Station, Major. Please come with me," Captain Diaz said.

"Last I checked, comlinks still worked," Sean replied.

Captain Diaz chuckled. "But they lack that personal touch, sir."

"Well, I better not keep them waiting," Sean said and started walking toward the door.

"Connor thinks the world of you, you know," Captain Diaz said.

Sean glanced at Diaz as they were heading back to the Command Center. "Becoming sentimental on me now?"

Captain Diaz chuckled. "It comes with being a father. And I remember seeing the look on Connor's face when he found you in that storage crate."

"He wouldn't have let me come otherwise," Sean replied, remembering how, seven years ago after being denied entry to the new Field Ops Search and Rescue team, he'd snuck into a storage crate bound for the remote training camp. He'd had no idea Connor intended to dump all the equipment and recruits out of the Hellcat transport for a low-altitude drop. Looking back on his actions, he realized how foolish a risk he'd taken. There were so many other ways he could have gotten to the training camp that wouldn't have required the risk of life and limb. Regardless, his life had been forever changed because of it.

Captain Diaz stopped in front of the door to the Command Center and looked at him. He leaned in. "Connor sent you back here to lead," Diaz said.

Sean frowned. "I know, but they aren't listening," he said.

"The CDF soldiers here will follow you. You just need to prove to the rest of them why they *should* listen to you. No one else here has faced the Vemus but you, sir," Captain Diaz said.

Sean remembered Juan Diaz being his superior officer when he was a fresh-faced recruit. Things had changed. Diaz had always insisted that he was only good for command at a certain level, while people like Connor operated at another level entirely. One thing Connor had instilled in the CDF ranks was to respect the uniform. The person who had that rank and uniform had earned it, something those outside of the CDF had trouble understanding. They judged by what they saw, and what they saw was a very young man who had attained a very high rank.

Sean gave Diaz a nod and then entered the Command Center.

Damon Mills, Director of Field Ops and Security Operations, glanced over at him. "Major Quinn, Phoenix Station has been destroyed. Transmitting the latest information from the station's data dump to you now."

Sean's lips pressed together in a white slash, and he used his neural implants to access the data. His internal smart lens projected the reports away from his eyes, so they were easily read by him, and the others around him couldn't see them. Sean quickly went through the preliminary report. The Vemus Alpha's primary weapon had been devastatingly effective.

"They were overwhelmed, but it looks like they did heavy damage as well," Sean said. "Call an emergency session of the city defense committee."

Director Mills relayed Sean's commands. "We can use the conference room over here."

Sean shook his head. "No need. We'll have the call right here. This won't take a lot of time."

"Most of the committee members are already here, and the ones that aren't can join in remotely," Director Mills said.

Sean frowned and peered over at the conference room. He saw his father pacing while speaking with other civilians around the conference table. Sean gritted his teeth and walked over. Damon Mills followed him.

"Why has Lunar Base gone quiet? These reports show that it hasn't used any of its weapons to engage that enemy ship," Parish said.

"We've been over this. General Gates' strategy was to keep Lunar Base in the dark to hide its presence from the enemy," Sean's father said.

"But with Phoenix Station—" Stanton Parish stopped speaking as Sean walked into the conference room. The committee members looked at Sean as if they weren't quite sure what to make of him.

"I see you've heard about Phoenix Station," Sean said.

"Yes, just a few minutes ago. We were just discussing it," Tobias replied.

Sean glanced behind him. "Captain Diaz," he said.

"Yes, Major," Captain Diaz replied.

"From now on, all CDF communications stay within CDF channels unless I give my express permission for them to be shared," Sean said.

Tobias frowned.

"This includes Field Ops and Security," Sean said before anyone could protest.

"Right away, Major," Captain Diaz said and left the room.

"What are you doing?" Tobias asked him.

"Yes, why cut us out?" Stanton asked.

Sean drew in a deep breath. "Why don't you all sit down," he said and glanced back at Director Mills, who watched him warily. "You too, Director."

The defense committee members looked at his father, who nodded for them to sit. He then regarded Sean for a moment before doing the same.

Sean looked at Stanton Parish. "You're not being cut out. The comms officer didn't follow protocol for CDF briefings. This lapse will be rectified."

"What difference does it make if we read the same briefing that goes to the CDF?" Stanton asked.

"Because you're not qualified to read them. There's a reason that filter's in place," Sean said.

"I beg your pardon?" Stanton said, flustered.

"You heard me," Sean replied crisply. "The status of Phoenix Station is a military matter and should have come to me first. I heard what you were saying when I walked in. Why didn't Colonel Hayes at Lunar Base fire his weapons at the Vemus Alpha? That's what you were pressing for, is that right?"

"It's a valid question," Stanton said.

"It's not what General Gates ordered," Sean replied.

"But he might be dead for all we know," Stanton said.

"Phoenix Station is offline, and the status of CDF personnel is currently unknown," Sean said.

His father cleared his throat. "Don't you mean destroyed?"

Sean's gaze hardened. "I meant offline. Destroyed implies that there are no survivors, which I don't believe until we can do our own reconnaissance of the area. As you're aware, I've been given operational authority for the CDF ground forces." Sean looked over at Director Mills. "Since this is a wartime situation, this includes Field Operations and Security forces as well. I expect you to comply with these agreed-upon orders."

Director Mills pressed his lips together. "When we made those laws, we assumed General Gates would be the person leading the CDF."

Several heads were nodding in agreement.

"He still *is* leading the CDF," Sean replied coolly.

"Sean," his father said, "Phoenix Station is . . . offline. Colonel Savannah Cross is next in the chain of command."

"Let me be crystal clear with all of you. General Gates assigned Colonel Cross to Sanctuary, and he assigned me to command our ground forces. I don't require your agreement with the commands of my superiors in order to carry them out," Sean said.

His father's eyes widened. "What are you going to do? Arrest all of us?"

"No, but I will have you shipped out to Sanctuary on the next available transport. Civilians have no place in this fight. You'll only get in the way of the soldiers," Sean replied.

His father's gaze narrowed angrily. "What about Director Mills? Are you going to remove him and anyone else who gets in your way?"

"Stop this right now!" Sean said, slamming his fist on the table. "I can't afford to waste time convincing you who's in charge. My job is to defend this city from the Vemus forces, not to waste precious time mincing words with all of you."

His father started to speak again.

"I swear, if this is another protest, I'll have a squad of my soldiers escort the lot of you out of here right now," Sean said, glaring at his father.

Director Mills cleared his throat. "I think we all need to take a moment to calm down."

His father took a steadying breath, and Sean looked at Director Mills.

"I'm not going to challenge your authority," Director Mills said and then glanced at the other committee members. "We have laws we all agreed on. One thing I have absolute faith in is that General Gates does nothing without careful consideration. He's sent Major Quinn here on his authority, and I will respect that."

Tobias cleared his throat. "Can you tell us your strategy for defending the city?"

"I think we're forgetting the fact that Lunar Base is there with enough firepower to finish what Phoenix Station started," Stanton said.

"They *don't* have enough," Sean said. "I was there. I saw what was coming for us. Colonel Hayes is following his orders."

"But he could—" Stanton began.

"I know you're scared and I'd be lying to you if I said things aren't going to get any worse. The fact is, we can't stop the Vemus from reaching New Earth. No matter what we do, we simply cannot," Sean said and looked at the defense committee members, giving them a few moments for it to sink in.

Stanton drew in a breath to speak again.

"Enough, Stanton," Tobias said. "We can't defeat this enemy with clever arguments. General Gates doesn't promote anyone who follows orders blindly. The CDF has seen the data and believe that keeping with General Gates' original plan has the greatest chance of success. Let's move on. Major, you were about to tell us about your strategy for defending this city."

Sean swallowed hard. "I've reviewed what's been done to bolster the city's defense here and also in the other settlements. None of you will like what I'm about to tell you."

An ominous silence took hold of the defense committee.

"We've been preparing for the worst. Why don't you tell us what you have in mind?" Director Mills said.

"We can't hold this city," Sean said.

The committee members divided their gazes between Sean's father and Director Mills.

"I don't believe this. After all the work we put in to make the city as defensible as possible, you come in here and say we've wasted our time?" Stanton said.

Sean shook his head. "I didn't say that. And the work that went into the defense of this city wasn't a waste of time. We'll use that against our enemy. I've faced the Vemus aboard one of their own ships. No doubt you're all familiar with the reports from that engagement. We don't have the numbers to meet this invasion force head-on. Connor knew it, and he often said that for all the Vemus's strengths, they aren't the most imaginative fighting force he'd ever encountered. They're powerful and can adapt, but in other respects they're slow to react. In essence, we need to outthink our enemy and be willing to sacrifice everything we've built in order to survive. Anything less won't be enough."

"You have our attention. Now share with us the rest of your plan," Tobias said.

Sean spent the next twenty minutes giving the defense committee the overview of his plan. To their credit, they listened quietly while he laid it out. During that time, Captain Diaz returned and Sean noticed the increased CDF presence in the Command Center. He hadn't wanted to resort to the use of force in order to take command of the city, but he would if he had to.

"Your plan doesn't include the colonial militia," Director Mills said.

"They're not soldiers. I'm not sure if using them in any capacity is going to help," Sean said.

"People have a right to help defend their homes," Director Mills said.

Sean frowned while he considered. "They do, but I cannot risk the lives of my soldiers on rescuing the militia if they find themselves in trouble. Do they understand the danger involved? At least CDF soldiers have been trained."

"How about as a compromise I suggest spreading the militia amongst Field Ops teams? There aren't enough CDF soldiers to be everywhere. We won't interfere with the work your soldiers are doing, but we need the militia's help," Director Mills said.

Sean knew Mills was right. He needed every able-bodied person who could hold a rifle. He'd love it if they were all trained like the CDF soldiers had been.

"You're right," Sean said, finally. "I just want it emphasized to anyone who remains that there will be no guarantee once the attack begins that we'll be able to get them away from the city. All the bunkers, as well as Sanctuary, will be closed to them. I won't risk sending another transport to any of those locations when the Vemus arrive," Sean said and looked at the others. "Now, this is all I have time for. I can be reached through CDF channels."

"One more question please, Major Quinn," Stanton said.

Sean really did need to go. "What is it?"

"Lunar Base. You didn't say how they'll figure into your plan," Stanton said.

"Colonel Hayes has been receiving the same updates we have here, and he'll assess the enemy forces and coordinate a strike against them. None of that will affect what we have to do here on the ground. In essence, we're hoping Colonel Hayes will find a way to blindside the enemy. Maintaining communications blackout with Lunar Base is essential in order for that effort to succeed. So, our job is to hold out as long as we can," Sean said.

His answer seemed to satisfy the former governor, and the committee members all left, except for his father.

"I know you have to go, but I need to talk to you," his father said.

"I'll be right outside, Major," Captain Diaz said and left, closing the door.

Sean looked at his father. They were alone. "Where's Mom?"

"She's helping to organize field hospitals throughout the city," his father said.

"There won't be many wounded. The Vemus aren't keen on taking prisoners or wounding us," Sean replied and glanced over at the door.

Tobias came to stand in front of him and put his hand on Sean's shoulder.

"It's been difficult for me watching you grow up. You're making your own decisions, and me questioning them is almost second nature. It comes with being a father. It's an old habit and I'm sorry," his father said.

"We can't be father and son in rooms like this. Not anymore," Sean said.

"I realize that. You're in command. I acknowledge that and promise to do my best not to interfere with it again," his father said.

Sean felt the edges of his lips lift. He hadn't realized it but there was still part of him that craved his father's approval and acknowledgment of the man he'd become.

"I have a request," his father said.

Sean pressed his lips together and frowned. "What do you need?"

"I don't need anything, but I'd like to stay at your side for the duration," his father said.

Sean's brows pulled together. "I can't allow that. I'm sorry."

His father lifted his hands in front of his chest. "I don't mean in combat, but everything else."

"I know what you mean, but I don't think you understand. Every place in this city is about to become a combat zone. I can't do what I need to do and worry about your safety. Can you please understand that?" Sean said.

His father's brows pushed forward determinedly. "I want to fight at your side, son."

Sean's throat thickened. "I know, but I'm going to be where the worst of the fighting is."

"You think that matters to me? You're my son. We may not have always seen eye to eye, but there's nothing I wouldn't do for you. You may be in command of the CDF, but I'm going to stay with you. You can order your soldiers to take me away and I'll still come back." His father's eyes became glassy and Sean felt himself being pulled into his father's arms. "I'm so proud of you. Please don't forget that. I've always been proud of you."

Sean hugged his father, feeling as if a great weight had been lifted from his shoulders.

"I won't order my men to take you away, but you'll have to explain yourself to Mom," Sean said.

His father chuckled. "I've already taken care of that."

Sean frowned. "What do you mean?"

"I mean that the last transport to Sanctuary will have your mother on it. Whether she's conscious for the trip will be another matter," Tobias said.

Sean's mouth hung open. "She'll never forgive you for it."

"At least she'll be alive to be angry. I'll take that over the alternative any day," Tobias said.

Sean nodded. He'd already made similar arrangements for his father. Some things weren't worth the risk.

22

Noah returned to the mobile Command Center at Sanctuary. They'd received notification that Phoenix Station had gone offline after its engagement with the Vemus Alpha ship. Not a good sign, but Noah knew that the CDF soldiers serving aboard Phoenix Station wouldn't be declared dead until the area was thoroughly investigated. Sean refused to believe Connor had died. Even if massive pieces of the space station had been destroyed, there were still pockets where people could survive. The official CDF update communication had come from Sean, who was commanding the CDF ground troops. Noah found himself looking at Colonel Cross for some reaction to tell him why she wasn't in command of the CDF ground forces.

"I see you looking at me again, Captain Barker. Is there a problem?" Colonel Cross asked crisply.

"No, ma'am, no problem at all," Noah said and turned his attention back to the latest analysis for the power converter. He'd tweaked the controller's sensitivity for the power regulator so that it could handle the greater range of fluctuations that the alien power station was prone to producing. These settings would greatly hinder the converter's life cycle, but he didn't need the equipment to last forever; it just needed to survive a few engagements with Vemus ships if they ever found Sanctuary.

After a few moments, he glanced over at Colonel Cross and she sighed heavily. "Since you can't seem to concentrate, I'll answer the question that's been burning in your mind since I arrived," Colonel Cross said.

"I'm sorry, Colonel. I really am. I'm trying not to think about my wife. She's stationed at Lunar Base," Noah said.

Colonel Cross raised her brows. "There are a lot of significant others serving on Lunar Base."

Noah frowned in confusion for a moment. "Oh, I hadn't realized."

"What? That I'm a woman as well as a colonel? Yes, there's someone important to me up there as well, so you're in good company," Colonel Cross said.

"Does that have anything to do with why you were sent here?" Noah asked and then immediately wished he hadn't. *Idiot,* he thought.

Colonel Cross glared at him and then a bitter half smile crossed her face as her gaze lost most of its venom. "Once again, if General Gates hadn't warned me about you, I'd have you dealt with severely."

Noah looked away, feeling embarrassed. He should have known better, but sometimes his brain just latched onto an idea and refused to let go.

"You know what? Fine, I'll tell you. General Gates sent me to Sanctuary because I'm pregnant and there are regulations against me serving in an active combat zone," Colonel Cross said.

Of all the reasons Noah had thought, Colonel Cross being pregnant hadn't been among them. He looked at her. "Congratulations, Colonel," he said.

Colonel Cross snorted and shook her head. "I think you're the first person who's said that to me. Thank you."

"I mean it. It's nice to have something like that to think about rather than always . . ." Noah's voice trailed off, and he pointed up toward the sky.

"I'm sure you'll make a wonderful father someday, Captain Barker," Colonel Cross said.

Noah noted the slight bitterness in Colonel Cross's tone. "Does your significant other know about the baby?"

Colonel Cross bit her lower lip and shook her head. "I didn't get the chance to tell him."

Noah perked up in his chair. "I'm sure I can find a way for you to get a message to Lunar Base. I could bury it in satcom—" Noah said.

"No," Colonel Cross said sternly, cutting him off. "We can't take the risk with the Vemus closing in on the planet."

"Yeah, but it would just be another broadcast signal among many. Difficult for them to track, even with an AI tasked with evaluating the signals," Noah said.

"No. And that's an order. The broadcast signals will have decreased now that the Vemus are here. If we keep up the broadcasts, sooner or later even the Vemus will start wondering why we would do such a thing, and it wouldn't take a large stretch of the imagination for them to conclude that we have someone listening on the other end," Colonel Cross said.

"I hadn't thought of that, Colonel," Noah said, conceding the point.

"No one can think of everything," Colonel Cross said.

They heard shouting from outside the mobile Command Center. Recognizing Lenora's voice, Noah sprang out of his chair. Her shrill voice became even louder through the thin walls of the center. She hadn't taken the news about Phoenix Station well. Noah couldn't blame her and was secretly thankful that, for the time being, Lunar Base was relatively safe from Vemus attention.

Noah hastened outside and Colonel Cross followed him. Off to the side, Lenora swayed on her feet, holding a glass bottle. Behind her, a huge berwolf watched her intently. The creature's large pink tongue lolled out of its blocky head, resting lazily over a row of impressively sized teeth. The tips of retractable black claws that could rend through steel poked out from the brown, hairy paws. Noah recalled that Lenora had cared for the berwolf as a pup and had even named him Bull. The CDF soldiers kept a wary eye on the creature.

"Colonel," Lenora said. Her slurred words and bleary-eyed gaze were indication enough that Lenora had had more than a few drinks before coming here. "They're here! They. Are. Here!" she said, stabbing her finger up at the night sky. "We've spent all that time getting that big cannon to work. Why haven't you used it yet?"

"Lenora, you know why," Noah admonished.

Lenora shushed him with an excessive hiss and a shake of her head. "I want to hear it from her."

"Dr. Bishop, you need rest. Please allow my soldiers to escort you back to your quarters," Colonel Cross said.

Two CDF soldiers stepped toward Lenora, but when one of them moved to grab her arm, a deep growl resonated from the berwolf's massive chest.

Lenora stumbled back away from the guards and toward Bull. "I don't think he'll like it if you try to touch me," she said, scowling at the soldiers and scratching the berwolf behind his ears. "At least *you're* still here," she said to Bull. The berwolf sniffed Lenora's breath curiously. No doubt it hadn't smelled anything like vodka before, or whatever flavored grain alcohol Lenora had been drinking.

Noah walked past the soldiers. "Come on, Lenora. You know we can't bring that weapon online. I know you *know* that."

Lenora glared at him. "Oh yes. All the colonists suddenly find one of my archaeological sites so interesting," she sneered and scowled at the crowd of refugees quickly shuffling away from her. "Oh yes, all of you come cowering here. Half of you thought he was crazy. Remember?" she asked scathingly of the retreating group. "There's no danger coming from Earth. There's no way something like that could happen. You scoffed at his efforts and made him plead for you to give him the tools he needed to defend you all. Now you cower here, looking up at the skies in panic," she said, stabbing a finger up at the night sky. "Now you give him your support, proclaiming he's been right all along. None of you deserve what Connor's given you. None of you!"

Lenora lost her balance and stumbled to the side. Noah stepped forward, ready to catch her if she fell but also keeping a wary eye on the berwolf. He couldn't tell whether the creature was going to attack him or not. For the moment it seemed preoccupied with watching Lenora's drunken rage.

She steadied herself with outstretched arms to keep her balance.

"Lenora, please. They're scared enough without you yelling at them," Noah said.

Lenora looked at him, her long hair in tangles, some of which were in front of her face. She pushed her hair out of the way and Noah saw her glassy, red-rimmed eyes. "How can you side with them? Don't you want to kill the Vemus?"

Noah took a small step forward. "Yes, I want to stop them, but this isn't the way."

"Then why aren't you firing the colossus cannon right now?" Lenora asked.

"Because it won't stop them. It will only alert the Vemus to our presence here," Noah said.

"Good! Then I can grab one of these rifles and put it to good use," Lenora said and looked over at Colonel Cross. "I'm not such a bad shot myself."

"Lenora, please look at me," Noah said.

Lenora blinked slowly as she turned her gaze to him.

"Connor wouldn't want this—" Noah began.

"I don't care what Connor wanted!" Lenora shrieked and glared up at the night sky. "Are you happy now? You got what you wanted. Killed in the line of duty. A soldier's death . . ."

Lenora muttered a few incoherent curses and tripped. Noah caught her in his arms and she pressed her face into his chest, sobbing. All he could do was hold her while she wept. He hadn't seen her since yesterday. She must have found out about Phoenix Station, and he cursed himself an idiot for not going to tell her himself. He should have checked on her. The mostly empty glass bottle clattered to the ground, and he lifted her up and started to carry her off.

"Put her in my quarters. They're closer," Colonel Cross said.

Noah changed directions, heading for Colonel Cross's tent. Lenora kept muttering off and on while he carried her. She needed sleep. He heard the berwolf padding along behind them. Colonel Cross opened the door to her tent and Noah carried Lenora to the small bed inside. He laid her down and pulled a blanket over her. Satisfied that there was nothing more he could do, he left the tent and went back outside.

"You should stay with her," Colonel Cross said.

"But I have to—"

"It can wait. She needs you. You should be here for her when she wakes up," Colonel Cross insisted.

"Thank you, ma'am," Noah said.

Colonel Cross and the CDF soldiers left him, and the berwolf settled down nearby. He grabbed one of the nearest chairs and sat down. The creature would swing its head toward Lenora whenever he heard her moan in her sleep but then would settle back down.

"She'll be alright," Noah said softly and hoped he was right. Lenora had kept so many things bottled up that he should have known something had to give. He crossed his arms in front of his chest and gazed up at the night sky where New Earth's rings cast a soft glow. He never got tired of that sight, but tonight he couldn't take any comfort in it. The Vemus were here and he had no idea how they were going to stop them.

23

The Vemus Alpha had settled into a geocentric orbit around New Earth, and after the cruisers finished taking out the structures on the lunar surface, they returned to the Alpha. The Vemus seemed to have ignored Lunar Base altogether, and Nathan had deployed small scanning drones from one of the comms satellites they had in orbit. The scanner drones were configured to do a single pass by the Alpha and then send the data through an IR channel to repeaters the CDF had placed nearby. Since the IR signal required a direct line of sight to send the data, there was very little chance the Vemus would detect it. If they did, they could only trace the signal to another repeater. In theory, the Vemus *could* be patient enough to track the IR signal, but they would have to be in close proximity to the actual repeaters, which they weren't. The risk was minimal and the CDF needed the data, as it was crucial data for their counterstrike.

Nathan had deployed armed CDF squads to secure all the locations throughout the base that had access to the lunar surface. He hadn't accounted for securing those locations when the Vemus arrived and had nearly been discovered. Less than a handful of people had made the foolish attempt to engage the Vemus, which would have put Lunar Base at risk, but luckily Nathan had more levelheaded soldiers in the area to avert disaster. What really frustrated him was that Dr. Kendra Robinson's death could have been avoided. Struggling to keep the disgust from his voice at the pointless waste of life, he sent out a base-wide update reminding all Lunar Base personnel that the communications receivers were still online and there was no need for anyone to be at the surface installations.

"It's the pressure, Colonel. Makes people do foolish things," Major Shelton said.

Nathan pressed his lips together. "I know. We just can't afford it."

It had been twelve hours since Phoenix Station had gone offline, and he hadn't allowed himself to think about Savannah at all. He'd checked the comms logs from the escape pods and her signature hadn't been among them. The escape pods had ceased broadcasting once the Vemus cruisers entered the area. Unless those CDF soldiers had been able to disable their beacons, it was probable that they'd been captured or killed by the Vemus. Given those options, Nathan hoped they hadn't been captured.

He turned his attention back to the main holoscreen. Despite the massive size of the Vemus Alpha, Phoenix Station weapons had bludgeoned it, rendering near-catastrophic damage. The probe scans revealed that the exoskeletal hull was thickest toward the rear of the massive ship where the engines were buried deep in the cavernous hindquarters. The twenty-two-kilometer ship must have had millions of personnel aboard, perhaps more, but those numbers had to have been seriously decimated. Connor had focused Phoenix Station's weapons on key soft areas that were revealed after the initial HADES IV-B missiles had sloughed off a few layers of the exoskeletal hull. He'd done a lot of damage, but the enemy ship was still flying.

Nathan had brought in his reserve watches and fed all the data they'd gathered throughout the base. He encouraged anyone with any ideas about how they could attack the enemy to bring them to their immediate superior officers, who would then decide whether the suggestion should be sent up the chain of command. Currently, his normal bridge crew, with the additional presence of operations and tactical units, was gathered in the command area.

"We need to hit the Vemus Alpha so hard that they can't recover from it, but we need to be cautious because we can't have that ship crashing into the planet," Nathan said.

Lieutenant LaCroix raised his hand and Nathan nodded for him to speak.

"Colonel, my team and I have run some preliminary firing solutions, but once we commit fully, there's no way we can mask our presence here," Lieutenant LaCroix said.

"Yes, the Vemus will become aware of our presence once we begin shooting at them, so what's your real question, Lieutenant?" Nathan asked.

"Our main objective is to take out the Vemus Alpha, but what about the ships that'll take their forces to the ground? I think we should be trying to prevent that as well, Colonel. What good is a surprise attack if everyone's dead by the time we come up with a plan to engage the enemy?" Lieutenant LaCroix said.

"Any minute now the Vemus are going to send in a landing force. We've seen them use Talon 5s to storm Titan Station, but they didn't use them on Phoenix. Please bring your attention to the main holoscreen. That large scorched area is roughly seven kilometers across, and recent scans show that there are separate ships inside. We think their landing crafts will use that area. How can we stop the landing crafts from reaching New Earth?" Nathan asked as his eyes swept over his staff. "This question isn't just for Lieutenant LaCroix. Once we reveal our presence, there's no going back."

"I have a suggestion, Colonel," Major Shelton said.

"What is it?" Nathan asked.

"We can't let the Vemus land any craft on New Earth completely unchallenged. They're in position, and perhaps they believe they've won. We need to keep them off balance by striking at the landing craft as they make their descent, letting them know they're not unopposed and reassuring the people on the ground that we're still up here fighting for them," Major Shelton said.

"Agreed. Given the distance, what could we use that would reach those targets in time?" Nathan asked.

"We could use our midrange Hornet missiles. They can close the distance quickly, and the Vemus wouldn't have much time to launch countermeasures, Colonel," Lieutenant LaCroix said.

"That could work. Put your team on coming up with a firing solution for that. We'll need to use a LIDAR burst to update PRADIS. Work off the assumption that as soon as we fire our missiles, we return to Dark-Star status. I agree with Major Shelton that if we can get the Vemus to look over their shoulders, it might give us some more time to find the soft spots in their armor," Colonel Hayes said.

An alert came to prominence on the main holoscreen. Several large pieces had broken away from the Vemus Alpha.

"Tactical, those are your targets. Comms, set Condition One throughout the base. Ops, commence LIDAR burst on my mark," Colonel Hayes said.

"Yes, Colonel, ready on your mark," Sergeant Martinez said.

Nathan waited for Lieutenant LaCroix, who, after a few moments, turned and said, "Firing solution ready. Hornets in the tubes and ready, Colonel."

"Ops, commence burst," Nathan said.

On the lunar surface, massive hatch doors opened and actuators pushed up a large sensor array, which sent out a sizeable scanner burst. There was no way the Vemus would miss the sudden activity. The PRADIS scope updated with targeting information.

"Fire missiles," Nathan ordered.

"Yes, Colonel, missiles fired," Lieutenant LaCroix confirmed.

The scanners showed the Hornet missiles leaving their launch tubes, racing toward the Vemus troop carriers.

"Ready second wave of missiles," Nathan said.

Finally, they were in this fight. The first wave of missiles blindsided the Vemus troop carriers, causing the ships to break apart during entry into the atmosphere.

"Colonel, two Vemus cruisers are inbound. They'll be in detection range within ten minutes," Sergeant Martinez said.

"Tactical, do we have time for one more wave of Hornets, with half of them targeting those cruisers?" Nathan asked.

"Affirmative, Colonel," Lieutenant LaCroix said.

"Do it. Fire when ready," Nathan said.

He watched the main holoscreen as their missile tubes were reloaded with the midrange Hornets.

"Firing third wave, Colonel," Lieutenant LaCroix said.

"Retract array and close all missile hatches," Nathan said.

Hornet missiles flew away from New Earth's moon, some darting off toward the inbound cruisers. Nathan watched as the cruisers took out the inbound Hornet missiles. One cruiser escaped unscathed while the second cruiser took multiple direct hits along the prow of the ship, taking out its forward cannons.

"Colonel, the last scans show that some of the bigger troop carriers got through and are heading toward the planet's surface," Lieutenant LaCroix said.

"What're their last known trajectories?" Nathan asked.

"Their trajectories are aligned with colonial settlements. None of the remote emergency bunkers are located at any of those areas, Colonel," Lieutenant LaCroix said.

"That's something, at least," Nathan said quietly.

"Passive scans show more ships heading our way," Lieutenant LaCroix said.

"Ops, I want the gun batteries hot and ready to go, but keep the hatch doors shut unless it looks like the Vemus ships are about to fire on us," Nathan said.

"Yes, Colonel, alerting fire teams now," Sergeant Martinez said.

Major Shelton glanced over at him. "How many do you think got through to the surface?"

Nathan watched the main holoscreen grimly. "Too many. Those troop carriers can hold thousands of soldiers."

"Yeah, but the cities have been evacuated. Only soldiers will be there to greet them," Major Shelton said.

"Maybe I should have used the few HADES IV missiles we have," Nathan said.

"No, you were right to keep them in reserve. Now the Vemus will expend some energy trying to figure out where we are, which buys our soldiers on the ground time to deal with the immediate threat," Major Shelton said.

"Colonel, the last scanner burst came back with some strange detections," Sergeant Martinez said.

Nathan glanced at her, but the sergeant's gaze was locked onto her screen.

"Colonel, I think our scanners detected faint power readings from the Phoenix Station wreckage," Sergeant Martinez said.

"You think? I need more than that, Sergeant," Nathan said.

"It's hard to tell because we had our array focused on the Vemus forces, but what we detected is at the edge of the scanner range. That area is where Phoenix Station was," Sergeant Martinez said.

Nathan looked at the scanner data on the main holoscreen and frowned. He didn't want to start hoping when it was likely to be nothing. "Send in a scanner drone from our Bravo installation on the dark side of the moon."

"Drone away, Colonel. Estimated arrival in ninety minutes," Sergeant Martinez said.

"Very well," Nathan said and continued to watch the main holoscreen while considering their next move.

"Colonel," Lieutenant LaCroix said, "would you and Major Shelton come over to Tactical, please?"

Nathan walked over to the tactical workstation where LaCroix sat with two members of his team.

"The HADES IV-Bs were modified to improve their effectiveness against countermeasures, which made them better able to reach their targets in a long-range engagement. We only have a few of them here on base," Lieutenant LaCroix said.

"That's right—only about twenty. Have you come up with a way to use them?" Nathan asked.

"Since this isn't a long-range engagement with the enemy, we're proposing to consolidate the HADES IVs' payloads, Colonel," Lieutenant LaCroix said.

Nathan narrowed his gaze while he considered it. "You guys came up with this?"

Lieutenant LaCroix shook his head. "No, the idea came up from one of the engineering teams—an engineer by the name of Kara Roberts. She said—and I'm quoting here, sir, 'I have a way to blow those SOBs out of the damn sky.' She had a few more expletives, but you get the idea."

"So, you want to take twenty of the HADES IVs and combine the payloads into one single missile?" Nathan asked.

"No, Colonel, Major Roberts is proposing that we consolidate them down to four missiles. We cap them with extra armored tips to increase their penetration effectiveness and use countdown detonators since the Vemus can block our command-and-control signals," Lieutenant LaCroix said.

"And you think that will be enough to destroy that ship?" Nathan asked.

"We can't be sure, Colonel, but it's our best shot at doing the most damage against them," Lieutenant LaCroix said.

Nathan glanced at Major Shelton.

"The idea has promise, Colonel," Major Shelton said.

Nathan drew in a deep breath and sighed heavily. "How long until they can be ready?"

"According to Major Roberts, six hours, sir. They need to break down the assembly and transfer the payload to the other missiles," Lieutenant LaCroix said.

"Alright, tell Major Roberts she's authorized to start," Nathan said. "Major Shelton, I need you to go down there and supervise the effort. No use blowing ourselves up while we're trying to save the colony."

"Yes, Colonel," Major Shelton said and left the command area.

Nathan swung his gaze toward the main holoscreen. Vemus cruisers were inbound, and they needed to hold out for over six hours.

24

CONNOR WAS SLUMPED over in his chair with the straps digging into his shoulder as red flashing lights reflected from the smooth surface of the floor. He blinked several times, slowly escaping his stupor. Swallowing the coppery taste of blood in his mouth, he raised his head to look at the main holoscreen. Amidst the flashing alerts was a long list of failed systems. Connor swung his head around and saw CDF soldiers slumped in their chairs. Other soldiers were lying on the floor, their helmets broken. He couldn't tell whether they were alive or dead. Connor unbuckled his straps, rubbed his shoulder, and stumbled to his feet. He turned and approached Major Elder, who had fallen halfway out of his chair, some of his straps having come unbuckled. Connor's neural implants showed that Major Elder was alive. In fact, his life signs were strong.

"John, are you okay?" Connor asked, shaking the man's shoulder.

Major Elder groaned as Connor pushed him upright in his chair. He opened his eyes and looked at Connor. "I'm still here, General," he said, wincing.

"Just sit tight for a minute and catch your breath. I'll get a medic up here," Connor said.

Major Elder pushed himself up and waved Connor off. "I'll be fine," he said and took in the state of the Command Center.

"Good, let's see where we stand," Connor said.

They started working their way around the command area. The soldiers that had been strapped in their chairs were alive but disoriented. There were more than a few critically injured soldiers lying on the floor, and Connor used his comlink to find Dr. Allen. Fortunately, Dr. Allen had been near the Command Center during the Vemus Alpha attack. The chief medical officer put whoever was standing around to work helping to assess the injured soldiers.

"Ops, I need a situation report. What shape are we in, Lieutenant?" Connor said.

Lieutenant Rawn rubbed his eyes and peered at his personal holoscreen. "General, I'm showing that sections four, five, and seven are completely offline and aren't attached to us anymore. We have critical failures in section six, but the bulkhead doors have sealed and are holding. Maneuvering thrusters are offline. Weapons systems are offline. We have life support and artificial gravity but we're tumbling out of control. We're leaking atmosphere from multiple impact points. Honestly, sir, I don't know how we're still together," Lieutenant Rawn said, his eyes going wide.

"Well let's not start counting our blessings just yet," Connor said.

They had life support for the moment. They needed to get the station stabilized so they could figure out where they were and then figure out where the Vemus Alpha had gone. He glanced up at the main holoscreen, which kept flickering due to power surges.

"Ops, try to reach someone from Engineering. I need to know what the state of our reactor is or whether we're on backup generators. Tactical, is our scanner array intact?" Connor asked.

Captain Thorne raced back to his workstation and opened his console. "Scanners are offline, General. The logs don't show that it was damaged, but with all the systems offline, I'm not sure we still even have the array."

They needed to restore main power and get those systems back online. "Understood, Captain. See if any repair crews can check it out. We're blind until we can get access to that array," Connor said.

Major Elder came back to Connor. "We still have people checking in, but preliminary reports indicate that we're missing a substantial portion of this subsection. Davis, down in Engineering, believes the Vemus Alpha's primary weapon cut right through our armor. The fact that we were out of control and spinning may be the only reason we're still alive."

Connor nodded. "Lieutenant Daniels, do we have any comms capabilities?"

Lieutenant Daniels had a cut on her forehead that one of the medics had just patched up. She peered at her console. "We have short-range comms capabilities, General."

"See if you can detect Bravo or Charlie stations. Don't broadcast right now, but see if you can connect to their systems that are online," Connor said.

"We saw them get destroyed, sir," Major Elder said quietly.

"We saw them go *offline*. There was so much going on that we don't have confirmation that they're gone. *We* shouldn't be here, and I won't count anyone out just yet," Connor said.

Major Elder nodded, considering. "There could be other sections with survivors, but they might not have any way to reach us."

"That might be a blessing because the last thing we need is to start broadcasting our position. The Vemus Alpha might've passed us by, thinking we were dead," Connor said.

Major Elder frowned. "Why wouldn't they just finish us off?"

Connor shook his head. "I'm not sure. My best guess is that they thought we were no longer a threat, which means they could send a ship back to finish the job or capture survivors."

Major Elder's face became grim. "Not the best position to be in. General, I'd like to assess the damage firsthand."

"That's a good idea. We'll split up. Send me an update via the comlink. We need critical systems back online. Hopefully a few maneuvering thrusters made it so we can at least stabilize our position," Connor said.

"I'll make that my first stop, General," Major Elder said.

They spent the next few hours doing damage assessments, and Connor started to put together casualty reports, as well as lists of CDF soldiers that were simply missing. Connor divided his remaining soldiers into search parties to look for survivors and check ship systems. He left the Command Center to lead one of the search teams. They were still alive but far from out of the woods. For the moment they were on borrowed time.

25

THE ONLY PEOPLE left in Sierra were the ones who were going to fight and those supporting them. The last transport to Sanctuary had left over an hour earlier. Sean's mother had been on it and he was told she was none too thrilled about it. His father had stuck with him ever since they'd learned the fate of Phoenix Station, but Sean was so focused on what he had to do that most of the time he forgot his father was there. They didn't have enough AR-71s to distribute to the militia, but they did the best they could. Some of them were armed with a CAR-74 semiautomatic hunting rifle, and Sean wasn't sure how effective they'd be against the Vemus. Certainly, the smaller Vemus soldiers would be vulnerable to the civilian rifle but definitely not the Vemus Alpha troops. Sean had seen those rise after being torn apart by incendiary rounds from an AR-71. The only time they stayed dead was when there was nothing left to come back to life. Even that wasn't right. The Vemus had remarkable healing capabilities that New Earth scientists were at a loss to fully understand.

Sean knew that fighting the Vemus would be like facing his worst nightmare, except this time he didn't get to escape in a ship. This time the Vemus wouldn't go away. The fighting would be close and he needed them to come into the city. There were only a select few who knew his plan in its entirety. He'd expected more resistance than he'd gotten, but it was no secret that Sean was amongst the foremost experts in dealing with this particular enemy. He didn't feel like an expert—not by a long shot, which was what this whole mission was turning out to be.

Sean powered off the small holoscreen in front of him and stepped away from the comms station. He'd established command units throughout the city so he wouldn't be tied down to one place. His M-Viper sniper rifle rested against the wall beside him. He was one of the best shots in the entire Colonial Defense Force.

Lieutenant Compton shifted his feet and looked at Sean as he turned around. "They're as ready as they'll ever be," he said.

"I just told Delphi and New Haven that they're essentially on their own. I don't know how Connor dealt with this every day for the past seven years," Sean said with a sigh. He felt as if his head was going to burst.

Lieutenant Compton nodded. "It's one thing to take orders and it's quite another to be giving them and making all the decisions. But I'm sure Majors Winters and Roberts will do their jobs."

"They'll hold their respective cities as long as they can," Sean said.

They stood on one of the taller buildings in Sierra, which gave them a bird's-eye view of the city. It was a few hours after sunrise and the Vemus Alpha was in geosynchronous orbit around New Earth. The ship had been there for hours, and Sean presumed it was identifying targets.

"Major," Lieutenant Owens called out to him. "My scope just lit up with a bunch of bogies, sir. We've got incoming."

Air raid alarms began blaring throughout the city and Sean opened a broadcast channel to his gun batteries. "Hold your fire until we have visual confirmation of the enemy. Conserve your ammo as much as you can."

Multiple cracks of thunder boomed throughout the clear sky and Sean peered up, along with everyone else. He felt his brows push forward as he squinted. The sky was full of large, fiery ships that must have come from the Vemus Alpha. The invasion had begun. Behind the ships were several large explosions that tore through the enemy vessels.

"What is that?" Lieutenant Compton asked.

Sean smiled. "That has to be from Lunar Base. Colonel Hayes must've authorized the attack, but he won't be able to attack for long."

"Why not?" Lieutenant Compton asked.

"He's just lending us some support and reminding the Vemus that they're not entirely unopposed. And now they'll have to expend resources in order to investigate where that attack came from—" Sean said and was cut off by the loud sonic booms of enemy ships clearing Lunar Base's attack.

Hundreds of enemy ships streaked down toward Sierra, and the rail-cannon gun batteries began rapidly firing on the approaching ships. Sean watched as the heavy rail-cannons tore into the enemy ships. The high-velocity projectiles were made from a sixth-generation alien alloy they'd found in the abandoned alien ruins on the planet. The components to make the hardened alloy were plentiful and were comparable to what the NA Alliance military would have used.

Some of the enemy ships began to lose control, slamming into each other as they veered off course.

"Owens, start broadcasting the Vemus control signal," Sean said.

"Yes, Major. Broadcasting Vemus disruption signal now," Lieutenant Owens said.

Sean watched as hundreds of ships approached Sierra. They stayed in formation, which meant the Vemus disruption signal was no longer effective.

"Shall I keep the signal going, Major?" Lieutenant Owens asked.

"Yes, keep it going just in case, Lieutenant," Sean said.

The Vemus landing craft never returned fire. They just kept coming despite the damage the rail-cannon batteries were doing. At first, they crashed outside the city, but they were drawing steadily closer.

"The ones behind the front line are breaking apart," Lieutenant Compton said, pointing.

Sean peered at the area, using his neural implants to temporarily enhance his view of the approaching ships.

"They look like pods," Sean said. "They're using drop-pods!" he exclaimed and turned toward Owens. "Alert all commands that the Vemus are using drop-pods with a heavy concentration of troops coming toward the western side of the city."

"At once, Major," Lieutenant Owens said.

"Should we send in the mobile infantry units to bolster the west side of the city, sir?" Lieutenant Compton asked.

"No," Sean said, shaking his head. "They're still coming down. The drop-pods are harder to hit and will only fire their retro-boosters at the last moment for a hard landing. Then, whatever's inside comes out."

Sean's father glanced at Director Mills before looking back at him. "How did you know all that?"

"Connor made sure—" Sean said, then frowned. "He made sure I knew about NA Alliance military tactics," he said, remembering how Connor would randomly drill him on military tactics that Sean wasn't convinced he'd ever use. Sean had thought the bulk of their engagement with the Vemus would be in space. He'd been wrong, but Connor had known better. He'd tried to account for every conceivable attack scenario and had trained the Colonial Defense Force accordingly. How long had Connor been grooming him to lead the CDF ground forces?

Sean watched as the rail-cannon batteries tried to target all the incoming drop-pods, but there were too many of them. He noted that many of the drop-pods were successfully landing in the areas outside the city.

"Comms, send out an alert for infantry teams to target the retro-booster assembly on the drop-pods to prevent their thrusters from working," Sean said.

"Yes, Major," Lieutenant Owens said.

Sean looked at his father. "I'd intended to get you out of here, but—"

"I'm not leaving, son," his father said.

"Fine, but I'm sending you to the east side of the city," Sean said.

Tobias opened his mouth to speak.

"That's not up for discussion," Sean said and glanced over at a nearby soldier. "Corporal, take a squad and escort the governor to the east encampment."

Sean watched as his father was led away. The sounds of the rail-cannon batteries, in their unrelenting barrage against the Vemus invasion force, hadn't slowed down. In fact, now the CDF infantry was firing their weapons at the drop-pods, which added to the sounds of wanton destruction. Drop-pods crashed into the ground and impact craters began to dot the landscape. The CDF soldiers hit the fuel lines, causing drop-pods to hit the ground in flaming wrecks, which became small explosions. Other drop-pods hit the ground without slowing down, the force of the impact shattering the pods and the Vemus soldiers inside them to bits. But still they came, and more of the drop-pods began to make it through to land safely. Some even landed inside the city walls. Upon landing, hatches opened up and large dark figures stalked out of the pods. CDF soldiers stationed on the rooftops above rained fire down on them. The Vemus returned fire, and white stun bolts blazed through the air. Some of the enemy were massive, easily twice as tall as Sean was. Their skin was a deep, dark purple that glistened in the light. Their rounded heads angled to a pointed snout, making them look anything but human.

CDF fire teams worked together to bring them down using kinetic weapons to stall their advance or otherwise immobilize them and then thermite explosive rounds to burn away whatever was left.

Multiple reports came in of Vemus forces gathering outside the city. A large explosion to the west snatched Sean's attention.

"That's not ours," Lieutenant Compton said.

"Order the mobile infantry unit to the west side of the city. Get the Hellcats in the air to give air support," Sean ordered.

He'd held the Hellcats in reserve. The Vemus drop-pods and troop carriers seemed to have stopped. The skies were clear for the moment, but that could change at any time. The high-pitched whine of multiple Hellcats flying overhead filled the air as they streaked toward the west. Updates from New Haven and Delphi reported the Vemus using similar tactics, but the bulk of their forces were here at Sierra. The Vemus had correctly surmised that Sierra would be the most heavily defended.

Carrying his M-Viper sniper rifle, Sean headed toward the barricade wall on the roof of the Field Ops Headquarters, which was centrally located in the city. He squatted down to set up his position and was immediately joined by a few other soldiers. He glanced at the soldier next to him and saw a wisp of blonde hair beneath the edges of the helmet.

"Boone?" Sean asked.

"I hope you're still as good a shot as you used to be, Bling," Field Ops Captain Donna Marten said. She'd been part of Search and Rescue and hadn't left Field Ops.

Sean hefted the M-Viper and rested the barrel on the barricade wall. "Better," Sean said.

Captain Marten arched an eyebrow. "Care to make a wager on it?"

Sean grinned. "Can we get a couple of spotters?" he said.

He'd ordered sniper units to the rooftops of the buildings and could already hear the distinct pop of an M-Viper being fired. They were three kilometers from the edge of the city and taking out a target at that range would be a challenge, but not beyond the capabilities of the M-Viper or Sean.

"Loser buys drinks tonight," Sean said.

"Oh, you're on, Major," Field Ops Captain Marten said.

Finding targets was relatively easy given that the Vemus were so big, and once on the ground, they moved toward the city in a dark wave. Sean peered down his scope, searching for a target beyond the edge of the city, but they moved so fast that he no sooner had a target than it was quickly out of sight. Sean focused ahead of one of the alphas and squeezed the trigger. The high-velocity round blazed toward the target at supersonic speed, and the head of the Vemus exploded like a melon on impact as the large body dropped to the ground. CDF soldiers who were much closer lobbed thermite charges to burn up the remains. Sean updated his nano-robotic ammunition to use incendiary rounds. This would give the CDF soldiers more time to mop up the remains so the Vemus couldn't rise again.

Sean picked another target and squeezed off a round, the incendiary ammunition streaking red through the air to reach its objective. The CDF infantry rotated between using incendiary rounds and regular kinetic rounds, which lasted longer. Sean had ordered them to conserve their ammo, but with so many Vemus storming the city he wasn't sure how long they could last. Field Ops Captain Marten took down at least as many targets as Sean did, probably more. It felt good to see the enemy fall.

Sean wasn't sure how much time had passed, but he started to get an itch in the back of his mind that he was missing something. Backing away from the barricade, he motioned for another CDF soldier to take his place and he returned to the command area where there was a holographic display of Sierra. Computer systems piped in updates from the computing core deep within the building.

Director Mills glanced at him. "What is it?"

Sean frowned. "I feel like I'm missing something. Something important."

The Vemus were primarily attacking certain areas of the city. The drop-pods that landed inside the city were quickly dealt with by the mobile infantry units.

He noted one of the seemingly quiet sectors of the city and picked one at random. "Ops, what's the status of our recon drones in sector three?" Sean asked.

Lieutenant Owens quickly brought up the status of the drones. They had so many deployed that they were grouped and tasked with specific sectors to patrol. The data provided from the drones were too much for any one person to keep track of, which was why they relied on the computer system to alert them to anomalies. Lieutenant Owens frowned. "Major, I'm showing a thirteen percent drop-off in drones reporting in from that sector. The drop-off occurred less than ten minutes ago."

"Who do we have in that area?" Sean asked.

Lieutenant Compton quickly accessed the information on his workstation. "It's mostly Field Ops and militia in that area, but Sergeant Brown is in the vicinity with a squad of CDF soldiers."

Sean opened a comlink to Sergeant Brown. "Sergeant, we've noticed a suspicious drop-off in recon drone activity in your vicinity. I need you to investigate whether there is enemy activity in your area."

The comlink channel opened, and Sean heard the sounds of a battle.

"Sir, we're under heavy attack. We need reinforcements. The Vemus are overwhelming our position!" Sergeant Brown shouted.

Sean looked at Lieutenant Compton. "Alert the reserve Hellcat squadron and send them to sector three immediately." He switched back to the comlink. "Air support is on its way."

"We'll hold out, sir," Sergeant Brown said.

"Why didn't they tell us they were under attack?" Director Mills asked.

"The attack probably came so suddenly that they didn't have time to report it in," Sean said. He studied the map of the city and the troop locations. "Send mobile infantry units thirty-six and thirty-seven to sector three. Do we have any satellite feeds? Can we track where the Vemus landed?"

Lieutenant Owens shook her head. "The satellites were taken out when the Vemus attacked. Backups were supposed to move into position, but none have reported in yet."

Director Mills nodded, finally understanding. "You suspect that in addition to the assault on the city, they landed a few kilometers away."

"It's what I would do," Sean said.

The recon drones failing to report in could only mean one thing. Those drones had been taken out so fast that they'd even failed to send in a destruction signal. Sean accessed one of the cameras on a tall building in sector three. Once it powered on, he put the live feed up for the rest of them to see. Vemus troops were staggering their approach, firing blue bolts of energy at Field Ops and militia soldiers.

"Good god! That's the east side of the city!" Director Mills said.

Sean stared at the video feed. He'd sent his father to that area of the city, thinking it was safer. Instead, it was being overwhelmed by Vemus soldiers. Sean recalled that the Vemus had used blue bolts to overcome the Nexstar combat suit defenses. They were shooting to kill.

The Vemus stormed the area, one group taking out the heavily armed soldiers while another pinned down the helpless combatants and spat a blackish goo onto their faces. They quickly moved on to the next person and did the same thing. The people with the blackish goo on their faces lay on the ground, their bodies going into convulsions that didn't let up.

Lieutenant Owens gasped. "What are they doing to them?"

Sean felt his mouth drop open. "That's how it spreads."

"But the data retrieved from the Vemus ship said the virus was airborne," Director Mills said.

"This is what we saw them do on the ship," Sean said and refreshed the CDF troop placements on the map.

Director Mills' face became pale. "How long does it take?"

"I have no idea. We fled the area," Sean said.

The holographic display showed the reserve Hellcat units moving into position to provide air support. Sean's mind raced and his mouth became dry. It was much too soon to implement the next phase of his plan. He tried to force an idea for some kind of backup strategy, but nothing came.

Director Mills' thick brows drew together in concern. "We can't hold this city, can we?"

Sean swallowed as he searched the map. He gritted his teeth. This was much too soon.

"What are your orders, Major?" Lieutenant Compton asked.

Sean looked around at the CDF soldiers and Field Ops people in the command area. They needed him to be strong. He wouldn't falter now. Connor had picked him to lead and that was exactly what he was going to do.

"We fight. We make them pay for every inch of ground they take from us, falling back to this position," Sean said and used his implants to outline the CDF headquarters. "This will be the secondary rally point. The primary is now highlighted." He looked at Director Mills.

"Those are tunnel entrances," Director Mills said, frowning.

Sean nodded. "They lead out of the city."

"Yeah, but how can you be sure there aren't Vemus forces in those locations?" Director Mills asked.

"Because we'll lure their forces in," Sean answered.

Director Mills studied the map again and then glared at Sean. "You never meant to hold the city."

"Only if it was feasible to do so. It's not," Sean said. "Comms, open package designation Siren-B and send out updated orders now."

"Confirmed. Siren-B package—" Lieutenant Owens' voice faltered, and she cleared her throat. "Orders sent, Major."

The holographic map updated, showing the intended troop movements for the updated orders.

"You bastard," Director Mills snarled. "Why didn't you tell anyone about this?"

Two CDF soldiers positioned themselves between Sean and Damon Mills.

"Because I needed your cooperation," Sean said coldly.

Director Mills glared at him. "I don't believe this. I don't believe you'd do this . . . were even capable of doing this. How many of them are going to pay with their lives for this plan of yours?"

Sean grabbed Mills and slammed him against the wall. "As many of them as it takes to stop the Vemus. That's why Connor put me in charge—because he knew I'd get the job done. Look out there!" Sean screamed and jerked his head to the side. "Just because you suddenly realized the level of sacrifice required so we can survive doesn't make it wrong."

Sean let go of Damon Mills and stepped back.

"I won't stand by and watch you destroy everything we've built," Director Mills said.

"No one will be standing by. The CDF will hold this position until it's done. Field Ops and the militia will escape in the tunnels. Then this city and every single Vemus inside will be blown up," Sean said.

Director Mills flung his arm toward the sky. "What about the rest of them? What are you going to do when the rest of them come down here?"

"I guess we better hope Colonel Hayes on Lunar Base comes up with a good plan. Now that you know, are you going to storm off, or are you going to help? There's more to operation Siren than what you've seen so far," Sean said.

Director Mills balled his hands into fists and sighed, then looked away in disgust. Sean felt the same way. He hated what he was about to do, but he couldn't think of another way to strike a crippling blow to the Vemus invaders. A lot of people were going to die, but at least others would get to live. Why else would he fight?

26

Colonel Hayes frowned at the three-dimensional holographic image of the Vemus Alpha ship. Everyone else in the mission briefing room remained silent as they studied the same image with the same perplexity Nathan felt. He was glad it wasn't just him, but when his engineers were confounded, that was serious cause for alarm.

"I need options, people. Anything you've got. Let's lay it all on the table," Nathan said.

Major Shelton forced her lips together in concentration, looking at Major Kara Roberts. "Can you go over that one more time, Major?"

"Particularly the part where even with the combined HADES IV missile payloads we'll still be unable to destroy the Vemus Alpha ship," Nathan added.

Nathan watched as Major Roberts sucked in a deep breath. "The explosive force of the additional payload isn't the entire issue. The problem is we can't penetrate the ship deep enough for them to do enough damage."

"When you proposed this idea before, I thought the issue of penetration wouldn't be a problem. What changed?" Nathan asked.

"We got updated scanning data from our recon drones, and the interior of the Vemus Alpha isn't as hollow as we hoped it would be. I'm sorry, Colonel," Major Roberts said.

Nathan shook his head. "Don't be sorry. I'd rather we find out now than after we launched our last missiles."

They'd been about to proceed with the launch of the original plan when Major Roberts stormed into the Command Center, demanding that they abort. Since she was the lead engineer largely responsible for the proposed modified payload, together with the fact that she insisted there wasn't a chance in hell her proposal was going to work, Nathan aborted the launch. Three Vemus cruisers patrolled the area, looking for the lunar base, and their window to launch was rapidly closing.

"We still need to keep moving forward. We managed to hinder their drop-ships, but we don't know how long that will last," Nathan said and switched the holographic display to show the main continent on the planet. "The Vemus managed to land a sizable force at Sierra, Delphi, and New Haven. As far as we can tell, they haven't discovered the bunkers or Sanctuary."

Nathan noticed Major Roberts' shoulders relax slightly at the news, her expression relieved.

"We need to focus, people. We all have someone important down on the planet, counting on us—wives, husbands, daughters, sons, friends, and the list goes on," Nathan said. "Who do you have waiting for you, Roberts?"

Major Roberts swallowed. "My husband, Noah."

Nathan frowned. "Captain Barker? Noah is your husband?"

"Yes, Colonel. The last communication I received from him was that they were sending him to Sanctuary to work on the power converter for the alien power station," Major Roberts said.

"They have a colossus cannon there. Very powerful. It should give them some measure of protection," Nathan said. He knew of Noah Barker. He was a brilliant engineer. Noah and Kara were the team that had updated the targeting systems of the HADES IV-B missiles. He would've liked to have had Noah here to work with Kara because two great minds are better than one.

He brought the Vemus Alpha ship back to prominence on the holodisplay. "How do we destroy that ship? If missiles can't do it because they can't get deep enough, then what will? Do we send four separate teams to do it? Use drills? Something . . . anything," Nathan said and looked around the mission briefing room, not liking what he saw. A long silence took hold of the room, with no one daring to speak. They were paralyzed by fear and he needed them to snap out of it. "Focus on the solution."

Major Shelton cleared her throat. "If we were to send in teams to storm the Vemus Alpha, they'd need to know the target depth they had to reach."

"We have four bombs, but the trouble isn't with the shape of the Alpha because it's not one big ship. It's made up of smaller ships that have somehow been absorbed into a jumbled mass. If we think of the Alpha as a large asteroid, then perhaps getting our bombs as close to the center as possible would do the trick," Nathan said.

Major Roberts shook her head. "It's not the same. Ordinarily, yes, that would work, but we're dealing with an unknown substance. The exoskeleton grows, and it's the real thing keeping that ship together. So while getting our bombs as far into the ship as possible is a step in the right direction, there's no guarantee it would work."

"What about sending the four missiles into the seven-kilometer hole General Gates blew in there from Phoenix Station? It's already a structural weak point," Lieutenant LaCroix said.

"Maybe, and that's a big maybe because we can't get any recon drones inside there to determine the extent of the damage," Major Roberts said.

"If it *is* a weak point, the Vemus would likely have it guarded," Nathan said.

He agreed with Major Roberts. They needed eyes inside the Vemus Alpha, but he doubted the Vemus would be cooperative about it. They had combat shuttles, but whoever he sent on that mission would likely never return. Nathan knew there would be no shortage of volunteers, but he'd only make that kind of sacrifice if he knew it was worth it.

"Someone has to go take a look then," Lieutenant LaCroix said.

"I'm not sure that would work," Nathan said.

"Why not, Colonel?" Major Shelton asked.

"If we start poking around, the Vemus will know we're interested in that area. If we're going to send a team in, they might as well take the bombs with them and finish the job. The rub is we don't know if the bombs would do enough damage to destroy the ship, and given its proximity to the planet, pieces of the ship could crash into New Earth," Nathan said.

"What if we draw them away from the planet?" Major Roberts said.

"To where?" Lieutenant LaCroix asked.

"Here. If we lure them here and destroy the ship, who cares if it crashes into the moon? Their ship would just make another crater but wouldn't do any real damage to the moon," Major Roberts said.

"How do we get them to come here?" Nathan asked.

"I think you said earlier something about all or nothing. We attack them with everything we have. Reveal our presence," Major Roberts said.

Nathan thought about it for a moment and then nodded. "I think you're onto something," he said and noted the somber expressions in the room. "Look, I don't like this situation any more than you do. Frankly, I'd prefer a solution that didn't end with all of us dying, but if Major Roberts is right and we do this, we'll save everyone on New Earth."

A comlink opened to the mission briefing room.

"Colonel Hayes, please report to the command area," Sergeant Martinez said over comms.

"I'm on my way," Nathan replied.

The comlink closed.

"I invite anyone to come up with a better solution, but I think Major Roberts' idea is the best we've got. We don't have time to endlessly debate this. Time is running out, so if anyone has serious doubts about our way forward, voice them right now," Nathan said.

The Lunar Base staff in the mission briefing room remained silent, if a little pale.

"Alright then. Let's get to work. We're essentially kicking a hornet's nest," Nathan said and headed for the door.

Major Shelton met him at the door. "Colonel, if it's alright with you, I'll stay in here and keep them on task."

"I'll be back as soon as I can," Nathan said.

He walked down the corridor, heading toward the command area. Two CDF soldiers on duty at the door saluted him as he walked by. Nathan entered the command area and walked over to the communications workstation.

"What have you got, Sergeant?" Nathan asked.

"Sir, we've just received a message from Captain Walker," Sergeant Martinez said.

Nathan frowned and peered at the message. Captain Walker had left them to search for the salvage team his brother was on. "Update the encrypted channel using what Captain Walker sent us."

"Yes, sir," Sergeant Martinez said. After a few moments, she added, "Relays are up. We're bouncing the signal so the Vemus will have trouble locking on, but it won't last that long."

"Understood," Nathan said and grabbed a headset.

A comms channel opened and he saw Captain Walker's face appear onscreen.

"Colonel, we tried to reach the base when we noticed three Cruiser-class ships orbiting the moon. We assumed they were Vemus, so we came up with this alternative way to communicate," Captain Walker said.

"What's your status?" Nathan asked.

Captain Walker's gaze looked pained for a moment. "We found the salvage team but they were contaminated. All team members have been killed. We encountered Vemus soldiers in one of the large pieces of wreckage."

"I'm sorry to hear that," Nathan said.

"Sir, my brother was able to learn more about the Vemus, maybe even a way to stop them," Captain Walker said.

Nathan's eyes widened.

"Colonel, Vemus cruisers are closing in on our position," Sergeant Martinez said.

Nathan nodded to her and turned back to Captain Walker. "Can you transmit what you've found?"

"We're running out of time. We'll work on getting the data to you—"

The comms channel was severed.

"What happened?" Nathan asked.

"The comms channel was cut on their end, Colonel," Sergeant Martinez said.

Nathan frowned for a moment and then blew out a breath. "Keep monitoring for them."

"Yes, sir," Sergeant Martinez said. "What did they find in the wreckage?"

"Brian Walker was a scientist who wanted to get a living sample of Vemus tissue. He might have discovered something about them," Nathan said and pressed his lips together. "See if you can get someone from R&D up here. Brian's team. Maybe they'll have more of an insight."

Sergeant Martinez said she'd get right on it and Nathan walked over to the tactical workstation where Lieutenant Johnson was on duty.

"What can I do for you, Colonel?" Lieutenant Johnson asked.

"We have a combat shuttle that has important information aboard and we need to get it back to base. Given that Vemus cruisers are in the area, can you think of a way we can get that crew back here safely?" Nathan asked.

Lieutenant Johnson bit his lower lip. "I need a few minutes, sir."

We all need a few minutes, Nathan thought but nodded at Johnson. "The key to defeating the Vemus might be aboard that shuttle, Lieutenant."

"Understood, Colonel."

The Vemus cruisers could move faster and shoot from a far greater distance than a combat shuttle was capable of and he wasn't sure that one lone shuttle could make it safely back to base. He racked his own brain, trying to think of a way to bring Captain Walker in. Nathan gritted his teeth. Nothing was ever easy.

27

CONNOR CHECKED the gray bulkhead door. The repair teams had done a quick patch and then moved on to another part of the station that required attention. It appeared that the partial remains of subsection six was all that was left of Phoenix Station. It had been the centermost area of Phoenix Station where the main Command Center was located, and the reinforced superstructure was the only reason any of them were still alive. They'd been leaking atmosphere in so many places that Connor had tasked every able-bodied person not working on repairs of critical systems to pitch in with patching up the holes. That included him. The lights from his EVA suit made it possible to see what he was doing. He reached inside the supply case and pulled out a repair kit containing liquefied material that could be applied in a vacuum. Once the repair kit material was activated, it quickly adhered and bonded to the surface, filling in the cracks.

Connor gave it a moment to set and then opened a comlink. "That should do it for this area. Try to pressurize the section."

"Copy that, General. You might want to move to the side in case the patch doesn't work," Captain Randle said.

Connor stepped to the side and waited. No need to tempt fate at this point, and besides that, he knew Captain Randle could see him through the camera feed from the nearby recon drone.

"Pressurizing now, General," Captain Randle said.

Connor watched the area he'd just patched and his suit sensors didn't detect any trace of escaping atmosphere. "Looks good from out here," Connor said.

"Same in here, as well. Pressure holding. Dr. Kim will be ecstatic to have his research lab back," Captain Randle said.

Phoenix Station had been home not only to Colonial Defense Force personnel but scientists and engineers as well. Each one of those scientists and engineers believed their work was crucial to defeating the Vemus. While Connor acknowledged the importance of their work, it didn't supersede systems like life support and thrusters. They were still focusing on surviving, and weapons capability was beyond them at the moment.

"That's all the repairs in this area, General. Now please come back inside," Captain Randle said with just a hint of exasperation.

"Understood. On my way back, Captain," Connor said. He packed up his repair case and headed for the nearest airlock. It had felt good to do some hands-on work for a change. The remains of Phoenix Station weren't quite as knocking-on-death's-door as they had been when he'd first awakened after the Vemus Alpha had nearly destroyed them.

"What's the status of the communications array?" Connor asked.

"They should be finishing that up soon, sir," Captain Randle replied.

The airlock doors opened and Connor stepped inside. Once the airlock doors were shut, he disabled his magboots. There was a blast of air as the airlock pressurized and then the interior doors opened. Captain Randle waited nearby. Connor used his neural implants to tell the EVA suit systems to retract his helmet, which then unclasped itself in the front and collapsed into the thick holding chamber at the base of his neck. Connor breathed in the station's air and could still detect trace amounts of smoke. The atmospheric scrubbers were working overtime to make the air breathable, but considering how many people had died, he felt lucky to be breathing at all.

He'd caught a glimpse of all the wreckage from the other subsections of Phoenix Station. Because his EVA suit helmet had excellent optics, he'd also been able to see the wreckage that was in relatively close proximity, but they hadn't made contact with either Bravo or Charlie stations. Connor hoped Captains Mason and Saunders and their crews were still alive.

Connor looked at Captain Randle. "If the communication array is almost up, that means a scanner array should be up soon as well."

"That's affirmative, General," Captain Randle said.

A short Asian man walked out of a nearby room. He looked over at them and smiled excitedly. "General Gates, thank you so much for repairing this section."

"You're welcome, Dr. Kim," Connor said.

Dr. Young Kim regarded Connor for a moment. "You don't realize what we have in this lab. There are samples of different viruses and bacteria we've gathered from New Earth that could be instrumental in our fight against the Vemus."

"I'm glad the redundant power systems were able to keep your samples alive," Connor said and looked up at Captain Randle. The bear of a man chuckled.

They'd been through this a few times. Connor knew research labs had their place, but of all the areas that could've survived the attack on Phoenix Station, he didn't think the research lab rated very high.

"You're still not convinced," Dr. Kim said.

"I meant no disrespect to you or your work, Dr. Kim. It's just that the Vemus Alpha is still out there and we need to find a way to stop them. I'm not sure how your samples of microscopic organisms are going to help us with that," Connor said.

Dr. Kim seemed unperturbed by Connor's answer. "Actually, General Gates, the best chance we have of defeating them is within my lab."

Connor frowned curiously. "Okay, you've piqued my curiosity. Want to explain it to me then?"

Dr. Kim's eyes widened with excitement. "I'd be happy to. If you'd follow me—"

There was an audible comms chime in the corridor they were in and Connor waited for the announcement.

"General Gates, communications and scanning capabilities have been restored. PRADIS is starting to update, sir," Lieutenant Daniels said.

"Acknowledged, Lieutenant. We're on our way," Connor said and looked at Dr. Kim. "Hold that thought, Dr. Kim. I'll be back down here later and you can tell me about what's so important in your lab."

"Of course. I look forward to it, General Gates," Dr. Kim said.

Connor and Randle started making their way toward the Command Center. A direct path from the section they were in was no longer possible, so they had to circle toward the outer fringes of the wreckage. Connor had to prioritize certain areas, and though they were intact, they had to conserve their power consumption. The overhead lighting had been so badly damaged during the Vemus Alpha attack that there were entire corridors without lighting, but there was limited power available. Repair teams had set up temporary lighting in those corridors.

Connor checked the reports from Engineering as they walked. "Doesn't look like we'll get much beyond emergency power."

"The main reactor is gone, so we're basically running on reserves and the backup reactor," Captain Randle said.

"Looks like one of the hangar decks isn't damaged," Connor said while still reading the high-level reports. "Even if we crammed everyone into the shuttles we have, it still wouldn't be enough to get everyone off the station. We could use the remaining escape pods, but that wouldn't get us back to New Earth."

"One thing at a time," Captain Randle said. "We've got comms and scanners back up."

Connor nodded and hastened toward the command area. When they arrived, they saw that the medics had moved the wounded to another location, but there was blood in some areas that hadn't been cleaned up yet. The main holoscreen was still only showing a partial window, so Connor went to his workstation and brought up his own screen.

"Comms, what's our status?" Connor asked.

"There are still limited broadcast signals from New Earth. But the Vemus attack has begun and these broadcasts are several hours old, sir," Lieutenant Daniels said.

"Ops, what's our current position?" Connor asked.

"We have limited thruster capability, but we've stabilized our position so we're not simply spinning through space anymore. At twenty million kilometers, we're still a long way from New Earth, but we're heading in the right direction, sir," Lieutenant Rawn said.

Connor nodded. "Comms, are there enough communications satellites still up to get a message to Lunar Base?" he asked.

"Yes, there are, General," Lieutenant Daniels said.

"Good. Send an encrypted message to Lunar Base letting them know our current position," Connor said.

If Colonel Hayes was able to, he'd open a direct comlink to their position, which should minimize the risk of the Vemus detecting the signal. He checked PRADIS, but it was still gathering data.

"General, I've received a reply from Lunar Base. They've sent us the coordinates to a specific comms satellite using a nonregulation encrypted channel," Lieutenant Daniels said.

Connor frowned. "Nonregulation?"

"It's not CDF-specific, but it's not NA Alliance military either, sir," Lieutenant Daniels said.

"Alright, connect us using that channel, then. Directly to my screen, Lieutenant," Connor said.

Connor waited a few seconds for the connection to establish and then saw Colonel Hayes on his screen.

"It's great to see you alive, General," Colonel Hayes said.

"You too," Connor replied.

"Before I bring you up to speed, I need you to know that this comms channel will only be secure for a short period of time," Colonel Hayes said and proceeded to inform Connor of what had happened.

"I didn't think the Vemus Alpha was going to attempt a landing on New Earth. The Alliance military couldn't even do something like that with their larger ships, and we all know how big that Alpha is. I think you did the right thing, Colonel," Connor said.

"General, you're pretty banged up. I'd really like to send out a few shuttles to resupply you until we can get a rescue mission organized," Colonel Hayes said.

"We could use those supplies, but we need to focus our efforts on stopping the Vemus," Connor said.

Colonel Hayes's eyebrows wrinkled in grim acknowledgment. "We do have one of our shuttles that was in the debris field when the Vemus attacked. With the Vemus cruisers in the area, we've been trying to find a way to bring it in without alerting the Vemus to our location. The crew was sent to investigate a salvage and recon mission to attempt to learn more about the Vemus."

"What did they learn?" Connor asked.

"We're not exactly sure. The salvage team was lost, but the rescue team was able to retrieve the data and the Vemus samples that were gathered. The lead scientist believed he'd discovered crucial information that would help us defeat the Vemus," Colonel Hayes said.

"That sounds good, but I'm sensing some uncertainty," Connor replied.

"We're dealing with combat shuttle comms. With the Vemus cruisers around we can't even establish a connection to the shuttle long enough to dump the data," Colonel Hayes said.

Connor nodded. "I'm beginning to understand. Who's in command of the shuttle?"

"Captain Jon Walker. He's a good man, but he's just lost his brother, who was part of the salvage mission. It was his brother, Brian, who made the discovery about the Vemus," Colonel Hayes said.

"Send orders to Captain Walker to bring his shuttle to me," Connor said.

"I was afraid you'd say that, sir, and I'd be remiss in my duty if I didn't warn you about the degree of risk involved. The mission report provided by Captain Walker indicates that the salvage team had become compromised by the surviving Vemus soldiers aboard the wreckage, so we can't be sure that Dr. Walker's claims about his Vemus discovery are really what we hope they are," Colonel Hayes said.

Connor leaned back in his chair and rubbed the stubble on his chin. "We don't have a choice. Order Captain Walker to come here and we'll see what we've got. We can't afford to leave any stone unturned."

"Understood, General," Colonel Hayes said.

They had to close the comlink after that because their time had run out and the risk of a Vemus cruiser discovering the signal would put both Lunar Base and the remains of Phoenix Station at risk. They agreed to reconnect again in a few hours' time.

"At least we haven't lost Lunar Base," Captain Randle said.

Connor looked at Captain Randle. "We're still in this fight," he said. "Ops, inform the hangar bay that we have a combat shuttle on its way to us."

"Yes, General," Lieutenant Rawn said.

Connor looked at Captain Thorne. "Do we have any weapons capability?"

"No, sir. We thought we might have had a few rail-guns and perhaps some point defenses, but those systems are too far gone. Essentially, we're a lifeboat at this time," Captain Thorne said.

Connor gritted his teeth for a moment. He supposed it would have been too much to hope for that they had any serious weapons capability. "Understood. Captain, I want you to continue compiling a list of our assets. I need an inventory of everything we've got."

"Yes, General," Captain Thorne said and went back to work at his terminal.

"Ops, when will PRADIS be back up and running?" Connor asked.

"The scanning array is up. We're running passive scans now and processing the updates we've received from Lunar Base. I can give you a snapshot of the Vemus location within the last two hours, but that's it for now, sir," Lieutenant Rawn said.

The system was taking its sweet time coming back online. He guessed the PRADIS designers hadn't thought of the impact of being cut off from the primary computing core. There were a lot of things they hadn't thought of, so he'd have to be patient. Connor gestured for Captain Randle to follow him. "It shouldn't take the combat shuttle long to get here. I want to meet them when they land."

They headed to the lower decks, and Connor ordered a team of CDF soldiers to meet them in the hangar. Later, Connor watched as a CDF combat shuttle entered the hangar bay. There were gouges on the hull and damaged plating. The hatch on the side of the shuttle opened and a battered crew stepped out. Once they reached the floor, they stood at attention and saluted Connor.

"Welcome aboard Phoenix Station—what's left of it, that is," Connor said.

"Thank you, General," Captain Walker said. "I don't think we could stand being on that shuttle much longer."

A team of medics came forward to check the shuttle crew.

"We followed decontamination protocols, and the samples that were gathered are in the biological containment unit right here, sir," Captain Walker said and gestured to the metallic case in his hand.

"Captain, I understand you've lost your brother. He was on the salvage team?" Connor said.

"Yes, he was, General," Captain Walker said.

"What did he find?" Connor asked.

"We tried to do our own analysis of the data, but we didn't understand it," Captain Walker said.

Connor gestured for one of his soldiers to take possession of the case. "Let's get you and your team cleaned up. Then we can talk."

"I appreciate that, sir, but my brother died for this data. I need to know if . . . I just need to know, sir," Captain Walker said.

Connor regarded Captain Walker for a moment. He clutched the case in a white-knuckled grip.

"Alright. We have a few working labs. Let's head over to them and let those scientists analyze what you've got. In the meantime, the rest of your team will be debriefed and cleaned up," Connor said.

Captain Walker nodded, relieved.

Connor led them out, the CDF soldiers walking behind them. "Not what you were expecting, were they," he said.

Captain Walker frowned.

"The Vemus. Colonel Hayes reported that you encountered Vemus soldiers," Connor said.

Captain Walker's expression hardened. "No, they weren't, sir. I have trouble believing they were once people."

Connor nodded, remembering his own encounter with them. "They might have been people once but not anymore."

They headed toward the biological lab where Dr. Young Kim waited for them.

"I hadn't expected you to return so soon, General," Dr. Kim said.

"Circumstances have changed. Captain Walker here has brought live tissue samples taken from Vemus soldiers. There has already been a preliminary analysis done by Dr. Brian Walker," Connor said.

Dr. Kim's eyes darted toward Captain Walker and then he glanced at the other soldiers. "Where is Dr. Walker?"

"He didn't make it," Captain Walker replied.

Dr. Kim's gaze softened. "I'm very sorry to hear that."

"I have his data. He died for it," Captain Walker said.

"Yes, of course. I'll take very good care of it. Please upload over here," Dr. Kim said and gestured toward the nearest terminal at the end of a long table.

Dr. Kim walked over to the terminal, completely ignoring the case with the Vemus samples. They waited a few minutes while he studied the information. Connor glanced around the lab. There were all sorts of instruments and containers marked as cold storage.

Dr. Kim looked up from his terminal. "This is remarkable."

"We're glad you approve, but we need to know if there's something in there we can use against the Vemus," Connor said.

"Brian said he'd found the key to destroying the Vemus for good," Captain Walker said.

Dr. Kim bit his lower lip and glanced down at the screen. His eyes slid into a look of calculation, as if he were weighing the possibilities, and then he snorted. "I can see why he thought that."

Connor's brows pulled together. "Do you agree with his findings?"

Dr. Kim frowned. "What Dr. Walker discovered was that the Vemus behave like a hive. There's a strict hierarchy," he said and looked at Connor. "I recall your reports on the Vemus included an opinion that they weren't very imaginative."

"That's right. They only seem to react to the immediate threat," Connor replied.

"How can they be a hive? That doesn't make any sense," Captain Walker said.

Dr. Kim shrugged. "Actually, a hive hierarchy is one of the dominant groupings of life. We've seen it on an insect level but also among microorganisms. So it's not much of a stretch of the imagination that the Vemus have this hierarchy as well."

"There's a lot that doesn't add up here. Hives don't work this way. They don't cross interstellar space to hunt humans," Connor said.

"No, they don't," Dr. Kim said. "What we're seeing is a parasitic organism that's in symbiosis with a very specific virus. One cannot survive without the other."

"If there's a hive, then there's a queen. Will the hive die if we kill the queen?" Connor asked.

Dr. Kim shook his head. "I may have oversimplified what the Vemus are. They're hive-like. I need some time to look at Dr. Walker's data and the samples he's collected."

"We're a little short on time. How much do you think you need?" Connor asked.

"This is where you expect me to give you a completely unreasonable timeframe because I'm a scientist who can't see beyond what's directly in front of him. But I assure you, General, I'm well aware of the stakes. Give me a half hour to look things over carefully and then I'll have more answers for you, or at the very least a reasonable estimate," Dr. Kim said.

Connor swallowed hard. "Thirty minutes," he said and left the lab.

Connor walked back into the corridor, his mind replaying what Dr. Kim had said. He really could have used Wil Reisman's help with all this or even Noah's—both were good at finding the devil in the details. He glanced behind him and saw Captain Randle and Captain Walker following him. They were good men, but they weren't Sean. He was surprised by just how much he'd come to rely on Sean Quinn's counsel. He didn't regret sending Sean back to New Earth, but he did wish he was still here with them. Connor closed his eyes and took a deep breath. He thought about Lenora and felt his chest tighten. She certainly had never pulled any punches when dealing with him. He wondered what she'd do if she were here.

Connor stopped walking and leaned up against the wall. "What do you think about what Dr. Kim said?"

"Honestly, sir, this is beyond my expertise. I don't know what to think," Captain Randle said.

"What about you, Walker?" Connor said.

"Brian wouldn't have made the claim that the data he'd found was important unless he really thought it was. He knew he was never getting out of that ship. He'd been infected, along with the entire salvage team. He even stopped the other team members from trying to escape. So if you're asking me whether I believe what my brother said is true, then I do, sir," Captain Walker said.

"The hive theory makes sense, but I'm not sure if that's because I *want* it to make sense. We know the Vemus were using some type of command/control signal for the fleet. We blocked that signal and it severely limited their fighting capability. So there's evidence to support that we're at least dealing with a centralized intelligence," Connor said.

"Sir, how do we go from a disease that spreads among mammals and then, when we try to fix it, it targets humans exclusively? That's what was in the data from the *Indianapolis*. I can understand how the virus spreads, but for it to become some type of collective intelligence, I'm not sure how we can defeat that other than by taking the damn thing out," Captain Randle said.

Connor sighed. "I think you're right. We just need Dr. Kim to confirm it, and hopefully those samples will give us something we can use against them."

Captain Randle frowned. "What's to stop this thing from spreading to creatures from New Earth?"

"There's no way to know for sure. The experts won't say. They'll only say something about life developing on different evolutionary paths. Plus, we know that Earth scientists modified the virus, which made it into something outside of nature," Connor said.

Captain Walker nodded. "I remember my brother mentioning that. But we can't afford to let any of them escape."

"You'll get no arguments from me on that. Let's give Dr. Kim some time and hope he'll give us some good news. In the meantime, we need to come up with a plan to take out that Vemus Alpha," Connor said.

"General, this station doesn't have any weapons capabilities," Captain Randle said.

Captain Walker arched a brow in surprise.

Connor leveled his gaze at them. "Yes, it does."

"We have no missiles or heavy weapons, sir," Captain Randle said.

"You're right, we don't, but I was thinking of something much more dangerous," Connor replied.

Captain Randle frowned in confusion.

"Never underestimate the power of what a soldier can accomplish with the use of only his rifle. There are a few hundred of us left here, and we have the element of surprise," Connor said.

28

Sierra was a war zone and Sean was at the epicenter. Vemus soldiers roamed the streets of the outer city, hunting for them. Sean was in the upper levels of a high-rise building, and the high-pitched whistles and clicks of the Vemus soldiers drew closer as a horde of them closed in on Sean and his team. The combined CDF and Field Ops forces had held the line for as long as they could before retreating. Civilian militia helped with the wounded, running them back to temporary safe zones so they could be transported away from the city.

Sean looked through the scope of his M-Viper rifle and watched a group of Vemus soldiers surround a fallen CDF soldier who was in a twisted heap, covered with a thick black liquid. The soldier squirmed, and for a moment, his face was free of the viscous liquid. He struggled to move his arms but the Vemus pinned him down to the ground. The soldier screamed. Something dark slithered along his body and went into his mouth. The soldier's eyes widened as he tried to cry out. Sean lined up his shot and squeezed the trigger. A lone shot of mercy rang out amidst the gunfire that raged throughout Sierra. The writhing CDF soldier jerked back and then was still. Sean moved away from the window. He'd lost count of how many shots he'd taken like that. Mercy killings. He preferred to think he was easing their pain, but it only slowed the Vemus down. They didn't abandon anyone on the battlefield regardless of whether they were living or not. All seemed to have equal value.

There was a muffled bang from several floors beneath them.

"We can't stay here. They're through the barricade downstairs," Lieutenant Compton said. "There's a Hellcat waiting for us on the roof, Major."

Sean followed Lieutenant Compton up the stairs. The Vemus had ignored the buildings unless they knew CDF were inside. He'd ordered CDF soldiers to remain behind beyond the line of battle to hamper the Vemus soldiers as they pushed forward. They'd conceal their locations and then strike the enemy from behind before escaping to the next building using temporary walkways.

The Vemus seemed conditioned to engage only with something directly in their path, and Sean exploited this weakness for as long as it was effective, but they eventually caught on. The Vemus always did, and in this case it didn't take them long to learn that they had to start clearing the buildings before moving forward. The longer the Vemus engaged the Colonial Defense Force, the more intelligent they became in the execution of their tactics.

Sean ran up the stairwell and heard a Hellcat troop carrier flying overhead. They didn't stop in any one place for very long. He'd tasked the Hellcats with transporting soldiers, removing them from hot zones but keeping them in the fight for as long as they were able. The Hellcats were armed with an M-180 gauss cannon capable of firing thirty-millimeter projectiles in rapid succession. When engaged, the M-180 was capable of mowing down whatever enemy force was in its path. The problem was the damn Vemus energy weapons, which were capable of bringing down even the Hellcats. But the Hellcats could provide air support for a limited time and sometimes that made all the difference for the mobile infantry units on the ground. No sooner would a CDF squad get picked up than they were deposited at another location within the city. The CDF still fought, even knowing they had no hope of pushing the enemy out of the city. Instead, they fought to kill as many Vemus soldiers as they could while drawing them farther *into* the city.

Sean and the others exited the stairwell and followed Lieutenant Compton onto the waiting Hellcat. As soon as he was aboard and the Hellcat pilot was flying away, a CDF soldier raised a rocket launcher to his shoulder and fired it at the building. There was a brief lull in the area before the interior of the building exploded, killing all the Vemus soldiers inside.

In an instant, the hard work of the colonists was ripped to pieces. Sean had stopped telling himself they'd rebuild it all someday. It didn't help. After destroying several buildings, it didn't feel as if there would ever be anything here but death and destruction. A deep-seated fury took hold of him each time a part of Sierra was demolished. They'd killed so many Vemus soldiers, but it was never enough. The brief euphoria at gouging the enemy's numbers was always short-lived. In the beginning, he'd relished the feeling. Striking the enemy down had sparked a deep satisfaction, knowing he'd hurt the things that were there to kill them. Then, bitterness set in at the reality of what they were facing. What good was a victory when they had to destroy their home in order to survive? But still, he would fight. He clutched his rifle—just as all the CDF soldiers had—and kept throwing himself into the fray. Survival required a sacrifice paid for in blood, and the colony as a whole was paying a terrible price.

Sean glanced over to the side and watched as another Hellcat flew toward a rooftop to extract soldiers waiting for a pickup. As the Hellcat approached the rooftop, a large group of Vemus soldiers stormed onto the rooftop of a neighboring building and threw themselves at the ship. The pilot tried to steer the ship away, but some of the Vemus fighters made it on board. Sean raised his weapon and called for help. He aimed and glimpsed the soldiers inside the

Hellcat, trying to fight the Vemus soldiers. Deadly blue bolts flashed inside the aircraft. The Vemus had long abandoned the less effective white stunner bolts. The blue bolts could penetrate armor and combat suits alike. Sean was about to fire his weapon when the Hellcat slammed into the neighboring building and crashed onto the street below. Sean ordered the pilot to bring them around so they could search for survivors, but before they could move into position there was an orange flash and the Hellcat exploded. As the Vemus began to turn deadly weapons toward their aircraft, the pilot quickly flew them away.

Sean clenched his teeth and glared at the building swarming with Vemus soldiers. "Sergeant Mitchell, take out that building."

"Sorry, Major, no more rockets," Sergeant Mitchell replied.

Sean blew out a harsh breath and sat down, using his neural implants to sift through the updates from his platoon commanders. The sun was waning in the sky and the Vemus showed no signs of slowing down. Their own equipment worked just fine at night, so it was safe for Sean to assume that the Vemus wouldn't be stopping to rest anytime soon. Did they ever rest?

"Sir, I have a comlink from Captain Diaz. He's on his way to the tower already," Lieutenant Compton said.

"Put him through," Sean said.

A new connection registered with the comlink interface.

"Major, the battle lines are collapsing. The CDF forces to the east are already at the central tower. They were hit pretty hard," Captain Diaz said.

Sean could hear the sounds of the battle on the other end of the comlink. "Understood. We need to hold that tower. I'll send reinforcements there now."

"Sir, I was hoping you would be among the reinforcements," Captain Diaz said.

Sean frowned. They were nowhere near the central tower. He glanced out the open hatchway to get his bearings, and his eyes widened. He'd completely lost his sense of direction. They'd been fighting and moving from building to building while drawing the Vemus steadily toward the central part of the city. A heavy toll had been extracted from the Vemus, but Sean couldn't quite believe that they were already near the central city line.

He looked at Lieutenant Compton grimly. "Order the retreat. All troops are to fall back to the tower. If they can't make it, they're to go to the designated extraction points for pickup," Sean said. "We'll see you shortly, Captain Diaz."

"Understood, Major," Captain Diaz said, and the comlink closed.

Sean went to the cockpit. "Change in plans. Take us to the tower."

"Yes, Major," the pilot said.

They didn't have far to fly. There were still a lot of Hellcats in the air, and when it became apparent that they weren't going to hold the city, certain members of the CDF requested permission to set up a few parting gifts for the Vemus. High-grade explosives were hastily deployed, waiting to be triggered by the unsuspecting Vemus forces. Those explosives would stop the Vemus fighters permanently.

It was then that Sean noticed the smaller Vemus fighters as they reached the tops of the buildings and attempted to glide to the next one. They had skin that stretched from their wrists to their feet. They were much smaller than the average Vemus fighter, at only five feet in height. But for what they lacked in height, they made up in numbers. They were astonishingly fast, but they were also easier to bring down. Sean saw a group of them try to reach the rooftop of a building where the CDF had an M-180 gauss gun nest. The soldiers fired the M-180, cutting the gliding Vemus fighters down, and their small bodies fell to the streets below.

The Hellcat took them to the landing area in the shadow of Sierra's tallest tower. Sean and the rest of the team climbed out and the Hellcat flew off to extract another troop. With his boots on solid ground again he felt weakness deep in his muscles. He was beyond the safety of consuming more stimulants, but it didn't matter. He didn't have time to rest. None of them did.

The landing area was a buzz of activity as soldiers were dropped off and wounded soldiers were taken to the tramway beneath the city. There was only one tramway working. All the other tunnels had been destroyed to prevent the Vemus from using them.

Director Mills walked toward him. His towering form allowed his long strides to quickly cover the distance between them, and his gaze no longer held the bitter disgust it had displayed earlier.

Sean looked at the Director of Field Ops and Security. "Are the trams still running?"

"They are. All these soldiers are being moved there for the final run before we blow the last tunnel," Director Mills said.

"Better make it fast. The Vemus forces are going to make a major push right for this area," Sean replied.

Director Mills frowned and Sean guessed that his father's friend wanted to ask how Sean could possibly know what the Vemus were going to do.

"We'll get it done," Director Mills said.

Sean continued to walk. He needed to get to the Command Center they'd established inside the tower.

"Sean, wait," Mills said.

Sean stopped and looked back at him.

"I'm sorry about before. I should have trusted you," Mills said.

"It's gotta be hard since you've known me since I was a teenager," Sean replied.

Director Mills nodded. "And one who excelled at getting into trouble."

Sean snorted. "We've come a long way," he said and glanced at Lieutenant Compton, who gestured that they needed to get moving. Sean looked back at Mills. "Make sure you're on that last tram. I need someone to get those wounded soldiers to safety."

Director Mills arched a brow knowingly. "And here I thought you just wanted to get me out of the way."

"That too. You're a pain in the ass," Sean said with a half-smile.

Director Mills became somber. "About Phoenix Station . . ."

Sean felt his throat seize up as he fought the emotion. "I wouldn't count Connor out just yet."

Director Mills pressed his lips together. "No, you wouldn't, would you? Connor and I clashed on a lot of things, but I know he was very proud of you. He saw something in you that your father and I both missed."

Sean regarded Director Mills for a moment. "This isn't goodbye, Damon. I'll see you later."

Damon Mills nodded. "Right . . . see you later."

Sean left the Director of Field Ops and Security, keeping a firm grip on his emotions. Thinking about Phoenix Station and the fact that Sierra was a heartbeat from being destroyed threatened to topple his resolve. He hastened toward the tower and took the elevator to the CDF mobile Command Center. He remembered when the tower had been completed, commemorating the colony's sixth anniversary. It was a time when belief in a hostile attack force that was on their way here was starting to wane in earnest. All the preparations they'd made by building Titan Space station, the beginnings of the CDF space fleet, and the missile defense platforms had lulled them into a false sense of security, which Sean hadn't been completely immune to. He'd thought they would have more time. The only people whose commitment never wavered were Connor, Wil, and Kasey—the most senior military officers in the Colonial Defense Force and men who not only had actual combat experience but who had made a career of neutralizing threats that operated outside the normal confines of society. Those men might not have been ideally suited for mankind's first interstellar colony, but they were the best men to see that the colony survived what was coming. Wil and Kasey had been killed during the colony's first battle with the Vemus, and Sean had to admit, if only to himself, the very real possibility that Connor Gates was dead as well. Sean hated that he'd ever had the slightest inkling of doubt that an attack force like the Vemus was coming for them. It all seemed so foolish now with the benefit of hindsight.

The elevator doors opened and the CDF soldiers in the Command Center glanced up, immediately looking relieved that Sean was there. Sean had seen this same thing many times when Connor walked into a room. There was a certain comfort that came when the burden of command rested on someone else's shoulders and that superior officer was someone like Connor. Sean kept expecting their gazes to shift to the side where Connor would normally have been standing, but they were all looking at him. The soldiers at the entrance saluted him, and Sean returned the salute as he walked past them.

Sean glanced toward the windows, where he saw multiple Hellcats flying in, dropping soldiers off. There were several flashes of light about half a kilometer from where the line of battle was still being fought.

"Major Quinn, I need you over here, sir," Captain Diaz called out from the CIC.

Sean turned away from the windows and walked over toward Diaz, who stood at the command table where the three-dimensional holographic display was focused in on the tower and the immediate surrounding area. Sean grabbed a canteen of water and gulped it down.

"Where do we stand, Captain?" Sean asked.

Captain Diaz regarded him for a moment with concern. "How many stims have you had beyond the recommended dosage, sir?"

Sean gave him a hard look, which he knew wouldn't change the pupil dilation in his eyes that had no doubt given him away. "Irrelevant, Captain."

Captain Diaz frowned but didn't press the matter. Sean knew he was beyond the maximum dosage allowed, but he also knew he could push the limits. He could hear his mother's voice in the back of his mind, scolding him for doing such a thing, but he ignored it. He had a job to do and had no time to worry about how his body would need to cope with the withdrawal symptoms from extended stim usage. If he survived long enough to experience the severe muscle cramping and the inability of his brain to determine reality, it would be a blessing.

"All CDF troops are falling back to this position. The Vemus have been pushing forward much harder than they were before. It's like they become more capable the longer they fight," Captain Diaz said.

"It's only going to get worse. Those bastards can smell blood in the water," Sean said.

Captain Diaz's face became a thoughtful frown. "Interesting choice of words. The last group of scientists we evacuated from here had a theory about the Vemus mimicking the behavior of ocean mammals, particularly predators, which might account for their appearance."

"Does it help us kill them?" Sean asked harshly, the stims barely keeping exhaustion at bay.

Captain Diaz's expression went back to business. "Well, they do seem to follow an alpha in their midst, which suggests they might organize themselves into packs."

"Which is why we've been targeting those alphas. It stalls their attack when we can take them down," Sean said.

"And they're the hardest to kill," Captain Diaz said.

"I don't care where the scientists think the Vemus came from. I only care about stopping them," Sean said.

"What about knowing one's enemy, sir?" Captain Diaz said evenly.

Sean shook his head and grinned. Connor had preached the importance of learning all they could about their enemy. "Point taken, but we really don't have time for a theoretical discussion," Sean said.

Captain Diaz nodded and brought up the Saber failsafe interface, which required Sean's authorization.

"It's a little too soon for that, don't you think?" Sean asked.

Saber failsafe was the CDF code for the self-destruct that would level the entire city.

"This is the authorization for it to be armed. Detonation has to be authorized by you or the next officer in the chain of command in the area," Captain Diaz said.

Sean took a long look at the authorization window that awaited his input. This was his plan for striking a crippling blow against the enemy, so why was it so hard for him to push the proverbial button? Sierra was their home and he hated seeing it destroyed. And what was worse was the fact that there was a Vemus Alpha ship filled with more soldiers, so was there even a point to the destruction? Sean gritted his teeth. Frowning, he looked away from the authorization prompt and sighed. He couldn't worry about the Vemus Alpha in orbit above the planet. The Vemus army in Sierra was what he needed to deal with. Sean used his implants to send his authorization codes, and the Saber failsafe armed. The authorization window flickered away and was replaced with the Saber failsafe status set to ARMED.

"You did the right thing, Major," Captain Diaz said quietly.

"Why does it feel so shitty then?" Sean asked.

"There are no perfect solutions," Captain Diaz replied.

Sean gave him a sidelong glance. "You sound like Connor now."

Captain Diaz snorted. "Who do you think I first heard say it?"

For the next ninety minutes, Sean helped coordinate the strategic withdrawal from Sierra. Wounded soldiers were loaded onto the tram and taken out of the city where ground support vehicles waited to take them to the gathering place. The secret encampment was located in a highly defensible position about a hundred kilometers from the city.

The Vemus pressed the CDF forces back to the tower. The strategic withdrawal of troops worked as long as their lines of soldiers weren't overwhelmed. Each group had to cover the retreat of the previous. There had been a steady stream of CDF soldiers making their way to the tower and then flying out on Hellcat troop carriers. Sean heard the fighting gain intensity down below as the Vemus stormed the landing field and ordered all soldiers in the tower to head to the roof. He glanced out the window and still saw CDF soldiers firing their weapons at the Vemus from nearby buildings surrounding the tower complex.

"We need to get those soldiers out of there before they're cut off," Sean said.

Captain Diaz contacted the Hellcat commander to relay Sean's orders. Sunset had long since passed and they were in the darkest of night—as dark as night could get on a planet with brightly lit rings around it. He saw the glowing points of the Hellcats' engines as they blazed by. There were more than a few CDF soldiers who had stayed behind, doing whatever they could to stall the enemy's advance. The city was being overrun, just as Sean had known it would be. If he'd kept all his soldiers in the city, they might have held it for another day, but the outcome would still have been the same. They would all be dead. The feeds from the recon drones that flew through the city showed Vemus fighters moving into the area, except for the groups that were busy lining up fallen CDF soldiers who were now covered in a viscous liquid that transformed into a dark pod. Something began to move inside some of them. Sean had taken his fair share of shots at them, as well as the Vemus in the surrounding area, but it only slowed down the metamorphosis happening inside the pods.

They headed to the roof and Sean caught the urgent chatter from the teams still making their way up the tower. Vemus forces were trying to cut them off by scaling the outer walls.

"J-Squad to the edge of the roof. They need covering fire!" Sean ordered.

He grabbed his M-Viper and ran to the east side of the roof, where CDF soldiers slid toward the low walls. The corded safety lines that prevented people from leaning over the side had already been cut away. Sean squatted and quickly crawled toward the edge. CDF soldiers joined him, and he felt someone grab hold of his legs. Sean glanced behind him.

"Give 'em hell, sir!" the soldier said.

Other soldiers quickly moved in and did the same thing, throwing themselves over the legs of the soldiers who were firing their weapons at the Vemus.

Sean leaned over the edge of the thirty-meter-tall tower, which was minuscule compared to the major cities on Earth but was the tallest building in Sierra. He aimed his M-Viper. The light sensor on his scope had already adjusted to the darkness and compensated for it. Sean had a clear view of the Vemus soldiers scrambling up the walls. The creatures' claws gouged into the sides of the tower as they quickly climbed upward.

Sean squeezed the trigger, sending high-velocity projectiles downward and taking the Vemus soldiers by surprise. The Vemus were knocked from the sides of the building. Some slammed into other Vemus soldiers, knocking them off as well. Several floors beneath them, Sean saw the flashes of Vemus weapons fire.

Sean looked behind him and saw Compton. "Make sure they have backup in the stairwell, Lieutenant."

Compton ran off and Sean scanned below, looking for more Vemus to kill. Hellcats flew to the rooftops and CDF soldiers clambered to get aboard. Another Hellcat circled the tower and used its main M-180 gauss cannon to tear into the enemy. The Hellcat stayed on the move, and the Vemus soldiers were unable to get a clear shot at it.

"Time to go, Major!" Captain Diaz shouted.

The soldier holding Sean's legs down pulled him back from the edge. Sean pushed himself up to his feet, thanking him, and they ran toward the waiting Hellcat. The tower was alive with the Vemus's high-pitched whistles and clicks, and it suddenly seemed like a spoken language that Sean couldn't begin to comprehend. All he knew was that he never wanted to hear that sound again. Sean reached the hatch on the Hellcat and gestured for the soldiers to climb aboard. A squad was covering the stairwell entrance. There were still CDF soldiers running through the door, escaping the hordes of Vemus inside. When the last soldiers came out, the nearest soldier threw a grenade and ran toward them. There was a bright flash as the grenade exploded.

"Your turn, sir," Captain Diaz said, gesturing with his thick, muscular arms.

Sean was about to turn and climb aboard when he noticed a dark shape scramble onto the rooftop. He reached out and grabbed Captain Diaz, shoving him aboard the Hellcat. Sean quickly followed while the Vemus opened fire on the Hellcat.

"Go! Go!" Lieutenant Compton bellowed.

Sean felt something hot singe through the armor protecting his shoulder, followed by intense pain. He cried out, and the CDF soldiers dragged him further into the Hellcat, away from the hatchway. The Hellcat's pilot maximized the thrusters and the troop carrier sped away.

"I'm fine. Let me up," Captain Diaz said.

He pushed his way to Sean's side and looked at his wounded shoulder.

"Get me a medical pack, ASAP!" Captain Diaz said and then looked at Sean. "Just had to be the hero, didn't you? Just lie there for a second. You're bleeding. That damn weapon of theirs cut right through your armor."

Sean gritted his teeth at the pain. "Now you owe me one."

Diaz snorted. "We'll see about that," he said and then glared at the nearest CDF soldier. "What the hell is taking so long? If you move any slower, you might be standing still, damn it!"

A CDF soldier hastened over, carrying a medical pack. Diaz reached inside and grabbed the medi-gun, which carried the treatment for severe burns.

"Alright, bite down. A lot of pain and then nothing at all. You ready?" Captain Diaz asked.

"Stop sweet-talking me and just do it already, Captain," Sean said through clenched teeth.

"You must have spoken to my wife. She likes to take charge, too," Captain Diaz said. He ripped open a sealed canister and shoved it into the medi-gun. "Alright, on three."

Sean didn't hear the rest because Diaz squeezed the trigger and medi-paste flooded the wound. Nanorobotic-filled paste swarmed over the wounded area and Sean's vision swam. He squeezed his eyes shut against the pain and then his shoulder became numb, but he was still gasping as he opened his eyes. He took several deep breaths and looked up at Diaz, who grinned down at him.

Sean climbed to his feet and looked at his shoulder. There was a thick, flexible mesh that looked like an extra layer of skin. He rolled his shoulder and felt a dull ache, but he knew better than to overdo it; his shoulder needed time to heal. At least the pain had lessened.

He looked at Diaz. "I thought you said you'd go on three?"

Captain Diaz smiled, showing a healthy set of pearly whites. "That's just so you'd relax before I got you."

"Thanks," Sean said dryly.

The cool night air came in through the open hatchway in the back of the Hellcat. Sierra was a sea of blazing fires. He could still hear the firing of CDF weapons from inside the city, but it was sporadic and spread out.

"There are men back there," Sean said.

"We can't get to them," Captain Diaz replied.

Sean pressed his lips together and clenched his teeth. The Vemus had taken the city. While they could chance a flyover high above the city, they couldn't risk going down there to extract the CDF soldiers they'd left behind. Sean walked toward the hatchway and watched. He'd gotten the Vemus to do exactly what he wanted, so why did he feel like they'd just lost the battle? The Hellcat raced past the edge of the city and over the dark forests beyond.

Captain Diaz came to his side. "All Hellcats still flying have cleared the city, sir."

Sean drew in a breath and held it, allowing his eyes to take in this last sight of the home they'd built. Buildings were burning, and many soldiers had died in defense of the city as part of their ruse to draw the Vemus in.

Sean used his neural implants to take control of the Hellcat's communications system. He sent out a warning signal to the other Hellcats, then counted to ten and sent the detonation signal for the Saber failsafe. Sean watched as a bright flash lit up Sierra as if a molten sun had just ignited in the middle of the city. He looked away from the bright light, but he couldn't block out the intense sound of the thermal nuclear explosion, which had enough force to level the city and the area surrounding it. One moment Sierra was there and the next it was gone, wiped clean off the face of New Earth. Sean wondered if they would later find a crater where the city had been or if it would just be scorched earth. He forced his gaze ahead, not wanting to look back at where Sierra had been.

The Hellcat was far enough away that they hadn't felt the kinetic forces from the explosion, and they experienced an uneventful twenty-minute flight to the away zone. The Hellcats and ground vehicles that had left earlier had made it to the coordinates. They were far away from the secret civilian bunkers they'd built, which Sean couldn't really think about at the moment.

Diaz came over and sat next to him. "You made the right call," he said.

Sean lifted his gaze and looked at him. "Would he have made the same call?" he asked.

Diaz nodded without even a hint of hesitation. "Connor would have done the same thing."

Sean sighed. "I guess that's something. The question remains: what happens when more soldiers from the Vemus Alpha come down here?"

Captain Diaz swallowed hard. "I'm sure Colonel Hayes and the rest of our forces at Lunar Base are going to take care of that."

Sean wished he had Diaz's confidence, but he didn't say that aloud. No need to spread disharmony in the face of losing their home.

The Hellcat landed and Sean walked down the ramp. The night air was fresh and cool, not at all like the acrid smoke they'd been breathing in Sierra. He glanced up at the deceptively peaceful night sky.

Lieutenant Compton walked over to him. "Major, they need you at one of the tents."

Sean shook his head. "Can't I get a moment, just one moment to get my bearings? Is that too much to ask!"

Lieutenant Compton looked over at Captain Diaz for a moment.

"Sir, it's your father. He's been hurt."

The exhaustion pressing in on Sean suddenly vanished. "Where is he?"

"Medical tent seven. This way," Lieutenant Compton said.

Sean followed the big lieutenant as they ran toward the CDF encampment. Tent seven was only a short distance from the landing zone. He ran inside the tent and saw his mother standing, grim-faced, beside a bed. Confusion and then surprise chased each other across Sean's face. His mother was supposed to be at Sanctuary. How'd she even gotten here? But as soon as the question formed in his mind, he realized his mother had probably bullied her way back. She looked up at his arrival, her eyes brimming with tears. Sean looked down and saw that his father was gravely wounded.

His mother wiped her eyes and walked over to him. "He doesn't have much time," she said.

Sean's mouth hung open. "What happened? Isn't there anything you can do?"

His father stirred at the sound of Sean's voice and opened his one good eye. The other was swollen shut. Sean could see that his father's torso was bloody and bruised beneath the white sheet. He lifted the sheet up and gasped.

"Sean," his father said.

Sean looked at his father and sorrow closed up his throat. "I sent you away from the combat zone. To make sure you were safe . . ."

The painfully grim lines of his father's mouth lifted. "I had to help, son," his father said softly.

The skin around Sean's eyes became tight and his vision started to blur. "You should have . . ."

"What? Gone to safety while other people died? That's not what you would have done."

Sean noted the stubborn gleam in his father's one good eye and recognized a similar view when he looked at himself in the mirror. He leaned closer to the bed. "Thank you."

His father's lips lifted for a moment and then his body arched in pain. He grabbed Sean and pulled him closer. "Survive," his father said in a harsh whisper, and then he collapsed to the bed, his body going limp. He heard his mother cry out and then slam her fist on his father's chest. She began administering chest compressions while calling out for medicine. None of the medics moved and Sean glanced at all the blood on the floor. There was no coming back from such a huge loss.

Sean reached for his mother and she snarled at him.

"He's. Not. Gone," she said, emphasizing each word with a compression.

Sean watched as his mother pounded on his father's chest. "He *is* gone. You need to stop."

Sean gently grabbed his mother's arms as they kept pressing on his father's chest. He brought his other arm around her shoulders, but she just wouldn't stop. "Please, Mom, you need to stop. He's gone."

Sean tried to pull his mother away but she drove her elbow into his stomach. He took hold of her firmly and pulled her back while she cried out, reaching toward his father. Sean held her as she sagged into his arms, weeping. He felt his own tears streaking down his face as everything he'd walled up inside burst forth. He clung to his mother and tried to be strong. It was what she needed. The people around them stepped back, giving them room. Theirs wasn't the only grief being felt that night, but Sean couldn't think of anyone else as his mother sobbed in his arms.

29

THERE WAS a heavy silence across the Command Center on Phoenix Station. Connor had just gotten an update from Lunar Base that Sierra had been destroyed.

"A nuclear explosion," Major Elder said. "We destroyed our own city."

Connor frowned as he reread the report.

"Major Quinn wouldn't have done this without careful consideration," Captain Randle said.

"He's right," Connor said.

"But, General, why would Major Quinn destroy not only Sierra but Delphi and New Haven?" Major Elder asked.

CDF soldiers in the Command Center craned their necks so they could hear Connor's response.

"We obviously don't have all the information, but my guess is that Major Quinn made a strategic decision," Connor said. "They couldn't hold the city, so he did exactly what I would have done—lure the enemy inside and then blow them to kingdom come."

"But General, there are people here who have families there," Major Elder said.

"The cities had already been evacuated and the most recent reports indicate that most civilians are safe at either the secret bunkers or Sanctuary. Look, I know it's tough being in the dark about what's going on back home. I get it. But we still have a job to do. We're still fighting for those same people," Connor said.

Slowly, the Command Center returned to its normal buzz of activity. He knew the war was far from over. With a ship that size, many more Vemus fighters were bound to begin the next stage of the invasion. The question remained: could the Vemus detect the bunkers they'd built, or Sanctuary?

"General Gates," Lieutenant Daniels said, "Dr. Kim has an update for you and requests that you join him in his lab."

Connor thanked her and gave a slightly annoyed glance at the main holoscreen, which was still broken.

"Captain Thorne, you have the con," Connor said.

"Yes, General," his tactical officer replied.

Connor left the Command Center and had Captain Randle send a comlink to Captain Walker to meet them at the lab. Major Elder followed them. Connor kept thinking about Sierra, trying to imagine just how bad the fighting must have been. The report he'd read indicated that the Vemus's fighting abilities had increased throughout the course of the engagement. Connor was familiar with soldiers becoming more adept at their jobs, but this was something different. If the war continued for a lengthy period of time, the Vemus would continue to become even more dangerous. Was this what had happened to the NA Alliance military? They needed to end this war quickly if they were going to have any hope of survival.

Connor walked into the Research and Development Lab. Captain Walker was already there and snapped to attention.

"At ease, Captain," Connor said and looked at Dr. Kim. "I've given you more than thirty minutes. Tell me you have some good news."

Dr. Kim nodded and then gestured one of his assistant researchers toward a clear container on the lab table. Connor glanced inside and saw a small puddle of dark liquid.

"What's in there?" Connor asked.

"It's them," Dr. Kim said. "Or at least it would be if it were to come into contact with humans. Watch."

Dr. Kim accessed one of the transference chambers and put a tiny ball of pinkish skin inside. The ball seemed to quiver. Dr. Kim closed the chamber door, pressed a button, and the ball of skin was deposited inside the chamber. The dark substance that was allegedly a Vemus had no reaction to it.

"That is a living tissue sample created from the DNA of a mouse. Observe how the Vemus sample has no reaction to it," Dr. Kim said.

Connor glanced back at the container. "We already knew the virus was modified to target humans."

Dr. Kim nodded and loaded another flesh-colored ball of skin into the transference chamber. "This was created from human DNA. Though it looks similar to the last sample, I assure you it's quite different," he said and then deposited the second sample into the container.

The dark liquid reacted almost instantly and began to move across the container toward the human tissue sample. It covered it completely. Connor glanced at Dr. Kim and then back inside the container. The Vemus sample was absorbing the human tissue sample and then it just stopped. The dark liquid sank back to the surface, becoming a pasty gray substance. The human tissue sample looked as if it had been only partially consumed.

Connor's mouth hung open in surprise. He leaned closer to the container, looking for some indication that the Vemus sample would begin to reform, but it didn't. He looked at Dr. Kim, who was smiling proudly.

"Please tell me this is something we can use," Connor said.

"Oh yes, General. We can kill them now," Dr. Kim said with an excited gleam in his eyes.

Connor swallowed. "You need to explain to me exactly what just happened. How this works. Everything."

"Earth scientists had been trying to stop the Vemus for years before they lost everything. You've had these samples for barely an hour," Major Elder said.

Dr. Kim waved them over to the wallscreen. "We've been collecting samples of microscopic organisms from New Earth since we arrived, cataloging them and their properties. What we found was a native virus that breaks down the proteins in other viruses—the very same proteins the Vemus uses to keep itself together. In essence, it sterilizes the virus and starves the parasitic organism. We break the symbiotic chain. We know the Vemus are highly adaptive and that the virus is capable of absorbing the DNA of an infected host. This is then transferred to the parasite that then takes over the host. It introduces new DNA to the host with a set of instructions that causes genes to express at a geometric rate. It's quite literally like being reborn. Think along the lines of a human embryo in its early stages of development."

"And this is possible because we modified the virus?" Connor asked.

Dr. Kim's eyebrows rose. "That's the really interesting part. We already knew the virus the Vemus uses had been modified and we were told it was modified to avoid humans, that it was their plan since they couldn't cure it. This was to buy the people of Earth time to come up with a more permanent solution," Dr. Kim said.

Connor narrowed his gaze suspiciously. "Are you implying that someone deliberately modified the virus so it would target humans exclusively?"

"Once they modified the virus, by its very nature it would take in new DNA to improve itself . . ." Dr. Kim shook his head. "My point is that once they modified the virus, it became a synthetic organism that was designed to behave in a very specific way."

"You mean a weapon. The Vemus are a biological weapon!" Connor said, hardly daring to breathe.

"Precisely," Dr. Kim confirmed.

Connor leaned back and tried to get a handle on his racing thoughts. He clenched and unclenched his fists while he paced.

"But who would do such a thing?" Major Elder asked.

Dr. Kim shook his head. "I'm sorry. I don't know who actually did this. It could have been anyone—government agencies, terrorist organizations, corporate research conglomerates, or some rogue agency. Take your pick, but the evidence is there. The most catastrophic event of our time is of our own making."

Connor couldn't believe it. He didn't *want* to believe it, but it all made sense. "Someone back home seized an opportunity to become more powerful and it backfired on them."

"My guess is that it simply got out of control," Dr. Kim said.

"I don't understand. How could it have gotten out of control? They modified the virus," Major Elder said.

"They must have had some way to protect themselves or thought they had a way to stop it, making themselves into heroes in the process," Connor said.

"They could have done that anyway without obliterating the population," Major Elder said and shook his head.

"Think about it. They found a way to remove any obstacle in their path, except they underestimated what they'd done. They tried to play God and the whole thing blew up in their faces. This whole thing makes me sick," Connor said in disgust.

They were silent for a few moments while they all digested what Dr. Kim had told them. Connor rested his hands on his hips and shook his head. One of the primary objectives of the Ghosts had been to stop things like this. Human ingenuity, which had spawned their most amazing creations, also came with the threat that the worst part of humanity could also rear its ugly head as well. If so, in a celestial blink of the eye, they would all be gone—just another intelligent, advanced race snuffed out of existence because of someone's blind ambition.

Connor looked at Dr. Kim. "You said we can kill them. How?"

"We can synthesize the virus. I've already spoken to Dr. Morgan. She's a nano-robotics engineer and she believes we can combine the two," Dr. Kim said.

"What good is that?" Connor asked.

"It will make our virus kill the Vemus faster. We can also do our own bit of manipulation to make it seek out the synthetic virus from Earth," Dr. Kim said.

"There has to be more to it than that. You said the Vemus operate like a hive. We've seen them function as if there was a centralized intelligence commanding them. Could you make enough of that stuff to take it out?" Connor asked.

"Most certainly, General," Dr. Kim said.

"How long will it take to make it?" Connor asked.

"We can have a batch ready in about seven or eight hours. Subsequent batches will be much faster as we perfect the process," Dr. Kim said.

Connor frowned as he calculated the time.

"What's the matter, General? I thought you'd have been pleased," Dr. Kim asked.

"We need it a lot faster than that," Connor said and opened a comlink alert message from the Command Center.

"We'll do the best we can," Dr. Kim said.

"You need to. The best way to stop the Vemus is to get aboard the Alpha ship, find wherever the hell this centralized brain is, and kill it at the source using whatever you come up with. You've got less than three hours to do it," Connor said.

Dr. Kim's brows drew up in a worried frown. "Why so little time?"

"Because we just got another update from Lunar Base. Colonel Hayes believes they're preparing for another attack on New Earth. Our best speed in the combat shuttles we have to reach the enemy ship is two hours. You've got one hour to prepare. We can bring whatever equipment you need with us," Connor said.

Dr. Kim's eyes widened. "Me? Go with you?"

"Will that be a problem?" Connor asked.

"We have a mobile lab that we can put on the shuttle, but we haven't perfected the process. I'm not sure we can do what you require in the time we have," Dr. Kim said.

"We don't have a choice. Lunar Base is reporting Vemus scout ships are searching the main continent. It's only a matter of time before they discover where we've hidden our friends and families," Connor said.

Dr. Kim's gaze darted around.

"General," Major Elder said, "why don't I stay behind and help Dr. Kim?"

"I think that would be best," Connor said. "One more thing. We need to send whatever method you come up with for creating this weapon to Lunar Base and they'll broadcast it to the colony."

Dr. Kim frowned in confusion.

"This way, if we fail, at least whoever's left will have a fighting chance. Some chance is better than none at all," Connor said.

Dr. Kim swallowed. "I'll do my very best, General."

Connor nodded and looked at Major Elder. "I'll see you in one hour in the hangar bay."

He left the lab, Captains Walker and Randle following him.

"General, I'd like to be on the away team," Captain Walker said.

"And there's no way you're going without me, sir," Captain Randle said.

"Don't worry, I'm not leaving you guys behind. I aim to bring everyone I can on this. We're going to end this thing one way or another," Connor said.

"Looking forward to it, sir. I'll head to the hangar bay and see about getting the combat shuttles we have ready to fly," Captain Walker said.

Connor and Captain Randle went back to the Command Center. They had a lot of work to do and very little time to get it done. Captain Thorne saluted Connor as he approached the command area.

"Captain Thorne, I need to know what we have left regarding infantry weapons and combat suits. Everything. Do we have enough to equip every able-bodied person left on this station?" Connor asked.

Captain Thorne blinked his eyes a few times while he processed Connor's request. "I need a few minutes to look that up, sir."

"Understood, Captain," Connor said and looked at Lieutenant Rawn. "Ops, I need an intercept course that will take us right to the Vemus Alpha executed at once. Best speed possible."

"Right away, General," Lieutenant Rawn said and began typing furiously on his holo-interface. "Course laid in. Best speed will put us there in five hours."

Connor frowned. Five hours wasn't the best time he could have hoped for, but it was what he had to work with. "Course correction, Lieutenant. Put us in geosynchronous orbit with New Earth. Should be about the same travel time."

"Yes, sir. Course correction updated," Lieutenant Rawn said.

"Very well," Connor replied.

"I have those figures you asked for, General," Captain Thorne said.

Connor went over to the tactical workstation with Captain Randle at his side. "Alright, let's see what we've got."

30

Nathan had hardly left the Command Center on Lunar Base, and instead of returning to the mission briefing room, he had his staff join him there. After spending the last several hours planning their attack on the Vemus Alpha, they detected multiple nuclear detonations on the planet where the cities of the colony had been. Delphi had been the first to be destroyed, and within a few hours, New Haven followed. It wasn't until ten hours afterward that there was a massive nuclear explosion at Sierra. He immediately sent an update to Connor on Phoenix Station. Lunar Base had later received an encoded message simply stating that the CDF ground forces were still intact.

Learning that the colony's three major cities had been destroyed was hard to take, but it was Connor who'd figured out what Major Quinn had done. There was brutal efficiency in the plan Major Quinn had employed in his fight against the Vemus. Nathan wasn't sure he could have even conceived it. Though he outranked Major Sean Quinn, Nathan knew the man was a brilliant strategist and he found himself wondering what Sean would do if he were in command of Lunar Base. There were times when Nathan felt his own promotion to colonel had been born out of necessity rather than achievement. But regardless of the reasons General Gates had promoted him, he would carry out his orders and achieve the objectives of the CDF to the best of his ability.

"Tactical, have those Vemus scout ships returned?" Nathan asked.

"Negative, Colonel. They haven't been seen since they entered New Earth's atmosphere," Lieutenant LaCroix said.

Nathan pressed his lips together. They could only guess how long those scout ships would take to locate the civilian bunkers and Sanctuary. The Vemus seemed to increase the complexity of their tactics the longer this engagement went on. If their previous attack had been them asleep at the wheel, Nathan hoped they could take out the Vemus Alpha before the damn thing became any smarter. He'd considered sending a few of their combat shuttles to New Earth to investigate, but they had little chance of escaping detection by the Vemus cruisers patrolling the moon. They were stuck between a rock and a hard place unless they wanted to begin their attack on the Vemus.

"Colonel Hayes, I have a comlink from General Gates," Sergeant Boers said.

"Put him on the main holoscreen," Nathan said.

The tactical readouts disappeared from the screen and were replaced by the head and shoulders of General Gates.

"General, we're showing that Phoenix Station is heading back to New Earth," Nathan said.

"That's correct. We couldn't send an update before this time due to the communications blackout. How stands the battle preparations?" Connor asked.

"We haven't seen the Vemus scout ships since they entered New Earth's atmosphere, so they probably haven't found our civilian safeholds. We have a strategy to bring the Vemus Alpha to Lunar Base," Nathan said and proceeded to tell Connor their plan for engaging the Vemus Alpha in an all-out assault. Before the attack began, he'd send out four assault teams that would attempt to sneak aboard the enemy ship while it was en route to the moon to plant the bombs they'd made inside.

"That's a good plan and it won't have to change all that much when you hear what I've got to say. But given the time constraint of this communications window, there'll be very little time for explanation or questions. We're sending multiple comms drones loaded with the relevant data that will validate what we're attempting," General Gates said.

"Just say the word and we'll do everything we can, General," Nathan replied.

"I know you will. We'll need to coordinate our efforts because your assault teams won't be the only CDF soldiers on that enemy ship," General Gates said and proceeded to lay out their plan of attack.

Nathan listened, and for the next fifteen minutes, General Gates informed him of the discoveries they'd made using the data and samples collected by Dr. Brian Walker. When he'd authorized Brian's mission, Nathan had had no idea of the potentially profound impact it would have on all their lives. If it worked. The comlink to Phoenix Station closed, and there was a stunned silence in the immediate vicinity of the main holoscreen.

"A way to kill the Vemus," Major Shelton said in a tone that suggested she didn't quite believe it.

Nathan's mind raced. He had so many questions he wanted to ask the general, but he knew there simply wasn't time. He knew Connor had glossed over many of the facts and he also accepted that he didn't need all the facts in order to achieve their objective. They were going to throw everything they had left at the Vemus and there would be no second chance.

"We need to settle down and focus," Nathan said.

The CDF soldiers in the command area went silent.

"Coordinating this attack won't be easy and the battle plan has just become a lot more complicated," Nathan said.

As Nathan began to put the entirety of the plan together in his mind, along with its implications, he faced the grim reality that much more sacrifice would be required if the colony was going to survive. He glanced around the command area at all the CDF soldiers. They didn't realize it yet, but when he caught Major Shelton's gaze and then Lieutenant LaCroix's, he saw that they understood. In a few hours' time, none of them would probably be around to see how their war with the Vemus ended. This had always been a possibility and was one they'd taken steps to prepare for should the worst happen. They still had a bit of time, precious little though it was. There were still preparations to be made, and what remained of mankind depended on the actions they'd take over the next several hours. It was a terrible burden to bear, but they'd do it together—just as they would die together so their loved ones could live.

Sergeant Boers called him over. "Colonel, I just had a comms drone report in from the surface."

Nathan frowned. "Where did it come from?"

Sergeant Boers swallowed. "It's from Sanctuary. There are personal messages from the people there. Sir, I need your authorization to send the messages out since we're officially still under Dark-Star protocols."

Nathan pressed his lips together while he considered. Messages from home could distract his staff from doing what they needed to do. He looked around the Command Center at all the CDF personnel and the scientists who had elected to come here to help with their fight against the Vemus. He had no doubt that some of the commanding officers could deny those final messages from home in order to achieve their objective, but not Nathan. He couldn't do that. He had more optimistic tendencies and believed it was those messages from home that would enable his soldiers to fight much harder because they'd have been reminded of what they were fighting for. He looked down at Sergeant Boers. "Send them on, Sergeant."

Sergeant Boers smiled in relief. "At once, Colonel . . . and thank you, sir."

Nathan gave her a nod and turned to go back to his own workstation.

"Colonel," Sergeant Boers called out to him. "There's a message for you as well. It has Colonel Cross's identification on it."

Savannah? Nathan thought. "Send it to my console, Sergeant."

Nathan went over to his console and put on his headset. The new message flashed in his inbox and he opened it. A video recording file opened, and he took a moment to savor Savannah's beautiful face. She'd let her thick blonde hair down and it surrounded her face like a lion's mane. He felt the edges of his lips curve up into a smile. God, how he wished he could be with her, but they'd chosen to keep their relationship a secret.

He started the video.

"I know the timing of this sucks, Nathan, but I have something to tell you. After we learned what had happened to Sierra and the other cities, I knew you would be neck deep in planning your assault." Savannah's voice cracked and she looked away from the camera. "Damn it, this is a lot harder than I expected, just like I didn't expect you to come to mean so much to me. At first, I thought it was only because we'd both just survived the Vemus attack and were aboard the *Vigilant* together, but it's more. It's so much more," Savannah said and reached toward the camera. Nathan felt as if she were reaching toward him and the breath caught in his throat. "I need you to come back to me. It's so very important that you do because it's not just you and me anymore . . ."

Nathan listened to the rest of Savannah's message, unable to keep his mouth from hanging open. The message finished playing and he leaned back in his chair, blowing out a breath.

"Is something wrong, sir?" Major Shelton asked.

Nathan looked over at her and saw Sergeant Boers watching him too. His heart was racing, and for a few moments he thought of keeping what Savannah had just told him to himself. He smiled. "I'm going to be a father," he said.

Major Shelton's brows drew up in surprise, but then she jumped out of her chair and came over to give him a hug. The news spread like wildfire, and through all the good wishes and congratulations, there were several sympathetic looks from those around him. He understood those looks all too well, given what they were about to do. He was going to become a father. The more he thought about it, the more real it became, along with the looming certainty that he would never meet his child.

Nathan swallowed hard and clenched his teeth to keep himself focused. When he'd authorized distribution of the messages from home, he'd never thought he'd receive the news he had. And now his thoughts went from elation at the thought of becoming a father to a flash of anger at the thought that someone else would be raising his child. He'd authorized those final messages because he thought it would remind people of why they needed to fight. He never would have believed the message he'd receive would remind him of why *he* needed to *live*.

31

Noah received a response from the comms drone he'd sent. The drone had needed to get within the vicinity of the lunar base receivers so the messages the people at Sanctuary recorded could be sent. It had taken a lot of convincing and assurances for Colonel Cross to allow him to send the drone. In the end, she'd sent a message of her own, which he hoped was a good thing. Recording his own message to Kara had been more difficult than he'd thought it would be. He knew what he wanted to say but felt that his message was woefully insignificant when compared with how he was really feeling. Despite his propensity for having long conversations, when it came to what he really wanted to say to his wife, he found that he wasn't as articulate as he wanted to be. He wanted Kara here with him right now—safe, or as safe as either of them could be—and not on some damn moon. That was it, and Noah felt it wasn't too much to ask.

He glanced over at Lenora. Grim lines of grief marred her pretty face. When she had finally awakened, she'd taken to a cold, brooding silence, but the comments she did make indicated she was acutely aware of what was going on around her. Noah hadn't thought it was a good idea to leave her alone so he had insisted she come with him to the mobile Command Center. She drank from a canteen, which was thankfully filled with water. No doubt she was experiencing the mother of all hangovers, for which there was no miracle cure other than simply rehydrating. She hadn't mentioned anything about her behavior the night before and made no apologies either. All night long Noah had sat outside that tent, his only companion the berwolf Lenora had named Bull. He'd finally put his feet up and gotten some sleep. When he'd woken up, Bull was nowhere to be found and Lenora was awake. They went to the mobile Command Center.

Lenora claimed a workstation off to the side and Noah started working from another station nearby. He reviewed the results of the latest simulations and stress tests of the power conversion system, and the changes they'd made had yielded a thirty percent increase in stability. This was a remarkable achievement since they were taking power from old alien technology and converting it into something they could use. The fact that they could do this at all was amazing, but was it enough? They could power the colossus cannon, which fired a powerful lance of electrons that was capable of reaching targets two kilometers away from Sanctuary. What they really needed to do was test-fire the weapon, but that also ran the risk of alerting the Vemus to Sanctuary's location. They had the weapon and a few CDF soldiers, but fighting the Vemus here would be the stuff of nightmares. Sanctuary's location had been picked because they could hide a lot of people, but it wasn't the most defensible position. There were no mountains nearby or natural barriers that would make a ground assault difficult—just an unearthed alien city nestled amidst rolling hills with forests in the distance.

Occasionally the recon drones would find a large herd of runners, which were long-legged herbivores that averaged close to twenty feet in height and galloped the great plains on their migration trails. The migration drew packs of berwolves, but they left Sanctuary alone. At least there weren't any ryklars in the area. Noah shivered. Ryklars were dangerous and cunning predators that many colonial scientists believed had been genetically altered to increase specific traits. Ryklars responded to certain frequencies and would protect alien sites such as Sanctuary. The ultrahigh frequency stimulated the ryklars' predatory instincts and put them into a heightened state of agitation where they became hypersensitive to their surroundings. Instead of hunting and killing in order to survive, they would start killing far more than they could eat. Prolonged exposure to the ultrahigh frequency even got the ryklars to hunt the colonists. Berwolves, on the other hand, while highly lethal, behaved much more like the predators from Earth. But after being around Bull, Noah was convinced that the berwolves were much smarter than an average dog. Berwolves were stocky like a bear, but they had a strong pack instinct. Colonial scientists believed that even the berwolves had been genetically altered, but not to the extent that the ryklars had been.

Noah leaned back in his chair and looked at Lenora.

"Any idea where he goes?" Noah asked.

Lenora glanced over at him. She sat with her knees folded in front of her chest and had been reading so intently that she probably hadn't heard what he'd asked.

"Bull. Do you know where he goes when he leaves you?" Noah asked.

Lenora shrugged. "He does what he wants and doesn't bother anyone."

She looked back at her screen, glaring at it. Noah had watched her off and on for the past hour and she seemed to go from rigid fury to just wanting to be alone. But being alone at Sanctuary was almost impossible now. Noah knew Lenora hadn't been thrilled at the idea of the CDF designating the archaeological site as a safe haven for the colony, but she'd gone along with it and had worked tirelessly to make sure people were as safe as they could be. Now she looked at all of them as if they were intruding on her own personal space, as if she had claimed the ancient alien city for her own.

"Do you want to get some air?" Noah asked.

"The air out there is the same as in here," Lenora replied without looking up from her screen.

"Alright then," Noah said and stood up. He'd tried. "I'll be outside if you change your mind."

He left the mobile Command Center. The skies were clear and the sun was shining. Even the rings that surrounded the planet weren't as visible as they normally were. By all evidence, contrary to this beautiful day, the cities they'd built had been destroyed over the span of twenty-four hours. Today was an awful, miserable day for the colony. Since the attack on their cities had begun, Colonel Cross had instituted a mandatory curfew, with only small groups of refugees allowed beyond the city ruins at any given time. Not ideal, but it did give the refugees a chance to stretch their legs before returning to the lower levels of the alien city.

Noah glanced back at the brown, prefabricated walls of the mobile Command Center. Through the doorway, he saw Lenora shaking her head at something on her screen and frowned. There was only so much irritated, cold fury he could take from one person, even if that person was family to him. He turned around and walked away.

The mobile Command Center was near the entrance to the archaeological site where the ancient alien city had been discovered. His boots crunched along the well-worn path to the left toward the grassy plains beyond. A group of displaced colonists were heading back to the alien city, and some waved at him as he walked by. After they'd received news that Sierra had been destroyed, only one other communication from the CDF forces had made it to Sanctuary. Noah knew Sean had made it out, but the only thing in the message was that they should remain hidden because the fight with the Vemus wasn't yet done. Of all the things Noah hated most, being in the dark about what was going on was near the top of his list.

He sucked in a breath of fresh air and blew it out. For the span of a single breath, he'd found a moment's peace, and it felt good to stretch his legs. But suddenly, an ear-piercing siren began to wail, catching him so completely by surprise that he actually ducked at the sound of it.

The colonists nearby looked up at the sky in alarm. Noah heard several people shouting, but he couldn't make out what they were saying. A pair of CDF soldiers drove out in an ATV, using the vehicle's PA system to order all of them to return to Sanctuary. The refugees were slow to respond and Noah began shouting for them as well. The nearby colonists looked at him, and upon seeing his uniform, started to head back into the alien city. They were slow to move at first but quickly increased their pace. Noah stayed out on the grassy plains to make sure the colonists were returning to the subterranean levels of the alien city.

The CDF soldiers driving the ATV headed toward him and stopped. "Can we give you a ride, Captain?" one of the soldiers asked.

Noah thanked them. The ATV only had two seats, so he had to hold on from the outside. He stepped onto the running boards and grabbed the handle. The driver pressed down hard on the accelerator and the ATV lurched forward. Noah held on as tightly as he could and they quickly made it back to the city entrance.

The last of the refugees were already inside and Noah saw CDF soldiers retreating to the interior of the city. Everyone knew the drill. They had to minimize their presence on the surface to avoid detection by the Vemus. Colonel Cross wouldn't have ordered the use of the siren unless there was a credible threat nearby. That meant there were Vemus ships in the area.

The CDF soldier slowed the ATV down near the mobile Command Center, and Noah stepped off the running board at a jog. They quickly drove away as Noah ran into the Command Center.

Colonel Cross glanced at him as he walked in. "Where've you been?" she asked.

"I went to get some air, Colonel," Noah said and went back to his workstation. "Are they close?"

"Whatever it is, it's at the edge of our scanning range," Colonel Cross said.

A central holoscreen powered up and showed a simplified PRADIS output. There was one ship at the edge of the range, just like the colonel had said, but there was no identification code being broadcast, so they knew it wasn't from the Colonial Defense Force. The unidentified ship wasn't heading directly toward them, but it was going to fly close enough that if they weren't careful, it might detect their presence.

A CDF soldier came into the Command Center. "Colonel, all colonists are inside the safe zones," he said.

"Acknowledged," Colonel Cross said and turned toward Sergeant Yates. "Ops, set Condition One. All CDF soldiers to action stations."

Noah heard Sergeant Yates repeat the order and then send a broadcast to all soldiers stationed in Sanctuary.

"Colonel, should we bring the colossus cannon online?" Noah asked.

Colonel Cross pressed her lips together. "Not right now, Captain," she said.

"When would be a good time?" Lenora asked.

Noah glanced over at her in surprise. She'd been so quiet that he'd forgotten she was there, and he wasn't the only one.

Colonel Cross brought her steely-eyed gaze to Lenora. "Dr. Bishop, I don't think your presence here is appropriate anymore. It would be better if you went to one of the safe zones," Colonel Cross said.

Lenora snorted in disgust. "The Vemus aren't far away. Why not use the cannon we've been working on so hard to shoot them out of the sky?"

The breath caught in Noah's throat. Lenora was completely out of line. He stood up and went over to Lenora before Colonel Cross had her forcibly removed.

"Come on, you can't be here anymore," Noah said and moved to grab Lenora's arm.

Lenore flinched away from him and stood up. She glared at him. "Fine," she said and walked toward the exit.

Noah looked at Colonel Cross, who nodded for him to go after Lenora. He went outside and called out to her.

Lenora spun. "I'm fine. Go follow orders, soldier," she said scathingly.

"That's not fair, and you're out of line," Noah said.

Lenora looked away from him and sighed. "They're coming. We've got to at least defend ourselves."

"We will, and we'll do it the right way, which doesn't involve you questioning the orders of Colonel Cross," Noah said.

Lenora rolled her eyes.

Noah heard Colonel Cross snap an order to someone inside and turned back to Lenora.

"What's the matter with you?" Noah asked.

Lenora jabbed her finger toward the sky. "They're what's the matter!"

Her shouts drew concerned glances from the soldiers passing by. Noah stepped closer to her. "We can't just start shooting at them. There's more than one ship, and if we shoot one down, it'll paint a giant target on us here."

Lenora's brows pulled close together. "I know," she said through gritted teeth and then her gaze softened. "I know. Go back inside. You can't stay out here and babysit me."

"You'd do the same for me," Noah said while backing toward the mobile Command Center doors.

There was a loud whirl of actuators moving something heavy, and Noah's eyes widened. He turned toward the heart of Sanctuary. Jutting out from the ruins was the long barrel of the colossus cannon. It was powering up.

"Barker, get in here!" Colonel Cross shouted from inside the mobile Command Center.

Noah hastened inside.

"We're locked out of the colossus cannon controls," Colonel Cross said.

Noah brought up the command interface for the cannon's weapons systems. He was completely locked out. He tried to take back control, but nothing worked, and he slammed his hands on the desk.

"I'm locked out, Colonel," Noah said.

"Comms, are the soldiers guarding the colossus responding?" Colonel Cross asked.

"Negative, Colonel. They're not responding," Corporal Blanks replied.

"Sergeant Gray, get a team of CDF soldiers down there now—" Colonel Cross said and stopped.

There was a bright blue flash over the skies above them. Noah's mouth hung open. Someone was firing the colossus cannon. He jumped out of his chair.

"I need to get down there to fix the lockout. I can't do anything from here," Noah said.

There was another bolt of blue-white lightning lancing overhead. If the Vemus hadn't known Sanctuary was here before, they did now.

32

THE LUNAR BASE Command Center had become a cauldron of renewed vigor and determination. Nathan was infused by its energy and he also heard it in the voices of those nearest him. He looked at one of the status holoscreens for the base. The smaller satellite CDF locations were home to rail-cannons that were peppered across the lunar landscape. Separate from those were the missile pods that were home to the midrange HORNET class missiles.

"All stations report status green, Colonel," Sergeant Martinez said.

Nathan glanced at the young officer. There was a slight catch to her voice, and she swallowed. "Acknowledged, Sergeant," Nathan replied.

Major Shelton shifted in her seat next to him.

"Tactical, any change in the Vemus cruiser's orbit?" Nathan asked.

"That's a negative, Colonel," Lieutenant LaCroix responded.

The three Vemus cruisers were orbiting the moon on different elliptical planes that were about to overlap. When his tactical officer alerted him to the possibility of the overlap occurring, Nathan had expected the Vemus to adjust their velocity because the targeting opportunity they were giving him was too good to pass up. They were essentially lining up for him to take them out.

"Let's show them our teeth. Execute firing solution Knock Out," Nathan ordered.

"Executing firing solution," Lieutenant LaCroix said—three simple words that carried with them a huge spike in activity.

Scanners became fully active and fed targeting data to the HORNET missile salvos that were launching from their pods.

"HORNETS away," Lieutenant LaCroix said.

The HORNET missiles were close-range weapons capable of bursts of speed that would crush a human, even with the inertia-dampening technology they had on their ships. Nathan watched as the missile marks on the main holoscreen showed them quickly closing the distance to their targets. The Vemus cruisers hadn't altered course or launched countermeasures.

"Ops, give our guys in the hangar bays the green light for launch," Nathan said.

They needed to get the assault teams away before the Vemus counterattacked.

"Confirm missile detonation, Colonel. Direct hit," Lieutenant LaCroix said.

Nathan watched the main holoscreen as the missiles pelted the Vemus cruisers.

"Tactical, target bravo salvo and task all mag-cannon turrets to target the cruisers. Light them up," Nathan said.

Lieutenant LaCroix confirmed the order. "Scanners show two Vemus cruisers completely destroyed. The third is severely damaged."

A live feed from the high-res optics showed the remaining Vemus cruiser being chewed up by the rail-cannon high-velocity projectiles. Nathan watched with grim satisfaction as the Vemus cruiser exploded.

"Colonel, assault teams are away—" Sergeant Martinez said and stopped speaking in the middle of her status update. Her eyes widened. "Colonel, sensors have detected colossus cannon active fire near Sanctuary."

Nathan's gut clenched. "Are there any Vemus ships in the area?"

"Negative, Colonel," Sergeant Martinez said.

"Comms, have there been any alerts from our CDF forces on the ground?" Nathan asked.

"No, Colonel," Sergeant Boers answered.

Nathan winced and looked at Major Shelton. "It has to be those Vemus scout ships we detected earlier. They've located Sanctuary."

"Colonel, Vemus Alpha is moving out of orbit from New Earth," Lieutenant LaCroix said.

"Put it on the main holoscreen, Lieutenant," Nathan said.

The Vemus Alpha was slowly moving away from New Earth.

"Tactical, ready the next HORNET salvo," Nathan said.

"Yes, Colonel," Lieutenant LaCroix responded.

"What about Sanctuary, Colonel?" Major Shelton asked.

Nathan frowned, trying think of something they could do to help. "Comms, send an encoded broadcast to CDF ground forces."

It was the only thing they could do. He had already committed his resources to the Vemus Alpha. There were CDF ground forces. They'd have to deal with the threat to Sanctuary.

Three new ships appeared on PRADIS. They came from the Vemus Alpha.

"Troop carrier class ships detected, Colonel," Lieutenant LaCroix said.

Nathan gritted his teeth in frustration. "Target the carriers," he said and watched the PRADIS screen update. The Vemus Alpha was moving faster now on an intercept course right toward them. There would be no hiding from the Vemus. Nathan knew he couldn't stop all the troop carriers from reaching Sanctuary, but he hoped that what they were doing would give them a fighting chance.

"Target all weapons on the Vemus Alpha," Nathan said.

The CDF had built weapons systems all across the lunar surface, and once they went active, they could be tracked by the enemy. Lunar Base was in this fight now. Hopefully, the assault teams were flying undetected, closing in on the Vemus Alpha. They'd have to execute emergency combat landings on the Vemus Alpha, but that was something his teams were prepared for. It was Connor and his team that needed to get inside that massive Vemus ship if they were to have any hope of stopping the Vemus permanently. He couldn't even warn them about the change in plans, but it wouldn't have changed anything. The Colonial Defense Force's final assault on the Vemus was just beginning.

33

A SMALL TASKFORCE of ten combat shuttles had left the remnants of Phoenix Station two hours before. To keep their approach hidden from the enemy, Connor ordered the taskforce to power off their main engines. He didn't want to give the Vemus any reason to suspect the combat shuttles were anything but wreckage from previous battles. Throughout their engagement with the Vemus, they'd proven to be more reactionary when the CDF switched tactics.

"Nothing like putting Sir Isaac Newton in the driver's seat," Captain Randle mused from the copilot's seat in the cockpit of the shuttle.

"There are worse ways to get inside an enemy ship," Connor replied, thinking of when he'd used a storage container to infiltrate a space station. The entirety of the Ghost platoon had been cramped inside that confined space with nothing but a whole lot of waiting to be offloaded.

"Final update from Phoenix Station. The comms drones have been sent off. They've staggered their departure and speeds," Captain Randle said.

The comms drones contained all of Dr. Kim's findings on the Vemus, as well as what they were about to try. Connor understood the theory that supported the scientist's belief that the Vemus were behaving with a hive hierarchy, but he couldn't help but think there was more to it. The evidence was there to support the scientist's theory, but there seemed to be some missing pieces that Connor couldn't quite wrap his mind around. Primary among those missing pieces was the fact that the Vemus had navigated across interstellar space to find them. They had followed the deep space comms buoy network like a trail of breadcrumbs. A two-hundred-year journey was no easy feat. How had the Vemus survived for that long? Connor was sure that, with time, colonial scientists could answer those questions, but ultimately he just wanted the Vemus gone without a chance of survival. The colonists were the last humans in the galaxy. He was disgusted that part of the reason humanity was in such a predicament had stemmed from an opportunistic human faction. Were humans always destined for such an outcome?

New Earth had been home to an alien intelligent species that had evolved to build a civilization, but the colonists hadn't figured out what had happened to them. They left behind cities and ruins. Colonial scientists had even detected an alien influence over the other species on the planet. Had they reached a point in their evolution where their own self-destruction was assured? Were humans just another species to follow along that seemingly well-worn path to destruction, paved by the intelligent species before them? In the hundreds of years that humanity had looked to the stars with wonder, they hadn't detected any traces of intelligent life.

"The final comms drone is configured to reach Sanctuary's vicinity in seven days," Captain Randle said.

"It's our failsafe in case we aren't successful," Connor said.

"Let's make sure it's not needed then," Captain Randle said.

Connor glance at Randle. They were heading into the belly of the beast. Given that their chances of survival weren't great, Connor was surprised to see a hopeful glint in Randle's determined gaze. He'd seen a similar look in Reisman's eyes right up until Connor left him to die.

"You've got that look again," Captain Randle said.

Connor turned back to the controls. "I was just thinking of Wil and everyone else we've lost during this war."

"Wil." Captain Randle snorted. "I liked him. He always came up with ways to keep you on your toes."

Connor let out a small chuckle. "It was what made him so good at what he did."

A comlink opened to the cockpit from the rear of the shuttle.

"General, it's ready," Dr. Kim said.

Connor sat up in his chair. "Excellent work. I'll buy you a drink when this is over."

"I'll take you up on that, General," Dr. Kim said.

The comlink closed and Captain Randle gave him a sideways look. "Here's what I don't understand. How is whatever the doctor is cooking up back there going to stop the Vemus?"

"I'm sure if you went back there and asked him, he could spend hours trying to educate you on it, but by then the mission would be over," Connor replied.

Captain Randle laughed. "I'm surprised you don't want to know."

Connor shrugged. "The way he explained it to me was that the basic function of a virus is to spread itself. He's just helping to speed that along, which is where the nanobots come in. The process will gain momentum as time goes on."

"Okay, but if the living exoskeleton is what's keeping that Vemus Alpha together, why couldn't we just insert the toxin on the surface and then get the hell out of there?" Captain Randle asked.

"The only way to be sure is to find the collective intelligence behind the Vemus and infect that first. This way, it will spread to all of them while crippling their capacity to fight," Connor replied.

Captain Randle shook his head. "You really think there's a hive queen?"

"Call it whatever you want, but I do believe there's a collective intelligence controlling the Vemus," Connor said.

Captain Randle nodded. "What about the Vemus forces that aren't on the ship?"

"They'll need to be stopped. Every single one of them," Connor said.

A passive scan alert appeared on the combat shuttle's heads-up display. Connor read the alert and frowned.

"Colonel Hayes has begun the attack," Captain Randle said.

"He's early," Connor said while rubbing his chin. "Something must have happened."

He'd kept the combat shuttle's systems on passive to avoid detection, which included the long-range communications systems. He opened the short-range comms channel to the other shuttles. "We need to move faster than originally planned. Start up main engines. We'll use the battle as cover to get aboard."

The other combat-shuttle pilots acknowledged his orders. They were close enough to the Vemus Alpha that they should be able to sneak aboard. Connor initiated the startup process for the combat shuttle's main engines. When the shuttle's engines came online, Connor engaged them and they darted ahead, flying toward the cavernous rear of the Vemus Alpha. Connor had estimated that this was the area where the Vemus Alpha's main engines were located. While not the safest place to fly, he also knew there would be maintenance hatches not far from the engine pods. Colonel Hayes knew the approach vector Connor was going to take, so they didn't have to worry about being caught in friendly fire.

They closed in on the Vemus Alpha, flying in close to the rear section of the hull. The hull of the Vemus Alpha was rough, as if it had been part of a large asteroid. Connor knew the Vemus had absorbed other ships in order to form the hulking mass that was the Alpha. As they approached the cavernous drop-off at the rear of the enemy ship, Connor used maneuvering thrusters to swing the combat shuttle around and then engaged their main engines to slow their approach. Even with inertia dampeners, Connor felt himself pressing into his seat while he used the main engines in a rapid deceleration maneuver. The other combat shuttles did the same, and once they reached the rear of the Vemus Alpha, Connor engaged the main engines in a burst that would take them inside. There was an array of engine pods, some of which Connor recognized from battleship carriers and others that looked like they'd come from civilian freighters used throughout the Sol system.

"How'd they even power all those engines?" Captain Randle asked.

Connor wasn't sure. He knew that, in theory, the reactors that powered NA Alliance military vessels could work for hundreds of years. They just needed a fuel source for their fusion reactor cores. Efficiency was a must for any ship to operate in space, and it didn't matter whether the spacecraft was civilian or military.

Connor angled their approach to avoid the engine pods, taking a circuitous route toward the center. They only needed one point of entry for all of them to board. Connor brought the active scanners online. There was little chance of being detected because they were just outside the inner hull of the ship. Scanning data started to show on the main heads-up display and a map of the hull appeared. He zeroed in on an area that looked promising and slowed the shuttle down. The exoskeletal hull became sparser the farther they went. Bare patches of the original ships' hulls became more prevalent, and Connor felt the edges of his lips curve into a smile.

"I don't get it. Why are there these bare patches here?" Captain Randle asked.

"It's the same as their other ships. They don't fully encase the entire hull with the exoskeleton. Maybe they just don't have the resources to cover it all or they think they don't need to. Regardless, that's where we're getting on the ship," Connor said.

Captain Randle glanced over at him. "You expected this to be here."

Connor nodded. "If it hadn't been, we'd have made our own hole and gotten on board."

Connor highlighted the targeted landing area on the heads-up display and transferred the coordinates to the other shuttles. There was no sign of the Vemus in the area. He deployed the landing gear and brought the combat shuttle to the hull. The landing gear hit the hull and he deployed the anchor bolts that would hold the shuttle in place. He powered down the engines and put them on standby.

Connor and Captain Randle left the cockpit and went to the rear of the shuttle, where Nexstar combat suits waited for them. The assault team already had their combat suits on and were waiting. The chest of the combat suit was split down the middle from the neck to the feet. Connor stepped inside and initiated the startup process. The Nexstar's systems came online and the suit closed up, encasing Connor in a protective shell. He saw Dr. Kim standing off to the side, wearing an EVA suit.

"What do you think you're doing, Dr. Kim?" Connor asked.

Dr. Kim glanced at the other CDF soldiers and then back at Connor with wide eyes. "I just assumed that I was going with you aboard that ship." He had a large metallic cylinder clutched to his chest.

"Is that it?" Connor asked, gesturing toward the cylinder.

Dr. Kim nodded several times. "Yes, this is it," he said in a shaky voice.

"I'll take it from here. Why don't you stay on the shuttle?" Connor said.

Dr. Kim's mouth rounded into a circle. "I can help you," he said.

"You've done enough. We'll take it from here," Connor said.

The warring emotions on Dr. Kim's face cycled through disappointment to stark relief. Connor knew that if he allowed the scientist to come with them he'd be among the first to die. Connor stepped closer to him.

"You've done enough. We wouldn't have this chance without you," Connor said.

Dr. Kim's brows pulled together in a tight frown. "I did nothing but pull together the pieces of other people's work. Brian Walker is the real hero."

"Stay on the shuttle and wait. That's all I need you to do," Connor said and reached out for the metallic cylinder. "I'll take this and ensure it gets where it needs to go."

The scientist reluctantly let go and stood there, unsure of what to say.

Connor turned to the assault team. "Open the hatch."

The rear hatch of the combat shuttle opened and the assault team began stepping off the shuttle.

"General, I just want to . . ." Dr. Kim began to say, and Connor turned back toward him. "I just wanted to say thank you. You're one of the bravest men I've ever known."

Connor gave him a long look and thanked him. "Good luck to you," he said.

As Connor left the combat shuttle, he didn't think he'd ever see the scientist again. He stepped out onto the hull of the Vemus Alpha and gritted his teeth.

"Final gear check!" Captain Randle called. "Check yourself and check the soldiers around you."

There was a flurry of activity as they all did one final check. Connor reached up and cinched the straps of the cylinder hooked to his back a bit tighter, making sure the cylinder was secured to the bracket on his belt. He sure as hell didn't want the damn thing firing off early. Dr. Kim had told him how to activate the nanobots inside.

The other assault teams from the combat shuttles gathered around. They were all heavily armed and were as ready as they could be to face what was inside. Connor sent the team ahead to check the maintenance hatch airlock.

"Sir, there's no manual override," Corporal Manis said.

Connor stepped forward and the corporal moved aside so he could access the panel. He used his old credentials from the NA Alliance military and the hatch unlocked. Connor gestured for the two nearest soldiers to go in first, and Captain Randle stayed at his side while he waited. They went through the airlock in groups.

The inside of the ship was dark and sparse, as if it had been abandoned. A minimal atmosphere registered from the sensors of Connor's combat suit—hardly enough to breathe in but it had an unusually high nitrogen content.

Once the CDF assault team was inside, they moved deeper into the ship. The dark gray corridors were empty and there was a buildup of a dark substance along the walls. It didn't look like anything he'd seen on the other Vemus ships. Connor figured the maintenance corridor wouldn't see a lot of foot traffic, but he had expected to see some sign that the Vemus had been in here. How did the Vemus maintain the engine pods if they never came down here?

Over the next hour, all seventy members of the assault team cautiously poked around the Vemus Alpha ship, but the exterior of the ship was over twenty-two kilometers across, and they barely scratched the surface. They left the maintenance corridor behind and headed to the main section of whatever this particular ship had been. That was when they began to see a brown sludge adorning the interior walls that was all too familiar to Connor.

"Stay away from the walls," Connor warned.

That brown sludge was the same substance that had begun to absorb Wil Reisman while they'd been aboard the *Indianapolis*. As they went farther into the ship, the sludge seemed to solidify, becoming a hardened substance. The buildup of the brown sludge rounded the edges of the corridor until Connor felt as if he were walking through a large tube.

As they continued, the Vemus Alpha was looking a lot less like an NA Alliance ship, or any ship Connor had been on. He knew from the last time they'd been on a Vemus ship that they couldn't use comlinks because the Vemus could sense them somehow. Their communications envelope was limited.

"General, perhaps we should consider splitting our forces to do some reconnaissance, then meet back up," Captain Walker suggested.

Connor nodded. He'd been thinking the same thing. "I think you're right. Let's split up and meet back here in thirty minutes."

Captain Walker took half the assault team and went off down a different corridor.

"Any idea what we're looking for?" Captain Randle asked.

"Ideally, we'd be seeing more signs of life," Connor said.

Captain Randle grunted.

They came upon another set of corridors and there was a soft amber glow emanating from the exoskeletal walls. There were glowing orbs inside that lined the corridor like shining pearls. They followed along until they came to a tunnel that spiraled down and to the left. The orbs glowed even brighter. CDF soldiers took point on either side of the tunnel, and Connor peered down into the gloom. There was a drop and then the tunnel twisted out of sight. The interior atmosphere had become increasingly humid, according to his combat suit's sensors. Connor leaned forward and took a small step. His foot slipped out in front of him and he went forward into the tunnel. Connor grunted as he rolled, completely out of control. He slid down the long, slimy tunnel floor and crashed into a wall. Connor was gasping, and it took him a few moments to get his equilibrium under control. Everything kept spinning. He pushed himself onto his feet and grabbed his AR-71 assault rifle, which had miraculously stayed by him as he slid down the tunnel. He reached his hand to his back and felt that the metallic cylinder was still securely in place.

Connor looked up the way he'd fallen and cursed. After a few moments, he heard the sounds of something else coming down, so he brought his weapon up and waited. Three CDF soldiers slid down the tunnel like Connor had and came to a stop nearby. Connor darted over and helped them up. The third soldier was Captain Randle.

"Are you all right?" Connor asked.

Captain Randle sighed and shook his head as if to clear it. "I'll live. I was just about to tell you to get back from the edge when you slipped. I ordered the team to find another way down, then followed you, along with Corporal Mathis and Sergeant Brennan here."

Connor opened an IR channel and tried to reach the rest of the team, but there was no response. Captain Randle turned and looked up the steep slope of the tunnel. The slope angled away from them, so they couldn't see to the top and there was no way to tell how far they'd come down.

"Should we try to open a comlink, sir?" Corporal Mathis asked.

'We can't risk it. The comlink would draw attention to us," Connor said.

"I think we already did that, sir," Captain Randle said and leaned in toward the glistening wall.

Connor frowned. 'What do you mean?"

The orbs inside the walls became brighter and the whole tunnel seemed to light up in an amber color. Captain Randle's helmet was less than a foot away from the wall, and Connor was about to tell him to step back when Captain Randle quickly backed away and glanced at Connor.

"It looks like a swirling mass of liquid is moving beneath the surface. I checked the corridor before we went down and I could've sworn that tunnel wasn't there before."

"Are you saying you think the tunnel just formed?" Connor asked.

"I wasn't sure. I'm sorry, sir. I should've said something sooner," Captain Randle said.

They were all a bit jumpy, and Connor couldn't fault Captain Randle for not speaking up. He started to get the feeling that they were being toyed with.

"Don't worry about it. Let's keep moving," Connor said.

They continued moving forward. The tunnel widened into a vast chamber, and the glowing orbs inside the walls pulsed brighter. Connor looked around the chamber, trying to find another way out but didn't see any near them. They walked into the chamber past massive columns made of the exoskeletal substance.

Corporal Mathis cried out and Connor spun toward him. The CDF soldier was trying to move the legs of his combat suit, which were sinking into the ground. Sergeant Brennan and Captain Randle grabbed his outstretched arms, trying to pull him free. Connor glanced at the floor and saw that the area by their feet had a swirling substance beneath the hardened surface. It was gathering underneath the two men. Corporal Mathis sank to his thighs and screamed in panic, firmly rooted in place. Connor shuffled to the side and squeezed off a few rounds into the swirling mass surrounding the corporal. The slugs penetrated the hardened surface but had no effect, and Corporal Mathis sank past his waist.

"It's in my suit!" Corporal Mathis cried.

Sergeant Brennan started to sink, and Connor saw the area beneath Captain Randle's feet begin to liquefy. Connor yanked Captain Randle backward. Captain Randle tried to grab the sergeant, but he sank too quickly. Within a few moments, the two men were completely submerged, with only the gurgling sounds of the dying men's screams escaping the viscous liquid. Connor stumbled back and pulled Captain Randle along.

"What the hell! How could it just swallow them up like that?" Captain Randle said.

It had all happened so fast that Connor could only react. He'd never seen anything like it.

They ran across the open chamber. "I don't know," Connor gasped. "We have to keep moving or the same thing is going to happen to us."

A shudder worked its way through Connor as they hastened from the chamber. He felt like each step they took would sink them into the exoskeletal substance. The amber glow continued to pulse along the corridor. Connor looked at the ground and there was no escaping the hardened substance. He risked a glance behind them and saw something swirling beneath the glowing surface, as if it were swimming through the liquid. Connor felt his heart pounding in his ears and his mouth went dry as panic gripped him. They came out of the corridor into another vast open chamber. Connor looked up and couldn't see the ceiling. There was only a thick fog gathered about ten meters above him. The glowing orbs inside the walls faded off to either side of them where the fog thickened.

Captain Randle clutched his weapon as he spun around, trying to peer into the gloom. Connor used the combat suit's systems to cycle through a visual spectrum range, and only infrared showed a huge circular shape in the middle of the vast chamber. Thick, rounded cables connected to it. Some he recognized as power cables and others were something he couldn't identify.

Connor moved forward and Captain Randle followed. The lighting in the chamber began to increase and Connor was beginning to make out details of what was with them in the chamber.

"Holy shit!" Captain Randle gasped.

Tall, dark shapes seemed to appear out of nowhere as the fog receded away from them. Their thick dome shaped heads seemed to angle downward aggressively and a harsh blast of air expelled from their mouths startling Connor. He pointed his AR-71 at one, and several of the Vemus fighters shifted their thick legs and clawed feet. The sound of that shift echoed throughout the chamber. There must have been thousands of them in that chamber alone.

Captain Randle's breath came in gasps. He clutched the AR-71 with shaking hands.

"Hold your fire," Connor said.

"Sir, they're going to kill us," Captain Randle said between gasps.

"If they wanted us dead, we'd be dead already," Connor said.

Connor felt a cold shiver rush down his spine as he made himself lower his weapon. He took a step forward and the Vemus soldiers didn't move. A thick amber cord was attached from the lower backs of the Vemus soldiers, went to the ground, and stretched in the direction of the central, amorphous mass in the middle of the chamber.

"There are too many. Too many of them. We can't . . ." Captain Randle muttered.

Connor felt terror grip his chest, but he forced it away. "Wayne, you need to calm down."

Captain Randle turned toward him with wild eyes, moments from panicking. Focusing on him, Connor felt his own fear subside.

"Bull, you can't freak out now. Come on, you've got to keep it together," Connor said.

Captain Randle continued to gasp and then started running. Connor glanced at the Vemus for a moment, but they didn't move or appear to pay any attention to him. Connor ran after his friend, who was heading toward the middle of the chamber. He'd gotten so far ahead that Connor couldn't see him in the gloom. Only a partial image of his combat suit appeared on Connor's heads-up display. He heard Randle grunt loudly, and it sounded as if he'd fallen.

"I'm coming," Connor shouted, hoping Randle would hear him.

Captain Randle screamed and Connor darted toward him. The CDF captain was tangled up in the cords along the ground. Connor squatted down as Randle was trying to push himself to his feet.

"Connor, they're crawling all over me. Get them off me!" Captain Randle said.

Connor tried pulling the cords away, but the ends sought out the fallen captain like snakes. Connor swung his rifle around and started shooting at them. The AR-71's projectiles chewed through the cords, and there was a hiss of vapor whenever they were pierced.

Bright overhead lights flared and Connor could see that he was only three meters from the giant amorphous mass. It was dark gray in color, with streaks of pink spidering across it like veins. Connor froze and his breath caught in his throat. Feeding into the mass were thick power cords over two meters in diameter. For each power cord, there was another cord made from the same exoskeletal material found throughout the ship.

A comlink established a connection to his combat suit.

"Colonel Gates, NA Alliance military," a deep monotone voice stated.

Thousands of high-pitched whistles sounded from the Vemus forces, and Connor felt his knees go weak. The Vemus collective had just spoken to him—using his old rank.

34

Noah raced to the colossus cannon, with Sergeant Gray and a security team following closely on his heels. A blue-and-white lance shot from the colossus cannon, and Noah glanced in the direction the shot had gone. A ship in the distance crashed to the ground and smoke billowed from the wreckage. The massive barrel swung overhead and was priming for another shot. Noah headed for the base of the cannon where the controls were—the only place he could end the lockout.

He heard someone cry out, and as he rounded the base of the cannon, he saw Captain Raeburn Gibson lying on the ground with Lenora standing over him. She had her stunner pointed at Barnes.

The large Field Ops and Security sergeant looked at Noah. Then he regarded the other CDF soldiers and raised his hands. "We had to defend ourselves," Barnes said.

Lenora looked back at Noah. "I tried to stop them, but it was already too late."

Noah nodded and then looked at Sergeant Gray. "Secure the prisoners," he said and went right for the colossus controls. He didn't have time to consider how Gibson and Barnes had managed to free themselves, but they must have had help. There was a tangle of wires sticking out from underneath the control panel, and Noah clenched his teeth.

Lenora came to his side. "What do you need me to do?"

Noah studied the wires and then looked at the command status of the cannon. It was locked on the Vemus scout ship heading toward Sanctuary.

Lenora reached for something behind the console and pulled out a small metal box. "This is Field Ops issued."

Noah's eyes widened. "Good work. That's causing the lockout. Here, let me see it."

Lenora handed him the box and Noah peered along the edges. Finding a slight indentation, he jabbed his thumbnail in and pried it open. Pain lanced through his thumb as his nail started to tear, but the box opened and Noah used his fingers to force it the rest of the way. He twisted the control chip and it split in two.

Noah opened a comlink. "Colonel, you should have control now."

Lenora took his hand and wrapped healing tape around his thumb. "I'm forever cutting my fingers on a dig, so I always have supplies on hand," Lenora said.

Noah nodded appreciatively.

"Colonel, can you confirm you have weapons control?" Noah asked.

"We have control," Colonel Cross said, finally.

Noah blew out a breath. "Glad to hear it, Colonel," he said and explained how Captain Gibson had taken control of the colossus cannon and that Lenora had stopped them.

"Thank Dr. Bishop for me, but Gibson shouldn't have been able to take control of the weapon using a secure authentication box," Colonel Cross replied.

"Normally you'd be right, but Gibson removed the hardwired connections that would have prevented it. It's a real mess and will take hours to clean up, ma'am," Noah said.

"No time for that. We need that weapon operational for as long as possible. We've got incoming ships headed right to our location," Colonel Cross said.

"I'll return to the Command Center at once, Colonel," Noah replied.

"Negative. I need you to stay there and keep that weapon working. Is that understood?" Colonel Cross asked.

"Yes, ma'am," Noah said.

"Captain," Sergeant Gray said, "where should we take them?"

Several loud pops from the sky drew their attention.

"Take them to the fortifications near the entrance. Then remove the shackles and give them a weapon," Noah said.

"Sir?" Sergeant Gray asked.

"The Vemus are coming here and we have to defend ourselves. That means we put every able-bodied person who can shoot on those fortifications. Now go," Noah ordered.

Sergeant Gray saluted Noah and took the Field Ops agents away. Lenora started to follow them.

"Where are you going?" Noah asked.

"I'm going to the fortifications. You said they need everyone who can shoot. Well, I can shoot as well as any soldier," Lenora replied.

Noah pressed his lips together and tried to think of a protest he could make so she wouldn't go, but he couldn't. "Stay safe," he said.

"You too," Lenora said and ran.

Noah scrutinized the tangle of wires. The colossus cannon primed for another shot, and the charged particles in the air made the hair on Noah's neck stand on end. He needed to see the status of the power converter, the console of which was down thanks to his good friend Raeburn Gibson. How much time could they save if they fitted the idiots of the world with shock collars to prevent their stupidity from affecting others?

Noah quickly got to work reconnecting the monitors for the power conversion systems. The weapon would still work without them, but he'd have no way of knowing if the entire weapon system would simply fail on the next shot.

Noah gathered his engineering support teams and stationed them near the power converter at critical systems. He needed to squeeze all the power he could from the old alien power station.

The colossus cannon fired another straight bolt of blue-white lightning surrounded by a blue nimbus. Noah looked up, knowing that the reason they'd put the cannon on such a high platform was to minimize radiation exposure.

Every time the colossus cannon hit its mark, it did devastating damage to the Vemus ships. The beam melted away the exoskeletal hull, wreaking havoc inside, but the Vemus troop carriers were entering the atmosphere almost on top of Sanctuary. Noah heard gauss rifles being fired and knew that some of the Vemus had made it to the ground.

Noah managed to keep the colossus cannon firing for an hour, then it failed. In the end, it wasn't the power converter but the alien thermal core taps that had completely melted away due to the severe overload of the system. The heavy barrel of the colossus cannon sank down as the mechanized support structure lost power. He'd been so focused on converting the power for the colossus cannon that he hadn't even thought of the effects the sustained power output would have on the old alien technology. Now that it had failed, it seemed painstakingly obvious and something he should have noticed. But he wondered if he could have done anything about it if he had known.

Noah ordered all his teams to the fortifications near the entrance of Sanctuary. There was nothing more they could do here. As he ran out of the heart of Sanctuary, he didn't pass many colonists. Colonel Cross must have had anyone who couldn't fight moved as far from the fighting as possible.

One of the first things Colonel Cross had the CDF soldiers do when she'd first arrived at Sanctuary was set up fortifications that could be quickly assembled if the Vemus were to discover their location. Noah hadn't given it much thought when she'd done it, but as he reached Sanctuary's entrance, he couldn't have been more thankful that Colonel Cross had prepared them for battle.

Noah was quite familiar with the sounds most CDF-issued weapons made when they were used, but it was the sounds the Vemus made that instantly grated on his nerves. He'd seen the video recordings of the Vemus from combat suit cams, but they sounded different now. The ear-piercing whistles made him clench his teeth.

Noah raced for the nearest fortification and found Colonel Cross looking at drone feeds.

"Put me to work, Colonel," Noah said.

Colonel Cross glanced at him and the people he'd brought with him. "We only have civilian hunting rifles left. Grab them and get up on that wall."

Noah grabbed the CAR-74 semiautomatic hunting rifle that was a common weapon for people who worked remotely, as well as Field Operations. While he knew the CDF had more powerful weapons, there hadn't been enough to circulate to everyone. He raced down the fortification wall and found Lenora wearing a CDF-issued helmet and firing her own CAR-74.

Noah took up position next to her, peeked over the wall, and wished he hadn't. There were thousands of Vemus fighters on the field. They fired their white stunner weapons that would completely disable a person if they were hit with it. Noah aimed his rifle toward the nearest Vemus soldier and fired a shot, taking him in the chest. The Vemus hardly slowed down. Noah fired off a few more rounds at it, hitting it on its large, rounded head. Gritting his teeth, he found another one and kept firing his weapon. He noticed that CDF soldiers were interspersed throughout the fortification and were firing incendiary ammunition at any Vemus that went down. Death by fire was the surest way to guarantee that the Vemus stayed down.

"What are you doing here? Don't you have a cannon to keep working?" Lenora asked between firing her weapon.

"I missed you," Noah said.

White bolts slammed into the fortification walls near them, and Noah jumped.

"You're the only family I've got," he said.

Lenora smiled and punched him in the arm. "Don't get sentimental on me now."

They continued fighting and the Vemus drew steadily closer. They kept coming over the nearby hills, and he had no idea how many of them there were. Runners had come by and dropped off ammunition blocks, but Noah was almost out again.

The Vemus fighters surged forward in an all-out run. Sanctuary's defenders tried to keep them at bay, but the Vemus kept moving forward. They could no longer get a clear shot to incinerate the fallen Vemus, and they rose again. Noah kept firing his weapon as panic seized his chest. He just wanted them to stop. He wanted it all to stop.

Lenora cursed. "I'm out!"

"So am I," Noah said.

Twenty meters away the Vemus fighters vaulted over the walls, overwhelming the CDF soldiers there. Noah grabbed Lenora's arm and started pulling her in the opposite direction.

"No, they're over there too!" Lenora said.

Noah looked behind them. Vemus fighters were storming the fortifications and there was nowhere for them to go. The way the Vemus moved, there was no way they could outrun them.

The Vemus finally noticed them and Noah's mouth went dry. He held onto Lenora. "Don't look at them," he said, but Lenora wouldn't turn away. She screamed angrily and flung her empty rifle at them.

To his left, Noah saw something moving toward the Vemus fighters and was shocked to recognize packs of berwolves racing toward them. They tore into the Vemus fighters and overpowered them in a rush. Noah watched as Vemus bodies were tossed into the air and then were torn apart by the berwolves' powerful jaws.

Noah wasn't sure whether the berwolves were vulnerable to the virus. Most colonial scientists didn't believe that the creatures of New Earth would be, but there was no way to be sure.

A scarred-faced berwolf padded over to them.

"Bull!" Lenora cried.

Noah watched as more berwolf packs entered the battle. A sonic boom sounded above, and soon after, seven more Vemus troop carriers came into view.

"We have to get out of here. More are coming," Noah said, knowing how futile it was.

The Vemus were regrouping after the berwolf assault. Noah was watching the approaching Vemus troop carriers when a salvo of missiles streaked across the sky and slammed into them. Flaming wrecks crashed to the ground.

A broadcast signal registered on Noah's comlink as CDF Hellcats flew into the area.

"This is Major Quinn. We saw that you have an infestation of Vemus soldiers and we thought we'd help out," Sean said.

Noah smiled and pumped his fist into the air. He had never been so happy to see a Hellcat in his entire life. The CDF Hellcats made another pass and began mowing down the Vemus on the battlefield. Meanwhile, CDF troop carriers landed behind the fortifications and dropped off reinforcements. Noah was choked with emotion and happy to be alive. He and Lenora picked up two fallen weapons and headed back to the fortification walls. They were still in this fight after all.

35

THE VEMUS ALPHA closed in on New Earth's solitary moon even as weapons of the Colonial Defense Force tore into its hull. The Alpha's primary weapon cut deep gashes into the lunar surface, taking out CDF installations.

Nathan looked at his two main holoscreens. At least no more ships were leaving the Alpha. They'd stopped as many as they could, but he knew a small number must have gotten through.

"Comms, has there been any reply from our assault teams on the Vemus Alpha?" Nathan asked.

"Negative, Colonel. We just had a partial broadcast," Sergeant Boers said.

He shared a look with Major Shelton. The partial broadcast they'd received earlier could be taken as a sign that the assault teams had successfully delivered their payloads and were moments from detonation.

"Colonel, the last plasma cannon has been taken out. Their next shot will be at our location," Lieutenant LaCroix said.

"Comms, send out the evacuation codes for all base personnel," Nathan said.

The ground shook beneath his feet as it had done every time the Vemus Alpha fired its primary weapon. They'd fired everything they had at that weapon and they just couldn't disable it. The CDF soldiers in the Command Center began evacuating the area. They'd try to survive in one of the underground bunkers they'd built.

"Aren't you coming, Colonel?" Major Shelton asked, her voice shaky.

Nathan kept studying the holoscreens that still showed sensor data coming in. He'd sent the detonation signal for the assault team's payload shortly after receiving the partial broadcast. Nothing happened. They could have set the bombs to use a timer, which couldn't be overridden by a detonation signal from Lunar Base, assuming the signal could even penetrate the Vemus Alpha.

"Colonel, there's nothing more you can do here. We have to go," Major Shelton said.

Nathan had done everything he could but it didn't feel like enough. Nonetheless, he began to back away from the command area. He didn't want to leave, not with the Vemus Alpha still out there, but Major Shelton was right. They had no more weapons and the Vemus knew their location. They'd been systematically taking out all CDF installations.

"Please forgive me," Nathan muttered and turned away from the main holoscreens.

He followed Major Shelton out of the Command Center. They ran to the nearest transit tube, which was almost full of CDF soldiers.

"It'll be a tight squeeze, but we'll get you in," said a soldier near the entrance.

Major Shelton went in first and Nathan followed. As the doors shut behind him, they were squished together like sardines. There was a loud pop and the elevated capsule they were in shot away from Lunar Base. The magnetic tracks had no friction, and aside from being pressed up against each other, Nathan could hardly feel the movement. Thrusters fired as they reached their destination bunker. The doors of the transit capsule opened, and once they started to get off, Nathan finally released the breath he'd been holding in. The lights in the area dimmed.

"Emergency power activated," a monotone voice said.

The main facility of Lunar Base was gone. Now all they could do was wait, hope, and pray.

36

CONNOR FELT an immense vibration from the exoskeletal floor and something rippled beneath him, heading toward Captain Randle.

"Stop!" Connor shouted.

Captain Randle tried to squirm away from the swirling mass under the ground.

"He will be brought into the collective. A soldier he will remain, but better," the voice said.

Captain Randle was pulled under the ground, and Connor screamed. He clenched his teeth and swung around, bringing his AR-71 up. The amorphous mass of the Vemus collective didn't react at all. With Connor's comlink activated, he began receiving broadcast updates from the lunar base assault teams. The bombs had been planted.

"No, he won't," Connor said. "He'll die, just like you will."

"You resist. Just like before."

Connor frowned. "What do you mean, before?"

Something glowed inside the Vemus collective. He imagined the gray mass was one huge infected sack of living tissue, and if he fired his weapon, the infection would ooze out of it.

"Your weapon will not harm me. I am everywhere," the Vemus collective said. The entirety of the vast chamber pulsed in rhythm with the words spoken. The glowing orbs flared brilliantly from deep inside the exoskeletal-encased cords. They went beyond sight, and Connor suspected that they went throughout the entire Vemus Alpha. The Vemus collective was the ship.

"You're nothing but a disease," Connor sneered.

How could a disease achieve anything resembling sentience?

"They used to believe as you do. They thought to stop us, but we are the same."

"What are you?" Connor asked.

"We're humans who've taken an evolutionary leap," the Vemus collective replied.

Connor shook his head. "That's impossible. You can't be human."

New network connections became available to Connor through his combat suit's system. Then a data dump began to download to his suit computer.

"Why have you come here?" Connor asked.

The Vemus collective didn't respond. Instead, words began to appear on his heads-up display.

::*Biological imperative*.::

A series of images flashed on Connor's internal heads-up display—mission briefings to research subheadings for things Connor had never heard of before.

"It won't succeed. There are bombs planted all over this ship," Connor said.

"We have the measure of your weapons. They will not stop us," the Vemus collective said, once again speaking aloud.

Connor glanced at the AR-71 in his hands and let it fall to the ground. Reaching behind his back, he moved to the side, next to one of the exoskeletal cords. Another ripple moved through the floor toward him, and he slammed into the cord. He braced himself against it and the shuddering movement beneath his feet stopped.

"You could just leave. You came all this way and for what? There aren't very many people here," Connor said as he moved away from the cord.

"Humanity is the imperative," the Vemus collective replied.

Connor swallowed as an image appeared on his heads-up display showing an NA Alliance soldier with his weapon pointed straight at him. The name *Col. Gates* appeared on the HUD overlay.

Connor's eyes widened. "What's this?"

Memories blazed through Connor's mind like wildfire. The image was from his last Earth mission. Everyone who'd been witness to it was dead, or so he'd thought. The Ghosts were gone, and there was only one other person who'd been standing in front of him.

"RJ!" Connor hissed. His eyes widened as he realized that buried within the Vemus collective was the leader of the Syndicate—a powerful group that operated above governments. They'd wanted to control everything and establish dominion over all people. The Vemus organism must have given them the opportunity.

The horde of Vemus soldiers behind him seemed to move all at once.

"You cannot harm us, and you will never leave this place," the Vemus collective said. "Your weapons are not strong enough to stop us, nor will you ever kill us—"

"I just did," Connor said quietly, holding up the cylinder that was attached to the canister on his back. Four large-bore penetrators were still deployed from one end, each dripping with thick amber-colored liquid. Connor watched the blackened area around the spot he'd shoved the injector into spread rapidly. The New Earth virus, coupled with the nanobots, spread away from Connor like a black wave. The Vemus soldiers still attached to the collective started convulsing violently, and the soldier nearest him fell to the ground, unmoving. Connor turned toward the giant mass and watched with grim satisfaction as it seemed to sag into itself. He heard the fleeting, high-pitched whistles of the Vemus stretch into an elongated tone that soon faded to nothing.

"General?" Captain Randle groaned.

Connor spun toward the call. The cords that had held Captain Randle had slipped off of him, and the CDF captain was trying to claw his way out of the murky liquid. As Connor ran over to Randle, his feet were sloshing through the exoskeletal surface. He barely made it to the captain before his legs could hardly move through the stuff.

"I'm here," Connor said.

Captain Randle turned toward him. "My comlink is online. The other team—"

"I know," Connor said.

The Vemus exoskeletal walls weakened, going from a hardened surface to a liquid form. A large section sloshed to the ground, upsetting the rest, and the glowing orbs within went dark.

The only lighting came from their combat suits.

"What happened? Did it work?" Captain Randle asked.

Connor stopped trying to struggle against the thick, viscous liquid and simply stood there. He looked over at Captain Randle and saw that his combat suit had been severely damaged by the Vemus exoskeletal sludge.

"It worked," Connor said and glanced at the timer for the bombs the assault teams from Lunar Base had planted.

"My suit is going offline. You should leave me behind. You might be able to get away," Captain Randle said.

"Like hell I will," Connor replied.

"But General," Captain Randle protested.

"We're about to die. You can use my first name, Wayne," Connor said.

"Well, don't stay on my account, Connor," Wayne said.

"You're not that pretty," Connor replied. He doubted he could crawl out of there anyway.

Wayne snorted. "I'm no Lenora Bishop, but I do like what I see when I look in the mirror."

Connor shook his head. "You would," he said, and his throat thickened. He closed his eyes, not wanting to watch the timer anymore. Instead, he pictured Lenora's beautiful face and long auburn hair with the rays of the sun casting her silhouette in shining brilliance. He wished he could be with her right now. He'd gladly live the rest of his life apologizing for the fool he was.

He slipped beneath the liquid surface of the Vemus exoskeleton as the New Earth virus broke it down, and he looked over at Wayne's darkened suit. The damage must have killed his power.

"Wayne!" Connor called.

There was no response, and Connor tried to wave to get his attention, but Wayne didn't move at all. His body just sank in the murky sea of liquefied Vemus exoskeletal material. He screamed to Wayne and there was no response. Wayne was gone. His vision blurred. This was it. He was going to die . . . alone. He felt a wave of panic seize his chest. Connor gasped for breath and glared at the sight around him. He was surrounded by the dark bodies of dead Vemus soldiers, sinking into their watery grave. They'd once been people and he hoped they were at peace.

Connor cringed inwardly as a flash of regret blazed through his thoughts, and he didn't try to stop them. Instead, he let all his regrets have their due. The darkness closed in all around him and he felt an overwhelming sense of loneliness. He didn't want to die here. He flailed his arms, trying to work his way through the murky liquid, but nothing worked. He just continued to sink among the still forms of the Vemus soldiers. Connor swallowed and glanced at the timer. Squeezing his eyes shut, he finally surrendered to the inevitable.

37

Colonel Hayes leaned back and closed his eyes. A cool breeze blew through the open doors of the mobile Command Center at Sierra's CDF encampment on New Earth. As the tension melted away, he sagged into his chair and his breathing became deep and regular with the allure of sleep. He'd found himself leaning over, succumbing to some much-needed sleep three times already, and by the fourth, he just gave in. There'd hardly been a moment's peace in the two months since the Vemus Alpha ship had been destroyed. Fragments of the ship had bombarded the lunar surface, and the careful cleanup operations he'd been overseeing for the past few months were starting to catch up with him. He'd slept when he could sneak it in, and he felt himself drifting away now. Would anyone notice if he just rested his head on his desk? Perhaps he could just lie down on the floor.

A woman's voice cut through his slumber like a cleaver, and an instant headache came over him, snapping him awake. Nathan winced, hearing her walk into his office. He cracked an eye open and glanced at the doorway.

"We do have a bed you can sleep in," Savannah said.

"I know, but if I take the time to go there, I'll just wake myself up," Nathan said softly.

Savannah snorted. "So, you don't want to join me for my four-month checkup with Dr. Quinn?"

Nathan's eyes snapped open, startled. "I thought that was tomorrow," he said and quickly stood up.

"It *is* tomorrow," Savannah said.

Keeping the days straight had become increasingly difficult when he hadn't had a day off in so long that he couldn't remember the last one. "I don't know how Ashley does it."

"Her appointment as governor is temporary. She'll serve out the remainder of Tobias's term, but she'll always be a doctor at heart," Savannah said.

Nathan arched his back and stretched. He glanced at the small swelling of Savannah's midsection and smiled. She was only just now starting to show her pregnancy. "Are you sure you don't want to wait to find out if it's a boy or a girl?"

Savannah arched a brow. "What? Is it suddenly five hundred years ago?"

"Well, technically it's a little over four hundred and twenty, but since we spent two hundred of those years in . . ." Nathan's voice trailed off and he raised his hands in front of his chest. "I was just asking."

Savannah stepped closer to him. "Does it really matter if it's one or the other?"

Nathan smiled. "No," he said.

"Good answer," Savannah purred and kissed him.

They left the mobile Command Center and he told Lieutenant LaCroix to continue monitoring the teams they had out in the field.

They stepped outside and Nathan's eyes widened. He was still waking up and his brain wasn't quite functioning yet.

"What is it?" Savannah asked.

"If today is your appointment, that means we should also be getting the results for the survivors," Nathan said.

"Colonel Quinn is already there," Savannah said.

Promoting Sean Quinn to colonel was something Nathan had pushed for recently. Sean had been doing the job since Connor had put him in charge of the CDF ground forces. Being the war hero of Sanctuary, he had a loyal following that starkly rebuffed anyone who questioned Sean's decision to blow up Sierra. Nathan had reviewed the reports and also supported Sean's decision. Given the overwhelming enemy fighting force they were facing at the time, it was the best choice to ensure their survival. It had taken CDF forces weeks to hunt down all the remaining Vemus that had made it to New Earth. Once the Vemus collective had been destroyed, they seemed to lose some of their fighting capabilities, including their highly adaptive fighting abilities. Scientists were still theorizing about how the Vemus connection worked. They wanted to collect samples for study, which Nathan had steadfastly refused. All Vemus and remnants of equipment modified by the Vemus were to be destroyed. No exceptions. Nathan was the most senior officer of the Colonial Defense Force, so the decision was made by him. On the one hand, he understood the scientists wanting to know exactly what had happened on Earth to spawn the Vemus, but on the other hand, the colony had just miraculously survived something that had claimed billions of lives, so why tempt fate? He wasn't convinced there was a real benefit to studying the Vemus, and some stones were better left unturned.

Nathan and Savannah took an ATV to the CDF secure location outside the encampment a hundred kilometers from where Sierra had been. With the threat of the Vemus lessening as the days passed, colonists were being transported from the bunkers to the encampments near the decimated cities. The "clean" nature of the fusion bombs used to destroy the cities allowed for immediate reconstruction, and temporary housing had already been established for the surviving colonists.

They were starting over, but the colony had paid a terrible price for the privilege. Nathan suspected that some of the new structures would incorporate a way to reverently honor the sacrifice of all those who had died in the war against the Vemus.

They went through the security checkpoints to enter the CDF base and drove to a secluded, heavily guarded warehouse. The driver of the ATV stopped near the entrance and Nathan and Savannah climbed out.

Standing outside the warehouse was a short, muscular CDF captain Nathan had come to know recently.

"Colonel," Captain Diaz said and saluted Nathan and Savannah. While Savannah's pregnancy had prevented her from service aboard Phoenix Station, she was still part of the CDF and a ranking officer, the same as Nathan.

Standing next to Captain Diaz was an older Asian man.

"Captain," Nathan said and turned to the other man. "Dr. Kim. Thank you for your discretion in this matter."

"I only hope that after all this time we get some good news," Dr. Kim replied.

Dr. Kim had been with Connor's assault team and had stayed behind on a combat shuttle. During the battle, when the CDF bombs were about to detonate, Dr. Kim had flown the combat shuttle away from the Vemus Alpha. He'd waited as long as he could, but Connor and his team hadn't returned.

It was Dr. Kim who'd detected the active combat suit signals from among the wreckage of the Vemus Alpha. CDF rescue operations had recovered nearly sixty CDF soldiers from the wreckage, including General Gates. Some of the CDF soldiers had been encased in the Vemus exoskeletal material and were in a state of being absorbed into the Vemus collective when the toxin had been released. There was nothing they could do for those soldiers. They weren't quite dead, but they weren't fully alive either. They were a biological contagion and had to be destroyed, so when the survivors had been discovered, Nathan had ordered it kept secret. The families of those soldiers already believed their loved ones were dead, and to reveal what had really happened to them would have been cruel. But for Connor's body it was different. His combat suit was perfectly intact, with only some minor damage, but the suit itself had been directly exposed to the Vemus collective. Nexstar combat suits were designed to keep their wearers alive through the harshest conditions. When exposed to a prolonged harsh environment, it would administer medicine that reduced the consumption of life support. The best way to achieve this was to put the wearer of the suit into a temporary coma.

Nathan had had Connor's body quarantined and made the knowledge of his survival confidential. Only a select few knew the CDF general was alive, but whether he was free of the Vemus was another matter entirely. They'd kept Connor in a medical coma while in quarantine. Ashley Quinn had injected nanobots into his system to evaluate Connor's cellular structure. They needed to know whether his suit's exposure to the Vemus had left him infected. The evaluation had taken weeks, and today they would find out whether they would lose one more friend to the Vemus.

They went through another security checkpoint. Even the CDF soldiers serving in this facility weren't aware that their commanding officer was being held in quarantine, fully sedated.

Dr. Quinn stood at the medical capsule, speaking with her son.

"You know him. If we wake him up and he suspects he's been infected, he'll take matters into his own hands," Sean said.

Ashley glanced at Nathan as he and Savannah walked into the room, navigating among the monitoring equipment that was connected to the capsule. Captain Diaz and Dr. Kim followed them inside. They were the only people who knew Connor was alive.

"Today is the day," Nathan said.

Ashley looked at Savannah and gave her a warm smile. Then she turned back to Nathan. "I was just explaining to Sean that no matter what these results show us, there's no way to know for sure whether Connor's exposure to the Vemus will have lasting effects, or even latent effects."

"And I was saying that when we do wake Connor up, we'd better be sure of the results or he might do something rash," Sean said.

"He's right," Diaz said.

"So what are you suggesting?" Nathan asked.

"That we don't make any snap decisions once we get the results," Ashley replied.

"I think it's time we find out the results of the test," Nathan said.

When they'd decided to run the full spectrum of tests, with the nanobots essentially examining every part of Connor's body, they'd used a lockout protocol that required all six of them to be present to get the results.

Ashley went to the capsule and opened the console. She inputted her own authentication and stepped aside so the rest of them could do the same. Nathan went last, but before he inputted his credentials, he whispered a silent prayer that the results would be positive.

CONNOR FELT a jolt and then something tugged him from a bottomless sleep. He became aware of the deep void he'd been in and felt as if he were being pushed through a doorway to the frigid outdoors. He felt a tingling pain in his hands and feet. There was something hard in his throat and he heard the sound of muffled voices speaking. Connor tried to cough as his throat muscles worked to expel the hard rod from his mouth. Then he felt the tube in his throat slowly being pulled out. He winced and coughed weakly, spitting out a foul-tasting liquid as someone helped roll him to his side.

"Just take it easy for a moment. You've been in a medically induced coma."

He recognized Ashley's voice and did as she said. Connor lay on his side and took a few breaths.

"Where am I?" Connor asked, his voice sounding hoarse.

"You're on New Earth," Ashley said.

Connor opened his eyes and blinked several times before his vision began to clear. The bed began to lift him into a sitting position so he was more upright and that helped clear his head. He looked around and saw Ashley standing near him. He glanced behind her and saw Sean, Nathan, and Savannah. There was a clearing of the throat to his left and he saw Dr. Kim standing there, smiling.

"Either you're all dead or I'm alive," Connor said.

Ashley smiled at him. "You're alive," she said.

Sean gave him a measured look. There was a hardness to his gaze that Connor recognized as something that came with the burden of command.

"Is someone going to tell me what's going on?" Connor asked.

"Barely awake for a minute and he already wants a mission report," Diaz said and grinned.

"The Vemus are gone," Sean said.

Connor tried to remember his last moments on the Vemus Alpha. "Were there any other survivors? Wayne Randle was with me."

Sean shook his head. "No one else aboard the Vemus Alpha survived."

Though Sean met Connor's gaze, he had the impression there was something they weren't telling him.

"You all suck at poker," Connor said and frowned. "Am I infected?"

There was a deafening silence in the room and their expressions became somber.

"According to the nanobots, there are no biological contagions in your system," Ashley Quinn said.

Connor gave her a level look. "But there's no way you can be sure," he said.

He looked at Dr. Kim. "What do you think?"

Dr. Kim sighed. "There's strong evidence that supports your continued health. But there's also a lot we don't understand. We only figured out how to stop the Vemus. We're not adept at detecting whether someone is infected."

"Well, if I were infected, wouldn't symptoms start to show by now? How long have I been in a coma?" Connor asked.

"Yes, they would," Sean said. "And you've been in a coma for two months."

Connor took a moment, considering. "So monitor me. Have the nanobots continue to monitor me for as long as it takes until we're sure. Any deviation and we'll deal with it then."

Sean's eyes widened and Connor watched as he glanced at his mother.

"They were worried you'd find a more permanent solution to the problem that involved you removing yourself from the equation," Ashley said.

Connor's mouth hung open as he looked around at all of them. Then he started to laugh—a chuckle at first and then a full-on, hearty bellow of a laugh.

"Maybe at one time I might have, but . . ." Connor shook his head. "No," he said and frowned at the thought. "No, definitely not."

He swung his legs off the bed and stood up. Ashley was closest to him, and he reached out and pulled her in for a hug.

She hugged him back and then pushed him away. "You need a shower."

"Where's Tobias?" Connor asked.

A pained expression showed on Sean's face. "He died fighting the Vemus."

The momentary elation he'd felt diminished. "I'm so sorry," he said.

Ashley gave him a nod and he finally noticed the pain in her eyes. She was still grieving. Sean met his gaze and Connor leaned on the bed.

"Alright, tell me the rest of it," Connor said.

For the next few hours, they brought Connor up to speed about what had happened since the Vemus Alpha had been destroyed. More than a few times he found himself glancing at Nathan. If there was anyone he'd appointed to the right post, it was him. Connor suspected there was much more they hadn't told him. He had the distinct impression they were pacing him in regards to how much information they were sharing.

"General, we'll need to tell everyone you're alive," Sean said.

Connor pressed his lips together. "That would be good, but you shouldn't call me that anymore."

Sean frowned. "What do you mean?" he asked and glanced at Nathan.

Connor shared a look with Nathan. "I can't be the general of the Colonial Defense Force."

"There is ample evidence that you've not been infected. The colonial government would certainly approve it," Sean said and glanced at his mother.

Connor looked at Ashley. She'd been his friend since he'd woken up from stasis all those years ago. "I know, but I'm resigning my commission."

Their reactions ranged from complete surprise from Sean, to relief from Nathan, and then to intrigue from Ashley. The others in the room had varying degrees of the same.

"But—" Sean began.

"Any one of you," Connor said, pausing to look in turn at Sean, Nathan, and Savannah, "are more than capable of taking command of the CDF. I'm going to take some time off."

There was a loud snort from Diaz. "Take time off? I didn't think you even knew how to say that, let alone do it."

Connor smiled. "I'm going to start right now, assuming I'm free to leave this place."

Nathan stood ramrod straight and saluted Connor. He was quickly followed by Savannah and then Sean. Diaz renewed his stoic features in an instant and followed suit.

Connor's throat thickened, and he returned their salute.

"I'll handle all the formalities of your . . . retirement," Ashley said with half a smile. "And there's a Hellcat that will take you anywhere you'd like to go, but I do suggest you put on some clothes. You can find them over there."

Ashley pointed to a metallic footlocker by the wall and the others left the room while Connor put on some fresh clothes. He walked out of the room and Sean was waiting for him.

"I can't believe you're going to just walk away from all this," Sean said.

"I'd like to think of it as walking toward something. The CDF is in good hands. You've exceeded all my expectations and I have no doubt that you'll continue to do so," Connor said. What he didn't say was that he needed to put a lot of distance between himself and the CDF. They hadn't shown up yet, but

Connor knew that the ghosts of those who were no longer with them would be felt in earnest before long.

"Thank you, sir," Sean replied.

"Your father was really proud of you," Connor said.

The skin around Sean's eyes tightened. Connor knew that, with time, the grief wouldn't sting quite so much as it did now. There was no shortage of that going around, judging by the somber expressions of those around him.

Sean escorted him out of the secure warehouse. The CDF soldiers had been dismissed so Connor's return wouldn't become public knowledge just yet. Ashley had assured him that they'd wait a few days to announce his miraculous recovery.

Sean walked with him to the Hellcat and went right for the cockpit, taking the pilot's seat.

Connor arched an eyebrow at him.

"You've been in a coma for two months. I'm not going to let you fly one of our Hellcats. Just tell me where you want to go," Sean said.

"I retire just a few minutes ago and you don't trust me anymore?" Connor asked.

Sean calmly waited for Connor to tell him their destination. Connor did.

THE HELLCAT LANDED at a remote site about as far away from the colony as they could get. Scorched craters could be seen from the sky, marking where the battle had been fought at Sanctuary. Connor saw the wrecks that had been the Vemus troop carriers, and Sean filled him in on the battle here. One day he'd return to Sierra, but right now he just wanted to be here.

"There'll be a supply run here in a day or so and I'll make sure there's a package for you," Sean said.

"I expect your mother will want me to return to the encampment in a few days for the formal announcement," Connor said.

"They might want to make you governor," Sean said.

Connor winced. "I hope not," he said.

"Good luck, sir," Sean said and made a show of looking past Connor. "You're going to need it."

Connor walked down the hatchway and stepped onto the ground. The hatch closed and Connor watched as Sean flew the Hellcat away. There were a few temporary structures, and the archaeological team had gathered outside. There were a few CDF soldiers there with them and one noticed Connor's approach.

Connor smiled as Noah walked over to him, grinning. "You're alive!" he said in a tone that sounded as if he couldn't quite believe it.

"They had me under lock and key for a while," Connor said.

Noah shook his head in disbelief. "I don't believe it."

Connor looked around at the people, searching.

"She's not here. She's in the dig site. They found a new chamber . . . well, one of the refugees did. I'll take you down there," Noah said.

Connor followed Noah into the alien city. There weren't many people there, but the few they passed gave Connor strange looks, as if they thought they recognized him from somewhere. They went down into the central city, and he heard Lenora's voice.

". . . and now that the refugees are finally gone, we can get back to our work here. We're a bit shorthanded with the new chamber, but the data archive we found should help us figure out who used to live here," Lenora said, speaking to a small group of people who looked over at Connor and Noah as they approached, and Lenora turned around.

Connor just stood there, taking in the sight of her. Her long auburn hair was tied back and her hands had dirt on them. She must have been digging. From the corner of his eye, Connor saw Noah motioning for the others to leave them alone.

"I heard you were looking for an extra pair of hands," Connor said.

Lenora narrowed her gaze. "It's been months and you show up now as if nothing has happened?"

She stalked toward him and then stopped. "You . . ." she hissed. "You're still alive?" she said accusingly.

"I was in a coma. They only just brought me out of it today," Connor said.

Lenora's mouth opened and she licked her lips. "That's crap. Ashley would have told me if you were alive," she said and walked away from him.

Connor sprinted after her. "I swear to you, it's true. They didn't know if I'd been infected."

Lenora rounded on him and shoved him away. "If you've come here to tell me you're dying, I swear I'll shoot you myself."

Connor shook his head. "I'm not," he said and then repeated himself. "They found me in some wreckage and kept me in quarantine."

Lenora glared at him. "And you thought what? You'd come back here and we'd patch things up until the next crisis?"

Connor had known she'd be angry with him, but the level of fury in her eyes wasn't what he'd been expecting. "I had to see you," he said.

Lenora held up her arms. "Great, you're alive. You've seen me. Now leave me alone," she said and started walking away.

Connor stepped toward her and grabbed her arm. "I'm sorry," he said.

Lenora snatched her arm away from him.

"I should have listened to you sooner. I'm sorry for leaving, for not being able to let it go. For everything," Connor said and reached out, taking Lenora's hand. "You were the first person I wanted to see when they woke me up and you were the last person I thought about when I thought I was going to die on that ship. You might hate me now, but I'm not leaving. I don't care how long it takes. I'm staying."

Lenora pursed her lips. "What if I've already moved on? Would you still wait?" she said.

A momentary doubt seized Connor's chest, but then he pushed it away. "Someone once told me I'd make a good archeologist," he said and stepped closer to her, "so I thought I'd work with the best."

Lenora snorted and her lips curved upward. He pulled her into his arms. There was no one else.

"It'll take years to become the best. A lot of work. A lot of time," Lenora said.

"Time is the one thing I *do* have," Connor replied.

Lenora shook her head. "You've got an answer for everything."

"Not everything. Just this," Connor said.

He knew the colony would carry on despite the heavy toll that had been paid for their survival. Throughout his whole life he'd been restless, always moving from place to place. He'd struggled to know where he fit in, and he'd found a home in the military. When they learned of the threat to the colony, he'd reacted in the only way he knew. He was familiar with that life, but now he was ready for something new with the woman he loved. He didn't know what was in store for him and he'd lost count of the many chances life had given him, but he was determined to make the most of this one.

DEAR READER,

THANK you so much for reading the first three books of the *First Colony* series. I sincerely hope you've enjoyed the story.

The series does continue with the fourth book, but before you grab the sequel, I'd like to offer you a free science fiction story I wrote. If you join my mailing list, I'll send you a free copy of **Crash Landing**, a story set in the *Ascension* series *(A difference SF series I wrote.)*

Click Here to download your **FREE** copy of **Crash Landing**

The series continues with the 4th book

First Colony - Sanctuary

THANK YOU FOR READING.

The series will continue with the **4th book**. If you would like to be notified when my next book is released please visit kenlozito.com and sign up to get a heads up.

The series continues with the 4th book

First Colony - Sanctuary

I've created a special **Facebook Group** specifically for readers to come together and share their interests, especially regarding my books. Check it out and join the discussion by searching for **Ken Lozito's SF Worlds**.

ABOUT THE AUTHOR

Ken Lozito is the author of multiple science fiction and fantasy series. I've been reading both genres for a long time. Books were my way to escape everyday life of a teenager to my current ripe old(?) age. What started out as a love of stories has turned into a full-blown passion for writing them. My ultimate intent for writing stories is to provide fun escapism for readers. I write stories that I would like to read and I hope you enjoy them as well.

If you have questions or comments about any of my works I would love to hear from you, even if its only to drop by to say hello at KenLozito.com

Thanks again for reading.

Don't be shy about emails, I love getting them, and try to respond to everyone.

ALSO BY KEN LOZITO

IF YOU WOULD LIKE TO BE NOTIFIED WHEN MY NEXT BOOK IS RELEASED VISIT
KENLOZITO.COM